"The Atomic Priesthood should be required reading for all humanity. Lillian Hall methodically describes the problem. But she does not abandon us. Instead she leaves us inspired with the solution of how we can live in beauty, health, and harmony on this great earth. She is truly a visionary of our time."

Sandra Ingerman, author of
Soul Retrieval and Medicine For the Earth

"This book is a must read for all. Lillian Hall has revealed a profound depth of understanding of the core truth within what is experienced as the circumstances of our lives and even ourselves. Beautifully and often poetically articulated, it will be a book that requires underling favorite passages and margin notes."

Elmarilla Bailey, author of
Bridges to Light and A Love Story

Stone People Enterprises Inc.
P.O. Box 56, Cleveland, GA -30528-
www.lillianhall.com

ISBN 0-9755083-0-X

Printed in the U.S.A.

Cover Design – "Exhibit Solutions," Richard L. Gabbert
Cover Art – Joanne Steele
Cover Photo – Lillian Hall
Interior Layout – Jim Thiel
Author Photo – Micheal H. Hall

THE ATOMIC PRIESTHOOD

LILLIAN M. HALL

STONE PEOPLE
ENTERPRISES Inc.

Even though this book is written in a fictionalized form, it is based on real world events that transpired during the Atomic Age, incredible and unbelievable as they may seem. The characters are based on inspiration and imagination, and are not meant to depict real people.

Prologue

Mild summers were treasured respites in the vast, flat, treeless expanse known as the "steppes" along the eastern border of Kazakhstan, near Mongolia. As with the indigenous flora and fauna, only the most hardy and stoic could endure the harsh winters and brutal living conditions in the land of the small, nondescript Soviet village at the outskirts of the city of Semipalatinsk.

The village was so small that when the night wails of birthing came, everyone within earshot knew whose time it was to be giving birth. They knew how many other children she had, how well she cooked and how her garden grew. It was a communal area—still full of ancient customs and ancient ways—and there were few secrets.

However, a crack had begun to penetrate the collective resolve of the villagers. For the previous two decades, when the sounds of childbirth had begun, each of them had learned to hold his breath. And wait. And listen.

What they waited for was the silent period that would follow the final searing pangs of the labor process...for the sound that followed that silence would determine the spirit of the village for many days ahead.

On this crystal clear, warm, quiet July night in 1970, there was nothing to muffle the sounds—no closed windows, no storm, not even a barking dog to distract the attention. Even the winds, which had whipped almost constantly across the steppes, were eerily still this night, and this night it was Irina Kundrata's time to fill the night air with the sounds of birthing.

Irina labored hour after hour, the black night punctuated over and over again with her intermittent moaning as it built to peaks of forceful and sometimes angry cries. Her sweat saturated her bedding. The midwife continually offered words of encouragement and wiped her face, neck and chest with a cool, water-soaked cloth. Irina's cries grew into screams, as they got closer and closer together, until at last there was the silence.

Most often the sound that followed the silent period was one of joy, laughter and, in more recent times, great relief. But sometimes...

And then it came—the thing that everyone had dreaded: a heart-rending scream of horror from the Kundrata house, a scream so filled with agony that it pierced the still night like a knife through the very soul of the village.

It had happened again. Another monster had been born.

* * *

Sometimes the mutated babies were born two-headed. Sometimes they displayed a combination of animal and human looking parts, grotesquely de-

1

formed beyond human imagination. Though the villagers near Semipalatinsk were aware that mutations occurred everywhere throughout the world, they also knew that they had been occurring there for the last two decades with an unholy regularity.

And they knew that whenever it happened—whenever the unnatural sounds filled the air of their village or one of those nearby—there were seldom any funerals. The attending midwife would almost always mercifully carry the small, offensive bundle away from the affected house. No one knew where the bundles were taken. They seldom even asked. They only knew that the occupants of the house and the rest of the villagers, as well, were relieved to have every trace of the horror removed from their midst, if not from their memories.

There were rare times when some of the families resisted. The Kazakhs were a strong people, a proud people, from a culture rich in heritage. Their ancestors had left their marks on the pages of history books. In centuries past their land had felt the presence of men of almost mythical proportion, men like Kubla Khan and Ghengis Khan. These Mongol leaders had charged across the steppes in conquest and glory with the force of tidal waves. At times when the winds shrieked madly across the plains, the land still seemed to echo with the sounds of thousands of conquering hoof beats.

So, when the agonized cries replaced the normal sounds that accompany joyful birthing events, instinct and ritual sometimes took over in spite of the trauma and grief. At those times, uniformed men with guns strapped to their sides appeared and carried the bundle away. There were even rumors of their digging up small graves and taking away the contents. Then they would disappear from sight as quickly as they had appeared—some said—into a mysterious red brick building in the city of Semipalantinsk, known simply by the sterile sounding name of Clinic Number Four.

On this particular night, the weeping from Irina's house continued long after the midwife had left, carrying the small bundle away with her. It lasted off and on for most of what was left of that July night. And the sounds pained everyone in the village—reminded them over and over again of the awful reality that had befallen their lives. A few of the other women cried silently, wiping tears from their faces with their hands, or muffling their sobs deeply into their pillows at the memory of their own painful birthing experiences.

But some of the villagers, angered by the wails, wondered why Irina didn't just suffer in silence like the rest of them.

Sometime, just before dawn, in the cloud-covered, pitch-black night, Irina—weak from exhaustion—let out the last of her pain-filled moans. In the silence that followed, the villagers, one by one began letting out individual breaths of relief, as one by one they realized that the sounds from the

Kundrata house were finally over. Some even relaxed enough to sleep.

Then the wind began blowing once more...quietly at first and then slowly, louder and louder. It shrieked across the steppes again as it had for so many centuries past. The sound of it was eerie, haunting...as though it was picking up where Irina's cries had left off. It moaned and wailed through the night air as though it was still crying out her pain, past the reaches of the village, into the universe and beyond...searching...searching for a place to rest.

Chapter One

Not a single Appalachian mountain breeze stirred the unseasonably dry heat that had settled over the small town of Clayton, Georgia. Trish Cagle cursed as she pounded the posthole digger again and again into the unyielding red clay.

"Stupid damn cows!"

Sweat dampened auburn ringlets clung to her face as she worked in the hot sun. Her arms ached. She stopped to catch her breath, and wipe the sweat from her forehead with her shirtsleeve as she surveyed the trampled remnants of several tomato plants. The neighbor's loose livestock had made short work of the fence surrounding her vegetable garden.

Breathing heavily at first, and then lighter and more slowly, she glanced around, listening to the sounds of cicada, their characteristic crackling crescendos from the tall, dry grasses at the edge of the woods signaling the hottest part of the day. Grasshoppers were making popping sounds like popcorn over a flame on the stove, and from time to time launched themselves noisily across the nearby meadow.

Trish stretched her shoulders back and then rotated them one at a time. The day had seemed brittle all morning, the result of a recent drought that had descended on the region with no let-up in sight, and she sensed that brittleness penetrating her body down to her bones, as though something deep inside her was about to snap.

As she closed her eyes, a gentle, unexpected wisp of wind wafted almost imperceptibly onto the moist skin of her face; she breathed it in unconsciously, deeply. When she tried to take in another breath of it, the light breeze was mysteriously gone, as though it had never been there. She opened her eyes and looked around. The air was still and quiet. At that moment she realized that there had been no sounds of rustling foliage accompanying the light draft of wind. Goosebumps erupted on her arms, her legs, and then on the top of her scalp. When they disappeared, she shivered involuntarily.

"What *was* that?" she asked out loud. Trish looked around again. The air felt as still as a vacuum. Had the ghostly breeze even been there, or had she simply imagined it? Or wished it?

She jammed the posthole digger into the ground once again and propped on its handles. Taking off her baseball cap with one hand, she tilted her head back and shaded her eyes with the other, scanning the garden. Was it really worth all the effort? The drought had been a continual focus of news and weather reports during that summer of 1995, and its effects, even in the mountainous area where Trish lived, had been bad enough to force her to start watering the garden every evening. Her vegetables did appear to be surviving, but not thriving, and she knew they needed rain—a good, slow, long gentle rain—one that would last for days, or possibly weeks. A squinted glance at the sky told her that wasn't likely anytime soon.

She took off her gloves and stuffed them into a pocket on her overalls. Thank goodness living and working on the family farm had kept her slim, agile and relatively strong the last two years she'd been back. Still, the constant chore of keeping things running—even marginally—was overwhelming at times.

Throughout her adult life she had nurtured a fairly acute sense of independence, which had served her well...most of the time. Since she didn't have a well in the meadow and couldn't afford to have one drilled, she'd come up with a stopgap solution to keeping her plants alive that summer by rigging the bottom of a plastic 55-gallon drum with a spigot and hose line, filling it with water on the back of her old blue truck, and gravity feeding the water to the vegetables. She was rather proud that her impromptu system had worked, though the evening ritual had become time consuming and tedious. That morning, however, when she discovered the broken fence from the neighbor's marauding cows, she felt discouraged. The deer, rabbits and other wildlife had always taken their share of the vegetables in the past, but this particular intrusion into her ordered world felt downright invasive.

After a few curses, she'd taken a deep breath and marched to the barn for some tools. There she glanced at the tractor. It would make quick work of the fencepost holes. But another glance at the broken auger propped in the corner of the barn reminded her that wasn't a possibility. So she'd grabbed the posthole digger and shovel instead and headed out, not realizing how hot it already was, and unaware of just how hard the drought had left the ground during the previous weeks.

On this day, of all days, the heat, coupled with the frustrations of yet another unnecessary obstacle to overcome, left her feeling tired...bone tired, physically and emotionally. She felt defeated. In the two years she'd been back in Clayton she'd come to feel trapped, discontented, restless and even a little bitter that she wasn't at all where she wanted to be in life. And since she was in the throes of middle age, she was painfully aware that she had less time and fewer chances to accomplish the goals she'd set. She was surviving in Clayton, Georgia, but, like the plants, she wasn't thriving.

Trish threw down the posthole digger. Maybe she'd just let the garden go. She headed for her thermos of water sitting beneath the shade of the big red maple tree at the edge of the meadow. As she gulped down several swallows of the ice water, she deliberately allowed streams of it to run down her neck and onto her chest. She uttered an involuntary "Whoo!" from the shock of the chill on her body, then sat down, leaning up against the trunk of the tree.

As a girl she'd climbed that same tree and looked out across that same meadow as far as she could through her girlhood eyes, as though, if she tried hard enough, she could see her future somewhere in the distance. She'd wondered about that future, dreamed about it, imagined it, time and time again. She couldn't have imagined then that she'd be sitting under that same maple tree at age forty-five, reminiscing about her past, unable to imagine a future beyond the job of repairing the fence.

She'd managed to keep the professional disenchantments that had bedeviled her for years at bay with a series of distractions for some time. But that was no longer possible. Now it was "in her face." It couldn't be ignored, denied or put off. And the arduous task in the meadow brought back all the frustrations of the previous few days with a fierce intensity.

How could she have ended up working for a small town paper, like *The Clayton Times*, after working with some of the biggest papers in the country? Why couldn't she have just been a reporter? Why had she had to fight her editors and publisher throughout her entire career to get out the real news?

• • •

When she was fresh out of journalism school, Trish Cagle had been so gung-ho about reporting that her enthusiasm seemed to actually annoy the other reporters. In time she began to get a few inklings of why many of them seemed so jaded. One of the main principles of journalism she'd learned in college was that the financial side of the media had to remain separate from the news gathering side, yet one incident after another flew in the face of everything she had ever been taught.

Years before, during one of her visits home to Clayton, she went to see her friend and mentor, Dr. Max Rogers. They'd met when she attended college at the University of Georgia where he taught literature, and had maintained a lasting relationship. His counsel had sustained Trish through many challenges in her adult life: the difficulties in her career, her one short-lived, failed marriage and eventually the deaths of her parents. She needed his advice badly that day as she paced on the front porch of his mountain cabin, railing about the frustrations of journalism.

"God, Max, I understand that money drives the news business. Hell, it's just a numbers game when you think about it. Subscriptions make up a smaller part of a paper's income, so it's the advertisers you try to keep happy. I get that. But what do you do? How do you work within that kind of atmosphere and remain a reporter?"

She turned to face him as he sat in his rocker, eyeing her over the top of his bifocals with his pipe held at the corner of his mouth. But before he had time to mull over an answer, she added that the first time she experienced the manipulation in her reporting she chalked it up to small town politics or an aberration in the industry. "I just knew it'd be better somewhere else." She told him that since she had fairly lofty ambitions, she simply bided her time until she could get a better job at a bigger paper in a bigger city.

"It didn't take long to land my second job." She grinned with pride. "I had a pretty good resume of clips handy." She held up a hand. "But, I get to the next place and find the same damn dynamics there." She vented that though the media constantly touted the public's right to know, their silence on some of the critically important issues was downright obscene. "When I stood my ground with that next editor, I found myself assigned to garden club variety stories. Nothing too meaty. Nothing too controversial." She told him that after a few weeks of what she finally realized was professional punishment, she just woke up one morning, feeling anything but repentant, and said, "To hell with this," and began looking for yet another job.

She propped onto the porch rail. "It was at that job, after a lot of heart-to-heart conversations with other more experienced reporters, that I finally had to admit it was probably the same at just about every paper...and I'm pretty sure in every media." She held up her hand. "So how do you survive in a business like this and stay true to your ethics?"

He took off his glasses and inhaled deeply as he looked out at the mountains. In that moment of silence, Trish noticed how calm he seemed, as his white hair and beard glistened in the sunlight. He set his pipe in its holder, then laced his fingers together with his arms across the front of his rounded abdomen. "Trying to be who you are," he began, "trying to be authentic within the constraints of a money making industry can be daunting at best a good deal of the time, Patty." He was one of the few people who called her by her childhood name. "Our culture is simply geared that way. I'm not saying it's right, and I'm not saying it isn't challenging, but it's what it is. I've faced it myself in the world of academia."

"But how do you compromise...or at least straddle that line? I can't envision going into another career after busting my chops for four years to be a reporter." She walked over and sat down hard in the rocking chair beside him. "And besides, this is what I want to do. Even in high school I knew this was what I wanted to do with my life."

"My dear, I'm afraid you'd find those same dynamics in most private industries and enterprises, anyway." He leaned forward. "And can you just imagine what it'd be like to work in a governmental setting?"

She let out a short breath. "No. Hell, I've covered enough local government and politics to figure that one out."

He rubbed his beard, then leaned onto the arm of his rocker. "Patty, all of us want to be who we are—or at least get a chance to try to figure that out. We all struggle to be the real self within all kinds of structures: families, schools, jobs, social situations. By the time we're around five to seven years old we all have a breakpoint—some critical moment or incident when we finally realize we can't be ourselves and get the approval we need from others. We can't get angry, can't get messy, can't ask embarrassing questions...even when they need asking. We can't feel what we feel. We have to 'behave' by saying things we don't believe and accepting things we don't understand.

"So we start putting on masks—the ones we've learned to project onto the world to be accepted." He slipped his glasses on again. "You know the ones: the good child, the good student, the good wife or husband, or good employee...or at least our culture's portrayal of it. The 'reality' of it is something else again." He snickered and shook his head. "We've been bombarded by Ozzie and Harriet type myths for so long in our society that it's like living in a drug-induced state. And those modern day myths are as seductive as hell. We know now that most families are dysfunctional. Why wouldn't they be? Our ideas of perfection are just facades that we try to project to the world.

"You go to college and are taught more idealized concepts and rules. Then you go out into the real world and find that it's the same old sham."

"That's it," she proclaimed, sitting forward in her seat. "It's like every time I learn the rules for whatever stage or circumstance I'm in, someone changes them. And they don't do it openly, either. There's just a wink and a nod...and sometimes not even that." She held out a hand. "There's this whole subset of unspoken rules that I never quite understand. Everyone else seems to get it without much trouble. Sometimes it seems like someone has told a joke that everyone gets but me. The main purpose of the news desks and newsrooms was supposed to be gathering and presenting the news...not making a profit. That was the business of the publishing end of it. It's practically written in stone in journalism schools." She shook her head. "I just don't know how to cope anymore with these hypocrisies and constraints."

"Well," he began, "over the years I've come up with a kind of personal formula that works fairly well for me."

"Yeah?" she asked, eyeing him.

He nodded in assent.

"Mind sharing it?" She propped her head on her hand.

"It's nothing earth shaking," he began. "Rather simple, in fact. I try not to take anything personally. That's a place where I used to lose a lot of energy." He grinned. "Believe it or not, I actually learned that one while being shot at in World War II."

"That seems pretty personal...being shot at."

"It was war, Patty. No one hated me personally. You go through a dead German's things and see the pictures of his family, the wife and kids smiling at you, and you realize he's just like you. He'd rather be home with his loved ones, too, than being blown away in some battlefield. We were all just trying to survive." His voice trailed off briefly. Trish looked up as he rubbed his forehead and sighed.

Then he cleared his throat and added, "A lot of people are going to take pot shots at you throughout your life, but it's their projections. It has nothing to do with you. Try to find understanding. Look behind the facades of anger and jealousy and judgment that people hide behind. We're all just in pain. It's easier to be compassionate when you can understand that."

He picked up his pipe again. "And I try to find the humor in things that punch my buttons. I usually find it if I'm really looking. Then, lastly, I try to be genuinely grateful every day for everything I have in my life...and I'm not just talking about material things. Everything in life is there to learn from...even the problems. I try to think of them as challenges to integrate into my life on my road to self-discovery, rather than obstacles to overcome or stifle.

"The truth is if we were all sitting on a bed of roses, we'd be bored silly." He smiled at her. "I can't imagine anyone with as much curiosity and determination as you have living a life that *wasn't* full of challenges, Patty."

● ● ●

Because there was no breeze blowing, even in the shade the heat was sweltering. Trish could feel drops of sweat running from her scalp again and underneath her braless breasts, dampening her T-shirt. She took off the outer cotton shirt she'd worn to protect her arms and neck from the sun, and wiped her face and the back of her neck with it. As she did, she caught the distinctive, acrid scent of a tomato leaf on her hand, lingering from having brushed up against one of the plants. She smiled to herself. That smell was one of her favorites, a scent full of promise, even before the first yellow blossoms appeared. Promises of that homegrown tomato flavor on sandwiches, salads or just sliced thick alongside a plate of fried okra, creamed corn, cornbread and green beans that had been cooked all day. She couldn't get that taste from a grocery store. How could she let it go?

Trish spread the shirt out on the ground and laid back on it. A few June bugs began buzzing around her. She envisioned herself in her childhood days out in the meadow with her best friend, Kathy Dunnigan, catching the noisy bugs. They'd deftly tie strands of thread on the bugs' legs and watch and giggle as they flew buzzing around in circles overhead like miniature, green, iridescent helicopters. One June bug flew to her left, and as her gaze followed it, her eyes fell back onto the garden...and the trampled fence...and her thoughts returned to her career.

• • •

    As Trish recycled the events of the previous week, her mind kept returning to one of her early attempts at challenging the status quo during her career. By that time she was working at a paper in Bowling Green, Kentucky. One morning, after deadline, the reporters were summoned into the newsroom. "Look, Guys," her editor had begun, "we've got a new policy on releasing information about new industries moving into town."

    A few months before, a local environmental group, the Bowling Greens, had discovered that a chemical company with a questionable environmental record was making plans to locate in the town. After further discovering that the company had applied for a permit to emit huge amounts of smelly pollutants into the air and water, the group quickly began questioning the company and writing letters to the editor.

    Though she hadn't had much background in environmental reporting, she'd been assigned to help the main reporter covering it. Researching the controversy surrounding the possible siting of the chemical company in her community had made her acutely aware of how lax environmental law enforcement was and what levels of highly toxic chemicals were legally allowable in a community. It had been enlightening.

    The legitimacy of an environmental permit bore no correlation to safety; they were in essence merely licenses to pollute. A simple check of the EPA's Toxic Release Inventory revealed how many billions of pounds of toxins where released annually into the nation's air, water and soil. She wondered how long the media could continue bragging about covering the globe while ignoring the planet.

    After the paper's much publicized scrutiny of the controversy, the company eventually withdrew their plans. The local Chamber of Commerce, along with one of the local banks—which routinely bought large shares of advertisements from the paper—were furious at what they considered interference in their business negotiations. Suddenly there was the new policy at the paper.

    "There's no need to release information about a company's plans to move into town until all the business negotiations are taken care of, everything's been set in cement and it's time for an official announcement," the editor continued. Then, with a pointed finger, he tacked on the caveat, "Unless it's discovered that the company negotiations are already being discussed in every coffee klatch around town."

    Trish realized immediately that the intent of the caveat was to try to save the paper the embarrassment of appearing too controlled to the public. "Oh," Trish had leaned over and whispered behind her hand to one of her colleagues at the time, "So we're going to be lackeys for the banks. We just don't want to look like total lackeys."

She turned around and headed back to her cubicle, where she shuffled papers and slammed them down noisily on the desk. It was supposed to be the job of the newspaper to find out what was going on behind closed doors—especially if it could have a detrimental impact on the community. But at least she was getting a better grasp of the financial dynamics surrounding media control.

After a few days she summoned enough courage to address her misgivings about the new policy with her editor. She waited until they were alone after a meeting. Attempting to ease into the subject, she offered an example that was far removed from the present situation: a story about a paper in the Northwest that had nixed a report about selling a house without a realtor. "You know how much a report like that would have benefited the paper's subscribers," she pointed out. "But it was apparently killed because some of their biggest advertisers were local real estate companies."

The editor looked at her as though she'd slapped him in the face. He'd instantly made the connection. With barely controlled seething, he bellowed red-faced, "No advertiser has ever tried to twist *my* arm about a story."

Easing into the matter had taken an abrupt nosedive. In the calmest tone she could muster, Trish said, "Look, Mike, you and I will be gone from here to the next job before long. Most of the people in this town are going to have to live the rest of their lives with what comes into it."

He glared at her and asked, "Why is it you think everything that makes money is evil? What's so wrong with these people having decent jobs and making a little money?"

She raised her hands and her eyebrows at the same time. "Why can't we just provide both sides of the story? Why can't we just let *them* decide if minimum wage jobs are worth the health risks to their families and community?"

"What makes you think you always know what's best for everyone else?" Then, without waiting for a response, her editor stormed out of the room.

Don't take it personally, she heard in her head. *Try to find the humor.* But, if the same pattern she'd experienced at papers in the past because of her non-conformist ways was any indicator, the likely prospect of being saddled with garden club reporting for the rest of her tenure in Bowling Green wasn't funny to her. And she knew that squelching stories was a much subtler dynamic than having a big advertiser use financial intimidation with an editor or publisher. Stories that might offend or anger them simply weren't done in the first place. That was one of the unspoken rules she had finally learned that hadn't been taught in journalism school.

• • •

Trish grabbed her thermos again and gulped down the ice water several times before her throat began to ache from the cold. She set it down and laid back again, looking up at the canopy of still and lifeless limbs and green leaves overhead. Breathing deeply several times and closing her eyes, she tried to relax her body from the frustrations that were swirling through her head.

Through sometimes intricate and tedious balancing acts, Trish had managed to have a few good stints over the years working for larger newspapers in bigger cities. Still, she always had that spark of hope that on the whole things could be different. But she often found out they weren't. She'd known in her head for some time, and eventually, had to accept in her heart that in the business of news, the bottom line was, and likely always would be the bottom line. It was a cold, cruel fact of life. No business could stay in business if it wasn't making money. She asked herself once again, in light of that reality, how she could ever be a reporter…how any reporter could be a real reporter. She'd struggled with that question for years. She still struggled. She was still a reporter. As of two days ago, an unemployed reporter, but a reporter, nonetheless.

All morning long she'd tried to figure out how things had gone so wrong, and what the hell had happened to her life. The thoughts and memories had come in a wave of glimpses and feelings that drifted into her almost unexpectedly, like the mysterious breeze she'd breathed in before she'd thrown the posthole digger down on the ground, what, maybe fifteen minutes before? She stood up slowly, taking in as deep a breath as she could of the hot, still air around her and then breathed it out again.

As she swept her eyes across the garden, Trish saw a rabbit at the far edge of it, sitting near the last of her pitiful crop of green beans. All of her anger and frustration suddenly had a focus. She looked down at the ground, picked up a rock and threw it as hard as she could in his direction. The rabbit had bolted before the rock ever left her hand. "Git out of my garden, you varmint!" she hollered, seething.

"Oh, Lord," she said, blanching at the sound of her own voice. The thick Southern accent she'd taken classes to overcome had come back with a vengeance after just two years back home.

Feeling parched on the inside, and altogether saturated from heat and sweat on the outside, she glanced at the broken fence one last time. It was simply too hot to work on it any more. Trish headed back to the house to cool off and get some iced tea and possibly a little lunch. Let the rabbit have his lunch in her garden.

• • •

As Trish trudged back to the house, she was surprised at how heavy the thermos seemed. Her efforts in the garden had been more strenuous than she'd thought.

Likewise, she hadn't realized how taxing the emotional and physical strain of her career had become over the years until she'd moved home and assumed the added burden of caretaking a farm. She'd reached the height of her discontent with her twenty-five year profession years before when the Berlin Wall was torn down and "glasnost" began creeping into the Soviet Union. It was then that she finally realized she would one day have to leave it. At the time she'd been excited, even on a personal level about the obvious magnitude of the monumental changes in world politics. She dreamed of being chosen to go to Europe and getting one of the first glimpses of what had been going on behind the Iron Curtain during the Cold War.

After all, she'd reasoned, the U. S. government had spent untold millions of tax dollars trying to find out what had been going on in the Soviet Union in the previous four and a half decades, and many billions more in preparing for a possible nuclear war. The Cold War had been an incalculable financial drain on the U.S., and clearly had driven the Soviet economy into the ground. It was an unbelievable opportunity for the media to finally shine a light on what, for the West, had been a very dark place…a chance to focus on a mysterious, secret spot on the planet, to go to the proverbial lion's den. She'd felt vibrant, almost dizzy from making plans in her head.

Her editor and publisher, however, didn't share her enthusiasm. Their excuses ran the gamut: budget constraints; the public really didn't care; other news agencies would cover it; they could get copy of stories over the AP wires.

She was dumbfounded.

On the phone with Max one night, she unloaded. "This is a chance to cover one of the biggest stories of the century." She lamented that they never would have made excuses about getting the inside scoop on the marital problems of English royals. They wouldn't have hesitated to send a reporter to dig up gossip on the tawdry affairs or divorces of any well-known politicians…or movie stars…or evangelists. "Throw in a little violence, and it'd be cinched. If it bleeds, it leads. It's stories like those that get labeled the trial of the century or the story of the century. Well, this really is one of the biggest stories of the century…and it's not like I was beaten out of it by another reporter. My editor and publisher just aren't interested in doing the story at all."

She told him that even the broadcast media, which must have recognized the enormity of the event and been willing to put some money into covering it, seemed to shift their focus away after a rather short time. Much too quickly for her, the whole episode was consigned to that mysterious netherworld of "yesterday's news."

"But, Max," she'd continued, "this story isn't going to go away."

"Patty, it doesn't matter if the press reports about it or not," he assured her, explaining that the international sequence of events that had been put into motion by the fall of communism couldn't be relegated to the closet for very long on the world stage.

"Why not?"

"Because, my dear, it's too much of a shift. Too much has been set in motion. Barriers have been broken. The Berlin Wall was simply a symbolic metaphor for the divisions in our world—and in our lives—coming down. Whenever you tear down a structure like that, things are going to come spilling out. That's what you need to be in tune to and watch for."

Trish couldn't understand why. What difference did it make what came spilling out if no one was given free rein to report it?

If nothing else, she thought it said reams about everyone's competency, both the media's and the government's, that they were caught completely off guard by the fall of communism. With all of their resources, they both missed the signals entirely. She thought that fact alone should have prompted a serious bout of soul searching.

But it didn't seem to.

● ● ●

While Trish walked, she rubbed the sweat from one of her hands on the side of her overalls, and in doing so, felt her waist. She'd promised herself she was going to lose ten pounds. Three years ago. She couldn't imagine how she hadn't sweated them away in the previous sweltering weeks.

The changes in her body had been on her mind for a long time and, along with the frustrations with her career, had evolved into a nagging worry. Even though she didn't think her physical appearance had changed that much since she'd been in her twenties—and though she still wore a size seven dress—she was well aware, whenever she looked in the mirror naked, that the gravity of the previous two decades was catching up with her.

She found herself devoting more and more time to exercise, to stave off the sag of her buttocks and the girth of her waist. Even her breasts were taking on a more pendulous curve, and she was thankful she was still having regular periods, with their accompanying monthly dosages of estrogen. In previous years she'd seen more than one friend or contemporary quickly become wrinkled and dowdy after an early menopause or hysterectomy. At least her ovaries were good for something, and at least—she tried to comfort herself—she didn't have stretch marks from any pregnancies. A hint of crows' feet when she laughed and a barely perceptible sag in the lower half of her face seemed to be the only outwardly visible vestiges of her years of hard work and struggle.

Trish had to laugh at the irony of her situation. Nothing at all had changed for her in the previous two and a half decades in spite of all her well-laid intentions to get off of the farm, to become a successful career woman and, eventually, a wife and mother. The children never came, and now she accepted that they never would. Her marriage had ended in divorce after only five years when she was in her twenties, and though she was aware that she could still turn heads on occasion—and never failed to take notice whenever she did—her romantic life had been anything but satisfying or stable.

The career as a reporter in the big city had been less than remarkable. And a couple of years before, when her parents had died only a few months apart—her mother in a car accident and her father six months later of a heart attack—they'd left her their land and farmhouse in their will. It was her only asset. So there she was, after all, back on the farm, the farm from which she had tried so hard to escape, feeling that all of the careful, thoughtful, meticulous planning she'd done in plotting her future life—all of it—was down the drain.

If it hadn't been for her parents' deaths, coupled with those years of professional disillusions, she knew that she might still be back in Cleveland, Ohio, pounding away at a computer, with no thought of leaving a job that paid a decent salary—even though she'd felt far from satisfied with her work for a long, long time.

Trish never understood why her parents distributed their estate the way they did in their will. They left her two older sisters their house in the town of Clayton and the family business—which was a furniture store on the square. And they left her the farm. She'd originally thought about selling it. Yet, when she mentioned that possibility to her sisters, they had recoiled in horror.

"You can't *do* that, Patty," Carol Anne stated with a look of disbelief.

"Mom and Dad would turn over in their grave," Marsha glowered. "You *know* how much the farm meant to them."

It was the final straw. She couldn't see alienating what was left of her family, so she'd quit her job in Cleveland, sold her condominium, and moved back home to lick her wounds. When she got there, she quickly secured what she thought would be a temporary job at the local paper. At the time she'd almost felt insulted that the local editor, Tom Buffington—a former upper classman from high school—didn't seem to notice or appreciate the fact that she was vastly overqualified for the position.

"He probably doesn't want to have to acknowledge that I'm also under-paid," she'd told her friend, Kathy. "Still, it's a job I know how to do. And I think the salary will sustain me in the short term. I never did try reporting before in my own home town. Maybe it'll be better here. We'll see." Trish paused in the shade of a tree to take another drink of water. *Well, we saw all right.* It was during the very first month at her new job that she heard Tom Buffington pose the question: "Hey, if a meeting takes place in town, and *The Clayton Times* doesn't cover it, did it really happen?" By the way everyone laughed she could tell it was a popular inside joke. There in that small newsroom, she realized with defeat that she'd come full circle in her career. Only the name of the small town was different...and the name of the local newspaper.

And she was twenty-five years older.

• • •

Trish couldn't believe it was only a week ago that she found out about a chemical company making inquiries about locating in Clayton. No one knew anything about them. And no one was asking any questions. She assumed that was the job of the newspaper and called Tom's attention to it.

He immediately waved off her concerns. "Don't make trouble where there's not any. Besides, you need to get busy on that story about the Chamber's fundraiser."

It was back to Bowling Green all over again. Only this time she wasn't green; she was a seasoned reporter with a lot more experience. And this wasn't a town she was passing through on her way to bigger and better career opportunities. This was her home town. She owned a piece of it. And what was left of her family lived here.

"Tom, how do we know there's not a problem with this company if we don't ask a few questions?"

"If the state of Georgia issues them a permit, that's good enough for me." He turned back to his paperwork.

She stood staring at his back. He couldn't be that naïve.

After taking a deep breath, she said, "Oh, really? Well, the state of Georgia issued a permit to a respectable, innocuous sounding company mak-ing watches in Athens while I was at college, and they'd gone bankrupt by the time anyone realized they'd left radioactive contamination behind in friggin' downtown. It turned into a damn Superfund site. I don't want to see anything like that happen in Clayton."

He swiveled back toward her slowly, scowling. "God, you're paranoid."

She simply stared at him a moment, infuriated that he'd turned his lack of a credible response into a personal attack on her. Then she stormed out of the room.

A few days later, after Jim Peterson from the Chamber of Commerce told Tom that she'd been calling the company and the state Environmental Protection Department asking questions about the company's inventory and permit application, Tom told her he couldn't put up with insolence from an employee.

"I wasn't asking questions as a reporter," she retorted. "I was asking them as a private citizen."

"Well, you can't be a reporter *and* an activist. I won't tolerate your becoming part of a story. It's unprofessional."

"*What* story?" she shot back. "According to you, there *is* no story." She let out a breath and added, "And maybe there's not. But how do we know if we don't ask a few questions? Besides, you seem to 'tolerate' my writing a column that's nothing but free advertising for the Chamber fairly well. If that's not taking a political position, I don't know what is."

From there, the conversation went rapidly downhill, with her demanding to know which local bank was negotiating with the company about financing and how financially dependent the paper was on that bank's advertising. She couldn't back down. Not this time.

By lunchtime, she'd lost both her appetite and her job. As the conversation had escalated, she'd thought about quitting, but before she got the chance, he'd fired her.

She'd never been fired before. The shock of it felt much like the divorce, like failure and humiliation. She knew that by the end of the week, everyone in town would know about it. And they wouldn't understand the dynamics. They wouldn't know that she'd only been trying to do her job.

After she got home, her shock shifted to a variety of other emotions. All of the frustrations of devoting her life to the industry, and being treated like another expendable cog in the wheel, left her feeling empty and angry. She was even angry for never taking a sick day in her two years with the paper, and that she'd always worked well over forty hours a week with no overtime. It had always simply been expected that she'd work off the clock—without even the acknowledgement of a "thank you."

She stopped and closed her eyes. *God, what was I thinking? Who did I think I was, anyway, to think I could come back into this environment and not meet some resistance?*

She opened her eyes again and looked up. How much more did the universe want from her? She'd lost her parents, given up a decent paying job with a large newspaper and now she'd been fired from an unknown, small town paper.

In her entire life, she couldn't remember ever feeling so vulnerable.

Chapter Two

When she topped the crest of the hill, Trish saw her house at a short distance. She was pleased with the way it looked, tucked in amongst the huge oak trees, with its fresh coats of white paint and new green shutters, much like a scene set on canvas. A small wave of pride swept over her; even though the renovations had been more costly than she'd expected, they'd turned out beautifully.

She stopped a moment, closed her eyes and took a breath. Just at that moment she felt a strange, ghostly waft of air like the one she'd felt earlier at the garden. She breathed it in again, and out. And again, when she opened her eyes and glanced around, it had vanished as though it had never been there. She shivered involuntarily, then grasped her upper arms, rubbing them vigorously. *What was that?*

Trying to dismiss the incident, she focused instead on getting out of the heat. She crossed the yard to the back porch and entered through the creaky screen door. As she opened and shut the inner door, the change from the ninety plus degree weather outside to the chill of the air conditioning inside felt instantly refreshing. Immediately she went to the kitchen sink, washed her hands, then cupped them under the faucet and splashed water on her face and the back of her neck. "*God*, that feels good," she sighed. She grabbed a dishtowel and dried her face and hands.

As her eyes began adjusting to the darker interior of the house, she glanced around and noticed her fluffy orange cat, Muffin, asleep on the chair. She walked over and reached down to pet him. He lifted his head from sleep in acknowledgment, uttered a brief chirp, then stretched and yawned. She scratched him under his chin and spoke to him in baby talk. "Yes, yes…I see how hard you've been working, too."

As she walked through the house, she glanced around. In her attempts to modernize it, she had struggled to maintain its charm and history. Family antiques still graced the rooms, juxtaposed with modern replica pieces she had purchased. The stark expressions of her ancestors still gazed at her from old, sepia portraits held in antique frames, contrasting with the more recent colored family prints that beamed constant smiles of approval.

Trish had converted one of the bedrooms into a computer room. There framed awards for her work as a reporter hung alongside her college diploma and other announcements of her accomplishments—all reminders of a life that she had lived and was living.

She'd taken great pains to assure that the house reflected the person she had become, while still embracing the person she'd been, and she thought she had accomplished that. But for all the displays of past and present that

19

surrounded her like a map of her life, she realized that there was no clue here of where she was going.

Still, there were those moments—those stories in the news that would grab her in the pit of her stomach, like the story she had watched on television just a few months before when her reporter's urge to dig had been re-ignited.

• • •

Trish walked over to the sofa, sat down and stared at the blank television screen. On the spring day when she'd first planted the garden, she'd watched a program on it that made everything in her body and her mind shift. As she looked back at the memory, she could still see the program playing out in bits and pieces in her mind's eye

Ed Bradley was talking on screen about a place called Semipalatinsk, a city in Kazakhstan, which was the heart of the Soviet's nuclear testing program during the Cold War. She'd stayed seated on the edge of the sofa as she watched, unable to take her eyes off the television.

Pictures of atomic bomb blasts flashed on the screen as Bradley spoke about the hundreds of explosions that had occurred near the edge of the city during the fifties and through the end of the Cold War. Person after person related stories on camera about the atomic testing and about the sicknesses—cancers and birth defects—that their families, friends and neighbors had experienced during the period of the atomic bomb testing. The camera panned a cemetery, filled with headstones, as Bradley noted that many of the markers from the decades following the fifties bore significantly lower death ages than previous grave markers from the past. People in Semipalatinsk were dying much younger than they had been before the beginning of the Cold War.

In one scene, clad in a protective white suit, complete with oxygen mask, Bradley stood beside what he called an atomic lake, as he related how it had become radioactive and would remain that way for many centuries into the future due to atomic bomb blasts. A Geiger counter was turned on and began clicking loudly to emphasize the point.

Trish hurried to the kitchen to grab a soft drink from the refrigerator. She returned to the sofa just in time to see Bradley interviewing a Russian doctor. English captions were blipped on the screen as the doctor spoke. He related that he and other doctors had worked in a museum during the Cold War, secretly documenting the health effects of the atmospheric testing on the local populace. They didn't treat the people, but simply documented any illnesses that might be attributed to nuclear exposure. The Soviet government wanted to gauge the effects of enormous amounts of radiation on local populations and on human DNA. The doctors were collecting data...and fetal genetic specimens.

At that point the camera focused on a section of the museum called Clinic Number Four, panning several rows of shelves holding wide-mouthed glass jars, each appearing to be two to three gallons in size. Each held a deformed human fetus. She knew that the grotesque sights would likely make most people flip to another channel, but her reporter's curiosity held her transfixed on the screen.

One specimen had a single eye in the middle of its forehead, and didn't look human or real, but rather like something produced in Hollywood for one of their high budget movies. Bradley spoke of other fetal mutants in the jars...one with two heads and one with the lower body like a fish and a human looking upper body. The doctors were now going public with the information about what happened in the clinic because the Cold War was over, because they were finally independent from Russia and because they wanted the world to know what had happened there.

When the segment was over Trish had turned off the television and sat for a long time in stunned silence. Max had been right. Things were starting to spill out.

The report had grabbed her in a way no other had. Since returning to Clayton and working with two environmental activists who were well versed in nuclear issues, Trish had come to believe that any other environmental issues paled in comparison to nuclear ones. This story drove that fact home. Her initial reaction was to find out more, but she knew she could never pursue it, not while working for *The Clayton Times*. Still, the story haunted her and kept her awake at bedtime. The images in the program struck her—not only on an obvious, surface level—but on a deep, almost ancient, psychic level. They stirred her blood and kept intruding on her thoughts, like a nightmare she couldn't shake.

It puzzled her that she couldn't relegate the story to the recesses of her mind and memory. But it refused to be forgotten, refused to stay buried. For that reason, it seemed this story—of all the stories she had seen and heard before—was her reporter's Holy Grail. She was convinced that the report had just scratched the surface, that there was an even more incredible story behind it—one begging to be told, screaming to be heard.

● ● ●

Trish was still staring at the blank television screen, caught up in her memory of the program, when she heard a car drive up in her gravel driveway. She pushed aside her thoughts, hurried to look out the kitchen window, and saw Kathy Dunnigan getting out of her car. Trish grinned sideways.

Kathryn Dunnigan had remained her best friend through grade school, high school and her entire adult life. Even though their lives had taken very different courses and a lot of time and distance had separated them over the years, they always managed to pick up right where they left off whenever they got back together. In short order they'd revert back to giggling like schoolgirls, catching up on the latest gossip and fixing each other's hair in different, new styles.

Kathy still called her "Patty," just as she'd done most of her life. When Trish decided in junior high school to adopt a more sophisticated version of her given name "Patricia," she never could get her to break the habit. She'd long ago given up trying to persuade Kathy to accept her new moniker, and had eventually come to view it as a sweet reminder of the days when they were just "Patty" and "Kathy," two little girls exploring the world together with complete abandon.

Trish thought of her friend now as a good-looking, earthy, irreverent, mouthy, Southern broad...and it was simply fun to be around her. Though Kathy had married straight out of high school and had three children—all practically grown—and though she was thoroughly ensconced in the rural lifestyle, she'd always taken pride in Trish's accomplishments in the big city. Renewing their friendship had been one of the few bright spots in her move back home...that, and finally being able to live close to her long time friend, Max Rogers.

He and his wife Rachel had moved to Clayton shortly after his retirement, and Trish had remained close to them, in spite of any separations of time or distance. Sharing their crises had made Max seem more like a father than a mentor.

Trish walked out onto to the back porch to greet Kathy, who was carrying a covered dish and two plastic grocery sacks. Trish took the dish, as they hugged in greeting, then drew back quickly. "Hey, you don't want to get any of this grime off my clothes."

"Oh, don't worry about that," Kathy responded, edging her way into the kitchen door with her load of edibles. "With three kids, I'm used to dirt. I just brought you a little lunch. I didn't figure you'd had a decent meal in a while...the way you hate to cook."

Trish noted how fresh and vibrant Kathy looked on such a hot day, as her friend wasted little time busying herself in the cool of the kitchen. Even after motherhood, Kathy was still incredibly pretty and trim for her age; still blond, with the regular help of bottled hair color; and—to Trish's great relief—she was still the Kathy she'd always known.

"Oh, Kathy, you know I don't hate to cook. It's just that it's hard to cook for one person. Besides it's too hot to eat. I've been out in the garden most of the morning, pounding a posthole digger. Those damn cows got loose from the Davis's farm again, and knocked down the fence this time…and I feel like I've about melted."

"Oh, this isn't anything too heavy. It's Mama's cold cucumber salad and a squash casserole."

While Kathy deposited items from the grocery sack into the refrigerator and freezer, Trish sat down at the table and lifted the lid off one of the dishes. She breathed in the aroma of Italian dressing, and reached into the bowl with her fingers and sampled a couple of cucumbers. "Mmm," she intoned, "this is perfect."

As Kathy pulled silverware and plates from the cabinets and drawers to set the table, she said, "Well, everybody needs to be pampered once in a while." Then she took glasses from the cabinets, filled them with ice and poured their tea. Trish kept seated at the table and watched her. She recognized Kathy's "in charge" manner whenever she saw it. At those times it was best to just keep out of her way. As she watched her, it was also clear that Kathy was avoiding the obvious. She'd called Kathy the day she was fired and assumed her visit was probably more about commiseration than making sure she was getting the proper nutrition. But she'd play along for a while.

"Seen Max lately?" Kathy inquired off-handedly, as she finally joined Trish at the table and spread her napkin in her lap.

"Yeah, we went out to eat a couple of weeks ago to celebrate his birthday," Trish responded, as she took one scoop each of the squash casserole and cucumber salad.

"How's he doing?"

"Great…as usual…keeps busy with his books and his computer."

"How's that book of his coming along?"

"Oh, he doesn't talk about it much. But I know it's not like the first two he had published. It's more of a compilation of essays and short stories and poems he's written over the years." Trish set the serving spoon back, smiled and leaned onto the table. "He still calls me 'Patty.' "

"Yeah?" Kathy asked with a slight smile.

"Yeah…thanks to you I guess. I wish I'd never mentioned that name when I first met him and Rachel at college."

"Hey, I never even *met* them till they moved to Clayton, so you can't lay that one on me."

The Rogers had begun calling Trish by her childhood name when she mentioned it early in their relationship. She wasn't miffed about it, the way she had been when she finally had to accept that her family and Kathy were never going to call her anything else, no matter how much she begged and reminded them. She never would have imagined being saddled with the name Patty again with anyone in college, but when the couple seemed to latch onto it, she simply accepted it. She'd fought all the battles she ever wanted to over her name. They, in turn, asked her to call them by their first names instead of the more formal "Dr." and "Mrs. Rogers." It was easy, as Trish had never been in any of Max's classes.

"How's he holding up in this heat?" Kathy asked, as she scooped salad onto her plate.

"He seems to be doing all right." She grinned sideways. "He's got more sense than I've got…going out working in the hot sun."

"Oh, Patty, why don't you just let that garden go?" Kathy asked with a hint of aggravation in her voice. "Lord knows, you give more of them away than you eat; it's not worth the time and energy you put into it. And, damn, I don't know how you're growing anything in this drought, anyway."

Trish grinned. "You know, I've just been asking myself why I don't let it go." She picked up her fork and left it suspended in the air a moment as she stared forward. "Maybe because Mom had it as far back as I can remember. When we were kids I always loved working in it with her." She pushed her food around in her plate. "You know how proud she always was of that garden."

Kathy nodded. Then, as she reached for the casserole dish, she said almost casually, "Say, Patty, by the way, I heard around town that Jimmy Hartwell got a divorce some time back."

Trish's hand brushed against her glass and almost tipped it as she was reaching for the salt and pepper. She managed to catch the glass just before its contents spilled across the table. "What? *Again?*" she replied, trying not to call attention to the slip of her hand. But she could see from her friend's eye movements that she had noticed it—without comment.

"Oh, come on now, Patty. Give that poor man a break. He was madly in love with you in high school."

"Yeah? If he was so crazy about me, why'd he get married to someone else as soon as I left for college?" Trish looked straight at her friend and cocked her head to one side. "This little tidbit of information wouldn't be the purpose of your visit, now would it? Now that I'm out of a job, you're trying to hook me up with someone?"

"Huh? Why, of *course* not, Patty. I'm surprised at you," she answered with a look bordering on indignation.

Trish ignored her disclaimer, with only a mumbled, "hmm," and continued eating.

Kathy told her that Jimmy had simply been on the rebound after she left. She leaned forward slightly. "You know that marriage didn't last six months. You were the one he really wanted. In fact, I never saw anyone as much in love as he was with you."

"Jimmy John loves *everybody*, Kathy," Trish shot back. Then propping her hands against the side of the table, she added, "Hell, he *marries* everybody."

"Oh, come on now," Kathy said, flipping her napkin. "He's only been married three times. And personally, I think he was just trying to find someone to measure up to you…and no one ever must have. By the way," she added, in a tone tinged with coyness, "have you seen him since you moved back to town?"

"Oh, I've seen him a few times," Trish replied, trying to sound as nonchalant as possible.

"He still looks good, doesn't he?" Kathy quizzed, with a mischievous grin.

Trish sighed wearily and stared toward the window. "Oh, I guess so." Then she looked back at Kathy with a slight smile and added, "…if you like that rugged, lean, *masculine* look."

Kathy chuckled, as Trish returned her attention to her food, smiling.

● ● ●

After they'd finished their lunch, Trish propped onto the table and looked directly at Kathy. "So, tell me, are you here to console me or cheer me up?"

Kathy grinned. "Which would you prefer?"

Trish let out a breath, then leaned back in her chair and stretched. She remembered that Kathy had put something in the refrigerator and freezer. A grin came over her face. "I don't guess you brought one of your Mama's pies for dessert, did you?" Trish and Kathy had spent so much time together when they were growing up that Kathy's mother often treated her like a second daughter.

"As a matter of fact, she did send you an apple pie when she found out I was on my way over here…and I stopped at the store and picked up a half gallon of ice cream to go with it."

They both squealed in unison as they jumped up and raced to the refrigerator together. Kathy got the ice cream out of the freezer section, while Trish pulled the pie out of the refrigerator. Then, as Kathy sliced and served the pie into bowls and dug into the ice cream, Trish told her seriously, "Now, I want lots of ice cream, Kathy. If you'd told me about the pie beforehand, I'd have never eaten any of the casserole."

Kathy swiveled toward her with her hand on her hip. "I swear, Patricia Cagle, you're worse than my kids."

As they sat back down and began eating their dessert, Kathy asked, "So tell me: what do you plan to do now?"

Trish set her spoon down and leaned onto the table on her forearms. "Shit, I don't have any idea. I was barely squeaking by on the salary at the *Times* as it was." She dabbed her mouth with her napkin. "But you know,

Kathy, I really would like to go to Russia to do some investigative reporting on something I saw on TV a few months back." She told Kathy about her desire to go there since the dismantling of the Berlin Wall. She lamented, however, that there was no way now she could manage it. "And, hell, even if I *was* working for a paper that could afford it, I don't think that kind of reporting—the Watergate kind of reporting—is even possible today." She told her that with the present atmosphere and dynamics that existed in the news industry, due to downsizing and consolidation, the range of "coverable news" was just too limited, the budgets too tight.

Trish sighed and rested her forehead on the back of her hand. "Oh, God, here I go again." Over the years she had shared so many of her frustrations related to her work with Kathy, that she thought she'd probably overworked the topic with her friend.

Kathy waved her hand. "That's okay. Anything bad you want to say about the news media is fine with me. They're right up there with lawyers and used car salesmen, as far as I'm concerned." She returned to her dessert, and Trish returned to the aggravation that had been needling her all morning.

Leaning outstretched over the table, she said, "Kathy, if you knew how many times I saw news stories slanted to keep from alienating the papers' biggest advertisers, and how many times I heard about my bosses socializing with the big-shot community power brokers, who they *should* have been putting under a microscope for some of the things they were involved in...well, it'd blow you off your seat.

"And," she continued, feeling as though she had to get it all off her chest at one time, "they write editorial after editorial condemning censorship, when they're the very ones engaging in the worst form of it." She waved a hand in the air. "They just do it by refusing to cover certain stories." She leaned back hard enough in her wooden seat to make it creak. At times she thought it was deliberate, and at others she thought it was out of sheer incompetence. She didn't think economic, environmental or social issues were covered the way they needed to be because offending advertisers came with a price tag. "Anybody who still thinks we've got a free press in this country is damned naive."

Kathy broke in for the first time. "Yeah, but we've got a better shot at it than most countries."

Trish sighed. "Yeah...that's been one glimmer of hope I've been able to hang onto for the last couple of decades...plus the few reporters and editors around who still care about the news." She added, "The problem is, they're not considered the cream of the crop by industry." She explained that the ones who still maintained a strong commitment to the public's right to know were often treated like troublemakers and were steadily leaving the profession, unable to maintain the energy it took to get real news published. Kathy wagged her empty spoon in the air toward Trish. "Like you?"

Trish shrugged her shoulders and pushed her bowl away, abandoning her remaining dessert. She told Kathy that most reporters were smart enough to figure out which advertisers were off limits. "You knew who wasn't supposed to be riled by the more probing questions, regardless of any conflict of interest they might be engaged in. Only positive, fluff stories could be written about them—the ones we called 'blow jobs.'"

Kathy raised her eyebrows and grinned.

"Well, I didn't give blow jobs, and I was damn tired of fluff stories every time I got into hot water over trying to follow the rules of journalism I'd learned in college." She held out a hand. "Hell, Mom and Dad paid a shit load of money for me to get that education. And then I get out in the real world and find out how manipulated the whole process is." She was irritated and demoralized by watching the "real" news replaced by distractions and gossip on a more and more frequent basis. The class was going out of the news business. Most of it had degenerated to appealing to the lowest public common denominator, with the lines between tabloid press and mainstream media growing more blurred by the day. "The majority of stories were the easy ones…'talking head' interviews, with no thorough, independent research behind them. No one wants to go out on a limb any more." Trish failed to add that she had been pushed back from that limb so many times that she'd almost given up trying.

"What kinds of things got squelched?" By now Kathy had abandoned her dessert, as well.

"Wait. Let's go sit in the living room. I'll clean this stuff up later."

● ● ●

Curled up at one end the sofa with her feet pulled up under her, Trish began her story, as Kathy faced her from the other end. "I had this colleague from Cincinnati. He'd been assigned to some of the first reporting on AIDS for his paper." The man firmly believed that if the media had sounded the alarm soon enough and loud enough, the epidemic might have been stopped.

"Really?" Kathy asked, tilting her head.

"Yeah. One night a bunch of us got together for drinks after a Press Association meeting. He told how he kept trying to get his editors to realize that the government and the CDC were engaging in a lot of whitewashing about the severity of the disease. But they kept treating him like Chicken Little. Hell, *he* didn't want to believe they were lying, either. But you dig long enough and you realize when you're not getting the straight skinny.

"Then by the time everybody realized the scope of the thing, he said it was too late. It was too widespread. He couldn't even remember the local stories that filled the front pages of the paper during that time. The guy took a drink from his glass after that and slammed it down hard on the table. Then everybody stayed quiet for a while till the topic turned to something else." She shrugged a shoulder. "Hell, we all had some kind of war story like that."

"So what's the deal with this chemical company? Are they really coming to Clayton?"

"It doesn't look like it. The word is that, just like in Bowling Green, the minute I started asking questions, they started to lose interest in locating here."

Kathy sighed audibly. "Well, thank God for that." She put her arm onto the back of the sofa. "So what's this story in Russia you want to do?"

"Well," Trish began, tilting her head, "I've always thought we should be looking harder at the environmental consequences of the Cold War. But hell, it's hard enough just to get them to look at the economic ones. Then, a couple of months ago I saw this program on "60 Minutes.""

Trish began telling Kathy about the report that had piqued her interest. After a few minutes Kathy suddenly sat up straighter and broke in. "Patty, I saw that one; it was horrid." Her eyes widened, and she added, "Hey…why don't you just go on your own, and sell the story…you know, like, freelance, or whatever?"

Trish let out half a laugh. "What I ought to be doing is freshening up my resume and sending it out to every paper around the country, instead of knocking myself out in the garden." She rested her head on her hand. "Thing is, it doesn't look so great to say that your last job was in Small-town, U.S.A., much less that you've just been fired from it."

Trish leaned forward and looked at her friend. "Even if I *got* another job with another paper, I don't know what I'd do about this farm…maybe rent it out or something. But I hate to think about doing that after all the money I just put in it." She leaned back. "Kathy, I really *do* like being back home. It's just this damn profession that drives me crazy.'

She tilted her head. "Believe it or not, I actually *thought* about doing a freelance story. But I don't know how I'd pay for a trip to Russia…or find someone to look after the farm for me…or even take care of Muffin." She motioned her head toward the big orange cat still asleep on the chair. "I don't have any assurances that I could peddle a story like that. And I doubt I could even make enough to cover my expenses, if I *could* sell it."

Kathy didn't respond, and Trish looked up and saw that her friend was eyeing her closely. Kathy kept her eyes on her a moment longer, then leaned forward. When she began speaking, it was slowly, as though choosing her words with careful deliberation. "Patty, I've loved having you back home.

It's really made my life seem more complete to have my best friend here to talk to and visit with." She shook her head. "But I know deep down in my heart that you haven't been happy with your work here."

She told her that she'd always believed Trish was destined for bigger and better things than working for the local rag. She'd observed Trish's insatiable curiosity about life for years and listened mesmerized at the wonderful ideas in her head. She smiled sideways and tilted her head. "Why don't you just *go* for it?" She leaned back. "You know you won't be happy till you do. So you don't make any money; you could always think of it as an investment in getting your name back in the market."

"But it's more than that, Kathy." Trish sighed, letting out almost all of the air in her lungs, then propping her head on her hand. "My whole life hasn't worked out like I'd planned. I feel like I'm just floundering through it. I've had some time the last few days to do some evaluating…and I'm still at loose ends." Trish folded her arms and stared at the wall. "You know, I always wanted to be an independent person, and now I just feel alone. I thought I was going to change the world, and I can't even change my own life. And you're right—I'm not happy, and I don't quite know why."

She looked back at Kathy. "I thought about selling just *part* of the farm to finance the trip, but Mother would roll over in her grave if I did that…and Susan and Carol Ann would croak over it." She added in a sarcastic tone, "They've made that perfectly clear on more than one occasion."

Kathy abruptly interrupted her. "Patricia Cagle, you're sitting here telling me all these reasons you can't cover this story, and all I'm hearing is a lot of boundaries you've constructed yourself. Hell, *I'll* take the damn cat. Now we've got *that* little problem covered."

Trish felt a little taken aback, as Kathy continued in her strident tone, "What do you think your mother would have wanted for you, anyway? As full a life as possible? Or one stuck here on this farm the rest of your life— filled with regret and bitterness." She motioned in the air and rolled her eyes upward. "Hell, she's probably rolling over in her grave right now because of your attitude. This just isn't like you."

By now Trish felt fully stung and somewhat defensive by her friend's sudden aggression. "And just how do you think I can manage the finances?"

"How the hell should *I* know?" she asked, shrugging her shoulders. "But I know one thing for sure: you're smart enough to figure it out. Besides, haven't you ever heard that a life without risk is a life half-lived?"

In a tone edged with bitterness, Trish said, "I'm already living half a life."

Instead of the sympathy Trish expected, her friend crossed her arms and turned on her again. "Please, not the old childless routine again."

Trish's expression shifted to one of controlled anger, but Kathy continued unintimidated. She uncrossed her arms and leaned forward, easing her tone somewhat. "Patty, these stories you do *are* your children, whether you know it or not. I've seen you in action. You plant the seeds and nurture them. You give them life and then present them to the world. God, I've got kids crawling all over me, and I envy the creative talents and abilities you've got at the tip of your fingers. They're rare gifts." She took a deep breath and let it out again. "If you had real children, wouldn't you be willing to *die* for them? Wouldn't you risk everything to give them life?"

She smiled sideways and let out a breath. "Come to think of it, whenever your mother showed me some of your columns, you'd have thought she was showing pictures of grandchildren—she was so proud." She reminded Trish she didn't have anyone she had to placate or even any boss to constrain her any more. "Most women in this town feel trapped. And some are jealous of the kind of freedom you have." Holding her hand out, she added, "I know it probably feels like you're at the end of your rope here. But, God, Patty— with no job, no solid relationship, no prospects—what have you got to lose? Hell, every door in the universe is open to you. You may never have this kind of freedom again.

"Good gosh, we're just talking about living expenses here—electric bills and crap like that—and a little old trip to Russia. I know you, Patty; you could swing something like that without even ruffling your hair…if you really wanted to." Kathy stopped long enough to catch her breath, then added tenderly, "I don't mean to be so blunt with you, but it just makes me angry when you don't appreciate yourself the way I do."

Trish sat silently and gazed toward the window a moment, allowing her friend's powerful and unexpected comments to sink in. Within a relatively short visit, they had managed to touch on three of the most sensitive topics in her life: her career, her childlessness and Jimmy Hartwell.

Finally, still staring toward the window, she broke the silence, "Kathy, sometimes I hate the things you say to me." Then she turned and faced her with a look of resignation, "But I know I need to hear them." She smiled. "You're the only friend I've got who'll risk kicking me in the butt when I need it." She leaned forward and tilted her head. "You wouldn't happen to be one of the women in town jealous of my freedom, would you?"

Kathy smiled sideways. "Oh, a little, I guess." Then she added, "But it may surprise you to know that I've really enjoyed this homebody thing: the kids, the husband, the Easter egg hunts. Mostly I think I just missed you." She grinned again and added, "But, there *are* a few who were just gourd green with envy that you were a successful, professional woman working in the big city."

Trish grinned back and asked, "Tell me…who?"

Kathy feigned an air of maturity, as she lowered her eyelids and turned her head slightly. "Now, Patty, that is *so* childish. And I don't have any intention in engaging in gossip with you."

"Since *when*?" Trish asked, raising her eyebrows.

Kathy wiggled slightly in her seat and leaned forward. "Well, since you asked, the truth is that Lavinia Mercer can't resist taking a pot shot at you every chance she gets."

"Really?"

"Oh, *yeah*," she responded. "Didn't you know she still resents that Jimmy Hartwell dumped her for you in high school?"

"No," Trish answered, fully surprised. "That's a long time to carry a grudge."

"Oh, I wouldn't give it a second thought," she said with a wave of her hand. "Hell, everything sticks in that woman's craw. She went to seed a long time ago, and she even resents anyone who's thinner than she is…and that's most of the town."

Trish giggled. "Kathryn Dunnigan, you're terrible."

Then, with a look of mock fear, Kathy added, "Her ass is so big, it's *scary*."

"Kathy!"

"You know what I mean, 'Be afraid. Be ve..e..ery afraid.'"

Trish laughed again, the room echoing with happy sounds.

The two of them continued reminiscing and joking about the good old days, then ended their visit with a hug at Trish's door. As she watched Kathy leave, Trish was acutely aware of how Kathy always seemed like a breath of fresh air when she needed it most. And the fresh air she'd breathed that day over lunch had begun blowing life back into her, along with a sense of direction and focus.

Just before going back inside to load her dishwasher, Trish felt that mysterious draft again. She breathed it in again, but this time, when it disappeared, she simply looked around with curiosity and returned to the kitchen.

But something felt strangely different as she went through the rest of her day. Something in her mind had started turning. Something brittle inside her did seem to have broken. Kathy was right. What else did she have left to lose? Maybe she *would* go to Russia and get her story. She didn't allow the thought to rise to the level of commitment, until she picked up the latest edition of *The Clayton Times* and reread the last column she'd written before being fired. It was a report on the fluctuating prices of gasoline in town.

She lowered the paper and shook her head. She was absolutely certain. That wasn't how she wanted to spend the rest of her life…not when another life was out there waiting for her…calling to her.

Kathy's kick in the butt had met its mark.

Chapter Three

As Trish began preparations for her trip to Kazakhstan, securing financing for the trip was her first consideration. Then she would focus on research, making contacts with people to meet and interview there, and creating an itinerary.

The first category proved less daunting than expected. Even when she factored in money for food, lodging, train and taxi fares, she discovered that a trip to Kazakhstan didn't cost nearly as much as she'd imagined. Though refurbishing the farmhouse had drained much of her savings, enough remained from selling her condo in Cleveland to cover her expenses. It wouldn't be enough to do broad investigation, but that didn't matter. The environmental consequences of the Cold War were her main concerns. She'd leave the financial costs of the War up to the bean counters.

Yet, as she began narrowing her focus out of necessity, it riled her that those bean counters never factored many of the real Cold War costs into any of their equations, such as the clean-up of contaminated nuclear sites around the world, which she'd learned from environmental sources could easily run into the hundreds of billions of dollars. She also felt a sense of frustration in the pervasive public belief that a nuclear "clean-up" was even possible. She'd learned from those same sources that the most anyone could hope for in a best-case scenario—with unlimited funds and total political backing—would only be nuclear "containment." Many of the contaminated sites would inevitably remain radioactive for tens and even hundreds of thousands of years.

• • •

Trish divided her subject research into two sub-categories. Within her time and budget constraints, she'd first lay out a map of everything she needed to know about Russian history, culture and politics. Then, on top of that background, she'd focus on the subject of the nuclear arms race itself and the history of the atomic age.

Late one afternoon when she first began her research, she sat reading and taking notes at a table in the main library at the University of Georgia with books stacked and opened before her. After a couple of hours, she looked up and ran her pen back and forth in her hand, feeling amazed on a personal level—and a little embarrassed, as a reporter—at her lack of knowledge about an area that had been of such strategic importance in the world, particularly during the Cold War.

That afternoon she learned that Kazakhstan had been one of fifteen Soviet Republics that had made up the Union of Soviet Socialist Republics.

Being located on the southeastern side of the Soviet Union, just south of Russia and north of China, left it sandwiched between two super powers. Its eastern side was bordered by Mongolia. The country encompassed over a million square miles with a population of over seventeen million citizens. She discovered that it had been the second largest republic in the Soviet Union, and though the Aral Sea lay at its southern edge and the Caspian Sea sat at its western, the middle part of the country was wide, extensive desert.

She also learned that from the fifteenth to the nineteenth centuries, Russia had embarked on a campaign of huge geographical expansion that encompassed vast areas of non-Russian populations. It was during that time that Kazakhstan became part of the Russian Empire. It became clear to Trish during her reading that the Kazakhs had probably resisted Russian domination harder than any other ethnic people. They fought valiantly for decades to maintain their independence and identity, but eventually—during the mid-1700s to the 1800s—what had been known as the "khanate" system was replaced by the tsarist regime of Russia.

Even then, for years, the Kazakhs had continued to rebel against Russian rule. Many of them were killed when they refused to serve in the Russian military during World War I. In spite of that, Russia maintained its control of the indigenous people.

As she sat in front of her stack of books, Trish read that the creation of the republics had been Lenin's idea. He expressly wanted ethnic, indigenous people treated more justly than they had been in the past. Their treatment under the tsarist regimes hadn't worked, so creation of the republics allowed the people to maintain their ethnic loyalties to a large degree. Trish leaned back in her seat and—as she see-sawed her pen between her fingers—silently reasoned that Lenin's idea had probably been a smart political change in attitude. The idea of the republics must have quieted a lot of discontent out in the hinterlands of such a large country—large and difficult and expensive to control.

When she began reading the accounts of Stalin's rise to power after Lenin's death, however, she again became disheartened. It was obvious that under his rule thousands of non-Russians were slaughtered if they showed any hint of loyalty to other than Russian socialism. Those massacres eventually became known as the "purges."

She also read how Stalin forced the Kazakhs into collective farming, even though for many centuries their culture had been one of nomadic herders of livestock—horses, sheep, camels and even native antelope. The transition was not only extremely difficult for the native, Muslim people; it was a total cultural upheaval, because, again, many thousands were murdered in the forced program. However, when Trish read that millions had died from mass starvation in the failed program—an estimated two and a half million—she realized that Stalin had taken a system that had worked for thousands of years and in a space of a few years had superimposed on it his own particular idea of how people should live, eat and breathe. It was no wonder that they had died like flies.

Trish stopped at one point in her reading and note taking, put her elbows on the table, her face in her hands and sighed loudly, without any concern for who might be sitting around her. Pushing her chair back with deliberation and another sigh, she stood up and stretched, then went to take a bathroom break. As she walked, she thought about the passages she had just finished, how Khrushchev came to power after Stalin's death in 1953 with a much more moderate stance in his treatment of non-Russians. By the time she read that part of the text, she'd become so absorbed in her research that she felt relief...almost as though she was reading a narrative and hadn't already known that fact.

Since many Russians had already migrated and continued to migrate to non-Russian republics, by the 1980s Kazakhstan's population was almost 40 per cent Russian, with Kazakhs only slightly more. The rest were a variety of other ethnic people—Germans, Uzbeks, Ukrainians and Tatars. While Kazakhstan's native people were still treated like second-class citizens, the country itself had become an important source of raw materials for the rest of the Soviet Union, rich in minerals—and most significantly during the nuclear arms race—uranium.

After Trish gulped down several swallows from the water fountain, she returned to her seat, paused a moment and then dove back into the books, as if plunging into an unknown sea.

With her focus returned, she read about Mikhail Gorbachev's arrival on the Soviet political scene. He had developed his commitment to "glasnost," or openness, after learning the full extent of Stalin's purges. The Kazakhs, as well as Soviet citizens, were apparently shocked to discover that millions had died or been killed in the purges. That bit of information had never before been disseminated to the Kazakh people by the government-controlled press or in their history books. Trish mused as she fingered the page of the book she was reading that it was that small streak of light cast by what was called glasnost that had propelled the darkened Soviet Union headlong into a dramatic and irreversible change in course. It caught the rest of the world completely by surprise.

Trish checked her watch. Her time at the library had run out at almost the same time as her tolerance level with the subject of Russian history. She gathered her notes and closed the books.

• • •

As Trish continued making research trips to both the public and the university libraries, she began concentrating on the effects of the Soviet nuclear testing on civilian populations during that period. That put her focus on the Republic of Kazakhstan, the heart of the Russian nuclear testing program.

Her social life—what little there was of it—had quickly been relegated to "later."

After she returned the books she'd finished to their proper places on the shelves of the libraries, Trish checked out the ones she wanted to study more thoroughly at home. It was there—curled up on her sofa late one evening—where she read about the attempted coup against Gorbachev in August of 1991. Even though the Soviet military leaders were determined to stop the dramatic changes that were occurring, Trish wasn't surprised that the coup was unsuccessful—even in hindsight. The sheer magnitude of the changes was inevitable once that crack of truth called "glasnost" began spreading through the land like a fissure in a tectonic plate. The realization of that fact made Trish even more acutely aware of the responsibilities of the press than she'd been before studying Russian history.

She read in the same book that the USSR was dissolved in December of 1991, when the CIS, or Commonwealth of Independent States, was formed with eleven republics joining, including Kazakhstan. The following year Kazakhstan was admitted to the United Nations.

With the introduction of glasnost, the Kazakh people began learning even more about what had taken place inside their borders, besides the purges. They clearly knew that they had become host to Russia's main nuclear testing program during the arms race. They also knew about uranium production in their republic, since it had been the source of a number of jobs and income. They must have also known that nuclear tests had occurred there. Trish realized that it was impossible to hide the over five hundred very tangible nuclear blasts had been set off in the area around the city of Semipalatinsk.

On the other hand, it was clear that the Kazakhs hadn't known the full extent of the consequences of the testing. Millions of tons of radioactive materials had been dumped into the environment, and the citizens had been used as guinea pigs to document the effects of atomic fallout on civilians and soldiers in a possible nuclear battle.

Trish set down her notebook and book and went to the kitchen to get a glass of water. She realized as she drank that she wasn't even thirsty; she'd just needed a break from the onslaught of cerebral overload. She poured the rest of the water out in the sink, turned out the lights around the house and went to her bedroom and flopped onto the bed. She felt like a sponge that had absorbed all it could for the time being. She hoped sleep would give her the respite she needed from too much of a dose of reality about Russian history and the Cold War.

• • •

The next day, Trish decided she needed to break the tension with something purely mindless. When she called Kathy to ask her to join her in some kind of activity and told her the nature of the invitation, Kathy let out a roar over the phone. "Oh, that's just great! You want to do something 'mindless,' and *I'm* the first person you think of?"

Trish chuckled. "No, no, Kathy. It's just you're always game for anything, so..."

"Oh, so now I'm mindless *and* easy."

If Trish needed a break, Kathy was always the one to call. "I thought we might just go out and get plastered," she told Kathy, "but with all this research I probably need to keep sharp."

"How about some weed?" Kathy asked. Trish chuckled again. Then Kathy asked, "How about pouring soap suds in the fountain in front of the bank tonight?"

"Maybe if I was a teenager," Trish responded with a judgmental huff.

"Well, how about going over and mooning old man Davis for letting his cows get loose and tromping up your garden?" Kathy asked, undeterred.

"Kathy, that's not just childish; it's gross." Trish paused. "Besides we can't do that anymore since you got that little tattoo on your butt in high school. You're too easily identifiable now."

"Nah!" Kathy retorted. "You and Mike are the only ones who know I've got it, and y'all wouldn't tell anyone."

Trish deliberately waited just a moment, then asked, "Oh, is that what you thought?"

After another brief moment of silence, Kathy demanded, "Patty? Patty!"

When Kathy went silent again, Trish said, "Trying to remember everybody you mooned back twenty-five years ago, aren't you?"

"Hell, no," Kathy replied indignantly. Then, as though pondering, she added, "I'm trying to remember everybody I mooned last *month*."

• • •

Nestled back on the sofa the next evening, Trish plunged back into her research. With the revelation of the facts about the health effects of the atomic testing seeping out into Kazakhstan and the resulting public outrage, Trish read how Kazakh president, Nursultan Nazarbayev, took the dramatic step of closing the nuclear test sites in his country. He took that action during the same month as the unsuccessful military coup against Gorbachev.

The next year his country returned 320 nuclear bombs to Russia. It didn't surprise her that anti-nuclear sentiment was high there, in light of the devastation to the environment from the nuclear program in Kazakhstan. She closed her book momentarily with her finger marking her place. The people must have suspected that the monster in their midst had been doing much more harm than was ever admitted before glasnost. Because of that, she wasn't surprised that the newly independent country had intended to become a non-nuclear state with a military doctrine committed to nuclear non-proliferation. She speculated, nevertheless, that at the same time they must have known that if they gave up all of their nuclear weapons, they'd be extremely vulnerable militarily. Because of their long history of being dominated, that was no minor consideration. When she returned to her book she learned that at that point in time Kazakhstan was retaining strategic nuclear weapons, as well as testing and production facilities.

Besides the obvious, practical implications of that decision, Trish assumed they had also realized that without nuclear weapons, the rest of the world might ignore them, that they might be relegated to non-entity status on the world stage, and that they didn't want to be forgotten. And—she learned as she continued reading—this paradox still dominated political decisions on nuclear weapons in Kazakhstan in that summer of 1995.

The more Trish read, the more painfully aware she became of Kazakhstan's need for outside help—economic and environmental help.

It was inevitable that as more and more information about Russia's nuclear arms program during the Cold War began to emerge, it would eventually begin filtering out to the rest of the world, as well. Though she had been attentive to those revelations as they began seeping past the barriers of secrecy that had held them back for so long, she hadn't become as transfixed by any of them as she had by what she'd seen on the "60 Minutes" program in her living room that day months before.

On occasion she would take notes about what she could recall about the episode. She'd tried to order a transcript, but had been told that videos of the program were not being sent out because of a pending lawsuit concerning it. She remembered the mention of the 500 nuclear bombs exploded in the area since 1949—more than 100 of them atmospheric tests that had blanketed the area with nuclear fallout. She remembered scenes of the Atomic Lake that had been created when one of those nuclear blasts had been set off to see if it could change the course of rivers. She'd heard that the lake would remain radioactive for 20,000 years. Soldiers, workers and local inhabitants had been routinely exposed to massive amounts of radioactive fallout and exposures. And she remembered the reactions she'd had to those facts, ranging from shock to sympathy to outrage…and finally intrigue.

But none of that had grabbed Trish's attention the way the pictures of the mutants in the jars in Clinic Number Four had. She didn't need a video to remember that. Her conviction of a deeper, more profound meaning behind those sights grew the deeper she probed the roots of the story.

It seemed to whisper to her in her dreams at night and on the wind during the day—as though the energy of the story was reaching out to her from around the globe.

Chapter Four

Since returning to Clayton, Trish had come to regard Peggy Craft and Mark Matheson as the best news sources on nuclear issues she had ever encountered in her career. Their volunteer environmental work revolved almost exclusively around nuclear weapons and energy. It was obvious that she was going to need their assistance with her research on the history, politics and science of the atomic age.

As a reporter, she'd long before discovered that volunteers were a special breed—much more generous with their time and information than other news sources, and totally devoted to their individual causes. Though their dedication could sometimes border on obsession—an assumption that held true for both Peggy and Mark—she genuinely admired their tenacity. But most importantly, after working with them, she'd come to find that the information they provided was impeccably accurate.

As soon as Trish had accumulated enough background information on Soviet history, she called Peggy at her home in Gainesville, Georgia, and told her about being fired and about the freelance project. She contacted Peggy first because she suspected that conducting an interview with Mark would prove to be a good deal more challenging.

"Trish, I'd be thrilled to work with you on this," Peggy responded with an enthusiasm Trish hadn't expected. "Hey, why don't you come on down tomorrow morning? I don't have a thing on my schedule for this week-end. I can pull some articles and papers together for you that might help, too."

The next morning Trish gathered her cell phone, recorder, tapes and a fresh notepad, then climbed into her red Jeep for the hour long drive. As she drove down the expressway with her air conditioner on full blast, she glanced at the tape recorder on the seat beside her.

The first time she'd used it to interview Peggy Craft was shortly after she'd moved back home and begun working for the Clayton paper. They met through Trish's friend, Jan, who thought Trish might be interested in hearing the woman's story and in getting it out in the newspaper.

Jan told her that Peggy had been an employee at the Savannah River Plant for a number of years, working daily with plutonium and tritium, but had been fired from her job and was going through the legal process of trying to get it back. When Trish first heard about her, she was a bit dubious about doing an interview. Reporters always tend toward cynicism. It was too easy to be seduced by a person's story.

Still, Jan kept pushing her. "Trish, this woman is legitimate. She was fired unfairly, and, I swear to God, she's got one humdinger of a story to tell." Trish finally agreed to meet Peggy and talk to her briefly before deciding if she wanted to conduct an interview. And, if she did, she'd also need enough information to persuade her boss to let her do a story for the paper.

When Trish was first introduced to Peggy at Jan's, she found herself shaking hands with a tall, well-proportioned woman with short-cropped, dark brown hair, an olive complexion and dark brown eyes. She appeared to be about the same age as Trish, and had a facial structure that was so well defined it seemed chiseled. Trish instantly focused on Peggy's husky voice, which had a strange hint of masculinity or seductiveness to it.

With the three of them seated at Jan's kitchen table drinking coffee, Peggy volunteered her personal information right up front. She was a married woman with two teenage sons, working as a secretary for a veterinary clinic in Gainesville, a job that Trish quickly noted was a far cry from her previous training and qualifications. With the basics out of the way, Trish began asking a few questions, which soon turned into many more. Within her first few minutes with Peggy Craft, Trish was hooked, and asked for permission to turn on her tape recorder.

Trish glanced at the recorder on the car seat again. Where did she put those tapes? She might need to go over them again when she got back home.

As the two of them talked in Jan's kitchen, Trish became more and more impressed by Peggy's determination and also by her obvious intelligence. "Trish, you need to know that during a lot of my career I was pronuclear." Then, however, she'd begun witnessing incidents at the plant that bothered her and tugged at her conscience. Corners were cut on safety, and she was stunned to discover that her original attempts to call attention to the problems—which she was mandated by law to do—were rebuffed by management. Still, she'd continued asking questions and pointing out deficiencies. "I just couldn't let it go…not with something as crucial as the safe handling of nuclear materials."

As Jan freshened their coffees, Peggy continued telling Trish about her frustration with the industry. Trish identified with her. There it is again, she'd thought to herself, those rules again, the unspoken rules that always over shadow the real rules.

"It didn't take me long to figure out I'd been branded a troublemaker by management…*and* by most of the other employees." Peggy pushed her seat back and crossed her legs. "After that conditions in the workplace became almost impossible."

"How so?" Trish asked.

"They put me in job settings where I had to stand on my feet all day…even though they knew I had problems with sciatica and my joints." She was ostracized by many of her co-workers, and the pressure and stress became so tremendous that at times her blood pressure soared. She took a sip of coffee, then set her mug back down. "I finally had to admit that they were trying to force me to quit."

But she didn't. Instead, she became more active, documenting violations and getting copies of her health files, where she discovered that the company doctor had diagnosed her complaints about her sciatica and joints as psychologically induced rather than real physiological problems.

During the interview—which the "talk" had turned into—Trish also found Peggy refreshingly candid. "To tell you the truth," she told Trish, "if it'd been something like water pollution, I'd have probably just kept my mouth shut and kept my job. But you can't afford to cut corners in *this* industry. That's why all the safeguards were built in; there no margin for error with elements that can alter human DNA and hang around for thousands of years doing just that." Those strict regulations were the only reason she'd believed the industry could work in the first place.

What she hadn't counted on was that the same human dynamics that exist in every industry existed in that one, as well: greed, incompetence, politics, simple human errors. "You name it. There's no way to control nuclear energy one hundred per cent, no matter how pure your motives may have been in the beginning. And we've got to find some way to protect whistleblowers. Otherwise, who'll warn the public?"

Trish hadn't found the comment self-serving, but had naively asked, "What about the NRC? Didn't they help?"

"Are you kidding? Don't you know what those initials stand for?"

"Nuclear Regulatory Commission?"

Peggy snickered. Trish furrowed her brow and then grinned. "Okay... I give. What?"

"Nobody Really Cares," Peggy answered, then added, "In fact, I've pretty well established that they're the ones who exposed me to the company when I started revealing some of the violations."

"But aren't they supposed to guarantee whistleblowers anonymity?"

"I thought so...but I found out differently. It left me so vulnerable. And when I looked at my health files and read that I'd been labeled a hysteric, I realized they were starting to build a case to fire me. I thought, 'If they really think I've got mental problems, why the hell have they let me work with plutonium and tritium all this time?' It didn't make any sense." Then she added with a hint of irony, "Come to think of it now, I probably *was* crazy to be working with those kinds of materials under the conditions in that plant."

Trish shook her head at the memory and returned her attention to the road. As she noted how the drought had left the grass along the expressway dead and yellow, she mused how—just like her—Peggy had stayed on in a profession she knew wasn't working, thinking she could somehow change it.

As Peggy related her experiences at the plant, Trish was reminded of the similarities to the story of Karen Silkwood. It wasn't until one point in the interview, when Peggy talked about being contaminated in the plant one day that she realized just how similar the two stories were. Almost at the point of tears and with her voice quivering at times, Peggy said, "There we were, late one night, with scrub brushes and all in the shower—just me and one technician. I wouldn't have believed it. It's not even in my files that the incident ever happened. And after I discovered that it hadn't even been documented, that's when I first began to suspect it had been deliberate."

As Peggy choked up, Jan got up from her seat and went to comfort her. Peggy put her hand to the side of her face and continued, "I went over it again and again. I didn't want to believe another human being was capable of deliberately contaminating me. But, once I got past my denial, I realized it was the only possible explanation." Peggy pressed her lips together and shook her head. "I never believed anything like that could ever happen."

As intrigued as Trish had been with Peggy's story, she'd never gotten a chance to write about it. It was a much bigger project than she'd imagined, and she was finally forced to admit, with the help of her editor, Tom, that a small publication like *The Clayton Times* simply didn't have the resources to tackle something that big and complex, not to mention time- and budget-consuming. As soon as she accepted that she couldn't do it justice, she tried to steer Peggy to former contacts at larger papers who might be interested in pursuing it.

Though nothing had ever materialized with any of those contacts, Trish and Peggy had stayed in touch. Over time, Trish began noticing subtle changes in Peggy's attitude. She'd initially seemed intent on being vindicated and in exposing the injustices that had been inflicted on her, but was beginning to focus less on her personal situation and more on the public implications of it. When Trish asked her about her shift in attitude on the phone one day, she said, "Well, you remember how I told you about meeting and working with other whistleblowers in the industry?"

"Yeah."

"It was a great support group. And I needed it. Outsiders just couldn't understand what we were going through." She took a breath. "But then one day after yet another session of carping about the way we'd all been screwed, I finally got tired of listening to the same old things and I blurted out, 'Hey, the real problem here is bigger than us and our personal gripes. Hell, we know what the dangers are. It's the public out there that stands to get really screwed; being radiated is a hell of a lot worse than losing your job; and they don't have any idea how much danger they're in.'

"And this guy says, 'Are you kidding? They don't want to know.' So I said, 'But they *have* to know if we really expect anything to change. And, damn it, we're in a position to tell them. We know the industry. We're not amateurs. If we don't tell them, who will? Maybe we should start using the knowledge and information we have to get the word out instead of worrying about ourselves all the time.'

"I tell you, it even surprised *me* when I said those things. I don't even know where it came from...but I guess deep down I knew it was true."

"Did any of the others agree with you?" Trish asked.

"Trish, it's hard to think of the public good when you're worrying about putting food on the table for your kids. It sucks all of your energy. Besides, once a whistleblower gets labeled a disgruntled employee, his message tends to get discredited in the public eye." The moment she'd said that, Trish had to admit to herself that she'd had the same initial reaction when Jan first approached her about covering Peggy's story. "Anyway," Peggy continued, "I finally got this job as a secretary. I knew I had better qualifications, but it was secure and it was sufficient...and I'd already been pretty much black-balled in the industry. So I did a little downsizing in my lifestyle, and now I've started spending my spare time as an activist on nuclear issues, rather than wasting so much energy trying to get my old job back or an apology— which isn't even realistic in the first place."

"Do you see your support group any more?" Trish asked.

"Oh, I went back a time or two after my little outburst, but I felt like an outsider. We were heading in different directions."

"Sounds like you were just evolving faster than they were."

"I don't know about that. You'd have to have been there to understand how bad it was for us. I had a husband with a secure job, so I wasn't under as much pressure as most of the others who'd been the sole breadwinners in their families. I don't feel badly toward any of them. All I know is that I feel better doing what I'm doing now. Hell, I don't even have high blood pressure any more."

Since her experience at Savannah River Plant, Peggy had done a lot of research on the nuclear age—how it had come about, what fueled it and how politics had shaped its evolution. She'd become active with several environmental groups, lending her expertise where it could help and educating herself on working with the political system.

Though Trish admired her long-term commitment and newfound pragmatism, she knew what an uphill battle Peggy had ahead of her. Still, her background research into the nuclear age was just what Trish needed, and she was grateful Peggy had spent so much time gathering it and, in the process, becoming a better source.

And she was glad Peggy was willing to share that expertise with her, after spilling her guts to Trish one time with nothing to show for it.

• • •

After Trish reached Peggy's house and received a warm greeting, they got settled into chairs opposite each other in her family room. Peggy had assembled reams of magazines, books and documents for Trish. When she pointed out the eight-inch stack of material on the coffee table between them, Trish jutted her head back, a bit overwhelmed. "Is that all for me?"

Peggy grinned. Then she addressed one of her growing concerns about the atomic age. It centered more on psychological conditioning than on what was happening to the environment as a result of nuclear experimentation. She told Trish she had come to view all pollution as a symptom of a much larger societal or perhaps spiritual problem. "The poisoning of a society begins long before it manifests physically," she said as she crossed her legs. Trish was surprised at how much more philosophical Peggy had become about man and his environment since the last time they'd talked.

After Peggy completed her brief exploration into that area of concern, Trish began the interview. "Like I told you that first time we talked at Jan's, just try not to let the recorder make you too self-conscious. I've found that using it makes people a little formal. Just relax and pretend we're having a normal, everyday conversation."

Peggy smiled. "I'll try."

With pad and pen in hand, Trish cleared her throat and began, "Tell me what you know about the radioactive contamination that went on in the Eastern bloc nations during the Cold War."

Peggy turned slightly in her chair. "Well, it's even worse than anybody in the environmental community could've imagined. Everybody thinks Chernobyl was the defining tragedy of the nuclear age, but that it's over. But, it's not over." She told Trish how the cement sarcophagus built immediately after the accident to contain it was beginning to collapse under its own weight.

"Really?" Trish asked, lifting her eyes. "I didn't know that."

"It is. There are cracks in the thing big enough for birds to fly through...and the reactor is still leaking radioactive wastes." She raised her right hand briefly in the air. "I don't know what on earth they plan to do when the thing falls in. The containment hasn't even held up for ten years, and it'll be radioactive for tens of *thousands* of years." She reminded Trish that the Pyramid was believed to be the longest existing structure on the planet, and its age was estimated at only six thousand years. And now, just a decade after the accident at Chernobyl, the Ukrainian government was warning that water was already dripping into the ruins of the sarcophagus and could very well set off another uncontrolled reaction.

"Yeah, and the Pyramid's already been penetrated," Trish couldn't help interjecting.

"Exactly," Peggy agreed. She lamented the amount of human indifference it took to use a product that would contaminate the world for that many thousands of years. "Any benefits it produces compared to that kind of legacy are purely negligible." She leaned back in her chair and shook her head slightly back and forth. "I can't believe I let myself be brainwashed into thinking it could be used safely. But," she continued, "that doesn't compare to the amount of arrogance by both the government and the scientists when they invented the bomb in the first place."

"Arrogance?" Trish asked. "Weren't they just trying to stop the war?"

"That was their reason when they started out…and, incidentally, I don't get caught up in the debate about the morality of dropping the bomb on Hiroshima…but when they exploded that first bomb at Alamogordo, they really had no idea what would happen. One of the scientists even made a bet that the whole of New Mexico would be obliterated. They had one theory— even though it was remote—that when the device was triggered, it would start a chain reaction that would ignite the atmosphere. And they triggered it anyway."

Trish raised her eyebrows, then quickly jotted a notation to get documentation on that incident.

With her hand outstretched Peggy continued, "Don't you think that the rest of the world might have had a few objections to risking the whole of humanity, if they'd known about it? I can't imagine intelligent, sane people blindly taking a risk like that, without understanding the magnitude of what they were doing. It was like, 'Hey,'" Peggy shifted her voice, ' Let's just trigger this here little gizmo and see if it blows up the planet.'" Trish shook her head, and then Peggy shifted in her seat, signaling a new topic. "Trish, have you ever heard of the 'Atomic Priesthood'?" she asked.

"No," Trish responded, looking up from her pad. "But it sounds fascinating."

"Well," Peggy began, gesturing with her right hand, "at some point it must have finally dawned on some of the intelligentsia that we were doing something profoundly critical to the planet. After all, we were leaving areas of contamination that could inflict major genetic damage on all living species and that couldn't be cleaned up." She explained that since that contamination would last for tens and even hundreds of thousands of years into the future, it was beyond the reach of present-day language and symbols. She sat back. "The implications were obvious. How do we warn future generations about the dangers? How do we communicate to them where the radioactive waste containment sites are, and warn them to stay away?

"It presented a unique problem in the history of the world."

Peggy glanced at the wall for a moment, and Trish filled in the space. "So how would we?"

"One think tank group came up with the idea of an atomic priesthood." She told Trish that the priesthood would be a group of people who would pass the information down from generation to generation by word of mouth in a ritualized manner, similar to oral traditions that had been passed down for thousands of years in primitive cultures. It would be akin to a religion, full of symbolism and parables, myths and metaphors. She said oral traditions were the only documented instances of ongoing information surviving for even close to that long a period. The Australian Aborigines were believed to have the oldest known surviving religion on the planet. "It's supposed to go back for at least 20,000 years, and some say for as long as 40,000 years—or even much longer."

"Jeez, this sounds like science fiction," Trish commented, wrinkling her brow.

Peggy smiled. "When Harry Truman was first briefed about the bomb, after Roosevelt died, he said it sounded like something out of Buck Rogers to him."

"But wouldn't that kind of information become corrupted over such a long period of time?" Trish half laughed. "I know in Clayton a story could get twisted backwards and forwards from sun up to sun down of the same day."

"Look, I'm not even saying this is a workable idea, but we have to do *something*. Maybe they thought the ritualized, religious nature of a priesthood would guard against corruption...and oral teachings would be preferable to, say, fixed written warnings or pictures."

"Why's that?"

Peggy explained that oral traditions are alive because they change and adapt to circumstances in life, and that change was inevitable in any culture over a period of hundreds or thousands of years.

"What kind of myth would begin to warn about the atomic age?" Trish asked.

"I don't know." Peggy glanced around the room. "Maybe something along the lines of a Pandora's box." Peggy looked back at her and asked," Would you like something to drink?" She stood up. "I know I would."

"Yeah, that'd be great...a diet drink, if you've got it."

Peggy went into the adjoining kitchen, while Trish took advantage of the break to check her tape and stand up and stretch. As Peggy got out glasses and filled them, she said, "But, you know, Trish, radioactive contamination isn't all that's devastated the Soviet Union. We've heard just horrific stories about industrial and chemical wastes that have turned some cities and communities into virtual wastelands, where the water is undrinkable and the air is practically unbreathable."

Peggy returned to the room with their drinks and handed Trish hers.

"Thank you," Trish said as she sat back down in her chair and took a few sips.

When Peggy got seated again, she said "When we first started hearing those stories after glasnost, I couldn't help but laugh at the bitter irony."

"Why's that?" Trish asked as she set her drink down.

Peggy set her glass down as well and sat back and crossed her legs. "I remembered how environmentalists were called communists for so long. Hell, I even did it myself years ago. And then with all we were learning, about what had been going on in the heart of the communist territory, it seems the polluters should've been labeled communists.

"And now—since communism is supposed to be dead—the new catch phrase that's applied to environmentalists is 'eco-terrorists.'" She raised a hand in the air briefly. "Can you believe it? I mean, I thought a word like 'eco-terrorism' would logically be applied to the ones who *poisoned* the earth, and killed people and made them sick with toxins—not the folks who were trying to prevent it."

"At least we had it better than the Soviets," Trish interjected.

"That may be true…but if you think we were guiltless in this little scenario, you'd be dead wrong." Trish looked at Peggy, tilting her head, and Peggy added, "We engaged in secret nuclear experiments, just like the Soviet Union. And we even conducted secret human experiments." Peggy said the experiments were simply unreported. It wasn't until Hazel O'Leary from the Department of Energy started declassifying tons of documents that had been labeled top secret during the Cold War that the public became aware of the enormity of them.

"Yeah," Trish responded, "I remember reading something about that."

"Believe me, I don't have any love for the DOE, but at least O'Leary instituted a form of glasnost we desperately needed in our own country, and I have to give her credit for that." Peggy stopped long enough to take a sip of her drink, then told Trish stories about pregnant women who were given radioactive iron during their pregnancies in a hospital in Tennessee, as well as other patients who were injected with plutonium. School boys in Massachusetts were fed oatmeal with radioactive trace elements.

Trish asked whether the experiments could have been a normal part of the Cold War hysteria, similar to the government's negligence with the atmospheric bomb tests before they realized the amount of harm being inflicting on the public. She suggested they didn't fully comprehend their actions and were operating out of fear and ignorance, believing that somehow the experiments were serving some greater good. "Couldn't they have just been trying to find a positive, medical use for this radiation they'd unleashed on the world?"

Peggy set down her glass. "But, Trish, in this case it wasn't just the government. It was the doctors themselves—doctors sworn to uphold the Hippocratic Oath—who joined in the experiments on their own patients. It's clear some of those babies had much higher death rates, and their parents weren't given a shred of necessary information or choice in the matter...no informed consent whatsoever. One little guy with leukemia was bombarded with enough radiation to kill several grown men, and his mother wasn't told the truth about it...just that the experiments were his only hope. In fact, agreeing to the experimental treatment was the only way she could *afford* to have him treated."

"But, Peggy, do you think they really understood the dangers?"

Peggy set her jaw and pursed her lips briefly. "Oh, I think they knew full well." She questioned what other reason the nuclear industry would have had for insisting on immunity from legal liability for the things they were involved in. "And besides," she added, "they knew from all the way back to the time of Madame Curie, when she first did *her* work in the field. She died from radioactive exposure during her experiments. In fact," she emphasized with a pointed finger, "her death should have taught us a lot more about messing around with radiation than anything else she did in her career."

Peggy told Trish about an incident during the early part of the century when young women working in a factory died from painting radium dials on watch faces, and how those in management had even told them to put the points of their brushes in their mouths to shape a finer point while painting. "Some of the ones who died actually had their bones crumbling. The studies they did on that—and others that they did on animals—gave them a damn clear idea of the dangers from radiation exposure. And they sure as heck knew after what was documented in Hiroshima and Nagasaki." Then, cocking her head to one side, she added, "And—by the way—a lot of the films they took there right after the war are still classified."

"Why's that?"

"I don't have any idea why the government does half the things it does," she answered cryptically, "but after over fifty years, national security seems like a pretty thin excuse to hang their hats on." Peggy nodded toward the stack on the table. "When you get into some of this material, you'll read how many Americans were exposed to radiation by our government during the Cold War. It wasn't just the atomic veterans and down-winders and nuclear workers." She told Trish that life expectancies of some of those on the front lines of the atomic program were cut by an average of twenty-two years, and that birth defect rates were four times higher than that of the national average.

"And some of the things the scientists and doctors did in their experiments with radiation violated the main principle of the Nuremberg Code." Peggy let out a short breath. "And they were the very ones who came up with the code in the first place—to make sure nothing like the Nazi medical experiments would ever happen again."

"What does the code say exactly?" Trish inquired as she jotted the heading "Nuremberg Code" on a fresh page. "I'm not familiar with the specifics."

Peggy told Trish the code states that each scientist or doctor has to give full disclosure of the consequences to a subject before that subject can agree to participate in any scientific experiment. Scientists and doctors can't pass blame or liability on to any other entity if they fail to do so. She added that she thought one of the most incredible ironies of the Cold War was that both Russia and the U.S. ended up killing more of their own citizens during that period than the enemies they were supposed to be preparing for. "I think the Cold War is the classic example of revenge being like taking poison every day and thinking that it's going to hurt the other person."

Trish sensed that Peggy was lapsing into a psychological evaluation of the nuclear age. She'd let her finish her thought before steering her back to the tangible facts she needed for her research.

Peggy continued. "But since the Cold War is over and we still haven't gotten any of the real so-called 'peacetime dividends' that we were promised, I think the real question we need to ask is whether or not we're capable of living without an enemy yet."

"Why do you say that?"

"That's the purpose an enemy can serve—as a projection of your own conflicts and faults and weaknesses, so you can work on them externally because you're not able for some reason to work on them internally. Maybe you're in denial or something," she expounded, "so focusing on an enemy lets you avoid the psychological self-examination you need to engage in, while still working on the problem unconsciously on another level."

"But don't you think we've learned anything psychologically from the Cold War experience yet?" Trish asked before she had time to realize she was getting caught up in Peggy's interest in the psychology behind the atomic age.

"I don't know, but I do think that's why we're seeing examples of domestic terrorism we've never seen before. I think we're still projecting, though…just closer to home now since we don't have communists or any other foreign threat to focus on any more."

Peggy believed that because the super powers still neglected to examine the psychological and spiritual aspects of their own collective and individual behavior, they were still poisoning themselves and the planet. "To me it feels like a slow form of suicide." Peggy shifted in her seat and added, "I think we're long overdue for a serious bout of soul searching."

Trish took a long breath and responded, "Well, I have to admit I see that same dynamic in the news industry. I'm so sick of seeing that precious news space and news time devoted to gossip and trivia. They say they're just reflecting what's happening in society today. But I think they really need to admit that they're manipulating the direction the mirror is pointing in. There are three hundred and sixty different degrees that the mirror could be held at. And none of them even thinks about pointing it up or down—or even backwards—at themselves." Trish lowered her forehead onto her hand. "Oh, God, Peggy, I didn't mean to get back on *that* band wagon again.

"I think I need a break."

• • •

After a short break, Trish started her recorder again. But as Peggy began talking about the Nevada Test Site, where the U.S. atomic testing had taken place for the previous decades, Trish's mind wandered. She felt much as she had as a girl sitting in church listening to a sermon, hearing, but not absorbing, except that this material wasn't boring; it was mind-boggling. Still, she kept fading in and out of the conversation, and finally abandoned her notepad. As she watched Peggy talking, she could occasionally focus enough to reply or ask questions, but she felt detached. Somewhere in her mind she was glad she'd remembered to restart the recorder.

When Peggy paused for a moment in her commentary, Trish sat forward and confided, "Peggy, I don't know if it's all the heat we've been having or this subject matter or what, but I'm having a little trouble focusing." She shrugged her shoulders. "Or maybe I'm just tired."

Peggy eyed her briefly, then pursed her lip. "Hmm…" She took a breath. "Trish, believe it or not, I've found that when people get into this subject matter at any length, it actually starts affecting them physically." Trish glanced to the left, trying on Peggy's words. She didn't know why, but that explanation felt right. As Trish turned back, Peggy continued, "When I first started digging into information about the atomic age, it was so intense and overwhelming that it was like I had to go to sleep just to digest it on another level. It's like, when the mind has taken all it can take, it starts shutting down." She suggested a longer break, then went to refill their glasses. After that, the two of them took their drinks outside to Peggy's back patio.

As soon as they stepped outdoors, the heat hit Trish full in the face. She tried to focus on Peggy's comments about her garden. "It's been such a hassle trying to keep these flowers alive. I've had to water them twice a day with dishwater from the sink because of the watering ban." She gently stroked her hand across the flowering tops of red salvia in one container. "I had to give up on my grass over a month ago because of the drought, but I'm hanging in there with these flowers."

Trish thought about her garden. She hadn't watered it that morning. When she began fanning herself with her notepad, Peggy glanced at her and commented, "Well, this isn't going to work. I was going to suggest a short walk to help you get grounded in this material you've been soaking up, but it's too damn hot to even stand here. I guess we'd better get back inside to the air conditioning."

When they got settled again in their chairs, they chatted a few more minutes about the drought, then the black and white photographs on Peggy's wall. Trish was surprised when Peggy told her she had taken the shots; they were excellent for an amateur. Trish talked briefly again about her travel plans in Kazakhstan, then took a few deep breaths. The lethargy was gone.

Peggy glanced at Trish and said, "Your eyes look clearer."

Trish grinned in response, then picked up her pad and pen and cleared her throat. She said that while she was aware Peggy wanted to focus on the psychological aspects of the atomic age, she was an invaluable source on the facts of it. "And that's what I need to keep focused on with this story: the facts."

Peggy smiled. "I don't think these facts mean a damn thing to the public unless it affects them personally."

"Why do you say that?"

Peggy exhaled forcefully. "Trish, even though I was concerned and even frightened about the conditions at Savannah River Plant, I wouldn't have gotten to where I am today if I hadn't been radiated that time."

"Well, from what you've been telling me, maybe a lot of people are more personally affected than they realize."

"Oh, I believe that. But I don't know how you're going to get past the denial part. That was a tough one for me."

Trish held up a picture of the Nevada Test Site that Peggy had shown her earlier. "With pictures like these. And like the ones I saw in that clinic." She put a fresh tape in the recorder and picked up her notebook again.

Peggy leaned forward and said, "Well, then, I'll give you a few *more* facts you probably didn't know about the Nevada site then...if you're up to it." Trish looked up as Peggy asked, "Did you ever hear that there was a major nuclear accident there the same month as the accident at Chernobyl?"

"No, I didn't. What happened?"

Trish flipped to a fresh page as Peggy began. "Well, in one of their tunnels they set off a bomb test they called 'Mighty Oak.'" She related how there were three huge barrier doors in the tunnel between the blast and the outside world to help trap some of the nuclear debris. She took a sip of her drink, set it down and cleared her throat. "Anyway, after the bomb was triggered two of the doors failed, and the explosion destroyed millions of dollars worth of equipment...but, thank heavens, the third door held."

"Is that in this material?" Trish asked, pointing to the stack.

"Yeah," Peggy answered, as she quickly rummaged through the stack and picked out a book. "I think it's in this one." She set it back down and continued, "But several days later they opened the third door and vented the gases into the atmosphere. The public wasn't warned or even informed about it." She explained that the jet stream carried the fallout northeastward, across the country, just as it had years before during the atmospheric testing. A few days later, the accident at Chernobyl occurred. At about that time a second release of the gases was vented into the atmosphere from the Nevada site. "Hardly anyone in the public knows about this accident even today. They only know that our government said, 'no cause for alarm' or 'all within acceptable limits,' about the Chernobyl accident...and Chernobyl was just assumed to be the source of any of the fallout that was detected in major U.S. cities."

Trish stopped writing. She didn't want to believe Peggy's information. That was the kind of thing that happened in Russia. "I've never heard anything about this before."

"Hardly anyone has. But the thing is Trish, acceptable to whom? The public isn't given any input into these standards or monitoring or announcements. And I tell you, the extra cancer deaths and deformities and miscarriages that follow these tests and these accidents sure as hell aren't acceptable to *me*."

Trish squirmed in her seat. "Peggy, has anyone ever attempted to calculate the number of deaths or health effects from the nuclear project since the forties?"

"Well, the risk model that the governments use right now estimate over a million deaths."

"Good gosh," Trish commented, as she wrote the figure down.

"But that model has been subject to a lot of criticism; it's considered flawed."

Trish looked up. "Why?"

Peggy told her that the estimates from the International Commission on Radiological Protection, or ICRP, didn't come from accepted scientific method, but were based instead on outmoded philosophical reasoning—cost-benefit calculations—which underestimated the risks. She said there was a 100-fold discrepancy between their model and actual studies, such as the one of the childhood leukemia cluster near the Sellafield complex in England.

Two studies from Chernobyl showed a 100- to 1000-fold discrepancy.

As Trish leaned onto the arm of her chair, she asked, "So are there more accurate figures anywhere?"

Peggy tilted her head sideways. "I hear there's a report in the works by the European Commission on Radiation Risk that uses a more scientific model. And I've heard they're going to be predicting over 61 and ½ million deaths since 1945."

Trish's face went blank. "Good God!"

"And, of course, you'd have to consider other casualties, too. Some may not appear as profound as the mutations you were telling me about when you called." She said some effects were simply as insidious as lowered immune systems, lowered fertility or some other form of diminished quality of life. "But we're just on the front end of the casualties." She told Trish that with the persistence of some radioactive materials for a quarter of a million years, death rates could easily run much higher for future generations. "*You* do the math."

Trish felt a wave of now familiar overload. "Peggy, I had no idea about some of these things."

"Neither did I," she responded, "till I started studying it." She leaned her head onto the back of her chair. "I guess you could say that I was blissfully and conveniently unaware. But the stuff is there; you just have to look for it. And," she added, pulling her head back up, "if you have a vested interest, you just don't look for it...or you try to rationalize it away." She edged forward and started digging again into the stack of material on the coffee table. "There's one more picture I want you to see." She pulled a magazine from it, turned to another double-paged picture and handed it to Trish. "Here."

In the magazine Trish saw eight small children around the age of seven standing in a row—all in their underwear and all missing their lower left arms. She read in the caption that they lived in two neighborhoods in Moscow where industrial contamination was extensive.

"See, Trish," Peggy explained as Trish looked and read, "after the mother of one of these kids discovered this same birth defect in other kids in her neighborhood, she started investigating and located over eighty other children in Moscow with the exact same deformity. She figured there had to be some kind of exposure at about the same time of the mothers' pregnancies, in the same part of the city, for this much coincidence."

This isn't coincidence, Trish thought to herself. Even with as little scientific background as she had, the powerful images convinced her. It couldn't be simply anecdotal. Her first instinct was to close the magazine and get back to the interview, but her reporter's curiosity took over, just as it had the night she watched the program about the mutations in Clinic Number Four. She began taking a closer look, allowing the images to soak into her consciousness. She noticed that, in spite of how innocent the children looked, they were all quite sad.

She stared at the picture, committing every tiny detail and every nuance of the images to her memory. She never wanted to forget one missing limb, one crooked smile, one curly, blond ringlet...or one bare toe.

Peggy finally broke the silence. "Trish, if you had a maniac in some city going around lopping off the arms of dozens of kids in town, everyone would be in a panic trying to find him and arrest him and punish him. It'd be on the front page of every newspaper in the world. But you do the same damn thing with chemicals and elements that screw up DNA, and nobody gives a shit about who dumped the poisons...or where...or how they need to go about stopping it and cleaning up the mess. What's the difference?"

Trish left the question hanging unanswered in the air.

Without lifting her eyes from the magazine, Trish asked, "How do you do it? How do you continue to fight this? Doesn't it depress you? Don't you want to just forget it and go on living a comfortable life without thinking about all this trauma in the world?"

Peggy's answer was instantaneous. "Trish, how could I *not* do it? How could anyone know about these things and do nothing?" she asked, motioning toward the stack of material on the coffee table. "The only time I ever get cynical and depressed is when I try to walk away from it...and, believe me, I did try to do that for a long time. But once you know about something, you can't ever go back to the luxury of not knowing."

She shook her head. "To tell the truth, after my trouble at Savannah River, I got so self-absorbed. I went through a really long period of self-pity...and I can assure you it wasn't a pretty sight. But then, when I started to realize that this thing was a hell of a lot bigger than just me—that it was universal—I knew I had to start focusing my energy outward in a positive way instead of inward in a negative way. It's still not easy, but it's the only thing that works for me."

At that Trish finally raised her head from the magazine and looked at Peggy, as she continued, "Who knows? Maybe it *is* all hopeless...but I do what makes me feel good about myself now. That's the only thing I *do* have any control of. I had to let go of worrying about the outcome of my work. To tell the truth, I don't even think I'll live to see the outcome of it." Her tone shifted to one of gentleness, as she added, "But maybe my boys will."

After Peggy took another drink, she began to squirm uncomfortably in her seat. Trish instantly recognized the body language as that which usually precedes a confession. She'd learned from years of experience, however, to first wait and see if the confession would come of its own accord. She returned her focus to her notepad a moment to allow Peggy time to summon the courage to say what Trish knew she was struggling to share.

Finally, Peggy took a deep breath, then stared at the floor and said, "Let me tell you something…that I've never told anyone before—not even my husband." Her voice was tinged with resignation. "I just figured that from the day I got contaminated in the plant that time, I was a dead woman."

Before Trish had time to react, Peggy quickly added, "Oh, it's not like I'm going to drop dead on the floor at any minute…but something told me that from that point on, I was dying. I don't know when or where. But I just figure that whatever I do with the rest of my time is going to be my legacy. I could spend the rest of my life enjoying my family and myself…and I do that, too…as much as I can. But, I'm in a position to do more, so I *have* to do more." She shook her head gently. "It may not mean that much in the big scheme of things, and I sure won't get a Purple Heart for it. But, it'll be more than just a tombstone left behind."

"Oh, Peggy… I…" Trish stumbled for words.

Peggy looked up. "Look, Trish, you don't have to feel sorry for me. And who knows? I might outlive you. But, when I did realize I was probably facing my mortality, and accepted it, there was actually a strange kind of relief to it, believe it or not. It was easier to see my purpose in life, and to follow it. Hell, it's a lot easier to feel courageous, when you figure you're already dead."

Trish looked at Peggy curiously. Was she right? Had she been talking to a dead woman? She didn't believe she'd ever interviewed a dead person before.

Peggy quickly returned to her meaty supply of facts about the atomic age. And Trish allowed it—without comment—as though nothing so profoundly personal had been broached between them.

After asking Peggy about technical information on nuclear jargon, so she could better understand the issues and material, Trish felt she had done as much as she could for the day. She brought the interview to a close and thanked Peggy for her help. The two of them walked outside—each carrying a portion of the research material Peggy had assembled. After exchanging some more pleasantries about Peggy's children and family, they loaded the material into Trish's car and said their good-byes.

As Trish drove away, she reflected on how much she really admired Peggy, and, yet—at the same time—she couldn't help but feel sympathy for her. How could she get any enjoyment out of her daily life, knowing what she knew? She was feeling a good deal heavier herself than she had when driving down. The overloaded feeling seemed almost tangible—like the heavy stack of material on the seat beside her.

It wasn't a feeling she'd often had before as a reporter, but she was beginning to think that it was possible to know *too* much about some things.

• • •

The next day was overcast. Trish hoped that meant rain, but when she walked out onto the porch, it didn't feel like rain. After she went back inside, the sky blackened and thunder began rumbling in the distance. As she worked around the kitchen, the sounds grew closer and louder, with lightening flashing menacingly closer, as well. But still there was no sense or sign of rain. It had happened before a few times that summer. It was as though the drought was teasing everyone. When she was a child, the old-timers called the phenomenon heat lightening, but Kathy was calling it "constipated sky." Trish joked about how professional that description would sound on a weather report.

"Well, it might not get the weather man a raise," Kathy retorted, "but everyone sure as hell would know what he was talking about."

Trish grinned at the memory, then looked out the window one more time. There was no break in the clouds. Maybe it would be a good day to transcribe some of the recordings from her meeting with Peggy.

She gathered the material she'd brought home, got settled on the sofa, then immediately reversed the tape in the recorder to the section when her mind had started wandering the day before. Peggy's voice was tinny but clear on the machine. "Have you ever seen a picture of the nuclear testing site in Nevada?" she asked.

"No, I don't guess I have," Trish heard herself respond. The sound of her own voice on a recorder always sounded strange to her, the Southern accent more pronounced.

Trish could hear paper rattling on the tape. It was when Peggy had pulled a large sheet from the thick stack of magazines, clipped newspaper articles and books she'd assembled. "Here you go," she said, as she handed her the paper.

When Trish took the double-paged sheet she'd found herself looking at a colored photograph, identified in the caption beneath it as the Nevada Test Site. The aerial view of the site showed a massive area of gigantic pock marked craters on the desert floor near Las Vegas. Even in its silence, the picture had impacted Trish. "God," she heard herself almost whisper on the tape, "this is such an awesome picture."

"I know," Peggy agreed.

"My God, it looks like the site of some ancient, catastrophic meteor shower, or something."

"Yeah, it does at that," she heard Peggy say on the tape, just as Muffin startled her by jumping up on the sofa beside her. "I think a lot more people ought to see what we've done out there," Peggy continued on the machine, as

Trish scratched her cat's neck. "National Geographic does the best job I've ever seen of capturing our reality in pictures." Her tone shifted slightly. "But even as dramatic as those scars on the earth are, they don't begin to tell the whole story."

"How's that?" Trish asked.

As the thunder continued louder outside, Trish turned up the volume of the recorder and took notes as Peggy talked about a weekly newspaper column in the Atlanta paper called "Earth Week Diary" that she'd begun reading years before. She began noticing in the column that every underground nuclear blast was followed by a report of a powerful earthquake or volcanic eruption in the same general vicinity of that particular part of the world. There was also a worldwide increase in earthquake activity. After following the events on a long-term basis, Peggy could see a definite pattern.

Trish could hear the doubt in her own voice as she questioned Peggy about what she considered a definite pattern.

Peggy explained that because of national security secrecy claimed by various nuclear powers, the public wasn't well informed about all of the nuclear testing going on. And because earthquakes and volcanic eruptions happened continuously and naturally on the planet, it wasn't always possible for the average layperson to even look for cause and effect—or even for a scientist.

Nevertheless, some scientists were researching the phenomenon. Peggy mentioned one in Canada, as well as one in Japan, and another in California. She reiterated that their data had to be incomplete due to the secrecy of the world's nuclear powers. But even with incomplete data, a pattern that was beyond coincidence was forming.

Peggy herself had eliminated the possibility of coincidence when she and her family members began predicting with relative accuracy the location and timing of the next earthquake and volcano after a nuclear blast.

While Trish looked out the window at the darkening sky, she rubbed her purring cat and listened as Peggy explained how she and her family would see the symbol for a nuclear detonation in the Earth Week column one week. Then they would speculate, not only on the location, but the strength of the earthquake for the following week.

Trish glanced back at the recorder as Peggy said, "And sure enough the next week there would be the symbol for an earthquake or volcano in the same general vicinity we'd guessed, and an increase in earthquakes worldwide. It went from being almost comical, in a macabre sort of way, to being downright spooky. I started feeling like someone with premonitions."

"But I can't believe the scientific community isn't broadcasting this…if there's anything to it," Trish stated.

"Who knows? Maybe they're trying to, and we just don't know about it. Things take time. Look at the ozone hole thing." She reminded Trish that even with all of the data that had been compiled, people still denied it. With different studies saying different things, the issue was becoming one akin to dueling experts. That put the public in a position of not knowing who to believe. "So, most opinions fall squarely down political lines. Until the latest NASA findings that finally confirmed: yes, it's there. And, yes, it's getting bigger. And, yes, we did it. If we didn't have the technology we do now, and people hadn't gotten focused on looking at the problem, we'd probably still be in the dark about that, too."

"I guess," Trish admitted on the tape. But at the time she hadn't fully grasped the implications of what Peggy had said.

Peggy told her that people would probably just notice one day how many people they knew who were getting skin cancer and cataracts. They wouldn't know how widespread it was, or make any cause and effect connection to the incidents of skin cancer going up 500 per cent. Trish expressed surprise at the figure.

Then Peggy went on to explain that since the nuclear industry was big business for a lot of powerful interests, there'd be very little motivation for them or government to even pose questions about a connection between the underground tests and earthquakes, much less look for answers. Since those were the main financial interests that could afford to tackle a project like that, it was unlikely that it would ever get the needed attention. She reminded Trish about all the years the tobacco companies conducted so-called studies into risk assessments from smoking, and about the assurances from doctors on television saying it was perfectly safe. It had taken a long time for plain common sense to turn the tide of public opinion on that industry.

Trish remembered that it was at that point she finally allowed herself to consider the possibility of the truth of what Peggy had just said.

"Jeez, Peggy, this is dynamite if there's any possibility at all that these underground explosions are triggering earthquakes and volcanic eruptions."

"Well, that's the atomic age for you…but you'll see for yourself." Peggy had nodded toward the stack. "It's *all* dynamite."

A loud crack of thunder reverberated through the house, drowning out the recording. Trish jumped involuntarily, as Muffin darted off the sofa. She turned off the recorder, but heard the last words from it again in her head.

"It's all dynamite."

Chapter Five

Several days later, Trish sat on the floor of her living room, surrounded on all sides by the books, magazines and papers Peggy had loaned her. Any tiny doubts she might have had initially about actually going to Kazakhstan were left behind somewhere in that rubble of material. If only a fraction of the information she had read was true, she'd wasted a lot time as a reporter pursuing stories that paled in comparison to the story of the atomic age. With her mind completely set, it was time to talk to Max Rogers and let him know what she'd been up to. She slipped on some shoes, grabbed her purse and jumped in her Jeep.

Driving through town toward the turnoff to Max's house Trish recalled the time during college when she'd first met him at a school musical. Her roommate was in one of his classes and introduced them at the performance. Later she ran into him at a University of Georgia football game. When they bumped into each yet again at a café in Athens, they struck up a conversation while waiting for a table to open up. By the time one finally did become available, they agreed to share it. During the meal they discovered that they shared many similar interests and ideas about life and current events. The friendship seemed sealed when he found out that she was from Clayton, since he and his wife, Rachel, had recently purchased some land on Tiger Mountain outside the town. They planned to eventually build their retirement home there, and he jokingly began calling Trish "Neighbor."

When he learned that she was familiar with the area where they'd purchased the land and with the former landowner, Max invited her to dinner one night. There he and Rachel pumped her with questions about the town of Clayton, Georgia, and she talked about her career plans. They had so much fun talking and laughing during the meal that it became the first of many such encounters.

Trish found it comforting and stabilizing to have older friends to turn to whenever she needed advice about a schedule change or a teacher selection at school. She sought out their advice about making the best contacts for her internship as a reporter, or where to go to get her car fixed whenever it broke down—which was often. Trish assumed their attraction to each other had to do with their being childless, coupled with her insecurities about being away from home for the first time.

Rachel, in particular, seemed to enjoy mothering her, though Trish never felt smothered by her—the way she did at times by her own family. From the first time she met Rachel, Trish thought she was a perfect match for the dignified Dr. Rogers—both in temperament and looks. She was charming, polite and at times bubbly. She was a short, heavy set woman, with close-cropped, peppered gray hair that was tightly permed. Trish learned that her heavy Southern accent originated from the New Orleans area.

For his part Max exuded an air of authority, coupled with gentleness, which made Trish feel safe and comfortable. Physically he was of medium build with a slightly rotund midriff. His face was round and ruddy, and his white beard was always neatly trimmed. Though a tailored dresser, at a distance he looked disarmingly like Santa Claus. The smell of his ever-present pipe tobacco always reminded her of her grandfather's cherry tobacco blend.

By the time Trish's college days were growing to a close, not only did she have a permanent friendship with the Roger's, she had enlightened them with every bit of history, advice and even gossip she thought they needed to know about her home town and the local townspeople. She'd even recommended a reputable builder for them to contact when they got ready to build, after Max's retirement.

Leaving the main paved road, Trish turned onto the steep gravel one leading up to Max's cabin. A column of dust trailed behind her due to the dry conditions, and coated the foliage alongside the road. She pulled into Max's driveway, got out of her car and walked up the stone steps to the porch. After receiving no response from knocking on the door, she rang the doorbell…again, with no response. She looked toward the garage and saw Max's car inside. Since his walking stick was gone, she assumed he was out taking a walk on the property and would be back soon. Max's tabby cat, Franklin, walked over and rubbed up against her legs, purring. She bent over and scratched him under his neck, then sat down on one of the rocking chairs on the porch and waited to see if he would show up.

A couple of years before, she had sat there rocking with Max on a day not unlike this one. She'd just returned to live in Clayton.

"Well, Patty," he told her, "I guess our best-laid-plans kind of fell apart on us, didn't they?"

"Yeah, Max. I guess they did." The deaths of her parents had been the impetus for the changes in her life. And Rachel's death five years previously had caught him completely off guard. During the time of her college days, the Rogers had felt as though they had their future plans pretty well set, that their path was going to lead them to Clayton, Georgia for what was left of their lives together. But, just as with Trish, their lives didn't follow their game plans.

After building their retirement home, they settled into the rural lifestyle quite comfortably, just as they had hoped. They stayed in touch with Trish through letters and phone calls and visits when she was in town, just as they had committed they would when she left college. The one thing they hadn't planned on was the cancer that invaded Rachel's left lung from her years as a former smoker. Trish had noticed her chronic cough when she was at college, but Rachel had always attributed it to allergies; whether through denial or misjudgment, Trish never knew.

Her battle with the disease lasted for a little over a year, and when Max called to tell her that Rachel had finally succumbed, she couldn't believe how broken he sounded on the phone. Even when Trish came home for the funeral, she was stunned at how lost and disoriented he appeared. She was accustomed to seeing him confident and dignified, "shoulders and head" above any chaos that might be surrounding him at any given time. At the time she wondered if he'd ever be able to recover from the loss.

After Rachel's death, not only did she and Max maintain their friendship, it grew stronger. His house was usually the first place she stopped when she came home for a visit, and his advice was usually the first she sought with a career problem, mainly because it almost always proved best.

Trish stopped rocking and looked wistfully at the roses that Rachel had planted. They were in full bloom. Max must have been watering them well in the drought. As she resumed rocking, she recalled Max reassuring her that day, "We've still got each other. We'll muddle through." He'd leaned toward her, beaming. "It's fantastic to have you living back in Clayton."

Though Max still had difficulty overcoming the loss of his lifetime companion, his and Trish's 'muddling through' their major disappointments continued to keep them close. His mentoring still supported her, and his companionship was a reminder of her younger, brighter, more idealistic days— a connection to the dreams she'd had and the ambitions she'd pursued. They nurtured their relationship with a quiet respect for their shared past and somewhat dubious futures.

Pursuing the freelance story in Kazakhstan was a marked change in that relationship, since before today, she would never have gotten so far with such a dramatic shift in her life...not without first consulting or at least informing him.

● ● ●

Trish heard a twig break and got up to look in the direction of the sound in time to see Max approaching, his walking cane in hand.

"Howdy, Stranger," he bellowed when he saw her. "What have you been up to lately?"

"Working on a project," she responded as he climbed the steps and hugged her warmly. Then he walked to the other rocking chair, breathing heavily and dropped the weight of his body into it. "Project, you say. What kind of project?"

Before sitting back down, she said, "Wait a minute. Let me go get us some water. It's hot as blazes and you look like you could use some."

He grinned. "I could at that. I've just been down to the waterfall."

"Max, that's a pretty good hike out in this heat," Trish observed before entering the house. When she returned to the porch a few minutes later with two glasses of water, she sat back in her rocker and proceeded to tell Max about being fired and of her plans to go to Kazakhstan.

He leaned onto the arm of the rocker. "Why, Patty, I can't believe you're already so far along with these plans." Then he quickly added, "Not that you have to get *my* approval, mind you. You're perfectly capable of making your own decisions. It's just that I had no idea you were even thinking of such a thing. I noticed your by-line was missing from several editions of the paper, but I just thought you were on vacation." He leaned back. "My...this has happened so fast."

"I know. I'm a little overwhelmed myself. But I knew if I gave myself time to think about it, I might not do it at all. I'm excited, too, though. You know?"

"Well, I'd imagine you are, and I can't wait to hear all about it when you get back. When are you leaving?"

"Right now it looks like sometime next month."

He stopped rocking and leaned forward. "You're kidding. That quickly?"

"Yes, everything is flowing right along. I've still got a lot more research to do. And I really haven't got any promising contacts lined up in Kazakhstan, yet. There don't seem to be too many environmental groups over there, or at least any organized ones I've found. But, I've transferred funds for my expenses, and I'm getting my passport updated now. After that, I'll start making reservations. Kathy agreed to take care of Muffin." She smiled. "I told her it was the least she could do after coaxing—or should I say goading me—into going halfway around the world."

Max leaned back in his seat, then stretched his arms out to the side. As he set them back onto the armrests of his rocker, he said, "Patty, it seems you're breaking a few patterns of behavior."

She tilted her head. "I guess I am."

"Well, you might want to keep something in mind while you're doing it."

She looked over at him. "What's that?"

He pursed his lips a moment, then took a breath and answered, "This is a marked change for you, Patty. You've been aware of inequities in the world for a long time. Now you're reacting a bit more strongly to that awareness...taking a greater risk." He took a deep breath. "However, societies are built on structure; that's what holds them together and makes them function. And that structure is so strong in most cultures that breaking their rules can make you feel uncomfortable and sometimes guilty even when you know the rules are wrong...even when you know the structure is only there for the purposes of control and manipulation, rather than support."

He shifted toward her. "I want you to trust your gut feelings on this one. Whatever you run into, I want you to trust yourself...your own instincts and your own feelings. Make sure that what you're acting on is coming from your own internal guidance rather than any external conditioning."

Trish looked quizzically at Max. There was always more to his comments than met the eye. "Okay, I'll try to do that."

The two of them talked a while longer before Trish rose to go. "I'm going to be up to my neck in research for a while, but I'll call before I leave."

"I'll look forward to it, Patty. But now, you listen to me." He pointed his finger at her. "I want you to be careful when you go over there. Do you understand?"

"Now, Max, it couldn't be any more dangerous than walking the streets of New York," she assured him.

"Perhaps not, but I'd caution you before you went there, as well."

"Well, don't worry about me. I'll be there and back before you know it."

As Trish drove back to town, she mused that she rather enjoyed having someone to worry about her, to care about what happened to her and what was going on in her life. Besides Kathy—and Muffin—she didn't think anyone else cared as much as Max did.

• • •

After spending all of her spare time the next few days absorbed in research, Trish needed another breather. She drove downtown to shop for comfortable walking shoes and clothing to take on her trip. Since she didn't know exactly what kind of weather conditions or situations she might run into, she wanted to be prepared for whatever she might encounter.

When she finished making her purchases, she made one more stop at the furniture store to see her sisters. She hadn't talked to either of them since being fired, and wanted to blunt some of the rumors she knew must be flying around town. Her oldest sister, Carol Anne, was the only one there, and after she'd told her about the incident with Tom Buffington, they talked briefly about Carol Anne's children, the weather, trivial things. Trish had what she thought of as a "tea-time" relationship with her older sisters. She'd always attributed it to their age differences, their years of separation, normal sibling rivalry, but—whatever its source—she'd come to accept that the lack of closeness with them would always would be there.

She told Carol Anne briefly about going to Russia—almost as an afterthought—to avoid drawing too much attention to the importance it had for her. Then she glanced at her watch. "Listen, I've got to get going here, but you and Mack come to see me when you get a chance." After she and her sister exchanged a hug, she left to take her packages home and return to her research.

Though Trish had some ambivalence about being back in her home town, she had to admit, as she walked toward her car with her packages, that there really were a lot of things she liked about Clayton and Rabun County. She took a wide view glance of the square and the green mountains surrounding the town, closed her eyes and took in a deep breath. If only she could find a way to support herself properly, she really could be content here. The familiarity and the continuity of the town and its people appealed to her on some maternal, romantic and even childlike level. She had a flash of a thought that, if she'd ever had children, she would've enjoyed raising them here.

As she approached the stone benches in the small shaded park near the square, she set her packages down and sat down beside them. Leaning back, she scanned the forested mountains, enveloping the landscape in almost every direction. In the soft embrace of those mountains, the city of Clayton seemed caught in a time warp. And, though at times that could be frustrating to Trish, at others it was quite comforting—the sameness and the dependability of it. The town hadn't lost its charm, identity or its peaceful tranquility, the way so many other communities had in their headlong rushes toward "progress." Rabun County still had the feel of home to it.

Trish wondered why she'd tried so hard to escape it when she was young. Now that she had some degree of choice about going or staying, it didn't seem quite so confining, somehow. It was her ambitions that drove her from her home town—not the town itself. And perhaps, she reasoned, her ambitions were still compelling her. Still, she knew that having left town and been away from it for so long, she had a completely different perspective and appreciation of it than she would have if she'd never left.

After those few quiet moments of reverie, Trish picked up her packages again and, as she walked toward her car, she thought about some of the town's historical sites. There was the old house on the hill that was once called the "White House," because it had been the first house in town to be painted, as well as the first to have windows. As a child, her parents had told her that, before the advent of air conditioning, trains brought people up to Clayton from Atlanta in the summertime, as they tried to escape the oppressive heat in the big city. The train tracks on the edge of town were still a reminder of that period of the town's history.

At some point all of Clayton's history, its historical sites, the events that had taken place there over the years, the shared memories and experiences, had become interwoven with her own life. She was part of the fabric. She'd always be one of the home folks. No matter what.

• • •

Trish was still absorbed in her thoughts and feelings, when she turned the corner and ran full force into someone and dropped all of her packages. When she looked up, she was stunned to find herself standing face to face with Jimmy Hartwell—her old high school sweetheart. At first he seemed as surprised as she was, but then they both broke into awkward laughter.

As they scrambled to pick up the packages, Trish dropped them again. This time they just left them on the pavement and laughed genuinely. When the laughter finally turned to silence, Jimmy looked at Trish intently. "Well, I have to say, that's about the prettiest smile I've seen in a long time."

She diverted her eyes from him, the least bit uncomfortable at being scrutinized so closely. "Well, actually, I think this may be the first time I've *smiled* a real smile and laughed a real laugh…in a while."

"Then, I'm glad to have been the cause for it."

Trish could feel blood rushing to her cheeks, and it embarrassed her even more that she couldn't hide the flush. "I'd better go. I've got some more things I need to do today."

As she started to bend over to pick up her packages, Jimmy reached out and touched her lightly on the arm. "Don't go." He pulled his hand back and added, "I've hardly seen you at all since you've been back in town, and we've never had a chance to really talk. Why don't we go get something cold and icy to drink over at the cafe?" He squinted upward. "And get out of this heat."

"Now, *that* would sure set tongues wagging around here for a while," she noted with a hint of sarcasm. Trish wasn't sure just what Jimmy's new single status entailed at the moment, and she didn't dare ask. She hadn't been this close to him since returning to Clayton, but she noted that he was as handsome as ever…still wearing blue jeans and looking just as good in them as he had in high school. His hair and ever-present moustache were peppered with gray, yet he was still slender and his hair was still thick. Though he had deep crow's feet around his eyes and equally deep laugh lines when he smiled, the years had treaded softly across his narrow, familiar face.

When he smiled his same beguiling, easy smile, Trish also sensed the same magnetism that had attracted her as a teenager. It was palpable. The smell of his aftershave brought a reservoir of memories and sensations flooding back, and she blushed again. Feeling off-balance and awkward, she backed up a couple of steps and glanced around, debating about going with him to get a cold drink.

He asked, "Do I make you nervous, Trish?"

"Huh? What?" She looked back at him. "What do you mean by that?" She could feel sweat beading around her face and dampening her shirt.

"You look like you want to jump and bolt or something. Do I make you nervous?" he repeated.

"Oh, no," she replied with a slight laugh. "I guess I'm just distracted by this project I'm working on."

He looked unconvinced. "Well, at least let me help you to your car with these packages." He smiled sideways and added, "Since I've gone through all this effort of knocking them out of your hands twice."

"All right," she replied, looking curiously at him, as she shaded her eyes from the sun.

He picked up her packages, and she motioned toward the location of her car. As they walked along, she asked, "How's your business doing?" She'd learned from Kathy and friends years before about Jimmy Hartwell's outdoor supply shop and thriving white water rafting business on the Chattooga River.

"It's fine. Almost runs itself now...but then, it took a lot of lean years to get it to that point. I really enjoy having free now time when I want it...after being strapped to it for so long." He looked over at her. "How about you? What's this 'distracting project' you're working on?"

"Oh, that? Hmm, well...it's just some freelancing I've been thinking about doing for some time."

He didn't press the matter.

When they reached the car, Trish opened the trunk, and Jimmy loaded the packages into it. "Hope you don't have anything in these packages that will melt."

"Oh, no...just clothes and things."

As Jimmy shut the trunk, Trish noticed a shiny 1957 yellow Chevrolet parked across the street that looked suspiciously familiar. "Say, isn't that your old Chevy from high school?" she asked, tilting her head sideways with half a smile.

"You'd better believe it," he answered, returning her smile. "It's taken me a lot of time and money to keep that thing going...but I never could bear to part with it. It just has too many good memories connected with it."

Since she and Jimmy had dated in that car and it held a lot of good memories for her, as well, his comment left her feeling off balance again. She was surprised by the vulnerability and awkwardness she felt in his presence; she'd always prided herself on being an "in control" person. And right now she was feeling anything but in control.

When they walked to the driver's door, Jimmy opened it, and as she turned toward him to say good-bye, he blurted out unexpectedly, "Are you happy, Trish?"

She was caught completely off guard by both the question and the total sincerity in his voice. Though she could feel blood rushing to her face again, she resisted the temptation to brush his question off with a nonchalant reply. She took time to think a moment before responding, "Oh, I don't know, Jimmy," she began, looking down toward the pavement. "To tell you the truth, I don't know how I feel about a lot of things anymore." She looked back up at him. "What about you?"

He smiled slightly, as though trying to control something. "I'm managing."

She brushed the hair back from her face and shielded her eyes from the sun to look at him. Trish knew there must be more to his response—just as there was a lot more to hers. But, as was typical for her, she didn't ask, and he didn't offer more. So she simply told him good-bye, thanked him and got into the car. He closed the door for her, backed up a step as she started the engine, and with his finger pointed at her and that familiar, crooked grin on his face, he said simply, "See ya."

As Trish drove away feeling shaken, yet excited, she wondered if the rest of her life she was going to be plagued by the things she left unsaid.

● ● ●

On the drive back home Trish couldn't keep the memories of her long ago courtship with Jimmy at bay. They'd known each other for most of their lives, but hadn't really noticed each other until high school. It was at the beginning of his senior year and her junior that they met at a high school football game and began dating. It wasn't long before Trish and Jimmy had become an "item" around school.

Trish remembered that time of her life as one of her happiest. She'd dated other boys occasionally—going out to a movie or to the local hangouts for a hamburger. But with Jimmy, she was completely and undeniably in love.

Besides the fiery chemistry that existed between them, the two had a genuine friendship. They devoted a lot of time to simply getting to know each other—sharing their histories and their plans for the future. They hiked mountain trails and went horseback riding on Jimmy's father's farm. On weekends they occasionally drove to Gainesville in Jimmy's Chevy to hang out in the "big city"—though the town wasn't that much bigger than Clayton at the time. Kathy and her steady, Mike Dunnigan, went with them on some of their outings, and Mike and Jimmy got along, as well. Though it all seemed perfect, there were other elements that affected their relationship, and at least one of them was beyond their control.

The Vietnam War was raging at the time, and it was hard not to think about its implications on their future lives. They both had older friends or relatives who'd been drafted into service, and the threat that Jimmy would be drafted, too, after high school was very real. Trish encouraged him to join the National Guard. She knew that if he didn't have an exemption—like going to college or getting married—he'd almost automatically get a draft notice. But Jimmy didn't seem interested in either going to college or in joining the National Guard. He wanted to simply go ahead and put in his year in Vietnam and get it behind him.

Trish couldn't believe he was being so blasé about the whole thing. "Hey, this isn't prison time, we're talking about here," she'd told him. "This is *war*." She knew the odds that Jimmy could get killed. Trish's father had a friend who worked on the ramp at the Atlanta Airport. He'd told them about how frequently they'd unload coffins from the planes from Vietnam en route back home for funerals. Those stories really drove the point home in clear and unmistakable terms that this wasn't a decision to be made lightly.

Added to that complication was the fact that Trish had always planned to go away to college. She wanted a career, and in her senior year she'd settled on journalism. Having that specific goal had whetted her appetite even more for continuing her education.

Jimmy wasn't thrilled about her college plans. He was afraid they'd drift apart if they were separated that long. And marriage was definitely a part of their personal discussions. They'd become intimate in Trish's senior year and knew they were meant to be together for the rest of their lives.

But there were all those complications.

In the fall following her high school graduation—after a lot of soul searching—Trish left for college at the University of Georgia. Jimmy ended up joining the National Guard. Their separation, coupled with Trish's heavy load of freshman studies, made the distance between them grow, just as Jimmy had feared. It was late in that first year when Kathy came to visit her on campus with the news. "Patty, I hate to be the one to tell you, but someone has to. Jimmy got married to Margaret Simpson a couple of weeks ago." Trish would never forget those words. They devastated her.

She couldn't believe he was capable of doing such a thing—throwing away all their plans, without even a word of explanation. Even though she later came to realize that he must have felt abandoned by her decision to leave town, she'd felt betrayed by him. But, for Trish, his unexpected marriage wasn't the worst of it. It was that they'd never had a chance to sit down face to face and talk about it, to put to rest all of the strong emotions associated with their intimate plans and his reasons for leaving her. There was too much left unsettled.

And that unfinished business had haunted her throughout her adult life.

As Trish turned onto the road to her house, she thought her present uneasiness with Jimmy Hartwell might also have to do with his being her first love. She'd always heard that people never recovered from their first love. That was the only explanation that made any sense. Otherwise, she couldn't understand why the street-smart, in-charge, professional woman she considered herself to be would suddenly get weak-kneed and awkward at the sight of him, the mention of him or the presence of him.

She couldn't deny that she also felt some residual anger over the way they'd parted company, along with the deeply embedded grief. But she finally had to admit, as she parked her car and retrieved her packages from the trunk, that when she saw him in town she'd gotten the same tingly stomach sensations she'd experienced when they first started dating. She even began wondering why he'd hung on to the old yellow Chevy. Was it because they'd dated in it? Or were other memories from high school attached to it?

Whatever the reason for her feelings, Trish was certain of one thing: she didn't like unfinished business. She wanted everything in her life that was relegated to the past neatly and thoroughly packaged away. It was the same with items that had served their purpose, but were no longer useful: they were moved out or boxed away to make way for newer things and newer and better ways.

As Trish walked into the cool of her kitchen with the memories of her former life still lingering on her mind, she decided to simply write off the encounter as a needling distraction. She knew she needed to return her focus to the work at hand.

Her heart said something else. But she didn't speak the language of her heart. And she couldn't understand it any more than she could understand that indefinable force she called her reporter's instinct. They were just feelings.

Chapter Six

After absorbing everything she felt she needed from the reams of material Peggy Craft had loaned her, Trish concluded it was time to contact Mark Matheson. She'd purposely planned to set up an appointment with him last; she knew she'd have to get up to speed on nuclear matters before having any hope of keeping up with him in an interview. Mark was obsessed with computers and technology and at times seemed like a walking encyclopedia when it came to the subject of nuclear issues, though his engaging manner and ever ready smile made him as human as they came.

Before calling him, Trish sat in her sunny computer room with her feet propped up on a foot stool. As she tried to refresh her memory of the interview with Peggy with her notes, her mind wandered back to the time she'd first encountered Mark. She set her notepad down in her lap, propped her head on her hand and gazed out the window.

Shortly after she met Peggy, Tom Buffington assigned her to cover an environmental forum on forest protection in Atlanta. She met Mark during the lunch break, when they sat next to each other and struck up a conversation. He was a tall, handsome, single, young professional man—apparently in his mid-thirties—with a long, blond ponytail and an easy smile that had an engaging, innocent quality to it. As they talked, he piqued her interest in what he called a "nuclear forest" in Dawson County, Georgia, where he resided. "Lockheed conducted nuclear experiments there back in the fifties. It's used as a hunting reserve now, but it's actually owned by the city of Atlanta."

"Really?" There it was again: another story about radiation.

At the time Trish remembered that there had been some talk about the city of Atlanta eventually using the area for a second airport outside of the metro area. But what she hadn't known—before she met Mark—was that there was a dirty little secret about the site that had gone virtually untold for years. Over lunch he told her, "The land is still contaminated with hot cells and Cobalt 60 dust. People don't realize it, so they hunt there and camp there, ride their horses and water them at the wells." He suspected that the decades of exposure to the radioactive contamination were causing an inordinate number of local residents to be adversely affected with cancers and premature deaths.

Intrigued by his story, Trish asked if they could talk a little more about it after the forum. He agreed, and she ended up spending over an hour with him asking questions and taking notes. Whenever she asked a question, he'd launch into a stream of facts that literally boggled her mind. He was over her head on almost everything, and seemed to assume that she was as well versed as he was on the subject of radiation. It was also difficult to keep him on track. A certain fact would remind him of another related incident or thought, and immediately he'd be off on another trail. He was all over the map, so to speak.

Though it was a strain for Trish to keep him focused on one specific topic, she nevertheless recognized that he was an invaluable news source. He had documentation for everything he said, and even carried boxes of it around in the trunk of his car. In all her career she hadn't known anyone— not even Peggy—who could begin to compete with his sheer knowledge of complex facts or his ability to grasp the underlying implications of them.

As Trish drove back from Atlanta that day, it was hard to think about forest protection in Georgia, not when she'd just heard such a compelling story about a *nuclear* forest in the state. As soon as she got back to the newsroom, she approached Tom about reporting on it for *The Clayton Times*. He immediately balked at spending the time and money, saying, "Nobody in Clayton would care about a story so far from Rabun County, anyway." It was the old "so what?" question, that often eliminated a host of good news stories. "Besides, it's just too big to tackle," he added. Trish had believed that about Peggy's story, but not Mark's. She knew she was capable of handling it, but her boss wouldn't budge on the matter.

At the time she'd steamed yet again over the fact that the same dynamics that had driven her from the big city newspapers thrived in her home town, as well. Her boss and co-workers were so caught up in the mechanics of getting out the newspaper, meeting a deadline and staying within budget that they didn't appear to have time for the news anymore.

After weeks of trying to get her editor to change his mind, Trish finally gave up.

Three months later, another newspaper in another town came out with the story blasted across its front page. Though he wasn't identified, it was obvious to Trish that Mark Matheson had been one of their sources. She was furious that her editor had let such an opportunity escape them. But if he was embarrassed at all about being scooped, he managed to hide it well.

For Trish, it was just one more career frustration that was slowly and surely building to some inevitable climax she could sense, but not see, somewhere in the distance.

• • •

That night, when Trish reached Mark on the phone, he agreed to help without hesitation. Like Peggy, he didn't appear to hold any grudge about her inability to get his story in print. They decided to meet at his apartment in Dawson County that week-end, since he had such a wealth of resource material there, and neither of them was sure just what she would want or need. She didn't mention the program on television or being fired, just that she was going to Russia. "Ah, *hah!*" he said, his voice tinged with excitement, "right into the belly of the beast. Good for you."

On Saturday morning, after Trish drove the long distance to his place, Mark greeted her at the door and immediately began complaining that the reporter who'd done the story on the nuclear forest had failed to return a good portion of the documents he'd loaned her. "Before I loan any more of my stuff out, I'm thinking about requiring a blood oath or promise of a first-born child."

Trish grinned at his comment and made a quick glance around his apartment. It was a typical bachelor's habitat: dishes piled in the sink, clothes tossed across the back of chairs, a couple of take-out pizza boxes left on the kitchen table and, of course, an impressive collection of CDs and tapes for his stereo system. But she also noted something most bachelors didn't have: reams of books, magazines and videos, stuffed like a mini-library into shelves that covered one entire wall of his living room and stacked around the room on the floor. Sandwiched in between that bank of books was a computer, which appeared to be used a good deal more frequently than his kitchen sink.

When Trish got seated on the sofa across from Mark in his easy chair, the first thing he wanted to do was familiarize her with some of the terminologies used in the nuclear industry. She pulled out her notebook, pen and recorder. Covering the same territory she had with Peggy didn't seem redundant. Whenever she worked with an unfamiliar subject matter, she wanted as many different perspectives as possible. And this particular subject was as complex as any she'd ever worked on before.

With those preliminaries behind, she began the interview in as casual a tone as she could manage. "Mark, what do you know about the environmental damage done in the Soviet Union during the Cold War?"

"Well," he began, pursing his lips a moment, "I don't think it'd be an overstatement to say that the country's environmental and economic damages were bad enough to actually bring an end to their Cold War machine."

"I guess I can see how the economic crisis brought it to a halt, but how do you think the environmental damage contributed to it?"

"Well," he began, "Gorbachev played the majority role in bringing it to an end." At that Trish looked up. He added, "Even though he's not on the political scene any more, for the time he was, he quite literally changed the world."

Trish noted, with a little amusement, how Mark was tailoring his responses in a more formal manner because he seemed overly conscious of the activated recorder. She was used to that reaction. It would wear off once they got going and he forgot about the recorder.

"You see," he continued," he'd been a dedicated follower of communism all his life." Trish listened as Mark talked about the younger Gorbachev's reverence and loyalty toward Stalin. He described Gorbachev as a typical, classic, patriotic Russian, who, as a student, had written a paper about the elder Soviet leader. Once in power as an adult, though, he had access to information about the condition of the Soviet Union and the actions of its former leaders that he hadn't known before. "It must have really done a number on his conscience." Mark propped his head on his fist as he told Trish that it was unclear what made Gorbachev take the bold step of revealing so much of that information to the Soviet public. "We may never know. Maybe it was the coal miner's strike...or Chernobyl...or maybe Chernobyl was just the final straw."

He told her that Gorbachev had watched the horrors of a nuclear war described by some American doctors on Soviet television shortly before his about-face and suggested that as a possibility. He asked Trish if she was aware that since Gorbachev was out of politics, he'd dedicated himself to working in the international environmental movement.

Trish looked up from her notes. "No, I wasn't."

"He's quite candid about why he does it." Mark held out a hand for emphasis as he explained that the former Soviet leader talked a great deal about military toxic wastes, saying that the citizens in both countries were still being kept in the dark by their governments about it. "He says that we don't know enough about what went on during the Cold War, and is still going on, to protest. He lays the blame for the environmental damage to the world squarely at the feet of the two super powers." Mark paused, as though waiting for Trish's next question.

Trish was intrigued. This was an aspect that she hadn't run across yet. She sat up more erect and veered from her prepared questions. "But what was going on in the U.S. that the people didn't know about?" she quizzed. "I mean, I realize some things were hidden...for sure. But we've got a democracy, and there's no way things could've been suppressed on the same level they were in Russia."

Mark grinned and shook his head from side to side. "Don't kid yourself, Trish. We hid a tremendous amount, and still do, under the guise of national security." Mark talked about the Rocky Mountain Arsenal, outside of Denver, which he described as one of the most polluted sites in the world, a veritable witch's brew of nerve gasses and pesticides. "They're even doing an FBI investigation about the way that thing was run. And the Hanford plant in Washington poisoned *thousands* of unsuspecting people downwind of it for years." He related how the people virtually screamed about their death rates and cancer rates long before information leaked out about how many and what levels of radiation releases were actually made from the site.

"They were deliberate releases, Trish. Some say that over the years there were radiation releases from that site twenty times higher than escaped at Chernobyl."

Trish commented, "I remember reading stories about the 'down-winders' a few years ago.'" She started to slip off her shoes and stopped and asked, "Do you mind?"

"Of course not. In fact, you'd better get as comfortable as you can. I'd recommend a seat belt if I had one handy."

After Trish got settled more comfortably in her seat, Mark continued, "Every time you turn around they release more and more data about what really went on at some of those weapons facilities. We just found out that they buried all kinds of high-level nuclear wastes in bottomless containers just a few miles from the Columbia River outside Hanford." It was believed to be the source of levels of radioactive tritium four hundred times safe levels in the groundwater. He related several stories about the facility, including the discharge of around 40 billion gallons of radioactive liquid wastes into the ground, and over fifty billion gallons of wastes stored in underground containers, a third of which were leaking.

Trish automatically made a quick glance at her tape recorder to make sure it was working properly, as it was becoming clearer by the minute that she wasn't going to be able to keep up with Mark with her notes. He was rattling off information at too rapid a pace.

"And the Fernald plant near Cincinnati… Have you heard about that one?" he asked.

"I heard a little about it when I was working in Cleveland," she replied, twiddling her pen back and forth. "But I know it wasn't nearly as much as you've probably uncovered."

He crossed the fingers of his hands behind his head. According to Mark, the plant had operated for years without the people living near it having any idea about what was going on inside. "Some of the workers were totally uninformed about the dangers of the products they were making. They referred to the place as a 'feed mill'…even had a red checkered symbol that looked like the Purina Feed logo. Hardly anyone knew the feed they were making was fuel for a nuclear bomb."

Mark lowered his arms. "I remember seeing a program about it a few years back." As he watched many of the local residents venting their frustrations over the rash of cancers and deaths that had occurred over the years near the plant, one old man stood up and said he wasn't afraid of the Russians; he was afraid of his own god damn country. Mark tilted his head slightly. "And then, of course, there's the Savannah River Plant."

"I know a little about that place," Trish told him. "I talked to a woman who was fired from there…Peggy Craft. You know her?"

"Yeah...sure. All of us activists end up at the same dog and pony shows whenever the government boys hold their public hearings."

"I've been going over some of her material the last week."

Mark let out a breath and leaned forward with his forearms on his thighs. "God knows, they'll never be able to clean up that place... and because they employ so many people, it's still not popular to criticize it—even now that the Cold War's over." He told Trish how in years past radioactive wastes were actually buried in boxes to dispose of them. "There were open pits, too, where wild life would cross the perimeters, get contaminated and then fly or crawl away. Hell," he added with a grimace, "you could track them by the radioactive *poop* trails they left behind.

"There were even cases where radiated turtles would crawl from the ponds and walk across the road, and a car would run over them and—bingo— radiated tires spreading the contamination up and down the roads for miles."

"Jeez...that's almost comical in a bizarre sort of way," Trish observed. With a wince, she added, "I mean, it kind of makes you wonder where the idea for Teenage Mutant Ninja Turtles might have come from."

Mark broke into spontaneous laughter at her comment, and Trish couldn't help but join in. Then she set her head in her hand and, with a touch of embarrassment, said, "Man, talk about sick humor."

Mark glanced around. "Hell. Maybe we needed a break. This subject matter doesn't exactly make you feel all warm and fuzzy." He stood up and asked, "Can I get you something to drink."

"Yeah...but make it water. I've been feeling dehydrated lately with all this heat."

"Coming right up."

• • •

After their break and a little informal chat about Mark's work with a local forest protection group, they got seated again in the living room. "Let me tell you something, Trish," he advised her. "About the turtle business, if you can't find some way to keep your sense of humor while you're working on these issues, you'd just as well quit now...'cause I promise you won't last long."

Trish had been pleased that Mark was staying on track with the subject matter a lot better than he had in their previous interview, though she wanted to get back to the Soviet Union. "Give me some specifics about the environmental damage in Russia." She flipped to a fresh page of her notebook and turned the recorder on again.

He leaned forward, propped himself on his thighs and cleared his throat. "Well, for one thing, sometime in the 1980's, an entire lake in the Urals totally evaporated from the thermal energy created by wastes that were put into it. And there's another that's so radiated that you can't even go near it, much less drink the water. It'll stay that way for thousands of years."

"I think that's the one I heard about on a "60 Minutes" program a few months back. There was something else about mutated babies born near the test sites. Did you happen to see it?"

"Yes, I saw it." He leaned back. "Well, actually I missed it, but a friend of mine saw it and taped it and brought it over for me."

"Do you still have the tape? 'Cause I couldn't get a copy. Something about a lawsuit."

He shook his head. "No…I gave it back to him."

Before Trish had time to give her disappointment more than a passing thought, Mark added with irritation in his voice, "But you know, I just can't understand why sights like that don't motivate people to get up off their butts and do something about these things. All most folks seem to worry about nowadays is damn tripe…like working on their golf scores or what's happening on their favorite soap operas."

Trish held out her hand. "But, Mark, don't you think most people are overwhelmed by the enormity of the problems…like they're just too big for 'little 'ole me' to do anything about? So they fill their lives with distractions that keep them from having to think about the starving babies in Ethiopia or the nuclear bombs they might be making in Iraq? I know this subject matter is pretty overwhelming to me, and I'm *trying* to focus on it."

"But then," he responded, pointing for emphasis, "these are the very same people who complain that their lives are hollow and don't seem to have any meaning…and how bored they are and disgusted with the condition of the world and politics. They just refuse to make a commitment…even a tiny one. At least you're trying."

Trish looked down and smiled. "Well, if it makes you feel any better, that show really motivated *me*." She looked back up at him. "In fact, it's the main reason I'm going to Russia—Kazakhstan, really—to research that story."

"Is that right?" He tapped his thigh. "Well, glad to hear it." Then he tilted his head slightly, wrinkling his forehead. "I can't believe your editor is letting you do this."

"He's not," Trish replied, setting her notepad down. "I'm doing a freelance story. In fact, I just got fired from the paper."

"Well, son-of-a-bitch."

She grinned. "Yeah, after I got home and got over the shock of it, that's pretty much what I said…with a few other good expletives thrown in to boot."

After she told him about the circumstances of her firing, she raised her arms and stretched her back against the seat. "By the way, you wouldn't happen to have any contacts in Kazakhstan I could interview, would you?"

"As a matter of fact, I might," he answered with an enthusiastic smile.

She lowered her arms, jutted her head forward, and asked, wide-eyed, "*Really?*"

"Yeah." He told her how in the previous few years he'd met several times with some environmentalists and scientists who'd come to the U.S. from some former Soviet states. "They wanted to learn about citizen involvement in environmental monitoring and how to work within the political system."

"Really?" she repeated.

"Yeah, some of them were from the Czech Republic, and some were from other countries." Mark put his index finger to his lower lip a moment and then stuck it up. "Hey, come to think of it, one of them *was* from Kazakhstan."

By now, Trish was on the very edge of her seat, saying with deadpan seriousness, "You're kidding."

He shook his head. "No. There was a guy from Kazakhstan in the group. Don't remember his name, but I don't think he was a scientist. Maybe an environmentalist."

"How did they get over here?" she asked.

Mark shrugged his shoulders slightly. "They evidently used money that was left over from the Marshall Plan after World War II. An environmental friend of mine from Florida—Stephen—called me up one day and asked if I was interested in meeting them and exchanging ideas and information, and putting them up for a couple of nights. And I said 'sure.' That's how we met. It was a great experience. They spoke English, so there weren't any language barriers. And it was fascinating to hear how similar their pollution problems had been to ours...except that we'd been a lot more political and vocal in our movement than they'd been, of course."

Trish could hardly contain her excitement. "Mark, that's probably why I've been having problems contacting people to interview. They don't have any environmental groups like Greenpeace."

"Do you wonder? That kind of organization at the height of communism would have guaranteed prison time." He shifted in his seat and continued, "But things are really starting to open up over there now." He wondered aloud if it might not be easier to start with shaping an entirely new system than to try to move one as entrenched as the U.S.'s, which was becoming more ineffective by the day. He shrugged. "Still, I realize that it's not all positive. They really are at a vulnerable and critical stage, and their pollution problems are a lot worse than ours."

He leaned forward. "And you won't believe how bizarre this is. Even with something as devastating as Chernobyl, the Russian government is actually encouraging the Cubans to finish building the Juragua nuclear plant there, just because they've got money invested in it that they want to recoup." He explained that the plant was designed like the Chernobyl plant, and that some of the engineers who worked on it defected, bringing back information that it was quite poorly built.

"Think about it," he said, frowning. "We were so damned concerned about nuclear missiles pointing at us from Cuba back in the sixties, and now we're going to have this faulty plant 180 miles away from Key West. Hardly anyone in the U.S. even knows about it. And the worst thing is that we've just found out that the U.S. government has funneled $300,000 into Cuba to help fund the damn thing."

Trish picked up her notepad again. "Are you serious?"

"Deadly. And, believe me, heads should roll over that." He shook his head, "Oh, well. Who knows? Maybe they were trying to get money to them to help make the thing safer, since they were going to finish it, anyway." Then he added sarcastically, staring at the floor, "But I doubt it."

Mark looked up at her. "Anyway, I'll give you Stephen's phone number. I'm sure he'll be glad to put you in touch with some people over there who can help you out." He got up from his seat and retrieved a pen and writing material, then sat back down and wrote the information on a piece of paper.

As he handed it to her—without any warning—he shifted to another topic. "You know, the genetic engineering they're doing today is a lot like what happened during the development of the bomb and nuclear energy."

Trish realized he was about to get off the subject matter, and she tried to steer him back. "I'm sure it is, but…"

"The only difference is that the biohazard and genetic research and experiments are cloaked behind the label of 'proprietary rights' instead of 'national security'…you know, 'we can't tell you what we're doing, 'cause you might steal our secrets.' They say they're afraid of industrial espionage, and the government is supporting their position, but it's all the same thing, whether it's proprietary rights or national security. It's just another way of operating in the dark—out of the glare of public scrutiny."

"But, what about—" Trish tried to interject. But Mark didn't even pause. He was on a roll.

"And, I tell you," he continued, wrinkling his brow, "some of the things they're rumored to be studying and experimenting with are like a horror movie: trans-genetic mutations, where you could cross primate genes with human genes and create a race that could be used for slave labor."

"Oh, no scientist would do that," Trish bluntly chastised, raising an eyebrow.

"Maybe not deliberately." He stretched out his hand toward her. "But once you invent the technology, then you always lose the ability to control it—even if you're Mother Teresa and have the best motives in the world. Anyone can corrupt it and use it for his own purposes." He related the possibility of cloning poisons such as snake venom with bacteria or flu viruses and infecting huge numbers of people. "They're talking about those kinds of things right now. And you've got to know that some of these rogue countries would love to get their hands on something like that."

Trish set her pad down again, waiting for him to finish, and attempting to show him that this information wasn't what she was there for. Mark didn't appear to notice, as he continued on, noting that there weren't any laws in the U.S. preventing scientists from conducting those kinds of experiments. He lamented that they were tampering with the very fabric of life for sometimes trivial, even cosmetic, and certainly profitable reasons, without understanding the long-term consequences of those kinds of dramatic alterations.

Mark reared back in his chair. "It's like our technology curve is surpassing our ethical and legal curves. Some of the scientists today are totally intoxicated with the power they've got. And whether they started out working in the war programs and switched to the industrial field or the other way around, it doesn't matter. They're still selling their souls to the devil."

Trish sighed and propped her head on her fist. But for the time being, Mark wasn't even slowing down.

He leaned forward. "And who says that they wouldn't do that? Years ago *our* government broke light bulbs containing Bacillus Globuli in the subways of Manhattan just to see how long it would take to spread through the subway system."

"But isn't that an antibiotic or something?"

"So what? If you were, say, allergic to penicillin, would you want the government to expose you to it without your knowledge?"

"I guess not," she conceded.

"Besides," he added, "I have a problem with the government just haphazardly using its citizens as guinea pigs for biological research without their knowledge or permission, *however* benign it may seem." Mark stood up, stretched his back and turned toward Trish, informing her how the American government conducted other studies similar to that one in thirty different sites throughout cities in the U.S., without telling the public. "Hell, in San Francisco they had to hospitalize eleven people when something went wrong with one of their little experiments. One person even died."

According to Mark, the Army experimented on their own men with different chemicals, and in the fifties the CIA conducted thousands upon thousands of LSD and mind control experiments on people without their knowledge, in the name of national security. First they used volunteers in prisons and on college campuses. Then they decided that the tests couldn't be scientifically validated if the subjects knew they were being given the drugs. So they started giving it secretly to members of the general populace. It began on the fringes of society; they paid prostitutes to slip the drugs to their johns. Then it moved to white-collar people, housewives, mothers.

He crossed his arms. "They systematically and deliberately wiped out these people's memories, just to see if they could. One guy even committed suicide by jumping out the window of a skyscraper. His widow didn't know what the hell had happened to her perfectly normal husband till years later when some of the secret data was made public."

He told Trish how eventually some of the victims sued the government over the experiments and how a few of those cases went all the way to the Supreme Court. "Unfortunately they lost…but only because the Army was immune from liability. And the dissenting judges even compared those experiments to what Nazi Germany had done.

He uncrossed his arms and looked at her. "And, Trish, they did this to thousands and thousands of our citizens. And you think *other* branches of our government suddenly got religion?" He didn't pause for a response. "Even Britain carried out secret biological warfare tests in the Caribbean in the 40's and 50's."

When he stopped long enough to catch a deep breath, Trish quickly interjected, "Well, let's get back to nuclear issues for now." She glanced at her watch. "It's getting pretty late." She picked up her pad again. "What caused them to ban the atmospheric tests?"

"Oh, *that*." He tilted his head back and smiled. "Well, that's an interesting story."

Trish didn't think there was much of any topic about the nuclear field with which Mark Matheson was unfamiliar, and he had a gift of recall that was impressive—even to someone like herself, who worked in a profession that demanded precise recall.

Mark got up abruptly from his seat and walked toward the front door. "Wait a minute. I've got some material on that out in the car. Let me get it."

Trish grinned. "Are you sure you can trust me with it? I don't have a firstborn child to put up for collateral."

Mark turned back toward her as he opened the door and shot her that easy grin.

Chapter Seven

When Mark returned, Trish had just finished changing the tape in her recorder. She turned the machine on again as he walked over and handed her a folder. "A couple of articles in these magazines might interest you when you get a chance to read them." He sat back down, leaned forward and rested his chin on his pointed index fingers. "Back in the '50s," he began, "when the tests were all above ground, the government had a lot of complaints about some of the effects from the fallout: ranchers complaining about dead sheep, cattle deformities and so on."

"One town even had a cluster of babies born with Down's syndrome. They couldn't remember another Down's syndrome baby being born there before, but all of a sudden they had enough to fill an entire classroom at school." He sat up straight and talked about the string of government denials of any connection between that event and the tests that had been conducted upwind from the town. "When they did a statistical survey and couldn't deny or explain away the results, the government simply labeled the event a statistical glitch." He tilted his head. "Can you imagine that?"

Trish shrugged.

"Anyway," he continued, "when the wind shifted unexpectedly after one of the tests and carried fallout to St. George, Utah, the political pressure really started to build." Yet the full magnitude of the tests didn't start coming to light until physicists conducting radioactive experiments in a university laboratory in Troy, New York noticed their instruments suddenly and unexpectedly surging during a drenching rainfall. "They figured the radioactive fallout from the atomic tests out West had been carried all the way there by the jet stream. Some of them even called home and told their wives to keep their kids inside. But they didn't bother to warn the public." Mark sat back in his chair. "It's like that with most scientists. Their studies can figuratively pinpoint where bodies are buried, but their contracts with government and industry forbid them from making any of it public."

Trish listened intently as she took notes.

"Even so," he continued, "scientists around the country and the world began doing tests that showed that fallout had touched practically everything on the planet. And worse, strontium 90 was being carried in the food chain along with calcium and was being stored in the bones of children by way of the milk they drank."

Trish looked up from her notes. She had been a child in the fifties. And she certainly drank a lot of milk on the farm.

Mark told her what a sobering realization it was to the scientists when they discovered that everyone on the planet had been part of the giant atomic experiment. "Now it wasn't limited to soldiers marched to ground zero right after a blast, or even the children or the pregnant women who'd secretly been given radioactive iron; the whole of humanity was involved in the experiment." He leaned forward again. "Maybe it was unintentional, Trish, but that's the whole point." He held out a hand. "You don't monkey around with things, or create things you don't fully understand and can't control, and then unleash them on the rest of humanity…especially when you don't even bother to involve them in the decision making process."

Trish let out a breath. She didn't know if it was Mark's comment about the strontium 90 or the seriousness of the entire subject matter, but she felt ready for another turtle joke.

Mark told Trish how a segment of the scientific community went public with the information, eventually creating enough public pressure to lead to the Limited Nuclear Test Ban Treaty of the '60s. "Then the government went underground with the tests, both literally and figuratively. Nobody wanted to talk about the environmental consequences of simply shifting the location of them. I guess because you couldn't see or measure them as well as you could with the atmospheric testing…and even that took a number of years to detect. But *any* atomic blast is going to have an ecological effect."

He looked directly at Trish. "Have you ever seen a film of one of those underground blasts going off?"

"Yeah," she responded, looking up. She raised her arms out in front of her to demonstrate. "It's like you see this tremendous wave of energy radiating out from the point of detonation." She lowered her arms. "The sheer force of it must be tremendous."

"Exactly," he agreed. "And it's such a simple common sense thing, when you think about it. We all know you can't have an action without a reaction. That's one of the most basic tenets of science. What the hell do they think those blasts are doing to the network of tectonic plates below the surface of the earth?"

After Trish repeated some of her conversation with Peggy on the same subject, Mark told her about a man with the U.S Geological Survey. He was the Chief of Seismology in Menlo Park, California, and had reached the conclusion from his studies of nuclear tests that they had gone further down into the lower mantle than previously thought. "And there were a few other scientists who were studying the relationship between bomb blasts and the earthquakes that followed them.

"Most people aren't even aware of the earthquake factor," Mark told her. "But a lot of activists are. Hell, the government and scientists even speculated about the force of the bomb cracking the earth's crust before they dropped the bomb on Hiroshima."

Trish set her notepad down firmly and leaned forward. "Mark, why isn't someone doing something about this?"

Mark laughed out loud, which puzzled and slightly irritated her.

"Trish, get real. You're not that naive. The first thing that really pisses an activist off is that very comment."

"What comment?" she asked, crossing her arms.

"The 'isn't-someone-doing-something' one. Hell, we know the only real question is 'why don't *I* do something?' "

"Sure, I know that." She uncrossed her arms. But..."

"Really," Mark interjected, "the truth is, that's the basis of any democratic government." He assured her that he wasn't trying to sound preachy or civic minded, but reminded her that democracy only worked when people made it work. It couldn't be left up to bureaucrats and politicians, but, unfortunately, most of the people in the country had forgotten that, because that was exactly who was running the country. He held his right hand up. "So this whole experiment we call 'democracy' may just collapse on us one day."

"Mark, I know all that." Trish set her hands on her thighs. "But aren't the people in charge aware of a possible threat to the earth's crust from these bomb blasts?"

Mark wrinkled his forehead. "They may well be. But if they were, they'd never acknowledge it publicly." He speculated that the government might simply work quietly behind the scenes to get unilateral international agreements to stop underground testing. "And that may very well be the reason right now behind the political move to do that."

"But, Mark, I don't see how a nuclear blast could do any more damage to the planet than say a normal earthquake."

He told her that while the earthquakes, hurricanes and volcanic eruptions that occurred normally on the planet might appear to be quite random and chaotic, they could, in fact, be one of the most delicate balancing acts imaginable in nature. "That's what the chaos theory is all about." He explained that underneath what appeared to be an orderly world laid an inexplicable and unpredictable layer of chaos, and that beyond that chaos there seemed to be another layer of order and perfect balance that scientists couldn't begin to define or understand.

As Trish rubbed her chin, he asked, "Have you ever heard of the chaos theory?"

"I've *heard* of it...but that's about it."

"Well, you might want to take a look at it, if you have time." Mark walked over to his bookshelves and fingered the backs of several books. "But the thing is that when we start disrupting that natural balance by *creating* earthquakes and tidal waves and volcanoes, it would be comparable to turning a two-year old loose in a room full of military computers, and then saying, 'Well, he's just pushing buttons like the big boys. What's wrong with that?'" He pulled a book from a shelf, walked over to Trish and handed it to her. "This is a good one to start with."

She took the book and looked at the cover briefly, while he continued. "Besides, when you keep hammering away at the same spot over and over again—like at the Nevada Test Site—something's *got* to give eventually. And it's a provable fact that there's been an incredible increase in 6.0 earthquakes worldwide in recent years."

Trish looked up and said, "I'm not sure I'll have time to read this before I leave for Russia, but, if I don't, I'll read it when I get back."

Mark picked up Trish's empty glass. "How about some more water?"

She smiled. "That'd be great. I think I need something to wash all this information down with."

● ● ●

Trish left the recorder running as she followed Mark to the kitchen. She leaned up against the bar, as he refilled her glass, and said, "You know, Mark, while you were talking before, I remembered a trip my family took out West during the mid '50s. We were visiting my uncle in New Mexico near a town called Grants, outside Albuquerque. A lot of those atmospheric tests were going on that summer. It was the talk of the town."

"Really? I wasn't even born then."

She smiled sideways. "Well, thanks for reminding me about my age. I was only in grade school myself. But I remember my uncle and some of the men around there had Geiger counters, and those things used to go off all the time."

"Really?" He set her glass down on the bar beside her.

"Yeah." She took a sip of water and continued. "My uncle was a brick mason, and at one point he had the thing clicking around the gravel on the driveway of a new school he was working on. I mean, nobody thought about it being dangerous or anything back then. They just thought they were going to get rich from uranium mining. They were prospecting for it. I remember they said the Geiger counters were just going off because the gravel in the driveway had tailings from the uranium mining in it."

Mark drew his head back. "Really?" She nodded in assent. "Jesus Christ," he said almost under his breath, "you were out in the middle of *that*?"

"I guess I was. I remember, too, that we all got really sick there that summer—throwing up and everything. We were just deathly ill, but my uncle said it was nothing to worry about, that everybody got it…that it was bacteria or something in the water. They called it 'Grants-itis.' Maybe it *was* just the water." She tapped her fingernails on the counter top. "But now

I'm beginning to wonder if it was bacteria or something else.

"Oh," she added, looking up, "and we took one of those uranium rocks back home with us." She looked toward the wall for a moment with her hand on her hip and added, "I *just* thought about that." She looked back. "It had this powdery, yellow stuff on it. And we drove all the way back with it in the car. I don't remember what happened to it…I think I kept it in my room…by my bed. I was such a rock hound back then. All of a sudden I remember that as plain as day." Her eyes moved away and then back to Mark. "Do you think it's possible we could have had radiation sickness?"

"I guess it's possible," he responded, shrugging. "Or it could have just *been* bacteria in the water. There's no way to know at this late a date, but I wouldn't worry about it. You seem healthy now, and your family didn't suffer any other effects, did they?"

"Not that I know of…but, of course, we weren't thinking in those kinds of terms back then." For the first time, Trish began to wonder if the long ago incident had left her with any lasting physical effects. And for a split second she even wondered if it had anything to do with her infertility. They talked a while longer; then she followed Mark back to the living room. The moment they resumed their seats Mark was back on his breathtaking informational roller coaster.

• • •

Trish continued flipping her notebook pages, trying to keep up with Mark's barrage of incredible facts. She kept reframing, then altogether abandoning the questions she'd so carefully prepared the night before, as he listed one example after another of catastrophic nuclear accidents that were avoided only by what he called dumb luck. "There was one in Alabama in the mid-seventies when a guy starts checking for air leaks with a damn candle and started a fire that spread from the control room to the reactor building and burned completely out of control for over seven hours."

"God, Mark," Trish finally interrupted, "you'd think *scientists* would have an incentive to try to stop this kind of thing, like they did with the atmospheric testing."

He told her that in spite of the "bad eggs" in the scientific community, there were some really courageous, vocal scientists who were speaking out on the issues—even if their messages tended to get drowned out by the financial concerns. "They sure as hell are outnumbered. There's an organization called Physicians for Social Responsibility and another called the Union of Concerned Scientists." Mark stretched his arms out across the back of his seat, as he told her about some of their work in nuclear issues.

"And, too, I met this scientist at a seminar once, who gave a fascinating presentation about the problems with nuclear power and why more scientists don't speak out. He was quite blunt about the problems." Mark told her about the man's speech in which he told the audience that there were a lot of scientists in the world of academia who shared his concerns and feelings, but that they didn't dare express their views until they got tenured. That was simply the way the whole academic system was set up in universities. After his speech, the scientist gave a slide show enumerating well over a dozen documented incidents of accidental criticality in the U.S., in which several people had been killed.

"That can't be true," Trish retorted, with doubt in her voice. "I heard it said for years before Chernobyl that there hasn't been a single fatality attributed to nuclear energy."

Mark half laughed. "Well, if the nuclear industry said it, it must be true." Then the tenor of his voice shifted. "Trish, of all people, you know how government and industry lie and twist facts to suit their own purposes. Think about what they actually say."

"What's that?"

"They say, 'No one in the *public* has been killed by a *commercial* reactor *in the US*.' If you change any one single word of that statement, it's false. But the public perception is that no one has been killed by a nuclear reactor, and that just simply isn't true. In fact, they ought to add that no one has been killed *instantly*…because you can bet your ass that lots of the people who got nuked in the clean-ups of those accidents died prematurely because of it." He leaned forward. "See, there was this one incident: the SL1 accident at Idaho Falls in the early sixties. You know about that one, don't you?"

"No, I guess not," she replied, feeling woefully inadequate, even after having plunged headlong into research about the atomic age for the previous weeks.

As she sat listening, she couldn't believe what she was hearing. Mark told her that the reactor was a small experimental military model, along with about sixteen others in the general area of Idaho. It produced only enough electricity to power about a dozen homes and could be set up in a remote area like the Arctic.

One night three military men were working in the reactor building, when there was an explosion, apparently caused when one of the men removed a fuel rod too far. After alarms began sounding, the emergency people quickly arrived and saw that one of the men was dead and another was almost dead. They retrieved the live one from the room, but he died on the way to the hospital. So they brought him back to the facility and covered both of the dead men with lead aprons to try to reduce the radiation, because their corpses were giving off around 400 rads.

Trish had abandoned her notepad and was staring at Mark as he told her how the authorities then realized that the third man was missing and went back inside the room and began a search for him. They finally found him skewered through his shoulder and groin by one of the rods onto the ceiling.

"Oh, my God." She involuntarily raised her right hand to her chest.

"Thing is," he continued, leaning back again, "after they concluded their investigation, they still didn't know had happened, so they suggested the possibility of sabotage. I mean, come on. Even if that were true, it doesn't say much for the people who'd put someone that unstable to work in such a sensitive and dangerous job. That's the kind of guy you'd hire to work in the post office, right?"

"Jeez, Mark," Trish asked, "what did the government do about it?"

"Nothing."

"Nothing?"

He shook his head. "Nope. And it didn't deter the nuclear power industry one bit—even though it was only in its developmental stages. It went full steam ahead like nothing had ever happened. It was like they just shook their heads and kept on truckin'."

Trish crossed her legs. "What do you think happened?"

"I think one of the guys pulled the rod out too far because the thing was stuck. That's what they were doing, anyway, exercising the rods because they'd been sticking and jamming. It'd be like you were trying to open a sticky drawer and all at once the whole thing comes all the way out onto the floor." He held out a hand. "And, Trish, their heads and hands were so hot they had to be cut off and buried in lead coffins when they were taken to Arlington for their funerals. They say you can take a Geiger counter out there to the cemetery and still locate the graves."

"Good God." Trish shook her head, but what he was saying wasn't that much different than what she'd found in any other watch dog agency. They were all too cozy with the very industries they were supposed to be regulating, whether it was the FAA or EPA or FDA. During her career, Trish and her colleagues had often talked about the dynamics of regulating an industry and promoting it at the same time. She'd come to the conclusion long before that it was humanly impossible to do both at once. No one could serve two masters.

When she mentioned that to Mark, he said, "But, Trish, you cut corners on safety in *this* industry, and it's not just a downed plane or two. God knows that's bad enough, but when something goes wrong in the nuclear industry, thousands can die, and that part of the earth can be uninhabitable for thousands of years." He sighed and tilted his head. "See, first of all they say it's perfectly fail-safe, with all the redundant systems built into it, and an accident is impossible. Then when they get the technology in place and an accident *does* happen, they say,' Oh, but accidents happen whenever you're dealing with human beings.'" He raised a hand in frustration. "It's back to the old 'shit happens' excuse. Only *this* shit can have global consequences for the whole of humanity."

He said that at some point people were going to have to start asking if the limited benefit of nuclear technology even came close to being worth the risk and expense. He believed the only reason people thought it might be, was because they'd been steadily fed on a diet of propaganda by both the government and industry and had no idea what was going on.

Trish picked up her note pad, but didn't resume note taking. She was beginning to feel spacey again as she had at Peggy's. Thank goodness for the recorder. She drifted in and out as he told her about other accidents, including two at Chalk River in Canada. At one of those, former President Jimmy Carter was involved in the clean up when he was a young man in the service. There was an accident at a place called Windscale in England, where the whole complex had to be shut down temporarily, and then was re-opened under the new name, Sellafield. He talked about a number of accidents at plants, the names of which she'd never heard, and about higher incidences of childhood cancers and leukemia near some of those plants.

When he mentioned Three Mile Island, all she could remember about the incident was President Jimmy Carter's appearance on television within days after the initial alarms, saying everything was under control. She hadn't known that it was six years before the full extent of the accident came to light, when technicians were finally able to see that there had been some core melting, nor had she known about the threat of a hydrogen bubble explosion.

Trish set her pad down yet again and put both of her hands to her face, then swept her fingers back into her hair. "God, Mark, I have this sickening feeling that you could rattle this list off all day."

"I could, actually, if I got into the details. The cover-ups alone could fill several books. In fact, they do. But I'll put together a nice stack of books and articles so you can get a sense of it for yourself."

He told her about some incidents that had occurred in the forties that he thought she might be interested in. But Trish felt disconnected from the conversation. Her mind wandered to plans for her trip, the books on the shelves behind Mark, anything that could keep her from focusing on what he was saying. Though everything wasn't getting through thoroughly, she grasped enough to ask questions from time to time.

Finally, Trish rubbed her forehead, then stood up abruptly. "Mark, I've got to take a break."

• • •

After the break, Trish and Mark returned to the living room, but Mark didn't wait for her to sit down before starting again. He didn't seem to want to miss a beat. When he slowed long enough for her to gather her thoughts, she straightened in her seat and glanced at the floor. "Mark, I don't know how you get even a sense of the magnitude of this thing out to the general public; it's all pretty...well...unbelievable." She looked back at him. "Even after all the research I've recently done, it's still hard for me to absorb it." She crossed her arms. "I've gotta' tell you, I have a hard time believing the U.S. government would do anything as incredible as refusing to treat its citizens from radiation, like the Soviets did."

Mark set his fist firmly on his hip. "What do you think, Trish—that the Russian scientists knew something ours didn't? It's no different than the Tuskegee experiments. You know about them, don't you?"

She admitted that she'd seen a program on television about treatment being withheld from a group of black men with syphilis so the government could document the development of their disease without the interference of medicine.

"And with that information coming out," he asked, "along with the other stuff about medical experiments with radiation, do you see any effective laws being passed to prevent it from happening in the future?"

"Not that I know of," she admitted.

"And don't hold your breath, either." He lifted his hand in the air. "Hell, those Congressmen won't even pass any legitimate campaign finance reforms. They're sure as hell not going to do anything legally to tie the hands of industry. They're all in bed together."

Again the interview began feeling like a barrage—just as it had with Peggy. Trish was beginning to realize that she could only deal with this subject matter in small doses. Then she needed to get away from it completely and focus on something entirely different for a while. However, it didn't seem that there was anything like a small dose with radiation. Everything she heard about it came in big doses.

So, at the next lull in the conversation, she thanked him for his time. As they stood up and began the process of going through his material to collect things she needed for her research, he said, "Now listen, I'm enclosing a lot of pro-nuclear material in here for you to go over, too," he said, as he put the last piece on the stack.

"Why's that?"

"You might learn more from that than you will from the anti-nuclear material. At least that's how I got to the point I did."

"I don't understand," she commented, eyeing him.

"Well, truth is, I almost went into the nuclear field. That was where I was headed when I first went to college. It was real seductive...the money and all." He told her that, however, the more he read about it, the more he realized that it was too dangerous a technology to have on the planet. There was no way possible to avoid accidents. At that point he started researching some of the accidents. "Then one night I had this real vivid dream. Still remember it. It was a real breakpoint for me. I'm not much at interpreting dreams, but I knew what that one meant. I knew I'd be prostituting my intellect if I didn't change course right then." He held up a hand. "So I changed course."

"I had no idea," Trish said. "That really surprises me for some reason." She told him she already had been collecting and poring over pro-nuclear material. "And I intend to do more when I get back from Russia...interviews, too." She put her hand on her hip. "But, I'm just trying to get enough information and background to ask some intelligent questions once I get there. I'll finish it when I get back. I'm not going to get any second shots at this. I only need enough groundwork to be ready for whatever I find in that clinic...if I can even get into it."

Trish didn't bother mentioning that the pro-nuclear material she'd already read smacked of commercially oriented propaganda, and had conveniently left out huge and significant gaps in the history of the development of nuclear energy and the bomb. She was confident that he was painfully aware of that without any reminder from her.

The two of them talked a few minutes about the canoe trip Mark planned for that weekend down the Chattahoochee River. Then after thanking him again for his help, Trish headed for the door. Just before reaching it, she swiveled around. There was one more thing she had to ask him, even at the risk of prolonging the conversation. "Mark, I'm curious about something. How on earth do you manage to maintain your sanity, saddled with this kind of knowledge for the rest of your life?"

He smiled. "Trish, if I didn't get out on my motorcycle or kayak or canoe once in a while, I couldn't." He shuffled a foot. "Sometimes when I'm out there on one of those mountain rivers all alone in my canoe, I'll almost come to tears. Half the time it's because of how much damage we've done to the environment, and the other half it's because of how beautiful it still is in spite of us."

At the car Trish promised profusely to return all of his material. "Even though I *don't* have a first born child, I'll make that blood oath, if it'll make you more comfortable."

Mark simply flashed her that easy smile again and replied, "I think you might be worth the risk."

• • •

Trish was glad she'd asked that last question. It made her realize that she was going to have to do something drastic to decompress from the thorough saturation of information she'd just heard. Each time she thought the scope of the atomic age couldn't broaden any more, it did.

As she began the long distance home, she ran some of the information over in her mind. What could she use? How could she compress it? How did it relate to Clinic Number Four?

She recalled when she and Mark went to the kitchen and talked about her childhood visit to New Mexico. He suggested she look into an incident that occurred around the same time she was out West. During the mid-fifties—when some of the larger atmospheric bombs were being exploded—a movie called 'The Conqueror', with John Wayne and Rita Hayworth was being filmed in the Utah desert, 130 miles from the atomic testing. Trish remembered seeing the movie as a child. He said that Wayne took his sons with him out to the set in the desert, where wind patterns and sandstorms were said to have carried the fallout from that summer's atomic testing over vast areas. Trish remembered the sandstorms from the summer she was out West. They'd felt like thousands of tiny needles when they hit. Anyone caught in one of those storms had no choice but to get to shelter quickly.

Trish pulled into a parking lot. There was something she wanted to listen to again. She rewound the tape in the recorder beside her to the point when they were in the kitchen, clicked it in the play position, and pulled back into traffic as Mark's voice filled the interior of the car.

"Well," Mark was saying, "some of the people who were out there then—including one of Wayne's sons, I believe—think they were exposed to fallout that summer and got cancer from it. In fact, of over 200 people, 90 got cancer and half of them died." Trish remembered shaking her foot back and forth nervously, as Mark told her how they'd trucked some of the sand back with them to a Hollywood lot to finish filming; how it was given away for school and park sandboxes when the studios were finished with it; how they realized later that the sand was radioactive.

"Jeez," she heard herself utter in a whisper on the tape.

"There was a book about it...Secret of the Sands, or something. I don't think I have a copy of it around here," Mark continued as he'd glanced over at his bookshelves. "Your trip out West reminded me of it."

"If you come across it, I'd like to read it."

"I'll keep an eye out for it."

Trish clicked off the recorder and stared ahead as she drove. She took a deep breath, and, for the first time, fully allowed the possibility that exposure to those atmospheric tests might have been the source of her infertility. Had she been silently contaminated and not known it simply because there'd been no blaring alarm as there had been for Peggy at Savannah River Plant?

As the possibility felt as though it was lodging into the very cellular structure of her body, a wave of emotion filled her. She took another deep breath and tried to push the emotions back. Without success.

At the next stoplight, she picked up her cell phone and punched in some numbers with a shaky hand. She waited through the ringing until she heard the familiar voice on the other end inquire, "Hello?"

"Max," she began, trying to control the quiver in her voice, "I'm on my way back to Clayton from Dawson County, and I was wondering if you'd mind if I went down to your waterfall when I get back to town in about an hour. I need a little quiet time alone."

"Of course not, my dear. Make yourself at home."

When she reached Clayton, Trish drove straight to Max's and got out of her car and walked the quarter of a mile to the creek and falls. There, hot and sweaty from the walk in the heat, she crouched down for a few minutes staring and listening to the roar of water over wet rocks. She rocked back and forth, holding her bent legs and resting her head on her knees, fighting back tears. This story wasn't supposed to be about her. It was about other dynamics and other people. She looked back up at the falls. It wasn't enough to simply sit and look at it. She took her shoes and clothes off, walked out on a rock ledge and thrust herself part way under the cascading, cold water. The shock of the change in temperature made her squeal involuntarily. She thrust the rest of her body under the torrent and squealed louder. Then she screamed. And screamed again. And again…until she couldn't scream anymore.

Then, curling up into a fetal position on the ledge at the base of the falls, she wept without restraint as water pounded her back.

• • •

The next morning, still a little numb from the previous day's events, Trish sat down in a chair in the living room and pulled her bare feet up under her, as she recalled Mark's comments about a procedure called 'tickling the dragon's tail.' At that point she hadn't been sure she wanted to know about it. She remembered needing to take a break or get a breath of fresh air at that point. But she'd let him continue.

She reached for her pad and pen and set them in her lap, then turned on her recorder, searching for that section of the tape. She finally heard his voice saying, "This happened at Los Alamos in the forties, around the time of Hiroshima and Nagasaki. They were doing critical mass studies with their bare hands—seeing how close they could move components of a table top reactor together before it went critical."

Trish remembered going wide-eyed and abandoning her note taking. "God, that sounds like playing with nuclear fire."

"That's exactly what it was," he agreed on the tape, "'cause the dragon won." He said that the needles started clicking louder and louder as one man moved the piles closer and closer. What was happening, however, was that the closer he moved them, the more exponentially stronger the reaction was becoming. "Suddenly there's this characteristic blinding blue flash when the thing goes critical, and this guy takes the full force of the blast right in his face."

"Oh, my God. What happened to him?"

Mark exhaled loudly on the tape, then told her that the man didn't feel anything at the time, since evolution hasn't given man that ability yet. Then within days his cells began disintegrating, and within twenty-four days he died a horrible death. "It was like the Ebola fever thing they talk about; it wasn't a pretty sight. I've got a copy of the autopsy report on that one."

"Where the hell did you get *that*?"

Mark had grinned and answered in a mock German accent, "Ve have our ways…"

"Jeez, Mark, I can't believe something like that could've happened and I've never heard about it before."

He began telling Trish about another almost identical incident that happened only a year later at Los Alamos. Again, a man moved the components too close together, and again there was the blue flash, except that this time several people were in the room. Realizing what was happening, the man lunged forward and grabbed the piles with his hands, pulling them toward himself and taking the full force of the critical reaction in his stomach to save the others.

"What happened?" Trish asked.

"Again, he didn't feel a thing—even though he'd taken ten times a lethal dose. But within days he went through the same process."

"Died?" she asked.

Mark had nodded reluctantly. "Yeah, had huge blisters…swelling…fever. It was bad." He sighed on the tape. "There are a lot of these kinds of things that you'll never hear about—unless you're in some kind of grapevine line, like the environmental movement or some scientific circles."

Trish clicked off the recorder. It was only then that she looked down in her lap at the unused pad and pen and realized that again she hadn't taken any notes. She went to the phone and called Mark Matheson's friend from Florida. Her appetite for the story was whetted once more. After Stephen McKnight answered the phone and Trish told him about her affiliation with Mark and her plans to go to Kazakhstan, he offered to help in any way he could. He had a youthful sounding voice. Trish thought he was probably around Mark's age. His friendly manner made her feel comfortable. With pen in hand, she made notations as they talked.

As soon as she mentioned going to Semipalatinsk, he said, "Trish, that's where one of those couples was from who came over here."

Trish sat up straight in her seat. Had she understood him correctly? "Did you say they're from *Semipalatinsk* or Kazakhstan?"

"Semipalatinsk. Yuri and Katrina Medvedev. Great couple. You'll love them. I'm sure they'd be anxious to help you. Their biggest concern is how people over there have suffered from the nuclear tests."

She took in a deep breath, almost afraid to ask the next question. Holding her body perfectly still, she asked, "Do you think they might have any contacts at that museum where Clinic Number Four is?"

"Couldn't say. No one even knew about that clinic when they were here. It's just recently that it came out in a few publications. I guess it was a pretty well kept secret."

That was all right. At least now she had a contact in Semipalatinsk.

As they continued talking, Stephen advised her, "The way I'd do it is fly to Moscow and then to the capital...Almaty." Trish twisted her pen back and forth in her fingers as he talked. "From there I'd take a train to Semipalatinsk," he continued. "I'm sure Yuri and Katrina will help you with lodging and any contacts you'll need." He told her that since the environmentalists over there were so eager to get out information to the Western world, they'd be her best sources for pointing out what she needed to see and in getting around in the country. "Any other way and you'd just get caught up in a bureaucratic zoo and spend days and days in a hotel room doling out whatever cash you have and never get a chance to see anyone or anything.

"Yuri and Katrina both speak English rather well...and that'll come in handy, too. I've been over there a couple of times—once to Czechoslovakia and once to Kazakhstan—and it's absolutely essential to have an interpreter."

"Stephen, I'm pretty anxious about this, you know...eager...but a little leery, too," Trish admitted, still twiddling her pen. "It's not exactly like hopping on a plane and flying to England, is it?"

"Well, no it's not...but then that's really what makes it so intriguing. This isn't going to be anything like your standard tourist fare."

She let out a breath. "I really think I'm prepared. I guess I'm just excited because I've wanted to do something like this since the Berlin Wall came down, and all of a sudden it's all coming together so quickly."

He told her that he'd like to go back over there some day, but that it would be a while before he could afford to. Then he advised her to keep in mind the very serious financial problems most people were facing there and to insist on reimbursing them for things that Westerners take for granted, like gas or phone calls.

"I'll remember that...and thanks for telling me."

She and Stephen talked several more times over the next few weeks, as he put her in touch with his friends in Kazakhstan and continued giving her advice on traveling and interacting with the people. He also told her anecdotal stories about the places he'd gone, the things he'd seen, and the routes he'd taken to various destinations. He advised her to be sure to board quickly when she flew from Moscow to Almaty on the Russian carrier, since all the seats would probably be full, and people quite likely would be standing in the aisles.

"You're kidding," she responded.

"Nope. And if you get up to go to the bathroom or something, you probably won't have a seat when you get back."

Trish snickered. "You're *kidding*," she repeated.

"Afraid not."

Trish continued her research, and, within a little over a month after deciding to go to Kazakhstan, she had all of her travel arrangements in order. She'd given herself just two and a half weeks, including travel time, to gather her story. All she had to do now was to wait for her departure date.

Chapter Eight

The day Trish left, Kathy drove over to say good-bye and give her standard maternal warnings about being careful and having a good time.

"Don't worry, Kathy, I'll be careful over there in Russia."

"Russia, hell," she replied with her hand on her hip. "I was *talking* about the Atlanta expressway."

Trish laughed and hugged her friend, got in the car and left.

When she reached Atlanta and turned off the interstate onto the airport exit, she felt the same sensation she'd had when she first went away to college—a strange mixture of excitement and fear of the unknown. Though accustomed to traveling alone, she was having a few reservations about traveling to a foreign country that had only in relatively recent years been opened up to the Western world—and where she'd have trouble communicating because of the language and cultural differences. She hoped Yuri and Katrina Medvedev would be able to provide all the support she needed to get her story.

They'd already reserved a small bungalow in Semipalatinsk for her and had arranged interviews with several people, including a scientist who'd done studies about the health effects of the nuclear program there. Stephen said he wasn't sure, but that he believed the man had actually worked at a clinic or dispensary during the Cold War, possibly Clinic Number Four. Trish couldn't believe she'd gotten that lucky, and she couldn't help but question the authenticity of the information. Was it really Clinic Number Four? If so, just how involved was he in the work there? Did he still work there?

And most importantly, could he get her in?

Yuri had told Stephen that the doctor was a neighbor of one of his environmental friends; that he lived in the city; that his name was Mirek Klavanis; and that he'd said he'd be glad to speak with a Western journalist. Though it all sounded quite promising and she felt she'd done everything she could have beforehand, and even though she knew worrying wouldn't make her preparations any more complete or better, she couldn't help but worry as she drove.

When she reached the long-term valet parking lot a short distance from the airport, Trish parked her car and rode in a van to the terminal. There she checked her luggage, went through security, and boarded the jet for her flight to New York. From there, her next destination was Moscow.

On the long trip, she reviewed some of the books and magazines she'd brought along to study. After pulling out an atlas and turning to a map of the Western U.S., she began making notes about her trip out West with her family in the fifties. Her sisters had filled her in on some of the details she'd forgotten. Their memories were a lot clearer, since they were older. One thing she'd forgotten was that they had traveled down through Texas on their way to New Mexico because her father had always wanted to visit El Paso. Then they'd driven up along the Rio Grande toward Albuquerque and finally to Grants, where her uncle lived. As she looked at the map, it was clear that they'd traveled almost parallel to the White Sands Missile Range and just east of Alamogordo.

Carol Anne had said, "Don't you remember when we took that wrong turn and got stopped by those men at a roadblock out in the desert? They told us the area was restricted, and we were going to have to turn the car around and take a different route."

"Yeah...sort of," Trish had replied.

"Mom and Dad were awfully curious about it. The thing I remember most about the men was that they were in uniform." Carol Anne's comments had convinced Trish that the incident was connected to the bomb tests that were going on that summer in the deserts of New Mexico.

After closing the atlas and returning it to her overnight bag, she stared out the window. Just what was she getting herself into?

Trish thought about the depressing nature of the facts of the story. She doubted anyone in the general public would want to read about nuclear contamination anymore than they'd want to read about starving children in third world countries. To make the story marketable, she'd have to come up with some kind of angle to be at all effective and make the story marketable. Even though she didn't have an inkling of what that angle might be for the moment, she had no choice but to trust that it would come to her at the appropriate time. All she had now was that indescribable, indefinable sense that there was much more to the story than met the eye...as dramatic as the sight of the mutants had been.

• • •

After arriving in the Moscow airport and finally getting through the customs line, Trish reconfirmed her reservations for the next day's flight to Almaty, then called Yuri to tell him the approximate time she'd arrive in Semipalatinsk. She promised to call again before boarding the train, so he'd know exactly when to meet her. Then she gathered her luggage and took a taxi to the hotel where she'd made reservations for the night.

Exhausted from the trip, she welcomed a shower and a good night's sleep in the modest hotel room. In fact, she was almost too tired to even worry any more. She regretted not being able to see the sights in Moscow her first time there. She'd always dreamed about visiting Red Square with its colorful onion topped buildings, but there simply wasn't enough time or money.

The plane trip to Almaty was even more exhausting than the oceanic flight—mainly because she spent so much time in the Moscow airport waiting to leave because of flight delays. Even though Stephen had warned her about the inefficiency of the Russian carriers, her anxiety and frustration continued building with each setback until she could almost feel adrenalin draining from her body before she boarded the plane.

After arriving at Almaty, she made train reservations for the next day and then got a room for the night. When she did manage to sleep, it was fitful at best. She kept missing her train in her dreams. She'd toss and turn and wake up in a panic, unable to go back to sleep for long periods. As it turned out, all of her worries were wasted, since everything went as smoothly as could be hoped for the next day. She arrived at the station with time to spare, called Yuri, and, to her relief, the train actually left on time.

Since childhood, Trish had dreamed of taking a long train trip. After settling in her seat, she slipped into her familiar observer mode, watching people's body languages and listening to voice inflections. With the language barriers, attempts at communication would be pointless. Soon enough, though, she realized that she was the object of a lot of observations in the train car. Her appearance: her clothes, hairdo, even her luggage were obviously as different to the rest of the passengers as they were to her. Her Reeboks, in particular, attracted a good deal of attention and commentary.

Once the train left the station she focused on the sights along the route. She soon noticed that when they traveled through the larger cities—especially the industrial ones— the buildings appeared coated in some kind of residue. There was a grayish look and a haze to almost everything—so much so that it gave her the impression of traveling through a black and white movie, instead of one filmed in Technicolor. It was depressing. What Peggy and Mark had told her about industrial pollution in the Soviet Union was not only true, but very visible, as well. She wondered if the fumes from the smokestacks were impacting concrete buildings so dramatically, what they must be doing to peoples' delicate lungs, hearts and kidneys.

But out in the countryside, a Technicolor brilliance returned. The landscape was breathtakingly beautiful, full of trees, rivers and mountains, and eventually wide expanses of plains, devoid of forests—areas she had read about called the "steppes." Interspersed with all of it were tiny villages, set like pastoral scenes from a period movie, or the afterthoughts of an artist on canvas. There were hardly any signs of modern technology—no cars, shops or paved roads, just farm animals and pens and clusters of small homes, real villages. She felt as though the train had been transformed into a time machine that had propelled her into another century.

It was difficult to sleep on the train. Almost every time she closed her eyes, the train whistle would sound, or someone would laugh or speak rather loudly, or the train would stop or slow down, breaking the rocking, rhythmic motion of the train car. The combined apprehension and excitement from being in a foreign country didn't help matters, and she was only able to sleep in short stretches at a time. Before long the combined and distinct effects of sleep deprivation and jet lag began catching up with her.

• • •

By the time Trish arrived at the train station in Semipalatinsk, she wanted nothing but a clean bed on solid ground and about ten hours to sleep in it. She was anxious about locating Yuri. The station was bigger and more crowded than she'd imagined it would be. Though she'd described herself to him in detail from the airport in Moscow—and Stephen had described Yuri to her—everyone at the station looked alike to Trish.

Yuri would definitely have the advantage over her. All the looks she was still getting told her she stuck out in the crowd.

For what seemed like an eternity, she stood around feeling lost, bewildered and excruciatingly tired. Finally, a tall man who appeared to be in his late thirties approached her with a questioning look and inquired in heavily accented English, "Patreecia?"

It was Yuri. She couldn't have been happier to see him if he'd been a long lost relative who was going to donate bone marrow to her. She actually hugged him, and then quickly drew back, wondering if she might have committed a cultural faux pas. He simply laughed and returned her hug with an even bigger bear hug. The ice was definitely broken. Yuri appeared almost as glad to see her as she was to see him.

"Well, let us collect your luggage, and we will get you to your bungalow," he said with a broad smile.

As they walked Trish said, "You don't know how great that sounds. I sure could use a long nap right now. And you don't know how great it sounds to hear English again."

"Well, I don't know if my English is so good, but we will get you to a nice place. A friend of mine owns the bungalow where you will be staying and rents it from time to time since more and more outsiders are coming over here now. It is quite a nice little house."

They reached the place where the luggage was being off loaded, and Trish inquired, "Outsiders? What kind of outsiders?"

"Oh, it seems that we are quite—uh—uh—popular—yes, *that's* it— with the rest of the world. They want to do business over here now, and we have all different people from around the world selling things and starting business enterprises. We have a few tourists now...and even oil companies coming over to talk to the government because we have so much oil and minerals."

"Is that right?" Trish asked as she spotted her luggage and went to pick it up. Yuri beat her to the bags and deftly swung the heavier one over his shoulder and picked the smaller one up with the other hand. As he led the way out of the crowded area, he responded, "Yes, they are speaking about doing some explorations in Kazakhstan."

"Are you sure they don't mean 'exploitation'?"

"Huh?"

"Oh, never mind," she replied with a wave of her hand. "I'm just being a little sarcastic."

"You must be patient with me, with my English."

"No, no, your English is fabulous, honestly," she assured him, gesturing. "A lot of people in the U.S don't speak it as well—even some of the ones who were born there."

Yuri laughed. She had already noted that he laughed easily.

When they reached Yuri's car, it was obviously an older model. His wife, Katrina, was waiting in the back seat with the windows rolled down. After he introduced the two women and they shook hands, she motioned Trish to get in the front seat.

As Yuri drove through town toward his friend's apartment to get the key to the bungalow, Trish became distracted from the conversation by the pitiful condition of the roads. They were pockmarked, patched and bumpier than any she'd ever seen before. The most poorly maintained gravel roads she'd driven on in Georgia weren't as bumpy as a couple of the stretches they were driving over. The city landscape had the same overall gray appearance as the other industrial towns through which she'd traveled on the train. If the financial profits from the Russian nuclear program had benefited anyone, it certainly wasn't the people of Semipalatinsk. Or at least they didn't appear to have gotten their fair share of it—even though Trish noticed with admiration that there was no sign of litter anywhere.

All of the buildings had an institutional look to them, even the apartment buildings. They appeared to have been built in the fifties, as though the entire city had sprung up at that particular point in time and hadn't progressed beyond it. Either the architecture hadn't changed or the buildings were the same. She was accustomed to Americans always tearing down and rebuilding and redefining themselves architecturally. Nothing ever stayed the same in cities in the U.S.

"Patricia," Katrina asked as she leaned forward toward the front seat, "do you work for a big newspaper in America?"

"No," she replied. "And please call me 'Trish.' In fact, I'm not working for any newspaper right now. I'm doing it on my own time and with my own money for what they call freelance reporting, and then I'll try to sell the story when I get back."

"Really? I never heard of something like that before. How does it cost...uh...how do you afford it?"

Trish laughed and rubbed the back of her neck. "I can't really. I've kind of extended myself on this financially, and it's a real gamble for me, to tell the truth. But I just felt like I had to come and research this thing. It felt more important than just a job."

"Yuri's friend where he works, Valary—the one who lives near one of the doctors from the dispensary—he said that the doctor was unhappy with some of the other doctors because they talked to reporters from America without telling him about it. So we think that is why he is glad to talk to you."

Trish gave a sideways grin. "I wondered how I got so lucky on that one. Before I knew I'd get to interview someone from the clinic, it was like a shot in the dark, but, really, so far, everything about this trip and this story has fallen right into place...like it was meant to be or something." Then she raised her eyebrows. "You called it a dispensary. Is it Clinic Number Four?"

Katrina nodded, as she corrected, "*Dispensary* Number Four."

Trish looked forward, still a little confused, but before she had time to pursue the matter, Yuri pulled up beside an apartment building, parked and got out. While the women waited in the car, Trish noticed a few children playing with a ball in the grass outside of the building. Children were the same everywhere. One little girl giggled when a playmate found her hiding behind some steps. From her happy sounds it was impossible to tell if she was Russian, French or American. The children were full of energy, and Trish wished in that moment that she had just a little of that energy.

She confided in Katrina how tired she was. "I don't know if it's jet lag or what, but I feel like I'm going to collapse if I don't get some sleep." She thought—but didn't add—that she also felt too tired to even talk.

"This will be a quite nice place," Katrina assured her. "It is a quiet area, and you will surely get some rest there."

When Yuri returned, he had an older man with him, carrying a shopping bag. As he climbed into the back seat with Katrina, Yuri interpreted an introduction between them. The man was exceedingly polite, nodding to her and smiling broadly. Trish gathered that he was either the owner or the caretaker of the bungalow.

They drove down several streets and turned into an alley that was little more than a dirt lane. Trish noticed that the dirt road was almost smoother than some of the pitted, paved streets they'd driven on. They stopped at a tall, weathered, wood fence with a hinged gate. The man got out and opened it. Trish was apprehensive about what lay beyond it, but she simply wanted to be alone and quiet, and get into a nice, clean bed. And it didn't have to be elegant. She had even started to doze a few times in the car.

They pulled just inside the wooden gate into a small courtyard beside a tiny house.

"This is it," Yuri said to Trish with pride.

"Yah," the man added, nodding.

Inside the house, the man gave Trish a short tour. It was a one-bedroom cottage with a bathroom, a small kitchen and a separate living area. Like all the other buildings, it had a fifties look to it, but to her delight, it was extraordinarily clean.

The man retrieved her bags from the car, set them in the bedroom and then started unloading the shopping bag in the kitchen. Trish knew she couldn't go another step or another minute without sleep. She went to Katrina. "I'm just exhausted. I've got to lie down for a while. You'll have to excuse me."

"Oh, of course. It is no problem. Go to your bed, and we will go out by ourselves. We will put the food in the kitchen, and then come back in the morning to take you to Dr. Klavanis' house."

"That sounds great." She briefly wondered, but didn't ask if Dr. Klavanis still worked at the clinic—or dispensary—and in what capacity.

"Do not drink any of the water from the faucets," Katrina quickly cautioned. "He is leaving you some bottled drinks and some food, so you can eat when you get up—and in the morning, as well. He will bring you more food when you need it."

"Do I pay for the bungalow now?"

"No, no. He said for Yuri to bring him the key and money before you leave. If he is not there, we will leave them in the slot of the door to his apartment."

Trish couldn't believe it. The man would never make it as a landlord in most major U.S. cities. She wondered just what kind of culture shock he and Katrina and Yuri would experience if they ever traveled to the Big Apple. Trish excused herself and thanked everyone. Then she went into the bedroom, closed the door, took off her shoes and crawled between the sheets.

Her body felt almost immobile as soon as she lay down. She literally didn't think she could move. She felt drugged. The bedroom window was open and a light breeze was blowing through it. The temperature was pleasant. Birds chirped outside the window, and just as she began to doze, she thought how they—like the children at the apartment—were like birds everywhere. The birds might sing different songs and the children might speak different languages, but they were all the same.

She could hear Yuri and the other man speaking in the kitchen as they finished putting things away in the small refrigerator. As her body became less relevant, her senses became somehow more alert—the sounds inside and out, the smell of the sheets, the feel of the wind through the window. Yet, she was barely aware of any of her surroundings when everyone left the house. She only heard the car engine, and didn't remember anything after that.

• • •

When Trish finally roused from her sleep, it took a minute or two to remember that she was halfway around the world. She looked at her watch. She'd been asleep for four hours. The position of the sun indicated that most of the day was already gone.

Though she was tempted to go back to sleep, she was hungry. So she got up and went to the kitchen. The man had left her a variety of foods— sliced meats, cheeses and bread—much more than she could have eaten, as well as bottled drinks and beer. She opened a beer and sipped on it, then made a sandwich and relished every bite as she ate. She went into the bathroom and stripped to take a shower. It took her a while to figure out the plumbing, but once she did, the water felt good beating against her naked flesh. Then almost instantly, she felt a film on her skin from the tap water. She couldn't wash it off, either. That was why Katrina had told her not to drink from the faucet. Whatever was in the water would have stuck to the inside of her mouth just as it was clinging to her skin, and she didn't want to even imagine what it was.

Still, the temperature of the water was refreshing, and she wrapped herself in her robe and went outside to the small, enclosed courtyard to relax and look around and let her hair dry. As she sat in an old metal lawn chair, her attention was instantly drawn to the beautiful roses in full bloom around the yard. She hadn't even noticed them when they'd first arrived. The blossoms were huge and their colors were brilliant against the mauve, magenta and orange hues splashed across the sky from the setting sun. It was obvious that someone had tended them well.

She wondered whose house it was, and where they were then...if the man who'd let her into the house was the real owner, or only an agent. She wished she could speak even a little Russian. She was becoming frustrated trying to cope with a completely unfamiliar language. Still, she was grateful to have Yuri and Katrina to interpret for her and guide her through the city. She wondered whether Dr. Klavanis spoke English as well as they did. She again questioned her good fortune about the interview with him. Was Dispensary Number Four the same Clinic Number Four she'd heard about? And, if it was *the* Clinic Number Four, could the doctor get her into the room containing the specimens?

She heaved a sigh, leaned over and smelled one of the roses, then went back inside and again fell into a deep sleep.

Chapter Nine

The next morning, Trish had just finished a few bites of breakfast when Yuri and Katrina drove up in their car. She waved from the doorway, and called out, "I'll be right there." Quickly gathering her notebooks, tape recorder and camera, she crammed them into a small backpack, slung it over her shoulder and hurried out to join them.

"We talked to Dr. Klavanis this morning," Katrina began, as Trish climbed into the back seat of the car, "and he said that he could get you into the dispensary even though it is a Sunday. He has a key, and it will be no problem."

"That's great," she responded, excited by the confirmation that Dr. Klavanis at least had enough of a connection to some kind of clinic or dispensary to get into it.

"Did you sleep well last night?" Katrina inquired.

"Like a baby." Then Trish added with a chuckle, "Except that I kept feeling like I was still rocking back and forth on that train."

As they drove from the house Trish was both excited and apprehensive. She felt much as she had when she was about to visit the Dachau Concentration camp in Germany on one of her vacations to Europe. Even though it wasn't the kind of place anyone looked forward to visiting, she'd still felt compelled to go, as had the many thousands of others who had preceded her. After hearing about the camp in history classes as a teenager, she'd felt strangely fortunate to have the opportunity to capture a little of the reality of the place. And just as she had expected, it had proved to be such a powerful experience that she'd never regretted having gone. She knew that Max had been one of the first American soldiers to enter the camp during World War II, though he rarely talked about the experience, even to her.

When they arrived at Dr. Klavanis' house, Yuri's friend was waiting for them just outside on the sidewalk. Yuri introduced him as Valary. Not only were he and Yuri friends and co-workers, they'd also shared environmental concerns for years—even before the fall of the Soviet Union. Trish thought their interactions were more like those between brothers.

After chatting a while, the four of them walked up to the house. Before Valary had a chance to knock on the door, Dr. Klavanis opened it and greeted them. "Come in. I've been expecting you. Good to see you, Valary." He shook his neighbor's hand. Trish was relieved. His English was almost flawless, though heavily accented. She noted, too, that he was somewhat subdued. He was handsome, apparently middle aged, with curly hair, dishwater blond and tousled, as though it belonged on a two-year old, instead of a grown man. His eyes were strikingly blue and his nose slightly bent, as if in defiance.

After introductions the five of them got seated in Dr. Klavanis's living room on the sofa and in chairs around the room. It was a small house and looked a good deal like Trish's bungalow—except that there were no flowers in the yard. A woman appeared at the door to the kitchen, smiling only slightly. Dr. Klavanis introduced her as his wife, Natalya. When she asked if anyone cared for tea, they all politely declined and thanked her. Then she left the room.

There was a silent period. Trish thought they might be waiting for her to begin the conversation, so she started by asking, "So, Dr. Klavanis, they tell me you work in a dispensary here. Would it also be referred to as Clinic Number Four? The one where the mutants are preserved?"

"Please, call me Mirek."

"All right then, Mirek. And call me Trish."

"Trish," he repeated, as though trying the name out for sound. "Yes, indeed," he continued. "It is sometimes called Clinic Number Four. And it does contain mutant specimens." At that Trish felt a wave of excitement course through her solar plexus. "I have worked there for years," he added. "And they tell me that you are a reporter."

"That's right. I wanted to see for myself how the Russian nuclear program affected the people here."

"We had a very important television crew from America here who did a story about the clinic already once," he commented.

"Yes," she replied. "I saw that report, but it only lasted a few minutes, and it wasn't reported anywhere else that I could tell after that, except for a few obscure publications. I'm afraid that most Americans still don't know anything about the clinic." Her comment had an immediate impact. Everyone looked at each other wide-eyed, obviously stunned. So she continued, "Of course, when I saw it, it had a powerful impact on me. And that's why I'm here…to do a more in-depth story." The looks on the faces around the room still denoted disbelief. Trish held out her hand and added, "It takes time for these things to get out. Sometimes a lot of time." The disappointment on their faces barely subsided.

Finally, after a short period of silence, Valary asked, "Did you have much effect on *your* environments from your country's nuclear programs?"

"Quite a lot." She proceeded to tell the group some of the things she'd discovered about the more notable places of contamination. They listened transfixed as she related the problems. "And, of course," she continued as she crossed her legs, "there's the Nevada testing site where most of the blasts were set off."

"Nevada!" Valary exclaimed, lurching forward. "We know about Nevada. We have a Kazakh poet who led an anti-nuclear movement he called Nevada-Semipalatinsk."

"Really?" Trish asked.

"Yes, he said that the name was to link the two places, because they were the sites where the two super powers conducted all their tests."

Yuri added that their president, Nazarbayev, took a lot of pressure for letting the protest movement continue. "Moscow wanted him to put a stop to it, but then after the Soviet Union dissolved, he closed the Semipalatinsk Test Site permanently." With obvious pride, he added, "We were the first country in the world to close a nuclear test site—even before your country— or Russia."

"Is Nazarbayev a Kazakh?" Trish inquired, reaching into her backpack to pull out her notepad and pen. "Do you mind if I take notes?"

"Not at all," replied Yuri. The others shook their heads as well.

"Yes, he is," Yuri then continued. He explained that Nazarbayev was actually appointed by Russia before the fall of communism, but that afterward—when he renounced his former political beliefs and his connections to the former Soviet regime—he was elected the country's first president.

Trish looked around the room and asked, "Are all of you Russian?"

They looked at each other and all nodded affirmatively. Then Yuri added, "But as they say in your country, that the rain falls on the rich and the poor equally, we sometimes say that the fallout fell on Russians and Kazakhs alike...even though it was Russia who made all of the decisions about the atomic tests."

"Have things changed for Russians here since the fall?"

"Well," Valary began, as he stood up and walked over to a bookcase and began fingering one of the books, "this was a Muslim country, after all." He said it was fortunate that the radical changes hadn't led to the kinds of conflict and killing that they had in some of the other countries, such as Yugoslavia. "But it *is* a different culture." He looked back at Trish, "And there is no clarity yet on how the country will evolve—whether they will tilt more toward Eastern or Western ways—or whether there will be a good balance of both." He looked around at his companions. "For myself, I think that I will eventually leave and go back to Russia. I never did feel a belonging here."

Trish noted nods of agreement. She turned in her seat to face Mirek. He was eyeing Valary's movements at the bookcase closely. "Do you feel that way, too?" she asked.

"I suppose," he answered, turning his attention from Valary to her. "I really wanted to wait and see what was going to happen here after the changes. I suppose the Kazakhs resent us...and who can blame them?"

"Yes, that is true," added Katrina. Trish realized that she had not participated in the conversation before that, and she took notes as Katrina talked about places where wastes had been dumped that now had higher radiation levels than those at Chernobyl. "And we have higher leukemia rates and mortality rates." She added that eighty per cent of the people in the area downwind from the test sites had lowered immune systems, and that maps showing the fallout patterns were kept secret from the people.

"Don't forget the birth defects," Mirek added, as he glanced almost furtively around the room. Trish thought that his caution might be a hold-over from the years when he was forbidden to talk about the things he did in his work.

Yuri continued, "The people here have paid a high price for the Russian nuclear program, and they were not asked for permission or told the truth about how bad it would be."

"At least you got to vote for your new president. That's a good start toward running your own country," Trish noted, as she rested her hand on her notebook.

"There was little choice about it," Mirek stated in a cynical tone.

"Well, you have to start somewhere," Trish reminded him. She told them that during the inception of the United States, when George Washington was elected the first president, there were people who wanted to make him king, even after what they'd been through with the monarchy in England.

The others smiled, and Valary turned his attention from the books in the bookcase and returned to his seat.

After a few moments of silence Mirek said, "Well," as he slapped his thighs. He tilted his head toward Trish. "Are you ready to go to the dispensary?"

"I've been ready for months now."

"Good. The others are going to stay here and wait for us. There is no need for many people there, you see."

She looked at the others. Katrina said, "It will be fine with us. You go ahead with Dr. Klavanis, and we will be here waiting when you get back."

As she stood to leave, Trish was surprised at how tired she still was, even after a full night's sleep. Mirek went to the bookcase where Valary had been standing, took out a book, then went to the kitchen door and said good-bye to his wife. They left for the clinic in his old rattletrap of a car, which spewed smoke from its tailpipe. Trish noticed that Mirek kept the book tucked partially under his thigh as he drove.

• • •

When they arrived at the large brick building, Trish noted that it was as architecturally elaborate as it had been described on the "60 Minutes" program, though there was nothing about its exterior to indicate what was inside. As they walked into the entrance of the huge interior hall of the medical institute, it echoed from the sound of the door opening and closing. There were no rugs or drapes to muffle sounds. No pictures hung on the green walls, though there were faded outlines of some that must have hung there previously.

A young man in uniform came to greet them just inside the front door. Mirek spoke to him in Russian, motioning toward Trish. The only word she recognized was the name, Boris. As they walked away Mirek leaned toward her and lowered his voice. "I told the guard that you were a colleague and we would be going to the dispensary for just a short while." Trish glanced back at the man who was eyeing her intently. He said something else to Mirek in Russian, to which Mirek responded with a wave of his hand. He leaned toward her again. "He said that if I needed him, he would be at the desk."

Trish wondered if she was supposed to be there at the clinic. Not wanting to question her good fortune, however, she didn't ask. She simply followed Mirek to an office with what she assumed were Russian names on the door. After they got seated at a desk, he opened the book he'd brought from his house. He turned to a page in it, and handed it to her without comment. She took it and saw several pictures of what looked like mythical characters, then turned to the front cover. It was written in English and the title indicated a book on Greek mythology. She glanced back at Mirek with a questioning look.

"That is what you will see in the jars," he told her in a serious tone, as he nodded toward the book.

Again she looked at him quizzically. She didn't get it. What did the book have to do with the specimens? "I don't understand."

He sat silently a moment, then said, "Wait. Come with me. You will see." He got up and led the way down the hall to a room, where he opened the door and turned on the lights. Trish followed him inside. The walls were lined with rows of shelves holding what looked like three- or four-gallon, wide-mouthed jars containing the mutants. There was a faint but unmistakable smell of formaldehyde, and she unconsciously lifted her left hand to her nose. The smell took her instantly back to high school biology class and dissecting frogs. But this wasn't biology class. This was something they didn't teach in biology class.

Though she felt prepared for what she was going to see, she soon realized she wasn't. There were fetuses with multiple limbs, extra arms and legs, some with missing limbs. Hands stuck out abruptly from shoulders, reminding her of pictures she'd seen of Thalidomide babies in England. The specimens were in various stages of development and various degrees of deformity, their faces frozen in expressions that looked sometimes deceptively peaceful, sometimes grimacing. A few even had a noble appearance.

Mirek nudged her elbow and led her over to a jar that held the baby she had seen on the television news episode. It had large ears and the one eye in the middle of its forehead. As she peered into the eye at a distance of about two feet, a wave of nausea began to engulf her. She closed her eyes a moment, then opened them, noting that the specimen had a grotesquely wide mouth, stretching across its entire face in an eerie, permanently fixed smile. Raising her hand to her face, she closed her eyes again. Then something seemed to take over, as though she had shut down one aspect of herself and her automatic functions had clicked on. She opened her eyes and pulled out her camera. "Is it all right if I take pictures now?"

"Yes," he replied simply, and without much enthusiasm. It made Trish wonder again if she was supposed to be in the clinic…if perhaps Mirek had taken it upon himself to bring her there without getting prior official approval. But she was determined not to waste one moment of an opportunity that she had invested so much in.

She began clicking pictures of the specimens as she walked up and down the rows of shelves. Several of them had large, bulbous, reptilian-looking eyes sticking out like ping-pong balls. They reminded her of the eyes of a chameleon. Some had what looked like scales on their bodies. Many of the specimens had incisions up the middle of the abdomen. The stitching was crudely done. She paused a moment with her camera to her cheek, eyeing the stitches. No wonder. They were autopsied. No need for precision. *Don't look too closely. Keep moving.*

One jar held twins who were placed with their backs facing forward. From that angle they appeared normal, except that the backs of their skulls looked as though they had exploded outwardly, leaving an open cavity. *How did they ever reach a stage of full development like that?* She looked closer. *No, their skulls must have been opened during autopsy, the brains removed.* She snapped three shots from different angles, straining to see their faces. She couldn't. Maybe it was just as well. *Keep moving, Trish.*

She stopped a minute, holding the camera against her cheek again, with her eyes closed. *Take a breath. Now open your eyes, and keep moving.* She kept clicking. Some of the fetuses looked like props made up for a Hollywood horror movie. *God! How did this happen? It looks like some sort of DNA crapshoot. How could they have known about this and kept on exploding those bombs?*

The only way she could deal with what she was seeing was because of its unreality. On a conscious level she couldn't connect what she was seeing to anything that came close to approximating the human species. But these were human beings.

Oddly, the specimens that looked most human, with milder deformities, were the ones that brought up the most visceral reactions. Still, she continued walking between the shelves, taking pictures, until she was back at the specimen she'd seen on television. She was standing there looking into its face, transfixed, when Mirek took her arm and guided her to yet another jar.

"Here, look at this one."

There Trish saw the specimen with a human upper body and the lower body of a fish, which had been mentioned on "60 Minutes." She clicked her camera yet again.

"See?" he said, nudging her with the open book. He pointed to the pictures in it. "They are just like the myths...the Cyclopes and the mermaids." He pointed to another of the pictures. "And here...here..." he said, as he continued turning pages and pointing. Trish saw that he was pointing out a picture of a two-headed Roman god. "You see?" he repeated, pointing then to yet another specimen on the shelf. This one had two heads.

It suddenly hit her. She saw exactly what Mirek meant. They looked exactly like mythical beings. Mermaids. Cyclopes. Human and animal hybrids.

Thoughts tried to form in her head, but wouldn't. Words tried to come out of her mouth, but didn't. *It can't be. How can this be? This is the twentieth century, for God's sake.* She felt at once mystified and horrified by what she was seeing. Then her logical brain began to shut down. Something else was taking over.

Suddenly she felt as though her consciousness was being propelled backward into an unknown time, and yet, all at once somehow, forward at an equa-distance, as though it was so far stretched that it might snap. Her senses ached with the disorientation. In that millisecond, something in her mind cried out, *What's happening to me?*

Then there was blackness...soft, weightless, fathomless blackness. It felt comforting in a strange yet familiar way. Her first thought was: *I remember this place. I've been here before.* She struggled to recall where she was, and in that moment she felt herself going deeper, deeper into what seemed like a vastness of distance without time. *Is this the Void?* It felt like an eternal sea of presence and potential, expansive and yet womblike. It felt like nothingness, no worry, no fear, nothing...and yet there was a sense of everything.

She attempted to look around, and then very deliberately stopped. Something told her that struggling would do no good. She felt as fragile as a puff of smoke on a windy day. Any agitation on her part might make her slip away. So she simply relaxed in the nothingness, and when she did, she saw a tiny light somewhere in the blackness and began focusing on it. The disorientation began fading. She felt better somehow, calmer, and she wondered, without panic, *Am I dead?*

In the distance she heard a voice calling her name. It sounded foreign. "Trish? Trish?" Where was it coming from? She heard it again, louder. "Are you all right?"

Her face felt cold at first and then flush and hot, and she felt someone patting it, softly at first and then harder.

"Trish," the voice said again. "Are you all right?" it repeated clearly.

Her body felt sluggish, almost drugged. She tried to move, but felt heavy, weighted. The effort exhausted her, and she moaned. The voice said again, "Trish?"

She moaned again, then tried to talk. "Where am I?" The words felt thick in her mouth.

"You're here, with me, in the dispensary. You fainted."

She felt confused, tried to focus, tried to open her eyes. When she managed to open them slightly, the light was blinding. She lifted her arm to her face to shield her eyes, and it felt as though someone else was moving it, disconnected from her body. But when her hand touched her face, she felt more oriented and began remembering where she was. "Mirek?" she asked in a raspy voice that didn't sound like it belonged to her. She opened her eyes more fully and saw him kneeling above her. She realized she was on the floor.

"You frightened me," he admitted, looking shaken. "Your face went white."

She attempted to get up, and he quickly cautioned, "Stay there a moment. You're still shaky. Wait until the blood gets completely back to your head."

He needn't have said it. She quickly realized that she couldn't get up yet, anyway. She relaxed a bit and marveled at the realization that only seconds must have passed. It had seemed like an eternity. When she became fully aware of what had happened, she said "Oh, my gosh...I can't believe I fainted."

"Don't worry. You will be fine in a moment or two."

"Oh," she moaned. "I can't believe I did that."

"No, no, it was my fault. I should have realized. I should have gone slower with you. I have been seeing these things for so long that sometimes I forget how I felt the first time I saw them. Stay where you are. I'm going to get you some water."

Mirek left the room and came back with a cup. He bent down on the floor and lifted her onto his chest. "Here. Drink this."

As she drank the water, she was pleasantly surprised at how good it tasted. There was no film in it like the water from her shower the night before. After a minute longer, she caught her breath and said, "I think I can get up now."

"Are you sure?"

"I'm sure," she said confidently. Mirek helped her as she leaned forward and slowly got to her knees. When she was completely on her feet, she felt at first lightheaded and then fully embarrassed.

"Let's go to the office and sit down," he offered.

"Okay. That's probably what I need to do."

He kept his hand at her back, as they returned to the office. When they were seated, Mirek examined her face. "Your color seems back now."

"I can't believe I did that," she said, resting her head in her hand. "It certainly wasn't very professional of me," she added, in an attempt at light humor.

"You must not apologize." He emphasized the words with his hand. "I should have prepared you much more."

She looked directly at him, suddenly remembering the profound horror she'd felt at what she'd just seen. "Oh, my God, Mirek," she blurted out quietly, "how on earth did you work in this clinic for so long? I don't think I could have taken it." She felt overcome with pity. "What you must have gone through." She felt tears brimming in her eyes, but she fought them back. Instead of answering her question, Mirek gazed at the floor without saying a word. Trish suspected he was feeling discomfort with the sympathy she was offering, so she didn't say anything else. She looked back at her cup, realizing that it was still in her hand, and sipped some more of the water.

Then Mirek asked, "Do you know what it means?"

"What 'what' means?" she asked a little confused.

"The Greek monsters in the book...and why they look like the specimens."

"Oh." With her sudden contact with the floor she'd almost forgotten about his book. She rubbed the side of her face, trying to think. "Well, Mirek, I don't know, really...but the similarities are pretty startling when you think about it, aren't they?"

"That's what came to me—and I thought that someone from America might know what it meant. Maybe you have studies that we don't have about these things."

For the first time Trish thought she understood why Mirek had been so willing to show her the clinic. He'd hoped that she could help him unravel the mystery he'd discovered in the book. "Mirek, mythology isn't my field. I'm a reporter." The disappointment on Mirek's face was instantaneous and intense. She stopped and took a breath, thinking a moment, then added, "But you know, I do have a friend back in Georgia who's well versed in that area. Maybe he could provide some answers."

Mirek's face brightened. "This friend, does he also have a background in radiation or genetics?"

She half laughed, "No, no. He was a professor in literature at the college I attended."

Mirek replied simply, "Oh."

"But he's very intelligent and well educated," she quickly added, "and I have other acquaintances who know something about the other subjects. Maybe together we could figure something out about this." Again, his face brightened, and Trish had the sense that Mirek was extremely fragile to be investing so much emotion in her comments. She decided to shift gears. "What do *you* think it means, Mirek?"

"Me?" he asked, seeming surprised by her question. "I only know that it means something. I have read the book time after time since I got it, but it explains nothing to me. It only seems like a child's story book."

Trish put her hand to her head again, as another wave of light-headedness swept over her. Mirek noticed and suggested they return to his house. She agreed without resistance. As a reporter she knew she should have stayed and asked a hundred questions and taken more pictures and notes until she had completely exhausted such a wealthy source of information for her story. But she was too emotionally distraught and too physically weak to pursue the subject further. And she didn't feel at all like a reporter at that moment. She only felt like a human being...a very fragile one at that.

When they left the building, she noticed Boris eyeing them intently, as he uttered what sounded like a formal good-bye in Russian.

After they returned to the house, Mirek kept fawning over her. Trish reasoned that he felt responsible for her collapse, but then wondered if, in fact, he was more focused on trying to get answers from her about the book— answers she simply didn't have. Seated on the sofa with the others, she sheepishly explained what had happened at the clinic. Katrina took the situation in hand by saying they simply needed to get Trish back to her bungalow for some rest, that she was probably more exhausted from her trip than any of them had realized. She would need some time before attempting any more interviews.

After Trish thanked Dr. Klavanis for his help and asked to finish their interview at a later time, she, Katrina and Yuri returned to the bungalow. When they arrived, Trish felt as relieved to get back as she would have to be home in Clayton. It had begun to seem familiar rather quickly—and, as drained as she felt both emotionally and physically—all she wanted was to be alone, cocooned in comfortable surroundings so she could begin the process of recuperating from whatever malady or fatigue was plaguing her.

Chapter Ten

Trish spent the rest of that Sunday and the following day resting, trying to recover from her ordeal. Whenever she slept, even during the day, she had fitful dreams that left her with only glimpses upon waking, and which disappeared altogether rather quickly after that. Then on Tuesday Katrina returned to the bungalow to see if she was ready to visit various locations around the city, and to start interviewing some of the residents who'd been affected by the radioactive fallout over the years.

Though eager to continue, Trish felt more cautious than she'd been before visiting the clinic. There had been moments in her career when stories had tugged at her heartstrings or made her angry; she'd even had the hell scared out of her a time or two. But this experience was totally different. Nothing in her life had affected her quite this way. Her instincts about the story months before had been right; this was the reporter's Holy Grail, except that she didn't have a firm grasp on it, nothing close to a focus. All of her preconceived notions about the story had evaporated in the clinic on Sunday.

She was going to have to will herself through her present discomfort and be as professional as she could; she had too much invested in the story to do otherwise.

As they drove away from the bungalow, Katrina informed Trish that Yuri had been obligated to return to work and that they would be going out alone for the rest of the week. She also told her that many of the people who'd experienced some of the worst health effects from their exposures refused to talk to anyone about their problems—much less foreign reporters—even though they were probably the best sources to help get their stories out. Still, she'd been able to locate a number of people who were not only willing, but eager to talk, and she'd made appointments with them.

For the first interview Katrina drove them to the little village of Balapan. When they got out of the car and approached a tiny house, which Trish could only describe in her notes as a hut, a woman who appeared to be in her sixties came out to greet them. They went inside and got seated in the only two chairs in the room. The woman sat on the edge of a bed where her daughter—a young woman apparently in her thirties—lay, silently staring out the small window beside it. The daughter's hair was solid white and the older woman stroked it as she spoke to her softly in Russian. The only word Trish recognized was the name, Maria.

Through Katrina, the woman told about several miscarriages she had experienced before finally giving birth to a severely retarded baby with multiple birth defects. All of her energies went into caring for her child. As the older woman motioned toward her and dabbed her eyes with her apron, she wondered aloud who would care for her daughter if anything ever happened to her. The situation reminded Trish of one of the interviews in the program she'd seen back in the states. Katrina told Trish, "She said that sometime when she first learned she was carrying the child, she was at work in the field. A strange haze came over the sky and her skin burned when the haze fell down on her. Then the child was born like this." Katrina looked toward Maria.

Later that day, at a town called Abai Sovkhoz, Katrina and Trish met in a small house with several neighborhood women who had assembled to relate stories about cancers their family members had experienced. As Katrina interpreted, they told stories about severe birth defects in villages on the outskirts of Semipalatinsk, Pavlodar and Karaganda. They said that Kazakh herders in the surrounding countryside were always coming down with strange maladies, but that they refused to go to the dispensary to be treated since they didn't trust the Russians to provide medical help.

"After all," Katrina told Trish, "they believe it was the Russians who *made* them ill. They say they saw the atomic tests. They felt them, too. They were told to go outside during the tests so their houses would not fall down on them. Some of them did fall down. And then people and animals began to get sick." Some of the women nodded their heads or said, "Ya," as Katrina translated.

At other times, when the tests were conducted, the government would tell them to leave the areas for a week or so, but nothing was done to protect their livestock. When they returned nothing had been done to decontaminate their homes or the livestock or the land where they grazed. Nothing was done to decontaminate the land where they raised their crops. No one had a dosimeter, so they had no way to measure levels of radiation.

At one point, one of the women leaned toward Katrina and whispered in her ear. She glanced furtively at Trish while she spoke, a hand cupped to the side of her mouth. Trish found the episode a little humorous, since she couldn't understand Russian anyway. She simply used the opportunity to take pictures of the other neighborhood women.

They had one more interview that day in another rural village. The stories she heard from the women assembled were familiar by now. Poisoned land. Poisoned livestock. Poisoned crops. And poisoned people. They talked about the Atomic Lake—or "Atomkul"—created on the Shagan River. Soon after it was contaminated, it was actually stocked with fish, which the locals caught and ate for many years. Now no one could approach the lake without protective suits when they had to conduct monitoring of radioactive levels. Even then, work in the zone was limited to a few hours. The women talked about deformed livestock and children, about mental retardation and mental disorders. For most of them there wasn't any treatment. There wasn't any compensation.

This had been a war all right. But it hadn't been cold. It had been hot. It still was. And these people were the ones on the front lines. If the bombs exploded had been American made instead of Russian, would the outcome have been any worse? The absurdity of it tugged at Trish, left her weak.

She noted that most reactions from the people she was encountering fell into two distinct categories. Some exhibited profound sadness, weeping openly as they told their stories. Others were obviously angry and struggled to maintain control of their tempers. Yet, all of them shared one thing: they all seemed helpless to know what to do about their plights.

Much to her own frustration, they all seemed to want her to do something for them. Like Mirek, they kept asking questions she just didn't know how to answer. All she could do was offer what seemed like totally inadequate sympathy and promise to do her best to get their stories out to the rest of the world.

During the second day of interviews, Trish felt each anecdotal story weighing her down more and more. It had been one thing to see the fetuses in the clinic—infinitely more shocking than it had been to see them on television. But it was an altogether different experience talking to living people whose lives had been directly affected by the mutations and diseases brought on by the atomic age. On some level she knew that she could have been one of those women, given the right circumstances. Who knew? Maybe she *was* one of them. Maybe in some circumstances infertility was a blessing. Trish was beginning to wonder how much longer she could go on. When they drove away from the next village, she told Katrina she needed to return to the bungalow and rest again.

Katrina headed back toward the city without hesitation, eyeing Trish occasionally as she drove. "Your color does look a little pale," she finally said. "And you appear not to have been eating much."

"Oh, I always do that when I'm working on an important story," she assured her, with a wave of her hand. "Sometimes I just forget to eat…and I haven't been out in the sun much this summer, since it's been so hot in Georgia."

Katrina looked unconvinced. "Do you wish to see a doctor?" she asked.

"Oh, no…no. I guess I'm still tired from the jet lag or something, and these interviews have been pretty depressing." Trish rolled her window down. A blast of air hit her fully in the face and she breathed it in and sighed. "I'm fine…really. I just need a little more rest." She stared out the open window on her side of the car, so deep in thought that she was barely aware of the sights they were passing or where they were until Katrina pulled into the driveway of the bungalow.

When Katrina turned off the engine, Trish invited her to stay and have a beer before she went home. The two of them sat out in the courtyard and engaged in the kind of small talk and conversations that all women share. They laughed and exchanged information about their private lives and didn't mention the story for a while. Both of them knew—without saying—that they needed a break. After a couple of beers, Trish went inside and retrieved a tape player she'd brought along on the trip. When she started playing music from an Enya tape, Katrina's eyes lit up. "That is beautiful," she commented in her thick Russian accent.

"Isn't it?" Trish agreed. "It's my favorite. It was actually popular a couple of years ago, but I never get tired of it. I don't keep up with what's popular that much. I just know what I like...and this tape really relaxes me."

"I can see your enjoyment. I, too, like it."

They continued to drink their beers, talking and laughing, before Trish approached the story again. "You know, as a reporter I should also interview people who are pro-nuclear while I'm here." She explained that in journalism, they tried to give balance to a story, no matter how they might feel about it personally. Presenting both sides gave people a chance to make up their own minds about issues. "And I do plan to do more of that when I get home." She closed her eyes and took in a deep breath. "But, honest to God, right now I don't think I could even be civil to anyone who was pro-nuclear."

"You will not find many here who are, anyway," Katrina responded as she set her empty beer bottle down. She explained that the quality of life in her country had diminished because the government's history of spending such disproportionately large amounts on the Cold War had rendered basic necessities—such as education, medical services and food supplies—primitive and inadequate.

Trish leaned forward and set her beer down as well. "You know, I've been wondering about something." She tilted her head. "Didn't Kazakhstan produce a lot of grain for the rest of the Soviet Union?"

"Yes, that is true."

"Are any of those croplands downwind or downstream from any of the blast sites?"

"Oh, that's possible, I'm sure. But, too, we have nuclear waste dumps all *over* Kazakhstan, and we have little knowledge about *those* locations."

Trish ran a hand through her hair. "I don't have the least idea how I'm going to approach this story. There's so much more to it than even I thought...and I thought it was pretty damn big before I came over here." Trish fell silent a moment, then took in a deep breath and let it out. She leaned forward. "Katrina, do you remember yesterday when that woman was whispering to you?"

Katrina looked puzzled briefly, then responded, "Oh...yes...the woman at Abai Sovkhoz."

"Yeah. What was she saying to you when she whispered in your ear? If you don't mind my asking."

"Oh…it wasn't such a huge thing." Katrina reached for another beer and opened it as she spoke. "It was just that the native people here have learned to be so secretive over the years that it is difficult for them to behave differently." Katrina sipped her drink before she continued, "She was speaking of her father once telling her how the shamans from the area warned the Russians not to dig into the sacred mountains for the uranium. They knew that it could be harmful if it was used improperly. But in the time of Stalin they would not allow any dissent. They killed so many people, and especially the shamans. They silenced anyone who might question digging into the mountains for the uranium. If you even owned a drum, it was like a death sentence."

"A drum?" Trish inquired.

"Yes…shamans use a drum…and a rattle in their work."

Trish perched her chin in her hand. "Are they like medicine men or something?"

"It is somewhat like that. They do healing and travel out of time for their people. There are still not many of them around even today. They have lost many of their old wisdoms. Part of these peoples' ancient heritage was lost during the time of Stalin."

"These people?" Trish asked. "You mean the Kazakhs?"

"I don't know how you say it. The ones before Russians."

"Indigenous people?"

"Yes, I believe that is how you say it." Katrina stared at her bottle a moment, then said, "Dr. Klavanis called last night."

"He did?" Trish perked up.

"Yes, he wishes to see you again for another interview."

"Great," Trish responded enthusiastically. "I *need* to see him again, and ask some more questions." She lowered her head, then glanced up, adding, "Our interview got cut a little short by my little fainting spell."

"I told him that you would call when you had time and felt better."

"Well, I'd better do that, then."

"There is something I must tell you first," Katrina began, with what appeared some reluctance. She fidgeted with the bottle opener. "You see, we have learned that Dr. Klavanis had no permission to take you into the dispensary. He took it for himself to do it. As I told you that first day, we think that he took you in because he was upset with some of his colleagues. Then when you collapsed and he supported you out of the building, the guard on duty became curious and mentioned it to someone."

Trish pursed her lips. "I was afraid of that."

"He is in what you call 'hot water.' You can not go back to the dispensary, and Dr. Klavanis will be fortunate if he does not lose his job."

"Well, well…" Trish crossed her arms. "I hate to hear that for him, and it's certainly a set back for me. But somehow it doesn't surprise me…with some of the looks I was getting from that guard."

"Trish, perhaps you should see it as fortunate to have been able to get in at all."

"You're right," Trish acknowledged, leaning forward. "I did feel lucky to get in, in the first place…and maybe I saw everything I needed to, after all." As they finished their beers, she told Katrina about Mirek's book on Greek mythology. Katrina's response was one of mild curiosity. *You had to have been there,* Trish thought to herself.

"Maybe I just need to do another interview with Mirek, and let it go at that." Trish slowly rose to her feet, stretching her body upward with arms over her head, and said, "I guess we'd better go to your place and call him."

Later at Katrina and Yuri's house Trish talked to Mirek on the phone. He suggested they go to a restaurant to talk the next night, and they settled on a time for him to pick her up. Katrina said that she'd prefer to stay at home, if Trish didn't mind, since she had a lot of things to catch up on, and since Trish wouldn't need her for translations. Trish quickly agreed. Then Katrina suggested a particular dish that Trish might enjoy at the restaurant where Dr. Klavanis was taking her.

● ● ●

Early the next evening when Trish heard Mirek's car pulling into the driveway of the bungalow, she hurriedly grabbed the oversized purse she'd packed with her tape recorder and notepad, slung it over her shoulder and walked out the door. On the drive, she noticed that Mirek wasn't in a talkative mood. Because of that she decided not to mention his employment problems unless he brought it up.

As they entered the restaurant, Trish saw that there was a show in progress. Young women in native costumes were dancing to lively music on a semicircular stage. It was delightful, but not the kind of atmosphere she felt would be conducive to an interview. She and Mirek were led to one of several booths which were positioned around the stage. As Trish slid across the vinyl seat, she scanned the restaurant. Even though there were a couple of large noisy groups dining and drinking, she and Mirek weren't seated close to any of them. Shortly after they ordered drinks, the show was over. She was relieved. She didn't want to have to compete with loud noise.

When the drinks arrived, Mirek quickly downed his vodka and ordered another one before she had taken even a sip of her wine. His demeanor suggested that he might have also had a few drinks before he'd picked her up.

After asking and receiving permission to use her recorder, Trish pulled it out, set it on the table and clicked it on. With her pad in her hand, she glanced at her prepared questions and began asking them. As soon as Mirek began answering, she realized what a complex man he was. He appeared quite intellectual on the surface, and with a bit of effort, she thought he could even manage to be somewhat charming...but he wasn't. The more he talked—and drank—the more brooding and distracted he became. At times he would withdraw from the conversation completely—focusing instead on his drink—and at others, he would gush personal and private information about his life and his profession.

Trish was uneasy with and unaccustomed to that kind of behavior. Yet, when she reflected on what he must have been through the previous years in his career, she realized that it would have been almost impossible for him to be otherwise.

"What they put me through at the clinic," he began at one point, after ordering yet another drink, "it was unbearable at times." He absent-mindedly scratched his tousled hair, then straightened it with his hand. "I didn't know what I was getting into. They only said that I would make more money, and that it was scientific work...highly secret government work. So Natalya and I moved from Moscow. She wasn't happy to move. I should have asked her before I made the decision...but she liked the house better than our cramped little apartment...and she liked the extra money. Still—" The sentence went unfinished while the waiter set a fresh vodka down. He gulped down a large swallow.

When the food arrived, it was on common platters, with individual plates for them to serve themselves. As they began filling their plates, Mirek continued, "There were three other doctors already working in the clinic, and the first glimpse I got of the..." he pursed his lips, "...the *specimens*... well...*you* saw them." He told her how they were instructed to document every local case they could of deformities and illnesses that might be related to the nuclear testing that was going on in the surrounding countryside. They were to keep records of every case of cancer—such as leukemia and thyroid cancer—that could be caused by exposure to radioactive fallout. But doctors were told not to diagnose cancer. They weren't even properly trained to treat patients for it. If someone died from it, they were to list heart disease or some other disease as the cause. The people were lied to...systematically, relentlessly.

At that point Mirek forced an exhalation. "It was made clear that it was not our province to tell people what was wrong with them." He jutted his chin out. "Just *say* the word 'gulag,' or labor camp. We knew the consequences." He laced his fingers together in front of him. "We were also told to collect specimens of any fetuses or stillbirths that were of any sig-*nif-*

icance." The last word he uttered slowly and with contempt.

Trish ate a few bites of food as the interview continued, but this was not the kind of conversation to stimulate an appetite. And Mirek was more focused on his drinks. He told her that he was chosen for the assignment because of his background in genetics, but that he was quite unprepared for the genetic freak show that awaited him that first day in the clinic. "They were things that I had never dreamed of even in nightmares." He leaned forward and gestured. "At first it seemed unreal…as though I was looking at faked objects." But slowly, it began to sink in that he was, indeed, looking at very real human—or at least partially human specimens. It looked more like a house of horrors than any scientific laboratory he had imagined it to be.

"After that first day in the clinic, I became a different man," he said with resignation, as he leaned back in his seat recounting how his internal energies became entangled and conflicted, his professionalism and his humanity in constant struggle. Complex political issues had never before concerned him. He took another drink, glanced around the room, then back at her, and continued, telling her that he was moderately aware of how Russian history and current realities were manipulated for political purposes. He pointed to his chest with his right hand. "But I am a *scientist*, not a politician."

As a scientist, he was totally unprepared for the manipulation he would be asked to take part in. He held out his right hand as he told her that he didn't have a place in his frame of reference in which to put the experience—either emotionally or intellectually, and because it was real, because he had to face it every day, it was the rest of his reference points that began to collapse around him.

In spite of Mirek's obvious pain and bewilderment, Trish couldn't help but notice, with a touch of admiration, how well he'd apparently grasped and diagnosed his own feelings about his experiences and the impact they'd had on him. She wasn't sure if he had identified the severe depression he'd slipped into, but he was certainly aware of his symptoms. She glanced at the list of questions she'd prepared the previous night. This wasn't what she'd come for. But he needed to tell his story.

While intermittently drinking vodka and picking at his food, he continued, telling her of developing sleep disorders that ranged from bouts of insomnia lasting for days or sometimes weeks, to occasionally sleeping around the clock on his days off. He couldn't bear to sleep—to dream—and he couldn't understand why, because nothing he dreamed was as bad as what he experienced awake.

"It would have been better for me if I could have shared my frustrations with Natalya. But I didn't dare." He often suspected that the other doctors talked about their work with their wives in secret, but he knew that Natalya didn't really care about his work, and he couldn't imagine her offering either comfort or support for his torments. If he made such an attempt, he was sure she would be only too happy to remind him that it was he who had insisted on moving to Semipalatinsk…and without consulting her.

Trish shifted in her seat, wondering how long it would take him to get back to the subject of the clinic.

"And on top of that," he continued, "she was angry that I refused to discuss the subject of having a child with her any more. But how could I even think of risking a pregnancy after what I saw every day? And I could tell Natalya nothing about it." The anguish on Mirek's face was impossible to conceal. He paused to pick at his food again. As Trish eyed him, she thought how he must have buried the secret so deeply inside himself that it eventually began to methodically and thoroughly eat him up alive…as surely as any deadly, microscopic plague virus.

Trish knew if he'd been treating a patient with symptoms like his own, he'd probably have instantly recognized the severe depression. But he hadn't truly been practicing medicine in the clinic. His main purpose had been documenting cases and collecting data. And, like most physicians she had known personally in her life, he'd most likely become an expert at denying his own pain, his own weaknesses, his own humanity. She'd always attributed that to the many life and death decisions doctors were required to make. She decided to ask Mirek about it.

As she fingered the handle of her fork, she drifted back into his words. Then at a pause, she looked at him directly. "Mirek, do you think the godlike decisions those in your profession are required to make affect the way you see yourselves?"

He looked up at her surprised, then relaxed and said stone faced, "God had nothing to do with what you saw in Clinic Number Four. And if there *was* a god," he added leaning forward, "why would he let those things go on?"

Trish didn't attempt to answer his question; she realized it was hypothetical. But she briefly wondered how many people within his circle of neighbors, co-workers and family suspected he was a man on an emotional brink. How had he managed to remain functional? How had he managed to maintain his intricately deceptive façade? She'd have to draw him out of his despair long enough to complete her questions about his role at the clinic.

● ● ●

After they'd abandoned their food, Trish asked, "Mirek, how did you become aware of the connection between the specimens and the creatures in Greek mythology?"

Mirek leaned back in his seat and grinned broadly. It was the first time Trish had seen any genuine expression of happiness on his face since she'd met him.

"Well," he began, "I must tell you—it probably comes as no surprise—that my marriage was in shambles." Trish shifted uncomfortably in her seat, though Mirek gave no indication of noticing. "I found myself taking too many sleeping pills for my insomnia, and I was so distracted at one time that I narrowly missed being hit by a bus when I stepped in front of it one day."

A brief thought went through Trish's mind that he might have been unconsciously attempting suicide. She continued listening, her notepad untouched on the table. The more he spoke, the more acutely aware she became of how much isolation there was in Mirek's life. It was clear that over the years of residing in Kazakhstan he'd become cut off, not only from his family back in Russia, but from his wife and co-workers, as well. And he was childless. He'd become suspicious of everyone around him. He didn't appear to have any close friends to confide in, or the will to even attempt to cultivate friendships. He was like a dog chained to a post year after year, unable to break free, that finally quits trying to struggle beyond the limits of its tether. She wondered if she was the first person he had opened up to in years…and, if so, why he had chosen her, a reporter. She didn't think it was the drinks that were loosening his tongue that night.

"The only relief from my pain came from reading," Mirek was saying when she returned her focus to his words. He had withdrawn into a world of words, ideas and thoughts of unseen authors, occupying his free time by devouring every book he could borrow or acquire. He said that in Kazakhstan—as in the rest of the Soviet Union—the supply of good private books had always been a scarce and precious commodity.

"I often swapped books with my fellow scientists and acquaintances. And I often read well into the night and early morning." It was a way to occupy his time, since he couldn't sleep for long stretches at a time, anyway. He had a place on the sofa in the living room where he alternately slept and read. Mirek took two long gulps from his glass and winced as he swallowed them. "I'd long before stopped sleeping with Natalya." He wiped his lips with the back of his hand. "She refused to put up with my nightly wake patterns and restlessness. And who could blame her? We were growing more and more distant with each other."

Trish squirmed uneasily again.

"But even if I could have reached out to her, I wasn't sure if that was what I wanted any more." He told Trish that bridging the gulf between them would have taken far too much energy, when there wasn't anything left for them to share after such an effort. They continued living their separate lives under the same roof. Divorce wasn't even an issue. It wasn't a financially or socially viable solution. Even though he had suspected for a long time that Natalya was having an affair—or several of them—he wasn't even vexed by that possibility. It kept her off his back, and relieved a good deal of the stress and strain between them.

Trish pushed her plate back. "Mirek, I need to go to the ladies' room a minute." He pointed toward it, and when she went inside, she went to the sink, let out a breath and looked at her image in the mirror. She had to maintain some sort of professionalism and distance from the personal demons Mirek was unleashing. As fragile as she felt, she couldn't allow herself to get emotionally drawn into his depression.

When she got back to the table, she was about to bring him back to her original question, when he refocused on it without help. "One day I borrowed two of a colleague's personal books. One was a Russian biography of Stalin. And the other was on Greek mythology." He read the biography first, finding it rather dull and boring because of the constraints and lack of creativity of Russian authors. With a look of disdain, he said he found the book so patronizing that he felt insulted by it. He lived every day with the real legacy of Stalin, and was exceedingly bitter about it.

"The book on Greek mythology was written in English, and I at least found that fact stimulating. It gave me a chance to brush up on the language." He leaned forward as though sharing an open secret. "As you probably know, many scientists in the world learn English as a second language." He explained that was so scientific papers could be shared better on an international level. "Constantly trying to communicate in different languages could produce a sort of scientific Tower of Babel, you see."

Trish nodded, though she hadn't been aware of that fact, and was grateful that he was so well versed in English. She'd wondered how he'd managed to have such a grasp of, not only the basic language, but idioms and colloquialisms, as well.

"You see," he continued, "that is the reason all international pilots in the world are required to speak English—so that they can communicate instantly with airport controllers anywhere in the world. Without that requirement, the results could obviously be disastrous."

"Ah," she replied, nodding in assent.

He told her when he got to the book on mythology late one night, he carefully unwrapped the book from its outer brown paper wrapping and then from an inner layer of tissue paper. "I remember feeling as though I was unwrapping a present." Trish wrinkled her brow, and Mirek added that books of any kind were so valued in the Soviet Union that they were usually cared for meticulously by their owners. "They still are. And I treated that book as carefully as I would have one of my own."

He read the first chapter, then marked it with a bookmark, and flipped through the rest of the book to look at the pictures. He found them interesting, and enjoyed anticipating the stories that went along. "Then suddenly I stopped dead still, with my eyes wide open. I sat bolt upright on the sofa and adjusted my glasses and looked at a few of the pictures again, stunned. I flipped back and forth to three of them in particular. Then I shut the book and stared into space, trying to think of what I needed to do next."

Trish was transfixed at Mirek's sudden animation and excitement at telling this part of his story. The former heaviness was lifted from his demeanor.

"I looked at the clock. It was three A.M. It didn't matter. I got up from the sofa and quickly started getting dressed." His eyes were wide open, as he said, "I could feel the excitement coursing through my body. I hadn't felt that alive in years." He often worked at the clinic at night. Because his insomnia was common knowledge, it wasn't unusual for him to show up in the middle of the night to work on a paper or to finish a report.

"I quickly scribbled a note to Natalya, then raced to the clinic as quickly as I could, with my book in hand. When I unlocked the door and stepped inside the entrance, I fumbled nervously with my keys and dropped them to the floor. They made a loud crashing sound in the hollow, echoing cavern of the large entrance room, just inside." He looked directly at her. "You remember it."

Trish nodded. Mirek was so caught up in what he was relating that Trish felt as though she was actually witnessing what he was telling her in her mind's eye. She glanced at her tape recorder, hoping there was enough tape left to capture what he was saying without interruption.

"Seconds later Boris came bounding around the corner, looking startled and attempting to look as alert as he could. 'Oh, Dr. Klavanis. Working late again tonight?'" Mirek laughed slightly. "He attempted so hard to hide that he had been sleeping…but the wrinkled pattern on the skin of his face gave him dead away.

"I told him that I needed to finish working on a report before morning, and that I wouldn't be long. Then I went quickly to the room where the jars were stored and flicked on the light." He opened the book and looked first at the pictures and then at the jars—back and forth. And there they were: the mermaid, the Cyclops, the two headed monsters, the half men, half beasts— all of them—the Greek mythological beings, right there in jars on the laboratory shelves…the myths and the monsters.

• • •

The next morning when Trish woke up, she glanced at her clock. She had plenty of time to get ready before Katrina arrived, so she stayed snuggled in bed, recounting the interview with Dr. Klavanis from the previous evening. She recalled how he talked about standing transfixed before the specimens in the clinic after he found the book on Greek mythology. He felt goose bumps from his head to his toes, and the hair on the back of his neck stood up. He wasn't sure how he should even feel—if he should be more horrified or perhaps excited by the finding in the book. The only thing he was certain of was that he had stumbled upon something of gargantuan proportions. And though he couldn't grasp the meaning of it, he understood enough to know that it had monumental significance to humanity.

He talked about devising a plan to trade the book on Greek mythology permanently with his colleague. Not wanting to raise suspicions by appearing too eager, he decided to offer the man any one book of his own collection in exchange for the book on mythology. But first he'd take his most precious books off the shelves, and leave one medical textbook that he didn't think the man would dare pass up.

Though Mirek regretted the deviousness, it had become a way of life in the Soviet Union for as long as he could remember. Trish thought it was no wonder that marriages and relationships soured under the oppressive conditions in which people were forced to live in those days.

When the man came to Mirek's house to swap the borrowed books, he took Mirek up on his offer, selecting the medical textbook he'd expected the man to take in exchange for the book on mythology. Still, Mirek didn't understand the connection to the pictures in it and the specimens. He told Trish that he hadn't been sure of much of anything for a long time. He was afraid he was losing his soul in Clinic Number Four.

Trish got out of the bed and slowly wandered into the kitchen. She opened the refrigerator door and stood before it several seconds before pulling out some cheeses, sliced meats and a loaf of bread. It wasn't the kind of morning meal she was accustomed to eating, but she had to force herself to eat something. The two cups of tea helped her wash down a few bites before her appetite waned.

She went to the bathroom, pulled back the shower curtain and hesitated briefly before turning on the water. She knew it was still contaminated, but all she could do was to make the shower a quick one.

After drying off and getting dressed, she thought about how Mirek's hope of solving his newfound mystery got caught up with a hope for the future, about which he had only dared to dream in the previous few years. Because of all the changes brought about in his country by the presidency of Mikhail Gorbachev, with his "glasnost" and "perestroika," he believed things might actually begin to change.

"But they have, haven't they?" Trish had asked him. "You've got to know how much they've changed. We're sitting here in this restaurant talk-

126

ing, aren't we?"

Mirek had only smiled weakly in response. But, at least he'd stopped drinking at that point, and seemed quite coherent for someone who'd just downed so much vodka.

He told her that the new independence from Russia had prompted the Kazakhstan government to allow Western reporters into the country to give them a glimpse of life in a former Soviet state, complete with many of their "warts showing." He thought the government could persuade the U.S. to establish trade relations and provide financial assistance to help their ailing economy, and possibly even help rebuild their cities and infrastructures, just as they had with other countries they'd defeated in war. Why should the Cold War be any different? All they had to do was show them their casualties…their cancer victims, their polluted lands. The clinic alone should have been enough to make them see the devastation they'd suffered at the hands of the Soviet government.

At that comment, Trish had looked at him curiously, wondering if he meant that Russia seemed like the enemy during the Cold War, rather than the U.S., or if that had become his consensus in more recent years.

Mirek talked about the American reporters being given access to the clinic and the medical museum. He hadn't found out about the interviews until the day before they took place, and realized that his colleagues had to have known about it for some time previous to that. He was offended that they hadn't included him in the discussions.

He speculated that their lack of trust in him might have been caused by suspicions that he was a spy for the Russian government, since he was the last one hired to work there before the fall. Still, he was delighted the reporters were coming. Once atrocities done to the civilian population were exposed, he knew help would be on the way.

Trish tidied up the kitchen and went to the living room and retrieved her recorder from her purse. She turned it on and searched for that part of the conversation as she sat on the edge of the sofa. When she found it, Mirek's voice was firm, though his speech was slow. "When the American crew got there, they filmed and interviewed people for days. I knew that the story must be as important to the reporters as it was to us."

Trish had shifted in her seat and sighed deeply before she spoke, trying to choose her words carefully. "Mirek, it's like I told you before, the footage they shot was edited down to just a few short minutes to fit into the time frame of one of the show's segments. It simply didn't get the kind of news coverage that you'd imagined it would. You have no idea how precious minutes of news space on the airways are in the states."

"Yes, I remember your saying that at the house." He'd eyed her intently at that point. "I must ask you bluntly what you intend to do with this story. Will it be buried along with the other? How will you get this information to the American public if your press is just as controlled as ours?"

She'd automatically raised her hand, prepared to defend her country's press, then slowly lowered it as she recalled the untold numbers of hours, days and weeks of news time and space devoted exclusively to two murders in California involving a famous American sports figure. The story on the clinic hadn't lasted as long as it took to drink a Coke. She'd felt a wave of defeat and an inability to answer his question. "All I can tell you is that I'll do the best I can."

Mirek asked her again if she had any idea about a connection between the mutations and the myths. She reiterated that she didn't, but felt strongly that there was one. "Look, Mirek, I'm just as hooked about this thing as you are," she heard herself reassuring him on the tape. She told him she'd try to contact people who might understand more about it when she got back home, and that she'd get back in touch with him if she discovered anything.

Though she'd felt grateful that Mirek had gotten her into the clinic and agreed to the interview, he reeked of desperation. She'd wondered what he wanted from her. What was it Max had said? Go with your gut on this one? She wondered if her conditioning as a reporter was keeping her from figuring the man out. He certainly had seen and been through enough over the years with his work to drive a normal man insane. But even drunk, he was intelligent enough to know not to share the kinds of personal and professional secrets he'd been unloading with, of all people, a reporter. So what did he want from her? Absolution? She wasn't a priest.

She remembered rolling her pen back and forth, staring at her notepad. If that was what the interview had been about after all—a confessional— maybe, like the good books in the Soviet Union, priests were in short supply. She'd looked up at him. "Mirek, you need to forgive yourself. You weren't responsible for what was in that clinic."

She could still see and hear him slamming his fist down on the table. "I was responsible for *telling* people." He'd raised his pointed finger toward her. "And now *you* are."

Eyes wide with surprise, Trish had leaned back in her seat and repeated, "Mirek, I'll do the very best I can."

"Good," he replied simply, "because the creatures in that museum deserve no less." He'd leaned forward, eyes wide and bloodshot. "Do you think I don't know that one of them could have been *my* child?"

When they left the restaurant later, Trish had briefly questioned riding back to her bungalow with Mirek after all the vodka he'd consumed. Yet, he'd walked to the car without difficulty, and she didn't think he was capable of speeding, with the conditions of the roads. *Oh, well.* She'd opened the door. She hadn't done very well as a priest and she wasn't Catholic, but she'd had some friends who were, and she knew a few lines of the Hail Mary. She'd paused a moment. *Hail, Mary, Mother of God, bless us sinners now and at the hour of our deaths...* Taking a deep breath, she'd climbed into the car.

Later, as they'd said good-bye at her door, Trish had somehow known that she would never see Dr. Klavanis again.

• • •

Meeting with Mirek had been so draining the previous night that Trish briefly considered asking Katrina to cancel the interviews for the day. Almost immediately, though, she remembered her financial investment, and repacked her backpack with recorder, camera and notepads. When Katrina arrived, she asked about the meeting.

"Let's just say it was illuminating in a number of ways...but tedious at the same time." Katrina glanced at her briefly, but didn't press for details. After they drove from the house, Trish told her, "I keep getting the feeling that he wants answers from me I'm not qualified to give." She rubbed the side of her head. "In fact, it seems like everybody I interview is looking to me for some kind of help, and I don't know what to say to any of them." She looked out the side window. "I feel like I need help myself. The scope of this story makes me feel so inadequate and helpless, and I'm not used to feeling like that."

Katrina spoke without taking her eyes from the road. "Trish, if you simply tell this story to the Americans, I think it will help. Maybe your people or your government will do something."

Trish propped her arm on the ridge at the bottom of the window and rocked her head back and forth on her fist. How totally and blissfully unfamiliar Katrina was with American apathy and government gridlock. She simply looked over at her companion and smiled, then looked back out of her window for a few quiet moments, thinking.

Suddenly, Trish looked back at her. "Katrina!"

Katrina shot her a sideways glance. "What is it?"

"Dr. Klavanis!"

Katrina wrinkled her forehead. "Yes?"

"His Greek monsters! That's the angle I'll use for my story."

"Yes, you told me about his book."

"But I've been wondering since before I left the states what kind of story angle I'd use for this report, and it's been staring me right in the face since I went to the clinic...Dr. Klavanis' Greek mythical monsters!"

Katrina tilted her head to the side. "I don't know so much about story angles."

"Well, it's a perfect one,' Trish began, turning sideways in her seat with her hand held out. "Except that…" She paused, dropped her hand and slumped. "Oh, hell, I don't have any more of an idea what it means than *he* does, though." She let out a deep breath. "I'm going to have to do more than a repeat of the television report. If I can't figure out the connection between the atomic age and Greek mythology, there *is* no story to tell."

"Why not?"

"Katrina, people in the states are so jaded they hardly care about what happens across the county line. You have to show them how something affects them personally before they'll get involved in anything." She thought about Peggy. Even she had to get nuked before she committed to trying to keep it from happening to anyone else. Trish held out her hand. "Maybe there's something more universal to this story than simply getting medical help for these people."

Katrina looked toward Trish. "These people *need* medical help."

"I know that. But what good will it do if global nuclear exposure isn't stopped? What good does it do to stop these tests if more Chernobyl's are waiting in the wings and an unending stream of radioactive wastes accumulating?" Trish let out a breath. "Katrina, I think the atomic age has just been ratcheted up to a whole new level with the appearance of these mutants on the world stage." She looked out the windshield. "But right now, I've only got a sense of it."

"Perhaps it will make more sense for you after you return home. Maybe it is like a coincidence, at any case."

Trish leaned her arm on the window again and put her hand to her head. "Maybe, but I don't think so. I think there's got to be something to it."

"Must it have meaning?" Katrina asked.

It was obvious Katrina didn't share her excitement. "Maybe not. Who knows?" Trish decided to approach another aspect of the subject. "Another thing I was wondering about is how complete the collection of mutations in the clinic could be."

"I don't think it is at all complete. Many of the nomadic Kazakhs must have had dead and deformed fetuses in their yurts out on the steppes…and simply buried them quietly." Katrina glanced at Trish on occasion as she explained that since those kinds of things were a cause for shame in their culture, it wasn't likely that they'd go around talking about it or presenting the Russians with specimens of their babies.

"I never even thought about that aspect of it. I just thought they couldn't possibly have documented all of the miscarriages and stillbirths—even under the best of circumstances." She shook her head, then added with resignation, "I guess I'd better just focus on these interviews and not concern myself with anything else right now."

The day was filled with more meetings with local people—most of them women—and it was filled with more oppressive details of diseases, strange maladies and deformities, all of it weighing heavier and heavier on Trish.

Later, on the way back to the city, Trish noticed Katrina eyeing her, without comment. Then Katrina finally said, "When we arrive in the city, there is a small pastry shop where we can stop. I would like you to taste some of our wonderful bakery goods before you have to leave next week."

When they reached town, Katrina drove down a little alley and parked. Upon entering the shop, Trish was instantly engulfed in the aroma of freshly baked goods. She breathed it in and looked around. The shop was quaint and charming, all of the rich wood trim glistening with layer upon layer of sealant. The windows and glass shelves were sparkling clean, and the tables were set with linen tablecloths, cloth napkins and fresh cut flowers. Trish couldn't understand why the pleasant sights and smells made her feel like bursting into tears. She took a deep breath to hold back her emotions.

They sat down and ordered coffee and pastries. When they were delivered by a smiling, gray-haired, grandmotherly lady, Katrina introduced her to Trish. As the two talked freely in Russian, it was obvious that they had known each other for a long time. Trish glanced at the fresh doilies set under the coffee saucers and china dessert plates. It was such a refreshing and marked change from the disposable, fast food culture she was used to. That was it. That was why she'd almost cried. It had the feel of home about it.

When they were about to leave, Trish had Katrina translate to the woman that she thought the pastry was the best she'd ever tasted. The old woman beamed and thanked her in Russian. As they walked back to the car, Trish told Katrina, "I'd weigh two hundred pounds if I lived near a shop like this. I'm a sucker for pastries."

"Wasn't it wonderful?"

Trish nodded. The outing had done a lot to lift her failing spirits, and Trish understood that Katrina had suggested it for just that purpose.

After that, each afternoon before they returned to the bungalow, Katrina took Trish to some local spot of interest or activity. One day they went to a local marketplace, where stalls full of rugs, foods and farming animals lined the street. She learned that people brought their horses to sell or trade, and that mare's milk was the favored drink. They saw a few cans of American colas being sold, with the same red and white logo as those in the U.S., except that they had large Arabic looking writing down the side. Trish eagerly bought two of them for herself and Katrina. She told Katrina, "If I had to, I'd pay twenty dollars for these drinks right now—and I'd give thirty for a juicy cheeseburger."

The bustling sights and sounds of the market with laughing children running around had a rejuvenating effect on Trish. She glanced at Katrina at one point as they drank their drinks and smiled at her briefly. In spite of the horrifying anecdotal stories they were collecting at the periphery of this particular culture, had Katrina realized how desperately she needed to be reminded of the normalcy that still existed in the world? That grandmotherly ladies still baked pastries and children still ran around giggling?

• • •

The outings were always preceded by trips into the surrounding countryside and interviews with local residents and activists, as the two women dutifully continued their work into the next week. Trish kept scrupulous notes and took numerous rolls of photographs.

Then, on a gray, drizzly, rainy Thursday—three days before Trish was due to leave—Katrina said, "Trish, I would not wish for you to think that all that has happened to our children has been bad."

Trish looked over at her and tilted her head.

Katrina appeared to be searching for words—not so because of the English involved, but more because she was having difficulty explaining something. "There are a *few* children...not many...ah...I don't know how to say this thing. They are quite, you might say special...no, gifted...no..."

Trish attempted to help her. "Do you mean they're brighter than most children?"

Katrina paused a moment. "Maybe."

"Well, in the U.S., children—babies in particular—have seemed brighter than they used to be. I hear parents and grandparents talking about it all the time. I used to think it was just bragging, but I don't anymore."

"No..." Katrina responded, hesitantly. "I know what you say...but that is not what I mean here. It is something else."

She paused again, and Trish filled in the empty space. "What, then?"

Katrina still seemed confused about how to explain what she meant. "There is a small village nearby...and there is a child who lives there."

Trish felt almost defeated. She didn't think she could take another deformed child at that point, but Katrina continued, "This little girl seems to have some kind of...well...power."

"Power?" Trish asked, wrinkling her forehead.

"Yes, I don't have the words to say it properly...even in Russian...but we could go to the village and you could see for your own."

"Well...sure," Trish commented, hesitantly, "Why not?" She looked out of the windshield as the rain began pelting down and the wipers squeaked noisily back and forth.

Katrina drove several more miles, then turned onto a one-lane side road. "This child, she does not affect everyone the same way," she continued.

"How so?" Trish asked.

"Well, some think there is nothing special about her...and some think she has a magic."

"Magic?"

"Yes." Katrina gestured with one hand, as she steered with the other. "It is difficult to speak in words. Some people in her own village are even afraid of her and chase her away from their houses."

Trish raised her eyebrows again, wondering if she had stumbled onto some kind of local urban legend. Katrina glanced at her and added, "But there are some who come from miles away and even bring their sick ones for her to touch."

Trish felt confused, but also intrigued.

"They call her 'Ilyani,'" Katrina added.

Trish responded with a simple, "Oh."

After driving the short distance to the village, Katrina pulled up to the edge of it and stopped the car. There had been a break in the rain shortly before, for which Trish was grateful. But when she opened her door, she looked down at the mud covering the ground and knew she had no choice but to slog through it. Hopping as gingerly as possible over the larger puddles, she fell in behind Katrina, as she led the way to a small weathered, wooden house with a thatch roof. Katrina knocked on the door. After a time, an elderly, stooped woman appeared and listened while she spoke.

As the two women talked in the now expected foreign language, Trish heard some children giggling and playing at the side of the house and took a few steps toward them to get a better look. She became more absorbed in their play than in the conversation going on at the door. The children were covered in mud and gleefully painted each other's bodies by dipping their fingers in the ample supply of mud on the ground.

Trish's attention was drawn to one little girl in particular. She appeared about four years old and had dark brown, curly hair and large dark eyes. As Trish watched her paint mud on the face of one of her playmates, she noticed she was missing the little finger of her right hand, and had a couple of open sores on her face. When the little girl looked over and noticed the women, she smiled at Trish and giggled, then ran over to her.

Without thinking and, in spite of the mire surrounding her, Trish automatically squatted down to her level to engage in the little girl's face painting play. The girl reached out with her deformed right hand and touched Trish's left cheek.

Instantly, Trish felt something similar to an electrical charge at the point of the girl's touch. It was a pleasant, almost indescribable feeling, as though sparks had entered her face, surging warmth throughout her body.

The sensation was overwhelming. Tears began involuntarily filling her eyes and running down her cheeks as a sense of peace that she had never before experienced in her entire life engulfed her. She tried to speak. But all that came out of her mouth was an, "Oh…"

Without warning her body felt as though it was vibrating warmth, and she found herself literally speechless. She felt like the universal mother and the child before her felt like the universal child. She could image and feel the energy of that connection spreading out around her, beyond the village, across the globe and encircling it.

Then she watched as the little girl ran giggling away out of sight with her playmates.

Trish stood up slowly after a time, still filled with emotion, still warm with whatever had entered her body. She had the sense that the warmth had been internal and had simply been awakened by the touch. Her desire to analyze what had just happened was quickly drowned out by her emotions. She could almost hear her mother saying, "Now, wash that off your face. You don't know what germs you might have picked up." But her own voice responded in her head, *How could I ever wash off that touch?*

She pressed her hand to her cheek, trying to hold on to the feeling. Almost in slow motion, she turned back toward Katrina. She could see that Katrina was eyeing her and had observed what had just happened. Trish took a few steps toward her, and Katrina met her halfway, stating, "That was Ilyani." She looked at Trish, as though reading her expression. "You were fortunate to have felt her touch. Not everyone does."

"What *was* that?" Trish asked, almost helplessly, as tears streamed down her face.

"It was what I was trying to tell you. But it is not possible to *tell* anyone about it. They must experience it for themselves…and many people see and feel nothing out of the ordinary. You were quite fortunate," she repeated.

On the way back to Semipalatinsk, Trish continued to wipe tears from her face. She finally regained her composure enough to ask, "How many children are there here like that, Katrina?"

"We do not know," Katrina responded, simply. "We know of a few, and they appear to have been recent."

She wrinkled her forehead. "Do you think they have anything to do with the *nuclear* pollution?"

"We do not know that, either. We only know that they are here. We do not know if there are others like them everywhere in the world, but some say there are others in Tibet and China and Japan." She turned briefly toward Trish as she drove. "Do you know of any in your country?"

"No. I mean, you hear weird stories a lot; but, honestly, I never paid much attention to them. I've seen stories about *adults* that seem to have some sort of strange…maybe healing powers. But I don't recall hearing anything about children having it."

Trish didn't ask any more questions; she simply stared ahead, and the two of them spent the rest of the drive back to the city in silence…a silence that Trish could only liken to reverence.

● ● ●

The two women never mentioned the incident with Ilyani again, as though speaking about it might somehow minimize it. Trish attempted to return her focus to the original story.

Late the next day, as they sat in the yard drinking beer and snacking on cheese and bread, Trish took notes as Katrina told her about a recent German article she'd come across having to do with the publication of a relatively new finding about life expectancies in Russia. They were plummeting at a rate unprecedented in history, particularly for men. "Infant mortality also is rising…at a very great rate." She said that it was the condition of those born that was most alarming; over ten per cent had serious birth defects and over half the children were chronically ill.

"Does that really surprise you?" Trish asked, looking up from her notes.

"Not at all. It is a surprise to me that the finding was published."

"Do the experts assign a cause for the changes?"

Katrina set her beer down on the table. "In fact, they do. Some of the Russian doctors are even saying such things as they have a disaster on their hands, that they can not continue to blame the numbers on life styles. They say that no life style could be the blame for the numbers they are seeing." She explained that the doctors were blaming the decades of radiation exposure. "They are beginning to look at their patients as Cold War casualties." The doctors also said that their geneticists had warned them back in the sixties that they were facing genetic damage to the population from the widespread exposures, but that no one was listening to them.

"I guess they're listening now," Trish commented.

"Perhaps. I am not so sure."

Trish asked, "What are they going to do? Have they got a plan of action?"

Katrina said that there were vested interests—like the government and private sectors—who thought they needed more studies.

"Right," Trish interjected, in a voice laced with cynicism.

"But," Katrina continued, "these doctors know there is no time to wait for absolute proofs. They know that radiation kills and causes genetic damage. They know their people have had massive exposure. And now they are seeing those exact same health consequences. That is all the cause and effect they need." Katrina arched her back, stretching in her seat, then leaned forward again. "You know after the Chernobyl accident, the Russian government did nothing for the people, except relocate them from their villages in the exposed zones to other sites that were just as radioactive."

"Why did they do that?

"This I do not know. Perhaps they had no knowledge of what to do with them, or how care for them. Or, perhaps they believed they had no money to care for them." She told her how the people were eating contaminated meats and vegetables and drinking contaminated milk because they didn't have anything else to eat or drink. They were also burning radioactive wood to keep warm—even though wood absorbs radiation like a sponge—because that was all they had to heat their homes.

She said that years later a woman in government—who'd been a journalist living in the fallout zone at the time of the Chernobyl accident—wrote about finding documents showing that the politicians had lied about how many people had been sent to the hospitals after the accident. In actuality, tens of thousands had to be hospitalized, and when the levels of radiation got higher and higher to unsafe levels, the government simply adopted new higher standards for safe levels. "They did this so they could keep telling the people that there was no danger to them." Katrina rubbed the side of her face. "The woman even found out that the meat that was produced in some of the areas of the fallout was distributed as widely as possible throughout the country, even though they knew it was contaminated."

Trish's face went blank. "Why on earth did they do that?"

"To save money."

"You're kidding!" she reacted, jutting her head back.

Katrina shook her head slowly from side to side. "I do not joke about such things." She told Trish that it was mixed with normal meat in sausages and meat products—tens of thousands of tons of it, and that permitted levels of radioactivity in milk were raised to avoid wasting it. Two million tons of it were distributed and consumed throughout the country, contaminating the people who'd been in safe areas as well.

"The government kept documents about that?"

"Yes, they also bragged about saving over a billion rubles by doing it."

Trish sighed. "My God, no wonder the people are dying." She stared at the cheeses and bread on the table in front of her. How would anyone know if their food was contaminated? She looked over at Katrina. "You know, even a man who robs a bank gets twenty years in jail. Just think how many years of life must have been stolen from the Russian people just to save a little money." She let out a forceful breath. "But what usually happens is they give the guy who saved over a billion rubles an award or promotion for coming up with such a fine idea." She took a deep breath and rested her head in her hand. "If they'd done it for genocide instead of greed, we might be talking about mass murder here."

"And," Katrina added, "because the effects are not immediate and it is not possible to assign direct cause, there is no one to point to for blame."

Trish stretched her hand out on the table. "Katrina, we've got to start rethinking the roles the different governments of the world are playing when it comes to national security. Over 61 million dead doesn't sound like *any* country is protecting its people. Has any *terrorist* come close to killing that many? Has any *war* ever touched and contaminated every living thing on the planet?"

Katrina stared at the roses in the yard a moment. "And it was not simply brave men at war who died and suffered," she added. "It was also women, children, the old."

Trish looked at the roses, as well. And just like Peggy said about the kids with missing arms in Moscow. If it had been overt, like a maniac or terrorist running around, everyone would be up in arms. But this had been a silent war, waged against unwitting people, by an invisible force, wielded by hands washed in greed, ignorance and patriotism.

• • •

On Saturday evening Trish packed her bags. Then, Yuri and Katrina came over and the three of them lounged around the bungalow, reminiscing about the events of the previous days. She took a few more pictures of them, because wanted to remember what the two of them looked like, though she knew she'd never forget their generous help.

The evening was filled with ambivalence for her. She hated to leave the friends she'd made—and even the little rental house that had become home to her in such a short time—yet she desperately wanted to be back in her own home in Clayton, the way anyone wants to be home, where everything is familiar and comfortable when they're sick or in crisis. And she was going to need time to recuperate. It didn't seem possible that she'd been gone only two weeks.

After she paid her bill for the bungalow, and, through Katrina, was able to personally thank the man who had rented it to her, she repaid Katrina and Yuri generously for all of the expenses they had incurred on her behalf— even though they protested. At the train station, Trish gave Katrina her tape recorder and batteries and all of the music tapes that she'd brought, including the Enya tape Katrina had liked so much.

"Oh, no, Trish, I can not take this." Katrina held up her hands.

"Katrina, I insist. So don't even argue. It's small compensation for all the help you've given me." She set the items firmly in Katrina's hands.

Katrina smiled as she took the articles and said, "The only thing we ask is that you tell the people in America what is happening here."

"I promise. I'll do my best."

Then Trish hugged Yuri and Katrina warmly and boarded the train back to Almaty. She waved good-bye from the window until she couldn't see them any more.

Chapter Eleven

The return trip to the U.S. was a reverse of the one over to Semipalatinsk: the train ride to Almaty, the flight to Moscow and then the one to New York, broken up by a night's stay at each main destination. There was one difference. Trish wasn't the same person who'd made the trip more than two weeks before...not the same person at all.

Her lingering exhaustion had made it almost impossible to even worry about the logistics of the trip; she'd felt as though she was operating in a fog the entire time. After arriving at Kennedy Airport in New York, she stood in the customs line still in a daze. When she approached the customs man, he appeared to be eyeing her suspiciously. She reasoned—with as much humor as she could muster—that he must have thought she was on drugs, with her tired, punch-drunk demeanor. But he simply smiled after a time and said, "Did you enjoy Moscow?"

"I guess you could say I had an interesting time."

"And where do you plan to go next, Australia?" he asked with a slight smile.

"No, no. I think my traveling days are going to be over for a while. I'm pretty exhausted from this trip...and broke, too," she added candidly, with a raised eyebrow.

He smiled at her with a twinkle in his eye and waved her on. She lifted her heavy suitcases onto a cart and continued on her way.

When her flight arrived at the Atlanta Airport that night around eight o'clock, she was so glad to be back in Georgia that she thought she would have cried if she'd had just a little more strength. She deplaned and rode the train to the baggage claim area. As she lifted her suitcases from the carousel, they seemed as heavy as if they'd been full of lead souvenirs. She had a baggage handler load them onto a cart and carry them to curbside, where she'd wait for the van to carry her to the valet parking lot.

When they walked outside the terminal, Trish was almost taken aback by the heat, even though the sun had just set. It was difficult to breathe, and she felt for a moment as though she would smother. "Wow. Now I remember why they call it 'Hotlanta,'" she commented to the baggage handler. "I'd almost forgotten."

"Yeah, it's been a real scorcher this year...and dry as toast," he agreed.

As he set Trish's bags near the curb, he noticed the Moscow customs sticker and commented off-handedly, "Moscow, huh? You must be some kind of world traveler."

"Not exactly."

"Where are you going next, Australia?"

She jerked her head around toward him. "You know, you're the second person to ask me that since I got back."

"Really?"

"Coincidence, I guess, huh?"

"I guess." He smiled, thanked her for her tip, wished her a good evening and then returned to the terminal whistling. But Trish thought she'd been bumping into quite a lot of coincidences in the previous few weeks.

After having her bags loaded into her Jeep in the parking lot, she headed north up the expressway on Interstate 85 toward Clayton. She was deep enough in thought that it wasn't until she reached the turnoff to Gainesville that she even noticed where she was. She drifted back into her thoughts and memories, unconscious of her location again until she drove into Clayton itself. When she reached her house, she carried her luggage just inside the kitchen door with what felt like her last bit of strength. The house was hot and stuffy. She adjusted the air conditioning to a lower temperature and headed for her bedroom. There she pulled back the covers on the bed, flopped down on the clean sheets and quickly drifted into a deep sleep.

A little after three A.M. she awoke and went to the kitchen, where she micro-waved a frozen dinner. After eating a few bites, she went back to bed and fell asleep again.

The next morning she was still in a daze. She knew she needed to unpack and organize her notes and do a million things, but she didn't have the strength to do anything. And she didn't. When she ate, it was sparingly. When she slept, it was fitfully. Awake, she sat zombie-like, curled up in her favorite, overstuffed chair in the living room, replaying bits and pieces of the experiences, sights and conversations of the previous weeks. Peggy was saying, "Trish, once you know about something you can't go back to the luxury of not knowing." She saw Mirek slamming his fist on the table. "I was responsible for *telling* people." Then he'd point his finger at her and bellow, "And now *you* are."

What was it he'd said after that" "Do you think I don't know that one of those creatures could have been *my* child?" *My God, he had a relationship with those mutants.* Trish sat staring at the wall. *Of course he did. They were the children of every scientist in the world from Oppenheimer on.*

Trish felt almost frozen in time with thoughts weaving in and out of her mind. But time was passing. Three days had passed before she looked at her caller ID to check the date. *My God, has it been that long?* Asleep, her dreams were full of images of Ilyani.

The little girl would always run up to her giggling, touch her cheek and then run away again, still giggling. She would briefly feel that same sense of peacefulness envelope her again. Then she'd find herself in the clinic, looking at the tiny creatures in the jars, and be jolted awake.

On some level she realized how debilitating the deep lethargy and fatigue were becoming, but her mind wasn't functioning clearly enough to figure out what to do about it. At times she felt almost catatonic—running things over and over in her mind, like a tape that someone might play and rewind, play and rewind. She was searching for some kind of understanding of her experiences. But her mind couldn't grasp it. The edges of her perception—the world as she had known it—had cracks in it. *Is this what Mirek went through?*

She was lying on the sofa, still running thoughts over in her mind one morning, when the phone rang, jolting her. She groaned and stumbled over to answer it, surprised at how unsteady she was on her feet.

"Hello?" Trish's voice—which she hadn't used in days—was croaky, weak and distant. It sounded foreign even to her.

"Patty, did I wake you?" Kathy's voice had concern in it.

"No, no. That's all right. I was just resting," she assured her.

"Well, when I was at the drugstore in town just now Margaret Ann told me she saw your car in your driveway this morning. I couldn't believe it, so I called as soon as I got home. Why haven't you called me?"

"I guess I've just been tired."

"Well, I can tell that from your voice. But I can't wait. Tell me all about it. I'm dying to hear everything that happened." Then in a feigned, snobbish tone she added, "And just where are you going next, Miss World Traveler...Australia?"

There it was again. It was too coincidental. But the events and people were totally disconnected. "Why did you say *that*?" she asked suspiciously.

"Patty, I was *just* kidding. Now, tell me. What happened over there?"

The distraction about Australia made Trish stop focusing on Kazakhstan, just long enough to realize how burdensome the memories had become. But suddenly it was all back again, and the weight of it felt like it would crush her.

"Kathy..." she began, with her voice cracking. She held her breath a minute, trying to choke back tears. "I can't begin to tell you..." She choked again, and then broke into uncontrollable sobbing. She could only hear bits and pieces of Kathy's words between the sobs.

"...Patty, what on earth... What's going on? ...I'm coming over..." Then Trish heard the dial tone, and she hung up the phone and retreated to her chair.

A short time later, Trish heard the crunch of gravel from Kathy's car as she drove up, and then her friend bounding through the creaky door.

When Kathy entered the room, she stood frozen in place a moment as she looked at Trish curled up in a fetal position, red faced and eyes swollen. "Oh, my God, Patty, what's happened to you?" she blurted as she rushed across the room and knelt beside her.

"Oh, Kathy..." Trish raised both her hands, covering her face.

Kathy embraced her friend, but Trish still couldn't talk, and Kathy simply comforted her while she cried. "Now, now. It's all right," she said, patting her back. "Whatever it is, it's going to be fine—just fine. You're home now. We'll take care of you."

For a long time Trish couldn't talk. Kathy went to the bathroom, then returned with a hand towel, soaked in cold water. She handed it to Trish. "Patty, you're really scaring me here."

"Oh, I don't mean to. I guess I'm just tired, too."

"Too? What 'too?' What's *happened* to you?" Trish realized that all kinds of things were probably running through Kathy's head, such as the possibility of her being raped or mugged in a foreign country. Trish wanted to reassure her, so she managed a half-smile and waved off her concerns with one hand, as she grabbed a Kleenex from the table beside her with the other, then blew her nose.

At that, Kathy stood up. "Look, I'm going to fix us both something to drink, and then we can talk. If it takes all day, we'll just talk till somebody makes us go to bed...like when we were kids." Trish managed to grin at her comment.

Then after sipping on their drinks, she began telling Kathy about what had happened in Kazakhstan, pausing from time to time to fight back tears. During the accounting she noticed that Kathy didn't probe much.

When she finally finished her story, Kathy leaned back in her seat. "Patty, I never should have pushed you into going to that place."

As they hugged again, Kathy joined her in crying. When they stopped, Trish said, "You know, Kathy, seeing those things in the jars...it was the first time in my adult life that I was glad to be childless."

"Oh, Patty..."

Kathy cried again, but by now Trish had better control. When she stood up to go to the bathroom, the weakness descended on her again, and she almost fell back down.

"What's the matter, Patty? Are you okay?"

"No, actually, I'm not. I was exhausted when I got there, and I've been even weaker since I got back. A few good nights' sleep don't seem to be pulling me out of it, either."

"Patty, you could have picked up a bug in Russia or something. I hear their water is pretty contaminated in places. You need to go see Dr. Smith right away."

Trish thought about the water in the bungalow shower. "You're probably right. I'll make an appointment in a few days if I'm not any better."

"A few days, my *ass*." She stood up and pointed at her. "Look, just stay right there. I'm getting you an appointment right away." Kathy went into the kitchen, where Trish could hear her friend's "in charge" voice on the phone. When she returned, her mood had changed completely. She'd become a woman with a mission. "They'll work you in as soon as you can get there, so get up and get ready. I'm driving you over right now."

"Well, that was sure quick."

"Listen, with all my years of sick kids, I know how to get into a doctor's office in short order."

• • •

Trish was being examined within the hour. When she finally returned to the waiting room, she found Kathy waiting impatiently.

"I'm sorry it took so long, but with all the blood tests and lab work...and we talked a long time..."

"Oh, I don't care about that," Kathy said, as she held the outside door for Trish. "What did he say?"

As they walked to the car, Trish answered, "Well, he poked and probed...and took a lot of tests, but he said if nothing came back from the lab, he was going to chalk it up to..." She stopped a moment, still weak. "Let's see now...he said 'a combination of jet lag, emotional fatigue and adrenaline let down.' *Or*, he said, 'it could be some kind of virus.' How's that for a diagnosis? Don't you love indecisiveness in a doctor?" When she reached the car, she leaned onto it. "Oh, and I'm supposed to call back immediately if I develop any more symptoms. He's going to call me when the tests come back, and let me know if they turn up anything."

"Well, that's a relief," Kathy exhaled, as she opened her door. "It sounds like we can fix that up with some rest and a few good doses of chicken soup." As they got seated in the car Kathy faced Trish. "You really had me worried there for a while. I thought maybe you'd even gotten some radiation sickness or something."

Trish faced forward, staring ahead. "I never even thought about that."

Kathy continued trying to uplift her as they drove back home. When they arrived, Kathy got her settled in bed, and busied herself unpacking bags for Trish and laundering her clothes. Before she left, she stuck her head back in the bedroom door and told Trish she'd return later with some good homemade food. "Now get some more rest and try not to worry about a thing."

Then Kathy came over and hugged her warmly. "You're going to be just fine. You'll see." Then she added, "Now get some sleep. I can tell that little trip to the doctor's just about did you in again."

But before Trish fell asleep, the realization slowly began entering her consciousness that nothing in her life was ever going to be the same again. She might look the same. She might even act the same in a lot of ways, but the person who traveled to Kazakhstan was gone forever.

• • •

Even though Kathy checked on her several times following her office visit, bringing groceries or a meal, Trish began slipping back into her depression and holing up in her house with her thoughts again like a wounded animal. She realized it was the worse thing she could do. At one point she considered seeing a psychologist, but she didn't think a psychologist would understand what she'd been through any more than she did. Besides, she was well aware that she couldn't afford that kind of expense.

Early one morning, as she pulled weeds from the dry flowerbeds in front of her house with Muffin by her side, Trish's thoughts kept wandering to one of her friends from college, who she hadn't thought about in a long time. Brenda Thompson had been her roommate during her junior year. They'd met in journalism classes at the University of Georgia and had become fast friends. Because Brenda was as gung-ho about being a reporter as Trish, she really enjoyed her company. Her enthusiasm was contagious, and the two of them spent hours together studying and talking. After college Trish was a bridesmaid at Brenda's wedding. In spite of always living far apart, they'd managed to stay in touch over the years.

After reporting happily for years at her home town paper, however, Brenda was assigned to cover a major local news story. A dam at Toccoa Falls in North Georgia had broken, inundating the college campus that was situated below it. Dozens of students were killed when the wall of water came flooding into their dormitories.

Completely inexperienced with disaster stories, Brenda had become emotionally drained by the experience. When she called Trish a couple of weeks after the incident, she couldn't talk about it without breaking down. Eventually Brenda quit her job and went into another profession. Though she became a successful realtor, it wasn't the job she'd dreamed of as a college student, and had enjoyed for much of her adult life.

As Trish pulled the last weed from around a shrub, she sat down on the ground and began wondering if that was what was happening to her—if she just wasn't emotionally equipped to handle the job any more—if the story was just too big for her to handle. She thought briefly about changing course completely, like Brenda had done. But another profession wasn't going to erase her memories. She was still going to have to deal with it. She'd never be able to put the clinic and Mirek's book out of her mind.

And then there was Ilyani. Where did she put that experience in her frame of reference? *Try sharing that with a psychologist, Trish. You'll end up in a clinic yourself. With a nice, white, long-armed wardrobe.*

But every time she tried to take notes or write something for the article, she couldn't manage to do that, either. "God," she said at one point, sitting and staring at the computer screen, "this is just great. Now I've got writer's block on top of everything else?"

Trish knew she was going to have to start pulling herself out of the emotional quagmire into which she was sinking deeper and deeper. But after several days of trying and still failing to deal with it on her own, she finally had to admit that she desperately needed some outside advice. She'd call Max Rogers and invite him to lunch. Even though he was the one person in the world she thought might be able to help, she'd resisted calling him when she first got home. She hated to admit to the father figure in her life that she'd gotten in over her head with her latest adventure.

In spite of that reluctance, coupled with her natural tendency toward independence, she had to admit that she needed Max more than ever...needed to see his face and hear his voice and have him reassure her once again that everything would be all right.

"Patty!" he almost roared over the phone. "Girl, I can't wait to see you. And I've been anxiously waiting to hear all about your trip."

"I can't wait to see you either, Max. I've missed your corny jokes."

He laughed one of his characteristic hearty laughs, and she could imagine him with his head flung backward. Just the sound of his voice and laughter made her feel better.

He accepted her invitation for lunch the next afternoon at a steak house restaurant that was one of their favorites—one that they usually reserved for birthdays and other celebrations. After their phone conversation, Trish began straightening up a few things around her house and trying to pull herself into some semblance of a normal routine. She was determined to will herself out of her depression, somehow.

Chapter Twelve

The next day when Trish arrived at the steak house, she went inside, paused at the hostess stand and scanned the restaurant until she saw Max already seated at a booth, drinking a glass of wine. Their eyes met at almost the same time, and she smiled and waved to him. He nodded and tipped his glass toward her. When she started toward him, Max stood up to greet her, beaming his familiar smile. But, the closer she got to him, the more his smile relaxed. His jaw finally went completely slack at her worn appearance. He embraced her warmly, then held her out at arm's length.

"Patty. My *Dear*. You've lost so much weight. And you look so drawn. Are you all right?" The expression on his face projected genuine concern.

As they sat down, Trish assured him, "Of course, Max. It's just a case of jet lag and fatigue—emotional fatigue, I think the doctor called it."

"Then you've been to a doctor?"

She nodded in response.

"Well, that's comforting. And he's sure it's nothing serious?"

"He gave me a thorough...and I do mean a thorough going over, and I'm fine, really."

"Well, that relieves me. The sight of you gave me quite a start."

The waitress brought menus, took Trish's order for a drink and then left.

Trish thought Max sensed her discomfort at having her appearance scrutinized, as he quickly dropped the matter and shifted to the purpose of their meeting. "So tell me, how was your trip to Russia...besides being exhausting?"

She drew in a deep breath, as she nodded her head slowly, then, "Ah, yes...Russia." She set her forearms on the table. "Well, Max, that's what I want to talk to you about...and it's important."

He smiled at her playfully, raising his eyebrows. "Well, I didn't think you'd be treating me to lunch at such a delightful place if it wasn't important to you, so fire away."

Trish sat up straight. "Max, what is the source of mythology?"

Max threw back his head and laughed one of his familiar, hearty laughs. "Oh, Patty, that's what I love about you. You're always so direct...and you always ask such simple questions."

She smiled slightly and lowered her head.

He stopped smiling. "You're quite serious, aren't you? Well, then." He tilted his head back. "Let me see. The source of mythology." He looked back at her. "Well, really we don't know the source. That's why it's *called* myth." He took a breath. "There are many who believe mythology is irrelevant in the present world, but I think it's more relevant than ever to the human condition." He paused to take a sip of his wine. "I hope you don't mind that I went ahead and ordered a drink before you got here."

She waved her hand in the air and shook her head briefly, as he continued. "I suppose you could say that our conscious belief systems are wrapped around—or possibly inside—another system of unconscious beliefs...and mythology talks to us on *that* level. I believe it reflects images of another reality that few ever explore, much less are aware of in our present society." Then he smiled. "Listen to me...teaching class again."

"No, Max, that's exactly what I'm after," she responded. "Tell me more...especially Greek mythology, and specifically Greek monsters."

"Ah, Greek mythology. Well," he began, "some think that Greek mythology more closely follows the development of the human psyche...and personally I like it the best of all the mythologies." He paused and looked at her as though reading something in her face. "You're not asking hypothetical questions, are you? You're on to something. What is it?" He leaned forward. "Just what have you gotten your pretty little self into in Russia?" But before she could respond, he added, "You know, they used to lock people up in Russia for asking too many questions."

"Oh, Max. I feel like I'm already in a prison, and I feel more trapped in it than if it had real bars...and I think the only way I'll ever be able to escape it, is if I *keep* asking questions."

Max leaned back in his seat and looked at her, as the waitress returned with Trish's wine. Max picked up his pipe and relit it. Then he puffed and puffed, as he continued studying her face.

After the waitress took their orders for lunch and left again, Max pointed with the stem of his pipe. "You know it's been fascinating watching you baby boomers grow up. You're an interesting breed—your generation. You always seem so compelled to throw open the veils, look behind the Iron Curtains...tear down the Berlin Walls...and dig up the family skeletons.

"But there's a price to be paid for opening doors that have been closed for years." He punctuated his words with his pipe occasionally as he spoke. "The mysteries you reveal might be shocking or depressing, or they might lead to even more mysteries—more closed doors—more questions to be answered. You might even get a glimpse into the abyss." He examined her face again. "Come to think of it, you look very much to me like someone who's stared into the abyss. Am I right?"

"I don't know. Maybe I fell into one," she responded as she fingered her silverware.

He rubbed his beard. "That's quite an interesting comment, you know."

"How so?" she asked, looking up at him.

He told her that many primitive cultures said that their shamans were people who'd had some psychological breakdown, or break-through or some near fatal illness that turned them inside themselves. There they began entering into another realm, an unconscious realm of existence.

"That's just what it feels like!" Trish exclaimed, pressing her midsection against the edge of the table. "It's like I'm falling into this thing and I can't stop it." She sat back in her seat and took a deep breath and let it out. She looked directly at him again and asked, "Max, what if I told you that I've actually seen a Cyclops and a mermaid?"

He laughed out loud again. "I'd ask you if you'd started drinks before you got here." When she looked down stone-faced, he added, "It's not like you, Patty, to be so cryptic."

"Oh, I don't mean to be mysterious," she responded with resignation. "It's just that it's so hard to talk about, and...well, I guess I should just start at the beginning."

And then slowly, over lunch, Trish began telling her friend all about her odyssey in Kazakhstan.

Max sat without any unnecessary movements, as though entranced by what he was hearing. Trish occasionally picked at her food and stopped to catch her breath or to choke back tears. She told Max about fainting in the clinic—about Mirek's precious, tissue-covered book on Greek mythology—about the pictures in it of the Cyclops and the mermaids—and about the contents of the jars in Clinic Number Four. She told him about the prolonged emotional trauma she was suffering because of everything she had witnessed and experienced in Semipalatinsk. And she told him about Ilyani. It was more difficult to maintain her composure at that point than it had been even about the mutants. She attempted to speak several times and choked up each time.

She finally said, "I can't...I can't..." Her eyes began filling again with tears and she dabbed at them with her napkin.

Max leaned forward and patted her hand. "It's all right. You can tell me about that at a later time."

"No. I need to say this." With tears streaming down her face, she added, "I can't get her out of my mind." Trish wiped her face and eyes again, glanced around the restaurant and in the process, she regained some of her composure. "If I'd known I was going to act like such a baby, I'd have suggested lunch at my place." She smiled slightly, then continued her story with more coherence. When she finally finished, she sat back and waited for Max's reaction...waited for him to play his role, to explain it all and make it all right somehow.

But he didn't. He simply said, "Oh, my. My, oh, my. I don't know what to say. It must have been a completely overwhelming experience for you. No wonder you look so tired and worn. You've been through a lot, haven't you?" He wrinkled his brow. "What do you intend to do now?"

Propping her hands on the edge of the table, she said, "I intended for you to explain everything so my life could return to normal."

"Patty, you don't *want* your life to return to normal, or you never would have gone to Russia in the first place. You were searching for something, and you found a bit more than you bargained for." He glanced at the ceiling momentarily, then back at her and added, "But I'm convinced that you're up to the challenge. Have you any plans from your reporter's perspective on how to proceed from here on your search?"

She shook her head slowly back and forth. "Oh, Max, I'm not a reporter anymore. I've totally lost my objectivity. How can any human being remain objective after seeing something like that—and still be human? I'm not an American anymore. I'm not a Presbyterian or Democrat anymore. I'm just..." she sighed. "I'm just a human being. I don't feel as though I owe allegiance or loyalty to anything but the human race any more...and the planet."

"But you've got to have some curiosity about it and plans on where to go from here. I know you better than that."

She looked directly at him and smiled. "Well, I've thought about going to Australia to look for answers. Don't ask why, but it's like some giant conspiracy or something that I'm supposed to go to Australia for the next part of the puzzle." She tapped her fist on the table for emphasis. "I just feel it in my bones—you know? Like that reporter's instinct."

"Now, that's the Patty I know," Max beamed.

After Trish related the incidents involving the comments about Australia when she first arrived back, Max said, "Well, it's good you didn't simply dismiss them as coincidences, because it sounds like Jung's synchronicity to me."

"Huh?"

"You know...Carl Jung. We talked quite a lot about him when you were taking psychology in college. Remember?"

"I know. I just hadn't thought about the synchronicity thing for years."

"Well, you can start thinking about it now, because I think you've just experienced a clear cut example of it."

"Wasn't that what he called meaningful coincidence?"

"It was, indeed."

The waitress came to take their plates and inquired about dessert. They looked at each other and Trish shook her head. Max glanced at their empty glasses. "Just some more wine for both of us, if you will."

She left again, and Trish took up the conversation where they'd left off. "Max, there was absolutely no connection between those three people, and for them to make the same comment was simply impossible. It was *too* much of a coincidence. You know?"

"Well, I happen to believe that there's no such thing as a coincidence...that everything in life happens for a purpose. Maybe those three people were totally disconnected. And then again, maybe they...maybe all of us are connected in a way that we can't begin to fathom at our present stage of development."

She asked him if he'd ever had an experience like that before.

"All the time, Patty...but it's not incredible that it happens to us; it's incredible that we notice it. And once we have an attention-getter as you experienced, and we start looking for them or noticing them, they seem to start popping up all around us...but they've really been there all along."

"But what does it mean?" she asked, tilting her head to the side.

"Ah...that's the next part of the puzzle...figuring out what it means." He sipped some wine and set his glass back down. "I think you've already pretty much figured yours out...that you need to go to Australia to look for answers. Unfortunately, many of the synchronicities aren't as straightforward as that."

After letting out a deep breath, she said, "Max, I don't understand any of this."

"Well, don't try to understand it for now; just continue noticing and focusing on it and accepting it. You accept your reporter's instinct, don't you?"

"Yes."

"And why is that?"

"Because I've seen over the years that it works."

"Experience, then...trial and error, right?"

"Right," she replied with confidence, as she crossed her arms.

"Well, I think you'll find that synchronicity will work for you, too. So, just accept it like you accept your reporter's instinct that you can't begin to explain, either...and then just plan your trip to Australia for now."

The waitress returned with more wine, set the glasses down and retrieved the empty ones, before leaving again. Trish twisted the stem of her wine glass back and forth on the table. "Yeah, well, the only thing is, I don't know where in Australia I'm supposed to go, or who I'm supposed to talk to—much less what questions to ask—or how I'll finance a trip like that. I've wiped out my reserves and then some on the trip to Russia, and I've still got all of those mundane things to worry about—like eating." She laughed, and he joined her.

Then, after a pause, he said, "Patty, you're curious about mythology right now—and rightly so. Have you ever heard the myth about Psyche and Cupid?"

"No, at least not in detail."

"Well, then, let me tell you the story."

"Wait," she said, rising from her seat. "Before you start, I need to go powder my nose. I know my make-up is a mess from all that crying."

● ● ●

When Trish returned to the table, refreshed, Max had re-lit his pipe. "I'll give you the condensed version of the myth," he said, leaning back. Then, while Trish sipped her wine, he looked briefly toward the ceiling and began. "It seems that when the princess, Psyche, was born, she was the most beautiful woman in all the land. People came for miles just to gaze upon her. The goddess, Venus—who was no slouch herself in the beauty department— was quite jealous of the mortal, Psyche. She was stealing her thunder, so to speak. People weren't worshiping her in her temple as they had before— instead favoring the princess."

As Max spoke, Trish noted that her friend had taken on the demeanor of a professor talking to his students. She'd become familiar with that de- meanor over the years and always looked forward to it, since it usually sig- naled very revealing, as well as entertaining information.

He told her how Venus went about convincing Psyche's parents that their daughter was doomed to fall in love with and marry a monstrous, ugly man. "Then she sent her son Cupid, the god of love, to make her fall in love with an ogre. Upon seeing Psyche's beauty, however, Cupid was hopelessly smitten with her. He pretended to his mother that he'd completed his as- signment, but instead, married Psyche himself and kept her hidden away in a remote and gloriously beautiful castle. There the couple lived happily."

Max moved his wine glass to the side and leaned forward on the table. "To conceal his duplicity, Cupid made his love promise never to look upon his face. No other desire would ever be denied her. He only came to her at nighttime in the darkened castle, where they made love and slept together night after night."

He told Trish how, even though Psyche was equally smitten by her mysterious husband, her two jealous sisters conspired and eventually per- suaded her that he was really the monster who would one day devour her. "So one night as her lover lay sleeping beside her, Psyche—determined to get a glimpse of the man with whom she'd been sleeping—quietly lit a lamp and held it over his face." Max held out his hands, cupping them like paren- theses. "And there she saw that, not only was this no monster, but Cupid himself—the god of love. She saw him in a new light and fell even more in love." He lowered his hands and raised his brows. "However, some hot oil from the lamp dropped on his shoulder and woke him."

Furrowing his brows, Max continued, telling Trish how Cupid was enraged that Psyche had broken her word and that he promptly deserted her, saying that no love could live where there was no trust. "She was heartbroken." Max tilted his head forward, adding, "...and also by now, pregnant." He raised his head back. "So she went to Venus for help in getting her husband back. But Venus, who was still jealous of Psyche, set out a series of impossible tasks for her to complete. Yet, against all odds and with help from different quarters, Psyche was able to complete them all...until the last one."

As Trish sipped more wine, Max inhaled a puff from his pipe and slowly exhaled it. Then he continued. "Venus told her that she had to go to Proserpine across the perilous River Styx into Hades." He told Trish that the purpose of the journey was for Proserpine to send Venus back a little of her beauty in a box. Once again, friendly forces helped Psyche by telling her to take two halfpennies in her mouth. They told her that when she came to the old man, Charon, who would ferry her across the river in his leaky boat, she was to give him one of the coins in payment, but whatever she did, she was not to give anyone else her other halfpenny. She would be tempted, but she was not to give the coin away. "It was her only way out...the only way she could pay for her trip back."

Max set his pipe down, sipped some wine and let out a sigh. "She got into Hades and retrieved Proserpine's box, and—just as she'd been warned—she was tempted by traps that had been set by Venus, including a drowning man. Through it all, however, she held steadfastly to her last coin, and was able to pay her fare to Charon and get back across the river, and ultimately she got her husband back. In fact," Max concluded, "Jupiter himself intervened and made her immortal. And she and Cupid lived happily ever after." He smiled. "The child they had was called Joy."

After he finished the story, Max's demeanor shifted back into the mode of a friend, as he leaned across the table and added, "Patty, Girl, whatever happens from here on out, remember never to give away too much of yourself. Hang on to that last coin—whatever that may be for you—to find your way out. Remember that you always have to get back to the world of the living. And remember, too, that with the marriage of the heart and the soul—the psyche and the cupid—one finds his true joy."

With that last comment, Trish felt a sense of peacefulness envelop her—not as strong as the one she'd felt with Ilyani—but similar. "What a beautiful story. I don't know quite why—I'm not sure I even understand it—but it seems like just the thing I needed to hear right now."

"Yes, well, myth is like that. It talks to us on that other level, and makes us feel good, or challenges us. It seems to touch that spot in our soul that needs touching." He sipped some more wine. "You needed to hear that story because you were drowning emotionally in your experience and needed to be thrown some kind of lifeline until you could learn to start swimming in it."

Trish half smiled at his comment. "It's not just drowning; I almost feel like I'm losing my grip on reality."

Max smirked. "They say that the word 'reality' should always have quotation marks around it...and I must say, I think you've been dearly challenged to redefine what constitutes reality. I think the *real* reality is so profound and so complex that human beings simply can't begin to grasp it with the conscious mind." He crossed his arms in front of him. "But our subconscious knows the truth. So we tell our truths with myths that seem like story tales. That's why I think they're so powerful...because our higher selves recognize the truth of them."

"But *could* there be any truth to mythologies?"

"Why, of course, my dear." He seemed surprised by her question. "Primitive cultures don't tell their oral histories as though they're fantasies. They tell them as deep truths. They believe them." He half laughed and told her, "One of my favorite books on mythology came from an antique store. It was in remarkably good shape, except for one handwritten sentence in the margin of one of the pages. The book said that no one today believes the myths in the book to be true, and some former owner had written boldly, 'I beg to differ!' I love that little inscription better than anything else in the book."

Max glanced around briefly at the emptying restaurant, then returned to the conversation. "I categorize mythology in with many other mysteries in life, and I believe it's dangerous for man to be too rigid in his thinking, and arrogant, as well, to think that he's somehow reached a point of having all the answers. Many intellectuals had accepted much of Greek mythology as purely symbolic, until one day a man named Heinrich Schliemann pronounced that the city of Troy was not a mythological place at all, but a very real location." He looked at her directly. "Do you know about him?"

"Only vaguely. He had something to do with archaeology, didn't he?" she asked.

"Indeed, he did." Max explained how in his youth, Schliemann had always been fascinated by the mythological stories he read. "Eventually he became convinced that there was a reality to them—that they were real histories that had simply been mythologized. As a result, he set out to prove his theory, and, by using Homer's epic poems as a roadmap, he retraced the voyage in The Iliad. Then sometime in the mid-1800's some say he actually found the ruins of the ancient city of Troy.

"He'd been scoffed at by his peers, but, as they say, no one could argue with his success. His methods were somewhat unconventional, to say the least." He held his hand out. "But can you imagine using a two and a half thousand year old poem as a roadmap to lead the way to what has become the system of modern archaeology?"

"No...I mean, I'd heard of Schliemann, but I never understood exactly what he did and how important it was."

Max raised up a hand. "The man was *nuts*, Patty...totally nuts. And *those* are the ones who change the world...the crazy ones who show the rest of us fools the way in life...the ones who see the world just the least bit differently than the rest of us. Don't ever question your crazy ideas about life. Sometimes I wonder if the myths are so real that we're all just reliving them over and over again until we understand them. When you tell me you saw mermaids and Cyclopes, I think, 'Heavens, that would put Schliemann's discovery to shame.'"

Trish rubbed her right temple with her fingers. "Max, after I saw what was in the jars in that clinic, I thought about the guy in the movie 'Jaws' who was throwing chump out the back of the boat trying to attract the shark. Then all of a sudden, the shark lunges up out of the water right at him, and he's stunned at the size of the thing, and the only thing he can say is that they need a bigger boat." She leaned onto the edge of the table. "Well, that's just how I felt—like this monstrous thing was coming up at me, and my boat wasn't nearly big enough to handle it. I couldn't contain it."

Max raised one eyebrow. "Actually, that's a very interesting analogy." He shifted in his seat, then added, "I think you're going to have to start asking yourself some questions here. First of all, will you let yourself be devoured by the monster? Or will you get a bigger boat? And what *is* the boat for you?"

"Well, I certainly don't want to be eaten by the *monster*...but how on earth do I get a bigger boat?"

"Well, since you used that particular symbolic analogy, it could very well be that you realize unconsciously that this story is bigger than any news report you've ever done before...or even perhaps done by anyone before." He pointed with the stem of his pipe. "However, it also seems to me at this point, that the small size of the boat--or possibly the limitations of it—are your own conscious belief systems. Maybe you need to expand your conscious mind, remove the boundaries of your preconceived notions about life and start over with a clean slate. That's the only way to get a bigger boat psychologically—one big enough to contain the monster."

He shifted again. "You're at a good point though; you're intelligent and curious, and you don't have much of a background in mythology—so you won't go into studying it with a lot of baggage, though you do need *some* frame of reference." He sipped the last of his wine. "I'm going to loan you my books on mythology for a start."

Trish could feel her mood beginning to lighten. "Max, I knew you'd help. I knew I could count on you."

"Well, this is exciting for me, as well. I find it quite stimulating. Besides, in mythology—even though the characters have to travel their journeys alone—they do have help along the way. I firmly believe that we have a duty in life to help wherever we can. We can't live other people's lives for them...or do their work for them. That would be cheating them of their own life experiences, but, where we can, we should help.

"Speaking of which," he added, "do you have your checkbook with you?"

"Well, yes, why?"

"Give me one of your deposit slips." He reached out his hand.

"Oh, no, Max, no, really, you can't..."

"Now, don't argue with me on the subject," he interrupted. "This is not negotiable." He looked sternly at her and repeated, "Now, give me a deposit slip."

Trish reluctantly pulled her checkbook out of her purse, tore out a deposit slip and handed it to Max. "This makes me feel guilty, you know," she said sheepishly.

"Well, it shouldn't. And it will only make you feel guilty in the future if you fail to pass on a helping hand to others whose path crosses yours at a time when they might need *your* help." He tucked the deposit slip into his pocket and said, "Now, come to the house anytime in the next few days, and load up on some of my books. We'll talk again many times, I'm sure, before you decide where you'll go from here...but I'm quite certain that the 'where' will be Australia."

"Max, it's always so good to see you." She reached across the table and touched his arm. "I feel so much better just talking to you. I always do."

"And it's always a pleasure to see you. I treasure our friendship more than you know." He took her hand, "You must realize that you've crossed over into the Land of the Dead to find your answers. Just be careful of the pitfalls along the way and hang on to your last coin." He patted her hand. "Continue listening to your instincts and watching for the synchronicities whenever you get stumped or come to a fork in the road. Those will be your roadmaps. You'll be just fine. I want you to think of this thing as a glorious challenge...a unique opportunity. Don't let it consume you. It's just like the monsters in our dreams. They're not meant to frighten us; they're just meant to get our attention, so we'll notice the dream message. It's gotten your attention. Now find the message."

They stood to leave, and after Trish paid the bill, they walked out to the parking lot into the brilliant sunlight and hugged good-bye. Trish got into her car, but didn't start it right away. She simply sat there in the over-heated interior, remembering Max's advice from years before about being grateful every day. Then—just as she had done so many times before in the previous weeks—she cried deep, heaving sobs. But these tears were of relief and release. They felt cleansing.

For the first time in weeks of unbelievable research and shock, Trish Cagle had begun feeling a sense of hope. And she paused in that moment in gratitude to consciously thank God for having such wonderful friends in her life, the kind who knew exactly when to comfort her, or encourage her...or kick her in the butt whenever she needed it.

Chapter Thirteen

Though still plagued by writer's block and occasional nightmares, Trish nonetheless was able to maintain an underlying sense of comfort from her conversation with Max for days. Feeling more motivated than she had since her return from Russia, she got dressed early one morning and drove to town to run errands before the mid-day heat descended.

Her first stop was at the bank to withdraw cash from the ATM machine. As was her habit, after retrieving her money, she glanced at the balance on the receipt to see if it was close to the one in her checkbook. Her eyes widened in surprise when she saw it indicated about fifty thousand dollars more than she expected. *This can't be right.* She rummaged through her purse for her reading glasses, then stopped and looked up. Had she punched in the wrong code? That didn't make any sense. And the screen had flashed, "Welcome, Patricia Cagle." Mystified, she pulled her car into the bank parking lot and went inside to check out the error with one of the tellers.

When her turn in line came, she approached the young woman at the window with a smile and a slight furrow in her brow. "Alice, there seems to be some sort of mistake in my checking account." She explained the problem. "Could you check it out for me?"

"Hmm," Alice muttered in reply. "Sure, Trish. It'll take just a minute."

After a few moments of typing on her keyboard, Alice looked up from her computer screen. "There's no mistake. Fifty thousand dollars were deposited in your checking account two days ago. Did you put it in the wrong account or something? I'll be glad to transfer it for you if you did."

Trish chewed on her lip. *Deposited, huh?* She gave Alice a slight smile. "Oh, no, no... That's all right. I think I might know what happened. Thanks for your help."

After returning to her car, she sat there a moment, thinking about Max and the deposit slip. She needed to talk to him right away. But there was still a fairly lengthy list of errands to run, so she drove to the downtown square and parked. As soon as she got out, she noticed Max's car parked on a side street and grinned to herself. What had he said about meaningful coincidence? She looked around and saw him exiting his doctor's office, then walking away from her toward his car. Good. She had him.

She quickened her pace to catch up to him. When she got close enough, she reached out and touched his shoulder. He stopped and glanced around as she said, "Well, well, if it isn't Dr. Max Rogers."

He turned fully toward her and smiled, then took off his straw hat and hugged her. "My dear," he said. "What a pleasant surprise."

"Well, *I* just had an interesting surprise at the bank regarding my checking account," she countered. "You wouldn't happen to know anything about that, would you?"

He gave a short chuckle and replaced his hat. "Did it give you a start?"

"Max!" she exclaimed. "Of *course* it did. I can't believe you did that. And I can't accept it. It's just too much, really."

"Now, now," he began in a calming tone, "we've talked about that already, and I've told you: it's not negotiable."

"But I had no idea." She looked down at the sidewalk. "I mean, I just can't..."

He interrupted, "Patty, that money was the advance I got on my last book." She looked back up as he added, "I didn't need it, so I just put it in the bank, and it's been sitting there ever since. And right now you do need it." He held out his hand and continued, "I've got no family. My life has been my books and my job. I've intended to leave the cabin and my things to you anyway, so you might as well have some of your inheritance now, while you have a real need for it. Besides, I still have more than enough resources to see me through my old age."

"Max, I honestly don't know what to say..." she responded as she glanced up at the tree they were standing under, grateful for the shade it provided.

"Well, I've needed to talk to you about this for a long time. I just never mentioned it before because the subject of wills always seems so morbid. So there's no sense in protesting; it's a done deal. I know you're going through a dramatic transition, and this will just be a little cushion to sustain you through it."

"Fifty thousand *dollars* isn't exactly what I'd call a little cushion," she responded, wide-eyed.

He smiled, obviously still enjoying his surprise. "Well, you're going to need traveling expenses...as well as money to tide you over in the meantime, till you figure out what you're going to do with this story...and, I suspect, about your career."

She shifted to the other foot. "Max, at the restaurant the other day you said something I can't get out of my head. You said I'd crossed over into the Land of the Dead." She tilted her head. "What did you mean by that?"

"Well," he began, smiling, "it's not as sinister as it may sound. It's quite symbolic, actually." He told her that even in the most ancient myths there were tales of heroes or heroines who journeyed to a place such as a dark cave of some type, or an abyss, or to the Land of the Dead, as in the Psyche and Cupid myth. He said that those tales represented journeys within the self. "A person *must* go within himself to really know himself, for that's where his demons lie," he finished, with a slight nod.

"I'm not sure I understand...at least not what that has to do with the story about Clinic Number 4."

"Patty," he replied matter-of-factly, "you will have to die to who you think you are—you *are* dying to who you think you are—in order to become the person who will write the story about that clinic."

Expressionless, she said, "I don't know what you mean."

Max took a deep breath. "This mystery you're attempting to solve and write about is not simply about that clinic. It's about you."

Trish wrinkled her forehead and tilted her head. "What are you talking about, Max?"

He pulled a handkerchief from his pocket, then wiped the perspiration from his forehead and replaced it. "As human beings," he said, pointing, "we must confront our demons and monsters in order to become self aware."

"But that clinic doesn't have anything to do with *me*," she responded, raising her hand to her chest.

He raised his brows. "Doesn't it? Why did it affect you the way it did?"

"Because it's a damn good story, that's why."

"Of course, it is. And I'm not attempting to diminish that fact. I'm simply suggesting that it might be as much of a personal quest as it is one of universal significance."

She darted her eyes to the side and back. "How so?"

He shifted his weight. "Well, Patty, in the restaurant the other day you said that you weren't a Presbyterian, a Democrat, or even an American anymore."

She shrugged. "Yeah?"

"Why is that? Those are some fairly substantial identities."

She took a breath. "Max, it's not that I reject or I'm ashamed of those identities."

"I didn't take it that you were. I simply think those boundaries may feel too limiting to you now." He repeated, "Why do you think that is?"

Trish exhaled forcefully. "Oh, I don't know. I think all that just melted away when I saw what was in those jars."

"And you said you don't feel like a reporter anymore."

"No," she answered with resignation, "not like I used to, anyway."

"And you risked all that was left of your savings to pursue this story," he continued.

"Yeah," she admitted, nodding.

"I believe that was truly a leap of faith for you…to risk financial security, perhaps even your career…to move out of that comfort zone—that shell— that so many of us can't seem to leave in order to grow and evolve. And I believe you'll be amazed at what else you'll sacrifice in order to follow this story to a conclusion."

Trish let out half a laugh. "What else do I have left, Max?"

He looked straight into her eyes. "Everything you think you are, Patty."

She sighed. "The old 'Who am I? Why am I here? What's it all about, Alfie' bit, huh?"

He snickered. "Something like that."

She touched her forehead with the tips of her fingers, as she shifted her weight again. "God! Why couldn't I have just settled for tennis or something?"

Max chuckled. "Tennis would have bored you."

Trish sighed. "Jesus, if I get into this thing any deeper, I think it might take a heavy-duty wrecker to pull me out of it."

He chuckled again. "Well, instead of a wrecker, why don't you come by some day soon and load up on some of my mythology books?"

She set her hand on her hip. "Do you really think that's going to be enough to unblock me?"

"It may. It may provide a new perspective that will help you start thinking and feeling about what you've experienced in a different way."

"Well, then, I'll do that. Right now, though, I have to finish some errands before it gets any hotter."

"Just give me a call and make sure I'm home."

Trish tilted her head. "By the way, what were you doing at the doctor's? If I'm not being too personal."

He grinned. "Just a check-up."

She was relieved. "I thought maybe this heat was getting to you."

Max looked skyward. "Well, it has been awfully hot." He looked back at her. "I'm glad I live high enough on the mountain to catch a few breezes."

"Well, we'd better get *out* of this heat before someone finds us melted right here on this sidewalk," she commented, then thanked him again as they walked toward his car.

He held up a hand. "Now, enough of that. I can't think of anything or anyone I'd rather invest in than you." He climbed into the driver's seat and looked back at her. "You know, most people don't have a concept of investing in themselves or in others. They like to see something tangible to point at, even if it's only a bank statement. I find it more stimulating to sit back and watch people grow instead of bank accounts or stocks."

Trish smiled. She felt less guilty about accepting the money. He was like that. Sincere. Nothing he said was a platitude. She leaned down closer to him. "Why are you so convinced I don't want to be a reporter any more?"

"Patty, my Dear, I've listened to you pour out your disenchantment with your profession for years now. It was only a matter of time before you steered your course in another direction."

"That's true," she admitted, as she shifted her purse to the other arm. "But I'm not really clear on what I *do* want to do with my life."

"Don't worry about that for now." He smiled at her. "It'll come in time."

He was always so confident in her. Sometimes that confidence was all that kept her going forward when all she wanted was to quit or go backwards. She backed up as he closed his door and waved good-bye.

She looked up at the sky once more. Damn, it was hot.

• • •

That evening, Trish carried her kudzu vine basket to the garden to pick some fresh vegetables for dinner. They would go great with some fresh buttered cornbread. That and a tall glass of iced tea. Though Trish hadn't asked her to, Kathy had watered the garden while she was in Russia. Trish was grateful she had, or nothing would have been left of her meager harvest.

After she'd picked all the vegetables that were ripened, she started toward the house, then abruptly turned back around to the garden and stood staring at it. To her it was a luxury. She could have bought anything she needed at the grocery. But homegrown just tasted better. What if the grocery shelves were empty most of the time? What if all you had to eat was what you grew yourself? What if the land all around your home was contaminated? The water, the soil, the livestock. She'd never thought about anything like that before. She'd never had to. Now she was thinking about a lot of things.

Could the U.S. government and scientists have known any less than the Russians did about the fallout effects on humans? Did they have maps of downwind patterns from their test sites and bomb factories that they'd kept hidden from their citizens as the Soviet government had?

As she stood there, her mind flashed to a comment she'd read just the previous day in one of Mark's articles. A down-winder from New Mexico said that during the bomb tests the government referred to the land he and his neighbors lived on as "virtually uninhabited." He stated that in just two words the residents had been reduced from human beings, and had begun calling themselves "virtual uninhabitants." Their lives weren't as important as other people's.

Trish looked down at her basket of food. God, she couldn't believe how much she'd taken for granted in her life before she went to Kazakhstan.

Later that evening, when she sat down to her meal, she said grace. She hadn't done that in a long time.

• • •

When Trish woke up the next morning, she stayed in bed a while with her thoughts. It was still difficult for her to entertain the thought that her

162

own government could have been as culpable as the Russian government in contaminating its own citizens, no matter how compelling the comparisons were and no matter how disillusioned she already was. Even in grade school when she and her friends discovered and finally had to accept the facts of life about sexuality, she still couldn't believe that her own parents had engaged in such activity. But even though grade school was far in the past, she felt like she was losing a lot of her innocence again.

After breakfast she called Max. She needed to talk about a possible career change. "I've been doing this reporter thing for so long, I'm not sure I even know how to do anything else," she lamented, as she sat curled up on the sofa in her robe, with her coffee mug in hand.

Max quizzed her about why she'd become a reporter in the first place.

"Oh, I don't know, Max," she began, as she set the mug down on the side table and stretched. "Now that you ask that, I guess I don't know exactly. I've been disillusioned with it for so long that I really have been wondering why I ever got into it. I thought I'd be looking for the truth, but it's all so corrupted now—like a business game or something."

"Then you became a reporter to find the truth."

"Well…" she answered, hanging onto the word, and then, "to find it…and to tell it."

"And you thought that you'd find it and be able tell it within the framework of a money making industry?" There was a tinge of disbelief in his voice.

She looked toward the window briefly and back again. "Look, I've known for years that money runs the media market, but I guess I just thought *some* of the real important stuff would seep through the cracks."

"Patty, it has…or you never would have found your way to Kazakhstan."

She sighed. "I guess so." Then she added, "But, you know, Max, if I'd been working for a paper when I went over there instead of freelancing, I never would have pursued it the way I did." She told him about how all of the "reporter rules" went out the window and how she'd let herself get emotionally involved. "I would have insisted on interviewing people from the pro-nuclear side of the issue. And I just couldn't. I just thought, 'Damn it. Some things are just wrong.' And now I feel like standing on a rooftop yelling, 'Don't you people know what the hell is going on in the world?!'"

He audibly took in and let out a breath. "Well, it sounds to me like you're taking a stand in life…like you're not content to sit on the sidelines anymore and observe. You sound like someone who's getting involved in life." He suggested that her professional adherence to objectivity was being replaced by her humanity and that she might find it difficult, if not impossible, to continue in life without taking a stand for something she believed in.

She shook her head and reached for her coffee. "Well, taking a stand seems foreign to me. Even when I felt my objectivity slipping away, I felt so empty and adrift. But I just couldn't dismiss what I was seeing with, 'Oh, well, isn't that a shame, but war is hell, you know,' or 'Well, gee, you might lose some innocent people along the way, but that's the price you pay for security or progress.' I just can't rationalize like that any more; I saw the price we really paid with my own eyes." She sipped the last of her coffee. "But, Max, it feels so strange to feel like this."

"Of course it does," he responded. "You've been trained and conditioned for years to be objective and follow rules...rules that were never really followed, from what you've told me. So, of course you're going to feel off balance for a while. But, Patty, you can't return to the life you once knew. You're too profoundly changed by what you experienced. You're a different person than you were before your trip. I could see it in your eyes in the restaurant. There's no going back for you. I suspect that any attempt to, will only frustrate and delay the inevitable changes that will be manifesting in your life."

"What changes?" she asked, as she glanced at her now empty mug and set it back on the side table.

"It's not for me to speak your truths, Patty, but I can see you coming into your power."

She dropped her arm to her side. "Well, I don't feel very powerful right now. I feel fragile and vulnerable."

"That's a natural part of the process. Change—even good change—always makes us feel unsteady for a while, until we get used to it." Trish could hear him inhaling from his pipe. "You've been through a life altering experience, and you're going to have to take some time to let it integrate. How that manifests for you, only you can determine. I suspect it will affect—not only your career—but also your relationships and a lot more."

"More?" What did he mean "more?"

"You may find that this experience becomes a frame of reference for everything you do for the rest of your life."

She leaned onto the arm of the sofa and propped her chin in her hand. "God, Max, there's this part of me that wishes I'd never gone to Kazakhstan...that wishes none of it had ever happened...that wishes I could forget it, all of it, so I can go back to who I was."

"Even the part about Ilyani?"

Trish smiled slightly. "No...no...that part was incredible."

He told her that as she researched the story and probed the depths of it, he thought she would find other jewels imbedded in the painful aspects of it. "I believe your depression is an indicator of just how hard and how deeply this thing has affected you."

She sat up erect. "How do you know I've been depressed?"

164

"Patty, you're *wearing* it…like a piece of clothing." He drew in a deep breath. "Each generation has a set of circumstances that challenges it. It's what we do with those challenges that make us who we are." He believed that the Great War the people of his generation fought was their own particular school for learning. "I was an infantryman in the 7th Army Division during that time, and there's one day I'll never forget as long as I live—April 29th of 1945—because my world and my life changed forever that day."

Trish could detect a distinct shift in her friend's voice. She suspected he was about to touch on a sensitive subject that he'd hardly mentioned in all of their years of conversations, and she sat still as he talked.

"I feel that it was similar to the day your world changed in Kazakhstan." He paused a moment, as though gathering his thoughts, then continued. "Even though I was still a young man, I'd seen a lot by then. I'd been in several battles…and it's odd the things that bother you most. For me, it wasn't the limbs blown off or the smell of death…as traumatic as that was. It was the little things—like going through a dead German's things. I think I've mentioned this to you before. You see the smiling faces of his wife, his kids, the people he loved most staring back at you from silent pictures, and suddenly you know how many people are going to be hurt by his death.

"You didn't realize you were putting a bullet through their hearts, too. You didn't go to war to destroy women and children, but that's what you were doing. Those were the things that brought me to tears. I didn't want to cry, but I wept like a baby over things like that whenever I was alone. War does that to you…strips away a lot of the defenses that you've spent a lifetime constructing." There was another shift in his tone. "But nothing prepared me for Dachau. I don't think anyone could have been prepared for Dachau."

He told her how bodies were stacked in deserted open boxcars on the tracks when they marched into the camp that day in April, covered by a late spring snow; how the snow made it difficult to really see everything; and how once they got inside the compound, there was nothing to hide the reality.

His voice cracked a little, and he hesitated. She heard him swallow deeply. "You've seen the pictures in documentaries. You know what it looked like. Well, believe me, it was a thousand times worse actually being there. You couldn't turn it off. You didn't have that buffer of time and space to insulate you from your emotions…but, still, what bothered me most wasn't the bodies stacked in piles or the skeletal figures walking around still alive, or even the smell, though I'll never forget it. It was the look on the faces of my buddies. I'd fought with those guys for months—some of them barely old enough to shave." He said they were the bravest men he'd ever known, and all of a sudden they looked so vulnerable, so pained and confused in spite of everything else they'd seen before. "It must have been the same look they saw on *my* face, as well."

He let out a sigh. "And that look was the same one I saw on your face the other day in the restaurant, Patty. It jolted me. I hadn't seen it in decades, but I recognized it instantly." He knew what she was going through and would continue going through. He still couldn't watch the newsreels and films about the death camps on TV. The memories came back as fresh as if they'd just happened. "For weeks after we arrived at the camp, we all walked around in a fog—a kind of surreal world…"

"That's what Clinic Number Four was like, Max," Trish interjected, "like some sort of surreal world."

"It sounds as though it was." He offered that she might be experiencing a bit more than the adrenaline letdown and jet lag that her doctor had diagnosed, perhaps a form of post-traumatic stress—just as he was sure he had experienced at Dachau—though there was no one to explain it at the time. "And—just like you—there was no one to tell any of us how to act or react, or what to do about it. Everyone else was as bewildered as we were. We'd seen up close what human beings were capable of doing to other human beings." He paused, breathing deeply a few times. "The experience depressed and demoralized me for years. I couldn't talk about it to anyone—not even Rachel. I didn't want to even think about it. I just wanted to block it out."

As Trish fingered her empty mug, Max told her how, many years later, he read a book about a man who'd found the meaning of his life in a concentration camp during the war. "It's amazing what that did for me." It began opening up the shell that he'd built around himself to protect him from the memories, and slowly—very slowly—he began to realize just how much the experience at Dachau had shaped him…how much a part of him it was. He hadn't blocked it out at all. He'd incorporated it into his very being, unconsciously. It had become his measuring stick for everything he did and said…every important choice he'd made in his life after the war, and—ultimately—he realized how much it had actually strengthened him and given him courage.

"How could any challenge or experience be worse than the one I'd seen and experienced there? I think that's when my search for knowledge in life took a dramatic turn."

Trish resisted her natural temptation to ask questions for fear of interrupting his train of thought.

Over the years Max wondered if it was possible for a small indiscretion or little white lie or lack of courage on his part in the face of a challenge, to in some way lead his community to a final end like the one he'd seen in Dachau, Germany. Could something he left unsaid at a critical juncture lead ultimately to a greater consequence than he could imagine? Whenever he was in turmoil in his personal or professional life, it always came back to him—even if it was unconsciously, but that it was as much a part of him as a leg or an arm…even though he'd taken it for granted for years.

"Patty, it shaped my life forever after. That's why I must encourage you not to retreat from the bad experiences in life. In an odd way, they can be the best in your life. Embrace them. Learn from them. Become a stronger person—a better person. Learn to be more in touch with your own humanity."

Trish rubbed her forehead and told Max that she was unsure of how to make that kind of transition.

He reminded her of the quote about people being spiritual beings having a human experience, rather than human beings having a spiritual experience. "When I first heard that, it shifted my perceptions of the world so dramatically that I could never feel the same about life again. I had experienced enough by then that I knew on some deep level it was true."

"Max, do you ever get over it?" she asked, resting her head in her hand.

"Oh, I hope not," he responded. "It gets easier to cope with it after a time, but if the pain ever completely left, I'm afraid I'd lose the part of it that I need so much." She could hear him inhaling on his pipe again. "You know, I'm convinced that at times we need our pain. We need to feel it, along with the joys, to remind us of those valuable lessons that have collectively made us who we are. If we didn't have the contrasts, how would we experience any of our emotions fully? It's just like your going to Clinic Number Four. Even though you'd seen it before on the television, and it intrigued and motivated and stimulated you intellectually, it wasn't until you went there and saw it with your own eyes and experienced it first hand that you got the full emotional impact of it.

"To truly learn anything, I'm convinced that we have to learn it on both an intellectual and emotional level…because the emotional part keeps it alive for us."

"Max, that's the most you've ever told me about Dachau," she commented, looking wistfully at the far wall.

"Well, I've always appreciated that a naturally inquisitive person like you never asked about it. But, Patty," he continued, "that's what I mean about facing the challenges of your generation. Ours was World War II." He suggested that it might be the job of her generation to process and learn from and come to terms with the Cold War. "Only instead of Midway and Pearl Harbor and Dachau, your battlefields were Alamogordo and Semipalatinsk…"

"…and Dawson Forest and Fernald and Savannah River," she finished. She speculated that because the battles were carried out in secret—because it wasn't on all the newsreels at night—they had been denied any opportunity to consciously and collectively work it out.

"Maybe that's your role now," Max suggested, "to add your voice to those trying to inform and warn the public what that war was all about and how many casualties there really were."

But, as high as the casualty count from the war was, Trish didn't believe it was over. It might just be beginning.

• • •

After hanging up the phone, Trish began reviewing the events of the previous days. As she did, she felt an inexplicable, yet familiar urge to clean her house. It was the same urge she'd often felt at times of change or crisis in her past...as predictable as rain that she could smell coming, even before it began to fall. The feeling was more welcomed than the immobilizing aspects of her depression. As she worked—scrubbing and dusting through layers of grime—the exercise also felt as if it was removing built up layers of thoughts and thought processes that had seeped into her consciousness from sources that didn't feel clean somehow.

The conversations with Max had stimulated previously unexplored reservoirs of questions, insights, and curiosity. And, as she tackled her kitchen, she thought about the monsters in Clinic Number Four, and how they'd seemed horrible and yet awesome. They had challenged her very concept of humanity—smashed all of her perceptions to bits and left her with no framework with which to understand what her eyes had seen. As she set the shiny, newly cleaned racks back into her oven, she realized that Max was helping her to create a new framework—one with which she could better understand the world. Maybe she was just experiencing growing pains, simply stretching and growing into another level of development. At least that thought felt more comforting and hopeful than the possibility of a prolonged clinical depression.

As she lifted the stopper in the kitchen sink and watched the dirty, soapy water being sucked noisily down the drain, she thought about the drowning man in his story about Psyche. As she briefly lifted her head and looked squinting out the sunny kitchen window, she wondered who that might be. It didn't take her long to focus on Mirek Klavanis. He certainly had all the characteristics of a drowning man. Both his pain and his presence had felt physically and emotionally draining. Since he couldn't seem to extricate himself from his demons, it was as though they were slowly and surely pulling him under. Trish was quite certain that anyone aligning with Dr. Klavanis would eventually drown with him.

Moving from the kitchen to one of the bedrooms—with furniture polish, window cleaner, and duster in hand—she paused at the doorway of the room and recalled what Max had said about her generation's unique perspective of the world. In that moment it occurred to her that theirs was the first to live their entire lives under the threat of the atomic bomb, and for the first time she began to fully appreciate just how burdensome it must have been for the children of her generation. *Hmm…baby boomers. They actually called us baby boomers.* The symbolism had eluded her before.

She went immediately to an old chest of drawers and pulled out what was designated her junk drawer. Everyone had one—filled with things they didn't know what to do with, but couldn't quite let go of. All of them were crammed to the brim, unorganized and the least bit dangerous; there was always something there that could stick or bite.

As she pulled out the drawer's contents, she made two piles—one for things to throw away and one for things that belonged more appropriately somewhere else in her house. In the back of the drawer she came across an old I.D. bracelet that she had kept since grade school. As she picked it up and fingered it, she thought how odd it was that she had come across that item of all items…and on that day. "No such thing as a coincidence," she almost heard Max saying in her head.

As she sat on the edge of the bed, she began recalling experiences from her time in grade school related to the new atomic age…how she and her classmates had gone through the instructions about ducking under their desks in case the sirens went off, signaling an impending atomic blast.

"Now, children, you *will* remember to look away from the windows and cover your eyes from the flash," Mrs. Newton had instructed as though it was just another lesson. *What a thing to teach children in school.* She stared at nothing in particular on the wall of the room. *And how completely useless it was.*

The day the I.D. bracelets were distributed to the students at school they eagerly waited for their name to be called in the lunch room. "Now, remember," the principal had said, "You must wear these at all times." Each bracelet bore the student's name along with other identifications. The girls in particular were quite taken with what they viewed as personalized charm bracelets. The glamour lasted until the day Tommy Ferguson pointed out their obvious purpose. "They just gave 'em to us so they could identify our bodies." Then the new charm bracelets lost all of their charm for her. She kept "forgetting" to wear hers in spite of Mrs. Newton's admonitions. Then one day months later she simply lost it completely.

As she rubbed the face of the old bracelet back and forth with her thumb, Trish recalled the rash of backyard bomb shelters people built during that period. During summers, as a child, she would spend one or two weeks visiting her cousins, Sharon Jo and James, in Nashville. One summer, when her cousins were in junior high, her aunt and uncle drove her past the house of a wealthy man who lived across the street from her cousins' school. They told her the man had the distinction of having the most expensive private bomb shelter ever built in the country. The final cost of over a million dollars was a significant amount of money for that period during the early sixties.

Trish's Aunt Rose gave her a clipping from the local newspaper so she could read all about the bomb shelter. For its time it was incredibly huge and complex, divided into male and female dormitories, complete with corresponding pink and blue sheets for the bunks. Enormous water and food supplies had been stocked, and it contained elaborate air systems, along with ham radio equipment that could communicate anywhere in the world. The man even built his three children elaborate houses on his estate near the shelter so they and their families would be close by in case of a nuclear attack.

Sharon Jo went to school with one of the man's granddaughters. On several occasions she had slept in the bomb shelter during slumber parties her friend hosted. "It felt creepy walking through those decontamination chambers," Sharon Jo had grimaced. Her older brother, James, was a friend of one of the man's grandsons. He talked about the two of them sneaking into the shelter to hide out and smoke cigarettes. "And look a *girly* magazines," Sharon Jo always added in a whisper behind her hand.

A favorite pastime for the children at the local school was speculating about who might make it to the bomb shelter in time...and who might be permanently locked out when the doors were finally sealed off like a vault from the outside world. James had always bragged that they would let him in because he was friends with the rich man's grandson.

The bomb shelters—like the I.D. bracelets—were intriguing and even provided little islands of hope...until, that is, Sharon Jo began posing some significant questions over dinner one night as the subject turned to the Cuban missile crisis. When James repeated his boast about getting into the shelter if he needed to, Sharon Jo flipped her napkin in the air, then placed it deliberately in her lap, and smiled smugly. "So what if you *did* make it to the shelter before the doors closed? What difference would *that* make if everything around it stays radioactive for thousands of years? How long could the food and water and air supplies last? I've spent a few nights in that thing...enough to know I don't ever want to spend the rest of my *life* there."

In just as long as it took for her to pose the questions, Trish realized that the best of bomb shelters would eventually become a giant tomb from which there was no possible safe escape. No amount of money could protect anyone from the effects of radiation for very long. It could only delay the inevitable.

In time the rich man's bomb shelter fell into disrepair—a monument to both the fears and false hopes of the atomic age. But to Trish, like the I.D. bracelets, it lost all of its charm at her aunt's dinner table that night.

Trish shut her eyes and put her hand to her head at the recollection of those childhood memories and the realization of what psychological impacts that kind of political and social atmosphere must have had on an entire generation of children. Was that why she and so many of her contemporaries had become cynical as adults? There'd been no real security about a future world for them. In the early formative stages of life they'd all grown up expecting to be hit by an atomic blast at any time. And, even though they hadn't been capable of fully understanding the shift, they must have known on some level that for the first time in the history of mankind, extinction of the human race was possible, as well.

Why hadn't she seen that before?

Looking at the I.D. bracelet again, she thought how small it looked. When she tried slip it around her wrist, there was a gap between the clasps. She glanced at the throw away pile and paused a moment. As a child, she'd crammed it in that drawer because she didn't have the ability then to do anything with that fear. She'd compartmentalized it in the back of her mind. But it was still part of who she was. It still had her name on it. And there were aspects of the child who'd first worn that bracelet that also carried curiosity, imagination, dreams and wonder at the world around her. She needed those aspects of the long forgotten part of herself in order to start facing her fears.

She went to put the bracelet in her purse. As she did, she recalled a time several years into her career when one particular incident involving ethics was distressing enough to make her consider leaving journalism altogether. But she felt as though she'd simply be running away to a new career just as she'd first run from one newspaper to another. When she talked to Max about it, instead of offering an opinion, he asked, "What are you afraid of?"

She paused only a moment before answering, "Losing my security."

"Patty, sometimes security can be a trap." That had been an eye opening moment for her. Then Max added, "Always identify your fear, Patty, then walk straight into it; it's a point of true power. That's why we fear it. We almost always fear true power. We confuse force with power, but on some level, we know that the greatest power on earth is not in any weapon, but, rather, deep within our own being."

Was the bomb and radiation her generation's deepest fear? Could it also in some way be the source of her generation's greatest power? Was going to Kazakhstan, and looking into the contents of the jars in Clinic Number Four, her own personal descent into the abyss? Or was it her entire generation's? What power was greater than a nuclear arsenal that could wipe out mankind several times over?

• • •

The next day, Trish wrote to Katrina and Yuri, and told them that she'd decided to pursue the story further, because she realized that it was much bigger than the newspaper report she had originally planned.

And she wrote Dr. Klavanis. After she told him how she planned to continue the research and promised to keep in touch, she encouraged him to begin looking for answers to the puzzle himself. She suggested that he might very well have resources and ideas that were better than hers or that might compliment hers.

Chapter Fourteen

When Trish arrived at Max's cabin a few days later to collect some books on mythology, he already had several of them stacked in a cardboard box in the living room. "Have you had a chance to think about the angle you're going to use for this story?" he asked, as he placed two more books in the box.

"Yeah, a lot, as a matter of fact, but I haven't gotten far enough along to really decide yet. I know the angle about mythology is critical to it, but I still don't have much of a handle on that. I guess I'm just relying on things to start gelling once I figure out exactly what area of Australia I'll be going." She picked up one of the books, glanced at its cover, then back at Max. "Why? Have *you* come up with something?" She'd had enough experience with her friend to know there was probably more to his question than idle curiosity.

"Well, I know some of the things you've told me about are pretty frightening. But if the purpose is to simply scare the hell out of people, I doubt they'll be interested in reading about it, much less be motivated by it."

She put the book back in the box and set her hand on her hip. "Max, I agree with you completely on one level. But, at this point, I think people *need* to have the hell scared out of them."

"Oh, for sure, they need to learn some of the facts you've uncovered," he began as he sat down in his chair and motioned toward the other chair beside him. She sat down, as he continued, "But my point is that...well...fear certainly can serve a purpose...sometimes a very valuable purpose. But I believe too much of it can sometimes immobilize and even paralyze people. If your objective is to motivate and inspire people with your story, then I think you're going to have to take a very different approach than simply the straight out facts. You may need to look for new perspectives and solutions. And I think you might consider committing to some sort of book at some point, as well."

"You mean a non-fiction book," she posed matter-of-factly, as she crossed her legs.

"Possibly...but, not necessarily."

"You mean *fiction*?"

"You may want to consider it."

He lifted his pipe from its holder and lit a match, as Trish wagged her head. "Now, wait a minute, Max. I'm not that kind of writer—never have been. I'm not a novelist. I'm trained as a reporter. I deal in *facts*."

After he blew out the match and tossed it into the ashtray, he leaned forward and remarked, "Well, my dear, in light of what you've just experienced and seen in Kazakhstan, you might just want to rethink your ideas about what constitute 'facts.' Do you think anybody would believe it, anyway, if you reported what you saw?"

"Hey, I've got pictures! I was *there*. There are witnesses. Even the Russians can't cover this thing up at this point." She realized her voice had become defensive.

"Maybe not, but think about it a moment," he began, as he leaned back. "You saw mermaids and Cyclopes and two-headed gods. Others could look at the same thing and just see mutants. They might say, 'Well, that's a nice coincidence, but it's just that—a coincidence.'"

"Look, Max, you take a creature with an upper body like a human and a lower body like a fish, and that's a mermaid, no matter *how* you want to cut it." She glanced at the floor a moment as she recalled Katrina saying the same thing. She looked back up at Max. "Is that what you believe…that it's just a coincidence?" She felt almost as though she'd had the wind knocked out of her.

"It doesn't matter what I believe, Patty. It only matters what you believe," he answered, pointing to her with the stem of his pipe. Then he leaned forward again and added, "And I believe in you, Girl."

She took a deep breath, looked across the room and wagged her head from side to side. "Oh, I don't know. Maybe this whole thing is just a wild goose chase. Maybe it *is* just an interesting coincidence. Maybe I'm blowing it all out of proportion."

"Patty, what does your gut tell you?"

She slid back in her chair, taking a moment to consider her answer. When she finally spoke, it was with confidence. "Max, my gut tells me I'm *on* to something, and that it's really big. Maybe even bigger than *I* think it is right now."

He smiled, and she noticed.

"You think so, too, don't you?" she quizzed.

"Indeed, I do. Indeed, I do."

"Then why all the questions?"

"Just wanted to introduce you to a little healthy skepticism from time to time. Do you think I would have invested $50,000 in your little puzzle if I didn't believe in it?"

Trish half laughed, then shook her head again. "You old fox! You had me going for a minute."

"Well anything to stimulate the glands…and the mind…and the heart muscles," he said chuckling. Then in a more serious tone, he added, "You may have to deal with a *lot* of skepticism when this thing is done, but just remember that you only have to deal with your own while you're pursuing this story."

"I am trying to stay skeptical. That much I've learned from being a reporter, but this isn't anything I expected to come across as a reporter." Her training hadn't prepared her for what she was experiencing. She added, however, that it would be difficult to focus on something other than a 'fear factor' since there was an ample amount to fear. She looked at him directly. "Don't you think so?"

"Why, certainly…but fear is what led to the Cold War to begin with, and fear isn't going to be what resolves the legacy of it." He reminded Trish that the men who invented the bomb were intelligent, well intended people attempting to end a horrible war. He was certain they couldn't have envisioned a massive build up of atomic weapons that would leave the fate of the world itself resting on a hair trigger for decades into the future.

"Max," Trish asked, tilting her head, "do you think Oppenheimer and his colleagues realized the enormity of what they'd done?"

"Oh, my, yes, indeed…eventually," he answered, repositioning himself in his seat. He reminded her that some of the most effective anti-nuclear activists in the world were some of the very ones who'd worked on the original atomic bomb program. He talked about Oppenheimer's quote upon seeing the first mushroom cloud from his own creation. "It was biblical, Patty— straight out of the Hindu Bhagavad Gita: 'I have become Death, the destroyer of worlds.'

He told her how in time Oppenheimer became embittered and disillusioned, feeling that the government had duped him. "He tried to undo politically what he'd done scientifically…attempted to stuff the genie back into the bottle, so to speak. But he knew it was too late." Max speculated that the scientist must have envisioned himself as becoming a scientific hero, who would save the world. "And in the end his very patriotism was under fire. He was labeled a 'commie' by the self same government that he felt had used and then corrupted his genius."

Trish shifted sideways. "But, Max, aren't all people innately curious? Isn't it human nature to want to figure out what makes things tick and how far we can go?"

"Yes, but there's a responsibility that comes with our curiosity," he responded, again pointing with the stem of his pipe. "We don't allow every human urge to run unchecked. We even put limits on wars now, because we've seen just how inhumane *they* can be.

"So, when we start tampering with basic life systems—like DNA and the atom, that we may not be able to control—we need to start asking some serious questions before unleashing their powers on our fellow man."

She sat back and grinned. "Yeah, one of my sources—Mark Matheson— said almost the very same thing before I went to Russia."

Max told Trish that it appeared as though scientists somehow felt they were more moral and high-minded than the rest of society. He raised his eyebrows. "And, mind you, it's my own colleagues I'm speaking about here. But I've seen it time and again. They suckle at the 'golden teat,' as I call it, for every contract or study for which they can qualify…whether the money comes from government or industry…and they seldom ask themselves moral questions. And even when they do, they're surprisingly adept at rationalizing. They'll manipulate their numbers and conclusions to suit the sources of their funding, simply to keep that grant money coming in."

He supposed that scientists did symbolize the curious component of the collective society, as well as the cerebral, thinking part of it, but offered that, in spite of that, they could be totally lacking in spirituality, and particularly in common sense. He tilted his head toward her. "The absent-minded professor is no myth."

She half laughed and added, "I'm beginning to think the *mad* scientist is no myth, either."

He smiled sideways, then told her he believed the spiritual component to the human equation had also been greatly neglected in society as a whole. "And I don't mean religious. I mean spiritual. That's why I believe that myth and art have never been more needed by our culture than they are today."

She looked at him wryly. "Well, that need may be being filled now, because it looks like some myths are coming back to life in Semipalatinsk. But I don't have any idea what they have to do with the atomic age."

At the conclusion of their conversation, they walked to Trish's car where Max set the cardboard box onto the front seat. Before Trish left she told him to come by and stock up on some vegetables from her garden, since she had an overabundance of them and didn't want them to go to waste.

As she drove back down the mountain, it was with a fresh eagerness. Maybe the answers she was looking for lay hidden somewhere in that box.

• • •

Trish went downtown to have lunch with her sisters and let them know a little about what was going on in her life and catch up on what was going on in theirs.

After that, she went home and pulled Max's books out of the box and stacked them. She wondered if the material inside them was as heavy as they were.

• • •

176

That evening Max came by. Trish met him at the door with her kudzu basket, and they walked down to the garden. While he picked some tomatoes, squash, peppers and cucumbers, she weeded between the rows. After they finished, they walked over and sat down under the maple tree, commenting on the vegetables and the drought.

Then Trish began telling him that, not only did she have no idea how to pursue the story, she felt totally inadequate to tell it.

"Tell me something, Patty," he said, turning toward her, "have you ever gone shelling at the shore in the early morning?"

She shrugged. "Oh, sure. It's one of my favorite beach activities. Why?"

"Well, if you notice people shelling, you'll see that each one is looking for his own unique find." He said that some looked for the unblemished, perfect shells, some for the unusual or rare finds, some for the most colorful. Some looked for the biggest. He cleared his throat. "Many aren't looking for shells; they don't even notice them because they're busy jogging…or they may be sunbathing." He said that some remained in their houses simply listening to the soothing sound of the surf, unaware that they were listening to the heartbeat of the universe. "Some people are sound asleep, completely oblivious to the wonder surrounding them."

"I think that's *most* people, Max."

He smiled. "Yes, Patty, I'm afraid that's true. And then there are those of us who sit in our dens and read books about shells…all kinds of shells. We see more of them. We learn more about them. But we experience less."

Trish tilted her head and smiled at Max. "You know, you're quite the philosopher."

He chuckled. "Yes, that's me all right: the armchair philosopher, the armchair environmentalist. You have me pegged perfectly. But, tell me," he prompted, "what are you looking for when *you* go shelling? The unusual, the odd, what? What are you looking for in life?"

Trish shook her head, grinning, as she picked a clover from the grass. "Max, it fascinates me how you move back and forth so easily between the literal and symbolic world."

"Well, *you* may find it fascinating, but I'm afraid most people find it irritating…and even infuriating. The only other person who seemed to enjoy it was Rachel." As he looked back at the garden, he told Trish how Rachel always managed to love him in spite of, and because of, every quirky thing that he was. He let out a deep breath. "I loved her so. I've never really understood why I wasn't allowed to spend the rest of my life with her. It's a point that I don't seem to be able to get past." He cleared his throat. "But I don't mean to digress," he continued, turning back toward her. "Really, what shells do you seek?"

Trish rubbed her temple. "I guess the unusual, the rare find." She also wondered about the shell's origins. Was it dislodged by an undersea storm and carried for miles? Did its live cargo struggle to stay in its watery environment or know it was doomed when that last wave tossed it too far up on the beach to ever return home again? Did it have a story to tell? "Sometimes I don't even know why I pick up certain shells, and then years later I might find that they're just perfect for angel wings on a Christmas ornament or something. And, too, I like to share my shells with friends."

"Those are interesting comments, Patty, very interesting, indeed." He sighed. "You know, the shore is a powerful place. It's where two worlds meet: the land and the sea. And it attracts people like a magnet. Symbolically, it's also said to be the meeting place of the conscious and the unconscious. I like to think of shells on the beach as gifts from our unconscious mind, and I believe the things we do with those gifts are critically important in our life's development."

The tone in his voice shifted almost imperceptibly. "There's just one thing I need to warn you about, though. Do you remember the myth about Cassandra?"

"Wasn't she the one who had the ability to see the future?"

"That's right." He told her that Zeus gave her that gift, but that when she reneged on becoming his lover, he was furious and wanted to punish her. "He couldn't take back her power to predict the future, so instead he cursed her by making sure that no one would believe her predictions."

"I remember that, now that you say it." She leaned forward, her arms resting on her knees, then looked at him. "Are you saying that no one might believe this story if I ever put it all together?"

"Worse. They may believe it entirely and not even care."

"But how could that be possible?" she asked, wrinkling her brow.

"Oh, Patty, never underestimate the human capacity for apathy. We've been so desensitized over the years that little or nothing moves us any more."

Trish looked back forward. She'd said almost the exact same thing to Katrina in Kazakhstan. Somehow, she didn't like hearing it said back to her.

She turned back to Max and abruptly said, "Max, go with me to Australia."

He threw his head back and laughed. "Oh, no, no. Don't think that I'm not tempted, and if I were a couple of decades younger, I'd be greatly tempted. But I've got enough white hair on my head and enough sense in it to know that this is your journey. And you have to make it alone. No, no, I'll be satisfied to sit back and read about it someday in that book you're dying to write."

She continued to pick clover, then asked, "What would be the point if no one was interested in it?"

"Patty, you must be clear on one point," he responded seriously, "and that's on why you're doing this in the first place. If you're doing it for anyone else but yourself, it's the wrong motivation. You won't find the answers you're looking for if you're looking for any other reason than pure personal truth and knowledge. Then, if you decide to share what you've learned with others, that's another matter. In fact, it'll be incredible, but this journey is no one's but yours."

He picked up a tomato and sniffed it, then said, "I envy your curiosity and your determination and energy. As an old man, I find it quite refreshing." He uttered a, "hmm," and then, "There's one more thing." He took a breath. "About my books—I don't know quite how to say this—don't take them too seriously. You'll see that there are many versions of the same myths, so simply try to get a feel for the essence of them."

He set the tomato back in the basket. "Also, I've felt for some time that you've gone past many of the old fogy notions of the past." It was something of a paradox to him in his years of teaching that the purpose of it all was to encourage young people to think and learn for themselves, and yet, they were forcing students to think within preconstructed belief systems. And they were using materials and texts and perspectives that might not be relevant to their world any longer.

Trish brushed her cheek with the handful of clover. "Max, why on earth hasn't someone already noticed the similarity of the radiated babies to myth?"

He leaned back onto the tree. "Well, a handful of people may very well have noticed it, and just dismissed it...but, basically, I think it's because we've become too compartmentalized in our thinking." He thought because of the current emphasis on specialization, few, if any, were capable of or inclined to make the connections from one field of thought to another. It was difficult for them to move from myth to psychology, or archeology to religion or science. The few who were flexible enough bridge the different areas of human perceptions were thought of as scattered, even though they might well be the greatest visionaries of current times.

"Well, I certainly don't feel like a visionary. Right now I just feel...raw...and vulnerable."

He tilted his head. "Of course you do. You've just had a few layers of perceptions about the world stripped away. You're shedding your skin of the past. How would you expect that to feel? Just don't let this thing devour you. It's an incredible opportunity to really *live*."

He took two long breaths. Trish glanced over at him. She started to fill the quiet void with another question, but something about the pause instinctively told her to wait. She sensed he was about to step out on precipitous ground to make a point that might help her as he had earlier that day.

"Patty, let's walk back to the house."

179

• • •

After he lit his pipe and Trish picked up the basket, they walked slowly back to the house. Max finally said, "I'm going to admit something that I never have to anyone before...except a handful of my old Army comrades.

"This is probably something a 'civilian,' as they say, couldn't begin to understand or relate to, but I think you need to hear this."

"Hmm..." He paused briefly, then started walking again. "Well...I have to tell you first of all that war truly *is* hell. I've never experienced as much fear, pain, trauma and grief in my entire life before...not even close. And I never have since, either...with the exception of the pain I've felt over losing Rachel.

"And, believe it or not—even with all of the negative emotions I en- dured—there actually were moments of pure joy." As he puffed on his pipe, he told her about giving candy bars to the dirty, shell-shocked kids they saw in the towns along the way—how their eyes would light up, instantly trans- forming them from dazed, lifeless looking waifs to happy, grinning, beauti- ful kids again. "I'd even beg and bribe candy bars from my buddies just to be able to give them out and see the looks on those kids' faces." Max's voice became animated as he recalled those events.

He talked about the time they marched through Italy, when Mt. Etna was erupting. It was the most awesome sight he'd ever seen. He went up to the edge of one of the flows at one point and collected a piece of lava that was still hot in his tin cup and pressed a penny down into it with his knife. When it cooled, the rock and the penny were melded together. He still had the lava rock and penny as a reminder of what a beautiful day that was.

"But those kinds of moments were few and far between. Mostly it was just the hell, with long stretches of drudgery in between...all the slogging through muddy roads up to our ankles, or sleeping on the ground, huddling against the cold and wind." He said that even during the drudgery, they were always tense, stressed, and afraid, dreading the unknown and expecting di- saster to hit them at any minute.

Max was silent a moment as they walked. Trish looked over at him.

He continued, "When the war was over, I never was happier in my whole life to be back home, back in Rachel's arms...and safe. When we'd said our good-byes, I'd thought...we'd both thought I'd be back in a matter of months. I never dreamed it would be years." He stared ahead, then said, "Sometime later, after I guess a lot of my emotional wounds had healed, I started reliving some of the experiences I'd had—in my mind—at the safety and distance of time, and I...well...I guess I started *missing* it." He looked toward her and quickly added, "I know how odd that must sound...maybe even crazy. But you know how, after Vietnam, some of the men who came back couldn't adjust to the 'real' world again?"

"Yeah."

"Some of them went off into the backwoods." He motioned with his pipe. "Lived out in tents with guns, trying to recapture their war years."

"Yeah, I remember those stories."

Max told her that he could relate to that on some level. "It's not like I wanted to go through the battles or Dachau or all the inconveniences again, but it was more that…well…that I missed the *emotions* I'd felt in the war…or at least, the intensity of them. Even though I was on this roller coaster with no control, the *intensity* of the emotions I felt and the risks I was forced to take—being constantly on the edge like I was—I tell you, I never felt more alive in my whole life. And I missed *that* feeling…or at least, the depth of it. It was so real, so genuine…almost like a sacredness of feeling.

"If I could ever recapture the depth of *that* feeling again, without the war, I'd do it," he stated with conviction. "I wouldn't even think about it. It was almost addictive. I felt so alive, and real."

Max took a puff from his pipe. Sensing that the pause marked the end of the narrative, Trish said, "Well, that *is* quite an admission. I'm not sure if I understand it."

"Patty," he broke in, as he looked at her, "the reason I told you this is because I feel as though, on some level, you're going through your own hell right now. I know how dreadful it must feel to you at this point, but at the same time you may never be this alive again in your whole life. You may even miss it when it's gone—when you've finally worked your way through it."

She half laughed. "Well…you're right about one thing. It does seem dreadful right now." She put her hand to her head. "But right now I can't imagine missing some of the feelings I'm having."

"Perhaps not…"

"Max, have you ever gotten any of that 'depth of feeling' again since the war?"

"Oh, yes, when I first got home—back to Rachel, of course. For a few months I felt like I'd died and gone to heaven. And there was one time when Rachel found a lump in her breast. When the biopsy came back negative, I had such a sense of relief that I can't begin to tell you." He crossed his hands behind his lower back. "Some of my army buddies, that I shared this with, said they'd had those intense feelings when their kids were born or at their children's weddings. Of course," he added quickly, "we never had children, so I can't relate to that."

His last sentence hung in the air a moment. Then Trish said, "Well, thanks for sharing that." It would never have occurred to her that she might miss something as heavy and debilitating as the depths of depression or shock.

He smiled. "I only mentioned it because I thought it might help with your depression." He uncrossed his hands and pointed with his pipe. "Just remember, Patty, be sure to watch out for the traps along the way while you're pursuing this thing. Learn to recognize them and don't let anyone talk you out of that last coin." Max waved his free hand. "Well, enough of my sermonizing."

"Max, you know how I love to listen to you." She told him she didn't know how to begin to properly thank him for all of his generosity.

"Now, enough of that. There's one thing I ask in return. I want you to learn to be kind to yourself—to rest and take care of yourself while you're preparing for this trip—or whatever you plan to do. Take a vacation away from the research and go out and simply have a good time. In fact, have *loads* of fun. I want to see that sparkle back in your eyes, and that color back in your cheeks. Will you promise me that?"

"I promise."

As they reached the house, Max said, "I have to tell you, I'm thankful now that you weren't in any of my classes at UGA. I probably would have corrupted you beyond repair."

"Max, you're the best teacher I've ever had in my life."

"Well, you're kind to say that, and I'll try to accept the compliment gracefully."

He pointed with his pipe. "When we talk about symbolism, I have to tell you that you symbolize hope for me, Patty. Hope for the future. It gets depressing watching and reading what's going on in the world today. We need a new ethic. I think we're about to rid ourselves of many of the old identity patterns and belief systems that might have worked for us in the past, but just don't anymore. I can't help but think that society is on the brink of some dramatic changes. And I believe they'll be good ones."

"I hope you're right."

As Trish watched Max drive away, she thought about their relationship. It had always been close, but she realized that in the last few days he'd opened up to her in a way he never had before.

Chapter Fifteen

For the next few days Trish pored over Max's books. First she focused on individual stories about Cyclopes and mermaids. While interesting, there was nothing in the texts that conveyed a possible explanation for the similarities between the mutants from the clinic and those from mythology. There were only the pictures. Maybe she was focusing too closely on the specifics or on the wrong things entirely. Or maybe she was taking things too literally, or too symbolically.

She was becoming discouraged when she picked up a book that addressed the origins of the world. The text stated that in the beginning there was nothing but chaos. Then when Uranus—who was Heaven personified—wedded Gaia, the Earth, they had children, some of whom were monsters, which Uranus buried in the earth. The monsters were Cyclopes and many-handed monsters and titans. That got Trish's attention—not only the part about the Cyclopes, but also the many-handed monsters. It instantly reminded her of a news item she'd read just a few months before about some school children in Minnesota who'd gone on a field trip in some wetlands. There they'd run across a cluster of hundreds of frogs that were grossly deformed with multiple limbs.

The article stated that the finding was a sign of some form of pollution that had entered the wetland environment. Soon after word leaked out about the Minnesota find, reports about multi-legged and deformed frogs started surfacing in other parts of the country and the world, as well. And while some of the frogs had multiple legs, others had entirely missing limbs.

Later in the day Trish read a myth about a Hindu goddess of destruction called Kali. She was depicted as wearing a belt made from dismembered arms. That instantly reminded her of the Muscovite children in the magazine she'd seen at Peggy's house. Then she found references to multiple-headed gods. One was a Hindu god who split mountains apart with his arrows and shattered them. "Hmm," she mumbled audibly, as she looked up from the book. Uranium mining during the atomic age certainly had split and destroyed mountains around the world and produced multiple-headed children and animals.

As she pondered the frog mutations, as well as those in the children, and in mythical creatures, she continued asking herself what could possibly be the connection between present day mutations and mythology.

But, each time she thought she was about to get close to an explanation, the mystery simply got deeper, the answers slipping further away.

• • •

One morning, after days of intense research, Trish felt so overloaded and frustrated with mythology that she had no choice but to put it aside. She hadn't contacted Peggy Craft since her return, so she called her to see about setting up another meeting. Peggy sounded anxious to hear about Trish's trip, and Trish was equally eager to see if Peggy could provide her with another puzzle piece.

They met for dinner that evening in downtown Gainesville at Mama Ruth's Café, which served the best country-cooked food in town. There, after ordering their meal, Trish began filling Peggy in on the details of her experiences, while Peggy pumped her with questions. When Trish finally finished her account—and her meal—she pushed back her plate, and told Peggy about her studies in mythology, particularly the myth about Uranus, Gaia and their children. She found that, like herself, this was a subject with which Peggy was only marginally familiar, and Trish began thinking she wasn't going to be much help in that area.

"Peggy, do you think there *could* be any connection between the mutants in Semipalatinsk and the ones in the Greek myths?" she asked, as she absent-mindedly twisted her watch back and forth.

"Why, of course," Peggy replied with surprise in her voice. Trish looked up, raising her eyebrows. Peggy folded her napkin, laid it beside her plate and held her hands out in front of her on the table. "Look, life didn't start on this planet until radiation fell below a level that could sustain it. For eons there wasn't even a protective ozone layer to keep out the ultra-violet radiation. Life began in the sea simply because water forms a kind of insulation or protection from radiation."

As Trish sat absorbed in Peggy's comments, she told Trish that it was perfectly conceivable that stories and myths about long ago mutations—that might have appeared in the early stages of man's appearance on the planet— still rumbled around within the human psyche. She told Trish that radiation levels had been steadily lowering since the planet was formed, but that the first humans, who developed long ago, closer to hot pockets that were still cooling, could surely have experienced clusters of mutations.

"But what's really the *most* significant—and this is critically important, Trish," she said slowly and deliberately, as she leaned forward with her forearms on the table, "Life—as we know it—exists on a razor-thin edge. Overhead we're shielded from *cosmic* radiation by an ozone layer that is paper-thin. And below our feet we're shielded from the planet's *internal* radiation by a layer of fragile soils. Our very *existence* is *dependent* on the viability of that narrow space between those layers.

"By disrupting these layers—as we have for the last five decades—for the first time in the history of humanity and the planet itself, we're *reversing* that cooling process." She motioned with her hands. "We're digging up the uranium that's been buried since the dawn of creation and dispersing it over the surface of the earth. And we're destroying that thin layer of ozone that protects us from atmospheric radiations with CF gases and nitric oxides from the nuclear testing…"

Trish put her hand to her head, stunned, and in a whisper, finished Peggy's statement. "And the monsters are coming back. Oh, my God." As she spoke the words, she felt goose bumps erupt on her body.

"Well, the mutations, if you will. And think about it, Trish, uranium being named after Uranus…well, the planet Uranus…but the planet was named after the god."

"My God, you're right."

"And think about the name Plutonium. Heavens, they named that after the god of the underworld. Don't you think there was some kind of psychic Freudian slip going on there?"

"That's incredible. I never *thought* of that before." Trish's eyes remained widened as she spoke. She held her arm up toward Peggy. "God, Peggy, look, goose bumps."

Peggy grinned sideways, then leaned across the table and said seriously, "Trish, I need to know something. Did you come across any children that were as profoundly mutated as the Cyclops and mermaid that lived?"

Trish shook her head. "No." Then she propped her arm on the table and added, "But it's strange you ask that, because I wondered myself if all those specimens were really stillbirths. Some of them were obviously miscarriages, but some of them looked full-term, and I did wonder if they'd been live births and had just been killed by someone right after they were born." She set her chin on her fist. "You're wondering if they were viable, aren't you, Peggy?"

"Yeah…if they were trying to adapt to an altered environment in a more viable form."

After she told Peggy that none of the deformities she'd seen on children and adults were as profound as those in the specimens in the jars, Peggy sat back in her chair and asked, "Did you know that mermaids were said to portend the future?"

Trish raised her eyebrows. "No…I didn't." She was surprised at how much insight Peggy was providing.

Peggy told her that pictures and forms of mermaids appeared, not only on ships and seafaring materials, but also in old churches and that they were somehow connected to religion. "I don't know *what* they're supposed to portend, but that's what they're supposed to do."

"Maybe their warning is that they *are* the future if we don't stop monkeying around with forces we don't understand." Trish turned her face toward the window of the café and stared for a moment. "*God*, this is some deep shit." Then she looked back at Peggy. "Where did you get your information on mermaids? Do you still have it?"

"Yeah, probably. I hardly ever throw written material away that interests me. It drives my husband absolutely crazy. The only problem is trying to lay my hands on what I'm looking for, but I'll give it a shot. I think I might know where it is."

"Also, would you happen to have any contacts with environmental activists in Australia?"

"No." Peggy half chuckled. "That's just a bit out of my range. Why?"

"Well, I was thinking specifically about any information about an environmental situation...one that might have to do with uranium or something along those lines."

"Yeah..." Peggy held a finger up in the air. "Now that you mention it, I *did* read about a huge environmental battle that took place in *northern* Australia—some sort of Aborigine lands, or something." She said that one of the richest uranium ore deposits in the world was located there, and that when it was discovered by a mining company that wanted rights to it, the Aborigines opposed any excavations. "They said their religion forbade anyone digging into this mountain."

"That must be it!" Trish said with undisguised excitement. "You wouldn't happen to have any material on *that*, would you?"

"Yeah, as a matter of fact, I do...and I know *exactly* where that is. Why don't you follow me home and I'll get it, and the mermaid material—if I can find it."

As Trish drove toward Peggy's house, she thought how ironic it was that Peggy had mentioned the Aborigine religion when she first told her about the atomic priesthood, since that was where her attention was focused for the next leg of her research. The prospect of finally figuring out a more precise destination in Australia excited and energized Trish more than she'd been in a long time. Maybe she was feeling what Schliemann felt when he set off on his quest for the city of Troy. Only her quest was an archaeological dig into the mind and soul of man and into the genetic patterns of flesh and bone.

• • •

As soon as Trish returned home, she began devouring the materials on the mermaids and on the controversy about the uranium mining in Australia. The mermaid material was a short magazine article, and had little more information in it than what Peggy had already provided. The rather lengthy magazine article about the mining controversy, on the other hand, was quite another story. She found it positively fascinating. The place was near Darwin. It was called Kakadu.

Trish curled up in her chair, a glass of iced tea on the table beside her, which she sipped on from time to time as she read. It was a large nature reserve located at the top end of the Northern Territory in Australia, about 130 miles east of Darwin. It had the distinction of being—not only a national park—but of being on the World Heritage list for both its cultural and natural significance worldwide.

It was a tropical region, home to a number of Aborigines and their rock art that dated back for tens of thousands of years, and also home to numerous species of birds, reptiles, fish and other wildlife. Its billibongs provided habitats for many types of water creatures, as well as an abundance of water plants. The vivid descriptions of the exotic environment left Trish feeling dreamy.

According to the article, in the 1970's, a mining company was conducting explorations in the area when they came upon what appeared to be an extremely rich area of uranium deposits. The find was so incredibly rich that at first the people from the mining company thought their equipment was broken because of the high readings. The article described them as off-the-scale. They soon discovered that their equipment was in perfect working order, and that the area contained the richest known uranium deposits in the world. Those and the gold deposits were estimated to be worth ten billion dollars. There was one little snag. It belonged to the Aborigines.

Trish glanced at the clock on the mantle. It was getting late. She reluctantly closed the magazine, and hurriedly went to brush her teeth and slip into an oversized T-shirt. Then she climbed into bed and took up her reading where she'd left off.

The Aborigines had been granted legal rights to the land rich in uranium under Australia's Northern Territory Land Rights law. Because of that, the mining company offered royalties to get control of it. Some of the Aborigines were tempted by the offer, but others refused it, saying that the land was sacred and was to remain undisturbed. The Aborigine elders prophesied a worldwide disaster if the lands in the Kakadu were disturbed. Trish looked up at that point as she recalled the woman in Kazakhstan telling Katrina that the shamans had warned the Russians not to mine the sacred mountains there

Trish continued reading about the political, legal, environmental and cultural battles which ensued. It was a classic war between financial interests and traditional values. It was only when the conservative government in power at the time enacted an exception to the land rights law, excluding an area known as the Ranger tract, that the mining company was given permission to start mining uranium. Even though they paid the Aborigines a share of the profits, many observers and interested parties had loudly proclaimed that it was disproportionate to the amount of wealth in minerals that was being extracted from the native lands.

Trish slapped the magazine down hard on the bed covers. She picked up her notepad and made notations of questions she would have asked if she had been researching the article herself.

When she picked up the magazine again, she read that three tracts, called Ranger, Jabiluka and Koongaria, were opened up for mining. Kakadu Park surrounded the tracts, but was not included in their boundaries. After the mining company received full approval for their operations, blasting and dynamiting went on for days on end, vibrating and shaking the surrounding area and releasing radon into the atmosphere. There were three and a half thousand blasts from 1981 until the time the article had been written. Seven countries were reported to have received the mined uranium—including Japan, France, and the United States.

The article stated that, since the tailings left over from the mining were too radioactive to be moved, a decision was made that they would be held where they were—under water—where they would remain radioactive for 100,000 years. When she read that, Trish recalled what Peggy had told her about water being a shield from radiation.

She read that the general public, as well as the Aborigines, had grave concerns about the tailing dams. The mining companies assured them there was nothing to worry about; the dams had been built to withstand a thousand year flood. Trish didn't believe it. It didn't take a genius to figure out—even if it were true—a thousand years didn't stack up against the hundred thousand that the tailings were supposed to remain radioactive. She squirmed in the bed and let out a hard breath.

She further read that during the rainy season in the Kakadu, floods poured over the top of the escarpments that surrounded parts of it, sending cascading torrents of water into the park. Just how many studies had the mining companies done on those annual events to be able to make that thousand-year projection in the first place? Future generations of the earth— particularly in that area—were going to *need* an atomic priesthood to warn them.

Toward the end of the article she read that eventually another government with a different agenda came into power, and in 1991 the mining company was denied permission to mine Coronation Hill, one of the most controversial areas in question. Trish pursed her lips. *Thank God.* The Jawan tribes, who had been displaced from their lands during World War II, had access to Jabiluka returned to them. It appeared that at the time the article was written only the Ranger tract was being mined. Mining stocks had fallen, and the mining company had been sold to another company that continued to fight legally and politically for the right to reopen and continue the mining.

When Trish finished note taking and reading, she put the material down on her night stand, turned out the light and nestled down in bed. It had been a long but productive day. While the information in the article had been unsettling, at least she knew with certainty that Kakadu was the place she was meant to go in Australia.

That night she had the first restful, most peaceful night's sleep in months.

Chapter Sixteen

Trish continued researching Australia for days. It was reassuring to have a direction for the second leg of her journey. Her writer's block was easing, and she was getting her drive back more each day. Though she felt better emotionally than she had when she'd first arrived home from Russia, she still wasn't feeling fully up to par. Occasional moments of weakness left her feeling light-headed and fragile, though she was consciously trying to take care of herself and eat properly.

From what she'd read about the area in the Northern Territory, it appeared a fairly rugged place. Since she knew she'd need to get in a good physical condition, she'd begun a mild exercise routine. But, she didn't need exercise, research or food; she needed a break. The familiar signs of overload were nagging her to get out of the house for a change of scenery before resuming the research.

She looked out the window. It was a gorgeous day—not the kind to be wasted with her nose in a book or in front of the computer. She got dressed quickly, grabbed her keys and headed out the door, unsure of where she might end up. "Out" seemed like enough of a destination for the moment.

At first she headed north up the main highway toward Highlands, North Carolina, thinking how beautiful a drive it would be, but before she reached the turn-off, she decided to go to downtown Clayton and shop for clothes instead. She hadn't done that in a long time, but at that moment all she wanted was a new outfit.

An entire afternoon of browsing leisurely through the dress shops around town felt good to her. And she enjoyed feeling good for a change, since the burden of knowing had slipped heavily around her shoulders. After making several purchases she headed to a nice restaurant for lunch.

When she got home that evening with her packages in hand, she hurried to try on one of the new dresses. She thought it looked even better on her than it had in the shop. "Great," she said to the image in the full-length mirror, then brushed her eyebrows, fluffed her hair and took a final look. It was just too nice to waste. On the spur of the moment she called Kathy to invite her out for dinner and drinks. The two of them would have a ball together out on the town, and they hadn't done anything with a "spur of the moment" quality to it in a long time. But Kathy wasn't home and her husband, Mike, didn't know when she'd be back, only that it would be late.

"Damn!" she said out loud as she hung up the phone and stamped her foot. "All dressed up and no place to go."

Determined not to stay at home working again or watching television, she grabbed her purse and headed out into the darkening night. It began drizzling enough to turn on her wipers, and she drove around town for a while, until she realized that she really didn't want to eat dinner alone. Instead of a restaurant she drove toward a small nightclub at the edge of town to have a drink and listen to some music. It simply wasn't a night to be alone. She wanted to be around people...music...noise...anything that felt alive.

Just before she reached the parking lot of the club, the drizzle turned into a downpour. Sudden, fierce storms of that nature had been popping out of nowhere in the previous two weeks. It was a dramatic contrast to the hot, dry days of the drought. Even though the storms were short-lived, and did very little to help the rain deficit in the state, Trish thought they had a strange feel about them.

She got drenched running from the car to the entrance of the club, and—feeling disoriented by the force of the shower—she stopped just inside the door to brush the beads of water off of her clothes and to flip what she could of it out of her hair. She could feel ringlets already forming around her face.

As she made her way to the bar, she attempted to brush aside an off-balance feeling that had swept over her as she'd run from her car to the club entrance. The seat she selected had a good view of everything and everyone inside, and she decided to stay there for a while. After she ordered a Margarita and started sipping on it, she made eye contact with several acquaintances and nodded briefly to them in acknowledgment, carefully avoiding striking up a conversation.

She had settled quickly and comfortably into her observer mode, a habit from her professional life that she never could quite shake. Still, she enjoyed watching other people, making note of their actions and body language as they conversed. She wondered about what was going on in their lives and in their relationships.

She was absorbed in her observations for almost half an hour, nursing her drink, when slowly she became distracted from them and started focusing instead on the music playing in the background. Practically every song she had ever heard about Georgia was playing in succession on the jukebox. Then she heard a string of songs from the '60's, all of them her old favorites from high school. She began feeling strangely nostalgic, as memories of her relationship with Jimmy Hartwell began filtering into her thoughts. But as she continued to focus on the music, she began to suspect that the selection of songs was far too orchestrated to be coincidental.

Just then, someone walked up to the bar next to her and ordered a drink. She instantly recognized the deep, husky voice and turned toward the source of it. Jimmy Hartwell was standing only inches away. He didn't even look at her until she had turned her head in his direction, as though he had bumped into her accidentally. But Trish realized that it had to be a ruse. She quickly deduced that Jimmy must have seen her or seen her car outside and come in and played the songs on the jukebox just for her benefit. She wondered how she could have missed seeing him in the crowd.

"Well, well," he said, apparently faking surprise. "Miss Trish. And what are you doing out on a rainy night like this?"

She tilted her head slightly. "Why, Jimmy Hartwell...I should have recognized the selection of songs."

He turned his body fully toward hers, as he leaned on his elbow against the bar and beamed a full-faced smile. "Like them?"

She gave a slight sideways smile, but didn't answer. Instead, she took another sip from her glass and—feeling bold from the effects of the Margarita—she swiveled her stool almost imperceptibly in his direction. "Jimmy John, are you out tomcatting tonight? Or are you just in between wives again?"

"O-o-oh. Miss Trish, you sure can be rough on an old country boy," he commented, wincing. "If you're not careful, someone's going to think you've gotten cynical."

She turned back toward the bar and took another sip. "Just realistic, Jimmy John. Just realistic."

"Now, when are you going to stop calling me 'Jimmy John'? Only you and my grandmother ever call me that anymore."

"And how *is* your grandmother nowadays?" she asked, as she turned back toward him again...this time, fully engaging in the conversation.

"As matter of fact, she just turned 90, but she still works in her yard and bakes biscuits and lives alone...and she's got a mind as sharp as a tack. Still cuffs me behind the ear if I cuss in front of her."

"Hmm. I always liked your grandmother."

"She always liked you, too." He twisted his glass back and forth for a moment, then said, "Trish, I was sorry to hear about your parents. I started to come to the funerals, but then thought I'd better not. I was having some, well...marital problems around that time, and it didn't seem like a good idea somehow. That's why I just sent the sympathy cards. I *did* come to the funeral home one night...when your father died. But there were people all around you, and you didn't see me."

She looked up at him, without questioning or pursuing his comment further, then began feeling the same jumpy feeling in the pit of her stomach that she'd felt the day she'd bumped into him in Clayton. She scanned the room with her eyes.

Immediately, he asked, "Trish, I'm not making you nervous again, am I?"

Trish looked directly back at him. "What do you mean by *that*? You don't make me nervous at *all*."

"Okay, okay." He held up a hand and backed up a step. "You just looked like you wanted to get out of here or something."

She took a deep breath. She knew he was right. Why was she letting her silly uneasiness with him throw her off balance? She downed the last of her drink and looked at him squarely in the face, with her hand on her hip, and asked, "And just what *is* you marital status at the moment?"

"I've been divorced for over a year now," he replied bluntly. "In fact," he added, "it was exactly a year since my divorce was final that day I asked you out for a Coke in town."

She was feeling braver. "Well, what happened? I thought the third time was supposed to be the charm."

"Ouch. You still go straight for the jugular, don't you?" he asked with a chuckle. Then he took a gulp from his glass and winced at the strength of the drink. "Actually, you shouldn't even count my first marriage. Hell, it only lasted six months."

"Well, if you don't count *my* first marriage," she countered, "then I guess I've been single all my life."

He grinned at her sideways. "Why don't we get a booth?"

She hesitated for just a moment, then grabbed her purse and her glass and headed for an empty booth without answering. In that brief moment she had decided that she wasn't going to run away from their unfinished business again. She'd follow the trail wherever it led and be done with it once and for all.

As she settled into her seat, Jimmy lingered at the bar long enough to order another round of drinks. When he joined her at the booth—and as she busied herself brushing her hair back from her face again—she could sense him staring at her. Finally, he commented, "You look tired, Trish."

Her reaction was instantaneous. "If *one* more person tells me how bad I look…"

"Hey, hold on," he retorted, holding up the palm of his hand. "Calm down. I didn't say you looked bad. I said you looked *tired*."

She exhaled forcefully. Why was she getting so angry at his comments?

"Hell," he continued with a boyish grin on his face, "I still think you're the best damn looking gal in Rabun County."

She lowered her head and stirred her drink, uncomfortable with the unexpected compliment. Then after a quick glance across the room, she returned his gaze and smiled, and they began a friendly banter as songs played in the background. There were quiet pauses in their conversation as they listened to the music. When Jimmy ordered another round of drinks, Trish initially refused. But at his encouragement, she began sipping on her third Margarita. They talked a little about her trip to Russia, but she had no intention of getting into the details of the experiences there or her plans to go to Australia. It was all too complicated.

Before they'd had time to get any deeper in conversation, Percy Sledge began belting out "When a Man Loves a Woman" on the jukebox. It was their favorite song from high school. The two of them looked at each other and grinned. Trish knew Jimmy had made that particular song selection just for her benefit. She leaned toward him and said, "Of course, you realize this is a classic, dysfunctional, co-dependent relationship he's singing about, don't you?"

Jimmy furrowed his brow, tilted his head and asked, "Trish, are you going to analyze the song to death, or are you going to dance with me?"

She didn't respond. She simply stood up, led the way to the dance floor, turned around and slipped easily into his arms. As they started to dance, it amazed her how natural it felt, how comfortably they both still seemed to fit together, how all those years just seemed to melt away. She could smell his after shave again. But this time, she didn't want to bolt and run. She merely nestled closer into his arms and enjoyed the moment, because—like the shopping—it was exactly and simply what she wanted to do.

The main refrain came up again, and the two of them looked at each other and sang the words out together spontaneously. Then they both laughed and held each other close again and continued dancing to the old familiar song. The smile quickly faded from Trish's face, however, as she realized that this wasn't just another dance. She could sense something more—something indefinable. She felt Jimmy tighten his embrace. "God, this feels good," he whispered in her ear.

Just then Trish stumbled a bit and stopped dancing, then put her hand to her head, "Jimmy..." She backed up a step or two from him.

"What's the matter? Are you all right? Did I say something I shouldn't have?"

"No...no...really..."

She turned and walked slowly and deliberately back to the table—feeling weak and slightly dizzy.

He followed her, and as they sat down, he placed his hand on top of hers and repeated, "What's wrong, Trish?"

"Nothing, really. I mean...well...I just haven't felt like myself since I got back from Russia. I've been really tired lately, like you said. I probably shouldn't have had that second drink...or, maybe I should have had something to eat first. I don't know."

She looked up at Jimmy. He was eyeing her, as if evaluating the situation. Then he turned serious. "I'm driving you home, Trish. You're starting to lose your color."

"No, really, I'll be fine in a minute." She tried to wave off his concerns.

"Maybe and maybe not, but I'm taking you home, anyway. You don't need to be driving in this storm in this condition."

She could tell there'd be no arguing over the issue, and she didn't want to argue about it. She stood up, and he slipped an arm protectively around her waist. At that moment—almost as though the timing of it had been orchestrated—"Rainy Night in Georgia" began playing on the jukebox. They stopped and looked at each other and exchanged a brief smile. It was another of their old favorites, and with the storm raging outside with its accompanying thunder, Trish thought it was exactly appropriate for the occasion. Jimmy had been extremely deliberate with his musical selections.

The song was still playing in Trish's head as they dashed through the parking lot toward Jimmy's truck. She carried her shoes in her hand, and was quickly soaked. Though she had doubts about leaving with Jimmy, she was too tired to put up any resistance. And she liked having someone else in charge of her well being for a change.

•   •   •

When they arrived at Trish's house, the two of them made another dash through the rain to the back door. They shook off under the porch and made their way inside. When Trish turned on the light switch, nothing happened.

"Lightening or a tree limb or something must have hit one of the lines. It happens a lot out here during storms with all these trees," she explained. "I keep flashlights and candles all over the place, just in case."

After locating a flashlight and matches in a kitchen drawer, she lit a number of the candles and old oil lamps that she kept strategically placed for just such events in her kitchen and living room. When the tiny flames were lit up all over the two rooms, they provided a warm glow. Just as Trish began realizing how soaked she was, she heard Jimmy say, "You'd better get out of those wet clothes."

"Well, I've heard better lines than that before," she retorted, with half a grin.

"Hey...you're not in any shape to be risking pneumonia right now." The tone in his voice was serious. And he was right. She carried the flashlight with her into the bathroom, looked around, hesitated a moment, then impulsively grabbed a large towel and returned to the living room.

"Here, this will probably fit you perfectly," she said as she tossed him the towel. He looked slightly puzzled before she added, "Don't worry, Jimmy John. I've seen you without your pants before." He grinned, but she barely caught a glimpse of it as she turned on her heels and walked back to the bathroom.

Trish lit several candles in the bathroom. Then she turned toward the full-length mirror on the back of the door and saw the image of her beautiful, new dress clinging tightly to her body, still dripping slightly. As she peeled off all of her wet clothes and piled them unceremoniously into the bathtub, she recalled how good she'd thought it all looked on her earlier in the evening. She dried herself and towel dried her hair, then grabbed her robe from the hook on the linen closet door and wrapped it around her.

Before walking out, she stopped and looked in the mirror again and wiped away the mascara smeared beneath her eyes. Then she whispered to herself, "What are you getting yourself into here, Trish Cagle?" Straightening her shoulders back and steeling herself, she took a deep breath and returned to the living room, wondering what she'd find when she got there.

Jimmy was standing at the fireplace, adjusting the flame on one of the oil lamps on the mantel. He turned toward her when she walked into the room. His clothes were draped on the fire screen and he had nothing but the towel wrapped around his waist. His hair was so wet that it looked black—even with the peppered gray, and it was combed back straight and slick against his head. A strand of it had come loose and was hanging at his forehead. The sight of him like that gave Trish an unexpected sensation. He looked so enticing…and yet at the same time she felt overcome with feelings of vulnerability.

She headed for the safety of her favorite chair, and curled up in it. "See? Didn't I tell you? Fits perfectly…one size fits all." She nodded toward the towel.

"Huh?" he asked, then followed her gaze. "Oh…the towel. Right."

Trish could tell he was as edgy as she was.

Just then a flash of lightening, followed almost instantaneously by a loud and long, rolling clap of thunder shook the house. Trish could feel the vibrations of it all through her body, as the windows rattled. "Ooh, *that* one was close," she commented, wincing and snuggling deeper into her chair. As disarming as the sound of the thunder was, the timing of it felt welcomed to her, as it actually seemed to break the ice that had begun building between them.

"I know," he responded, as he walked over to the sofa next to her chair and sat down. "That storm a couple of nights ago took out several huge hardwoods on my farm. And Clyde Bledsoe lost six of his cows last week when lightning hit a tree they were standing under."

"*Really?*"

"Yeah, these summer storms the last few weeks have been fierce. I don't ever remember the weather being as unpredictable and destructive as it's been the last few years…all over the country, as a matter of fact."

"Yeah, I know." Trish stared at the floor a moment.

Then Jimmy's words took a softer tone. "Trish, what's going on with you?"

His concern appeared genuine, but her first instinct was to look away and brush off the question. In a quick glance across the room, however, she recalled the resolve she'd made at the nightclub, and instead looked back at him, took a deep breath and answered directly. "I had a bad experience over in Kazakhstan, Jimmy." As soon as she spoke the words, she noticed a troubled expression on his face, and quickly added, "But it's nothing serious…really. I've been to the doctor and as far as he can tell it's just a combination of jet lag and emotional fatigue."

"But what caused it? I mean, what's gotten you so upset? You didn't get *mugged* over there or anything, did you?"

"No, nothing like that. It's just that…well, I think the story I went over there to get, got me instead."

"What?" he asked, wrinkling his brow. "What do you mean?"

"Oh, I don't know how to tell you exactly," she began as she repositioned herself and retied her robe, "but things are really bad over there, Jimmy." She explained that, not only had the economy crashed with the accompanying upheaval, but that the Cold War had left a lot more contamination in places than the public had been led to believe. "I mean—some of it was *really* bad. I think I got caught off guard by all of it, emotionally and physically, too. I actually passed out at one point…which wasn't a very professional thing for a reporter to do, I can tell you."

"Tell me about it, Trish," he said, fully focused on her. There wasn't any hint of morbid curiosity in his voice. But how she could ever begin to tell him? She could tell Max or Peggy or maybe even Mark. But how could anyone who hadn't been there understand any of it? She didn't understand it herself. She fiddled with the sash of her robe again, trying to think of what she could share even marginally, but all she could see in her head were the jars on those shelves. She couldn't share that. She felt suddenly overwhelmed with the frustration of trying to convey her experience to anyone.

Then she thought about Ilyani. No one who hadn't experienced her could understand that, either. For a moment she could almost feel Ilyani's little hand on her cheek again, and a rush of sensations filled her body. As she tried to speak, tears began filling her eyes. She couldn't stop them. All of her efforts at control, distraction and rationalization fell by the wayside in those brief moments. She covered her face and began to weep.

Jimmy got up from his seat and knelt beside her chair, putting his hand on hers. "Go ahead and cry, Trish."

Through the sobs, she said, "But that's about all I've *been* doing for the last few weeks."

He half laughed. And then after trying to console her for a few more minutes and without saying another word, he lifted her out of the chair and carried her to the bedroom, still crying. After he laid her down on her bed, he went back into the living room, returned with one of the oil lamps, and set it on the nightstand. Trish turned over face down on the bed and continued sobbing. It was the most thorough, surrendering cry she'd had since returning from Kazakhstan.

Jimmy sat next to her on the bed and put his hand lightly on her shoulder. Then he leaned over and whispered in her ear, "I don't know what happened over there, but it's going to be all right, Trish. It will; I promise. You're going to be fine. You just need to try to relax." Then he began massaging her shoulders lightly. "I don't remember ever seeing you this tense before in high school."

Trish was surprised at how refreshing and familiar his touch felt after so many years. "Jimmy, that feels so good."

"Just relax now. I'm not trying to get fresh with you or anything. Okay?"

She nodded, and she believed him. She attempted to relax...and slowly stopped crying out loud, only snubbing from time to time, as he massaged her shoulders and then her arms, back and neck. A sense of mellowness swept over her, as she felt herself letting go of some of her defenses. She let out a moan when the manipulating began to feel deep and achy, because it was the kind of aching that signaled a contact had been made with a point of soreness that needed to be reached.

As he continued, Trish began to think that at that moment there was nothing in the world she needed more. She didn't know if it was because the tension in her body had built to such an incredibly high level or if she had just been hungry for the touch of another person for so long. Or maybe it was because Jimmy Hartwell was the one doing the massaging. Whatever the reason, she felt intoxicated by it...that, and the lingering effects of the Margaritas.

She didn't know why, but she sincerely trusted him and gave herself over to his touches. He moved to her legs and only spoke to ask her if something felt all right. But at that moment it all felt "all right" to her. At the same time she felt both relaxed and stimulated...aroused. It felt delicious. Strains of "Rainy Night in Georgia" wafted through her head again, and—with the storm still raging outside and the soft glow from the flame in the room—the whole atmosphere seemed surrealistic, even magical.

She began slipping in and out of other times and other places as sleep began to softly and sweetly envelop her consciousness. Finally, she lodged in its embrace completely and continued on her journey to other worlds.

• • •

Several hours later, a roll of distant thunder jolted Trish awake, leaving her momentarily disoriented. When she finally cleared her head, she saw that the oil lamp was still burning a tiny flicker of a flame, providing enough light to check the clock. It was three A.M. She looked over and saw Jimmy Hartwell asleep on the other side of the bed, still wrapped in her towel. "Oh, God, Trish, what have you gotten yourself into?" she whispered under her breath. It wasn't like her at all to go to a bar and end up with a man in her bed. She wasn't that kind of person. But this wasn't just any man. He was the one who'd occupied more of her thoughts and dreams for the previous years than she liked to admit, even to herself.

Besides, even if she wasn't "that kind of woman," she didn't know exactly what kind of woman she was any more. Things had been changing so dramatically and quickly in her life in the previous few months that the old familiar inhibitions, survival techniques and defenses, on which she'd relied in the past, didn't feel quite right. In fact, she was beginning to believe some of them might have actually deprived her of more than they had protected her.

But she wasn't sure exactly who Jimmy Hartwell was anymore, either. The person she'd fallen in love with so many years before had been little more than a boy, and now he was clearly a man, with years of experiences and changes and ideas that hadn't included her. She ran a hand through her hair and sighed quietly, then looked at Jimmy again. Unable to see him clearly in the darkened room, she turned up the flame on the oil lamp, then looked back again.

She was surprised by what she saw. And felt. Asleep, as he was, she thought he was the most handsome man in the world. She realized in her heart, completely for the first time, just how much he really meant to her. Whatever paths their lives had taken while they'd been apart and whatever time had slipped between them, she was certain of only one thing: she still loved this man.

Just as that realization occurred to her, Jimmy began to stir in his sleep, and she heard him murmur, sleepily, "Trish?"

She whispered, "Jimmy, I'm sorry. I didn't mean to wake you."

He moaned audibly and stretched his arms, and, in a husky voice still heavy with sleep, he told her, "Don't worry about that, Lady. I've been waiting over twenty years to wake up next to you."

It was as though an iceberg had suddenly melted inside her. She didn't even think. Her tendency to analyze every situation suddenly evaporated, as she slid over to him, snuggled up to his chest and laid her head on his shoulder. "I've missed you so much, Jimmy."

As he held the arm she'd draped over his chest, he pulled his head up and kissed her forehead. Then he brought the palm of her hand to his face and kissed it, too. "I didn't think I could go one more day without you, Trish.

I've never stopped loving you." Then he turned over and positioned his body where he could embrace her and kissed her fully in the mouth.

There was no resistance at all on Trish's part, and as they continued kissing slowly, thoroughly and passionately, a huge storage of memories of long ago sensations and feelings flooded Trish's mind and her body. She wanted to say something, but words seemed completely inadequate. She momentarily pulled away and untied her robe, then returned to the embrace, feeling her naked breasts against his chest. She couldn't believe how good it felt just to be touching his skin.

Jimmy continued kissing her. He moved to her neck and then to her breasts. He slipped the towel from his waist. And as Trish succumbed to her passions, she released herself from years of defenses, years of inhibitions and years of doubt.

● ● ●

Trish was the first one awake the next morning. After she got up and went to the kitchen and started the coffee maker and breakfast, Jimmy came into the room, wearing the towel around his waist. "Kind of starting to like that style, huh?" she teased, glancing at it.

"Hey, I can take it off again, if you like," he answered with his hands out to the side and a smile on his face.

She laughed lustily, with her head thrown back. "No, no...I think both of us could use some *nourishment* this morning." Then she added, "But I have to warn you, I'm not much of a cook when I'm half awake."

"Hey, with your talents, who cares if you can cook or not," he responded, walking up behind her and slipping his arms around her waist as she stood at the stove.

"Jimmy!" she said with mock indignation.

He nuzzled her neck. "Hey, Lady, I'm talking about your writing abilities."

"Right," she replied in an unconvinced tone. She clasped her hands around his. "I've got your clothes drying now. They were still a little damp this morning."

"Who needs clothes...or food, for that matter?"

She turned around to face him, and they embraced. She didn't know what to say, so she didn't say anything; she merely held him as he nuzzled her neck. Finally she turned back around, and said, "Look, we really do need something to eat...at least *I* do. In fact, I'm famished...and for the first time in weeks, too."

As Trish made toast to go with the scrambled eggs and Jimmy sipped his coffee, they engaged in some small talk about things going on around town and about their old friends, seemingly to avoid the dramatic turn their lives had just taken.

As they were eating, Trish would stop to look at Jimmy and see that he was looking at her as well, smiling. Each time it happened she'd break into a grin and return her attention to her food. After it had happened the third time, she broke into laughter and he joined her. "Stop it. You're making me blush," she said, as she put one of her hands over the side of her face.

He reached over and pulled it down, then cupped the palm of his hand on her cheek and said, "It's time we were back in each other's lives, Trish. We've been apart way too long."

Later, after she'd finished her food, Trish put her fork down and abruptly asked, "Jimmy, do you have a philosophy about life?"

"A *philosophy* about life?" he repeated, as he set his coffee mug down.

"Yeah, you know…a way you live or see the world."

He took in a breath, and responded, "Well, now, let me see…a philosophy, huh?" He leaned back. After a moment he replied, "I don't know if I do or not. I've never given it much thought, really. But my grandmother always used to say that people who worried about those kinds of things usually didn't have much time to just live and enjoy their lives."

"Is that how you feel?"

"Well…I guess it is."

"Then *that's* your philosophy."

"I suppose so."

She set her elbows on the table and laced her fingers. "See, Jimmy, I don't ever remember you worrying what makes things tick. I don't think you do now…and I always did. I still do, I guess. That's the reason I went to Russia."

"Yeah, that's something I've been wondering about." He pushed his chair back slightly from the table. "Just why *did* you go to Russia?"

"Well," she began slowly, as she sat back in her chair. "I went to do a freelance story. But it seems to be turning into something else."

"Something else?"

"Yeah." She pursed her lips. "And I'm not sure exactly what, yet."

"So you're not working for another paper now?"

"Another paper? No. Why do you ask that?"

"Well, I heard around town that you'd been fired…and I thought you might be planning to move out of Clayton again, back to another job in the city."

"No, Jimmy, I'm not planning to move. Is that what you thought?" Trish began wondering if that was why he'd shown up at the bar the night before.

"That's exactly what I thought." He leaned forward onto the table.

"And when I heard you'd just up and gone to Russia out of the blue, I decided right then that I wasn't going to let you get away from me again...not twice in one lifetime."

"Oh, Jimmy..." Trish got up from her chair and walked over to him. As she did, he pulled his chair back further from the table, and she slid into his lap and put her arms around his neck. "I'm not going anywhere. I don't know exactly what I *am* going to do." She half laughed. "But I'm not going anywhere...not now, anyway."

As they continued holding each other, Trish was reminded of one of the things that had made Jimmy so appealing to her as a teenager. It was his tenderness. He'd always been so gentle with her. And it always seemed so authentic that she'd been thoroughly charmed by it. Snuggled in his lap like she was, the memory of that part of his nature—and the fact that he still had it—filled her with emotion.

They made love again that morning. Then they got dressed and went to retrieve Trish's car from the nightclub parking lot.

Over the next few days they spent an inordinate amount of time together. Then for the following weeks it seemed that they were either at one another's house or talking on the phone. Jimmy never brought up the subject of Trish's trip to Russia again, however, and she never mentioned it, either.

One day as they lay in bed she commented, "Lord, I didn't know two people could engage in as much unbridled, passionate sex as we have, at our age."

"Well, we've got a lot of years to catch up on," Jimmy responded with a boyish grin on his face. "Besides, what do you mean, 'at our age'? Hell, I don't know about you, but I feel like a teenager again."

While they continued to see each other every chance they got, they attempted to be discrete about it. After all, Clayton, Georgia was a small town, and they both wanted privacy in their renewed relationship. Still, in her quiet moments Trish couldn't deny the supreme and unparalleled happiness she was experiencing in her life.

Chapter Seventeen

Trish was working at her computer one day, when she heard a knock at the kitchen door, then heard it open. "Knock, knock. It's me," the familiar voice shouted.

"I'm in the bedroom…working on the computer, Kathy. Come on back."

"Are you decent?" Kathy asked, just outside the door.

"Of course, I'm decent. What do you mean by that?"

Kathy sashayed through the door, twirling her key chain, as she looked around the room with a facial expression that had a "cat-that-ate-the-canary" quality to it. Trish realized instantly that she knew about Jimmy and her. But, peeved that she was going to be deprived of telling Kathy about it herself, Trish didn't say a word.

She was also peeved that there didn't seem to be any secrets left in the little town of Clayton, Georgia. She couldn't imagine how Kathy could have found out about it so quickly, when she and Jimmy had been so careful.

"Have you been banging away at this computer all day?" Kathy asked.

"Pretty much."

"Am I disturbing your train of thought?"

"As a matter of fact, you are," Trish replied turning toward her.

"Well, *good*, 'cause you need to take a break and get out for a while. You never did know how to pace yourself. You're always such a fanatic when it comes to your work." She sighed, and, in a tone of mock resignation, said, "I guess it's always up to me to make you get out and change the scenery once in a while." Then Kathy brightened up. "Hey, why don't we go downtown and have some lunch…and maybe do some shopping?"

"Well, that does sound good right about now…but just let me finish this last paragraph first." She returned her attention to the computer.

"Go ahead. I'll just look in your closet while you're doing that and see if you've gotten any new clothes that might fit me."

"Help yourself."

Trish was continuing to type away, when Kathy suddenly burst out, "God, Patty, where did you get this *dress*?"

She looked up. "Oh, that one. I splurged a few weeks ago at that new little dress shop downtown. I can't think of the name. Oh, you know the one."

"You mean the Victorian Lace Boutique?"

"Yeah, that's it."

"Good God, Patty, that place is expensive as hell."

"I know. Like the dress?"

"I love it." She held it up to her and looked at her reflection in the mirror above the dresser. "This would look great on me at that picnic next week."

"What picnic?"

"Oh, you know—that reunion thing I told you about, with Mike's high school class."

"Oh. Well, sure, take it, if you like."

Kathy lowered the dress. "Patty, aren't you glad we didn't get fat like some of the girls from school?"

Trish swiveled in her chair toward her. "Are you going to be catty today?"

"Me? Catty? Whatever do you mean?"

Trish didn't answer. She just snickered, and started closing down the computer. She'd never get another thing done until she got dressed and went out to lunch with her friend.

When the two of them got seated in Kathy's car, Kathy began probing again. Before starting the engine, she turned and looked directly at Trish. "What's with you going out and buying such an expensive new dress? That's not like you. Something special coming up?" Then tilting her head, she added, "Or going *on*?"

Trish couldn't ignore the inferences any longer. "Kathy, is there anything at all that goes on in this town that everybody doesn't know about?"

"Not that I know of. Why? What's going on that you don't want people to know about?" She was still being coy.

"Kathy, I was going to tell you about it before long. I just didn't want to say anything till I'd had some time to sort it out a little myself."

"Then it's *true*? You and Jimmy Hartwell! It's not just a *rumor*? Hot damn!" Kathy's face lit up as though electrified, but Trish couldn't share her enthusiasm.

"Kathy! Just how many people around town are talking about this?"

"Oh, pretty much everybody," she replied matter-of-factly.

Trish winced and threw her head back with her hand to her face. "Oh, God."

But Kathy, unable to allow one moment to pass without continuing to probe, said, "Okay, Patty, give...I want to know everything. Tell me all about it." She finally started the engine.

"Why are you asking *me*?" Trish asked with sarcasm in her voice. "Why don't you just go ask someone over at the drugstore or the grocery, if you want to know something about my *personal* life?"

Kathy laughed as she backed out of the driveway, but Trish simply put her hand to her face again and shook her head in disbelief at how far the details of her intimate life had traveled around town...and how quickly. "Look, I don't know where this thing will lead. I'm not sure exactly how I feel about everything yet, much less how he does. We're taking it slow."

"That's not what *I* heard."

"Well...at least on an emotional level."

Trish couldn't hide the blush in her cheeks when Kathy glanced over at her. "Patty, you're in love. I can see it in your face. Who do you think you're kidding here? You never have gotten over him."

All of her pretense was over. Trish wrinkled her face in mock agony and almost gushed as she told her friend, "Oh, Kathy, in a way it's just like it was in high school. And in a way it's all fresh and new and exciting. Oh, God..." she finished, words failing her. When Kathy kept pumping for more information, she said, "Kathy Dunnigan, if you breathe one word of this to anybody, I'll...I'll..."

"Patty, you know me better than that."

"I guess so. But *someone* is out there blabbing all over town."

"Well, if you must know, somebody saw Jimmy's truck parked at your house one night and then again early the next morning. And several other people saw y'all leave together from the nightclub. Hell, Patty, your jeep was parked there all night. And the two of you haven't exactly been on buddy-buddy terms since you moved back. So it was hard to miss the signals." Kathy pulled onto the main road toward town. "It really didn't take much for folks to start putting two and two together...but I just couldn't believe anything was going on and you hadn't told *me* about it."

● ● ●

When they arrived downtown, they walked to the Clayton Square Café and got seated in a booth. As Trish glanced around, she noticed what she thought was an unusual number of people nodding and smiling at her, with knowing looks on their faces. She leaned forward and in a lowered voice asked, "Kathy, does it seem like everyone is looking at us?"

"No, it doesn't." she responded without looking up from her menu. "You're just being paranoid." After a moment Kathy peered over the top of her menu and looked around. Just then an older woman from Kathy's church caught her gaze and nodded toward her with what Trish felt was an overly sweet smile. Kathy nodded back, then leaned toward Trish. "Hmm. Well, maybe they are at that." She held her hand out. "But I don't know what you're so upset about. In high school everybody knew y'all were dating. So, what's the big deal now?"

"Kathy, damn it, at least in the big city you have a little anonymity. Everybody doesn't know everything about your private business."

"Yeah, and they don't even know who you *are*, either," she answered, as she sipped her water. "Hell, you could die in your apartment and no one would know it...till you started to stink."

"Oh, Kathy, that's gross."

"Yeah, but true."

"Well, maybe so," she acknowledged, grudgingly.

They ordered lunch, and when it arrived, Kathy asked Trish about her work. "It's actually going great. I've never done so much research on a single topic."

"Speaking of which, it sounds like this thing has gotten bigger than a news story."

Trish smiled. "Well, yeah, it has, at that."

"What are you going do with it, a magazine article or something?"

"Maybe. I don't know right now. I'm just following it where it leads for the time being." She set her glass down and laced her fingers in front of her. "It amazes me how big this story is. And, Kathy, if I didn't know it as a reporter, then hardly anyone in the public does."

"Then, why on earth don't reporters write about it more often, if it's so big?" Kathy asked, nibbling on her fries.

Trish shrugged. "I've thought a lot about that. I guess one of the main reasons is that it's so complex and intimidating."

Kathy dabbed her mouth with her napkin. "How so?"

"Well, when you talk about Cobalt 60 and Cesium 137 and isotopes and radio nuclides to most people, it's like speaking Greek. And reporters aren't specialized in highly technical issues. They just know a little about a lot of things. They still have to research things and interview people and ferret out a story."

Kathy sipped her drink and asked, "So, why isn't the media investing some time and money doing that?"

"I don't know. And that's what bothers me." Trish leaned onto the table on her forearms. "I mean, how much would it take to get even a little basic fact out about it?" She said she was beginning to believe that the invention of the atomic bomb and nuclear energy and what they had done to the planet and man's psyche made the previous fifty years the most significant in the recorded history of mankind. "I really mean that."

"Really?" Kathy seemed surprised by her friend's comment.

"Yeah, and how many people are even aware that we almost nuked the entire city of Detroit because of an accident at a nuclear reactor?"

Kathy set her glass down and swallowed hard. "Almost nuked *Detroit?* What are you talking about?"

Trish leaned back in her seat to relate the story. "Back in the '60s we almost lost the entire city because of an accident at a breeder reactor. They came close to spraying plutonium all over it. And if they had, the whole city would have been uninhabitable—from now on really—like Chernobyl."

"You're kidding. I've never, ever heard about *that* before."

Trish leaned forward again. "See what I mean? There are so many cover-ups about this thing that it's hard to keep rationalizing about the reasons for them. National security and proprietary rights just don't cut it for me any more."

"I don't even know what a breeder reactor is," Kathy admitted, with a look of sheer innocence on her face.

"Well, I'm not that clear on nuclear engineering myself, but evidently it's a reactor that uses uranium to produce plutonium; plutonium's probably the most deadly element on the planet." She told Kathy that instead of cooling the fuel rods with water, as they did in other reactors, the one they built near Detroit, called the Enrico Fermi plant was cooled with liquid sodium. She explained that if sodium in its pure form ever came in contact with air or water of any kind, it would explode.

"They put *that* in a nuclear reactor?"

"Exactly. You can't risk any leaks or any kind of explosion in a reactor core. In fact, they *did* have a sodium leak and flare-up at the plant with one of their initial trial tests, but the fuel hadn't been loaded yet so there wasn't any catastrophe. But there *could* have been if the thing had been fueled."

"Good God, Patty." Kathy was wide-eyed.

Between eating, Trish explained that the more she studied about nuclear energy the clearer it became that when dealing with it, one hundred per cent of everything had to go right one hundred per cent of the time. Since that was an impossibility and since nuclear energy was such a complex field, the rash of nuclear accidents was inevitable, though the public relations people for the nuclear industry preferred to call them "incidents."

"So what happened at the Detroit plant?" By now Kathy was focused completely on Trish's comments.

She told Kathy that in October of 1966, when the engineers and operators were trying to bring the new plant up to criticality, something went wrong. Alarm horns suddenly began sounding every three seconds for a Class I alert, indicating something critical was happening. No one knew what. They were certain of a radiation leak, and high temperatures in the core of the reactor vessel, but there was no way to know if any fuel rods were melting, because they couldn't see into the vessel.

"So they didn't know if they were facing a runaway melt down, or what. At a time like that, things can go terribly wrong in fractions of a second…in micro-seconds." She told Kathy about another nuclear accident at Chalk River in Canada where they'd come within half a second from either a meltdown crash down or a nuclear runaway.

Kathy said, "Wait, back to Detroit."

"They got the thing shut down, but they *did* have a fuel meltdown."

207

She told Kathy that they also had some sort of fuel shifting, which meant a secondary accident was still possible. Things the industry had said couldn't possibly happen, were happening, and the potential for even worse was still hanging over everything. Trish paused for a minute, sipping her drink.

"And? *And?*" Kathy prodded.

"Well, they didn't warn the citizens of Detroit or the surrounding areas…said they wanted to avoid a panic."

Kathy drew her head back. "Seems like a damn good time to panic to *me.*"

Trish told her that the people at the plant had to keep a close eye on the weather after the accident while they tried to figure out what had happened and how to contain it.

"The weather? Why?"

"Because, Kathy, when something like that happens, all that matters is which way the wind blows."

"Huh?"

Trish explained that in a nuclear accident people downwind of the radioactive plume get a full dose of it. "If you're upwind, you don't. It's that simple. If the wind is blowing toward a city during an accident, the city gets nuked. And the second day after the accident, that's exactly what happened; the wind was blowing toward the city…and there remained the potential for a secondary accident."

"So what happened?"

Trish took another drink from her glass and told Kathy that experts from all over the world flew into Detroit, where they finally reached a consensus that they had to get the melted fuel out.

"Did they?"

"Yeah, and luckily, without any secondary accident." She explained that it took three months to figure out that four of the subassemblies had melted, and another four months to remove them. It was two years later before they removed the part that had caused the accident.

"So what caused it?"

Trish leaned back and crossed her arms. "Some little safety afterthought that they'd installed at the last minute, that wasn't ever put in the blueprints. All of the redundant safety features they brag about installing in these reactors to make them safer turn out to be the very things that make things go haywire."

"Did they shut it down?"

"Eventually. They still didn't tell the public about what had almost happened. And there was still a push from the industry and the workers to reopen it."

"You're kidding. *Their* families didn't have any immunity to radiation."

"I know, Kathy. But, it's just like at Chernobyl." Trish twisted her glass back and forth on the table. "They want their jobs. So they keep buying the safety assurances, even when know how hollow they are. In fact, four years after the accident, they tried to start it up again and had another sodium explosion."

Kathy put her hand to her forehead. "Jesus Christ, Patty," she almost whispered.

"Then they started building *another* reactor to replace the first one." She told Kathy that even though over a hundred and twenty million dollars had been wasted on a reactor that had hardly produced any significant amount of electricity and had left radioactive wastes that would last for thousands of years and that would never be used again, they simply went ahead with construction on another one. "In fact, *billions* of dollars started pouring into the industry.

"With a near disaster like that, they should have shut the entire industry down, instead of investing half a trillion dollars into it. And with an investment like that to recoup, you can be sure they'll cut a lot of corners on safety to make sure they get their money back. Hell, the insurance industry wouldn't even touch it."

"They wouldn't?" Kathy raised her shoulders and hands and asked, "So, who's insuring it?"

"We are."

"What do you mean 'we'?"

"I mean, the government is insuring it because the insurance industry wouldn't." Trish pushed back her plate and told Kathy that it was necessary to do a risk assessment study to gauge the possible costs of a nuclear accident. When one was contracted, it came back with alarming results. She explained that the study was a limited one—not even close to a worse-case scenario—but that it still came back with 27,000 dead, 73,000 injured and seventeen billion dollars of damage. "*And* a portion of land the size of Pennsylvania nuked," she added.

"Good God." Kathy closed her eyes and lowered her face into her hand.

"The study was so bad that the industry and government both tried to hide the results…and they *did* for a long time." She said that after a lot of arm-twisting and threats, they were finally forced to release the study conclusions. "Then the insurance industry said, 'Hell, no, we're not going to insure them.'" She told Kathy that even Lloyds of London—a company known for taking risks—wouldn't touch it. At that point the government passed a law with a cap on any accidents of 560 million dollars, 495 million of that from government and only 65 million from private insurance. "And that's *it*."

Trish leaned forward again with her hand out. "I mean, even if you don't give a rat's ass about the environment—even if you're in complete denial about the health effects of something you can't see, taste, hear or detect, what about the financial impacts alone? Look how many businesses and industries and homes there are in Detroit. You nuke a city that size, and how many billions and billions of dollars worth of businesses and real estate do you think would be wiped out?"

Trish didn't wait for an answer. "Just how far do you think 560 million would go toward compensation? And that doesn't even take into account the deaths, either immediate or long-term from cancers." She talked about an independent university study that put estimates of the dead from an accident at Fermi at 133,000.

Kathy's face went blank, and she sat speechless.

"But even without that," Trish continued, "wouldn't you think the business community would've been raising hell about the dangers to their investments?"

"You'd think so. So, why weren't they?" By now Kathy was listening so intently that she had abandoned her food.

"Who knows?" she responded with her palms held upward. "Maybe they didn't understand the risks. But the financial aspect of the nuclear industry *alone* makes no sense." Trish explained that failing to hold the industry liable for any mistakes they made was the only way nuclear energy ever got off the ground—that, combined with the fact that it was tax dollars that developed the technology in the first place. "And holding them liable is the *only* way you'd get any semblance of reliable safety from them."

"So, then are you saying that if they *were* to nuke a chunk of the U.S., like at Chernobyl, there'd be no compensation for the people?" Kathy asked.

"Well, let's see," Trish responded, glancing at the ceiling, "five hundred and sixty million, minus thirty per cent for lawyers' fees, and you might be able to buy everybody a cup of coffee." She looked back at her friend and added, "...and maybe some aspirin."

"But I heard a Chernobyl type accident isn't possible here because of our containment domes, or something."

Trish half snickered. "Yeah, just like a Fermi type accident wasn't possible?" She rubbed the side of her face and leaned forward on her forearms again, explaining that even though most U.S. reactors did have containment domes, tons of used fuel rods were being held at the facilities that weren't under containment and could melt down in the open environment.

"Besides, if one of the containment domes *didn't* hold during a reactor explosion—and I don't think they've proven that they even could in a worse case scenario—the shell enclosure *itself* could create the biggest atomic bomb you could imagine...sort of like a giant atomic bullet."

Kathy's sat staring, as Trish continued, "You know, I always wondered why environmentalists piggy-backed nuclear weapons and nuclear energy together. It didn't make sense. They're for two totally separate purposes. But now that I've been doing this research, I realize that they developed together, sharing material, technology, routes. Besides that, the radioactive *effects* are the same."

Kathy looked puzzled and Trish added, "I mean, if there's a nuclear accident—no matter *what* the cause—you'll still have the same health effects as in a deliberate strike. Maybe not nearly as many initial deaths, but the same fallout effects: genetic damage, cancer and birth defects...even if the government and industry *together* denied any connection. So building these things so close to major cities is just insane."

"So why *did* they?"

"Because the cost of transmission lines is so expensive. To cut costs, they upped the risks even more by locating them near the big population areas they'd be powering." Trish took her napkin from her lap and laid it down beside her plate. "I didn't mean to ruin our lunch with my new obsession."

Kathy smiled. "In a weird kind of way I find it fascinating. Maybe because I'm in denial or shock or something." Kathy sat up straighter and gestured with her hands as she continued, "But ever since you got back from Kazakhstan, I feel like I'm hearing the greatest news story in the world for the first time...kind of like I've got this front row seat."

"Yeah, you always *were* a little nuts."

• • •

When the waitress came to take their plates, Trish and Kathy had their glasses refilled and continued talking.

"Now Max is telling me that I shouldn't use fear for my main point in this story," Trish told her friend.

"Good grief, it sounds like it's *time* people got the shit scared out of them."

"That's what *I* said. And I'm hoping another angle will pop up before long; it's getting a little heavy digging into this stuff." She tilted her head. "And here I am dumping it on you, after you brought me here for a change of scenery."

Kathy waved off her comment. "Hey, I *want* to know what's going on with you." Then she added with a glint in her eye, "Even when you try to keep things secret."

Trish grinned and let the comment pass, quickly returning to the main topic. She told Kathy that, though she knew she was going to focus on the mutants in the clinic in her story, she still didn't understand the connection to myth. She also wanted to write about what happened with Ilyani, but didn't know how to go about describing it. "I don't think people would believe it unless they'd experienced it."

Kathy cocked her head sideways. "Just what *was* that about with that little girl?"

"I don't know, Kathy. I've never experienced anything like it in my life. Katrina said there may be clusters of these kids around the world." She told Kathy that since she'd gotten back she'd found and read stories about "Blue Ray" children and "Indigo" children, who were purported to have some kind of psychic or intuitive knowing about spiritual realities that the rest of humanity didn't consciously have.

"You know, I've heard something about that myself…from Mary Ann Parker," Kathy said. "You know how she's always into spiritual stuff and psychological stuff. Hell, she even talks about quantum physics sometimes. I like to listen to her, but half the time I don't have a clue what the hell she's talking about, and the other half, I'm just fascinated."

Trish grinned. "Kathy, I don't think there's much that goes over *your* head."

"Are you kidding?" She gave a wave of a hand. "Hell, I don't even bother trying to deny it anymore. But sometimes I just stand there listening, 'cause I guess I like to feel the wind in my hair."

Trish chuckled, and then sighed. "Well, if you'd told me a story like what happened with Ilyani two months ago, it wouldn't have just gone over my head; I'd have thought you were *nuts*."

"Patty, do you think any of that is connected to the atomic age?"

"I don't know, but something tells me it is. If this is a widespread thing, why are the mutants and kids like that appearing at the same time?" Trish shrugged her shoulders and slapped her right thigh, "Oh, well. Who knows?"

"Patty, why don't you go talk to Mary Ann about it?"

Trish looked up. They'd been in touch a few times over the years since high school. "You know, I might just do that."

• • •

When they left the café, Kathy suggested they check out a new antique mall that had recently opened. As they drove, Trish told her she'd like to focus on something positive for her story, but that every day of research brought another incident or accident that she never knew anything about.

"Like?" Kathy asked with genuine interest.

"God, you really *are* a glutton for punishment."

"No, I'm not," she responded with feigned indignation. And then with a kind of innocence, she added, "I'm just curious. That's all."

Trish smiled. "Well, you know that new movie they're talking about? The one called *Broken Arrow*?"

"Yeah, I can't wait till it comes out; I lo..o..ove John Travolta," she purred as she stopped at a stop light.

"Do you know what a 'broken arrow' is?" Trish asked.

Kathy looked at her. "Well, I gather from the previews that it has to do with a nuclear accident or something."

"Right. It's military code for a lost nuclear weapon. And you know what?"

"What?" Kathy asked, checking the light, then looking back.

"There have actually been dozens of them that the military has acknowledged. And there are others they say are too sensitive to be discussed publicly."

"What kinds?"

Trish nodded forward. "The light's green now."

Kathy drove on as Trish told her that in 1961, a B-52 pilot on a training maneuver had to jettison two nuclear bombs over Goldsboro, North Carolina because his jet got into trouble and was about to crash. When the bombs descended to earth from parachutes, one of them came apart on impact, scattering radioactive debris all around the site. The other came down in a tree. "When that happened, five of the bomb's six safety switches released."

Kathy glanced at Trish. "What would have happened if the last switch had released?"

"Well, you could have kissed a good chunk of North Carolina goodbye. That bomb was hundreds of times more powerful than the one they dropped on Hiroshima." She let out a breath. "Hell, the Hiroshima bomb is considered a low yield, *nominal* bomb."

"Good God, Patty, I've never heard *anything* like this before."

Trish held out her hand. "See what I mean? These things should be common knowledge, and they're not. And what about all the other incidents and accidents the military's keeping secret because of so-called national security? You can bet your ass those are a lot worse than what happened at Goldsboro. And I seriously doubt they're too 'sensitive.' My guess would be they're just too embarrassing, and the public wouldn't put up with it, if they knew the truth." She took a deep breath. "God, I think once a government takes up nuclear weapons and energy it *has* to start lying to its citizens. The truth would just be too unacceptable to them."

"Jeez, Patty...you've got to *tell* people about this."

"If I can ever figure out how, I'm going to do my best." Trish rubbed her jaw line. "Because I don't think people have any idea of the vast amounts of radiation that have been unleashed on the planet since the 1940s…or just what that exposure has done, and *is* doing to us as a species."

Trish looked over at Kathy and shifted her tone. "Do you remember when we were kids and I went out to New Mexico with my family?"

"Yeah." Kathy grinned. "I've gotta' tell you, I was jealous as hell that I couldn't go, too."

"Be glad you didn't." Trish proceeded telling her friend how during that vacation, atmospheric testing was going on in the southwestern U.S. and how she suspected it had affected her. Then she added, "And see, our parents didn't have any idea back then that there was anything dangerous going on."

Kathy reached across the seat and laid her hand gently on her friend's. "Patty, do you really think that's why you never got pregnant?"

"Who knows?" Trish answered almost flippantly. She looked out the window.

Kathy sighed. "Well, at least we didn't grow *up* anywhere near that bomb testing."

"But, Kathy," Trish began, looking back at her, "the jet stream carried the stuff right to us…right through North Georgia and across the country. We didn't escape anything. In fact, we probably got a heavier dose back in the '50s and '60s because we were living in the path of the prevailing jet stream currents. And here our parents were encouraging us to drink milk to stay healthy. They didn't know Strontium 90 was being carried up into our bones along with the calcium, and that it'd stay there till the day we die, releasing tiny amounts of poisons into our systems."

"Is that what was happening?" Kathy was wide-eyed with disbelief.

"I'm afraid so…and I've just become aware of that in the last few months. And that's the whole point. Because these things are undetectable, you're not aware of the dangers."

"But don't they do studies to determine that kind of thing?" she asked as they pulled into the parking lot of the antique mall.

"Yeah," Trish replied, "but the ones generally paying for them are the polluters themselves…or the government. And *they're* in the back pockets of big industry. You know they aren't going to provide evidence of a smoking gun for someone to use against them, or sue them." Trish tilted her head and gestured with her hand. "Don't you know about studies they've come out with in the news that don't make any common sense? I mean, did you ever believe those tobacco industry studies they did years ago that said smoking was safe?"

Kathy unbuckled her seat belt and took her keys from the ignition, holding them in her hand a moment. "And you know—come to think of it— they have this one study that pops up every now and then about how kids don't really get hyper from eating too much sugar. And, hell, every mother alive knows *that's* a damn lie." Kathy looked curiously at Trish, and asked, "You mean that it would probably be someone with an interest in the sugar or candy industry that would come out with a finding like that?"

"Most likely. Or by someone with some other vested interest in the outcome."

With an indignant expression, Kathy stated, "Well, all I know is that the guy who came out with *that* one ought to have to spend a day locked in a room full of kids on a sugar high." Then her expression changed completely to one of girlish curiosity as she coyly commented, "But, back to this romance of yours."

Trish threw back her head and laughed. "Kathryn Dunnigan, you're incorrigible. I can't believe I've kept you off that subject this long."

They exited the car and went and browsed through the mall as Kathy prodded her friend for details about her budding romance. They joked and laughed as they walked along. Then, after another stop at a clothes boutique, Kathy drove her friend home.

Trish thanked her for getting her out for a breath of fresh air, and admitted how much she'd really needed it. As Trish watched her back out of the driveway, she felt a sense of gratitude that Kathy had always seemed like a breath of fresh air. And she realized that it was her friend's candidness, prodding and confidence that had helped determine the direction her life had taken in the previous months.

But she wasn't sure she wanted to thank her for all of those changes. Not just yet.

Chapter Eighteen

After days of having little success at grasping any new insights from her studies of mythology, Trish returned her attention to Australia. Research into facts and figures was something she could grasp. Just as she had months before with the subject of Russia, she began at the campus library in Athens. Even though she could have used any number of sources, there was something about being surrounded by books that always appealed to her. Even the smell of a library heightened her sense of anticipation about uncovering some missing link to a story which might tie a dozen loose ends together.

After gathering a number of books on the continent's history, culture and mythology, and even one on tourism, she found a secluded spot with a lot of table room, and pulled the book on tourism from the stack. As soon as she opened it she felt captivated by Australia; the pictures alone would have been enough. The sight of the unique flora and fauna, which had evolved without contact with the rest of the world for so many millennia, made it seem steeped in wildness and mystery.

First on her agenda was deciding when to go to Australia. That fact would determine how much time she'd have to devote to her research before leaving. In the book she discovered that the land was not only "down under," but in some ways, opposite from the U.S. Australians drove on the opposite side of the road. Because the continent was south of the equator, water—everything from sink water to cyclones—spun in the opposite direction than it did in the Northern Hemisphere. And when it came to climates, their seasons were also opposite. Their southern areas were temperate, whereas their northern areas were tropical—complete with monsoon seasons. Since it was the Northern Territory where Trish planned to go, she focused on weather conditions there.

She quickly determined that April and September were the best months to travel there; those were the in-between months—in between the "wets" and the "dries," as they were called. Traveling was quite limited during the wet periods of monsoon flooding that inundated valleys and lowlands. Then after those storms subsided, the rivers began a slow retreat. As they dried up, pockets of lakes and ponds called billabongs were left behind, which became havens for all types of wildlife, and especially crocodiles. The dries, on the other hand, seemed just as oppressive as the wets. The heat and lack of rainfall turned that part of the country into a scorched, barren land that would show little mercy to any hapless person who might find himself stranded away from civilization during that period.

Since it was the months in between the wets and dries that Trish needed to target for her trip to the Northern Territory, and since she felt that leaving in September wouldn't give her enough time to prepare thoroughly, she began focusing on the month of April for her departure.

With that decision made, she relaxed. She could study about the land and the history of the continent at a more leisurely pace.

Still scanning the book on tourism, Trish also began formulating the semblance of an itinerary. It didn't take her long to decide that her first destination would be the city of Sydney. As long as she could remember, she'd associated Australia with that city. The pictures of the Opera House's architectural "sails" on the skyline of Sydney Harbor made it even more appealing and magnetic. Max's "little cushion," and his encouragement to take a vacation from the work, would give her some opportunities she hadn't had in Kazakhstan. She also wanted time to get a feel for the continent, to talk to the people and get to know more about the land and its customs and attitudes toward the environment before getting to the heart of the research in the Northern Territory.

She let out a sigh. And thank goodness they spoke the same language and she wouldn't have to constantly rely on an interpreter.

After about a week in Sydney, she'd fly north to Darwin, and from there, she'd drive to Kakadu to learn about the environmental battle between the uranium miners and the Aborigines.

Though she'd been mildly aware that the Aborigine inhabitants hadn't fared well under the influence of white Europeans, it wasn't until Trish opened the second book that she began learning to her dismay of the extent of that cultural upheaval. Like the Native Americans, the Aborigines were at first a curiosity, then a nuisance, and then an obstacle to the invaders. Very quickly they had been relegated to a subhuman category—savages—seemingly unworthy of the basic considerations afforded to the rest of humanity. And just like the Native Americans in North America, they had no resistance to European diseases.

As Trish sat with her head propped on her hand, she read how the Aborigines had died by the thousands. They would have died from European diseases even if the white invasion had been totally peaceful, which she found it was not. She felt dismayed as she read the account of the tumultuous settlement of the island of Tasmania. The entire race of Tasmanians was wiped out, leaving them extinct.

She marked the page she was reading and stared across the expansive, quiet room, trying to recall any other account of an ethnic cleansing that had been so quick or so complete. She couldn't. As she returned to the book and continued to read, each new anecdotal account emphasizing the injustices inflicted on the native people in the early days of European settlement left her more disheartened.

Trish let out a long breath, then, stretching her bent arms up, she arched her back in the chair and slumped back down again. Why did it always have to be like that? Why did indigenous population have to be conquered or killed or assimilated or banished? It was all too familiar. Even predictable. *God, doesn't it just get **boring** after a while?*

Trish closed that book and went to a third. There she read that the Aborigine race itself was unique in the world, in fact, so much so that it had to be classified as totally separate from other races. The people were ultimately labeled "Australoids," and—as with the flora and fauna—once they had been labeled or categorized, they seemed to lose some of their mystery. The more Trish read about Australia and the Aborigines, however, the more she doubted that either the people or the continent were capable of being defined in European or white terms, that they existed on their own terms, and that to define them or label them was to devalue them. She wondered if they could ever be fully understood from an outside perspective.

She closed the book and stacked them all together to check out at the desk. She'd finish the research at home. The wooden chair was becoming as uncomfortable as some of the material inside the books.

● ● ●

The next day, when Trish called Max to share the information she was accumulating, he related a strange story about the European discovery of the duckbill platypus. He explained that the professionals in England—and scientists in particular—didn't believe that such a creature existed when the settlers wrote home about it. "They knew that it was totally ludicrous," he told her, "an animal with a bill like a duck and fur like a mammal, and one that laid eggs, yet suckled its young." The scientists were quite certain that someone was trying to pull a joke at their expense. Such a creature was impossible in the world of biology.

But, the stories persisted until someone from Australia finally shipped a specimen of a dead platypus to England. "Even then the scientists claimed it was a hoax. They announced that someone had stitched or glued body parts together to come up with the freakish creature, and that as reputable scientists, they weren't going to let themselves be taken in by such an obvious hoax."

"Yeah, Max, that's just what I thought people might believe about that mermaid."

After hanging up, Trish realized that Max hadn't told the story simply for entertainment purposes. He was trying to convey how much time it took for anomalies in nature to become "real" to the rest of the world.

When Trish returned to her books, it became clear that many of the beliefs of the Aboriginal people were still scoffed at by modern man. The creatures of the continent—unbelievable as they were—were impossible to deny any longer, but she knew that unseen belief systems were not. Even the anthropologists, whose works she perused, gave the Aboriginal tales of the "Dreamtime" about as much credence as children's bedtime stories. They were taken in an entertaining, but otherwise light manner. They certainly weren't given the same respect as even Old World mythologies.

Yet, they intrigued Trish. She was finding herself more open-minded about every possibility in life since her trip to Kazakhstan. And she remembered what Max had told her about the primitive cultures of the world telling their myths as though they were real, not just symbolic. Maybe Australoid myths of Dreamtime were only as impossible as the platypus.

• • •

As Trish curled up with her books on her sofa one morning, she focused on the city of Darwin, and discovered it a fascinating study all by itself. A city of about 70,000 people, it was located on the very northern tip of the continent on the Timor Sea. It was named after the famous botanist, Charles Darwin, who'd based some of his best-known studies on research of the continent. In every account she read about the city it was described as isolated...isolated from the rest of the country—not even in a state of its own—but a territory, closer geographically to some Asian cities than to Sydney.

The attitude of the people toward their parent government was described as feeling like a stepchild, who at times was ignored and abandoned, or when not ignored, abused. Their isolation was political, geographical, social and environmental. Not many modern cities were surrounded by dinosaurs.

Still, from what Trish read, the people of Darwin had developed a healthy respect for and a peaceful co-existence with the crocodiles. They had enacted laws to protect them from hunters, and simply captured the occasional wandering "crocs" that turned up in areas zoned for people and carried them off to crocodile farms to entertain the tourists.

It didn't seem as easy for them to adjust to their geographical and political isolation. And it didn't appear that the feeling was born of paranoia, either. Trish was surprised when she read that Darwin was the only Australian city attacked and bombed during World War II. During sixty-four forays, over two hundred people had been killed. The city had been evacuated a number of times during that period, and the scars from the attacks remained on the city's buildings for years after the war. Trish assumed that many of those scars must have been as much psychological as physical.

Trish closed the book she was reading, went to the kitchen window and stared out of it. She thought about her future relationship with Jimmy Hartwell. And she thought about a future career choice. She sighed, feeling overwhelmed with the number of basic changes she had to resolve and deal with all at one time in her life. Yet she sensed that all of the issues were interconnected somehow.

She glanced back at the pile of books, realizing that the more she focused on Australia, the more she felt drawn to it. It was like a giant magnet whose power to attract her increased exponentially the more she gave herself over to it. Clearly, this was the direction in which her energy was going. It wasn't that she didn't care as much about Jimmy or a career; it was just that she sensed from some deeper level that she'd never be able to have a complete relationship with him, or anyone else, or be happy in any profession until she resolved in her mind the issues that had been raised in Semipalatinsk.

It was just that simple.

● ● ●

When it came to Jimmy Hartwell, Trish felt she was constantly juggling conflicting emotions. Whatever excitement she experienced was always tempered with a mixture of apprehension. And though their romance was on a fast track, she still vividly remembered the years of emotional pain she had suffered as a result of their break-up...or lack thereof. She both dreaded and anticipated the talk she knew was going to have to take place sooner or later: the talk about their past and about their future.

That talk with him wasn't long in coming.

One night, after she'd put away her books and turned off her computer, Jimmy showed up at her house. The sight of him walking through the kitchen door excited her, and yet filled her with tension. She sensed from his body language and the look on his face that their conversation wasn't going to be small talk. Soon after they settled into their seats, Jimmy picked up the remote control from the side table and pointed it at the television. "Do you mind if I turn it off?"

"No." She turned toward him. "What's up?"

He switched off the television. "Trish, we've got to talk."

"Okay," she responded. She could feel a tightening sensation in the pit of her stomach.

He took a breath and let it out slowly before saying, "Well, I've been doing an awful lot of thinking. And what I've come up with is this." He inched forward in his seat and reached over and touched the side arm of her chair and looked directly at her. "I want you in my life...not just for a while, but from now on...however long that may be. I've always wanted you with me, and that's the only thing I'm sure about right now."

Trish took a short breath, about to respond, but before she could, he quickly added, "I think I might have been trying to hold on to you too tightly when we were kids, and that may have been what drove you away. I didn't want to give you enough breathing room, and you felt smothered. I know you need your freedom to be your own person and do the things that are important to you."

Trish could feel the tension in her stomach easing slightly.

"Trish, I *want* you to be your own person. I've realized that that's one of the things that fascinate me about you—that fire and passion you've always had about life. I want you to continue doing your own thing...but I want to be a part of your life, too. I want a commitment. It's that simple." He leaned back in his seat. "Maybe I lost you once because I couldn't love you with an open hand...or I was too proud and impatient. I didn't know how to love anyone at that age...but I think I do now. And if I don't entirely, then, damn it, I'll learn. But I don't want to lose you again."

Though Trish was glad to hear what Jimmy was saying, she felt content with their relationship as it was. The idea of marrying a man who'd been married and divorced three times didn't inspire her with confidence and had weighed on her heavily in some of the quiet times between their meetings. Unsure of how to respond, she blurted out, "Look, I'm not leaving till April, so we have plenty of time to talk about this."

"What? *Leave*? For where?"

She knew by the tone in his voice and the look on his face that it had been a mistake to wait this long to tell him about her plans to go to Australia. She wondered briefly why she hadn't already told him about something of such significance.

"I'm going to Australia in April."

"*Australia*? You're not planning to go there for *good*, are you?"

"No, of course not...I don't know..." And then with conviction, she finished, "I mean—no, no...of *course* not."

"Man, I didn't think you were going to put me to the test *this* quick."

His voice had a hint of testiness to it that Trish couldn't avoid noticing, but as his voice trailed off, she realized that she was saying all the wrong things, and in the wrong order. So she stopped, took a deep breath, straightened the sleeves of her shirt, and began again. "Jimmy, look, we *do* have a lot to talk about. I haven't begun to tell you what's going on with me professionally."

The look of confusion on his face made her realize that she was simply making things worse. "Look, I haven't been as happy in years as I have these last weeks. I guess I didn't want to put a damper on our happiness. I haven't felt like this since we were in high school...but I'm scared, too. And on top of that I've been dealing with some kind of short term depression and a lot of conflicting emotions...too many to handle at the same time."

"Trish..."

"No, Jimmy, let me say this." She held up her hand, then continued, "It devastated me, too, when we went our separate ways. I don't think I ever really got over it. I threw myself into my work, and in the end I realized that the career wasn't going to satisfy me through the rest of my life. There's this part of me that wants to throw myself into your arms and stay there...but there's this other part of me that still wants to go out and...and find the meaning of life and figure it all out." She held a hand out. "I mean, I spent years looking for that story of the decade. And all of a sudden I feel like I may have stumbled onto the story of the *millennium*, and I don't know what to do with it. I'm overwhelmed. But I know I won't be satisfied if I don't follow it to its end."

She reached over and laid her hand lightly on his forearm and looked at him pleadingly. "Jimmy, this commitment thing. I want it, too, but I feel so unstable right now," she added. "There are too many changes in my life, and I feel off balance and vulnerable." She raised an eyebrow. "Truthfully, it's the first time I've ever felt like this."

He leaned forward and touched her hand. "Look," he said tenderly, "we won't go too fast with this thing. I'm scared myself. Hell...I'm a three time loser." As she nodded in agreement, he added, "I'm not going to put any pressure on you before you're ready. I haven't asked you a thing about that night when you cried so long about your trip to Russia."

Trish grinned slightly. "I know. And I appreciate that, but I guess it's time to tell you what happened."

"Listen," Jimmy began, shifting his mood. "It's late tonight, and I've got to get some orders out in the morning, but I'll have the rest of the day off, and it's supposed to be beautiful tomorrow...and a little cooler. We could hike up Blood Mountain with a picnic lunch and talk." He smiled and added, "You know, like we used to do in high school. It's not a hard hike to the rock face, and we'll take it easy. What do you think?"

She smiled back. "Yeah, Jimmy, I'd like that. I need to get out of the house more than I have been lately."

"Then get your hiking boots ready," he said, slapping his thigh lightly, "and we'll get started around eleven. We'll stop by the deli and pick up sandwiches and drinks on the way."

Trish could tangibly feel the tension evaporate with his light-hearted suggestion, and she became acutely conscious that Jimmy had always had that kind of effect on her: to lift her spirits at just the right time, to comfort her when she needed it, to give her goose bumps by just walking into the room and looking at her. And to break her heart. And he still affected her almost thirty years later. She wondered if it was too much power to give over to any man.

• • •

The next morning it took almost an hour and a half to drive to Neil's Gap at the foot of Blood Mountain. It was Trish's favorite section of the Appalachian Trail in Georgia. As she climbed out of the truck, she glanced toward the sky. It was clear blue with hardly a cloud. They loaded their things into Jimmy's backpack, and Trish turned toward the trail and breathed in the fresh mountain breezes with an appreciation that the heat had subsided significantly. "You were right. It *is* a beautiful day."

"Yeah, the Indians would say it's a good day to die," he said, smiling.

She tilted her head and smiled back. She remembered how he'd often said that when they were in high school.

They took their time hiking up the mountain because of Trish's still fragile condition, and made several stops to rest and admire the scenery. When they finally reached the rock face where they'd spent so much time during their months of dating, they walked out over the top of it to a broad sloped area and spread a blanket out in an area partially sheltered by the shade of several pine trees. Trish was relieved that there weren't any other hikers around, and that they'd have some privacy for their talk. Breezes had started blowing lightly, which helped to soothe and mellow her state of mind.

After lunch, which included light conversation, they laid back on the blanket to relax and enjoy the solitude. Trish was keenly aware that Jimmy hadn't questioned her at all and was apparently leaving it up to her to select the right moment to address the subject from the night before.

She pulled herself up to a sitting position, and began telling her story about Kazakhstan and the things she'd seen and experienced there, and about her subsequent plans to go to Australia. Jimmy listened quietly. The only time he interrupted her was when he had questions about a technical issue or needed more information. At one point she showed him some of the pictures from the clinic. He shuffled through them and—except for closing his eyes briefly a few times—without expression.

Trish still had difficulty trying to control her emotions as she related parts of the story. She looked away from him and stopped a few times to wipe away tears at the recollection of those more sensitive memories, especially the one about Ilyani.

When she'd finally finished her accounting, she turned to him directly and added, "So you see, I can't just walk away from this story and act as though none of this happened to me. I don't know why it happened to me, but it did. And I can't go on with my life as though it didn't. I *have* to pursue it. That's just how I am. I have to go to Australia…and wherever else this might lead."

He allowed a few moments to pass, then leaned the weight of his torso on his right arm and said, "Well, this is pretty heavy stuff, Trish. I'm not sure what to say exactly, but it does give me a lot better idea of what you've been going through, and how you've been acting. It's had me stumped a few times."

She looked down. "I guess I should have told you about this sooner...but I just didn't feel like I was ready. Max and Peggy and Kathy were easier to talk to because it wasn't going to affect my relationship with them."

Jimmy sat up and wrinkled his brow. "What makes you think it's going to affect *our* relationship?"

"Well, it has everything to do with the direction my life is taking...with my career, and I think my personal life, too."

"Look, Trish" he began, "I really think we're on the same wavelength here. When you get back and get finished with this story, maybe then we can start focusing more on just 'us.'"

"Jimmy, I don't know what I'll find over there or what else it might lead to. Besides, I'd say we've been focusing quite a bit on each other already, wouldn't you?"

"Well, sure, but it'll just be nice when you don't always have your nose in a book or when you're not banging away at your computer all the time."

She turned toward him. What did he mean by that? She'd just explained what she was doing and why, and why it was so important to her. Her face was still damp from tears. She didn't have any idea how long the search would take or how far she might have to go for answers. "Is this that philosophy thing about life?" she finally asked.

"Huh?"

"You know, your philosophy about just living your life and not worrying about what makes things tick."

He shrugged his shoulders. "No...I just meant it'll be nice when we have more time for each other, when you don't have all these distractions going on."

"Is that what you think this is? Distractions?" Before he had a chance to answer, she added, "Look, if I needed distractions, I could think of a lot cheaper, easier and less painful ways of doing it." She couldn't hide the strident tone in her voice. She got up and faced the forested vista for a moment with her arms crossed and then sat back down, facing him. "Jimmy, do you find what I just told you the least bit interesting?"

"Of course I do, Trish."

"Do you find it *fascinating*?"

"Well, yeah, sure. I guess I just don't know if you'll ever find the answers you're looking for...and...well...you seem more committed to this thing than you are to us."

So there it was. He saw her work…no…her passion as competition. Had they come full circle? Were they right back where they left off years before when she wanted to go to college to pursue a career before marriage, and he wanted to get married straight out of high school? Was he going to run again, if she didn't fully commit to him over the other things that were important to her?

She ran her fingers through her hair. "Well, Jimmy, I guess we're making progress. We're barely into this relationship again and we've already got issues." She half laughed and stood up again and stretched her legs. "Maybe we'd better head back to Clayton. The temperature seems to be heating up again."

He reached up and touched her arm. "I'm not trying to push you, Trish. I just want you back in my life."

"I'm *in* your life, Jimmy. Haven't you noticed?"

He stood up and kissed her lightly on the temple. "Yeah, I noticed."

As they walked back down the mountain, she felt as though she was seeing an old pattern emerging. Maybe the events in her personal life *were* cyclic. But how could she change them? If she continued pursuing her passions in life, would he abandon her again? How could she trust the relationship? Why did she have to make a choice between him and her real self?

And, if it was true what Max said about the story ultimately being about her, then how did any of this relate to Clinic Number Four?

The questions came and went in her head all the way back to Clayton. But the answers eluded her.

Chapter Nineteen

During a trip to the square in Clayton one afternoon the next week, Trish stopped by the drugstore to pick up a few items. On her way out, she glanced up after retrieving her keys from her purse and saw someone who looked a lot like Mary Ann Parker. It had been a long time since she'd seen her, and she wasn't sure if it was her. She started to continue on, but thought briefly about Max and his "no such thing as a coincidence" comment. "Mary Ann?" she called out.

The woman turned around, looked at her and beamed a smile. "Trish! Why, Trish Cagle." She walked toward Trish and the two of them embraced briefly. "I haven't seen you in ages."

"Not since the last class reunion I don't think," Trish responded.

"Well, how've you been? I heard from Kathy that you just got back from…Russia, wasn't it?"

"Yeah, Kazakhstan."

"Well, how was it?"

"Hmm," Trish began, lowering her eyes and half smiling. She looked back up at Mary Ann. "I'd like to talk to you about that if you've got a few minutes."

Mary Ann didn't hesitate. "Well, sure, Trish. I don't have a thing on my schedule this afternoon." She looked skyward and squinted her eyes, as she shielded them. "But why don't we get out of this heat?"

A few minutes later the two of them sat in a booth at the Clayton Square Café drinking soft drinks and eating fries, while Trish filled Mary Ann in on some of the highlights of her trip, focusing mainly on the incident with Ilyani. "Kathy said that you might know something about Indigo children, or something like that."

"Well…yeah. I've read one book about them."

"Yeah?"

Mary Ann shifted back in her seat. "Yeah. But I don't think that's what you ran into in Kazakhstan."

"No?"

"No. It sounds more to me like that little girl might have been one of the Psychic children."

"Psychic children?"

"That's what they're being called. I've been getting material from friends recently about these special kids being born around the world who seem to have this incredible power, like they're just so full of love and compassion that they exude it to everyone around them…lift everybody's spirit just by being there."

Trish's eyes widened. She fidgeted in her seat and leaned forward. "Mary Ann, I can't begin to explain how that little girl affected me. She just touched me, and everything inside me sort of glowed and vibrated." She leaned back. "Love? Hmm. I don't know if that was what I felt or not." She tilted her head. "Maybe it was...and I couldn't tell if it came from her or if she just awakened something that was already inside me...dormant, maybe. But there was definitely some kind of energy exchange. It was palpable. My interpreter, Katrina, told me that not everyone was affected by her, and that some people were actually afraid of her."

"Hmm. It sounds as though you were just open to her at that moment."

"Maybe." Trish took a drink, then asked, "But what's this psychic thing?"

"Well, that may be why some people were afraid of her. These kids seem to know things before they happen...like they have a connection to people's thoughts and to the future." Trish raised her eyebrows, and Mary Ann asked, "Trish, do you know anything about quantum physics?"

She half laughed before answering, "No, science was never a field I was that interested in."

"Well, it's quite complex. I struggle with it myself. But there was a movie out a few years ago called <u>Mindwalk</u>, that you might want to take a look at. It tried to explain it in layman's terms." Mary Ann finished the last of her soft drink, and leaned forward on her forearms. "See, Trish, scientists know from mathematical models that matter is made up of vast regions of empty space."

"You mean not solid."

"Well, no. Picture a hydrogen atom." Mary Ann gestured with her hands. "It has one proton nucleus and one electron. If you enlarge the atom so that the proton is the size of a golf ball, the electron is one football field away. Everything else between is empty space. The electron moving around the nucleus is moving at incredible speeds...roughly at the speed of light."

"What keeps it from flying off? What holds it together?"

"Some kind of energy maybe. I think of it as a life force...maybe different than other energies. I believe it's what Eastern cultures refer to as chi or prana. They've known about this life force for untold centuries, and use it in medicine." She told Trish that Eastern cultures believed that anything that disrupted the life force affected a person's health because everything was connected by it. "It surrounds and penetrates everything." She leaned back. "I think of it in terms of a God force."

Trish propped her chin on her fist as Mary Ann continued. "To me it's as though nothing *exists* without everything else. If you think of life in those terms, then being psychic, or knowing about something or connecting to something on the other side of the globe or with someone else's thoughts or emotions is really just a natural phenomenon...one we just don't use consciously. These kids come into the world using it. I've read that they talk to people with their minds and don't understand when people don't 'hear' them, because *they* hear other peoples' *thoughts*. So the school systems end up labeling them with A.D.D."

"A.D.D.?"

"Attention Deficit Disorder, or some other learning disability, and then they put them on drugs, and the kids get *really* messed up." Mary Ann explained what a brutal time the children had trying to function within the educational system and in the world in general because they couldn't be who they are. "At least not in this culture. I read that some are cloistered in monasteries in places around the world."

"Katrina said something about that, too," Trish commented. "China and Japan, wasn't it?"

"Yeah, and I heard of a place in Bulgaria...Tibet, too, I think. I believe the Chinese and Mexican governments are actually working with these children, helping them to enhance their abilities. I'm afraid I can't give you a lot more information than that. I can get my hands on some articles though if you're interested."

"You bet I'm interested." Trish placed the palms of her hands on the table. "Well. This really has turned into quite an interesting little conversation. Could you send me some of that material?"

"Oh, sure." She retrieved a pen and paper from her purse and wrote down Trish's address. "I'll get it to you right away."

She put the paper back in her purse and looked up and smiled. "Say, didn't I hear somewhere that you and Jimmy Hartwell are dating again?"

Trish's eyes widened, and then she half smiled herself, closed her eyes and shook her head from side to side. Well, well. Kathy hadn't been simply talking about *Russia* to Mary Ann Parker.

• • •

The material from Mary Ann arrived in Trish's mail two days later. She read through it after lunch and found mention of a child who was communicating psychically through a man in the U.S. They were simple messages about love, compassion and enlightenment, which said that being loving was man's true nature and that humanity was at a critical juncture of choosing love or fear. They encouraged people to open their hearts and allow love to flow in and out, to become as children and learn to pretend again. They said that children's pretense became their truth because of the purity of their faith and belief. People were encouraged to pretend the truth of love within and remember who they truly are.

Another article reported that there were thousands of these children around the globe working together in unison with this simple message of love. Trish set the material down. Just months before, she would have thought it was all too childish and simplistic to waste time reading. But during the reading she'd begun having some of the same sensations she'd experienced months before in the small Kazakh village with a mud covered little girl on a gray, rainy day.

Almost afraid to move, she sat quietly on the sofa for a long time while a warm inner glow began filling her. She wondered how long she could hold on to it.

After a few minutes the phone rang, jolting her out of her reverie.

● ● ●

"Hello?"

"Patty?" Kathy's voice sounded sheepish.

"Yeah."

"Were you asleep? You sound like you just woke up."

"No…no. I was just reading some material I got from Mary Ann Parker, and I guess I got sort of zoned."

"Oh, you saw her?"

"Yeah…yesterday. I ran into her on the square." Trish filled Kathy in on their discussion, about the material, and about her outing with Jimmy. "Jeez, Kathy," she lamented, "what if Jimmy and I are just back where we were in college? God, I don't see much future for us if we are."

"Why not? You're both several decades older and have a lot more insights and experiences and resources to work with than you did when you were kids."

"Yeah, but the dynamics are the same. He wants me to give up who I am…what I do. One minute he says he can love me with an open hand and admires my passion, and the next he's squeezing me to hurry up and get it over. He sees this story as competition. And, Kathy, I just don't see how things are going to change this time, either."

Kathy exhaled deeply over the phone, and said, "Patty, if you don't think things can change, then why the *hell* are you wasting your time on this story?"

"What do you mean by that?" she bristled.

"Why are you even bothering to try to bring this information to the attention of the public?" She told her it wouldn't matter, anyway, if collective and personal patterns of behavior couldn't change. "Good God, Patty this thing you're doing is all about changing outcomes…showing people they've got a different choice—maybe lots of them—that they aren't bound by the past, that they can change their future, right now."

Before Trish could respond, Kathy continued, "Do you think *you* haven't been changed by what you experienced in Kazakhstan? Hell, *I've* been changed just listening to you. What good is all the information in the *world* if people can't do something with it? Is that who you thought your readers were all those years? A bunch of sheep? Are you trying to entertain or scare them? Or are you trying to motivate and inspire them?"

Trish leaned her head back on her seat and took a deep breath. *God*, Kathy liked kicking her butt. And damn it, she was right.

"Kathy, that's the same thing Max said when he told me that using fear for my main focus wouldn't work."

"Well, I get a little overwhelmed with the things you tell me sometimes myself, but I know there's *got* to be something we can do about all of it."

"Sometimes I wish I had your optimism…and your aim."

"My aim?"

"Yeah. Every time you kick my ass, you always hit your target."

Chapter Twenty

After another week passed Trish set up another meeting with Peggy. Before leaving the house, she gave herself enough time to call Mark Matheson and fill him in on her experiences in Kazakhstan, and on what she'd been doing since her return. Though he didn't know of any environmentalists she could contact in Australia, he suggested she contact the Greenpeace offices there.

For their meeting that day, Peggy had suggested Trish join her in a forested area north of Gainesville, where she had planned to take a break from her job and activist role by taking photographs in an area near the banks of the Tesnatee River. Peggy suggested combining the interview with the outing, not only to save time, but because she thought Trish might enjoy brushing up on her own photography skills.

Trish welcomed the chance. During her career, she'd been required on numerous occasions to get spontaneous shots on her own. Though she'd taken a few photography classes and had good equipment, she realized that photography was an art form; either a person had a special talent for it or they didn't. After viewing Peggy's work on the wall of her living room before she went to Kazakhstan, she'd realized that Peggy had that special talent. Even following behind Peggy and snapping pictures in the same vicinity, Trish knew Peggy's eye would see something that hers hadn't.

It was the same way that Peggy had seen the correlation between underground nuclear blasts and earthquakes that hardly anyone else had noticed.

The two women met late in the morning at a cut-off from a gravel road near the river. Dressed in boots and long cotton pants for protection from poison ivy, they hiked into the woods to a spot where a number of shoals skimmed noisily over the rocky shallows. After pulling out their cameras, they began snapping pictures as they walked.

After about an hour of taking pictures, the two of them settled on a couple of fold out mats for lunch. When they had finished their meal and small talk, Trish pulled her recorder out of her pack. Before she turned it on, she dropped her arm. "You know, I can't get over what a coincidence it was that you told me about that atomic priesthood thing and its connection to Aborigine oral traditions, and now that's where I'm going next."

"Yeah, pretty weird, huh?" Peggy responded.

"Well...maybe," Trish responded as she retrieved her pad and pen. "Max Rogers has just about convinced me there's no such thing as a coincidence."

"I tell you," Peggy agreed, "I'm to that point, too. I've had so many things happen to me since I got into the environmental movement that I can't explain away with logic anymore. Sometimes it's too much coincidence, you know?"

"I think so." Trish related Max's comments about Carl Jung and his thoughts on meaningful coincidence, or "synchronicity." "I think I'm beginning to get it on a personal level now. I've had this incredible feeling that some things that have happened to me the last few months—as bad as some of them were—have been guided or directed, and have had a deeper meaning." She couldn't remember going through so much change in such a short time before. "And the weird thing is—even though I feel overwhelmed at times—it feels so right."

Peggy dusted off the knees of her jeans. "Trish, you were just *ready* for a change, just like I was when *I* started. I couldn't keep quiet about the safety violations at that plant any longer."

Trish looked up from her pad and pen. "Well, let's get this show on the road." She clicked on the recorder, turned to Peggy, and asked, "If an atomic priesthood *were* formed, what kind of information would be handed down? How would it be disseminated? And how would that information protect humanity from radiation in the future?

Peggy shifted to a more comfortable position and cleared her throat. "First of all, it would be critical to be absolutely honest with future generations and tell them straight out that we'd fucked up, that we'd made a terrible mistake—maybe with the best of intentions—and that, unfortunately, they're going to have to pay for those mistakes."

She said that all of the known contaminated sites would have to be identified and marked. They'd have to attempt some kind of containment of the affected sites with the hope that one day they'd be able to find a technology to neutralize the radiation. "Obviously, the sarcophagus at Chernobyl isn't working."

She told Trish about government plans for an underground repository out West to store some of the nuclear wastes. "Thing is, it's not safe and won't even begin to hold it all. *And* it'll be obsolete before it's finished because they're not even slowing down with *producing* the waste." She said eventually the government would have to continue siting other repositories. Consequently, they'd also have to transport highly hazardous nuclear material every day from then on, some of it near and through highly populated, major cities. She held her hands out in front of her. "This is a *solution*?"

"I've heard something about that."

Peggy said that when the crypts were full, the buildings at the complex would be torn down and warnings left to keep future generations away from the site. "They've toyed with several ideas...like a field of huge metal spikes to deter people from going near the place, or sculptures with scary images.

"And they plan to leave warnings in several languages, which is pretty pointless, since they can't endure that far into the future. The only thing that *would* come close to reaching that far into the future *would* be some future atomic priesthood."

"But, it's what they propose to say in the warnings that gets me."

"And what's that?"

"Things like 'this is no place of honor,' and 'nothing valued is here.' Think about it. They dare to tell the future generations the truth, but they don't dare tell us the truth. We keep pumping out nuclear wastes like there's no tomorrow. And people won't know what the hell's going on till it's too late. Why do we always try to bury our mistakes?"

She sighed. "Oh, well."

She explained that radiation exposure wasn't the only thing that affected genetics. "Chemicals do, too." After she took a drink from her bottled water, Peggy told her about the thousands of chemicals being released into the environment worldwide, many of which were mutagenic and carcinogenic. She added with sarcasm, "And we wonder why the hell cancer rates are so high."

She took another drink and said that there was usually no evidence of an unsafe exposure until a cluster of unusual cancers or birth deformities showed up. By then, the culprit chemical or chemical soup may have already moved through the area months or even years before. "Talk about the perfect crime."

She swept a strand of hair back from her face. "It's just like those kids in Moscow with missing left forearms." Peggy also told Trish about a cluster of babies in England born without eyes, believed caused by pesticide exposure when the mothers were pregnant. There was a cluster of babies born without brains near the Mexican border where industrial pollution was incredibly high from chemicals such as benzene. "You'll find these clusters in places all over the world. It's like *we've* become the detection devices, instead of guinea pigs in laboratories and yellow canaries in the mines. It's not just the people in Kazakhstan."

"Trish," Peggy began as she shifted again, bending her knees and resting her arms on them, "it's important to remember that we're just on the front end of this disaster. That Cyclops you saw was only born a few years ago, years after the atmospheric tests stopped." She said that the effects of the atomic age—as bad as they were—were just beginning.

"You know," Trish began, leaning on her arm, "years ago I read somewhere that if there ever were a nuclear holocaust, cockroaches would survive very well. In fact, it was speculated they might become the dominant life force on earth."

"I remember reading something like that, too. It's something they have in their bodies that other species don't. Chitin, or something.

"Who knows? Maybe rats and cockroaches will inherit the earth."

"Rats?" Trish inquired.

"Yeah, I've heard that rats are somehow able to physically detect radiation when we can't." She took a deep breath. "But, the thing about the human mutants is that they'd likely become the warning signs for future generations." She explained that other Chernobyl-type accidents were almost inevitable in the future, with equipment at other plants worldwide continuing to get old and wear out. As that happened, deformities and mutants would develop around the worst contaminated areas, which might serve as a warning to stay out of those areas. "You know, 'Wherever you see cancer clusters or large numbers of mutants, stay away.'"

"Like at Clinic Number Four?" Trish asked, arching her eyebrows. Then she sat bolt upright, as Peggy's comment triggered another memory. "Peggy."

"What?"

"You know how I've been reading all this material on Greek mythology?"

"Yeah."

"Well, there was this one story about a Trojan named Aeneas, and after the Trojan Wars, he and his followers were sailing through the seas, looking for a place to settle and build a new city." She told Peggy how they came close to the place where Ulysses and his men had encountered the Cyclopes, and were almost killed by the monsters themselves. "Then the gods—or a prophet or someone—warned them to avoid the areas where the Cyclopes and harpies or sirens lived. I've got to go back and read that again. But it sounds like what you just said—avoiding areas where clusters of monsters or mutants live."

"Hmm..." Peggy intoned, "It does at that."

Trish stared off in the distance and rubbed the side of her face. "Why does it always seem to get back to Greek mythology? What in the world did they know that we've lost?"

Peggy picked up her camera and fiddled with it a minute and said, "Well, Trish, you know how myths and religions can get corrupted over the years. The versions we get may just have elements of truth in them; but you're starting to convince me that there's some kind of factual basis for them, too. And maybe it's not just Greek mythology. Maybe that's why you're headed for Australia. It could be that you might find similarities in some of those myths, too."

She told Peggy that, though she was finding common threads in the mythologies, she was still confused by them. "I mean, experts in the field really puzzle over the references to, say, Uranus burying his monster children in the earth as though they were actual people and then they take on characteristics of nature as though they weren't. Like when Uranus gets into a battle with his children, their weapons are natural forces like earthquakes, volcanoes and natural phenomena."

"Well, I'm not that familiar with specific mythologies." Peggy took another drink from her bottled water. "By the way, Trish—before I forget—I've been meaning to ask you if you heard about France's plans to conduct that series of nuclear tests in the Pacific."

"Yeah, I read about it."

"They'll be breaking a three year moratorium. Everybody is protesting it. Even their own people are opposed...almost two thirds of them. But, by golly, they're going to do it, anyway."

"What do you think will happen?" Trish flipped to a new page in her notepad.

Peggy stood up and stretched her back and looked up into the canopy of trees around them, as though searching for another photograph. "Oh, they'll set the bombs off, all right. They act like they're oblivious to the public outrage. But there's going to be a consequence."

"Earthquakes?"

"Of course," Peggy replied, looking back at Trish. "Just like science has taught us: no action without a reaction." She sat back down and told Trish about a vulcanologist in France from the Volcano Research Center who was warning that the tests could destabilize a submerged volcano in the atoll that had been inactive for around 9 million years. "I mean, that's all that atoll is anyway: the exposed top of a submerged volcano. And he says that if that happened, it could release huge amounts of radioactive pollution into the water and air, which is just common sense when you think about it."

"Is anyone paying attention to him?"

"Oh, yeah. A lot of people are. It's just not the ones who have the power to stop it. President Chirac sure as hell isn't listening." Peggy shook her head from side to side and talked about how baffled she was at the callousness of some national leaders toward environmental issues. She stretched again, and added that considering that the French government actually blew up the Greenpeace ship in New Zealand and killed a photographer to stop the protesting of their last series of nuclear tests, it was clear just how paranoid, insensitive and determined they were.

"I don't know how you keep from getting demoralized," Trish commented, as she momentarily set her notepad aside and propped her chin on her hand.

"I don't sometimes," Peggy replied. "That's why I'm out here with my camera today."

Trish dropped her hand and looked over at Peggy. "You know, it helps keep me from getting discouraged when I see people like you and Mark continuing on and on in the face of so much resistance—and such incredible odds."

"Oh, hell, I'm just stubborn," Peggy responded, smiling. "Besides, I figure my odds are better than they are with the Georgia lottery." Trish grinned, and Peggy added, "Speaking of help with information, Trish, there's this one activist I think you might want to get in touch with. She's quite a character. I didn't tell you about her before you went to Kazakhstan because she was out of the country then...to Australia."

Trish eyes grew large, as she sat up more erect.

Peggy snickered. "I thought that would get your attention. Her name is Gladys Hartley-O'Hara, and when I heard through the grapevine that she got back home last week, I immediately thought of you." She dusted some dirt off the side of her pants. "Maybe this is another one of your coincidences...except that her trip didn't have anything to do with the uranium mining. I think she was just visiting friends, or something. But she might be able to put you in touch with the right people who *are* involved in it. And she might give you a few helpful pointers with nuclear issues here in the States, since she's worked on them for years."

"Look, I need all the help I can get."

"Well, she's English, and has worked on nuclear issues for decades. Some people think she's somewhat eccentric. But then, people say that and lots worse about me. I'll dig out her number when we get back to the cars."

• • •

After chatting a while about their personal lives, Trish picked up her pad again, and said, "Peggy, back to this atomic priesthood a minute...what else would they do besides warning about the radiation and containing those areas? And what would be so difficult about finding some simple way of conveying the information, even if we couldn't communicate through language and symbols?"

"That's a good question." She told Trish that even with well-intentioned and dedicated oral traditionalists, relating the enormity of the dangers and identifying the contained areas would pose serious problems. She said that at one time there was thought given to some type of pictograms of a person breaking the seal on the containment. Then in the next picture the person would be seen dead. Then in the third he would be seen deteriorated to nothing but a skeleton. "But they had to abandon that idea."

"Why? That sure sounds like a lethal warning to me. What would be wrong with it?"

"Trish," Peggy answered, "some cultures read from right to left instead of left to right. Some future generation might read a pictogram like that backwards from what we'd intended, and think it meant that if they dug up their dead and exposed them to what's in the contained areas, they'd come back to life like magic."

Trish arched her eyebrows. "Oh, my gosh, I wouldn't have thought about that."

"You see? There are all kinds of problems with the warnings. And we can't say whether technology will advance in the future or collapse, so we can't depend on any mechanical device—like a Geiger counter—to warn people. But there is this one flower called a spiderwort that reacts to radiation by changing colors in its stamens."

"Really?"

"Yeah, it's been documented and everything." Peggy picked up her camera and looked through its lens back at the canopy of the trees she'd been studying before. "I grow them in my garden at home. You're supposed to be able to count the number of color changes and actually calculate the degree of radiation exposure." She set the camera back down without using it.

"I've never heard of that before."

"It's not such a surprising thing, really." Peggy related how scientists now know that plants have communication systems and are much more complex than they'd ever thought before. She reminded her that plant lovers had known for years that playing soothing music helped their plants grow, which suggested some form of hearing—or vibrational reception. "It's not much of a stretch from that to thinking they could detect earth or environmental changes. Some Indians say that before an earthquake there are different types of plants that will actually drop all of their leaves."

"You're kidding."

"What's so surprising about that?" she asked, shrugging her shoulders. "We recognize that some animals become agitated and run off right before an earthquake. Even some insects are supposed to be able to detect them."

Trish twisted her pen back and forth. "Kind of makes you wonder what we're missing out on when bugs and plants can detect things we can't, even with all of our sophisticated technology."

"Exactly, Trish. The difference is—I'm convinced—that we just aren't connecting with our own instincts the way the simplest of life forms are. Oh, there are a few 'earthquake sensitives' around the world, but they're not taken very seriously by society as a whole." Peggy held out her hands. "It's like we're making huge technological strides, but we're sacrificing our most basic instincts in the process…almost like we're evolving toward a more robotic form. And where is it taking us? I mean, think about it. We can't predict an earthquake with our most sensitive equipment, and a bug can. And we sure as heck can't stop one."

"You say we can't predict an earthquake." Trish tilted her head. "But you think we can *cause* one?"

"Oh, sure, when you can measure one of those atomic blasts on the Richter scale with the magnitude of an earthquake, of course we can. We don't have any trouble altering our environment, but the environment always reacts. It's that simple." As Trish took notes, Peggy told her that natural occurrences in the environment that people thought of as a disaster, like an earthquake or volcanic explosion, might merely be nature's way of evolving or possibly trying to heal itself, similar to an animal shaking off fleas when they become thick enough to start threatening their host. She also compared it to a place on a person's body erupting into a boil from some internal infection that needed to surface...or stretch marks on human skin during rapid growth stages, such as pregnancies.

"Then you believe earthquakes will follow the nuclear tests?" Trish asked.

"Wait and see. And, believe me; I take no pleasure in that fact."

Trish could feel one of her legs going to sleep and stood up and stamped it and shifted her weight back and forth from one leg to the other. Then she put her hands on her hips and said, "But, Peggy, you say that technologies may not survive into the future. What about that spiderwort plant? I've read that we're destroying species today at a rate never before in the history of mankind that we know of."

"Yeah, over a hundred a day."

"So who's to say that the spiderwort won't become extinct, too, and we'd lose that detection device?"

Peggy leaned forward. "You've just hit the nail on the head. That's a real possibility." She said that man might well be presently destroying plants which could help with cancer and a host of other diseases, even though it was known that plants were the medicine cabinets of the world. "And with all the new diseases cropping up nowadays that have no cures, we probably never needed them more."

She sat back up. "So, the spiderwort—or other plants with similar properties—would have to be, not only protected, but revered by the priesthood. If we lost those kinds of detection devices, the only warning system we'd have might be the mutants...or the monsters."

Peggy glanced at her watch. "Oh, my gosh, I didn't realize how late it was. We'd better wind this up for today. I've got a doctor's appointment this afternoon."

Trish checked her watch, too. "Holy Cow, I can't believe we've been here this long."

They quickly gathered the remnants of their picnic and their camera equipment, and walked back to their cars, where Peggy gave Trish the phone number for the English activist. After Trish thanked Peggy again for her help, Peggy mentioned that she'd be away on vacation for a couple of weeks.

"Well, have a great time. I guess I'll talk to you when you get back."

As she drove back toward Clayton, Trish thought the day had been productive. But she also felt that—as with all the other information she was accumulating—the more she learned, the more complex and challenging the puzzle was becoming.

Chapter Twenty-One

Shortly after breakfast one morning, and after going over her notes of the meeting with Peggy, Trish curled up on her sofa and called Max to fill him in on their conversation. As she sipped her second cup of coffee, she told him about the connection she'd made with the Aeneas myth, and then vented her frustrations over her continued confusion over the myths. "Max, I can't get a handle on it. I know you said some of the myths are different, but that's putting it mildly. I swear, I think if I read a hundred books on it, there'd be a hundred different versions...and some of them even contradict each other."

"Does that surprise you?"

"It sure does. Why? Shouldn't it?"

"Well, history is like that, too, you know." Trish could hear him inhaling on his pipe. "It's the same with myths...and religions, too, for that matter."

"But, Max, how do I know which ones to believe?"

"Why do you have to choose? Why can't they all be right? Or all wrong?"

"You're not helping me here," she stated flatly.

"Patty, my dear, I believe you've reached a barrier with the myths through which your logical mind can't pass." He told her he believed that the more she could release her logic, her expectations and her skepticism, the smoother the process would be for her.

"I don't know how to leave my logic behind." She propped her head on her fist. "I've relied on it too much and too long. And I'm not as raw and open as I was when I first got back. I've already started constructing defenses again."

"As long as you know that, they shouldn't be too difficult to penetrate." He let out a breath. "Also, I guess I'm really trying not to influence you too much." He said that since she had a perspective of the story that he didn't, he wanted her to preserve that uniqueness. "If you come to a fork in the road with your research, you'll need to decide for yourself which one to choose. You'll need to learn to listen to your heart and trust your own inner guidance."

She shook her head back and forth. "Oh, Max..."

He took a breath. "Look, Patty, stop focusing on the differences in the myths a moment. Focus on the similarities, and on the stories and aspects that make sense to you in relation to your own experiences. Why don't you break it down first? Tell me what you've learned about the Greek characters that resemble the mutants in the jars. Start with the Cyclopes."

She straightened her robe, cleared her throat and began, "Well, you see them in creation myths...sons of Gaia and Uranus. So I think they must have appeared in man's earliest developmental stages. In fact, in a lot of the creation myths, some of the first men are monsters or mutants. But then as time went on, men started developing and evolving toward the form we now know.

"Peggy says that makes sense when you think about life evolving in direct proportion to the cooling of radiation levels on the earth and in the atmosphere. She says that there would logically be some areas of hot spots as the cooling continued where you would see what we call mutants. Only as the cooling trend went on, man would evolve toward his present state, and what we think of as mutants would finally disappear."

"Hmm...interesting."

"But, Max, has man been on the planet that long?" she asked, and took another sip from her coffee.

"Who knows, Patty? Our knowledge in that area is limited to our present scientific findings. And we're constantly being forced to recast the mold in archeology. But go on. Don't let that stump you for now."

She let out a breath and continued, by telling him about the Cyclopes in later myths, such as the ones with Aeneas and Ulysses. "The thing is there seem to be colonies of them...and Peggy's been telling me about clusters of mutations that are showing up all over the world now. I saw this picture of kids in Moscow who were all missing their left forearms. There were dozens of them. And there was another cluster of babies without eyes. She's told me several stories like that. So the colonies of mutants in mythology sort of remind me of these modern day clusters that are cropping up."

Again, Max commented, "Interesting."

Trish told him what Peggy had said about man reversing the cooling process of radiation for the first time in recorded history and her assertion that that might be the reason behind the reappearance of mythical monsters on the planet.

"Well, Patty, you surprise me...and you don't seem to be unfocused at all." Max cleared his throat. "Now, go on. What about the mermaids?"

"Oh, the mermaids." She told Max how the mermaids were known as tritons in some myths, and were listed along with some of the inferior deities. "And that's about all I know about them generally—except that they were supposed to portend the future. There are worldwide myths about them, like there were several in Hawaii...one about Pele's younger sister who lived in the ocean off the coast of Maui and played with the whales."

She rested her chin on her hand. "But there was this one myth I ran across the other day that really grabbed my attention. It was about a merman named Glaucus. Originally he was human...a fisherman."

"Ah, yes. I remember Glaucus," Max broke in.

"Well, do you remember how he became a merman?" Trish asked.

"Yes, indeed." He told Trish that in his recollection, Glaucus one day saw his catch of fish starting to move about in the grass after he'd thought them dead. When the fish moved enough to slip back into the water and swim away, he thought there must be some magical power in the grass. So he ate a handful of it to see what would happen, and was irresistibly drawn to the sea. When he plunged into it, he was transformed into a god by the other gods of the sea, and became a merman with an upper body like a man and a lower body like a fish.

He told her that sometime later Glaucus fell in love with a woman who came to the shore one day to bathe, but that his love proved to be futile, since the sight of him was repugnant to humans.

"Max, I know how that felt. The sight of that mermaid in the jar was so...so *unnatural* to me that I can't begin to describe it. But the thing is, " she began, twisting the cord of the phone, "when the myth said there was a strange power in the grass that led to his transformation, I couldn't help but think about the Strontium 90 that accumulated in the grass during the atmospheric testing." She explained how the isotope got carried into the bones and bodies of the human population through the food chain. She started wondering if that wasn't exactly what led to the genetic transformation of the mutant she saw in the jar. "You see the similarity?"

"Well, girl," Max began with a slight chuckle, "I see you've been stretching your boundaries again. Did you also read that Glaucus had power over the waters after his transformation?"

"Yeah, I did...*and*," she added with a tinge of sarcasm in her voice, "I wondered if he might have a relative out there in the Pacific Ocean today named El Nino. It sure would seem fitting with all the atomic testing that's gone on there the last few decades."

Max addressed her comment with another, "Hmm," then returned to his original line of questions, "Now, tell me what you discovered about the two-headed monsters?"

"Oh, yeah..." She pulled her robe tighter around her and snuggled her feet under the sofa cushions. "I finally found a reference to two-headed men in some African myths...but the one that was probably best known was Roman. In fact, there's no counterpart for him in Greek mythology, like there are for other gods." She said his name was Janus, and she was surprised when she found that he was given as much status as Jupiter. "They sure didn't view him as a monster."

"Ah, yes, Janus." She heard Max inhaling on his pipe. "And what did you find out about him?"

"Well, he seems to be connected with the origins of everything...the god of 'good beginnings,' they called him." She told Max that his faces pointed in opposite directions to symbolize the beginning and the end of everything. He also held a key in his hand that showed that he opened in the beginning and shut at the end. "He's connected with doors that open and shut or something."

"Patty, did that description put you in mind of anything?"

She put an index finger to her chin and tapped it. "Yeah...it did...now that you mention it. It made me think of that passage in Revelations. You know the one: 'I am Alpha and Omega, the beginning and the ending.'"

"Very good. I've always thought the same thing myself. Now then, has anything else about the myths come to you?"

The line of Max's questions made Trish suspect he was designing them to guide her to some destination. "Well," she began, "so many of the creation myths talk about the beginning coming out of chaos."

"That's quite true."

"Well, Mark keeps talking about this chaos theory. Are you familiar with it?"

"Somewhat. But tell me your perception of it." Again, he appeared to be trying to help her to find her own answers.

"Well...now, I'm not sure I'm getting this right at all." She picked up her pen from the side table and tapped it absent-mindedly several times on her notepad. "It's so complex, and I'm just beginning to get into it...but it seems that it's a relatively new idea in science that may eventually reshape the way we think about classical science." She explained that the theory looked at the whole instead of the individual parts, similar to holistic medicine. The main premise seemed to be that there was a perception of order to things that disappeared once science got beyond the facade or the illusion of order.

"Everybody who knows anything about the theory knows the example of the butterfly flapping its wings in Peking."

"I don't," Max stated frankly.

She explained the concept of the simple energy of the flapping of a butterfly's wing, when extrapolated across the globe, ultimately causing rain in Central Park the next week. "Or if you throw a snowball in one direction from the top of a mountain, nothing may happen. But by throwing it at a slightly different angle or with a little more force, you could start an avalanche. That's the unpredictability—not just in complex systems—but in simple ones, too."

Trish took another sip of her rapidly cooling coffee. Then she told him the theory made it seem impossible to predict long-range consequences by using limited models. "Aerodynamics may not matter worth a hill of beans if you're building a footbridge, but if you're building a bridge that spans an ocean channel, it might matter a whole hell of a lot. Remember those films of that bridge in Washington, I think it was? They called it 'Galloping Gertie.'"

"Yes...yes...now that you mention it. I do." He told her how fascinating the sight of a concrete bridge with cars on it was, waving like a ribbon in the wind, right before crashing down.

"See? Unexpected consequences to long range circumstances that you can't predict with the limited models, or perspectives, that we use routinely." Trish sipped again from her coffee mug. It was almost too cold to drink. "They even dare to talk about intuition in chaos," she continued. "And then, behind the layer of seeming order, and the layer of chaos that they're just starting to see, there's a sense of another weird, indescribable layer of order..."

"Hmm..." he repeated.

"The thing is, Max," she explained as she shifted in her seat, "the more I study about it and think about it, the more it sounds like *divine* order to me."

"Interesting analogy."

She continued on without breaking her stride, telling him that Mark believed the reason the underground nuclear explosions were causing so much damage was because they were disrupting intricately complex systems of balance that exist in the natural world.

"That sounds fascinating, but what do you think all this has to do with mythology?"

She shrugged her shoulders. "Oh, I don't know. I just thought it was curious that the chaos theory pops up about the same time we start seeing mythical monsters reappearing, and that so many of the myths say the world *begins* out of chaos."

"Even synchronous, maybe?" he prodded.

"Maybe. It just seems like layers of chaos and then order and then chaos, and on and on."

Max took a breath, then explained, "You see, Patty, I'm not familiar with environmental issues. Oh, I care about them deeply, but I just don't have the background and information your friends Peggy and Mark do."

"But you know about mythology."

"That's the point."

She propped herself on the arm of the sofa. "What is?"

"You're finding the knowledgeable people you need in all of the various areas, and making connections between these things. You're acting as connective tissue to bring this all together in some recognizable whole form for other people to see...and that's quite a remarkable talent."

"Then you think I'm still on the right trail here?"

"Dead on it, girl," he answered without hesitation.

"Well, that reassures me. I keep getting frustrated because I can't quite get a handle on this thing." She held a hand out. "And yet I keep thinking I'm close, you know? Real close. And it does still feel right."

She touched her coffee mug again, realized it was too cold, and abandoned it. Then she added with a bit of hesitation, "Which reminds me…my personal life seems to be taking a very right course lately, too."

"I heard about that."

"*What*?" She leaned forward. "Max, does everybody in this town know *everything* about everybody else?"

"Well, pretty much, I suspect," he answered with a chuckle.

She closed her eyes and took a deep breath as Max added, "I'm told that Jimmy Hartwell is a really fine man." Then he added, "But I have to admit that I was surprised to hear that he's been married three times."

She grinned sideways. "Max, you sound like a worried father."

"I guess I do, but I can't help it."

"Well, Kathy says…You remember Kathy."

"Yes, I saw her just the other day."

Trish sat back hard on the sofa. "Then *she's* the one who told you!"

"Actually, I heard it from several other sources first."

"*First*?" Trish slapped the palm of her hand to her forehead in exasperation. "I'm going to kill her." Max chuckled again, and she added, "Anyway, Kathy says that he was always trying to find someone to replace me, and never did. But the honest to God truth is," she admitted as she let out a long breath, "I guess I'm having the same misgivings about his marital history that you are."

"Well, I'd like to meet this man."

"Max! You really *are* beginning to sound like a worried father." Then she added, "I think I kind of like that." She thought a moment, quickly formulating an agenda, then said, "Look, tell you what; I'll call and get Jimmy's schedule and get back with you, and we'll set up a time to go out to dinner one night. Or we could have dinner at my place. How does that sound?"

"That's fine, Patty. I'll be looking forward to it."

With that out of the way, Trish could return to another issue that had been bothering her.

• • •

While Trish stood up, picked up the coffee mug and went to the kitchen counter, stretching the phone cord almost as far as it would reach, she said, "Max, back to mythology a minute. I'm still having a hard time trying to sort out whether parts are symbolic or literal and what may be corruptions of the myths, and all those variables." She poured the cold coffee into the sink.

"And, Patty, you also need to keep still another dimension in mind. Remember I told you that Greek mythology follows the development of the human psyche?"

"I remember." She cradled the receiver between her ear and shoulder as she took the hot carafe from the coffee maker and poured a fresh cup.

"So have you come up with any new insights in that area?"

"It's funny that you'd ask that." Trish had given a lot of thought to how people incorporated the atomic age into their language and social behavior. "You know, it's like this whole Armageddon attitude you see nowadays. What if we're enacting the structure of a mythology for the distant future right now?"

She walked slowly back to the sofa, thinking, when he prodded her to continue. "And? What did you come up with?"

As she stood by the sofa, she told him how she wondered what form a future mythology might take if the future was so remote that it couldn't relate to the present world. Since there was no way of knowing the direction of evolution, a literal story of such an infinitesimally short span of human history might seem like a fairy tale to future generations. She speculated that the thought of an atom bomb might seem as symbolic, but unreal as the River Styx did to people today.

"Well, Patty, I can see you've been doing some soul searching in this area. I appreciate it when students do their homework."

After taking a careful sip of the hot coffee, Trish sat down. "And, Max, I thought about your reference to my going to Clinic Number Four as my 'descent into the abyss.' Well, what did I see in the abyss? Monsters. So a story about monsters in a pit of some sort might not seem real, either, to a future world. They might have no concept of genetic mutations from radiation exposure. Or hopefully they won't."

She set her mug on the side table. "Or if most of humanity did evolve rapidly in some mutant form because the problems got worse instead of better, mutants might seem normal. So, from that perspective, what would the so-called normal humans today seem like to a distant, future generation? Gods? Like Janus? Or would they seem like monsters themselves?" She looked toward the ceiling. "God, I can't decide if exploring these possibilities is more fascinating or frustrating."

"I know what you mean," he agreed with a slight chuckle. "And I think viewing our present situation from a distant possible future might give you a clearer perspective of our distant past than trying to figure it out from the present."

Trish repositioned herself in her seat. "But, Max, the time line thing has me stumped. I know you said not to worry about that for now." She said, however, that she was baffled about the time frame of the evolution of man and how it related to the research she was doing.

"Well, Patty, I know that must seem like no small issue to you at this point. In fact, you're on the periphery of delving into one of the most contentious debates of our day when you get into that area: the whole creationism versus evolution argument."

"Well, which one do you believe?"

"Why do I have to choose? Why can't they both be true?"

She wagged her head. "There you go again, Max...with your riddles."

"But, Patty, they both very well *could* be true."

"I don't see how," she responded.

He took in a breath and said, "Well, you see, some real geniuses of our time—like Carl Jung and Einstein—toyed with the concept of time being relative." Trish picked up her notepad and began making notations as he told her that they and others came to believe that time wasn't linear, as it was normally perceived, and that it was known that speed and gravity could actually alter time. "So when you truly break down the two theories to their basic parts, time may very well be the only point of contention. Cosmic time may seem instantaneous—from a distant perspective. But from an earthly vibration—to us—it may seem much slower. Rather evolutionary, in fact."

Trish lowered her notepad into her lap. "Now, Max, I've heard the 'time is an illusion' concept before, but honestly, I can't grasp that one."

"Well, don't attempt to for now. And don't let it throw you, either. Just don't let it be one of your frames of reference at this point." He advised her to get beyond the time constraints and into the timelessness of it, and to continue looking for different perspectives. "That's truly what we need in the evolutionary process—new perspectives—just as I mentioned before—perceiving a round earth instead of a flat one...and just like Copernicus, when he had the audacity to suggest the earth wasn't the center of the universe, that it was the sun, by golly."

He chuckled lightly. "Then Galileo comes along and nearly gets fried by the pope for furthering his concept. Can you imagine how that kind of new idea must have confounded and enraged the people of his day who'd all grown up believing the universe revolved around them? Can you imagine how that much of a conceptual shift must have shaken them up?"

Without waiting for a response he continued, "We don't seem to be focused on new ideas about life in society today, except in the field of technology." Trish leaned back and stretched her legs out on the sofa, continuing to take notes as Max told her that she was doing something that society needed to do more: re-framing questions and trying new perspectives. He said he didn't see truth as an absolute commodity—that as man continued to learn and evolve and develop as a species, his 'truths' would necessarily change as well. "After all, as I told you, archeology is nothing but an exercise in constantly *disproving* our previously held beliefs, as we continue discovering new truths about our past. Our future will undoubtedly continue to be a similar exercise in discovering new truths."

He let out a quick breath and inhaled slowly. "Human beings resist new truths for the same reason they resist change. The more profound the change, the longer it takes to adjust to it...to accept. It's a process—sometimes long, sometimes painful—but a process, nonetheless."

As Trish picked up her mug and took a few sips, Max continued, "However, I believe society is ready—more than ready—for a new truth...a new paradigm. I honestly believe that's the source of all the chaos we see in our world today. Chaos always precedes great advances in history, as I've told you.

"So I see the turmoil—while painful—as the forerunner to a new way of life, a new way of thinking. This chaos may simply be ushering in a new renaissance for mankind—a beginning—like the creation myths."

As Trish set her mug back down, he added with an edge of embarrassment, "Well, here I go preaching again."

"No, no, I love it," she assured him, as she curled the phone cord around her finger.

"Well, I always heard that you're never truly a good teacher until you start learning from your students. And, I have to hand it to you, I don't think anyone else could have stimulated an old fogy like me into re-examining his thought processes the way you have."

"Max, there's one more thing, before I have to go. I can't find any myth that helps me understand my experience with Ilyani, and I've searched like crazy. I thought the child of Cupid and Psyche might have some similarities, but I can't find much at all written about her after she was born."

Max mumbled, "Hmm," and took a deep breath. "Well, I'm not sure where to point in the myths on that one...but...you might consider looking at her from the archetypal viewpoint."

"Archetypal? We're back to Jung again?"

"It would seem so."

"Max," she said, tilting her head forward and scratching her forehead, "Honest to God, psychology class was so long ago that I can't remember that much about it. I'm not sure I got it even back then. I barely remembered about synchronicity." She let out a breath and straightened her head back up. "Why don't you pretend this is <u>Jung for Dummies</u>?"

Max chuckled. "Well, Patty, it's very difficult to define archetypes. The simple act of defining them limits them. I suppose you could think of them in terms of limitless, universal energies or patterns...perhaps shared cellular memories that demonstrate in form the human aspects that dwell consciously or unconsciously within all of us."

"Come again."

He chuckled again. "Let's just say that these archetypes are played out very well in mythologies. You know the ones: the heroes, victims, betrayers, warriors, the prostitutes...*and* the child. The divine child seemed to resonate with me when you first spoke of Ilyani."

Divine child, huh? That resonated with Trish, as well.

As she was about to ask him another question, the doorbell rang.

"Max, I'm afraid I have to go. Someone's at the door. I'll call you back about getting together for dinner."

"Great, Patty. Talk to you later."

• • •

Trish hung up the phone and retied the sash of her robe as she walked to the front door and opened it.

Jimmy was standing there, leaning up against her porch column, with his thumbs in his jeans pockets and his ankles crossed. "Hey, Trish."

She couldn't have hidden the smile or the flush on her face if she had tried. And she didn't bother trying.

He didn't say another word before backing her into the living room, wrapping his arms around her, and kissing her deeply and passionately in the mouth. When he'd stopped for a moment, she asked, "What? Not even flowers or conversation?"

Jimmy didn't answer, and she found her attempt at humor quickly giving way to her own passions, as he continued kissing her on the face and neck, while holding her head with his fingers entwined in her hair. She moaned almost involuntarily, "Oh, *God*. Jimmy..."

He eased her down on the carpeting and untied the sash on her robe. She had nothing on but panties underneath. He moved from kissing her neck to her breasts, and she moaned again.

It didn't take her long to slip out of her panties, and Jimmy quickly removed his clothes. As they returned to their embrace, Trish relished in the feel of her naked body against his. She matched his intensity, kissing his neck and chest. Her passion continued building, washing over her until it culminated with the two of them making love on her living room floor.

Afterward, and after Trish had time to compose herself, she turned to Jimmy, lying next to her on the floor, and, with a grin on her face, said, "Talk about being swept off your feet. What brought that on?"

"I'm not sure," he said as he combed his fingers through his hair. "But I was downtown talking to some guys at breakfast, and instead of listening to them, I started thinking about you and about how happy I am again after so many years…and I just put my coffee cup down, left everybody there at the table and got in the truck and headed for your door."

"And what if I hadn't been here?"

He turned toward her. "I'd have tracked you down if I'd had to go to the ends of the earth, Woman."

She laughed lustily, tilting her head back.

Then after a moment she looked back at him and commented off-handedly, "By the way, Max Rogers wants to meet you?"

"Meet *me*? Why would he want to meet me?"

"Because you're involved with his favorite student; that's why."

"His favorite student? *You*?" He pulled his body up to a half-sitting position, resting on his elbow.

"That's right, Buddy Boy," she answered, looking up at him sideways, grinning. "You're about to get sized up by the Papa figure in my life."

"Oh, that's just great," he said, rolling his eyes as he lay back down. He looked over at her. "And just when is this meeting supposed to take place?"

"Whenever it's convenient for you. All I need to know is a night you'll be free."

He rubbed the side of his face with his hand, and said with a sigh, "Well, I don't have any plans anytime soon, except for going down to look at some new equipment in Atlanta Thursday. But I should be back before five, even then." He dropped an arm to his side. "Oh, God, Trish, do I have to get dressed up and inspected like a side of beef?"

"Yeah, that's pretty much the way it works," she responded matter-of-factly. "So how's Tuesday night sound to you?"

"Okay, I guess," he answered with resignation. "Next *year* would be better."

"Now, Jimmy, you're just going to have to take your medicine like a man."

He leaned over and grabbed her and started growling and pretending to bite her neck. "I'd rather take a bite out of *you* like a man."

She giggled. Then he stopped and held his head further back to get a better look at her, and said seriously, "Trish, I really do love you. I've probably loved you longer than any other man in your life."

"Don't be too sure," she teased. "Clyde Bledsoe dated me before you did, you know."

"Clyde Bledsoe?" he asked with disbelief. "Give me a break. He's as country as any hayseed I know."

"Oh, and you're not?"

"No, I'm not."

"Well, I didn't say he was suave or anything, anyway. I just said that he might have loved me longer."

"Mm..." Jimmy rubbed his chin. "Well, that might be true. But, he couldn't love you any more." He slipped his hands under her body and held her as he rolled over until she was on top of him. She rested her head on his chest, as he stroked her hair.

Trish broke the silence. "Oh, Jimmy, this is all so perfect," she almost gushed, as she snuggled against him. "I never thought I'd ever be this happy again in my entire life."

"I know, Baby. I know."

When she turned her head to the side, her vision fell on the pile of books and notes by her sofa, and the doubts started creeping in again. No matter how much happiness she had with him, why were the doubts always so close at hand? Why couldn't she simply trust her happiness?

• • •

Trish didn't waste time making arrangements for the three of them to meet at her house for dinner the following Tuesday. After she'd confirmed the plans with Jimmy and Max, she started sprucing up her house to get ready. As she planned the dinner and shopped for things she needed from the grocery, she could feel her energy level and spirits improving. Tuesday morning Trish collected all of her paperwork and stacked it neatly in the bedroom. By that evening, her house was almost immaculate.

When he arrived, Max had a bottle of wine, and he and Trish drank some while they waited for Jimmy. When he arrived a little later, Trish greeted him at the door. As he presented her with a bouquet of flowers, he gave a sideways grin and raised one eyebrow. "I think I owe you some flowers for the other day."

"Well," she replied with a knowing grin, "how sweet of you."

Trish introduced the two men. After they all sat down in the living room and engaged in some light conversation, Trish noticed Jimmy tugging at his collar. His demeanor reminded her of a rough and tumble schoolboy who'd been made to dress up for some special occasion.

"Well, my dear, what's on the menu tonight?" Max inquired, turning toward Trish.

"Shrimp scampi."

"Oh, that's my favorite dish," he replied, beaming.

"That's why we're having shrimp scampi."

"How sweet of you to remember."

As the three of them continued drinking wine and talking, Trish sensed that the men were becoming more comfortable with each other. Max inquired about Jimmy's work, and Jimmy in turn, asked about Max's choice of Clayton, Georgia for a place to retire. The conversation turned to recent events around town, then to a local artist. They discovered that they both had prints of his works.

When Trish saw that Max and Jimmy had settled into a longer conversation about another mutual interest, she excused herself to go put the finishing touches on dinner. She glanced into the living room from time to time and realized—much to her delight—that they appeared to be hitting it off.

"It's ready, folks," she finally called to them. "Come on in and get seated."

"My, my," Max said as he entered the kitchen and glanced at the table, "it certainly does look wonderful...and smells divine."

"Why, thank you," Trish responded, as he held her chair out for her.

As both the dinner and conversation progressed, Trish found that she was thoroughly enjoying her meal. Max noticed, as well. "Glad to see you've gotten your appetite back," he commented, then added, "And glad to see that you've gotten some color back in your cheeks."

Trish lowered her head slightly, pressed her napkin to her mouth and glanced around. From the looks she got from the others, it was clear that they all had an idea of what had helped to get her color back.

Then Max and Trish began discussing the French nuclear tests, as well as other environmental issues. Jimmy sat watching and listening as they conversed.

At one point Max sat back and said, "Listen to us talking about nothing but shop." He turned toward Jimmy. "We must be boring you."

"Not at all," he responded, setting his fork down and leaning onto the edge of the table on his elbows. He laced his fingers together over his plate and said, "I may not know that much about the technical stuff, but it's fascinating to listen to the two of you talk about it. And, besides—even if I don't know much about science and mythology and the ozone hole—I sure as heck can see for myself some of the weather changes you've been talking about. The weather everywhere has been crazy as hell for a while now. And it doesn't take a scientist to see that."

"That's for sure," Trish agreed, as she refilled their glasses with wine.

Jimmy took a sip of wine and set it down. "Just look at these storms we've been having," he continued, fully engaging in the conversation, "and that heat wave on top of it." He sat back. "I mean, who would believe that over five hundred people would die from a heat wave in Chicago? *Chicago*! And those hurricanes. Man, they just keep coming out of Africa like freight trains lined up or something. Everybody I talk to thinks something weird is going on with this screwy weather. They just don't know exactly what it is."

"Well, I think our girl here may be well on her way to figuring out what's behind a few of these environmental situations…and I must say that I'm rather proud of her." He tipped his glass in her direction. "In fact, I've always been proud of her." Trish responded with a self conscious smile. "Hope you don't get too attached to Australia when you go," he added. "We want you back here in Clayton eventually, you know."

Jimmy folded his napkin, set it down beside his plate and pushed his chair back. Trish glanced at Max just as he was looking at her. "Well, maybe we can have our chocolate mousse in the living room," she quickly suggested.

After the table was cleared and the three of them had retreated to the living room and finished dessert, Max indicated that it was time for him to leave.

"Don't go yet. The evening's still young," Trish protested.

"Well, it's young to you because it's for young people. I'm an early to bed man myself," he said, rising to his feet.

Max told Jimmy how glad he was to have met him and shook his hand, then turned toward Trish and thanked her for the meal and the delightful evening.

"I'll walk you to your car," she responded.

As they walked, Max leaned toward her and said quietly, "I rather like your young man."

"I'm glad you do. I like him a bit myself."

"It's serious, isn't it?"

"Yes, it's quite serious."

"Well, I'm very pleased for you then. I can see from your face that you're happy."

When they stopped by the car, Max asked, "Did I detect some misgivings from him about your trip to Australia?"

Trish looked down at the ground, grinning sideways and shuffled some gravel with the toe of her shoe. She looked back up. "Well, well, nothing slips by you, does it?"

"I hope I'm not prying."

"No…no…" She exhaled forcefully and set her hands on her hips. "I guess I've been trying to ignore it."

"Is it working?" Max asked, peering over the top of his glasses.

Trish threw her head back and laughed. "Nope. As a mater of fact, it's not."

He smiled and said," My Dear, it's really none of my business."

"It's okay, Max. I'm well aware of the friction about this." She exhaled again. "I guess I just don't know how to deal with it, so…" She raised an eyebrow. "I just haven't been dealing with it."

"Well, I have to say that you seem happier than I've seen you in years, and it's obvious that he adores you." He grinned. "And why wouldn't he?" They hugged good-bye. "Dinner was simply delightful," he said before climbing into his car.

After he drove away, Trish returned to the house, where Jimmy told her, "You know, I've seen him around town before, and people always talk about the professor who lives up on Davis Gap, but I've never really known that much about him. He really *is* an interesting character. I can see why you like him so much."

"Well, I think he was impressed with you, too."

Jimmy raised his arms above his head and stretched. "I guess it's time for me to be going, too."

"No, don't. Why don't you stay here for tonight?"

He beamed his familiar sideways grin and said, "I was hoping you'd say that."

Chapter Twenty-Two

While Trish spent many of her days the rest of that summer and fall with her research and exercising, she'd also begun talking more about her upcoming trip with Jimmy Hartwell; still, she avoided sharing any more of her research into the Cold War. And even though they were sharing many of the life experiences they'd had during the years they'd been apart, Trish still avoided asking him directly why he'd married his first wife—the one that "didn't count"—while she was away at college. And why he'd done it without even a word to her. She'd thought he would bring up the subject himself eventually, but so far he hadn't.

Her pursuit of the story was the first "issue" in their relationship, and the unspoken issues of trust and betrayal were becoming the next. On some level she sensed that it was the things they didn't talk about that were beginning to threaten their future.

She was forced to face the fact that none of Jimmy's relationships with women had worked for very long in his life. And he had abandoned all of them. His abandonment of her was simply the first, or maybe it was Lavinia Mize from high school. She wasn't sure. She was only sure that she didn't want to become the latest in a string of his failed relationships. She had to start asking herself some other questions: Was the story she was pursuing really paralleling an aspect of her own personal life as Max had said? And, if so, what were the similarities?

At times she felt as though she was dealing with too many emotional extremes all at once...but she had the feeling that might be necessary in the process, as Max had said he experienced in war. With all of the pain, joy, conflict, excitement, confusion and chaos she was going through, she felt that she was being stretched and challenged to grow in a way that she never would if she hadn't taken that "leap of faith" into the unknown regions of her world.

To maintain her energy level through the changes she was experiencing, she decided to prioritize and pace herself in the same way Peggy Craft had. She took time to get out more, hike in the woods and horseback ride with Jimmy. And she took time to simply rest whenever she needed to.

Through that time, she also kept up with the news about France's nuclear test plans. She read in the papers and watched on the news as opposition to those plans built worldwide, in Japan, France itself, and especially the areas near the test sites. There were demonstrations at the French embassies in Australia, New Zealand and Papua, New Guinea, as well as worldwide calls for boycotts of French products.

On the news one night, she watched as scenes of the Rainbow Warrior

II setting sail for the location of the test site played out. As Trish listened to the account, it amazed her that the deadly sabotage of the first Greenpeace ship years before hadn't deterred the organization. There were reports of riots on the French islands nearest the test sites and of French troops being sent in to quell them. The Nobel Peace Prize was awarded to an anti-nuclear scientist, and there was speculation that it had been done partly as a slap at the French for planning to resume their nuclear testing.

The French government, however, seemed oblivious to the worldwide condemnations, and at the appointed time that summer, the first blast was set off.

For a day or two after the blast, Trish was busy with travel plans and wrapped up in several outings with Jimmy. Then, on a Saturday, she picked up her Atlanta paper and turned to the Earth Week section that Peggy had talked about, and her eyes grew wide in disbelief. Not only had a volcano erupted in New Zealand, the news account described Mount Ruapehu Volcano as springing back to life with a mushroom cloud that mimicked an atomic bomb. It was the largest eruption of the 9,190-foot mountain in 50 years.

"My God!" she muttered under her breath. She ran to call Peggy and got a recording before she remembered that she was away on vacation. She looked at the world map in the article again, and a second thing became clear. Again, as Peggy had said, there was what appeared to be a disproportionately large number of earthquakes worldwide.

The next week Trish read the Earth Week diary again. A number of earthquakes in New Zealand and other areas of the Pacific Rim followed the previous week's volcanic eruption, and she wondered to herself why no one but environmentalists—and possibly a few scientists—had noticed a possible connection between the atomic blasts and the rash of earthquakes.

She called Mark several times, and left messages when he didn't answer his phone.

• • •

"Sorry to be so long getting back to you," Mark said when he finally returned Trish's calls, "but I've been busy with some folks on the Etowah River with a zoning matter. And occasionally I do have to try to make a living," he added with a chuckle.

"Oh, I understand. What I called about is these earthquakes and volcanoes following the nuclear test," she said, sinking into her chair and reaching for her pad and pen.

"Oh, yeah, that. Pretty predictable, wouldn't you say?" he countered almost nonchalantly.

"Yes, *now* I would. But why the hell isn't anyone else? Mark, this is just phenomenal stuff."

"It takes time, Trish." He reminded her that science, politics and public opinion sometimes could move at a snail's crawl; that it took some twenty years for the reasons behind the expansion of the ozone hole to become publicly accepted; and that the first scientist to suggest the cause was ridiculed by his colleagues for a long time.

"Yeah, that's what Peggy said. But why?" she asked, pulling her legs up in her seat and wrapping her arms around them, still clutching her writing material.

"Because," he explained, "there were seriously vested interests in *not* believing there was an ozone hole caused by manmade products, that's why. And I'm talking about some wealthy, powerful companies."

Trish thought Mark was remarkably unruffled by the whole affair, less emotionally invested than she'd expected, or at least he didn't show it. Maybe it just seemed that way because it was all so new to her. And since Mark and Peggy had both been aware for a number of years, it wasn't "news" to either of them.

"Mark," she continued, "I've also noticed a large number of *other* earthquakes around the world, and volcanic rumblings—even at Mt. St. Helen's." She tilted her head. "Could that be connected to the atomic tests?"

"*I* think so—from common sense alone—but the thing we can say for sure is that it is a remarkable coincidence." He let out a breath. "Trish, science is only the science we know today. Tomorrow we'll know something else. And by the next generation or so, they'll laugh at most of our present ideas."

Trish smiled. "Yeah, I have another friend who says that," she said, thinking of Max.

"Hell, they didn't know the fault from the Northridge quake in California even existed before it struck last year…and they've discovered a whole series of what they call 'blind thrust faults,' one of them directly beneath downtown Los Angeles, for Christ's sake." Trish dropped her legs back to the floor, propped the phone between her shoulder and her ear and started taking notes. "But science isn't really looking in this direction," he continued. "It isn't motivated to. It takes time. Eventually it'll start filtering through to the rest of society."

Trish switched the receiver to her other hand so she could take notes better. "Mark, how could the quakes that aren't close to the test site be connected? I mean, it looks like a *swarm* of quakes to me, but they're not all close together."

"Well, Trish," he began patiently, "this is an extremely simplistic example, because when you're talking about the earth, you're talking about a living entity, not an inanimate object. But just imagine taking a hammer and hitting a sheet of glass with it." He told her that it was impossible to determine in which directions those cracks were going to radiate outward, but that the effects continued far out from the point of impact—not just at the impact site itself. He told her that some seismologists believed that earthquakes triggered other quakes, which suggested that a 5.5 or 5.6 seismic event, like an underground nuclear bomb, could also trigger quakes, especially ones being set off in an already fragile zone, like the Pacific Ring of Fire.

"Do you think the eruption of Mt. St. Helen's could have been related to the underground testing in Nevada?" she asked, raising her eyebrows.

"Possibly. Who knows? When they dropped Little Boy and Fat Man on Hiroshima and Nagasaki *above* ground, they speculated to the plane crews about the possibility of the bombs cracking the earth's crust. Back in the seventies, the governor of Nevada released an ad hoc committee report warning about the growing risks to his state from earthquakes." He sighed. "There's just so much we don't know right now. But, it's a fact that worldwide in 1976 we had some of the worst earthquakes we'd had in fifty years. There were *huge* quakes in China and the Soviet Union...and it was the year of a major one in Guatemala."

"Hold on, Mark. Slow down a minute. I'm trying to get all of this down."

After a few seconds of silence he told her that that same year there were also a huge number of underground nuclear devices set off. "It's not surprising that China and the Soviet Union were hit hard; they were setting off explosions in their countries' testing grounds like crazy." He paused again, as though giving her a chance to keep up, before adding, "But, like the atmospheric tests—when all the radioactive fallout was carried on the jet stream around the world—you had to wait some twenty years before you could start plotting the thyroid cancers along that same jet stream and see a definite cause and effect."

He took a quick breath and continued, "And if you think a possible connection between the bomb tests and earthquakes and volcanoes are scary, take a look at the natural quakes whenever you're thinking about nuclear *power*."

"Why's that?" she asked, looking up.

He told her that in Armenia a reactor was about to be started up which was built in the center of an active quake zone; it was an old-model type reactor that even the Russians had mothballed years earlier because of the area's instability. He said that the U.S. also had reactors in quake zones. "There's California, and along the New Madrid Fault here in the Southeast." He told her that scientists were predicting a mega-quake there some day similar to the one that struck in the 1800's. "Do those seem like smart places to put reactors?"

Trish shook her head and inhaled and exhaled slowly. She set down her pad and pen. Finally, she said, "Mark, I have a confession."

"What's that?"

"Well..." she began slowly, rubbing her forehead, "I've been a reporter all of my professional career...and I hardly knew anything about these things. Oh, I was interested in nuclear issues, but I never did any real investigative research on the subject. And now I feel overwhelmed and inadequate...ashamed that I never focused on it like I could have."

She held out a hand. "I mean, that was my job: to let the public know what was going on in the world and what was really important. And the scope of this thing...it's *enormous*. Why didn't I see it before? Where was I?" She let out a sigh. "I've criticized my colleagues up and down for not going after stories about critical issues, and the whole time I find myself guilty of the same thing."

"Now, Trish," Mark responded in a sympathetic tone, "don't let that get you down. Your publishers and editors probably wouldn't have let you spend the time and money on it, anyway. It's like that nuclear forest thing. I could tell you were hot to do that story, but your editor wouldn't let you touch it. We run into that all the time in the environmental community."

"I *have* run into brick walls over the years. But now I'm beginning to think I should have struck out on my own sooner."

Mark's non-judgmental attitude about the inadequacies she was feeling was only mildly comforting. She didn't think she was going to be able to be as kind to herself for a long time to come.

• • •

Trish shifted her position and picked up her pad and pen again. She needed to remain focused on the research. "Mark, Peggy gave me some material about the animal mutations near Chernobyl that I came across the other day, and I was wondering if you knew anything about that."

"Yeah, I've read about mutations in farm animals. And human birth defects have doubled in the affected areas. The cancer rates have people over there more worried than anything else." He told Trish that some of the activists and mothers with children suffering from leukemia claimed that over 60,000 kids had gotten sick as a direct result of the accident at Chernobyl.

He explained that, even though the Ukrainian government initially estimated only 8,000 deaths directly related to it, those numbers only included the cleanup workers—or liquidators—and that the overall documentations were completely inadequate. Trish remembered what Katrina had told her about Chernobyl that hadn't made the news. She was taking notes as rapidly as she could, when Mark added, "But there's something about the mutagens that has me even more concerned," he added.

She looked up. "What's that?"

"Well, sure you can see mutations in mammals when they're exposed to radiation or mutagenic chemicals. It's hard to deny a two-headed calf or pig—or what you saw in Kazakhstan. But mammals are high up on the food chain. What about the mutations that are occurring in the living things we *can't* see?"

Tilting her head, she asked, "What are you getting at?"

"Like bacteria, Trish. All living things are made up of the same elements. So, wouldn't mutagens affect all living things? And viruses, too?"

"I've never thought about that."

"Not many people have." Mark cleared his throat and told her that when insects were bombarded with pesticides to keep them off crops, they simply adapted and developed resistance to the poisons. And the chemical industry kept changing to new forms of pesticides because the insects kept developing defenses to those poisons and getting stronger. "It also keeps the chemical industry financially viable, because it's a never-ending cycle.

"And we know we're over-prescribing antibiotics," he added. "Take a look at what's happening as a result." He explained that while antibiotics were killing off weaker bacteria, they were leaving stronger, mutant bacteria, and that those were actually thriving.

As Trish feverishly took notes, Mark talked about the resurgence of pneumonia, E. coli, salmonella and other new strains of bacterial and viral infections. Medicine was less effective, because the strains were becoming drug resistant—more virulent—and because of that, people were dying from diseases that were easily cured in the past. "We thought we were going to wipe out infectious diseases with antibiotics, and now it looks like we may have just been making things worse. We can't begin to develop new antibiotics fast enough to catch up. And, that also keeps the *pharmaceutical* industry thriving financially."

"Where's the radiation connection?" Trish asked, confused with the new angle.

"Same principle. When we introduce something that can alter genetics into the environment, stronger, mutant forms of viruses and bacteria are bound to develop—sometimes at an incredible rate. And it's not like humans or animals that have longer life cycles. These have extremely *short* life cycles and can mutate rapidly."

At this point Trish didn't grasp enough to even ask the next question. Mark filled in the silence. "Think about AIDS, for instance. Right now, it's not airborne. But what if it suddenly were to start mutating that way?"

"Don't even *think* that, Mark," she admonished. Then after a moment's hesitation she asked, "What you're saying is that radiation could alter the agents that cause infectious diseases and make them more deadly?"

"Possibly. Who knows?"

"You know, Mark, while you were talking I remembered this illness they had in Kazakhstan that attacked the immune system, just like AIDS."

"That doesn't surprise me." He told her that he'd wondered for a long time if all of the so-called new diseases weren't simply opportunistic diseases that had been around for a long time on the planet and were simply hitting the human and animal populations at that point because their systems were simply weaker than ever before. He speculated that people might simply have less resistance to them because of the toxins that had accumulated in their bodies from the previous five decades of chemical and radioactive exposure.

Trish squirmed in her seat as he added, "We're exposed to dioxin—the most toxic substance ever synthesized by man—and PCB's, and all kinds of pesticides in our foods and water...heavy metals...you name it. They've even found PCB's in the fatty tissues of polar bears, and they haven't had *any* known direct exposure.

"We walk out into the sunlight and our bodies are like a prism of chemicals that no other generation of mankind before has had in his body. And we have no idea of the long-term effects of these alterations on the human race and the planet. We talk about fighting the drug epidemic all the time, and, hell, we're *all* on drugs. For most of us, it's just involuntary."

Trish squirmed in her seat again and absentmindedly started drawing squiggles on her notepad.

"And what about these deadly emerging viruses like Ebola and Marberg, Trish?" Mark continued. "Do you know anything about the Ebola virus that got into that monkey house in Maryland a few years ago?"

She stopped drawing squiggles. "Yeah, a little bit. A friend of mine covered that story for her paper."

Mark told her the background of the story and that the only reason there wasn't a major epidemic was because that particular virus had mutated to a form that wasn't lethal to humans. He said that it was airborne, however, and that it killed every monkey in the facility. The virus had even infected some of the handlers. "It's just that it had mutated enough that it didn't harm humans. We got lucky—really lucky. I'm telling you, thousands or even *millions* of people could have been wiped out."

She sighed. "That's what my friend kept trying to impress on me, but I don't think I understood it until now." She rubbed her forehead nervously.

"And, Trish," Mark continued, "here we are dumping thousands and thousands of *tons* of chemicals into the environment—many of them mutagenic—and radiation, and somehow we don't seem to think it's going to have an effect on us?" He explained that mankind had spent millions of years evolving and adapting to the planet's bacteria and viruses, besides every other life form—and to the planet itself—and that in a short fifty year span man had done more to alter his own environment than ever before. "I tell you, it's like global Russian Roulette."

She held a hand out in front of her. "But, Mark, why would chemicals and radiation have a weakening effect on *us* and make insects and bacteria stronger?"

"I don't know. That would be a good question to ask...maybe because they *can* mutate so rapidly. Did you hear about the mice mutations around Chernobyl?"

"No." By now she wasn't sure she wanted to know. Not only was Mark an invaluable source for information, he had an uncanny knack for overwhelming her with it.

While Trish began taking notes again, Mark explained that whenever an environment was altered sufficiently to threaten a species, that species either had to adapt or become extinct—the process called mutation. "It's just like your creatures in Clinic Number Four. Anyway, here we are with possibly the greatest laboratory in the world with all the direct contamination at Chernobyl and hardly any scientists are doing major, long-term research there."

Trish set her pen hand down. "Why not?"

"It's not something the moneyed interests of governments or nuclear power and uranium cartels are interested in focusing a lens on." He cleared his throat. "I talked to one of the few American scientists doing research over there, a guy from the University of Georgia. He said the mice around Chernobyl are mutating and adapting rather well. In fact, he said the gene variation between normal mice and Chernobyl mice is more than the difference between mice and rats."

"What's the significance?" Trish asked, looking up from her notes.

"Trish, those two species diverged around fifteen million years ago."

"Holy shit," Trish reacted. "Then that's a dramatic change in a very short period, huh?"

"It's mind boggling. The guy kept doubting his numbers and kept getting the study out over and over again, pulling data from it.

"Then there was another guy I talked to doing studies. He worked for the Department of Energy. When I asked him why he wasn't studying *human* mutations, he said he really wasn't interested in that—that it might sound cold, but that the etiology was gone and those instances were just anecdotal."

Trish looked up again, holding her pen aloft. Anecdotal? Is that what the specimens at Clinic Number Four were? Anecdotes? "I don't mean to sound stupid, Mark, but what is 'etiology?'"

"Well, simply put, it's the cause."

"Oh...okay."

"But, Trish, you can't just ignore accounts like that." Mark told her about a collective farm near Chernobyl where they'd experienced three mutations in their herd of cows and pigs in the five years preceding the accident. In just two years following the meltdown, they'd had 140.

"Wow."

"Yes, 'wow.' And you can't just dismiss those kinds of numbers as anecdotal, unless you're working for the Department of Energy, like that guy." He added in a sarcastic tone, "Or the nuclear industry."

"What kinds of mutations did they have on the farms?"

"The same kinds that you saw at the clinic, missing limbs or eyes. They'd have one born without a head, and then one nearby would be born with two heads...*weird* stuff."

Trish set her pen and pad down, closed her eyes and rubbed her forehead between her eyes. She exhaled and said, "Look, I'm not a scientist or anything, but what if everything that happens to mammals exposed to radiation isn't detrimental?"

"What do you mean?"

Trish told Mark about Ilyani and the other children she'd heard about around the world. She told him that in the Soviet Union and in other parts of the world that she'd read about, many of the lands rich in uranium were considered sacred by the indigenous people. She couldn't understand that, because they also said that it would be dangerous to dig up the uranium. "But I don't understand those kids like Ilyani appearing at the same time as the mutants, either. And I don't need any study to know that what I experienced with that little girl was real."

"What *do* you think you experienced with her?" he asked in a level tone.

Trish leaned her head back onto the back of her chair. "Mark, I don't know. I only know it was powerful." She pulled her head back up again, and added, "A friend suggested that it might have been love."

"Hmm..." he mumbled, then took a breath. "That just reminded me of something I've been meaning to tell you."

"What's that?"

He told her that a couple of years before, a number of prominent scientists from around the world had issued "an urgent warning to humanity" that the media failed to focus on.

She quickly turned to a fresh page to record what he was about to say.

"There were over 1500 scientists from 50 different countries, and over a hundred of them Nobel Prize winners."

"Jeez."

"Yeah, well, the information in the warning itself—about the water and air and loss of species—was nothing new to me. Hell, I'd been preaching it myself for years." He told her that they also said that man was on a collision course on the planet, that people had to change their ways and discover what they called a "new ethic" for dealing with people and the earth. They said it was the only way to avoid "vast human misery" and an irretrievably mutilated planet. They talked about humanity's alteration of the living world, saying that eventually it would be impossible to "sustain life in the manner that we know."

Trish let out a quick breath. "Frankly, at this point, I'd have to say that doesn't seem like an overstatement."

"But what really got to me was what they advised about the crisis."

"Why?" She shrugged her shoulders. "It sounds pretty logical."

"Trish, scientists are traditionally conservative people. They don't like to go out on limbs. And they avoid absolutes like the plague. For them to even issue a warning like that was incredible in the first place. But what they advised us to do it sounded almost like a spiritual message—a spiritual plea: develop a new ethic in dealing with the earth and people. It was like a cry to love each other and love the earth."

"Back to the love thing again, huh?"

"Yeah…well…unfortunately, most people interpret their Bibles as saying to conquer the earth instead of loving it or being good stewards of it."

"Why do you think that is, Mark?" Trish asked, resting her head on her hand.

"I don't know. Something's missing, I guess. But to me, it's basic: God created the earth, and we should revere his handiwork, not destroy it. I think the creationists ought to be out on the front lines of the environmental movement, if they really believe the earth is God's creation. Primitive cultures seem to have that kind of reverence for the earth."

Trish put down her pad and pen again and shifted her body. "Mark, I've kept you long enough. Once again you've given me more than enough to chew on. Let's keep in touch. If you have any more ideas, give me a call. I'm not leaving for Australia till spring, so I'll be here."

"Sure thing, Trish. I really do think you're on the right track with the questions you're asking."

"Thanks for saying so."

Max had told her the same thing. But more importantly, her instincts were telling her that she was on the right track, and she was listening to them and getting in touch with them more and more every day. And every day she was getting stronger physically and emotionally.

She sensed that she was going to need all the strength she had, and that the roller-coaster ride she was on, professionally and personally, was far from over.

Chapter Twenty-Three

The summer drought ultimately gave way to a dry, parched autumn in Clayton, Georgia. To Trish's dismay, most of the leaves on the trees began simply turning brown on their branches. She missed the brilliant bursts of red, orange and yellow that had always blanketed the mountains around the town every fall, signaling the influx of "leaf watchers" from Atlanta and the approach of winter. It was the time of year when she enjoyed that last bit of Indian Summer, visiting the fall festivals at Hiawassee and Clarkesville, and stocking up on cider, apples and preserves. It was also a time for putting in a final load of firewood for her wood stove and fireplace.

When Jimmy came over with his chain saw to help cut up some fallen trees on her property and stack the wood in a pile in her back yard, she'd put up a small protest, but it didn't deter him. And the fact was that she enjoyed having a man around the house, taking charge and watching over her…and occasionally keeping her bed warm.

Early one morning, before Trish had time to dress or turn on the computer, Jimmy surprised her by showing up at her door to take her out on a rafting trip down the Chattooga River with some of his rafting guides. It was close to the end of the tour season and one of the final warm days that were left. She didn't hesitate and hurried to get dressed.

After they arrived at the facility, the guides provided her with headgear and other equipment, and gave her preliminary instructions on rowing and following their guidance. The particular river stretch they'd be rafting on was classified a Category Four, which meant that it was perilous enough to require assistance.

Trish found the experience exhilarating, as they were pummeled over several rapids, trying to steer the raft in the right directions to keep it from turning over. She was beaming from ear to ear when they pulled the rafts up on the banks of a sandbar just past the last stretch of rapids. Beads of water trickled down her face from her dripping hair. She took off her helmet and life jacket and flopped down hard on the sand, panting and trying to catch her breath. She looked up at Jimmy. "Oh, my gosh, that was better than any Disneyland ride I've ever been on!"

"Well, I should hope so. We don't exactly have any mechanical tracks out there in the river. You pretty much have to take what you get on this course."

"Oh, Lord! My heart is racing ninety miles an hour." She threw her head back and laughed, then shook the excess water out of her hair. When she shielded her eyes from the sun and looked up, she saw him standing over her, smiling. In that moment she realized how much she liked his eyes on her, as well as his hands. There were a lot of things she liked about him, and like the river, their relationship seemed both exhilarating and unpredictable.

Later, as they drove back to Clayton, Trish stared out the window of the truck, still comparing the similarities between their relationship and Jimmy's wild river. The only "tracks" in it were the conditioned responses they both had from their culture and upbringing, the kinds that made every situation or "ride" come up with the same predictable outcomes. The one that had been playing silently in her head for months was not to make waves. The adrenalin rush from shooting the rapids made her realize that making waves might not be so bad after all.

She had hoped Jimmy would bring up the incident in college, but so far he had barely alluded to it. If she didn't bring it out into the open, she would be guilty of skirting the issue, as well.

Jimmy glanced over at her and asked with a grin, "You're awfully quiet. What are you thinking about?"

"Jimmy, we need to talk about 'us' again."

He leaned forward and turned the radio off. "Okay. Shoot."

"I've been waiting for you to come to the table with this, but..." She looked straight ahead and took a breath. "Jimmy, when I went to UGA...I know it was a long time ago...but when you married Margaret Simpson...I never saw that coming. I didn't have any idea you were seeing someone else." She closed her eyes. "It hurt me more than you know, and I've carried it around for years." She opened her eyes and looked at a fixed point on the dashboard, focusing on keeping her voice even. "I honestly don't know if I can trust a future for us. Because I don't know why that happened, I don't have any reason to think it won't happen again. I know both of us *must* have changed over the years, but there are patterns I think we both need to look at."

She finally looked at Jimmy. He was staring straight ahead at the road. After a few seconds it was obvious that he wasn't ready to respond, so Trish continued. "So, why did you marry Margaret Simpson when *we* were talking about marriage? Why didn't you tell me you were dating her? Why did I have to hear about it from Kathy?"

Jimmy fidgeted in his seat. "Trish...I know I should have talked to you first." He twisted his hands on the steering wheel. "When your calls and letters slowed down, I figured you were seeing someone else."

She felt heat rising in her face. "Jimmy, *I* wasn't seeing someone else. I was just working my ass off with my freshman load. Besides, if I had been, you still could have called and told me."

"I know, Trish. I know. I've felt guilty about it for years." He looked at her with a pained expression on his face, then back at the road. "Honest to God, I regretted it so much I think it's what broke up the marriage."

"And what broke up the others?"

He answered simply and calmly, "I don't know...I could tell you a lot of reasons, but they're just window dressing."

"Don't you *want* to figure it out before you start talking with me about another commitment?" She took a deep breath and closed her eyes again. "And, Jimmy, in all those years, why didn't you ever look me up?"

He raised one of his hands from the steering wheel momentarily, grasped it again, and then calmly replied, "I guess I just felt so bad that I didn't want to face you. Trish, that marriage to Margaret was just a rebound." He let out a breath. "I realized almost immediately it was a mistake. I left after six months. She wanted to work it out, and I felt so bad after what I'd done to her that it took a year to bring myself to file for the divorce."

She glanced at the roof of the truck cab. "Jimmy, there was no break-up, no clue." Looking back at him, she added, "Things slowed down and then, *wham*, you were married. It's like you just plugged someone else in where I'd been...like I didn't mean that much to you."

"It wasn't that, Trish." Again, he looked straight ahead.

"Then what was it?" She waited.

"I just don't know...maybe I thought I didn't deserve you."

She let out a sigh. "Look, Jimmy, I'm not trying to put you on the spot..."

"Well, it feels like an interrogation...like you're a reporter and you've got me under the microscope."

He was right about that. She wanted answers, but even as a reporter she'd never have used such direct tactics. She hadn't been that kind of reporter. She'd never been that direct in any relationship before. And that had been her pattern. But Trish wasn't a reporter anymore. This wasn't just any relationship. And she wanted answers for herself, not for some nebulous public. It was time to break some patterns. She repeated, "But you never even looked me up."

He nodded his head. "I know that. I thought you'd come back to Clayton after college, but then I heard you'd moved to another city to start your career and you'd gotten married, and I just decided to get on with my life."

She looked back at him. "Well, I'm back in Clayton now. And we need to talk about this. I need to know why things happened the way they did. And now I feel like you don't really want me to pursue this story, or that you don't see or care how important it is to me...just like college was important to me."

"Am *I* important to you, Trish?"

"Of course you are. But why do I have to choose...to choose you over college or you over this story?"

He blurted out, "I thought I'd lost you to college; and sometimes I feel like I'm going to lose you to this story."

"How?"

He wagged his head slowly. "I don't know. It's just a feeling I have."

She let out a long breath. "Please don't make me choose, Jimmy. I have to do what I think is right. And I don't know how to give anything but one hundred per cent in my work."

After a few awkwardly quiet moments, he said gently, "I know it may seem hard to believe, but I do love you. I always have."

A few more silent moments later, Trish leaned over and patted his hand. "Thank you for the rafting adventure, Jimmy."

He smiled weakly, and they rode the rest of the way home in silence.

• • •

Early in October, Trish read that France had just set off its second nuclear test in the South Pacific. At 100 kilotons, it was much larger than the first, and had a 5.5 magnitude force. Again, reports of protests from environmental groups followed, as well as reports of feeding frenzies from sharks at the shoreline of the ocean, where huge numbers of fish had been killed by the first French blast.

Trish waited. Then, within a week of the blast, the Earth Week Diary—which she'd begun watching carefully—stated that there was a proliferation of seismic activity worldwide. The quakes jolted Alaska, Mexico, Japan, and all along the Pacific Rim. A huge earthquake with a magnitude of 7 hit Sumatra, northwest of Australia. Mt. St. Helen's had a number of small tremors beneath it, and hiking trails around the mountain were closed.

Within a couple of weeks, Southern Mexico had no less than four large quakes. Then a volcano in Java began showing an increase in seismic activity, while the New Zealand volcano continued erupting. A volcano in Japan erupted for the first time in 257 years.

Finally, Mount Pinatubo was rocked by four explosions that sent clouds of ash thousands of feet into the air, and another Philippine volcano on the island of Mindanao came to life with predictions that it could erupt with the force of the one that first shook Pinatubo in 1991.

She wondered if what she was reading was simply cause and effect, and she wondered if it would be foolish to believe otherwise.

Chapter Twenty-Four

On October 27th, Trish read that France had set off its third nuclear bomb in the South Pacific.

As she had come to expect, for two weeks following that third blast, the earth was impacted with a large number of earthquakes. There were quakes from Alaska to Chile. They continued in southern Mexico. Japan, Taiwan, Africa and Italy were hit. They continued throughout the world in Kyrgyzstan, Iran, Bosnia, and in western China's Tanggula Shan mountain range.

There was also one near the border of China and Kazakhstan. As she read about it, Trish wondered if Yuri and Katrina had felt it.

The test stimulated Trish's enthusiasm to return to the research. She decided to call the English woman that Peggy had mentioned. Trish's hope was that Gladys Hartley-O'Hara might be able to provide her with some contacts in Australia. She was certain that the woman wouldn't have that much new information for her since Trish felt that she'd learned about all she wanted, or at least all she needed to know about nuclear issues.

After placing the call, it quickly became apparent how wrong she was.

The heavy English accent Trish heard on the other end of the phone seemed warm and earthy, but initially hesitant. It was obvious the woman was cautious about opening up to her. To get past those defenses, she assured her of her intentions, about her background as a reporter, and of her relationship with Peggy and Mark. Mrs. O'Hara was familiar with both of them. Once Trish got past that hurdle, a wealth of information came pouring out, every bit as new and fascinating as her previous research.

The woman first outlined some of her work over the previous decades, most of it quite impressive. It didn't seem boastful, but rather an establishment of her credentials to pave the way for their conversation. She had worked in the nuclear movement for over thirty years and had traveled to Russia during the Cold War years, when she helped organize a march that began in the U.S. and went around the world from California to Moscow. Upon hearing that, Trish set her head in her hand. Damn. Why hadn't she been able to establish contact with the woman before she went to Russia?

"But of course," the woman answered when Trish asked if she knew about the earthquakes and volcanoes. But she knew much more. Trish thought it amusing that Gladys, as she asked Trish to call her, began most of her comments with, "Of course, you know…" But, of course, Trish soon realized that she didn't know most of it.

Gladys talked about a host of nuclear accidents that Trish had never heard of before, in spite of what she'd considered fairly thorough research on her part.

"Of course, you know about Chelyabinsk," Gladys commented at one point, as she continued with her litany of nuclear accidents.

"No," Trish admitted almost sheepishly.

"Well, my dear, there were over two dozen towns totally destroyed in that accident...wiped completely off the map."

"Where was that?"

"In the Urals. But, you see, there have been *terrible* accidents over there for years—just dreadful—*massive* accidents. In Kazakhstan every sixth child is born with birth defects.

"Yes, I saw some of them."

"And the Russians finally began protesting—*thousands* of them protesting about it, and the coal miners backed them up. They began their strike—stopped mining the coal—and said to Gorbachev, 'Look, we're not going to give you any coal for your harsh winters.' Of course, they weren't getting paid either. That was what really led to the changes in Russia. The people just finally took back their power." Almost as an aside, she added, "Really, they had it all along, but just like most of us, they didn't *know* they had it. And, of course, if you don't use it, you don't have it. Right?"

"Huh? Oh, yes. Right...right."

As they continued talking, Trish's hand began cramping from feverishly trying to keep up with her notes. It was impossible to take in everything. She simply struggled to keep track of the high points, so she could get back to them more thoroughly when she got off the phone.

"Are you saying the Russian miners were responsible for the end of communism to a large degree.?" She asked.

"To a large degree," she repeated. "A lot of things went into the mix."

"Then I guess we should be grateful to them, too, that the nuclear arms race is over." Trish shifted around in her chair, put her pen down and added, "Peggy says that the nuclear industry is dying, too, that it's like a dying elephant in a china shop. It can cause a lot of damage thrashing about in its death throes, but that it *is* dying."

"I know Peggy and a lot of other activists believe that, and that the arms race is over, but they couldn't be more wrong."

"Why do you say that?"

"Because, my dear, it never *was* a nuclear arms race."

"What do you mean?" As the woman sighed in exasperation, Trish began feeling a sense of inadequacy.

"This was never about national security. It was about *money.* You were a reporter. You know the drill. Follow the money! Who got rich off the Cold War and nuclear power?"

"Who?"

"The mining and uranium cartels, the defense industry. Fabulously wealthy. And it was in their best interest to see the arms race continue to grow at any cost; it was never politically driven. It was financially driven. The rest of us fools were just dancing on a string, thinking we were improving national security and saving the world from communism...or Western decadence, if you were Russian or Chinese. They used fear to manipulate all of us." Then she added almost under her breath, "And I must say that it worked rather well."

Trish could feel a healthy dose of skepticism kicking in for the first time since their conversation began, but Gladys continued, "You see, these cartels all have different names and different subsidiaries, but they're interlocking."

As she spoke, Gladys wove a web-like string of information about uranium cartels around the world—in England, South Africa, Australia, America and Canada. It was a subject that no one had introduced to Trish. She explained that it was the complexities that kept reporters and activists from pursuing the money trails.

"I've been doing this for decades, all over the world, from South Africa to England...and there's a worldwide network of activists who stay in touch with each other. But you'll never read anything about it in the paper. Never. You have hardly anything but tabloid journalism anymore." She thought the press purposely kept the public distracted with trivia, sensationalism and gossip, so they wouldn't have time to ask the real questions that needed asking. "It's the whole Rupert Murdoch thing. It's infectious, I tell you. The media is so controlled and inept." She caught herself almost in mid sentence and added gently, "Sorry, Dear, I don't mean anything personal by that."

"That's all right," Trish assured her, shrugging. "I've been disillusioned with my profession for years now."

Trish picked up her pen again, as Gladys began talking about the rich gold mining areas out West that she said were being exploited by a Canadian mining company.

"Is that where the Interior Secretary...uh... What's his name?"

"Bruce Babbitt," Gladys answered.

"Yeah, Bruce Babbitt. I remember he said it was worse than any gold theft in the history of the U.S...said it was a bigger heist than even Butch Cassidy and the Sundance Kid could have pulled off."

"Exactly. And it's not just gold." Trish continued taking notes as rapidly as possible, as Gladys told her about the U.S. government also selling silver, copper and other resources to the mining companies for about five dollars an acre, without requiring royalties on what they dug up and hauled away. "They're absolutely raping the land, taking down whole mountains. And why do you think the government lets that continue?"

"Why?"

"*Money*, my dear! Money! It's *all* about money." While full of conviction, her voice was also laced with frustration. "They're practically giving that land away, and foreign countries and corporations are making *billions* off our resources…and it's like that all over the world.

"These cartels are getting cheap land, cheap labor…just deplorable conditions in some of these third world countries. They're trashing the environment, and the governments are letting them get away with it for the same reason governments protect any big financial interests. Corruption keeps governments working for them, not the people. These uranium cartels are fabulously wealthy, and most people don't even know they exist. That's what the arms race was really about."

Trish let out a breath and set a hand on her hip. "Gladys, are you suggesting…"

"My dear," Gladys interrupted, "I'm not suggesting anything; I'm very clearly stating that the fear surrounding national security has been encouraged and manipulated to make a relatively small number of people fabulously wealthy at the expense of the vast majority of the people and the planet."

Trish looked across the room with a stymied expression on her face. "But, why the hell would these wealthy people be so stupid as to risk their own health and security…no matter how much money was involved?"

"Ms. Cagle," Gladys began, momentarily leaving informality behind, "enough money can make people feel immune to anything common, ordinary people may be forced to consider: morality, the law…"

"And radiation?" Trish finished, in undisguised disbelief.

In a calm tone Gladys asked, "Have you ever heard of denial?"

Before Trish had time to answer, Gladys told her how the wealth of the world was held in the hands of a small number of people and families. "That's who's behind the decisions being made in the world."

"Gladys, I'm a little confused. Are you saying it's foreign countries or ours or corporations making this money?"

"Trish, when you get to the level of profits we're talking about, there's a whole different structure in place. It's almost like a dynasty. Borders dissolve. Nationalism is non-existent. The main agenda is to manage the wealth of the world. Politics are *used* to manipulate the way the money and resources flow, but the main objective is to keep these families in positions of power.

"Taxpayers of *all* countries have suffered. In *our* country we've funded the development of technologies out the yin-yang—technologies that the private sector couldn't have begun to finance. Then what happens? Things like uranium production get commercialized by Congress, under the guise of the efficiency of the free market. Hell, that's not free enterprise. Nowhere close.

Then, we, the people, have to pay again and again for the very things our sweat and labor brought into fruition. Things we can't control. Things we don't even want."

Gladys didn't miss a beat in her commentary. "If the public had any idea how this cabal of power is manipulating the world economies, commerce and living conditions, they wouldn't put up with it for a minute—not *one* minute. And you'd be astounded to find out who some of these corporations are." She paused just long enough to take a deep breath and added, "And then, of course, there are the banks."

"The banks?" Trish quizzed, arching her eyebrows.

"Of course, Dear. They have to put all those profits somewhere. It's a full circle operation, and banking and investing are part of it, as well. And, of course, you know about the Georgia connection with the BNL and BCCI banking scandals."

"Well, I know about BCCI and BNL."

Trish could tell by the tone in Gladys's voice that she was becoming more and more exasperated with her. She continued to explain, nevertheless, with what seemed like controlled patience, "Look, you always have self-sustaining industries. If these money boys are any good at all, they figure a way to work both ends of a deal—for example, the chemical companies that have polluted the environment. The government devises a Superfund program to clean it all up because the public is screaming, and who gets the job?"

"Who?"

"Subsidiaries of the companies that did the polluting in the first place. Pretty good deal, huh? You rake in record profits by cutting environmental corners. The land and the people get contaminated, and then you get paid to clean up your own mess. Where's the incentive to protect the environment?" Gladys didn't pause for an answer. She told Trish that the public paid for the company's products, and that they then paid with health problems so the companies' profit margins could be even bigger, a fact which she said never got factored into the so-called risk-assessment equations that were being touted. "And then the public pays more in taxes to them to clean it up. Close to ninety per cent of the budget at Savannah River Site goes for environmental management and clean-up now, and who do you think is running it?"

"Who?" she asked again. She shook her head and thought, *Damn, I must sound like an owl.*

"The same ones who were in charge when some of the polluting went on in the first place." Gladys answered. "How do you like *them* apples, Dear?"

"I guess I'm not well versed on this topic."

"Well, you need to be."

Trish felt stung by the terse comment. But before she had time to react fully, Gladys continued, "And the nuclear reactor at Georgia Tech..."

Trish sat up. Reactor? She didn't even know there was a reactor at Georgia Tech. She was beginning to dread acknowledging how much she didn't know.

● ● ●

After Trish took a couple of deep breaths to compose herself, she asked, "They've got a reactor at Georgia Tech?" But before Gladys could respond, she added, "That's in downtown Atlanta."

"Most people *in* Atlanta don't know there's a reactor there, much less that it's been leaking."

"Leaking?"

Trish took a deep breath and started rapidly taking notes again, as Gladys answered, "Of course. They've had all kinds of problems with it over the years, and it absolutely needs to be shut down. With the Olympics coming next year and all the media focus, why, it's a perfect target for terrorists."

Trish began to feel real skepticism at that point. "Terrorists?"

"My dear, didn't you see that TV magazine show last week about those reporters walking right into the Georgia Tech reactor site without any security there to stop them."

"No." She wondered how she could have missed it.

"Well, they walked right into the facility...even got a picture right through the window of the control room and walked around on the roof of the reactor building itself."

"My God. Nobody tried to stop them?"

"Someone questioned them, but they didn't attempt to check them out or stop them. They were doing a story about the lack of security at a potentially dangerous reactor site in the middle of a densely populated area." Gladys stopped long enough to take and release a deep breath. "I'd say they made their point."

"Yeah, I'd say so." Trish rubbed her head.

"If someone with cameras can get in that easily, what do they think a bunch of terrorists at the Olympics or from the Middle East could do? In fact, who do you think was *trained* at Georgia Tech?"

Before Trish could ask "who?" one more time, Gladys answered, "Students from all over the world...*and* the Middle East."

It was difficult to absorb everything so fast. Trish felt like she was eating too much food with no time to chew. At this point she was barely able to formulate questions. "What's Tech's excuse for the lack of security?" she finally asked.

"Oh, right now they're giving mea culpas about how embarrassed they are, and how they'll be sure to get that security tightened."

"God," Trish responded, rubbing her right temple, "it doesn't sound like there was any security."

Gladys told Trish that she didn't know how the people in charge of those kinds of facilities could take the dangers seriously when the government itself was constantly trying to assure the public how safe it was. "Talk about mixed messages." She said that the reactor at Tech was ancient to start with, and had a history of problems. "And there it sits in the middle of downtown Atlanta, for Christ's sake. With the Olympics coming, they just need to get the damned thing out of there for once and for all. It's not worth the risk. Never has been. And not with the Olympic Village right there. The finest athletes in the world will be there."

Trish realized she'd been so focused on the nuclear problems in Kazakhstan and Australia, that she'd ignored a situation in her own backyard.

As she flipped her notepad to a new page, Gladys began telling her about the history of the reactor. It was started back in 1963, for research, teaching, and testing. From the beginning, however, the mindset had been that it was simply another learning tool, like a computer—expensive and important—but not a security concern. There were other nuclear reactors like it at other universities around the country, as well, but the one at Georgia Tech had all kinds of problems.

"What kind of problems?" Trish asked. "Serious ones?"

Gladys talked about a contamination that occurred in the 70s during the re-containerizing of some radioactive Cobalt-60. In 1983 there was a spill of 3,000 gallons of water contaminated with it into Atlanta's sewer system, and the very next year a Cobalt-60 shielding pool overflowed. "It seems like Cobalt-60 is as big a problem as the reactor itself, and it will be radioactive a long time."

Trish continued taking notes as Gladys talked about one of the workers being contaminated with cadmium-115 after a spill in 1987, which he tracked onto a MARTA bus and then back to his home. "They didn't even report that incident. When the press finally picked up on it, the NRC was forced to shut the reactor down for two years. They had one leak that they patched with epoxy, and later the leak started again—only that time it didn't hold. As far as I know, that leak has been going on for years." Gladys took a deep breath. "I'd call that serious problems, wouldn't you?"

Trish sat in amazement. "Are you kidding? It sounds like Homer Simpson was running the place."

"Trish, *no* college officials or campus police are equipped to manage or guard something as sensitive and dangerous as a nuclear reactor." Gladys took and released another deliberately deep breath and explained, "You see, at least at nuclear plants they have monitors to alert them if they've been contaminated. At most of these university reactor sites they don't even have monitors. That's how that MARTA bus got contaminated. No one should have been able to walk out of that facility 'hot'." Trish thought about Peggy setting off the alarms at Savannah River Site when she was contaminated.

"At another university reactor," Gladys continued, "a professor contaminated his own lab and didn't know it. He walked out the door to go to the bathroom and didn't know his hands were 'hot.' He grabbed ole' Mister Potato Head at the urinal and contaminated it, too."

"You're joking," Trish responded in disbelief.

"No, I'm not. Can you imagine trying to decontaminate *that*?"

"No," Trish answered wincing. "Jeez, that even makes me hurt to think about it, and I don't have one." Then she added, almost without thinking, "My friend, Kathy, would probably say that the guy had a real 'fission pole.'"

Gladys laughed out loud right into the phone, and Trish chuckled a little as well. "Oh…God…I can't believe I said that. I guess I've been hanging around Kathy too much. She's starting to rub off on me."

"It sounds like one of your redneck jokes," Gladys added, still chuckling. She attempted as Southern an accent as she could with her heavy English one. "You know, if you think fission material involves a pole and bait, you be might qualified to operate a nuclear facility.'"

Both Trish and Gladys laughed out loud.

After a few more moments of levity, Gladys returned to the topic explaining that the reactor was scheduled be shut down and the fuel rods taken out the next few weeks, but it was just a temporary measure, until after the Olympics. After that they would be up for re-licensing, and if the college got it, the reactor would be restarted with a lower grade of uranium. "But, Trish, it'll *still* be in downtown Atlanta with the same security problems and an aging reactor to boot. And no one in authority, *no* one is focused on the fact that the Cobalt-60—the one they've had so much trouble with—is still there. If they think the thing's not safe to operate during the Olympics, then it's not safe to operate in downtown Atlanta *period*."

She told Trish that when a well respected expert in the nuclear field, Rosalie Bertell, was provided with information and documents about the situation, she said that a terrorist attack there would be worse than Chernobyl. Trish's eyes grew wide, and Gladys added that that information only went out in the German media, on a program similar to the U.S.'s "60 Minutes."

"Holy shit," Trish muttered.

Gladys told Trish that only one small publication in Atlanta's alternative press printed anything about the ongoing problems and the critical, upcoming re-licensing process. "And listen to this. *This* is how Tech began their response to the TV revelations." Trish could hear paper rattling. Then Gladys quoted, "'Despite the fact that the Neely reactor has operated without incident for more than 30 years...' Can you believe that? And no one has challenged it publicly. It's even amazed *me* how quickly this whole episode has fallen under the category of yesterday's news."

Trish was all too familiar with that category. It always amazed her how quickly any story could be replaced with the daily servings of anything that bled. And no one ever bled from radiation exposure.

Gladys suggested that Trish get in touch with a reporter who attempted to get the Georgia Tech story out. "He got the okay to research it from his boss, but after he started documenting all the cover-ups, they tried to pull him off the story."

"Why? What cover-ups?"

"All the violations and accidents...the employee who got fired when they reported the MARTA contamination...and the NRC inspector who had his report altered."

"Altered?" she asked in disbelief. "That's a serious accusation, Gladys."

"Well, don't take *my* word for it. Take a look at the lawsuit he filed against the NRC. He refused to change his report, and when they altered it behind his back, he objected, and they started harassing him from that point on."

"I'd like to talk to this guy," she said with a hint of doubt still in her voice.

"Fine. Got a pen?"

Trish grinned sideways and snickered. "Of course."

When Gladys provided her the name, address and phone number of the inspector and the name and overseas number for the reporter, she added that the reporter was in Germany.

"What's he doing over in Germany?"

"That's where he had to go to get his story out."

"What are you talking about?"

"When he wouldn't let go of the story, they fired him...and he eventually had to go outside the country to get it published. He even shipped the documents separately from his clothes, he'd gotten so paranoid."

"Gladys, do you know how crazy that sounds?"

"Maybe...but just check it out for yourself."

• • •

After the Georgia Tech revelations, Gladys moved on to other topics in rapid-fire order. At times Trish would stand up and pace to keep her circulation going and to release some of the tension building in her body. Gladys recommended books for Trish to read and told her exactly where to get them, because, she said, some were rather obscure, not the everyday kinds of reading materials to be found at a bookstore. She knew the authors of some of the articles, and of one book in particular, that the author had spent fourteen years putting together, while documenting the complex financial connections and actions of the mining cartels.

The woman went on and on, and Trish kept taking notes and asking questions—trying her best not to sound stupid. Then finally she paused and asked Trish, "Your interest in this topic, is it personal?"

"Not really... Well, I *do* have some suspicions that I might have been exposed to some radiation out West when I was a kid during some atmospheric tests back in the '50s." As Trish sat back down, she filled her in on some of the basic details that she could remember from the incident during her visit to Grants, New Mexico.

Gladys sounded stunned. "Grants, New *Mexico*?"

"Yes. Why?" she asked, straightening in her seat. It seemed unlikely that Gladys could be familiar with such a small and remote town.

"I have friends out there, fellow activists. And we went by there on another walk we did on nuclear disarmament out West. They've had a lot of cancer deaths since the tests. Heavens, they even used uranium tailings in gravel around town, even at the school. And it was in building materials, as well."

"You know about that?" Trish was genuinely surprised, and even briefly speculated that the woman might also be right about some of the other things she'd mentioned, things that she'd treated with skepticism.

"Of course, I do," Gladys responded. "Did any of your relatives out there ever get cancer?"

"Come to think of it, my dad's cousin died from it. And the last I heard, his wife had cancer. I don't know about anybody else. We never really kept in touch like we should have over the years," she answered, her voice trailing off. A momentary pang of what felt almost like panic seized her in her solar plexus as her mind replayed her suspicions about her infertility. But it was too personal to share with a voice on the other end of a phone line.

"You know," Gladys was commenting with half a laugh when Trish returned her focus to the conversation, "it's almost comical; whenever those nuclear tests were being set off in Nevada, those idiots in Las Vegas never worried about anything but their gaming tables shaking in the casinos. What a bunch of fools.

"But it's the *Indians* who've suffered most." Gladys told Trish that what happened to them was just another example of a super power taking land away from indigenous people, because they realized that their lands were rich in minerals, oil and uranium. "And then they contaminated them with fallout...but the land was *sacred* to them."

Trish reacted instantly. "Gladys, would you happen to know anything about Indian myths about those sacred lands?"

"Certainly. Some of the Indians marched right onto the test site out in Nevada in the early days. They knew the land wasn't supposed to be dug up because their myths warned them to protect their sacred lands."

But the woman quickly dropped the subject for some reason and returned to an earlier focus. "If you haven't already, sooner or later, you're going to come to the realization that nothing about the use of nuclear power today makes logical sense. Nothing economically. Nothing environmentally. Nothing. It's only from the standpoint of those getting rich off the supply of uranium that it makes any logical sense. So, you will remember, you must get a copy of <u>The Gulliver File</u> to learn about the cartels. That's a given, if you're going to research this angle at all. You shouldn't even get into it, if you're not going to do a thorough job."

Trish felt a twinge of resentment. She always intended to do a thorough job in her work, but, like most reporters, she didn't like her sources telling her how she should do it.

Still, the woman fascinated and mesmerized her. Trish had a feeling that if she could wade through the ocean of facts with which she was being presented, she might find some of the reference points she needed for her own journey through the atomic age.

It was the wading through it that had Trish concerned.

As the lengthy conversation came to a close, she thanked Gladys for her help. Unfortunately, the only activists Gladys knew in Australia were from the Sydney area and weren't involved in the battles going on in the Northern Territory. Just like Mark, she suggested that Trish contact the Greenpeace office. Trish expressed a hope to meet Gladys some day, thanked her again and told her good-bye.

• • •

Before the day was out Trish called the NRC inspector. His story was just as Gladys had described. Additionally, he told her that only one small newspaper article had ever been printed about the lawsuit, and there was no follow-up.

Then she called the reporter in Germany. "Do you mean to tell me they fired you because you wouldn't let go of a great story?" Trish asked as the man finished his account. "Hell, it sounds like Pulitzer prize potential to me, if it's all true."

"That's what *I* thought. And trust me, it's all true. I've got documentation out the wazoo. I couldn't afford to take any chances on this one. They were just waiting for me to make a slip-up. In the beginning, when I started asking questions, everyone tried to convince me that Gladys was a plumb off center. I thought so, too, from some of the things she was telling me, but everything she said was right on the money. And I dug out even more."

The man let out a long, loud breath, then added, "Mrs. Cagle, you know the methods the government uses to try to discredit someone…if she's a woman, she's either crazy or she's a slut. Who the hell cares if she's a raving loony, if the facts are accurate? Follow the information, and if the documentation is accurate, who cares about the source?"

"But they fired you because the story started getting better?"

"I'm sure that's not what they'd say…but figure it out for yourself. If I'd been unprofessional in some way, why didn't they just assign it to some-one else after they fired *me*? Why didn't another publication or network pick it up? And if it *wasn't* a valid story, why did the newspaper here publish it?"

Trish took a deep breath. "I'd be the first one to criticize the way the media works, but this is even hard for me to digest. Could it be that they were worried about scaring people away from the Olympics? Or giving some terrorist an idea he wouldn't have otherwise thought about?"

"I doubt it. Shit, they even had one TV news program where they literally gave any potential terrorists a blueprint on how they could order infectious bacterial agents through the mail and spread them at the event. That was goddamned insane. Besides, they'd already removed the fuel rods, and they could've eliminated any other potential risks by simply removing the Cobalt 60."

Trish set her head in her hand. "I'm still having a hard time accepting that a respected news network would, not only ignore, but suppress a story like this."

"Come on, Mrs. Cagle. Let's be honest. If you were a reporter for any time at all, you know there were some important news stories you wanted to investigate that your bosses wouldn't let you."

She thought about being fired herself from *The Clayton Times*. She'd come close to being fired several times before, but that was the first time she'd refused to let go.

The reporter promised to send Trish a copy of his story. When it arrived in the mail and she read it, something became immediately clear. The reporter had been right. Just like the stack of material Peggy had first given her, the story was pure dynamite.

When she set the article down in her lap, she remembered thinking how frightening it must be to live in a modern city like Darwin, surrounded by crocodiles. Yet Atlanta was a metropolitan city living with an invisible monster in its midst, and its citizens were totally unaware of it. Thyroid

cancer, leukemia and bone cancer weren't the kinds of things you could identify to a source cause, like being bitten or devoured by a shark or a crocodile.
She wondered how many other cities and towns in the U.S. were living unaware of the monsters among them.

The U.S. media never followed up on the report, even when Reuters ran
with it briefly. But the Japanese and Swiss did. Trish learned that both
Japan and Germany said they were considering not allowing their athletes to
stay at the Olympic Village, that they felt betrayed by the U.S. for not telling
them about the contamination on campus. Even though the U.S. press did
report that the Germans and Japanese were considering other housing, they
failed to mention why.

After those unexpected developments Trish called Max.

• • •

"Max, I think I just had a monkey wrench thrown into my research. I
actually think I may be getting too much information," she began, as she
shuffled through the pages of notes she'd taken while talking to Gladys, the
inspector and the reporter.

"How's that?"

She proceeded to tell him about Gladys, about some of the new angles
she'd presented concerning the Cold War, and about the uranium cartel. "Her
stories were unbelievable."

"Well, do you believe them?"

"I don't know." She shook her head. "I have to admit to some serious
doubts about the real motives she thinks were behind the nuclear arms race
and nuclear energy, but she sure seemed to know her facts. She was right on
about the reporter who got fired. She even knew about the uranium tailings
in the schoolyard in Grants, New Mexico." She told Max she didn't know
how anyone could be aware of that kind of obscure information, if they weren't
deeply involved in the mountain of details related to the topic of nuclear
arms and energy.

"So you think her facts are accurate?"

"Yeah," she replied hesitantly. "Of course, I'll have to do a lot more
follow-up and verifying. But the conclusions she's drawn from her facts are
hard to swallow—the whole mining cartel thing and how insidious she says
it is, how the whole nuclear arms race was about money instead of national
security. And the banking thing…I don't know about that. But, still, Max, I
never did think the media investigated those BNL and BCCI stories as thoroughly as they should have."

"Patty, I have to admit I don't know much about that."

She told Max that BCCI was the acronym for Bank of Credits and

Commerce, International. BNL stood for Banca Nazionale del Lavoro. There were two books that described the banks as fronts for influencing U.S. policy in the Middle East and told how the White House armed Iraq. "There was a copy in one of the books of a telex to BNL in Atlanta from the Rasheed Bank in Baghdad. They were asking them to open a $5.4 million credit to finance yarn and wool shipments to the Iraqi Atomic Energy Commission."

Max let out a "hmm" on the phone, and Trish continued, "I remember reading in the paper about the judge, Marvin Shoob, who presided over the BNL trial of the only guy who was ever prosecuted. He said that the man was just a low level scapegoat and that the real culprits were walking free." She told him about a statement the judge issued saying the international bank might be a front to help pay for Iraq's military build-up. "Max, shortly after that, the media practically dropped the whole affair. And I *know* how reporters can get pulled off of stories when they start uncovering things that might embarrass the paper's advertisers. I *know* how intimidated they can get by government and by the threat of lawsuits."

She took in and released a full breath. "What I don't know is what all this has to do with the uranium cartel…and I don't know what wool and yarn have to do with atomic energy, either. Still, Gladys's ideas seem a shade far out to me." Trish rubbed her temples with her hand. "Then I think, maybe it's because she's out on the cutting edge of something, instead of just a kook, you know, like you said about Schliemann and the nut that said the world was round…and yet…" She wondered briefly just how far-out some of her own ideas and conclusions might sound to someone unfamiliar with nuclear issues at that point.

"Maybe there is some truth to it," Max began, "but really, Patty, what's the problem with finding out too much information from a source?"

"That's just the problem: 'too much information,'" she answered with frustration as she stood up and began to pace, with her free hand set defiantly on her hip. "I mean, I could go in fifty directions with these nuclear issues— if I wanted to—and spend a lifetime gathering information, I suppose—like the guy that spent fourteen years on a book that nobody ever heard about, anyway…and probably no one will ever read. It's not that I don't think it may be valid. It may very well *be* valid. It's just, how much of this thing can I handle? How much of a load can I carry?" She stopped pacing and dropped her arm in defeat.

"I don't know, Patty," Max began. "That seems to be the paradox of all learning. The more we learn, the more we realize we don't know. As I've said before, it's a process, a continuum of learning new facts and knowledge. We can never really learn all there is to know. And if we did, where would be the mystery to life?" He inhaled loudly on his pipe. "You may want to consider separating the facts and theories from conclusions you've drawn, and then decide exactly what you need for your own purpose. You seem focused mainly on the mythologies. Do you want to lose that focus? Are the issues interrelated in a way that they can't be separated? Or are they merely important, but peripheral, to the one on which you're working?"

She laughed out loud, as she felt the tension in her body beginning to ease. "Max, your questions always seem to answer themselves." With resignation in her voice, she added, "I guess I'll continue with my main focus and whatever other issues come up related to it, well, I'll just work them into the time frame I have left before Australia...and then the next leg after that, if there is one." She sat back down.

"Next leg?" he asked. "Are you planning another trip after Australia?"

"Yeah, I'm beginning to think so. That's one thing Gladys talked about that grabbed me in my solar plexus." Trish said that when she got back from Australia she might go out West and talk to some Native Americans there, and perhaps do some reconstructing of the history of what happened between them and the government when they opened the Nevada Test Site.

She was surprised by what she was saying, realizing she was formulating plans almost as she spoke. "And I want to take a side trip to Grants, New Mexico, too," she continued, again making her plans on the spur of the moment. "I think I might have lost something there when I was a girl, something I can't get back. It's for me, that personal quest that you talked about."

"Well, you still seem focused to me, Patty." Then he added with what sounded like glee in his voice, "Just keep that glow on your face."

"Max, you old fox!"

As Trish hung up the phone, she thought how Max always had the ability to unblock her when she felt stumped. And she thought how nice it was to be able to rely on him without feeling dependent.

Still, Gladys Hartley O'Hara's distinctive English voice and words echoed in Trish's ears for days on end. She couldn't shake them. They were haunting.

Chapter Twenty-Five

Standing at the kitchen window one morning, watching leaves falling from the hardwoods around her house, Trish heard the sound of a motorcycle in the distance. The sound grew closer and closer until she heard crunching gravel as it moved up in her driveway. She went to the back door and walked out onto the porch just in time to see Mark Matheson dismounting from his bike. She called out, "Mark Matheson. What are you doing up in this neck of the woods?"

"Hey, Trish. Hope you don't mind some drop-in company."

"Are you kidding?" she asked, smiling, as she walked toward him. "Where do you think you are? This is Clayton, Georgia. Folks don't usually wait for engraved invitations to stop by and say, 'hidey.'"

He beamed his boyish smile as he took off his helmet and gloves, then pulled a folder and book from his knapsack on the side of the cycle. When she reached him, they hugged briefly. As they walked to the house, he said, "I decided to spend the day driving around the mountains, since all the leaf watchers from Atlanta have gone home for the season. I wanted to bring you some material I came across that might be helpful. I was already planning to come by Tallulah Gorge and thought I might catch you at home."

The gorge and the falls just outside of Clayton were popular tourist attractions. "How were the falls flowing?" Trish asked.

"Well, with the drought, not as much as usual."

Just before they entered the house, Mark handed Trish the material and dusted off his pants with his gloves. "I appreciate this," she said as he followed her into the kitchen. Then she added, "And you're just the one I wanted to see. I've got some questions…but first let me get you something to drink. How about some iced tea?"

"Sounds great, thanks. Is it sweetened?"

"Of course," she replied with a grin. "Is there any other way in the South?"

After Mark sat down at the kitchen table and Trish prepared drinks for both of them, he quickly gulped a few swallows of his tea, and said, "Listen, I tried to call you the other night, but your line was busy."

"Well, it stays busy a lot these days," she said as she sat down across from him.

"I wish I could've gotten through, 'cause there was this phenomenal report on TV." He raised an eyebrow, "And it was right up your alley."

"Oh, really? What about?" She took a sip of her tea.

"Well," he began, setting his glass down and interlocking his fingers, "it was just a short segment, but it had to do with a rash of reports from some natives in Papua, New Guinea, who say they've been seeing mermaids in the ocean."

Trish's eyes widened, and her expression almost froze. "You're kidding."

"No. I mean, the scientists and skeptics have dismissed the reports by saying that the natives just mistook sightings of native fish, but the natives insisted that they have seen them, that they sure as hell know what their own native fish look like. In particular, they said they've seen a woman with long flowing hair and a man and a baby—pretty specific stuff—not like something you'd mistake for a fish"

"Mark. That's right in the area where the atomic testing's been going on for so many years."

"Yeah, that was my first thought, too. And I thought that someone who'd seen a mermaid herself might be interested in it." He took another drink.

"You bet I am," she said. "It kind of makes you wonder if there were any mutants that actually survived in the open environment...before they got put into jars...or buried." Trish looked directly at Mark. "Do you think that's possible?"

Mark sighed deeply and told Trish that he'd read about mutations in the South Pacific that seemed downright gruesome—even worse than those in Kazakhstan.

"Worse?" Trish asked, wrinkling her forehead. "Like what?"

"Like the women in some of those islands giving birth to what they call 'jellyfish' babies.

"Jellyfish babies?"

"Yeah. Some of them didn't have spines. I don't know what other kinds of mutants were born. I never got into the information too deeply; it got pretty depressing."

Mark's demeanor indicated he didn't want to pursue the subject. He stretched his leg out from his chair and massaged his knee briefly, as he added, "Sorry I didn't tape it for you, but by the time I realized what it was, there wasn't time before the program was over.

"The thing is, though," he continued, straightening back up and facing her, "when you think about the fact that the ozone layer is paper thin, and that and the magnetic field are all—and I mean *all*—that make it possible for us to live on the land instead of the water, it really sets you to wondering if the only way we can survive in the future is to go back to the sea...you know, adapting by mutating."

"Mark, that reminds me of something I've wanted to ask you about since the last time we talked."

"Fire away," he said, leaning back.

"Well, you talked about bacteria and viruses and insects mutating because of all the poisons and antibiotics they've been exposed to…you know, adapting and becoming stronger."

"Yeah."

"Well, could that be what's happening to human beings? Could we be just mutating and adapting to the dramatic changes that have taken place in the fifty years since the atom bomb and all the synthetic hormones and pesticides and chemicals have been introduced to the world? I mean, if the mermaid family story out in the Pacific is true, like the one in the clinic was, maybe…" She stretched her arm out. "Well, maybe that *is* the only way we can survive without a handle on all the contamination. And, really, couldn't we just be getting stronger, and couldn't these changes actually be good, in an odd sort of way?"

He shook his head from side to side. "I don't know, Trish. It may be the way the planet works, but I don't buy into the 'good' aspect of it. Maybe it's a *scientific* reaction, but I can't believe the abnormal looking results are what we *want* to happen." He shifted his weight in his seat and leaned onto the table. "Trish, if our appearances as a species in our evolutionary process are a reflection of our actions, tell me something: do you really *want* us to look like the mutants you saw in that clinic?"

She looked down at the table and shook her head. "Of course not. I mean…" she continued, rubbing her jaw, "mermaids always look so mystical and glamorous in the depictions we see in books and art, but the things I saw in those jars certainly didn't look appealing." She sat up straight. "Anyway, I'm glad to learn about the program. Maybe I'll catch a re-run of it one day."

"Now, about your other questions," Mark began, leaning back. "What else is on your mind today?"

"Wait," she said, as she got up from her seat. "Before we get started, I need my notebook and recorder."

When she returned to the room and set her recorder down, she asked, "Do you mind?"

"Not at all."

Trish sat down, clicked it on and began with, "Look, I always thought that even though nuclear energy was destructive as hell to the environment, at least it was cheap. Now, in the last months I've discovered that it never has been cheap. What gives? Why is the public impression about that issue so skewed?"

Mark straightened in his seat. "Well, first of all, the calculations that industry and government have put out are all wrong. Some of the most expensive costs are never factored into their equations."

"How so?"

He told her that, years before, when nuclear energy was in its formative stages, the industry promised clean, safe, cheap energy. They promised that it would be so cheap that it wouldn't even have to be metered, and people were positively intoxicated by that kind of talk. "But the industry just hasn't delivered, and it never will. It never *can*. The cost overruns at the plants are in the neighborhood of about a hundred billion dollars."

Trish wrinkled her forehead as she looked up from her pad. "Good God."

"Yeah, and now that the licenses for the plants are running out, nobody wants to extend them, because it'd cost too much to keep the aging equipment up. And decommissioning the plants is a real unknown. Some cost estimates are staggering."

"Like how much?"

He leaned forward. "Estimates for three of the larger plants have come in at over five hundred million dollars each. And personally," he added, "I think that's way too low. It could easily run into the billions—especially after everyone gets through taking their cut."

He shifted in his seat and clasped his hands, pointing his index fingers together. "But, here's the thing. Where are they even going to put all the waste? Nobody wants it." He told Trish about a place called Yucca Flats in Nevada that the government was considering using as a repository for the wastes. Around a billion dollars had been spent simply studying the site, and there were plans to spend five billion more on studies. It was far from certain that the place would ever be acceptable. "They had an earthquake in the area a few years back that shattered windows in the field building, which was pretty embarrassing because they'd said the area should be safe from earthquakes for at least ten thousand years.

"Right now they're even looking for a Native American tribe to take the waste on their land on an interim basis in return for millions of dollars a year. They think they've found one in New Mexico that might do it."

"New Mexico?" she asked, looking up from her notes.

"Yeah. Why?"

"Well, that's where I plan to go when I get back from Australia…and that's where I think I might have gotten exposed to fallout when I was a kid."

"Yeah, I remember when you told me about that, but I didn't know you planned to go there, too."

She shrugged. "Actually I just recently made up my mind about it. I think I might find the answers to some questions I have, like why so many of these sites are referred to as 'sacred' by the indigenous people." She twiddled her pen in her hand. "But back to nuclear energy a minute. Why haven't we spent more money on the development of renewable energy sources, if nuclear energy is a failure?"

Mark finished his tea, then explained that the nuclear industry had about a twenty million dollar annual budget to spend on public relations, and that they had spent over twenty million dollars since the mid-eighties on PAC contributions. "That'll buy a lot of friends in Washington. And those friendships keep a lot of government subsidies going. Tax subsidies can shield you from a lot of the consequences of bad business decisions." He told her that the bulk of the research and development money—over half of it—was still being poured into a failed program, instead of toward developing and refining some well-known—and vastly cheaper—energy sources.

"If the industry had had to make it in the market place on its own merit, it would've gone bankrupt years ago." He held up a hand. "And we're not even talking about the legacy of thousands of years of radioactive contamination all over the face of the planet."

Mark explained how solar and wind energy were already working in various places out West. Solar collectors were being used in the Mojave Desert that heated synthetic oil to produce steam, making up to ninety per cent of all the solar energy produced in the world. Wind power produced in the U.S. offset five thousand tons of air pollutants that conventional energies produced. "There's even a town called Soldier's Grove, where they aren't just experimenting with these ideas. They're actually making passive solar energy work right now.

"But the real irony to all this," he continued, leaning forward, "is that the nuclear energy movement really is in full swing right now—like some born again revival movement. Those nuclear interests aren't going to let *anyone* kill their golden goose, no matter what the hell it's done to taxpayers or consumers or the environment. So there's this big push to start building more reactors in China because they're not as politically acceptable here anymore." He snickered. "Hell, that may be one of the reasons we were so damned eager to open up trade with China. Where else would you go if your markets were drying up? The most populated place on the planet might be your best bet for any future expansion."

He sipped the melted remnants of his iced tea. "See, Trish, you've got me on my soapbox again."

She grinned and got up to refill his glass.

• • •

When Trish returned to her seat, she reached for the stack of materials Mark had brought and spread them out on the table. There were several magazines called "Bulletin of the Atomic Scientists" and newsletters from different anti-nuclear groups. She picked up the book Mark had brought and read the title, <u>Nuclear Disaster in the Urals,</u> on the front cover. "Hey, I heard about this one, Mark—the accident at Chelyabinsk?"

"Yeah, that's the one."

"I talked to this woman about it...Gladys Hartley O'Hara. You remember her."

"Gladys? Oh, sure. Everyone in the anti-nuclear movement knows about her." He grinned slightly, and Trish noticed it.

"Okay, Mark. Give. What do you think about her? Truthfully."

"Actually, Trish, I'm not sure. I mean, no one can question her for her sheer knowledge about facts on the nuclear era, but..."

"But?"

"Well," he began slowly, as he squirmed in his seat, "I'm just not sure if she's a little fanatical or just damn brilliant...or both."

"I had the same reaction," Trish agreed.

"I tell you," he quickly added, "when she testifies at some of those DOE and NRC hearings, she literally captivates the audiences."

"I know what you mean. She had me spellbound."

"The truth is," he continued, "that some of the statements at those hearings get dull as dirt after a while, even if you agree with the speaker. But then she'll get up there to the podium—where they have this green and red light to let you know when your three minutes are up—and she'll start by telling how many millions of people she's speaking for who aren't able to be there and speak for themselves."

He told Trish that at one hearing she took a glass case out of her purse and put it over the red light to let everyone know she was ignoring the time limit. "Then she turned to the guy operating the microphone and said, 'And don't you *dare* turn this mike off.' The audience went wild, clapping and cheering and whistling, and I tell you, no one dared to mess with her." Trish grinned and sipped some of her tea.

Mark told how Gladys captivated the audience with her English accent and her delivery. "She talked about war crimes the super powers committed on their own people, especially on indigenous people in the South Pacific, out West and in Siberia, during the Cold War. She told them that she was holding each and every one of them accountable, you know, taking names and kicking ass. And if anyone dared to suggest that she sit down, the audience just went berserk. She didn't sit down till she'd finished what she had to say."

"You're kidding,"

"No, and not only that, but she so moved people at that hearing that this guy who'd been hired to operate the video adjusted the camera for automatic, and went down to the podium to speak his mind."

"What'd he say?"

Mark leaned forward slightly. "He said he was just there to operate the camera, but he couldn't keep quiet any longer. He said he was deeply concerned about what he'd heard and wanted to add his lone voice to those who were opposing the use of nuclear weapons and energy, and that he was ashamed as an American that he hadn't been more aware of what had been going on in the world."

Trish pulled her head back. "Boy, I bet he never got assigned to operate the camera at any *more* hearings."

"I don't think he cared."

She got up and freshened her half-empty glass and then settled back into her seat. "Mark," she began, as she picked up her notepad again, "Tell me about this book on Chelyabinsk."

"Well, it was written by a Russian scientist who was over here in the U.S. He mentioned the accident at a speech he was giving or something. It's been a long time since I read it." He nodded toward the book. "But it's all in there. Anyway, the government people—the spy types—think he's nuts. Nothing of that magnitude could have happened without their knowledge. Right?"

"And exactly what did happen?" she asked, looking up from her notebook.

Mark told her that the place was actually known as Chelyabinsk 40, near a town called Kyshtym, and was sometimes referred to as the Kyshtym disaster. At the time, during the fifties, the Russians were storing their high level wastes from their bomb making in some steel tanks. One of the tanks exploded, and the result was a massive zone of contamination that covered miles and miles. Thousands of people were evacuated from dozens of towns.

He told her that one of the rivers there, the Techa, already had high level radioactive wastes dumped in it from the previous years of secret plutonium production, and that though people were told not to use it, they weren't told why. And no barriers were ever constructed, so thousands of them— tens of thousands of them—continued to use it for drinking water and to water their farm animals, just as they had for centuries.

Mark shifted in his seat. "Of course, leukemia and other cancer rates just soared. Their hair fell out. Their teeth fell out. And they didn't know why. They knew enough to call it 'river sickness,' because they eventually made *that* connection, but they didn't understand why people were all of a sudden dying so young. And even though the doctors were documenting the health cases, no one told the people why they were testing them or what had caused their illnesses."

"Just like at Clinic Number Four," Trish interjected.

"Exactly."

She wondered, *And just like the people at Grants calling their illnesses from the water "Grantsitis," instead of "river sickness?"*

"So, anyway," Mark continued, "the Russian scientist told these spook types that for intelligence people, they weren't very intelligent, that it *had* happened, and he set out to prove it. He compiled a bunch of scientific studies, and asked them why they thought this and that showed up in the studies. Finally, he concluded that the spies were conditioned to just look for secrets, that they were ignoring a world of public information out there that anyone could put together."

Trish wrinkled her forehead. "Do you think they were they really that inept?"

Mark tilted his head. "I guess you could make a case for some pretty remarkable ineptness—especially when you consider all the news lately about double agents who were working inside the CIA itself for so long. Those jerks ignored even the most obvious evidence it was going on, and you can just imagine the amount of damage it caused. So it could have been ineptness—which is bad enough by itself. But I'm also sure Gladys would say it's more sinister than that."

He paused and Trish prodded, "How so?"

He half chuckled and leaned onto the edge of the table. "Well—knowing her—I'm sure she'd say that the CIA knew full well about the accident, but kept it from the public—not for national security reasons—but because they didn't want anything made public that would negatively impact the nuclear program in this country. I guess she'd say that our government will do anything to keep the uranium complex—or cartel—alive and well, that national security never has been their main agenda. It's been keeping private industry financially healthy."

Trish pointed with her pen. "You know, Mark, that may not be as much of a stretch as you might think."

"Why not?"

She inhaled and leaned back. "While you were talking I was thinking about the accident at Chernobyl. Our media didn't cover it like the European press."

"I know they didn't cover it very well, but how was it different?"

She leaned back forward toward him. "At first I bought into the 'no cause for alarm' company line that was being put out. I guess everyone just wanted to believe it. Anyway, one day right after it happened I went to my doctor for my annual check-up, and casually asked him what he thought about the accident, and if he thought it was serious enough to affect us here.

"He lowered his voice, glanced around and said, 'Look, just don't drink any milk or eat any milk products for a while.'" Trish crossed her arms on the table. "It really jolted me." She told Mark that a couple of months later she was talking to a woman who was visiting a friend of hers. She'd been living in Germany at the time of the accident, because her husband was stationed there, and Trish asked her what her experience of the event had been.

"You know, the different perspective bit that reporters like to do about any big news event."

Mark nodded.

"Anyway, she stuns me about as badly as the doctor did." Trish repeated the woman's story about the public warnings that were issued in parts of Europe about staying out of the first rains that would fall. They had to clean their shoes and clothes before entering their homes. They couldn't touch the surface of anything while they were outdoors or go swimming in the lakes, rivers or swimming pools. "The average person had to take all kinds of decontamination steps."

Trish held a hand out. "She told me there was a run on iodine tablets for the kids because that was supposed to keep their thyroids from absorbing the radiation. She almost panicked because she had to go to twelve different drug stores before finding one with pills in stock. The grocery stores even put labels on the foods about radiation counts.

"And I'm thinking to myself, 'Jeez, this isn't anything like what *we're* hearing.' So I go to my editor and tell him I want to do a story on Chernobyl from the European perspective, and tell him what my doctor had said about not drinking milk and all that, and he says, 'Trish, we're not in the business of panicking the public. And, besides, this isn't even your beat.'" She pulled her hand back. "And that was it.

"I mean, I tried several times more to get him interested, or just get him to assign it to another reporter with more of an environmental background, but it got to the point that if I even mentioned it, he'd get furious, and I finally dropped it." She set her elbow on the table and propped her head on her hand.

Mark raised an eyebrow and exhaled. He said many activists had the same experience trying to get some of their media contacts to do more in-depth accounts of the accident. "Trish, we all know by now how much paranoia there is in the news industry about this topic. It's easier for them to write us all off as a bunch of alarmists. But just about any reporter who wants to follow through with a story like Chernobyl hits the same brick walls we do."

He put his hands up in the air briefly in exasperation. "Hell, they hadn't believed anything else the Russian government had said for the previous forty years. So why were they all of a sudden buying into the company line about 'no cause for alarm?'" He told Trish that environmentalists later learned that the nuclear industry had spent millions of dollars on damage control right after the accident, trying to rehabilitate its image.

"That's probably one of the reasons electric rates shot up so high around that time, huh?" Trish asked, snickering.

"Yeah…don't you just hate to have to pay fees and taxes for your own damn brainwashing?" Mark added.

"Look," Trish said, "why don't we go sit in the living room where it's more comfortable? We're through with this material for now, aren't we?" she asked, nodding toward it.

"Sounds like a good idea."

● ● ●

Trish carried her pad and pen to the main room, where they got comfortable in their seats. Mark quickly took up where he'd left off. "Trish, *everything* was hot in those zones: cars, planes, ships, cargo. And it was worse the closer you got to Chernobyl. And who was checking them? Commerce and travel didn't just suddenly shut down. People were radioactive, too. Would *you* want to take in your own relatives if you thought they might contaminate your children?"

Trish touched her forehead, her eyes widened with disbelief. "Heavens, I'd never thought about that."

"Not many people do," he responded.

"But didn't they cool down?"

"Yeah, everything starts cooling down once you eliminate the source of the contamination. But the thing that happened was that the people in the Ukraine weren't removed from the sources, so they were eating contaminated vegetables, meats and milk, and it built up in their systems." Trish remembered Katrina telling her about that aspect of the Chernobyl contamination. "We're part of the environment," Mark continued. "It isn't something separate and apart from us. Even being thousands of miles away doesn't protect you from exposure when it comes to contaminants like radiation."

He leaned back on the sofa and, gesturing with his right hand from time to time, told her that the jet stream carried the radiation around the globe at various levels depending on other weather patterns. He said that it came down in the U.S. at Point Reyes Station, just north of San Francisco during a spring rainfall, and that bird hatchings there plummeted by more than half.

"But what gets me most," he continued, "it wasn't until the fall of communism that a lot of the stories about what really went on in Russia after Chernobyl started filtering into the mainstream media. And that's been only a trickle compared to the stories that get most of the news space, like gossip about the rich and famous."

"Don't even get me started on that one," she admonished, glancing up from her notes.

"But, see, Trish," he assured her, tilting his head, "you did try to do a story on Chernobyl, but it was like the Dawson Forest thing; your editors wouldn't let you."

"Well…I don't know. Maybe I should have pushed harder."

"If you don't have enough information to ask the right questions, it's pretty hard to know where to even start researching a story." He raised a hand and shifted his voice. "Like, what about these cattle mutilations? That would be a good place to start asking questions and doing some in-depth reporting. But the mainstream press won't touch it."

"*Cattle* mutilations?" she asked, pulling her head back.

"Yeah," he replied simply.

"What the hell does that have to do with nuclear issues?" Trish couldn't conceal the look of disbelief on her face.

"Look, Trish," he began as he leaned forward again, "do you believe the mutilations are happening?"

"Yeah, I guess they are…*sure* they are."

"And do you know how many have occurred over the years?"

"I know it's been a lot."

"There have been thousands of them. And it's been going on for years. No one can deny it's real; there's too much documentation. It ought to be a damn good story, so why isn't it?

She shrugged her shoulders. "I don't know. What do you think?"

"Because," he began, gesturing with his hand, "you introduce a little element like extra-terrestrials and everybody starts running for cover. They don't want to touch it. They don't want to talk about it. They don't want to hear about it."

"Well, it does sound a little crazy, you have to admit."

"Only the extra-terrestrial part…and that's the part that keeps the mainstream press away. The story may be bizarre, but it's real, and that ought to be enough."

"Do *you* believe in the extra-terrestrial angle?"

"Hell, no."

"Then what do you think it is? And what on earth does it have to do with nuclear issues?" she asked again.

He held out a hand. "Trish, look where the mutilations are taking place."

"Out West?"

"Yeah…mainly in portions of four states, to be exact. You can actually plot the perimeter of the affected areas fairly well on a map. The highest concentration of the mutilations takes place *inside* that perimeter."

She shrugged. "So?"

"So the only way to approach the issue is to ask what else is—or *was*—going on inside that perimeter."

"And what else was?" she asked transfixed and completely abandoning her note taking.

He leaned further toward her pointing, and said, "That exact same area—with the exact same perimeter—forms the downwind boundaries of the government's nuclear testing sites."

He relaxed back in his seat, crossed his legs and added, "And I guarantee the place you took your vacation when you were a kid also falls in that same geographic area." Trish remembered Katrina telling her how the Russian government plotted the downwind patterns of the nuclear testing, but wouldn't tell the people living downwind that they were in the fallout zones.

Again, he leaned forward gesturing and added, "See, people are reporting the black helicopters and precision excisions that indicate laser tools. There's some pretty sophisticated equipment being used there, I'll tell you. And who else could fund something as expensive as that?"

She raised her eyebrows. "You think it's the government?"

"Who else? Maybe some wealthy business could pull it off, but why would they? Unless they were being *commissioned* by the government to do it."

She scratched her elbow. "So, why would the government be doing it?"

"Secret studies," he replied almost nonchalantly.

"But now, Mark," she responded, looking at him sideways, "conspiracy stories scare off the press, too."

He snapped back, "Then they shouldn't have touched the Watergate story." His tone softened quickly. "Look, the government does secret studies all the time. You know about the LSD studies, and I've told you about some of the others...that we *know* about. They even hid risk assessment studies before private industry ever started building nuclear reactors, they were so bad."

"Yeah, I read about that," she admitted.

He told Trish that the Atomic Energy Commission denied those studies existed until someone got wind of it at a seminar or press conference, where they were asked directly for a copy of it, and they continued denying their existence. He said that at some point a few politicians started screaming and holding hearings. Then the court system finally got involved.

"Even then they didn't release the studies until they finally had to. It'd be the same with these cattle mutilations. You'd have to pull something like that out of them kicking and screaming. They don't want to admit how bad things were. Hell, they were the ones who gave it their blessings, and said that there wasn't any danger from the tests. The government itself probably introduced the extra-terrestrial angle as a cover story to keep what's left of the legitimate press at bay."

Trish was confused. "Why would the government be studying *cattle* in the downwind areas?"

He sighed and nodded his head. "I think they know a hell of a lot more about genetic damage from the bomb program than they've ever begun to admit." He looked up. "You know how I told you about the calf mutations on the collective farms in Russia?"

"Yeah." She started taking notes again.

"Well, they were going on over here, too. We aren't any more immune than the Russians. They might want to determine just how extensive the genetic alterations have been. Cattle out in the open environment would be a likely subject matter. They're large mammals, high up on the food chain. Their main food source is grass, which was highly contaminated by the atmospheric tests. They're right next to us on the food chain because of the milk we consume and the beef we eat." He said that the kinds of organs that had been removed from the cattle—eyes and reproductive organs, etc—were exactly the kinds of tissues a scientist would want to examine to determine genetic cause and effect from exposure to radioactive isotopes. "And besides," he added, "references to those kinds of studies already have leaked out at some scientific seminars."

Trish raised her eyebrows. "Really?"

"Yeah, and you'd probably have some public health agency involved in analysis of the specimens. In fact, the public health facilities at the CDC at Emory University down in Atlanta would be *my* guess."

"So, why doesn't someone just file a Freedom of Information request and see what's going on?"

Mark chuckled and brushed the side of his head. "Not that simple, Trish. They wouldn't let a little old Freedom of Information request intimidate them into rolling over on something they were trying to keep under wraps. They'd have the thing housed under a national security operation. It's just like Gorbachev said—there are tons of things *both* counties are still hiding from their citizens about what went on during the Cold War. And he was in a position to know."

Trish rubbed her scalp with the tips of her fingers. "God, Mark, this is starting to sound like something Gladys would say."

"I know," he admitted, "and I never mentioned this angle before, because I don't like getting into speculations with anyone who hasn't gotten beyond being naïve about the government and private industry. The facts you can document fairly easily are bizarre enough. Getting those out into the public domain is hard enough, much less getting people to believe them."

"To be truthful," she confided, "I still don't want to believe a lot of it. As jaded as I've become, especially in the last few months, it's still hard for me to accept that my own government would deliberately expose its citizens to that kind of contamination." She let out a sigh and shifted her body. "But, Mark," she began, "there's something else that's been bothering me," she began slowly, "I'm not a scientist or a nuclear engineer, and I don't pretend to grasp some of the technical points." She let out a breath. "Mark, I've started wondering if I'm really qualified...if I'll ever be qualified, to try to convey this story to the public."

He took a few breaths and pursed his lips before responding, then propped his hands on his thighs. "Trish, there are a lot of experts in the nuclear field who could dance circles around you and me both, when it comes to details. But even those experts disagree about the application of nuclear energy and weapons. The science is the science. The political issues and the moral issues are something else entirely." He reminded her that some of the most vocal, active opponents of nuclear use were people who once worked within the system and finally realized it was suicidal.

"I can tell from the questions you ask that you're getting a firm grasp on the overall meaning and background of this subject. So don't let yourself be intimidated by the complexities of the science. That may well be what's kept a lot of people and the media from getting involved in the first place." Mark looked at his watch, straightened up and slapped his thighs. "Look, I don't mean to rush, but I've still got a way to go, and I want to get home before dark."

They both stood up, as Trish set her pad and pen down one last time. "Mark, I don't know how to thank you for your help. Things are coming together and making more sense all the time." She told him that trying to cram fifty years worth of subject matter that complex into a few months would have been impossible without a lot of help.

They walked outside to say their good-byes. At his bike Mark turned to Trish and said, "You know, you remind me of the guy who left his camera at that hearing and went down on the stage that day."

"Why do you say that?" she asked, smiling.

"Because you've made a conscious decision to stop merely observing and go down to the stage of life and get involved. And now you don't care if they hire you to observe or act as a camera again."

She laughed self-consciously, then said, "You may not realize it, but you've just hit on something else that's been bothering me."

"What's that?" he asked, propping against the cycle.

She shifted her weight to one foot. "Well, you're right about my taking a position. I've pretty much abandoned the so-called 'objective' view. But, still, it bothers me that I'm not interviewing people from the opposite side— even though I've read all of the pro-nuclear material you gave me and more." She stared at the ground. "I mean, I feel confident in my position, but it'd be stupid to abandon *all* of my training." She looked back up. "And as a reporter, I'd have been looking more at the other side, whether I agreed with it personally or not."

"Hmm…" Mark began. Then with a pointed finger, he said, "Look at it this way, Trish. You've viewed nothing *but* the other side for most of your career."

"How so?"

He told her that for the previous five decades there had been nothing but the company line. He said that at the inception of the nuclear age there were some serious public debates going on in the country, but that the minute people started looking seriously at the risks and public opinion started shifting, it was all shut down. At that point, anyone who opposed nuclear weapons and energy was labeled a communist.

"And, fresh on the heels of McCarthyism and blacklisting, that label was no small threat." He said that then the program went full steam ahead, without the input needed from the ones who would eventually have to foot the environmental and economic bill, and who could have provided balance to the discussion.

He told her that for decades the taxpayers had been subsidizing the industry with untold millions in taxes and electric bills, and trying to contain the continually mounting nuclear wastes—not to mention the billions of dollars in medical bills from nuclear exposure. The industry had spent millions on their PR campaigns, while the other side had only volunteers, small donations and very limited access to the media to get out a trickle of information.

Mark put his helmet on and strapped it. "Why don't you look at what you're doing now as trying to put a little balance back into the debate? Don't you think it's about time truly objective people did that? This is a friggin' democracy we're living in, for God's sake." He held out his hand for emphasis. "And, Trish, you talk about this being such a complex issue. And, I suppose you're right from one standpoint. But it's really not all that complex in the final wash. It's as simple as right and wrong. When you looked at those creatures in Kazakhstan, didn't you just know in your soul that it was wrong?"

She flashed a half smile at Mark. "Now, you're preaching to the choir."

He grinned, put on his gloves, climbed on his bike and started the motor. She thanked him and waved as he drove away, disappearing before a column of dust from the gravel driveway. She thought he'd seemed a lot less scattered with his comments and answers than he'd been in the past. The ride through the mountains must have cleared his head. Or maybe she had finally accumulated enough data that she was simply beginning to understand it better.

Back inside the house, she cleared the glasses from the table, then glanced through some of the material Mark had brought. She couldn't focus on anything. It was too much for one day. She set it aside for later, and went to check the mail.

As she stood at the mailbox, going through the expected menagerie of bills, flyers and magazines, she came across a letter from Katrina. Trish hurriedly opened it and read on the first page that Dr. Klavanis had died. Her body stiffened and her eyes focused sharply as she quickly read and tried to digest the details. His wife had found him dead on the sofa one morning. They thought he'd had a heart attack. Natalya had said he took too many sleeping pills again.

Trish dropped her arms to her side and stared out across the woods. It didn't matter how. He was dead.

She felt an unexpected wave of compassion flood through her for the man who had lost much of his spirit long before his body died. She dropped the mail and cupped her hands to her face as she wept. He'd carried the guilt of the world for so long, and in the end he'd had no priest there to help him cross over. She alone had heard his deathbed confession in the restaurant that night.

She'd be his priest once again.

In her mind she projected herself back in time to his small house and the sofa she'd sat on months before. He was lying there with his eyes closed, a book across his chest. The title was in Russian. Was she imagining this? She looked at his face again. It was peaceful, peaceful enough to calm her doubts. She crossed herself with her right hand and then crossed him, as well. Was this the way it was done? *Hail, Mary, full of grace, Mother of God, bless us sinners now and at the time of our deaths.* Was a part of her really there in that city of secrets and mystery and pain? How much more pain had been born by the women of that city than even Mirek had endured? She held her hand outstretched before her. *Hail, Marys, mothers of Semipalatinsk, blessed art thou among women and the fruits of thy wombs.*

She closed her eyes and then felt herself back in her body, standing in her driveway in Clayton, Georgia. She looked skyward and called out, "I'm doing the best I can, Mirek. I don't understand this anymore than you did, but I'll figure it out somehow." She held her right hand up, clenched in a fist. "I refuse to drown with you."

She looked down, then bent over to pick up the mail. He was gone. And now she felt all alone with the responsibility.

Chapter Twenty-Six

The days following Mark's visit, Trish didn't have the inclination to focus on his latest batch of articles and magazines. Every time she tried, her mind kept returning to Mirek Klavanis. Instead of facts, she needed guidance. It was time to go see Max.

When she drove up to the cabin, he was outside working on the handrail to his front steps. He smiled and waved as she got out of the car. "Doing a little carpentry, I see," she commented as she walked toward the front porch.

He chuckled. "I'm afraid that as a carpenter, I make a very good professor."

She grinned in response.

"Come sit on the porch with me," he said, motioning toward the rockers. As he set his tools down, he added, "This is too lovely a day to waste inside…just the right amount of chill in the air to keep the senses crisp." He took in a deep breath and glanced around. "And I don't think we're going to have many days left to enjoy rocking on the porch before winter sets in for good." After they hugged and sat down, he asked, "Have you got enough firewood stocked up for the season?"

"Plenty. Jimmy helped out in that department."

He smiled. "You know, I really do like that young man."

"I'm sure he'd be flattered to hear that…especially the part about young."

"Well, the fact is almost everyone looks young to me nowadays." He straightened the hair on the side of his head. "Tell me, what's on your mind? How are your travel plans coming along?"

"They're falling into place. I've decided to leave in May instead of April because some sites I want to visit in the Territory don't open till then. I plan to contact Greenpeace as soon as I get to Sydney." She smiled. "I guess I'm going to let synchronicity take care of some of the itinerary." She looked down at the floor and took a deep breath before adding, "But I'm feeling bogged down right now." She looked over at him. "Katrina wrote that Dr. Klavanis died."

"Oh," he began, reaching over to touch her arm. "I'm sorry to hear that. Was it an accident?"

"No. He died in his sleep." She rubbed her temples. "Max, I tried so hard to figure him out. He was so far removed from the decisions that created what was in that clinic, and yet he felt such a tremendous responsibility for it." She looked over at him. "And now I do.

"I went through a little of Mark's material the other day and couldn't focus. It feels like too much information again." She closed her eyes. *"God.* I feel like I'm drowning in it."

"Patty, you might be caught up in your reporter's identity again. You know, you let go of that one for a while in Kazakhstan. Maybe you need to let go of it again in order to write the story."

"Old habits are had to break, Max. Besides, I want to be accurate. I want to be thorough."

"But this isn't about being a reporter. It's about being involved."

Trish propped her chin on her fist and smiled. "Mark said something like that the other day—about leaving the camera and going down onto the stage of life." She let out a breath. "So…" She smacked her right thigh with her hand. "If I'm not a reporter, then what the hell am I?"

With a slight smile, he said, "I believe you've moved to the stage of a seeker."

"What's the difference?"

Max picked up his pipe and began cleaning out the bowl of it. "You aren't simply researching a story here. You're seeking understanding of it. If we don't use knowledge to attain wisdom and put it to use, we're just spinning our wheels." He pointed briefly with the pipe. "And in the process of seeking wisdom, you musn't lose sight of the fact that this story is about you as well—a search *into* yourself. If you keep focusing outwardly, your external reach will only and always be as far as you're willing to go internally."

She sighed. "Well, I've been probing internally a lot lately." She closed her eyes and put her hand to the side of her head. "And it's painful, I can tell you."

"Patty, *go* to that point of pain, just to the edge of it, and then back off a little. Each time you do, you'll trust yourself to go further the next time. And consequently each time you'll be stretching your boundaries and your reach."

She leaned her head onto the back of the rocker. "I don't know how I'm going to reach anyone, if I can't even interest someone like Jimmy in a story like this. I told him about it—even showed him pictures from the clinic—and he wasn't curious at all…just wanted me to get it over with, like he didn't care."

"Do you think people would want to look at *my* collection of pictures from *Dachau?*"

She glanced over at him. "I didn't know you had any."

He looked over the top of his bifocals. "Oh, I have them. But I never even showed them to Rachel. Rarely look at them myself." He pointed to his head, "They're up here." He took a slow, deep breath. "A lot of people aren't ready for what's in *your* head and *your* pictures, Patty."

Trish looked down at the floor of the porch. "Max, I'm not sure how to tell a story like this without the reporter rules."

"This kind of story requires more responsibility, and responsibility is scary."

She looked back at him. "When I tell you I'm overwhelmed with these issues, I'm not telling you I'm going to run from them."

"I know. It's not an easy path you've chosen. When you ignore or deny or run from the dark side of yourself or of humanity, you empower it. It's only through acknowledging and exposing and revealing those areas that healing can occur, and our world is in great need of healing. I'm proud you've walked into darkness with your eyes wide open."

Max set his pipe on the ashtray and interlaced his fingers in his lap. "When you explore the global misuse of power, at some point you're naturally going to ask yourself: 'Where was I when all this was going on? What's been my contribution to the equation?'"

Trish nodded her head. "You've got that right."

"It's natural," he continued, "when you go through some of these profound changes you're going to go through emotional, personal and physical shifts, as well." He told her she needed to be aware of that to maintain a semblance of equilibrium. He didn't want her to be blindsided by the side-effects those internal shifts might produce. He leaned toward her and said, "You shake something up in your perception of the world around you, and it's like an earthquake in a metropolitan city. It's going to make you start feeling things you've never felt before, questioning things you've never questioned, and your resistance to those changes will be intense."

Max picked up his pipe and began tamping tobacco from his pouch into it. As he did, he asked. "Do you remember the times I've compared cultural conditioning to living in a drug induced state?"

She glanced toward the ceiling of the porch for a moment and then back at him. "Yeah…I do."

"I wasn't speaking entirely figuratively." He turned toward her and told her that people frequently negated or completely dismissed the internal chemical and hormonal responses their bodies produced to events and experiences in their lives, and that some of those chemical reactions could be quite potent. He reminded her that they could numb people during physical traumas, sedate them in emotional ones and heighten senses during significant events that demanded attention. He suspected scientists were merely on the threshold of discovering how vast those internal, physical medicine cabinets were.

He lit and puffed on his pipe, then blew out the match and tossed it in the ashtray. "When conditioning—particularly collective, cultural conditioning—the subtle kinds like television can produce—are prolonged and insidious enough, it may just be that our brains, our bodies, react chemically to what we unconsciously know is pure horse manure. I've come to suspect that once we recognize some of the belief structures we've relied on to function in society are false, our bodies literally have to go through a detoxification process."

He inhaled again on his pipe. "Once our spirits can no longer tolerate false external data and stimuli, the body stops producing sedatives that have allowed us to cope during this period—that have allowed us to numb ourselves to our deep psychic lacerations." He tipped his torso slightly forward and tapped his thigh several times for emphasis, adding, "And we have to start *feeling* again."

He leaned back. "No one wants to do that, Patty. No one wants to start the process of feeling that kind of pain. I experienced it at Dachau. It woke me up. Sometimes it *takes* something that profound to wake us up. You experienced it in that clinic. It woke *you* up."

Trish half laughed. "Well, it knocked me out first."

"I don't wonder. Your body and mind are incredible instruments of survival, passion and emotional expression, and will do whatever they have to do to survive. But once you start to examine the illusions that have been constructed for purposes of mass control and begin shifting what you think, you have to totally re-examine *why* you think the way you do."

"Sometimes I think I just think too much."

He held his pipe aloft. "We all do, Patty, but thought isn't the enemy. Instead of relying on it completely, it behooves us to examine how we *feel* about things first. We have to get our thoughts and feelings to work in cooperation."

"I don't know if I even know how to do that. I think I've lost control of my emotions since Semipalatinsk."

"Well…" He drew out the word, then pointed with his pipe. "I think you may have been simply getting in *touch* with your emotions." He told her he suspected that the crying she did upon returning from Russia was a kind of hormonal release of toxic build-up from years of dissatisfaction with the state of the world, her life and her profession. "I told you once we're all coming from pain. We all became trapped in some trauma, neglect or disappointment going back to our childhood—whether familial, cultural or spiritual—that we couldn't face or escape. So early on we started learning how to numb ourselves. We wanted unconditional love so desperately, but couldn't get it from our parents or culture."

He looked out at the forest. "Oh, our parents loved us, but they unconsciously projected onto us the versions of reality that had been passed down to them. We want to be our true selves and to be loved, and we don't have any idea that the only way to get love is to feel it inside and then allow it to flow from us."

Trish looked over at him a moment, and in a soft voice said, "I felt that love once, Max…unconditional love." He looked over at her. "It was with Ilyani. I know now that's what I felt when she touched me." She clasped her hand to her mouth and tried to fight back tears.

"Patty, she was just a reflection of you. The reason you felt that emotion—when others sometimes didn't—is because you allowed it in. You wanted answers." He suggested that she didn't want to believe that what was in that clinic was all that humanity was about, that she needed to see and experience a side of man's true spiritual nature. "It was no accident you found her. You found a part of yourself that day. Something was ignited, and it's stayed with you. It's still there. I can see it in your tears."

He pulled a tissue from its holder on the table beside him and handed it to her. She dabbed her eyes as he continued, "That part is in all of us, Patty."

He explained that no one wanted to look at their shadow side or that of humanity. "But we have to look at it…and own it. We have to embrace it…love it…heal it. That's all healing is: focused, unconditional love. We have to accept who we've been and what we've done before we can fully come to who we truly are. We have to take off all the masks, the encasements and weapons of words and war." He thrust his torso forward. "And that makes us feel vulnerable as hell." He leaned back. "But vulnerability isn't a weakness; it's a strength."

Max puffed on his pipe while Trish continued composing herself. "We're living in awesome times, Child," he continued. "I believe the potential for human growth has never been greater, even with all the chaos we see…maybe *because* of the chaos. Sometimes it takes chaos of this magnitude in order to motivate us to evolve to something new and better."

Trish wiped her nose and looked at him red-faced and said flatly, "Max, I'm having a little chaos in my personal life right now." Trish's face contorted involuntarily, and she covered it quickly with her hands. Choking back a fresh stream of tears she said, "Max, I'm having trouble in this relationship with Jimmy."

"I'd be surprised if you weren't."

"Can I have another tissue?"

Max grinned and handed her a few more. Then he stood up. "I'm going to get us some water."

● ● ●

When he returned to the porch, Max handed Trish her glass and sat back down. She drank a few swallows, then took a deep breath as Max started rocking slowly in his chair. "When you were in college Rachel mentioned a heartbreak you were experiencing over a young man. I suspect that was Jimmy." Trish nodded. "Patty," he said, "relationships seem to drive people crazier than anything in the world, but they're rich and fertile ground for growth, both personal and collective. *And* they help mirror aspects of ourselves."

"Mirror?"

"Yes…just as with Ilyani and the mutants." He told Trish that no relationship or experience was an accident, that they mirrored the parts of people that they needed to acknowledge. "When you went to Kazakhstan, I believe your determination allowed you to see the monsters within humanity as well as the divine within it. You made a global stretch to help facilitate some sort of healing process. And it may well be that Jimmy has re-emerged in your life now because you're ready to heal some of the personal wounds from your own past, as well.

"And if you weren't going through past issues with Jimmy, then I'd imagine you'd simply be going through them with someone else."

Trish straightened up in her seat, intrigued. "I've heard of mirroring before, but I'm not sure I know enough about the concept to understand it."

"Well, to give an example, we might admire a talent in someone without realizing that the reason we may admire it is because we have that same ability as well, one that might be begging to be expressed. We might have negative issues that we refuse to look at, so we project them onto someone else to work them out. Relationships are great catalysts for growth, and the people we choose to have in our lives say a lot about us, whether they're friends or enemies."

"Never thought about it like that before."

Max relit his pipe and puffed a few times, looking out across the forest. He told Trish that people usually defined themselves in relation to or in opposition to other people, and that they could learn more by asking what the presences and actions of those around them were reflecting. He turned to her. "You might want to ask yourself what you admire about Jimmy…what it is about him that drives you crazy or punches your buttons." He pointed the stem of his pipe in the air. "What if relationships are like the story you're pursuing? What if the deeper and further you go into them—into un-chartered territory—the more you discovered about yourself?"

"Well, I like to probe. It's my nature."

"You also like to shake things up, so I'd say you're something of a risk taker. Does Jimmy have qualities like that?"

"Are you kidding? With that white water rafting business?" Trish snickered. "In fact, I didn't realize just how much of a risk taker he was, till we went rafting the other day."

"Patty, it takes a lot of courage to challenge your culture's beliefs about relationships, as well as politics, religion, science…" He tilted his head. "…and myth. It takes courage to dare to view the world and your life differently."

"I don't know about that." She closed her eyes. "Sometimes I just want to crawl in my bed and pull the covers over my head and hide from all this stuff—this chaos I'm stirring up in my life."

"Haven't we talked about creation coming out of chaos in the myths?"

"Well, sure, but…"

He leaned onto the arm of the rocker. "Patty, you're recreating yourself right now. You've given up numerous aspects of your former identity in order to become a new person, a more authentic one. I know this must be painful for you, but you can't go back…unless you intend to start drinking and drugging."

Trish snickered and shook her head no.

Max held his pipe aloft. "I believe it was Nietzsche who said you *must* have chaos in your life to give birth to the dancing star."

"Well, I've definitely got the chaos."

"But that's how growth happens. And it's stimulating…keeps us alive. Most people don't have the courage to shake things up in their own lives. We're all hiding from something—pains from our past and fear of our future. We sacrifice our happiness in the present on those altars every time we deny our pain instead of walking through it."

"Why, Max? Why do we do that?"

"Because it takes hard work." He told Trish that he thought the real irony was that people generally spent more time, energy—and even money—denying, distracting and numbing themselves from their problems than it would take to simply go ahead and acknowledge and fix them.

He looked toward the forest and said, "But, when we deny our pain and problems, our emotions get trapped inside. I honestly believe that that's the source of a lot of diseases." He took a deep breath. "We have to do the healing work to get to the real joy and meaning in life…not that artificial, instant, condensed stuff that's being peddled today in our culture."

Max smiled tenderly at her. "Patty, I've been convinced for years that it takes a lot less energy to be happy than it does to be unhappy. In fact, I think it's our nature to be joyful. And I'm not talking about facades her; I'm talking about being genuinely joyful because you're being authentically who you are, and you're aligned with your purpose in life."

"Of course no one wants to see what's in Clinic Number Four. But we can look there easier than we can in our *own* closets. We can't seem to grasp that the front lines aren't on some battlefield or on some vague frontlines, like they were during the Cold War. They're right here." Max held his hand in front of his chest. "These are the front lines. And it's what we see right in front of us, the relationships we experience every day that really matter."

She stood up and lowered her eyes coyly. "I'm going to powder my nose."

• • •

When Trish returned to the porch, she stood by the rail and propped against a support beam. "Okay, Max, so I'm a seeker trying to understand the story *and* myself, and the only place I know to look is the myths. But, damn it, the myths don't explain anything to me...like why we did it. And nothing will change till we figure that out."

Max stopped rocking a moment, puffed several times on his pipe, then resumed rocking. "Patty, do you remember reading about the beginning of the Trojan War in your research?"

"Yes."

He asked if she remembered how the Greeks couldn't leave for battle because their fleet was stranded in the harbor because of fierce winds that wouldn't stop.

"Yeah."

He stopped rocking. "What do you remember about that part of the myth."

"Well," she began, as she folded her arms and gazed at the ceiling of the porch, "as I recall, Helen ran off with Paris, and the whole country was enraged because they thought it was such an insult. So the people called for war and the leaders started preparing for it. They assembled a thousand ships at...ah..." She looked toward Max. "I don't remember the name of the port."

"Aulis."

"Yeah, Aulis," she repeated, and then continued. "But the northern winds wouldn't stop blowing, and they couldn't launch the ships." She told Max they discovered that one of the goddesses had been angered by a slight by one of the Greeks. Because of that, she had kept the north winds blowing as punishment. "Wasn't it Diana?"

"It was. She was angry because a Greek had killed one of her animals."

"Well, they found out that only the sacrifice of a royal maiden would appease Diana." Trish related how, under the guise of arranging a marriage, Agamemnon sent for his daughter and had her sacrificed, which stopped the winds from blowing so the ships could sail for battle at Troy.

"Very good," he commented with a smile. "Now, tell me: why do you think a man would sacrifice his own innocent child to go to war for ten years over the honor of another man's unfaithful wife?"

"I don't know. The version I read described them as 'battle-mad.'"

"They *were* battle-mad. And I think that particular myth best describes the lengths to which man will go when emotions and hurt pride have been whipped to a fever pitch...when he operates from the ego. Once war has been declared, or even undeclared—as in the case of the Cold War—it's almost impossible to turn the tide. Even a goddess like Diana couldn't do it. Even the love a child couldn't do it.

"And do you realize what the Greeks sacrificed in order to go to war?" he asked, leaning forward.

"The daughter?"

He leaned back. "In the literal context, but in the symbolic, it was the feminine. And from what you've told me about the Cold War, that's what the U.S and Russia did, as well: sacrificed their feminine principle, or the earth, along with their innocent children."

"My God, Max, you're right," she said, standing up straight.

"Remember how you told me about all the sacrificed land since the beginning of the nuclear age?"

She stared into the distance, then turned back toward him and asked, "But I don't understand why our governments didn't stop once they saw what they'd done."

Max took another puff from his pipe and said with resignation, "Patty, men have been just as screwed up by the repression of women as women have been…because they've denied those inherent, nurturing, intuitive, receptive qualities in themselves. In our homophobic, macho world, it takes a tremendous amount of courage to own that."

He stretched his legs out, crossing his ankles, and told her he thought the reason those things happened was simply because God gave man free will, and that meant people were free to make wrong choices. "But free will means we'll experience the consequences of our actions, the first time and every time. And it doesn't matter how smart or rich we are; we experience them because it's the only way we learn. God and Mother Nature don't punish us. We punish ourselves."

He leaned onto the arm of his rocker. "When a toddler sticks his finger in fire, it burns him. It doesn't matter how innocent or cute he is. It burns him each and every time he does it. In fact, it's such a powerful lesson that he almost never does it twice."

"But what about nuclear fire? Why haven't we learned about that yet?"

"Perhaps it's the 'lag time.' The effects of nuclear fire aren't as instantaneous. And then there's the invisible factor—things that are undetectable to the five senses—and," he added with a pointed finger, "there's the fact that the people making the decisions aren't the ones getting 'burned'—at least they're not on the front lines. So they can deny, rationalize, minimize and justify."

Trish frowned slightly and said, "Max, it seems so unfair that babies have to suffer for what we did. They didn't do anything."

He peered over his glasses, "Sometimes it takes something as powerful as sins against the innocents to wake us up and make us pay attention to what we've done."

"Well," she said, sighing, "carrying this load was starting to feel heavy again. That's why I'm here today."

"Then, why don't you try to clear your head of some of these issues for a while, and not take so much of the responsibility? Don't beat yourself up over not knowing things you weren't ready to know." He smiled. "And don't restrict yourself to research while you're in Australia. Turn it into a vacation, as well. You deserve it. And don't have too many expectations about it. Enjoy it. You've been through a lot these last few months, and clearing your mind and lightening up a little might be just the ticket you need to find that new perspective you're searching for."

He tilted his head. "You need to relax. When you do, maybe you'll find that you don't have to find the answers. Maybe they'll come to you."

Trish smiled slightly and said, "I hope so."

Then she walked over to the rocker and sat back down. "Max, I'm not sure why, but Jimmy seems to think he's going to lose me to this story."

"He *is*, Patty."

She looked at him, and he added, "The person he fell in love with a few months ago wasn't even the same person who went to Kazakhstan. You've been changing so rapidly that he's threatened by it."

"Why?"

"Because he doesn't know who you'll be next month or a year from now."

She snickered. "Hey, I don't, either."

"Of course not. You're losing *yourself* to this story." He smiled sideways. "But sometimes you have to lose yourself to find yourself."

Trish smiled back at him. "Max, your talents are wasted on this mountain."

He gave his familiar jovial head back laugh. "Really, now? And, if I weren't 'wasting away on this mountain', where would you go when you wanted advice?"

"Your point is well taken," she answered, still smiling.

They both rocked slowly a while in silence as they looked out across the landscape. The outlines of the surrounding mountains were much more visible since the leaves had fallen. Trish never grew tired of the constantly changing views or of the comfort she always found at Max's cabin.

"Are you getting chilly?" Max finally asked. "We can move inside by the fire, if you are."

"No, Max this is perfect."

When it was time for Trish to leave, she hugged Max good-bye. From her car she called out, "It's a good thing I have a four-wheel drive to get up and down this mountain. I hate to think what the roads are like when it gets icy up here."

"That's why I always have a good supply of wood and food up here in the winter," he called back. "When it gets icy, you don't go *anywhere* till it melts.

"And, besides," he added, "what other kind of car would a rugged, mountain girl like you be driving but a four-wheel drive?"

She laughed and waved goodbye to him, then headed back down the mountain, marveling at how differently she felt than she had on her way up.

Chapter Twenty-Seven

After her conversation with Max, Trish spent so much time studying mythology, it felt as though she was immersing in it. She studied myths from Asia, the Middle East, the Pacific Islands, the Americas and Africa, though she could only find a limited number of Australian myths.

As she read, she looked for common threads as Max had suggested. Once she did, they popped up everywhere. The universal myths about a worldwide flood indicated a widespread—if not global—catastrophe of that nature. She reread the Old Testament about Noah escaping in his ark, and read Incan stories of a man and woman who survived the flood in a box. Indians from the Northwest told stories about some of their people escaping in a log, and she assumed that was a reference to a hollowed out log canoe.

The theme of a Sky Father and Earth Mother in myths from primitive, indigenous cultures was so common that she wondered again why Christianity didn't focus more on an Earth Mother. She recalled Mark lamenting the lack of reverence for the earth in their Western culture.

There were worldwide myths about spirits that lived inside mountains. While that aroused her curiosity, she didn't have any grasp of the meaning behind it, and wondered if, instead of human spirits or spirit beings, the designations were simply primitive symbolisms for natural phenomena, such as magnetic or radioactive fields.

Though the mythological research was fascinating, it was still confusing. At times Trish began wondering again if she might not be on a wild goose chase. She was hitting that barrier again that Max had talked about—the one her logical mind couldn't go past. But she didn't know how to leave logic behind. She'd relied on it all her life.

Then small references began attracting her attention. In a book she found in a used bookstore, she located an Armenian myth that told of a mermaid that lived in the river. In one of Max's books, she discovered myths of Cyclopes and mermen and other strange creatures from the Indians of the Northwest coast in North America. She realized that myths were truly universal—and timeless—as Max had said. They all incorporated tales of hybrid beings, both human and animals, very similar, if not identical to Dr. Klavanis' mutants.

Trish slowly began getting her focus back. Since returning from Kazakhstan, she'd been convinced of a link between events of the ancient past and those emerging from the atomic age. She was also convinced that the legacy of any human event with impacts like those of the huge radiation releases from the Cold War would eventually become incorporated into some future mythology.

Now if she could only figure out how to leave her logical mind behind, or at least suspend it for a while.

• • •

In late November, Trish read that France had detonated its fourth nuclear bomb on the Moruroa Atoll. At about the same time a powerful earthquake struck the Middle East. It was centered near the Gulf of Aqaba. Egypt, Israel, Jordan and Saudi Arabia were hit the hardest. Estimates of the magnitude ranged everywhere from 5.3 to 7.2.

In the Earth Week Diary the next week there were reports of a volcanic eruption in Nicaragua. The Cerro Negro began exploding in a huge fire display that sent columns of lava a thousand feet into the air and sent fifty-pound rocks flying. There were continued rumblings at Mt. St. Helen's. Some one hundred earthquakes had occurred there since the month of September, the same month France had begun its nuclear tests. There had been a number of quakes along the California-Nevada border since September, as well.

Then she read that there was a worldwide increase in earthquakes. There was a string of large quakes all along the Ring of Fire in Argentina, Chile, Mexico, Alaska and the Aleutian Islands. They were also felt worldwide, in Iran, Spain, New Zealand and Pakistan.

Trish put her hand to her temple and rubbed it while she read that the Kuril Island chain in Russia was hit with intense seismic activity for the week following the blast, and that there were no less than seven earthquakes there that week alone, with one as high as a 7.2 magnitude. That one was documented as having been centered at a depth of around thirty-one miles undersea. It was followed by another quake thirty-seven miles below the bed of the ocean.

She was encouraged to read that world condemnation increased against the French government for its continued testing in the South Pacific. The ten-nation Western European Union leveled a fresh string of criticisms in a report it issued. At the European Music Awards in Paris, a few days after the blast, President Jacques Chirac was criticized over and over again for the nuclear tests, and Greenpeace was presented with the "Free Your Mind Award" at the event, for its ongoing efforts to stop the assault on the French Polynesian Islands and its inhabitants. However, the French government seemed to remain oblivious to the growing world criticisms.

Trish also noted in the Earth Week Diary that there had been an important gathering in Madrid that same week of scientists and government officials from around the world to discuss global warming. It was called the Intergovernmental Panel on Climate Change. The panel had concluded that, not only did global warming exist, but the worldwide rises in temperatures could not be attributed to natural climatic changes. Human influence was the only possible cause.

The article stated that ecologists had feared that the group would be pressured to conclude otherwise by what they termed "The Carbon Club." That club was identified as lobbyists for major oil companies. Trish remembered what Mark had told her about the attempts by some companies to keep certain scientific conclusions from being drawn that might impact their financial interests. When Trish read the account, she mused that six billion tons of carbon dioxide released into the atmosphere every year from burning fossil fuels were taking their toll on the world's climate, whether it was acknowledged or not.

But there was something else in the diary that caught her eye that week. She read that the earth's ozone hole over the Antarctic had grown to an area twice the size of Europe at its height during the month of October, and that it had grown at an unprecedented rate that year.

When she talked to Mark Matheson about that fact on the phone one day as she sat in front of her computer, he told her he was aware of it. He cautioned her to take plenty of sunscreen with her to Australia. "And take UV sunglasses and hats, and be sure to use them." He told her that skin cancer rates were around ten times higher there than in any other country because of Australia's proximity to the ozone hole.

He also reminded her about the scientist who'd warned that the nuclear tests were going further down into the earth's mantle than previously believed, when she mentioned the quakes in Russia centered so far below the sea.

Then Mark told her, "I have to tell you that lately you've got me thinking about a lot of things I never thought about before, Trish."

"Like what?" She punched the Save button on her computer and leaned back in her swivel chair.

"You know how you're always talking about this mythology angle?"

"Yeah."

"Well, it has to do with the invisible part." He told her how frustrated he felt that people had difficulty taking something like radiation seriously because they couldn't see or feel it, and had no way of knowing if they were exposed since there was no immediate evidence of damage. Even then, he said, it was impossible assign a direct cause and effect connection. "Then I remembered what you said about plutonium and uranium being named after Pluto and Uranus."

"Yeah." What was he on to?

"So one day, out of curiosity, I looked up Pluto in the encyclopedia, and I discovered that in mythology he had a special helmet that made him invisible."

She leaned forward in her chair. "Hey, that's right."

"I read, too," he continued, "that he hardly ever left his realm in the underworld." He told Trish that Pluto wasn't made welcomed by the other gods on earth, nor at Olympus, because he was such a terrible god—not really evil, but simply pitilessly just.

"Man, I never thought about that aspect before." She rubbed the side of her head. "God, I study this material all the time, Mark, and I can't believe how I keep missing the obvious."

"I just started noticing it myself because you keep talking about it. Then, when I started looking at the symbolisms, I started thinking that maybe…maybe because the dangers are invisible, that since the atomic age began, we've unconsciously been trying to give some kind of form to these dangers—like with movies about giant, mutant rabbits or ants. Remember the one about giant ants?"

"Yeah, I saw that one when I was a kid." She snickered. "Scared the *shit* out of me."

"It's always a giant thing in the movies, sort of like a collective consciousness, where we're trying to say, 'This thing is big—*really* big.'"

She swiveled in her chair. "Hmm…interesting."

"And the Japanese have Godzilla for a mutant nuclear monster in their movies."

"Uh huh…" Trish stopped swiveling and asked, "But why would Western versions of nuclear monsters be giant mutations of common, ordinary animals, while the Japanese created a fictional, almost mythical monster like Godzilla?"

"I don't know, Trish. Maybe because they're the only ones who've had a nuclear bomb dropped directly on them." Mark reminded her that Godzilla did the same thing the bombs did to Japan, by destroying entire cities. He speculated that Godzilla might have been a mythically created version of the bomb—a personification of something too terrible to look at directly. "How else could they deal with those films of children with burned flesh and digest that kind of horror?"

"Hmm," Trish intoned. But before she had time to formulate a question, Mark continued by explaining that in the movies Godzilla was a holdover from the Jurassic period and had lived for eons undiscovered and undisturbed at the lowest depths of the ocean. He said that in the movie version, when they began testing the H-bombs, the monster was contaminated with Strontium-90 fallout and began rampaging on land. Anyone who wasn't killed outright got radiation sickness.

"Hmm," she repeated. "I didn't realize all that. I'm not that familiar with Godzilla movies. But it's curious. It sort of makes you wonder even more about the source of monsters in mythologies. Maybe they're just metaphors for dangers or something." And just maybe Mark was getting past some logical barriers that were still stymieing her.

"Trish, don't you see?"

"What?" she asked, leaning onto the desk beside the computer.

"We create fictional monsters as metaphors, and the monsters are already here in the forms of Cyclopes and mermaids...and animals with multiple or missing limbs. We don't even seem to be able to make *those* connections—even when our myths are replete with the exact same kinds of creatures."

"But we've talked about that. People don't know they're here yet."

"I know, and I know you're going to take care of that. But don't you think that for a long time it was easier for us to deal with on an entertainment or fictionalized level because it was such an overwhelming, unknown danger? Maybe we did it because unconsciously we *knew* how dangerous it was. And now we're starting to see the real consequences of the atomic age because we're finally ready to deal with it on a conscious level."

She picked up a pen and tapped it several times on the desk. "I guess so. Or maybe it's just that more of the consequences—or mutants—are beginning to show up, and they're more dramatic, more like a smoking gun than, say, cancer rates that you could always attribute to smoking or life style. I think a lot of the mistakes of the atomic age just got buried—except at Clinic Number Four." Trish let out a forceful breath. "You know, Mark, we ought to be grateful to the Russians for collecting and preserving the evidence."

"Kind of like finding new evidence from a cold case file, huh?"

"Seems like up until that clinic, it was like Peggy always says: the perfect crime."

"But," Mark continued, "the main thing about the Godzilla movies is how they've evolved over the years."

Trish sat back in her chair, swiveling back and forth again. "You're going to have to explain that one to me," she said, "'cause I'm only marginally familiar with Godzilla. I'm not exactly a connoisseur of Japanese movies. They might build good TVs, but making great movies is definitely not their forte."

"Okay, then." He cleared his voice and explained that in the original movies Godzilla was an atomic mutant monster who destroyed cities and posed a threat to humanity. For some reason, after that he evolved into a monster that actually fought other more dangerous monsters, such as robotic aliens from outer space.

"In essence, in the later movies he eventually evolves into something of a hero to mankind. And do you know why I think that might be?"

"Why?"

"Because eventually the Japanese government and industry came to embrace nuclear energy."

"That's right." Trish stopped swiveling.

"See," Mark continued, "they've created such a dependency on the nuclear industry now for energy, and the public is beginning to have more and more misgivings about its safety. It's like they're saying, 'See, Folks, this monster's not so bad, after all. Look, he can save the planet.'"

Trish picked up her pen and tapped it several times. "Interesting, Mark...but do you think their government and the nuclear industry could actually be that involved in making their movies?"

"Are you kidding?" he asked with half a laugh. "Can you think of any other reason they're so bad?"

Trish chuckled. "Everybody's a critic."

"Hey, it wouldn't take an expert to critique those movies." He also told Trish about a cartoon character introduced to Japanese school children called Pluto Boy. The character said what a shame it was that he was used in bombs because he really loved to work for peace—and that even though there were nasty rumors around about him, he wasn't really a monster.

Trish exhaled. "Man, talk about propaganda." Then she added, "And, God, how transparent can you be?"

"Yeah...Brainwashing 101." Mark let out a deep breath. "See how you've got me thinking now?"

"If you're not careful, Mark, you're going to end up as crazy as me...or Gladys," she added. She took a deep breath. "But, you know, Mark, of all people the Japanese ought to be concerned about nuclear disasters. When that place is so dammed earthquake prone, why would they embrace nuclear energy?"

"You've got me on that one. Hell, I can't figure out the logic of any of these things." He told Trish that there were no less than four major tectonic plates that converged in the area of Japan. "And with that quake at Kobe last year, you'd think they'd get serious about these issues. But all they ever seem to talk about is building stronger buildings and having better drills."

Trish took notes as he continued telling her, "If they think over a hundred billion dollars worth of damage and over 5,000 dead is bad, they ought to imagine a quake that size where they've got a reactor. It'd make Kobe seem like a picnic. And who'd want to buy nuked products?"

Then in a slightly shifted tone, Mark said, "By the way, Trish, one more thing before I have to run. Did you see where some nuclear scientists restarted the Doomsday Clock the other day?"

"The Doomsday Clock?"

"Yeah. You never heard of that?"

She tilted her head. "I don't think so."

He explained that in 1947, after the atomic age began, a group of scientists came up with what they called a Doomsday clock. It was located at the University of Chicago because that was the site of the first sustained nuclear chain reaction. "It was supposed to be this symbolic thing that essentially said that if the hands ever hit midnight, it would signal the end of humanity in a nuclear holocaust."

As Trish took notes Mark said that the scientists decided to start the clock forward toward midnight again because mankind hadn't taken advantage of the end of the Cold War by reducing the threat of nuclear annihilation. "They also said that nothing had been done about treating the wounds on the earth that were created during the Cold War."

Trish said, "Kind of reminds me of what Gladys said about the nuclear threats being alive and well and that we shouldn't let our guard down."

Mark told her that he was sending her some more material in the mail that might help with her research. Trish hated to tell him that she didn't want any more data. She'd really enjoyed his speculations about the connections between the atomic age and mythology and movie characters. So she simply thanked him. She'd skim the material and send it back as quickly as possible.

The two of them made a commitment to talk after the remaining two blasts in the South Pacific to compare notes. Then Mark added, "Oh, Trish, in case you missed it, the French announced that after they've completed their testing, they're going to sign onto the global test ban treaty."

"Yeah. Right."

She didn't even try to hide the sarcasm in her voice.

Chapter Twenty-Eight

On Christmas day Trish read in the newspaper that tremors from a strong earthquake shook the city of Darwin, where she planned to go the following spring. It was centered under the Banda Sea.

Unnaturally cold weather was striking various parts of the world. Japan, Scotland and England were racked by snowstorms. UN troops who'd been sent to ensure the newly negotiated peace in Bosnia were, as well. People as far south as Mexico died from exposure, as did millions of migrating Monarch butterflies. Nearly a hundred people died from the cold in the steppes of Kazakhstan.

The Northeastern United States was hit hard by unusual and early Nor'easters. Storms with winds over one hundred miles an hour hit the Northwest and Texas. Minnesota had wind chill temperatures of seventy-five below zero. And while much of the country suffered under the unseasonably cold, severe weather, California basked in summertime temperatures.

A number of scientists were predicting even more extremes in weather for the future. They explained that those extremes, which were by-products of global warming, would lead to more droughts in some areas and more flooding in others. They cautioned that there would be increased tornado and hurricane activity, and increased wind velocities. But all the while, world-wide average temperatures were continuing to rise.

Even Georgia was taking an unusually early and cold hit from the winter months. Trish thought that the only thing that could be said with a certainty about the weather anywhere, anymore, was that it was unpredictable. She was glad Jimmy had insisted on stocking a large supply of firewood at her back door for the season. She was using it faster than she'd imagined she would.

• • •

In late December, Trish heard on the news that France had detonated its fifth nuclear blast in the South Pacific. French officials said that it was only slightly larger than the Hiroshima blast, registering 5.2 on the Richter scale. They failed to mention that the Hiroshima bomb had been detonated above ground.

Within days, she read that Sulawisi was rocked by a huge earthquake with a magnitude of 7.7 on the Richter scale. It was centered in the ocean, with resulting aftershocks and tidal waves. Two volcanoes suddenly erupted there. A new volcano sprang to life off a Russian peninsula, shooting boiling water more than a mile into the air, and sending smoke almost four miles high. Several other powerful earthquakes in the region followed the quake in Sulawisi, and there were quakes in Venezuela, California and Vancouver Island, as well as in Japan and in the Philippines. Japan's Kuju Volcano, a volcano that had previously been dormant for over 260 years, began erupting.

During the next two weeks Trish clipped out accounts from the paper about quakes around the world, from Guatemala to China to Austria, even in Southern California and Utah. Many were in the range between 4.5 and 5.5 on the Richter scale, the same as the nuclear blast in the South Pacific. There were also reports of whales beaching themselves in Australia.

There was a mention in the Earth Week diary that the ice pack in the Antarctic was badly polluted with radioactive tritium from four atmospheric tests that the U.S. had conducted back in 1963. The levels of radioactivity were 500 times higher than normal. Trish sighed after reading the account. After three decades, it had finally been scientifically confirmed that those atmospheric tests had indeed contaminated the entire planet. But just as with the expose' about the Georgia Tech reactor, the dramatic news was hardly mentioned elsewhere in the media.

One morning, as she read the paper, she came across a very small account on the lower half of the sixth page. France had publicly admitted that they had experienced leaks of radioactive materials in the lagoon near the Mororoa test site. They came from the previous French nuclear tests in the South Pacific—well before their current string of tests. The admission was made only after word of the leaks was unintentionally made public at a scientific seminar. The French government quickly and casually stated that the leaks posed no threat to the environment. Trish thought the only leaks that concerned them were press leaks.

She slammed her paper down and called Mark again. As she stood by the phone in her living room, she fumed about the media's lack of focus on those revelations. "Why the hell isn't someone taking any of these issues seriously? If over thirty years after the fact, we're seeing conclusively how much damage we've caused to the planet, wouldn't you think *someone* would stop and say something like, 'Hey, wait a minute here. If we nuked the entire friggin' planet with those atmospheric tests, maybe we ought to take a closer look at what these underground blasts might be doing to the earth's tectonic plates.'"

She slipped down onto her chair. "Mark, I've completely given up on the print media on this one, but *screw* the print media, why aren't they reporting anything on the television networks?"

"Well, gee, Trish, let me think about that one real hard." The sarcasm in his voice was unmistakable.

"So?" she asked. "Why aren't they? Do you know something I don't?"

His sarcastic tone continued, "Now, could it just be that the owners of two of the three major television networks just also happen to *build* nuclear reactors?

"Duh... That's a real no-brainer, Trish."

Trish rose slowly to her feet, her hand to the side of her forehead, and almost whispered, "Holy shit." She slid her hand down to the side of her face. "I never realized that before."

"Well, just paint me plumb cynical, I guess."

Trish was mystified. Where had she been in her research? Maybe she should have paid more attention to the money angle, like Gladys had said. "Mark, I can't believe I didn't notice this," she continued. "It should have been obvious." She glanced sideways a moment, then back, wrinkling her forehead. "Why didn't you say something about this before now?"

He heaved a sigh on the receiver. "I've come to realize that sometimes it's better to let people find out some things on their own. Then it doesn't seem so much like you're preaching to them—or worse, trying to brainwash them."

She shook her head from side to side and slipped back onto the edge of her seat. "Why didn't I put this together? Of all people, *I* should have noticed. It's so basic: 'Always follow the money.'" She put her index finger to her chin and rubbed back and forth. "You know, I just couldn't understand why world governments would put something as crucial as the health of the human race at stake...not to mention the economic consequences, and now it's starting to make a little more sense." She stopped rubbing. "I'm beginning to wonder if Gladys might be right about some of her other conclusions."

"Trish," Mark said, "if you look at it strictly from the general health and economic standpoint, it won't ever make sense; it'll just look pathologic. And it may be a little of that, too. But if you look at it from the standpoint of who got rich during the Cold War, it makes sense." He let out another, more moderated sigh. "There's something essential you need to know, about the real power brokers in the world...not the politicians most people think are running things."

He told her that there happened to be an extreme minority of people who were wielding most of the power in the world, a handful of families including bankers and industrialists who were essentially running the world. He said that the only reason that so few could run the world economy was that the masses weren't using their own power. By allowing themselves to be controlled by the fears the small minority had planted in them through the media and other institutions, their labor was being exploited and their environment raped.

Gladys had touched on that same subject, but Trish had dismissed it,

320

not wanting to take the time to pursue it. Maybe it was time to do that. She reached for her pad and pen. "How are they controlling things?"

"They set the agenda for the world's economy…not openly, of course." He took a breath and then used as an example a group called the Bilderburgers who were influential people from around the world—not elected officials—but closely connected to them. He told her that their original meeting took place in Europe right after World War II in a hotel called the Bilderburg, hence the name of the group. They met on a fairly regular basis, and it was rumored that they were one of the groups that got together to discuss and begin implementing the economic marching orders from the world's financially elite.

She sat back further in her chair and looked up from her pad. "*Is* it a rumor? Or true?"

"Hard to say when things are done behind closed doors. They even had a meeting recently over at Lake Lanier Islands above Atlanta."

"Really? I never heard about that."

Mark let out a humph. "Of course, you didn't. The Atlanta press didn't touch it. I even called one of my reporter acquaintances and asked why they weren't covering something like a gathering of world famous people that included the likes of Hillary Clinton and the queen of the Netherlands—a damn 'Who's Who' gathering of the rich and famous—especially when this particular one was being held right in their own back yard." He snickered. "You know what he told me?"

"What?"

"That these weren't elected officials and they had a right to meet without being harassed or disturbed by the public glare."

"Jesus Christ, Mark."

"Doesn't sound like the press *you* know, does it?"

As Trish mumbled an expletive under her breath, Mark asked, "What do you think? They were just getting together for a little social fare?"

"Not likely." Trish twisted her pen back and forth.

"Hell," he continued, "the European press would never have given them carte blanche like that. They'd have been waiting by every closed door, asking questions…and at the very least letting people know a secret meeting was taking place and releasing photographs of who was there." Trish couldn't imagine a legitimate reason the American press wasn't doing that. "Shit," he continued, "people here probably wouldn't have given a crap about it, anyway. They'd just pop a beer top and flip on over to the sports channel."

Trish held her hand out into the air. "Mark, I know what you're saying. I ran into some of these dynamics during my career, but this is global…and it's complicated…and *hidden*. People are just trying to make a living and take care of their families the best they can. They don't have the time or energy or where-with-all to even think about all the peripheral implications you're talking about…much less do anything about them."

Mark told her that it wasn't uncommon for people to get concerned about environmental issues when they landed on their front doorsteps. It was only after looking at the issues through their own personal lenses, without having their vision clouded by the filter of media control that they began to see clearly what was going on. It was only then that they realized the old "jobs versus the environment" debate had never started out with a legitimate equation. He continued with a litany of examples of exploitation of workers, taxpayers and their environment.

"And look at all the chemical agents we have stored in Arkansas," he added. "We're so worried about what Iraq has in their chemical arsenal, and I doubt anyone on earth has more of the stuff than we do. Hell, those drums are corroding and leaking, and now the government has this plan to burn the damn stuff, and they don't have any *idea* what kinds of synergistic reactions those incinerations are going to produce out in the open environment." *God,* Trish thought, *do I even want to take notes in this area?*

"Folks in Arkansas are up in arms about it," he added. "*They* know what happened to the people downwind from those weapons plants during the Cold War. The government was saying, 'No cause for alarm,' the whole time they were deliberately releasing massive amounts of radiation on them."

Trish shook her head. "What do you expect people to do? It's too overwhelming."

"They can start by screaming," he shot back. "They can get up off their butts and start exercising their democratic rights, instead of waving the flag and thinking that's all there is to patriotism. They can get out of their foxholes and take a little responsibility for their lives and their government, instead of taking potshots from cover when their living conditions don't go to suit them. They can take a look around and take a look at what the hell is going on in the world around them instead of relying of the television or newspapers or politicians to tell them what's what and how to think and act." He inhaled and exhaled forcefully. "They can start taking a little of their own power back."

Trish fidgeted uneasily in her chair. In the previous months even she had underestimated the unpredictability of nuclear technology and the unintended economic and environmental consequences from the application of that technology. Her research into those unintended consequences from the release of massive amounts of radiation onto the face of the planet kept relentlessly piling up in her notes, her head and her consciousness.

Now it wasn't just radiation. It was chemicals, biological weaponry, bio-engineering—technologies being developed so rapidly that the public couldn't even keep up with the names of them, much less the understanding of them.

When Trish refocused on Mark's commentary, he was saying, "Trish, I don't mean to change the subject, but there's something else I've been meaning to tell you about that might help with your understanding of the environment. Have you ever heard about the Gaia hypothesis?"

"No." She set her pen down momentarily, "but I know that Gaia was supposed to be the feminine earth in Greek mythology. I didn't know there was any 'hypothesis' named after her." *Finally.* He was getting back to mythology.

"Well, all your talk about mythology made me start thinking about it again."

Good, she thought, then asked, "What's the hypothesis about?"

"Essentially it says that the earth is a living, breathing entity—a truly living organism."

"Now I've heard *that* concept discussed, and I've read about it in a lot of myths, but I didn't know there was a name for it."

He told Trish how indigenous cultures had believed it for centuries, but that it was just beginning to filter into the thought processes of Western culture. He said that a lot of people believed the earth would survive almost anything humans did to it, that it could even survive the detonation of all the nuclear weapons in the world. "Basically that's because it's been more radioactive in its history than it'd be from anything *we* could throw at it."

Trish stretched out her arms for a moment, then picked up her pen and scribbled down the heading, "Gaia Hypothesis." Mark told her that as an organism the earth would do whatever it had to do to survive. The concept was that when the earth was first formed, certain laws of nature were laid down to protect it from the effects of any life forms that might evolve over time and threaten its existence. "It's something like an immune system of the body that fights any microscopic organisms that threaten it…like parasites or bacteria or cancers. And the ways the earth fights those threats to *its* existence are those predetermined laws of nature."

He let out a breath. "We know something in the rain forests is the source of a few of these new, emerging viruses, like Ebola." He told her that—since the rain forests were the lungs of the earth and were being threatened by mankind—some people believed the forests were striking back. And they were doing it with the new dramatic, contagious and rapidly lethal viruses that were built into the system eons ago as one of its checks and balances. "Plants do have defense systems, you know, so the concept of a built-in defense system for an entire plant ecosystem isn't really that hard to grasp, when you think about it."

"Hmm," she mumbled as she tapped her pen on the paper. She failed to add that it was a concept that she wasn't quite grasping.

"Well, the organism doesn't fight *all* living systems, only the ones that threaten it." He explained that overpopulation of the planet—or too many people using the earth's finite resources—might be threatening to the host planet. Some people thought these viruses were emerging now because, as top dog on the food chain, man had few predators to keep him in check. And since he was threatening the world's environment, it was possible that the tiniest of organisms—bacteria and viruses—were the earth's built-in checks and balances to keep man from destroying it. "That may be what's behind the emerging viruses and drug resistant diseases we're seeing."

"Hmm," she repeated, as she curled her legs up into her chair.

Mark continued explaining that the earth's systems worked for all the organisms when they were all in balance. "It's only when they get out of balance that the defense systems kick in, or when the systems stop working *for* you, and begin to work *against* you."

At that comment Trish perked up, and with a touch of pride, said, "I think I may actually be starting to grasp this."

He told her he thought of global warming as a fever the earth had developed to fight the infection, which was mankind, since he'd gotten out of balance with the earth. He said that the warmer temperatures could eventually make people start dying off, or thinning out, similar to a fever that killed invading bacteria in the body. It had been documented that the warmer temperatures were causing infectious diseases, like malaria and dengue fever, to spread through world populations as the warmer climates spread. He thought man was bringing this on himself—just like most cancers, which were environmentally caused.

There was no need for Trish to ask questions; Mark was on a roll. As she scribbled notes, he said, "See, primitive man knew how to live in harmony with the earth. He took no more than he needed to survive, and whenever he took for survival, he gave back in reverence and gratitude to the earth. But as modern man has evolved, worldwide population rates are exploding."

Trish continued to busily take notes as Mark explained that in the process of spreading and using the world's resources to such an insatiable degree, man was destroying the surrounding, healthy systems—forest ecosystems, river systems and other species. "Any doctor would call living cells with those kinds of characteristics cancerous. And if you've ever seen any of the high altitude shots they take showing heating in the cities, I swear, they look just *like* pictures of melanomas on a person's skin."

"Really?"

"Here I go—getting into your symbolism again. See what you've done to me?"

She had time for half a laugh before Mark continued. He believed ozone depletion and dead zones in the seas and lakes were a part of that same destructive process. It was as though the planet actually was fighting a cancer on its surface, one that was metastasizing to its underbody from the decades of underground atomic blasts. "If you think of the earth as a cell in a much larger galactic body, that's the way individual cells behave. Survival is a powerful motivating force."

Trish took a breath and dove in. "It sounds like you're saying we're the disease, and these global phenomena are the planet's way of curing itself."

"That's pretty much it."

She twiddled her pen back and forth. "Interesting perspective."

"What I'm getting at here is that environmentalism isn't about the survival of the planet. That's not what's at stake here. Mother Nature can take care of herself very well, thank you very much. It may well be simply the survival of mankind that's at stake. It's not a save the earth or the environment kind of issue. It's strictly a save humanity movement when you get down to the bottom line, and I mean the *real* bottom line, not the one the bean counters always talk about. *That's* what the Gaia hypothesis is about."

Trish propped her chin on her fist. Mark had made things come into focus.

"And strictly from the economic standpoint," he concluded, "this is a doomed system we've created. If you look at environmental resources as assets in a business, I don't care how big and resilient the earth is, when you're using your finite resources up quicker than they can be replenished, sooner or later you're going to go bankrupt.

"God, Trish, it's just a matter of simple math. We're not just depriving our kids of their inheritance; we're bringing them into the world in debt up to their eyeballs. And it's not just financial; there's a health debt they'll have to pay, too. Just go take a look at the St. Jude Hospital in Memphis. Go plot the clusters of kids taken there from contaminated locations. Map it. Take a look. Some of the mothers actually car pool their kids there."

Trish looked up from her pad. "Mark, you've made this easier for me to grasp today, somehow."

"Well, glad I could help."

Chapter Twenty-Nine

In January of the new year a winter storm hit the Northeast, reaching as far south as Northern Georgia. It hit particularly hard in the mountain areas of the state, closing Rabun County schools. Because of her ample supply of firewood and food, the storm didn't seem like more than an inconvenience to Trish. In fact, she welcomed the opportunity to simply read and relax.

Some areas of the county were without power, and when she called and found out that Max's electricity had gone out, he assured her that he was well stocked with firewood and food supplies. His generator was powering the pump on his well whenever he needed water, or to run the heat for a few hours. "Don't worry about me," he told her, "I plan for events like these all year, even get a little disappointed if they don't happen, to tell you the truth. That mild winter last year seemed like a total dud to me."

On the second day of the storm, Trish was surprised to hear a car driving up and looked out the window in time to see Kathy and Mike exiting their vehicle. Kathy was waving what looked like a box of chocolate mix.

After hurrying to open the kitchen door, Trish hollered, "My gosh, Kathy, what on earth are you two doing out in this weather?"

Kathy and Mike shuffled through the snow and stamped it from their boots on the back porch before entering the house. "We just came by to watch the news with you on TV," Kathy answered breathlessly, as she and Mike walked into the kitchen and hung their coats, hats and gloves on Trish's oak hall tree.

"The *news*?" Trish repeated, as they removed their boots.

"Yeah, that's the best part about these storms," Kathy continued, "watching all those fools down in Atlanta playing bumper cars every time it snows."

Trish simply shook her head as she went to the stove and turned on a burner to heat some water. "You nut."

"Don't you just love it," Kathy continued with child-like glee, as she set the chocolate mix on the counter and got mugs out of the cabinets. "I mean, the weather guys say, 'Don't go out unless you absolutely have to, and stay away from the bridges and overpasses,' and it's like this giant signal for everyone to jump in their cars and head for the closest overpass or bridge. Man, it's the best sport on TV!" She looked toward the living room. "I see Jimmy's here."

After Kathy and Mike exchanged pleasantries with him, and Kathy and Trish had passed around the hot chocolate, they all sat down in front of the fire. As they watched the weather reports on the television, Kathy motioned toward the set. "Listen to this," she began, "'Stormwatch '96.'— complete with drum roll. Give me a friggin' break. It snows *two* flakes and the entire state goes berserk. Don't you know those Yankees laugh at us every time this happens?"

"I don't think they're laughing today," Jimmy observed. "They're too busy trying to dig out themselves. Where we get inches, they get feet."

"Well, it blows my mind how silly everyone down South acts about a little snow...*Oh*...Look at *that* one!" she squealed, pointing.

They all turned toward the screen and watched a shot of cars sliding into each other on the incline of a street in Atlanta. "Don't you just love it?" she added, grinning from ear to ear, giggling.

"Kathryn Dunnigan! You are one sick puppy!" Trish mockingly scolded.

Kathy kept laughing, and Mike and Jimmy joined in as well, as scenes of vehicles sliding into each other continued playing out on the television screen.

"Y'all just encourage her when you do that," Trish admonished the men.

Jimmy turned toward Mike. "Did you have any trouble getting over here?"

"Nah," Mike replied, with a wave of his hand. "That four-wheel drive will take you about anywhere you need to go."

Then Kathy added, "Yeah, they close the darn schools, and all the kids are out in their four-wheels spinning doughnuts on the streets. Their parents don't seem to be worried at all about that, but they would have had a *fit* if they'd kept the schools open." She shook her head in exasperation. "Go figure it."

The four of them talked, laughed, watched television and drank hot chocolate until it was lunchtime. Then Kathy and Trish went into the kitchen to set the table and heat up the big pot of chili that Trish had previously prepared. As they worked by the counter, Kathy leaned toward her friend and said quietly, "Seems like old times, huh?"

The two of them looked back into the living room at the two men sitting on the sofa talking. When Mike starting flipping the channels, Kathy reacted instantly. "Hey, don't y'all be turning that to any *ball* game now, you hear?" she cautioned with mock consternation in her voice.

Mike simply waved her off.

"Who the hell would be playing ball in this weather, anyway?" Jimmy asked.

"Oh, don't you worry," Kathy replied. "Mike could find a rerun somewhere if he put his mind to it." Then she turned back to her friend. "Well, what do you think? Does this all seem familiar and comfortable, or what?"

"It does at that," Trish admitted with a smile.

"Remember that time in high school when we were double dating," Kathy reminded her, "and we were all over here having dinner with your folks? Remember how we turned on some mountain music and the two of us did that little clogging routine in the living room?"

"Lord, that really was a long time ago, wasn't it?" Trish stared ahead at nothing in particular, then turned toward Kathy and grinned. "I also seem to remember generous applications of blue eye shadow around that time."

"Think we could still do that little number?" Kathy prompted, nudging her.

Trish looked squarely at her friend. "Kathryn Dunnigan, don't even start that."

When Kathy began setting the table, she asked, "Hey, what do you want me to do with this box on the table?"

Trish glanced at the box, which was stuffed with all of her notes and clippings and printouts from her computer. "Oh, just set it over there," she said, motioning toward a stool.

As Kathy picked it up, she remarked, "Good heavens, this thing is heavy. You could write a *book* with all this material."

"Are you kidding? I could write ten. The only problem would be sifting through all of it to find something to stick together in some kind of cohesive form...and, jeez, I'm probably not even half through."

"Then what *do* you plan to do with it?"

"Oh, I don't know yet. I'm still just riding along with it for now."

"Patty, why *don't* you write a book about what's happened to you?"

"Are you kidding? No one would believe it. Hell, I have a hard time believing it myself half the time."

"What are you talking about? *I* believe it."

"That's 'cause you're my friend, and you trust what I tell you, no matter how far fetched it seems, but I don't think the general public would. She picked up her serving spoon. "You know from what little I've told you how staggering some of this is. Frankly, most people don't *want* to know about these things."

"Why not? I find it fascinating, myself."

"I think it's because it makes them feel helpless." She started spooning chili into bowls. "They don't think they can do anything about it. So they just don't want to think about it or hear about it."

"But there *are* things we can do, aren't there?" Kathy asked.

"If I didn't think so, I wouldn't be doing what I'm doing. In fact, if I didn't think there were some solutions or answers somewhere at the end of this trail, I don't think I'd have been able to bear traveling down it."

"Well, there you have it, then," Kathy responded, confidently. "Just come up with some answers and write about *that* along with the bad."

"Kathy," Trish began, shaking her head, "you always make things seem so simple."

"Yeah...well...*Mike* would probably just tell you that's because I'm simple *minded*."

Trish laughed and tapped her friend lightly on the shoulder with her fist. "You nut."

They called the men to lunch, and the four of them eagerly dug into the steaming chili and continued enjoying their afternoon together snug and warm, while the winter storm began raging again outside.

• • •

On January 27th, Trish saw on the news that France had just exploded its sixth nuclear blast in the South Pacific at Fangataufa Atoll. The straight-forward report wasn't followed by any in-depth questions or background reports, and for the first time since Mark had told her about the ownership of the television networks, she thought she finally understood why. She read in the paper that the test was by far the largest of the six in the series, almost 120 kilotons. It had registered a 5.9 on New Zealand's seismographs. The Australian, New Zealand and Japanese governments publicly stated that they hoped it would truly be the last in what they considered deeply irresponsible actions by the French government.

Worldwide condemnations continued. Actor, Pierce Brosnan, boycotted the opening of his new James Bond movie in France and was speaking out publicly against the bombing of the islands.

Within days after the sixth blast, Trish read that a flurry of earthquakes had shaken the Hawaiian Islands, and that rivers of molten lava were flowing toward the sea, destroying huge tracts of forestland in their path. Another report stated that dangerous and unprecedented releases of sulfur dioxide gas were coming from the Kilauea volcano.

An earthquake of a magnitude 7 struck in Southwestern China, killing hundreds and injuring thousands. A quarter of a million people were left homeless. Within days there were almost a thousand aftershocks, and the Red Cross made urgent appeals for international aid for the area. The quake was reported to be the worst to hit the region since the fifteenth century.

Quakes continued worldwide in Alaska, California and Nebraska. She read that a powerful tremor struck in Indonesia, which was alternately reported as a magnitude 7.5 or 8. Some called it a 'monster' quake. A resulting tsunami swept over the country's Biak Island, killing almost a hundred people outright. Others, who were swept out to sea, were listed as missing. Thousands of buildings were destroyed, leaving uncounted numbers of people homeless.

A powerful undersea quake off the coast of Peru also produced a tsunami that swept through a coastal town killing people and swamping homes.

There were quakes in the North Island of New Zealand. Volcanic activity rumbled Mount Etna, producing a huge column of smoke that loomed over nearby villages. Over a hundred tremors in the Mammoth Lakes area of the Sierra Nevadas led to a low-level volcano alert. The last volcanic eruption there had occurred in 1446.

There were reports that people on a cruise ship near Vanuatu had sighted an erupting underwater volcano, which they described as emitting constant steam with intermittent eruptions of dark water. When Trish read that account, it reminded her of the French scientist who'd warned of a possibility that the blasts could destabilize an underwater volcano.

By now it was clear to Trish that earthquakes were global events. It was also clear that the last and largest French nuclear test had produced the largest global consequences for the planet, as well.

Shortly after France's announcement that the sixth blast would be their last, Trish read that President Chirac was traveling to the U.S. to celebrate the fiftieth anniversary of the U.N., and ostensibly to deliver a speech to America's leaders about the morality of continuing aid to developing countries. "Damn it!" she uttered out loud with her paper in hand. "Who the hell are *you* to preach about morality to *anyone!*"

In February, Trish read that after twenty-three years of applying for licensing, the Watts Barr nuclear plant in Tennessee was given approval from the NRC to operate—even though questions about faulty wiring in the reactor core and defective radiation monitoring systems were being raised. It was the first time an operating license for a nuclear power plant had been granted in years.

Around the time the license was granted, Trish read another very small item in the paper. Scientists had detected fresh radioactive fallout during the previous month over Scandinavia. Levels of cesium 137 and iodine were detected. Its source was unknown. Because of the prevailing winds, it was assumed that the source was possibly a nuclear reactor either in Russia or the Baltic states. Trish was stunned by how little fanfare there was about it. It seemed that the media was continuing its silent co-operation with the nuclear industry to quell stories that might turn public opinion against nuclear energy. And the tiny news space devoted to something as monumental as the licensing of the Watts Barr plant astonished her.

• • •

After the rash of snowstorms that had hit throughout the U.S., Trish noticed an unprecedented and record breaking number of days of warm temperatures across the country. Places in Texas reported temperatures of 100 degrees, even though they had battled ice storms just weeks before. The unusual heat, coupled with strong winds, was blamed for fires that swept across thousands of acres in the state. Even Rabun County was basking in shirtsleeve weather, as daffodils and tulip trees began blooming prematurely.

While Trish enjoyed the welcomed break in the weather, she couldn't help feeling a sense of apprehension, as a few scientists continued to warn that the extremes in weather they were experiencing were a predictable result of global warming. As if to emphasize the point, there was a television program one evening about the thinning ice pack in Antarctica, which sat directly beneath the ozone hole. As it continued melting, unusually large chunks of it were breaking off, one the size of Rhode Island. One scientist was quoted as saying that the formerly solid ice pack was turning into a giant slushy.

• • •

After French President Jacque Chirac arrived in New York for the fiftieth anniversary of the United Nations, Trish read that he had addressed a joint session of Congress to deliver a speech. Reports said that only a handful of the House Democrats attended. The rest boycotted it. Ushers and others were rushed in at the last minute to fill their seats, to avoid embarrassing the French president. In his speech Chirac called for a test ban and said that, "Together we must promote disarmament and combat the proliferation of weapons of mass destruction."

Trish was dumbstruck. Weapons of mass destruction? The past months he'd been exploding the most powerful weapon of mass destruction in the world on defenseless islands in the South Pacific, explosions which had also probably impacted the tectonic plates of the entire globe. Were people blind to this hypocrisy? Maybe not. She continued to read that representatives of various countries around the world also boycotted his speech before the United Nations.

One evening shortly after reading that account, Trish turned her television to the Larry King Live program and discovered that he was interviewing the French president. She turned the sound up louder with her remote and grabbed her pad and pen. The subject of the French nuclear tests in the South Pacific was bound to come up, in light of the worldwide controversy about it. When King finally brought it up, Trish sat stone faced as Chirac proclaimed that all scientists said the testing was perfectly safe for the environment. Chirac was surely either badly misinformed, delusional, or he simply believed that most people were ignorant enough to believe him. She couldn't keep quiet. "You lying son-of-a-bitch! If it's so friggin' safe, why the hell don't you detonate it off the coast of France?"

When King quizzed Chirac further about the condemnations from so many other countries, he responded by lamenting that the Australian leaders and others were excessive with their criticism of the tests.

She blanched again. "*Excessive?* Is bombing a ship and killing an innocent man excessive? How about criminal? How about homicidal?"

Trish continued listening while Chirac praised the democratic process in the interview, while conveniently ignoring the fact that two thirds of his own countrymen had also opposed to the nuclear testing. She was infuriated that King appeared to whitewash the controversy, by giving almost obligatory attention to it and then quickly moving on to topics less "embarrassing" to his guest. *This is news?* she thought to herself. *Damn! It's not even very entertaining.*

She thought that Chirac needed to see what she had seen in Kazakhstan, needed to read what she had read...needed to feel what she had felt. Her level of frustration rose to that of pure rage.

When the interview was over Trish clicked off the television set, grabbed a glass from her side table and sent it crashing into the fireplace.

● ● ●

A few days later, after shutting down her computer, Trish heard tapping at her kitchen door, and the familiar deep voice. "It's me."

"I'm in here at the computer, Jimmy."

He peeked around the door. "I'm not disturbing you, am I?"

"No, no. I need to take a break." She stood up, stretched her back, then walked over and threw her arms around his neck. "I think I'm about ready for another massage."

He laughed as they hugged and said, "God, it always feels so good to hold you after a long day."

"What have you been up to all day?" she asked, as she released her embrace and backed up a step.

"Oh, you know how seasonal the rafting business is. Most of that's been taken care of for the winter, so I just made some last minute additions to the orders for the shop before they went out. And I had some things to do at the farm...fed the horses and worked in the barn a while. What about you?" he asked, glancing at the computer. "Did you spend the whole day hammering away at that thing?"

"Yeah, just about...that and reading." As she sat back down and closed down the computer, she added, "You know, it might sound funny, but when I was working as a reporter, I loved the adrenaline rush I got from working on a daily deadline. Some of my co-workers got ulcers and migraines from it, but I thrived on it...thought it was stimulating." She looked back at him. "But even at that, I almost always wished I had more time and resources to do the stories better. So this isn't as dreary as it might seem. I've finally got a chance to do a proper job, with no time frames or bosses to constrain me."

"It must be nice to have a benefactor like Max so you can *have* the time."

She grinned. "Well, I won't be able to rely on his financial generosity forever. My days as a breadwinner aren't over yet, I'm afraid."

"They could be," he said, raising an eyebrow, "if you'd just come over to my place permanently."

Trish gave his comment a simple sideways glance, after which, he quickly dropped the subject.

"Want to go out to that new restaurant tonight?" he asked after a few awkwardly quiet moments.

"Oh, I don't know," she replied, stretching and yawning. "I think I'd rather just have a quiet night at home. Why don't I grill a couple of steaks and throw a salad together?"

"Sounds good to me. Want me to get a fire going in the fireplace?"

"Yeah, that'd be great."

While she headed toward the kitchen to start getting food out of the refrigerator, Jimmy went to the living room. She heard him rattling with the poker and then, "Hey, Trish, there's broken *glass* in this fireplace."

She winced, and innocently questioned, "Oh, really?" Then she walked into the room and added, "Well...uh...I had an accident with a glass the other night while I was watching Larry King Live."

"Huh?"

She wrinkled her face slightly and added, "Don't ask."

Chapter Thirty

When her departure date to leave for Australia finally neared in May, Trish felt as physically fit as she had in years. Exercising and walking two to four miles a day had given her a lean and tight body. As she packed her bags and made last minute checks on her reservations, she experienced occasional, nagging surges of apprehension. She attributed them to residual emotions from her experiences in Kazakhstan.

Saying good-bye to Jimmy proved more difficult than she'd imagined. It felt as though they were closing a chapter on their lives. Not knowing what to say, she simply shuffled her foot in the grass as she stood by the open door of the car. It was Jimmy who broke the silence.

"Don't let those crocodiles get you."

She grinned. "It's only two weeks; I'll be back before you know it." They hugged one last time.

After driving to the Atlanta airport, she boarded her plane and settled in with a book and a glass of wine. Reading for entertainment was a welcomed change. But, as she read, she couldn't help thinking that her book wasn't nearly as exciting as what she'd experienced the previous few months.

As the oceanic flight stretched, she was glad she'd decided to break it up with a layover in Hawaii. By the time the plane landed in Honolulu, she was ready to get out, stretch and sleep in a bed.

She took a cab to the hotel, where she'd made reservations deliberately close to the beach. As soon as she got checked into her room, she walked out into the darkening night toward the shoreline. She took off her shoes and felt the warm sand on her bare feet. Then she sat down and looked out, listening to the surf beating rhythmically against the shore. As she sat there, feeling a synchronization between the sound of the surf and her own breath, Max's comment about the shore being the symbolic meeting place of the conscious and unconscious surfaced in her mind, and she began wondering about the soul's connection between those realms.

She gazed up at the full moon rising on the horizon. If it affected the tides, couldn't every planetary body and event affect mankind? The weather and setting felt so rejuvenating that Trish wished she'd planned to stay more than just one night.

The next morning, after a sound sleep, she got ready and left for the airport. In route, as she finished reading her book, she noted a few riveting moment in it. However, it didn't come close to the experience she was living already. Maybe nothing could.

As the plane neared the Sydney Airport, the sight of land alone excited Trish. As she deplaned with the other passengers—not only was she relieved to be in a foreign land where she could speak the language—she was thoroughly charmed by the Aussie accents.

When she picked up her rental car, she got a map, and—concentrating on staying on the left side of the road—she drove to the condo she'd rented. She wasted no time making her call to the Greenpeace offices. A recording stated that, due to a national holiday, they were closed until the following Tuesday. That gave her three and a half days to see the sights in and around Sydney, and a chance at the vacation she felt she so desperately wanted. The small terrace of her condo had a clear view of Sydney Harbor and the Sydney Opera House, which she enjoyed a few moments before showering, changing clothes and preparing to go back out.

Even though she felt drained from the long flight, she knew not to give in to the temptation to take a nap. The nap would turn into an eight-hour snooze, and she'd get up wide-awake in the middle of the night, and take forever getting acclimated to the time zone. After rubbing sunscreen over her exposed areas, she hopped back into her rental car, map in hand, and ventured out onto the streets of Sydney.

Driving on the left side of the road didn't prove difficult, except when she turned corners. Then, out of habit, she almost automatically tried to readjust and get back on the right hand side. If the traffic was heavy, it wasn't a difficult transition; she simply fell in line with everyone else. But if there weren't any other cars around, she always tried to make that adjustment at the corners. However, she was adjusting. The added confusion of being in a strange city, to boot, made her super vigilant.

Trish had just enough time that first day for a complete outing at Taronga Zoo. There, she hurried to see all of the animals she'd thought for her entire life she would only see in pictures. Her first stop was the duckbill platypus exhibit. Then it was on to the Tasmanian devils, the wombats and echidnas. She felt like a kid in a toy store, hurrying from exhibit to exhibit, and then back again to her favorites. Her eyes sparkled with excitement. When she stopped to get a drink and catch her breath, she sat down on a bench and glanced up at the huge bush overhead, full of red flowers. She instantly recognized them as poinsettias.

My God, this place is simply heavenly.

• • •

After a refreshing night's sleep, and after a large Aussie breakfast, Trish engaged unabashedly in all of the city's touristy activities. She walked around the old part of Sydney called the Rocks, drove to the Circular Quay for a ferry ride across the harbor to visit an aquarium, and toured the Sydney Opera House. She ate meat pies and other samples of Australian cuisine, quickly developing an appetite for them.

Venturing out of the city, she visited the Blue Mountains and various wildlife parks. Even though the ever-popular koalas and tiny "Joey" kangaroos enchanted her, the sulfur-crested cockatoos quickly became her favorites. Each had its own individual repertoire and each said, " 'Allo," with a distinctively Australian accent. One surprised her by saying, "'Allo, Dawlin'," as she approached it. She couldn't help but laugh out loud. She thought about cockatoos in the South having Southern accents.

One of her free days in Sydney she made reservations to visit a sheep ranch, a short distance outside the city. When she pulled her car into the car park, the tour was just beginning at the old homestead, and she joined a group of Japanese tourists already there. Following the tour, they went to the stables for a horseback ride in the outback, then to the wool shed for a demonstration of sheep shearing. After that, there was a "bit of tupper" in the dining area.

Then all of the Japanese piled into a huge bus and left the ranch for the next location on their tour. That left Trish the only tourist there. One of the stockmen came over and spoke to her in a thick Australian accent. "G'day, ma'am. I'm Jim."

"Hi, Jim, I'm Trish," she responded as she stuck out her hand and engaged in a hearty handshake. He was middle-aged, tall and tanned, with muscular arms, and wore typical Western style jeans, boots and hat. "I'm going to be your guide for the rest of the day."

"Sounds great." She liked the idea of having her own personal guide for the rest of the tour. After following him to one of the barns, Trish got to feed a baby lamb from a bottle. She'd always had a weak spot for baby animals. As she stroked the suckling lamb, she heard a ruckus from a large tree behind the barn. She looked up and saw that the tree was beginning to fill with noisy white cockatoos. The sight reminded her of a Christmas tree slowly being adorned with white bird ornaments.

"Wow, Jim. How incredible." He seemed unimpressed. "You probably see this every day, but they're beautiful."

"Yeh, they come in to roost every evening about this time—just like mates showing up at their favorite bar."

"Did you know that in the states just one of them would probably sell for hundreds or even thousands of dollars?"

"Yeh? Well, 'round here, they're just part of the scenery."

After that, Jim escorted her to a corral area, where he demonstrated sheep herding with a sheep dog. Then—out in an open area—he taught her how to throw a boomerang. When he asked if she'd like to milk a cow, she snickered slightly. "No, thanks, I did enough of that as a kid. I'd rather just talk, if you don't mind," she said, as she leaned against a nearby wooden fence.

"Sure. What's you want to know?" he asked, as he propped his foot on a lower rail and the sheep dog curled up beside him.

She didn't want to slip into her reporter's mode, but it was a habit that was sometimes difficult to break, like trying to get back on the right hand side of the road when driving in a foreign country with left side rules. So, she focused on being more conversational than in an interview. "I'm going up to Darwin next. You ever been there?"

"Once when I was a kid. Me family took me. We drove all the way up in a car, and then back down to Alice Springs to see Ayers Rock. It was hot…and dusty. We musta' ate a ton of dust apiece. We didn't have air-conditioned cars back then, and I ain't never been so bored or miserable riding in a car in me life." He leaned onto a post on the fence. "But when we drove up to that rock, it was sunset, and the thing was glowing all red, like it was on fire or something. And, I tell you, up till then it was the most beautiful sight I'd ever seen."

"I've read it's awesome. The only thing we've got like it where I'm from is a place out of Atlanta called Stone Mountain. They say it's the biggest piece of exposed granite in the world. But, I've seen pictures of Ayers, and I've read that it's huge. I wish I had time to visit it, but I'm afraid I don't have the time. I bet it's a sight to see."

"Yeh, just like its beatin' red heart, it is. They say it's sacred to them Aborigine. And seeing it that first time, I could almost see why."

"Didn't they recently give that land back to the Aborigines?"

"Yeh, it was part of them land rights they been passin'. Been all the talk round here for years. They've been givin' 'em back their sacred lands. At least they say they're sacred. But some folks don't hold with it."

"How's that?"

"Well, they says, 'Why should the black fellow get so much land, when he only makes up one per cent of the population?' And others says, 'Cause the black fellow owned all the land before the white fellow came along and stole it from 'em.' "

"What do you say about that?"

"Oh, it don't matter what I say," he responded, lowering his eyes and shaking his head. "But, I guess if you lives in Sydney, it might seem okay to give back land in the Territory. If you're a Territorian, it might not seem like such a bloody good idea."

"I think I see your point." She put a hand on her hip. "Speaking of land rights, what about the uranium mining in the Territory? You know anything about that?"

"Same thing there, you know. There's a fight between the Aborigines and the mining companies, and them that wants jobs in the mines."

She didn't want to acknowledge any familiarity with the mining controversy. She wanted to hear his personal view of it, unencumbered by any of her preconceived notions.

"The black fellows say those lands are sacred, too. Say it's against their religion to mine them. Say they got myths that forbids it."

"Myths?" She perked up.

"That's what they say."

"You know anything about them?"

"Nah. Some folks say they made them up...or they're holding out for a better deal. Anyway, the government blokes has put a stop to some of the mining."

She crossed her arms. "What do you think about that?"

"Well, it don't matter 'bout my thinking." He hooked a thumb in his pants pocket. "But the blokes in the Territory thinks it's bloody damn generous of the government here to tell them they can't mine the uranium, when they ain't got any uranium of their own to mine. It ain't gonna' to be any skin off their noses, now is it?"

"I guess not."

Trish glanced at her watch. "Look at the time. I guess I'd better head back before it gets dark."

"I'd be worrying more about the Sydney traffic than the dark, if I was you."

She half laughed, "It couldn't be any worse than some of the traffic jams I've been in back home." She reached her hand out to him, "Jim, it's been nice talking to you—and having you show me around the place."

"My pleasure, ma'am," he said as he shook her hand, then tipped his hat.

She walked to the car park, while Jim headed back to the wool shed with the sheep dog following closely at his heels. After starting the car, she sat for a moment and realized that she had just spent several of the most incredible days of her life, all on her own. Her mind was clearer than it had been in years. She was beginning to feel alive again. Maybe Max was right. Maybe if she relaxed, she wouldn't have to look so hard for her answers. Maybe they would find her.

Chapter Thirty-One

The next morning, Trish spent a couple of hours at a three-story shopping mall in Sydney, stocking up on numerous souvenir items, including books on Australia and Aborigine myths for herself and Max. Then she made her way to the Greenpeace offices to discuss the environmental battles in the Kakadu.

When she entered the outer office, she scanned it and the adjoining offices briefly and noted a kind of structured chaos in the activities. After being greeted at the front desk by an attractive, young secretary, and after a brief exchange about the reason for her visit, the woman led Trish to an adjoining room. There, she introduced her to a young, blond man named Patrick O'Conner. Her first impression of him, as he stood behind his desk to shake hands, was that he was tall and almost too young. Maybe, as for Max, everyone was beginning to look young to her.

Almost as soon as they sat down to talk, Trish realized that, despite his youth, Patrick was very intelligent and well informed.

"What kind of research are you planning to do in the Territory?"

"For now, I'm just gathering information. I'm not sure what form it will ultimately take. It started out as a freelance news story in Kazakhstan last summer, but has grown into something else. I guess you could say I'm hooked."

"Environmental research can do that to people. It first hooked me when the French bombed the Rainbow Warrior in New Zealand. Made me madder than a cut snake. And I've been working all my spare time in the movement since then. Before that I never gave a thought to the environment. I was busy surfing and chasing girls." He grinned, adding, "Still do a bit of that now and again, eh?"

She smiled, then asked permission to tape their conversation. Unlike so many people who got second thoughts about talking to a reporter when her note pad or recorder came out, Patrick quickly agreed, as though he was an old hand at dealing with the press. After turning on her recorder and retrieving her notepad and pen, she began her questions. "Tell me, do you know of any genetic damage from any of the atomic testing in Australia?"

"You mean 'bombing'?"

"Well, bombing, then."

"You see," he said with his hand out on the desk, "'testing' sounds like something you do in a classroom. We like to use the proper words. What they're doing is bombing the hell out of the planet."

"I get the picture."

Patrick leaned back in his seat as he began. "When it comes to genetic damage, back in the '50s the Brits did some bombing in South Australia. It's a forbidden zone now, called the Woomera Prohibited Area…though I don't know how they think they can keep the Aborigine out of it. They posted a few signs, but so many of the Aborigine can't even read them. Anyway, some of their kids there were born with missing or malformed limbs."

Trish looked up. "Really?"

"Yeh."

"Patrick, there are a number of kids in Moscow who have missing limbs."

"That doesn't surprise me. They say they've located a bunch of radioactive waste sites in and around Moscow recently."

"You're kidding. I hadn't heard that," Trish responded, wondering how she had missed that little tidbit. "Patrick, just how long has France been bombing in the Pacific?"

"They first started back in 1963, but they didn't go underground with it until…oh…around the mid-seventies. They've conducted them at Moruroa since then. Everyone around here has been up in arms about it—even as far away as Tahiti. The French government still has this mindset that it's a bit of all right to dump on natives whenever they feel like it."

"Yeah, I saw an interview on TV last winter with Jacques Chirac, and it kind of blew my mind when he said there was absolutely no scientific evidence of environmental damage from the blasts."

Patrick instantly and unexpectedly lunged forward on his desk and narrowed his eyebrows. "Then, Chirac is ignoring evidence from his country's most famous son, because, no less than Jacques Cousteau has publicly described all the damage that's been done to that place: the sinking of the atoll, and the radioactivity he found in the lagoon. And Chirac sure as hell is ignoring the health effects to the *islanders.*"

Trish raised her eyebrows slightly at his visceral reaction to her comment. She was glad he didn't have a glass in his hand…or a fireplace nearby.

He sat back and continued by telling Trish that while the French government was expert at covering up, workers and islanders managed to get out a lot of information. He said there had been two accidents that they knew about, as well as a typhoon.

"What accidents?" she asked, with her pen posed in the air.

"They had an explosion in a bunker that contained plutonium. And the other one was when one of the bombs got stuck part way down the shaft. They couldn't dislodge it, so they exploded it anyway."

"You're kidding."

"No. The thing registered a 6.3 on the Richter scale. And a huge chunk of the atoll just dropped off into the ocean, causing a tidal wave. Of course, the French said that the explosion had nothing to do with the tidal wave."

"Jesus." Trish took a breath, held it a moment, then exhaled. "You mentioned a typhoon?"

He told her that during the storm, radioactive wastes were swept into the sea, and buried barrels popped out of the ground. He added that asphalt—which had been used to pave over radioactive wastes on one of the beaches after some previous contamination—was peeled off by the typhoon, and the contamination was washed into the lagoon.

"What did they do about it?"

"What do you mean? They didn't do anything. It's still there. Oh, they retrieved the barrels, but how do you retrieve stuff that's not containerized?" He didn't wait for a response, but shifted in his seat and then stood up. "Look, I'm going to get myself a fresh cup of tea. I'm not sure if that's what you Yanks like to drink, but we have some soft drinks and a little instant coffee somewhere, too, I believe."

"Tea would be just fine."

Patrick left for a few minutes and returned with their tea on a tray. He deftly set it on the table, as he told her about Greenpeace taking a ship to try to test in the lagoon after they'd found traces of radioactivity in the ocean near the island. When the activists got close to the lagoon, French commandos stormed the ship and arrested them.

He handed her a cup of tea, sat down and added, "They just can't stand any independent testing to show the world what they've done there. They can talk about security concerns all they want to, but when they bombed the Greenpeace ship in New Zealand—which isn't anywhere near the atoll—I knew they were just covering up and trying to silence any critics. Actually killed a journalist, you know."

"Yes, I know," she responded, stirring cream and sugar in her tea. "It's a risky profession." She took a sip. "Mm…"

After Patrick sipped his own tea, he continued, "The islanders didn't want the bombing. They objected fiercely at first, but it didn't matter." He said the French took scientists with them to assure the natives that everything was perfectly safe. During the sixties, French President de Gaulle went out on a ship to watch one of the explosions. On the scheduled day, however, the wind was blowing in the wrong direction toward some of the inhabited islands. After postponing it for a day, they were still blowing in the wrong direction. De Gaulle grew impatient and ordered them to detonate the bomb anyway. Patrick said the winds blew the fallout over several islands.

"Which ones?"

"Oh, I don't know all of them, but Cook Islands, Fiji, Samoa…"

"How do they keep getting away with it?"

"I don't know. But that's why I'm in this office today, instead of on the waves, surfing."

Trish sipped her tea, while debating how much to open up Patrick.

He continued, "Truth is, it's not much different than what the U.S. did in the Marshall Islands in Micronesia. They exploded dozens of nuclear weapons there and left the islands virtually uninhabitable."

"But they've tested...uh, *bombed* mostly in the last few decades out West in Nevada. Right?"

"In recent years, yeh. But in the beginning they did the same number on the natives there that the French are doing in the South Pacific. Same scenario." He told Trish how the Rongelaps had to leave the islands permanently because of cancers, miscarriages and other health problems they'd developed.

"Of course, the U.S. told them back in the '40s that it was all perfectly safe, just like the French did at Moruroa." He told Trish that even after the U.S. had finished their bombing in the 50s, they continued their safety assurances, but that the radiation levels continued climbing so high that they finally had to recant. They told the islanders over twenty years later that they were going to have to abandon their northern islands.

"The islanders weren't stupid, though. They knew the birds and fish they ate were still navigating through the entire atoll, and they'd still be exposed, even if they never went to the northern islands again. So they decided that they had to leave their home entirely." He told her that a Greenpeace ship carried them off their islands, and that he'd seen films of the evacuation, and didn't think any modern person could fully grasp the impact of taking a native people from their lands. "That alone was almost as bad as the radiation to them. Native people hold their lands to be sacred, just like the Aborigine, and your Native Americans."

Trish glanced up. She set her cup and saucer down on the desk. "You know, Patrick, I have this theory about primitive sacred lands around the world."

"What's that?"

"It may just be a coincidence, but out West in the Indian Territory, and in Kazakhstan, and here in the Aboriginal lands, a lot of the sacred lands are also rich in uranium and gold."

"Well, you might have a rough time with that theory, as far as the Aborigines are concerned."

"Why's that?" she asked, crossing her legs.

"Because to them, the whole earth is sacred."

"Well, I know that, but aren't there some areas that they'd consider more sacred than others...or that might have a different significance to them?"

"That may be true." He looked at the ceiling and rubbed his jaw. "I guess it'd be like thinking the body was sacred, and yet some parts of it, like the heart, would be more vital than others. That could be."

Trish remembered Jim's description of Ayers Rock as the red heart at the center of the continent, but since Patrick didn't seem to have any interest in her theory, she returned to her former line of questions. "Would you have any material on the battles between the mining companies and the Aborigines in the Northern Territory? That's where I'm going next."

"Oh, sure. There were a few magazine and newspaper reports that managed to really capture the essence of it. Let me get you some copies."

He opened a file cabinet beside his desk, pulled out some papers, and then went to a copying machine in the main office. The phone rang beside him, and she could see him talking while he made copies. She looked around at everyone else in the outer office. They were working at warp speed. It reminded her of a newsroom just before deadline, and she wondered if the hectic pace of the activity was part of the normal routine, or the result of some specific event.

After sipping the last of her tea, she got up and strolled around Patrick's office, looking at the magazines, pamphlets and papers stacked on the shelves. She picked up a page from one of the stacks. It was a copy of an article from the Sydney Morning Herald. Someone had handwritten across the top "Green Giggles." It stated that a French Foreign ministry official was trying to appease protesters of the testing at Moruroa Atoll by telling them that the area could be turned into a resort when his country had completed their nuclear tests.

A few of Australia's advertising agencies had come up with some tongue-in-cheek suggestions for names for the resort, such as: "Ill Paradiso," and "Club Ded." They suggested catch phrases for the advertising, like: "For the tan that radiates," and "Holiday in the Tropic of Cancer," and "Radiant smiles, glowing hospitality," and "Have the holiday of your half-life," and even "Bomb Voyage." Trish smiled as she read the article.

When Patrick returned with the copies and handed them to her, his phone rang again. He held up a finger. "Excuse me just a minute."

Trish began feeling as though she was intruding on the office routine. When she was a reporter, it always irritated her to be concentrating on a story and have someone call or come in, and interrupt her train of thought. She thought the people in the office were probably mostly volunteers and needed all the help they could get with their own work. She decided to get the information on the Kakadu battle and the names of some contacts from Patrick and cut the interview short.

"Sorry about that," he said as he hung up the phone. "Always something. But these articles should give you a place to start."

"I appreciate it. And, one more thing if you don't mind, would you have any contacts with environmentalists in the Darwin area I might reach for more information?"

"Sure."

He punched some keys on his computer, turned on his printer, and made copies, as he finished the last of his tea. He handed her two sheets of paper with names and phone numbers on them. "These are some local people near Darwin who worked on trying to close down the mining. Don't know how much help they might be to you now, though. A lot of the ones who were active back then have tried to get on with their lives. Blokes can burn out pretty quickly in this game."

"I'm sure of that, but every bit helps."

"You ever been to the Top End before?"

"No, I've never even been to Australia before."

"Well, most Yanks find it to be a dinkum place."

"It's certainly that," she replied, proud that she had recognized one of the local colloquialisms.

As she stood to leave, she pocketed her recorder and note pad. "I really appreciate your time, Patrick...and the tea."

"No worries."

Just then Patrick's phone rang again.

She smiled and reached out and shook his hand. "Let me get out of your hair. And thanks again."

"G'day to ya.'"

She left him talking on the phone.

● ● ●

Trish didn't want to spend her last day in Sydney stuck indoors studying, so the next morning, she took a warm jacket and a blanket from the condo to protect her from any winter chills and drove to a nearby beach. There she watched a few determined surfers in wet suits skimming across the waves. Her last day was relaxed, and she knew she'd miss Sydney when she had to leave for Darwin.

Chapter Thirty-Two

The flight to Darwin was smooth and uneventful. When Trish deplaned, claimed her luggage and walked outside to the car rental, the sight of the exotic local flora and the tropical temperatures instantly captivated her. After driving to the hotel and getting settled in her room, she sat down by the phone, pulled out the list of names Patrick had given her and began trying to contact some environmentalists.

She was having little success. Most simply weren't home, and the ones who were, seemed disinterested, as Patrick had told her. Some told her candidly that they were tired of the environmental battles, and wanted to just move on with their lives. She was feeling disheartened, and began to wonder if her trip across the globe was going to prove rather fruitless.

After about an hour of phoning people, she made contact with a young woman named Jenny Caldwell, who sounded enthusiastic and full of energy. She had a heavy Aussie accent, and identified herself as a schoolteacher in Darwin. When Trish told her why she was in Darwin, Jenny began volunteering details of her work in the uranium battles on Aborigine land with very little prodding. She had a lot of material she'd saved from that time, and maintained contact with some of the Aborigines with whom she had worked. In particular there was an old man called simply, "Old Tom," and a few younger Aborigine women from the same tribe.

"Do you think we could get together with them and talk?"

"I'll ring some people up and see if I can locate them," Jenny replied, "But I don't know what I can promise."

"Why's that? Can't we just set a time and drive out to meet?"

"We could do that. But it doesn't mean they'd be there."

"Well, I know they're nomadic, but…"

Jenny chuckled and asked, "You know how they talk about Australia being the land time forgot?"

"Yes."

"I think Aborigines are the people that forgot about time. It doesn't mean anything to them like it does to us. They don't have the concept of, say, a schedule."

"Oh."

"You see," Jenny elaborated, "they don't think like we do. I worked with these people for months on end, and I tell you, they live in a different world. Don't get me wrong. I don't think I'm superior or anything. I came to truly respect them when we worked together. It's just that I had to learn not to count on them necessarily being there at a designated time or place. They followed their instincts, not their clocks."

"Could *you* tell me anything about their myths?"

"I could try, but I'd probably get it all wrong. It's hard to explain, and they've got their own way of telling things; sometimes I just don't understand it. It'd be better for you to get it from them." She told Trish she'd ring up an Aborigine ranger she knew who worked in the Kakadu and see if he could locate the women and Old Tom and try to set up a meeting with them. She said they might have to get a permit, depending on where they were, and if they did, it could take some time. "Besides, with everything I've got going on, I really couldn't get to it before then. It'd give us all day Saturday if we wait. Would that be soon enough?"

"Sure. In fact, it'd be ideal, because I'd hoped to be able to do a little sightseeing in and around Darwin, anyway, while I was here. It'll work out great. I can't begin to thank you, Jenny, for offering to help."

"Oh, no worries. I really enjoyed the experiences I had during that time. They were life changing. And it's always nice to see my mates from back then again, and talk about old times and catch up on things. It'll be fun. Why don't I ring you up at your hotel as soon as I find out something for sure, and we'll have a go of it from there?"

"Sounds great."

She gave Jenny the name and number of the hotel and her room number, and they said good-bye. Then she went down to the lobby to start making reservations for tours in the area. In particular she wanted to visit the sites of some of the Aborigine rock art, which was reputed to be the best in the country.

The first two days Trish concentrated her sightseeing in the Darwin area. After a trip to a crocodile farm, she spent some time in downtown Darwin. Trish noticed that architecturally it had a rather modern looking appearance. From the tourist literature she discovered that it was due in large part to Cyclone Tracy, which had flattened much of the city on Christmas day in 1974, killing sixty-six people. Because of that event, much of it had been rebuilt within relatively recent years. In spite of the modern appearance, Trish thought Darwin definitely had a frontier feel. Several men with long scraggly beards, who looked as though they had just emerged from the outback, walked the streets of the modern downtown areas. Trish even noticed a few people walking around in public barefoot. With the tropical heat, she had been tempted to do the same thing.

Most of the Aborigines she saw were dressed in modern clothes, which gave her an inexplicably uncomfortable feeling. Before arriving in Australia she'd only seen pictures of them in their native dress, natural and untamed. After she saw a few of them staggering around in an obviously intoxicated state, she could identify the feeling; they seemed corrupted by the modern world of the white man.

346

While in the city Trish visited an aquarium, an art gallery and a museum, housing numerous examples of Aboriginal art and stuffed animals. One display showcased a huge sixteen and a half foot long crocodile. She was glad it was stuffed.

She discovered a place near Doctor's Creek, where people gathered every evening at high tide to feed the fish that came in from the ocean. As they threw stale bread out into the water, Trish delighted in watching the feeding frenzy that ensued. At one point she summoned enough courage to feed some of them by hand herself, and squealed like a small child when the furious splashing unexpectedly doused her.

After she had exhausted what she considered the main points of interest within the city limits, and with time still to spare before her meeting with Jenny Caldwell, Trish signed up for a cruise in a riverboat down the Adelaide River. She soon discovered that insect repellent was as essential as sunscreen. The mosquitoes were as voracious as any she had ever encountered. Though the heat was uncomfortable, she delighted in watching the crocodiles being fed right in the river at the side of the boat from fishing lines. She watched as the big monsters emerged from the murky surface of the water, gliding heavily upward with their limbs to their sides, like graceful ballet dancers swimming in mid air. Then after they grabbed their snack, they dropped back down into the water with an accompanying, thunderous splash.

Trish couldn't imagine living in a place where such dangerous creatures roamed at will, but, not only did the people of Darwin seem to enjoy their unique status, they took pride on protection of the crocodiles that had been hunted almost to extinction in years past. Yet, it didn't seem that the authorities in Darwin took their close proximity to the wild animals lightly, either. She observed how guides, as well as publications, constantly reminded tourists to take the crocs seriously. Virtually every billabong and creek she passed on her tours was posted with warnings not to swim in the waters. The guide on the boat told them that the few tourists who'd been killed by the crocs in previous years, had all ignored the posted warnings.

After taking in numerous sights of interest near and around Darwin, Trish was able to concentrate the rest of her sightseeing in the Kakadu National Park itself. She read that some of the parkland was Aboriginal land, and that, like Ayers Rock, it had been deeded back to the Aborigine. They, in turn, leased it back to the government.

Almost as soon as the tour began Trish was astounded by the number of bird species that filled the park. She stayed busy taking pictures of storks, magpie geese, cormorants, and some species with which she was completely unfamiliar. Her favorite was the lotus bird, which actually walked on the surface of the water, where water plants were prolific. What looked like huge anthills dotted the landscape. Some were as tall as a man. The guide informed them that the anthills were in reality termite mounds.

There were two spectacular falls in the park named Jim Jim Falls and Twin Falls. As she stood at the base of Twin Falls, she tried to imagine what it would be like to see the same breathtaking display multiplied by hundreds of times during the wet season, when walls of water came cascading over the escarpments that ringed the valleys. She realized that the sight she was viewing, as impressive as it was, was just a trickle of the area's annual monsoon events.

Trish was determined to get pictures of every bit of the rock art in the park she could. Only a few of the over 5,000 sites where they were located were available for public viewing. Their guide told her group that many of those sites were considered sacred by the Aborigines, and that at others the Aborigine said there were dangerous beings or spirits who the white men couldn't approach because they didn't know how to with safety. "Only the initiated can visit those areas," he informed them.

When the guide talked about the sacredness of the land, Trish thought, *There it is again. What makes these sites sacred? And who are the beings that live there?* The Aborigine warnings about dangerous spirits reminded her of the common worldwide myths about spirits that lived in mountains. She wondered if they were references to periodically high levels of background radiation near pockets of uranium in mountain caves.

As Trish took pictures of the art, she felt drawn to the human handprints and the pictures of native animals. At one site, drawings of masted ships and white men with long rifles recounted the invasion by the Europeans. At others she saw stick men and X-ray type pictures of animals, which showed the animals' skeletal features. The tour guide pointed out that the art had been dated back for tens of thousands of years because of the pictures of some now extinct animals, such as the Tasmanian tiger and a species of anteater. There were also examples of giant species of animals, which were believed to have been extinct for several millennia. The guide said that because of this, some experts believed the art went back even further than that.

At one location Trish became wide-eyed when she noticed that one of the older pieces of art included pictures of beings with human bodies and animal heads. *Hybrids*, she thought, *mythical hybrids.* She hadn't seen them depicted in any books she'd studied about Australia previously in Clayton. As she took numerous pictures, she became more and more convinced that the dating of the rock art was even more vastly underestimated than the guide had indicated.

There was something about a few of the paintings, however, that seemed oddly familiar. It kept nagging at her, like a name she couldn't quite remember, but she couldn't get any kind of reference points to formulate in her mind.

• • •

After returning from one of her tours one evening, Trish found that a message had been left from Jenny Caldwell. As soon as she got to her room, she called her.

Jenny told her that several of the women had agreed to meet them at one of the villages just outside the park boundaries, and that they were trying to contact Old Tom, as well. Jenny said she would pick Trish up at her hotel early Saturday morning, and warned that it would be a long drive to the village, with no guarantees that Old Tom would be there. "We'll just have to trek on out and see what happens." When Trish offered to drive, Jenny snickered and replied simply, "Trust me. Mine will be better than a rental."

Chapter Thirty-Three

It was still dark Saturday morning when Trish's travel alarm started buzzing. As she hurriedly got dressed, she felt the familiar excitement of going after a major story and working on a deadline. She crammed notebooks, a tape recorder and camera equipment into her small backpack, then rode the elevator down to the lobby. There, a lone, young woman stood checking her watch. Trish approached her and asked, "Jenny?"

The tall, tanned, blond woman, with California girl looks, smiled and stuck out her hand. "That's me." Trish recognized her heavy Aussie accent instantly and marveled at how quickly the California girl façade dissipated with the sound of it. Trish was surprised at how young and pretty Jenny was. If she'd seen her on the street, she would have labeled her a model rather than a school teacher.

The two of them exchanged the briefest of introductions, then immediately went to the car park, where Jenny led Trish to an older model four-wheel drive car. It was weather worn, seriously in need of a paint job and had a badly damaged grill. A faded bumper sticker still proclaimed, "No Mining on Sacred Lands!"

As Jenny drove toward the outskirts of the city, the two of them exchanged bios, as though to get them out of the way so they could talk about the subject at hand. Jenny, a native of Darwin, admitted to being a bit of a maverick, or a "larrikin," as she put it. She'd done her share of "kicking out the cobwebs" when she was younger, but had finally settled down and gone to college, where she chose teaching for a profession. It was one of best jobs available to women that involved working with children.

She'd entered the environmental arena over the mining controversy several years earlier, after accompanying a friend to a few initial meetings. Her friend's interests waned after a short time. Jenny, however, was hooked. She'd been active as an environmentalist since that time—a fact which she said initially didn't sit well with a number of her other friends or her parents. They considered her interests a continuing part of her rebellious nature. But once they realized how dedicated she was to it—that it wasn't just a fad—they eventually supported and even admired her work.

Jenny talked about her long time boyfriend, who she said wasn't interested in marriage just then. She wondered out loud how much longer she was willing to wait for him to make up his mind about a commitment. Jenny turned toward Trish and asked, "And you?"

"What?"

"You got a fella' in your life?"

"Oh, yes, yes...my old high school sweetheart, as a matter of fact. We've just been back together for a few months now."

"Now that's interesting," she commented in a tone piqued with curiosity. "Thinking about marriage?" she quizzed.

"We're thinking about it." Trish nervously rubbed her hands up and down her thighs, then asked, "Jenny, how long have you known the Aborigine women and Old Tom?"

"A few years now."

"I couldn't help but notice that a number of the Aborigines I saw in town seemed...well..."

"Shiftless?"

"I was thinking of another word."

"Drunk?"

"Well..."

"Spiritless?"

"I guess."

"It's okay. I know what you're saying." Jenny gestured with her free hand as she spoke. "A lot of them are all those things and more, and you can rest assured that a lot of people in Australia despise them for it. But the truth is that they also have the worst schools and health care in the country, and, not only have we stolen their land, we've treated them like third class citizens. How would anyone expect them to behave after that kind of cultural upheaval?" Jenny reminded her that the European treatment of Aborigines was remarkably parallel to that of the Native Americans in America and mentioned the similarities between the two races' health problems, high rates of alcoholism and depression.

Trish nodded. "Yes, I'm afraid it's all too familiar."

Jenny talked about an Australian program similar to "inculturazation" in the U.S. Aborigine children were forcibly taken from their families to live, forbidden to speak their own language and taught domestic skills, all in an attempt to breed either their race or their culture out of existence.

Trish turned sideways in her seat. "Really?"

"Yeh. They still did it as recently as the seventies...*nineteen* seventies."

"You're kidding."

"Not bloody likely. Never considered that a joking matter." Jenny swung the car onto another road, and continued. "Any time you take a native people and rip their land away from them, you rip out their hearts. They're connected to that land. We may not understand it, but it's part of them. That's why their suicide and alcoholism rates are so high. They don't know where they fit in any more. It's just devastated their spirits. The ones who fare the best are the ones who stay out of the towns and reject the white man's value system altogether—the ones who've maintained their culture—like Old Tom."

"Is he a custodian?"

"Old Tom? I think he's considered an elder. Beyond that, I really don't know." She didn't understand that much about Aborigine customs and social structures, and had given up trying to. She simply interacted with them on that little piece of common ground they shared over the uranium mining. As she propped her head on her free hand, she told Trish that some people claimed to understand them completely, but she doubted any white person really did or even could. "It'd be hard for them to open up fully to any white, to be frank." She related how the English treated the Aborigines like animals when they first came to the continent, and how they were hunted down in Tasmania, along with the Tasmanian wolf, as though they were animals.

"I remember reading about their extinction," Trish responded.

"Yeh, only I think you blokes call it genocide. They even laced flour with arsenic to kill some of them."

"They *did*?" Trish queried.

"Yeh." Jenny told her that the last pure blood there died in the late1800s, and that the last Tasmanian wolf died in the 1940s. The white man's goal seemed like an attempt to kill everything wild, to tame the land and conquer it by destroying the wild. "And the Aborigines today are still looked down on and mistreated by a lot of whites."

Trish let out a full breath, as she turned her gaze toward her window and at the city streaking by.

After they stopped by a café to get some take-out breakfast, and lunch for that afternoon, they climbed back in the car and Jenny began telling Trish about the early days of the British government's development of the atomic bomb. As she alternately sipped her coffee and ate, she told how the British were about to sit down at the bargaining table with the Russians and were impatient about completing their first atomic test beforehand. They intended to wait until the winds were blowing out to sea to set off the bomb. On the day of the test, however, the winds were blowing inland toward Aborigine lands. "Instead of putting off the test, they went ahead and set off the bomb...just so they'd be able to tell the Russians that they had it. They couldn't wait one or two lousy days."

"I just heard a similar story about the French testing in the South Pacific," Trish told her, "where the wind blew the fallout inland."

Jenny swung onto a two-lane road that stretched toward the horizon. The sight made Trish feel as though they were leaving the so-called "civilized" world behind. "You see," Jenny continued as Trish ate, "that was the whole problem with atmospheric testing. Every country that had the bomb was experiencing it. You couldn't tell where or how far the winds would carry the radiation. It happened in the States, too. It wasn't till the winds carried it over populated areas that they realized how fragile and unpredictable atmospheric testing was, or how far it was being spread."

Trish remembered the radioactive contamination from the 60s recently discovered at the Antarctic.

"You've heard of feng shui?" Jenny asked.

Trish tilted her head. "Yeah."

"In the West, people tend to dismiss it by saying the Chinese are inscrutable." Jenny glanced at her. "That's just fancy for, 'I don't get it.'" She looked back at the road. "But what they're saying is that energy matters. Where wind blows, fire goes. It's the same with radioactive fire. They say that during some of the atmospheric tests, a few of the Aborigine actually got vaporized."

"Vaporized?"

"Well, some of them disappeared without a trace." Jenny moved her visor to the side, adjusting for the direction of the sun. "Never even found their bodies." She told Trish that prior to the testing the authorities sent only two patrollers to check out and sweep an area of thousands of kilometers for Aborigine that might be in the area. "And you know there's no way possible a couple of blokes could have cleared an area that large. It makes me mad as a cut snake to think about it." She looked briefly at Trish, "So you can see why the trust level the Aborigine have for whites is pretty low." She looked back at the road. After a few moments she glanced back at Trish. "Tell me, what do you hope to learn from the women and Old Tom?"

Trish wiped her mouth with her napkin, deposited her food wrapper in the empty carry-out bag, then repositioned herself in her seat. She told Jenny about the idea of forming an atomic priesthood to warn about radioactive hot spots into the distant future and that it was based on the long-standing Aborigine oral traditions. "So I hoped to find out how they did it, how they've maintained their legends and religious beliefs by word of mouth without corrupting them over so long a period."

Trish gestured as she spoke. "I really believe the idea of a priesthood may be the only way to warn humans thousands of years into the future. I'm even toying with the idea of a correlation between uranium deposits and what indigenous people call sacred land…except that I don't have much of a grasp on that. None of the books I've read have been very helpful in that area." Trish drank the rest of her coffee and stuffed the cup in the paper bag.

"Interesting. Well, we'll give it a go and see what they can tell us."

The truth was that Trish didn't know exactly why she was there. How could she explain reporter's instinct, blind faith and synchronicity?

As she drove, Jenny filled Trish in on some of the background of the political battles with the mining companies in which she had been involved, and Trish took notes as she talked.

Many miles later, Jenny looked down at Trish's notepad.

"You sure take a lot of notes."

"Oh," she replied off handedly, "It's just habit."

"Well, I don't care myself, mind you. But, since the Aborigines have been so exploited over the years, I'm not sure the women or Old Tom would appreciate it. Everybody likes to come here and take pictures of the Aborigines and write about them, like they know all about them. They make a lot of money with their books and their movies, but, well, it's a sensitive thing with them. You can understand."

"No problem. I'll leave the notebook in the car."

"Good idea."

Trish didn't mention the camera and recorder.

● ● ●

Long after they left paved roads, and the ride had turned dusty, the women finally arrived at the little village. Trish was almost grief-stricken by her first sight of the place. Old rusting, tireless cars sat immobile on their axles in the sand, while naked or mostly naked Aborigine children played in and around them. The houses were merely shacks. A couple of old rusted and corroded trailers sat at one end of the compound. It was obvious people were living in them.

Some of the children walked up to their car and stared curiously when they exited it. Jenny walked alone toward one of the huts. After she called out to someone inside, two dark-skinned women emerged. They conversed with Jenny a while, then looked over at Trish and waved shyly. Trish waved back. Then the three of them walked over to her, and Jenny introduced everyone.

The women, who Jenny introduced as Jilley and Evi, appeared around the same age as Jenny. She told Trish the women had been friends since childhood, and had come to the village to visit Jilley's cousin while they waited for Jenny and Trish to arrive. They actually lived much further out in the bush, inside the park boundaries. Both were dark skinned, and both had black, wavy hair and easy, white-toothed smiles. Jilley was tall and thin, whereas Evi was more average in height and heavy set.

"Look, Trish, Old Tom isn't here. We thought we'd go over to one of the billabongs to talk. He might show up later."

Trish tried to hide her disappointment, but she felt as though it was seeping out of her pores. Jenny must have noticed, as she quickly added, "Look, it's the best I can do."

"Oh, sure...sure." But it was difficult for Trish to accept that she might not get to talk to one of the Aborigine elders after having traveled halfway around the world.

"He may show up," Jenny repeated, as the four of them piled into the car.

• • •

When they arrived at the billabong, several miles away, Trish found the atmosphere refreshingly natural, in stark contrast to that of the village. There was simply the land, in all its richness. The billabong had shrunken to little more than a large pond since the end of the rainy season, but the trees surrounding it provided an abundance of cooling shade. Combined with the lush cover of lily pads on the surface of the water, it was an oasis in the dry spinifex covered landscape.

The Aborigine women immediately plunged into the water to cool off. Jenny and Trish spread out the mats and food they'd brought along for lunch, then sat down to rest from the long drive. As Trish watched the two women giggling like schoolgirls in the water, their deep friendship was obvious. She watched as they picked lily pads and splashed each other as playfully as children might. A wave of homesickness washed over her, as she thought of her own best friend back home.

"Aren't they afraid of crocodiles or snakes?" Trish inquired.

"Do they look afraid?"

"No...but...oh, well." She leaned back on the mat on her elbows. "I guess they know what they're doing."

"Trish, they catch snakes with their bare hands."

"You're kidding!" She said, raising her eyebrows.

"Not at all. I wouldn't go near that water, but they've done it all their lives. In fact, the only thing I've ever seen them afraid of was the uranium mining."

After a while, the women emerged from the billabong, dripping trails of water behind them. They approached the mats where Jenny and Trish sat, and plopped down alongside them, with an accompanying squishing sound from their water soaked clothes. They appeared ready to eat, and to talk. Trish never got a chance to ask her first question.

"You know," Jilley began in her thick Australian accent, as Jenny passed around meat pies, "when them mining people first came, we told 'em we didn't want none of their money. And the elders warned 'em straight out that them was sacred lands and not to touch 'em...but they just kept comin' back and comin' back."

"Yeh," Evi added in between bites.

"The government people—you can't count on them. They keep changing their minds. First, they gave us back our land. Then they said we didn't have no right to keep 'em from mining it. Then they came back again, after them miners did all their damage, and told 'em they had to leave. Strange people," she said, shaking her head.

"Yeh," Evi added again, the word spoken as a period at the end of a sentence.

"Thing is, we couldn't get our people to stick together. Some of 'em held to the old ways. And some of 'em just got greedy from the miners promising 'em all that money. 'Royalties,' they called 'em. Told 'em they'd get richer than the white man if they just signed the papers." Jilley wiped the side of her mouth. "The people never worried about money before the white man came. Before that, they trusted their mother to take care of 'em all their life."

"Their mother?" Trish inquired, as she looked up from her meat pie.

"Yeh, their mother...the earth. The earth had always given the people water to drink and food to eat, and shelter and a song to sing. What else did they need? Then the whites, they bring in their money and take our land away from us, and some of our young people—and even the older ones—can't sing or dance anymore. They drink the liquor the white man brought and don't want to work anymore. They fight with each other all the time. They caught the white man's disease."

"Disease?" Trish inquired. "You mean alcoholism?"

"Nay," Jilley replied. "His greed."

"Oh," Trish uttered.

As she wiped her hands on her clothes, Jilley continued, "Them mining fellas, they came and told everyone it would be safe to mine the lands. They wouldn't listen to the elders at all."

Jenny broke in. "They told them that there was already background radiation at Kakadu, anyway, so it was just normal, that it occurred naturally."

"This one fella,' he said it was perfectly safe and wouldn't cause no genetic damage," Jilley added.

"That's a damn *lie!*" Trish stunned even herself with the outburst.

Jilley and Evi covered their mouths and giggled.

"They know that, Trish," Jenny said. "But I'm afraid people like Jilley, Evi and the others are in the minority now, even with their own people."

"The others are blinded by the money," Jilley said.

"Yeh," Evi added, as she finished the last bite of her meat pie.

For the next hour, the two women and Jenny continued telling Trish about their battles—not only with the mining companies and the government—but with their own people. Trish tried to commit as much of it as she could to memory so she could take accurate notes later.

Then Trish commented, "You know, this reminds me a lot of the battle going on in the U.S. in the Native American community between the traditionalists and the progressives."

"With mining?" Jenny inquired.

"No. Well, there's that, too. But also they're building casinos on Native American lands." She explained that even though some of the tribes were getting fabulously wealthy from it, the traditionalists said that the tribes needed to keep to the old ways and old traditions, and honor their lands and heritage. They were warning the people not sell out to the white man. "The government's even trying to bribe some of the tribes now to take a lot of the nuclear waste on their lands."

"Yeah, I've read a little about that in some of the literature I get from Greenpeace," Jenny responded.

Trish turned to ask Jilley and Evi a question, but the two of them were getting up to return to the billabong.

"Was it something I said?" Trish asked, turning toward Jenny.

She gave a slight laugh. "No...they just probably wanted to get wet again."

• • •

Trish and Jenny sat on their mats and watched for over half an hour longer as the Aborigine women alternately picked stems from lily pads and looked around in the water. After a while Evi splashed her hand into the surface of the water and let out a whoop. She pulled up a turtle by its neck, and laughed, holding it aloft for Jenny and Trish to see. The animal had a long snakelike neck.

"Well, they'll eat well tonight," Jenny commented. The two of them smiled and waved to the women in approval. "I guess we'll have the company of a turtle on the way back to the village." She added, "I sure hope they don't catch a snake."

Trish's eyes widened, and she winced at the thought of dead reptiles sharing seating space with them in the car—especially snakes. At least she hoped they'd be dead.

After a while the women came out of the water again and sat back down on the mats, with Evi's turtle in hand. Trish found herself genuinely enjoying the leisurely pace in the outback. She could almost imagine time standing still out there, if she stayed long enough. But as that thought passed through her mind, she noticed some movement in the bush and shaded her eyes, squinting toward it. She saw the distinct figure of a man—an old man.

A wave of excitement swept over her. "Jilley, there's someone over there behind that clump of spinifex on the ridge. Could it be Old Tom?"

"'e's been there for almost an hour," she answered smiling, without looking up.

"Really?"

"Yeh." Evi was still punctuating Jilley's sentences.

"Is he coming over?"

"If 'e'd a been, 'e'd a been 'ere b'now." It was the most Evi had said all day.

Trish looked around. Then Jenny said, "Why don't you go on over and talk to him, Trish. I think he wants you to go to him."

"Are you sure?" she asked to no one in particular.

"Sure," said Jilley. "Go'wan."

She started out, and Jenny quickly cautioned, "Wait. Take your hat. You're not used to this sun."

Trish bent over to take her hat from Jenny. Then she turned to Jilley, "I'm sure glad you were able to reach him. I was afraid he wasn't going to come."

"Oh," Jilley responded, "we never did reach him. No one knew where he was."

"What?" Trish inquired. "Then how did he get here? How did he know where we'd be?"

Jilley shrugged her shoulders, and Jenny responded, "Don't ask, Trish. I ran into this all the time with them. Somehow the elders always seem to know when and where to be. They just magically show up at the appropriate time."

Trish didn't pursue the matter. She walked out into the blazing sun toward the old man, while securing her hat on her head. As she drew closer, he didn't look up, but sat against a large rock, continuing to work intently with something in his hands. A long, thin walking stick was propped on the rock beside him. His skin was dark like an American black's. He had black eyebrows and mustache that were peppered gray, but his scraggly beard and tousled hair were blond, with tinges of white. She thought it was no wonder that Aborigines were classified as an entirely different race. His features and coloring were unique.

As he pulled something white and pulpy out of what looked like a twig or root of some kind, Trish stood quietly beside him. Unsure of the proper etiquette in such situations, she quickly and discreetly surveyed him, waiting for him to make the first comment. His hair was held in place across his forehead with a burlap-colored twine, and he was dressed only in shorts—no hat—and sandals for shoes. His deeply wrinkled forehead bore testament to the harsh living conditions of the bush.

He finally looked up. "Witchetty grub."

"What?" she asked, surprised.

"Witchetty grub. That's what these are. You want one?" He held the white object toward her.

"Oh, no," she replied, holding up her hand. "Thank you, though. I already ate."

Then, to her horror, he popped the worm in his mouth and started eating. He looked at her and chuckled, and she wondered if the old man wasn't simply having a good joke at her expense.

She felt awkward. "I hear you're Tom."

"Old Tom," he corrected.

"Well, I'm Trish. Patricia Cagle." She wasn't sure why she'd used her formal name.

"What's you here for, Patricia Cagle?" His pronunciation of her name was flawless.

"Well, I was wondering if you could tell me about some of the Aborigine myths and how they've been passed down for so many thousands of years without being corrupted. You know, like the one about the mountain at Coronation Hill."

"You mean the one God Bula lives under?"

"I guess that's the one."

He motioned his head toward the women at the billabong. "They told you about them mining fellas, did they?"

"They told me."

"Well," he said, "It's simple enough. Bula lives under the mountain, and he can't be disturbed. No one can dig in the mountain or disturb it in any way. It's a sacred place, it is." He brushed off one of his hands on his shorts, picked up the walking stick and propped himself on it, as he continued. "We are the ones who must guard his peace, and if we fail to protect him from being disturbed, we will face death for that failure. We are here to tell anyone who tries to disturb him that to do so will bring great misery to all the earth—not just here—but all over the world. He is a powerful god." He motioned his free hand in a circular fashion. "He can go anywhere."

He fell silent as he set the stick back and returned to his Witchetty grubs. As Trish scanned the landscape, she realized that the man was telling her that if anyone dug into the uranium rich mountain and disturbed it, there would be a worldwide catastrophe. She was about to ask him another question, when something struck her like a bolt. Her eyes widened, and she swung her head around and stared straight at him.

My God, she thought to herself in silent, fully formed words. *He is an atomic priest!* She realized that there, standing before her, was a living, breathing member of an ancient atomic priesthood. He and his predecessors had known exactly where the dangerous, radioactive areas were, long before any white men had come to the Australian continent. And they had been standing guard, giving these warnings for tens of thousands of years. The whites simply hadn't been listening to them.

Then, almost as quickly as the thought came to her, she began to doubt it. How could any primitive people possibly know those kinds of things? Where would they get information that would require highly sophisticated equipment to detect, a chemical background and a working understanding of the periodic table? Where would a primitive culture—just decades removed from the Stone Age—get that kind of knowledge?

But, then, hadn't Peggy told her about animals detecting earthquakes before they happened?

Her mind raced with thoughts that led nowhere and questions that wouldn't quite formulate. How could some think tank group have come up with an idea that had already existed for eons? It couldn't be. Who was God Bula? And how could he go everywhere? Could they really have been communicating with spirits that lived inside the mountains? And, if so, what kind of spirits were they? She wanted to ask more: the reporter's questions, the appropriate questions. But nothing seemed appropriate. She didn't have enough of a grasp of what she suspected to know where to go next.

Trying to clear her head of the confusion, she took a deep, cleansing breath and then bent down and lightly stroked a strand of spinifex. She gazed out across the dry, barren landscape. What other mysteries and ancient wisdoms might this land and these people hold for mankind—and for her, personally?

Looking up at the elder, Trish shaded her eyes and asked, "Old Tom, why do your people still keep some of the rock art secret from the white man?"

The old man smiled at her and rubbed his chest, then wiped his face with his hand. "Missy, the white man ain't ready to know what's in our pictures."

God, hadn't Max said the same thing about his pictures of Dachau, and hers of Clinic Number Four? Trish let out a breath and thought a moment. "If he was ever ready to know, then would you show him?" she asked, still shielding her eyes from the sun.

"Sure. We're brothers, ain't we? But if the white man was ever ready to know what's in our pictures and songs and stories, we wouldn't need to show him, now would we?"

"Why's that?"

"'Cause he's got his own bloody songs and stories and art, and he ain't even payin' attention to them, now is he?" He scratched his shoulder. "I used to think the white fella' didn't have pictures and stories, but I been talkin' to some of them white fellas, and I found out that they got 'em—same as us. They just ain't hearin' or seein' 'em. The white man hasn't paid attention to 'em for so long that he's even forgotten who he really is."

The comment reminded Trish of the biblical quote she'd heard as a child: "None so blind as those who will not see. None so deaf as those who will not hear." Maybe her culture simply wasn't seeing it's own art clearly, or hearing it's own history correctly. Maybe they were reducing the warnings and stories from primitive cultures to fanciful, childish gibberish.

Even though her mind felt bombarded, she was certain she wouldn't have entertained the same level of possibilities and realization anywhere else than she did at this exact place and this exact moment.

Trish tilted her head. "Are there any other people like you around Australia?"

Old Tom motioned with his hands. "There are ones of us around the world."

"There are?"

"Yeh. I speak to them from time to time."

Trish was puzzled. "On the phone?"

Old Tom chuckled, and his eyes swept the landscape, as though to say, "What phone?" Then he said, "There are many of us who guard sacred land. We have done this for all time. We will do it until there is no time."

Trish stood up slowly. So there were more of them. She looked directly at the old man's wrinkled, weather-beaten face, "Old Tom, I'm ready to know some of your stories. I'd like to know why you've been guarding these sites around Australia for so long...if you're willing to tell me."

He crossed his arms and perched his right foot onto his left knee. He stood there in the one-legged pose silently for a moment, looking out across the land. Then he set his right foot back on the ground, and, still looking across the landscape, he began. "Long time ago, in the Dreamtime, there were seven beings who tried to stop creation." He told her that the beings waged a great battle with the people, and the beings were finally captured and buried in the Earth. Before the last one was buried, he cried out a sound that had never been heard before by man. The people went to the elder in the village and asked what to do to keep the beings in the ground.

The elder told them to go to a certain tree, cut a limb from it and hollow it out. Then they were to blow into the log. When the people did this, the sound it made was the same that the being had made. "This log we call the didgeridoo. Its sound keeps the beings trapped and reminds us of our duty to stand guard over the places where they dwell. I have remembered my duty to guard these spots since I was a young man. They are sacred and forbidden places, but the mining companies are digging them up."

Trish stood motionless for a moment, trying to absorb what the elder had just told her. If the myth—or some form of it—was true, the implications could be incalculable. She took in a breath. "But, Old Tom, you call these places sacred...and yet forbidden. What's sacred about them if they're guarding such dangerous beings?"

He crossed his arms and said, "To us, they are sacred…but to those who do not understand this sacredness, they are forbidden."

His answer left her more confused—too confused to even pose questions, so she stretched her shoulders back, took another deep breath, and asked simply, "Old Tom, what is my job here?" She didn't know the source of the words she spoke. They had tumbled out of her mouth without any thought behind them.

He smiled a knowing smile. Then, as he stared straight into her eyes, his own eyes seemed to shift to a wild look that left her feeling as though he was looking straight through her, or maybe into her. She felt stripped naked, as though there was nothing she could hide from that gaze. The old man leaned forward and touched her lightly on the forehead with his index finger. The simple movement felt as though it was happening in slow motion. Then he replied simply, "Missy, it is your job to remember."

It was his last comment before he turned and walked back out into the bush and out of her life, without even a good-bye or a backward glance.

The suddenness of his departure surprised her. She had neither the time nor the inclination to call out to him, though she knew that he would never leave her memory—that his image and words would haunt her for a long time to come.

Even after he was gone, she could still feel the pressure of his finger where he'd touched her on the forehead, as though it was still there. She could only liken it to times when she'd wear sunglasses all day, then take them off at night and still feel the impression of them at the bridge of her nose and the tops of her ears. But that didn't make any logical sense; he'd touched her for such a brief time. Or had it been? It had seemed like it happened in slow motion. *Had* time stood still for her, after all, in that foreign, magical land?

She had no idea of the meaning of his words. Remember? Remember what? His words indicated that she already had the answers, and she'd been looking for them everywhere—across the globe, in fact—outside of herself. Was she like the white race that had its own answers, but refused to hear or see or understand them?

• • •

After Old Tom had left and Trish—almost in a dazed state—had returned to the shade of the billabong, Jenny reminded her that they were going to have a long trip back to Darwin and that they needed to get started soon. Though in agreement, Trish felt a little lethargic, as though she had just awakened from a night's sleep and needed to shake her consciousness back into the dimension occupied by the four of them and the concerns at hand. And she didn't think it was the heat of the sun that had brought about that feeling.

Jenny must have noticed. "Are you all right, Trish?" she inquired, as she lightly touched her shoulder.

"I'm fine…just fine," she replied, waving her hand dismissively. She looked one last time in the direction of Old Tom's departure from her life, then helped the others gather the remnants of their picnic and pile them back in the car—with the additional occupant of Jilley's turtle. When they arrived back at the village, Trish thanked the Aborigine women for their help with background information on the mining. She asked them to thank Old Tom, as well, when they saw him again, since he'd left so quickly she hadn't had a chance to do that. Jenny hugged Evi and Jilley good-bye, and she and Trish started the long journey back to Darwin.

Trish was quiet and pensive for a long time as they drove, staring out the window. She was mulling her encounter with Old Tom over and over again. Jenny finally broke the silence. "You're awfully quiet. What were you and Old Tom talking about, anyway? Was he able to help you with what you're looking for?"

"To tell the truth, I think he may have raised even more questions for me than he answered."

Jenny half laughed. "I know what you mean. I don't think anyone has caused me to question my life more than those people. Really shook my world up for a while, they did. That's one of the reasons I was so eager to see them again when you called. I feel this strong need to be around them and talk to them whenever I've been in the city for too long a stretch. It gets me grounded again…puts things in perspective or something. Or maybe they're just connected to something that I need to be."

"Like what?" Trish asked, as she turned to face her.

"Oh, the wild, I guess. I think we get too disconnected from it in our modern world. I'd wager that my family would tell you I'm wild enough. But it's a different kind of wild I'm talking about. My rebellious days were just rambling and unfocused…didn't accomplish anything. But with Jilley and Evi and all of their people, I feel connected to something bigger than my job or family or apartment…lots bigger. And it just feels good. It feels right. You know?"

Trish took a deep breath and began sharing the details of her experience at the billabong with Old Tom, and her epiphany about an ancient atomic priesthood. When she finished her accounting, Jenny said, "Say! Now that you mention that, I do recall reading something once about a sacred site here in the Territory, where the Aborigines told people to stay away because anyone who went there would get sores all over their bodies. Then later, they discovered levels of radon gas there that were dangerously high." Then she added, "It didn't seem to bother the Aborigines, though."

The two women talked more about the possibilities and the implications of a long forgotten priesthood. When they had exhausted much speculation on the subject, Jenny said, "Look, it's going to be a long drive yet. Why don't you get some sleep, and when I get tired, I'll wake you up, and you can give me a break driving. You still look tired after being in the hot sun for so long."

"Thanks, Jenny. I *am* awfully sleepy." She felt as though her sluggishness was coming more from the lingering effects of her conversation with Old Tom than from the hot sun, the time of day or their long journey from Darwin. She yawned and re-shifted her body into the most comfortable position she could, while still strapped into her seat belt. Soon her body began relaxing as she drifted into thoughts of an Australia that lay beyond the time and place of her conscious state.

● ● ●

After what seemed like a short time, Trish awoke to Jenny nudging her gently for her turn to drive. The car was stopped just off the pavement, and no other cars were in sight on the long stretch of road. When Trish saw that the sky had turned dark, she realized how much time must have passed and how far they must have traveled. "My gosh, how long have I been asleep?"

"A while."

Just then an incredible display of lightning lit up the sky, followed by crackling thunder, which broke the evening quiet. "My heavens," Trish said, wide-eyed. "That was awesome."

"Yeh, that's one of the things I love about this place. They say we have some of the most spectacular storms in the world here at the Top End of the Territory. We call 'em 'knock-'em- down' storms. They say it's because of all the heat and humidity here."

Both of them exited the car to trade places, pausing to stretch their legs for a while. Trish noticed the change in the air and the wind beginning to build. She turned to face the wind and breathed it in deeply, as it blew through her hair. "Oh, I love storms. Always have. It used to drive my mother crazy, but when I was a kid, I could literally smell a storm coming. And when I did, I'd run out in the yard and twirl around and around like a ballerina, just enjoying it. It energized me. Mom always had a hell of a time getting me back inside. It was a real battle of the wills between us. Nowadays, they say it's the ions in the atmosphere, or something. I don't know. But I still love it."

"I know what you mean. It affects me the same way."

Just then they heard a barking sound. "What's that, Jenny? A dingo?"

She chuckled. "No, actually it's an owl. Sounds like a dog though, doesn't it?"

"It really does. Oh…" she gushed, "it'd take me a lifetime to get used to all of the sights and sounds here."

Another brilliant flash of lightning streaked across the horizon bringing the sky alive again in the distance, with its accompanying roll of thunder. "God…sometimes don't you just stand in awe at the power and majesty of the earth?" Trish almost whispered. "I love this place. If I didn't have people waiting for me back home, I think I'd seriously consider trying to find a way to stay."

Jenny tilted her head. "You know how you said you could smell a storm coming when you were a girl?" Jenny asked.

"Well, I sensed it somehow. Smelling it was just one of the ways."

"But that's the connection the Aborigines have that I was talking about—that connection to the earth." Jenny leaned back against the side of the car, crossed her arms, and stared out across the darkened landscape. "Only the Aborigines seem connected to it all the time." She told Trish they knew when there was going to be flooding or drought, when to leave an area or when to stay, where to find food and water, when most whites would simply die in the desert. They lived on the marginal areas where no one else could because, as Jilley had said, they loved and honored their mother, and their mother took care of them. "It was only when some of them stopped trusting their mother that their lives started turning to shit. They let doubt and greed creep into their lives…fear, really. I don't know that I'll ever understand them."

As they talked, the storm was growing louder and closer. Jenny stood up straight. "We'd better get back in the car and get going."

After Trish got the seat and mirror adjusted on the driver's side, Jenny gave her some brief directions, before she settled down in the passenger seat. The next time Trish glanced at her, she was deep in sleep.

Later that night, after Trish drove to the front door of her hotel in Darwin, it took her a while to jostle Jenny awake. "Boy, when you sleep, you really sleep, don't you?"

"Never had any trouble in that department, I can tell you," Jenny responded, rubbing her face and stretching her neck back.

"Well, I can see that. And it's awfully late. Why don't you stay with me here at the hotel for the rest of the night."

"Oh, that's okay." She rubbed her face again vigorously. "I'm awake now, and it's only another fifteen minutes to my apartment from here."

"Are you sure?"

"Yeh."

As Trish began collecting her things—including copies of the material Jenny had brought about the mining battles—she said, "You know, even though

I'm still a little confused, I feel like I got a lot of information today. It may take me a while to digest it, though."

Jenny smiled. "I know that feeling."

Trish added, "I really appreciate everything you've done. I know how lucky I was to get a chance like this."

They both exited the car and met at the back of it to say good-bye, where Trish repeated, "I don't know how to begin to thank you for your help, Jenny."

"Oh, no worries about that one, now."

Trish slipped an envelope into her hand.

"What's this?"

"It's for gas and such."

"Oh, no." She started to return it, but Trish held up her hand in refusal.

"No, really, it doesn't begin to pay you back. It was so generous of you to take a chunk out of your week-end like this for a complete stranger, who just happened to call out of the blue. This is mostly for your expenses. Anything left over you can use for the environment, if you like."

"Well, I must say I think you're really on to something here. And we need all the publicity we can get about this thing in the Territory. The threats and dangers are still here. You can truly pay me back by doing a smashing job at writing about this thing."

"That's a deal."

The two women hugged good-bye, and Jenny added, "You know, I think women like you and me and Evi and Jilley share some kind of bond. And I think there are millions of us around the world who are beginning to realize that something just isn't right on this earth…that we've gotten out of balance with it somehow. And we know deep down that we need to do everything we can to get that balance back."

"I did feel a sense of sisterhood when the four of us were together at the billabong." She shuffled her toe on the pavement, then, "Well, let me get on to my room so we can both get to bed for what's left of the night."

Jenny got into her car and started the engine. "Have a safe trip back to the States. You've got my address, so write when you can and let me know how things are going."

"I'll do that. And, again, thank you, Jenny. It's been a real pleasure."

Jenny smiled and waved as she drove back out onto the empty streets of Darwin.

• • •

Two days later, after documenting everything she could remember about what had occurred on her trek in the outback, Trish was at the airport boarding a jet back to Hawaii.

Even though she was tired from her adventures, she was almost as excited about returning to Clayton as she'd been about going to Australia. She couldn't wait to tell Jimmy, Max and Kathy all about her trip.

As she had on the way to Australia, she made a stopover in Honolulu for the night. The next morning, before boarding her plane, she made a quick stop at one of the shops to select another book to read on the way back. She was trying to find one with a little more excitement in it than the one she'd read on the trip over, but a quick glance at her watch made her hurry. She quickly grabbed one with an interesting cover, then went directly to her gate.

Though the final leg of her trip was uneventful, she found the non-fiction book she'd selected for the flight fascinating, if somewhat unconventional. By the time she got to Atlanta, the jet lag and time zone changes were finally catching up with her.

She rode the airport bus to the valet parking lot, picked up her Jeep, got her luggage loaded and then headed north up the interstate. By the time she reached the Rabun County line, she was struggling to stay awake.

Chapter Twenty-Four

When she pulled into her driveway, Trish half expected to see Jimmy's car there. When it wasn't, she was actually relieved. She needed a chance for a short nap before facing anyone. After unloading her luggage, she collapsed on the bed and was asleep within minutes.

The next thing she was conscious of was the sound of the kitchen door opening and shutting. But it wasn't enough to rouse from her sleep-state. It was as though on one level, she was reasoning that there was nothing to worry about—that the person coming through the door was probably Kathy or Jimmy—but on another level she wanted to continue sleeping. She couldn't even move her body, and didn't want to. She felt surrounded by a cocoon of warm, healing energy. All she wanted was to continue dreaming. She was dreaming about Old Tom. He was repeating the myth he'd told her, except that his lips weren't moving, and he was talking to her in her mind.

Some time later, Trish's dreams were slowly replaced by conversation in the next room. It took a long time to fully rouse. When she finally looked at her clock, she couldn't believe the time. Her nap had lasted four hours. She felt drugged. And it was dark outside. She got up, put on her robe and walked slowly into the living room, rubbing her face. Both Kathy and Jimmy were there sitting on the sofa.

"Well, Sleepyhead!" Kathy began, as Trish came through the door. "We were starting to worry about you."

"Hey, Sweetheart," Jimmy said, as he walked over and embraced her. "I can't tell you how much I missed you," he whispered in her ear.

As she hugged him back, she thought how good it felt to be back in his arms. "God, I can't believe I slept so long."

"Why didn't you call when you got home?" Kathy asked. "You must have been dead. I've been here for almost an hour, and Jimmy's been here for two." Then she added with child-like pride, "Aren't you glad we didn't wake you up?"

"Kathy, I don't think you could have."

"You must have been exhausted…and you must be famished, too. Jimmy went and picked up some barbecue, and we were just about to eat."

"Barbecue sounds so good right now."

"I bet it does after trekking around in the outback, eating goanna, huh?" Kathy teased with a mocked, squeamish expression and a faked shiver. Trish grinned and headed for the table, while Kathy filled glasses for everyone and added, "I hope you took lots of pictures."

"You don't have to worry about that. I took tons of them," she replied, as she helped herself to the contents of the take-out bags on the table.

As they ate, Trish filled them in on her adventures in Australia, about the people she had met, the places she had gone and the things she had seen. When she tried out some of the Aussie dialects she'd picked up, Kathy giggled. Both Jimmy and Kathy seemed as excited to hear the tales as she was in telling them.

After the meal, she pulled souvenirs from one of her suitcases. Kathy immediately began playing with them. "Man, this is just like Christmas morning," she gushed. Jimmy tried on a hat Trish had bought him. It fit perfectly. Then he took it off and leaned over and gave her a thank-you kiss.

"Now, the bullroarer and boomerang are for the kids, Kathy," Trish cautioned. "So you let them play with them once in a while. You hear?"

Jimmy leaned over and put his hand at the back of Trish's neck and nuzzled the side of her head. "It sure is good to have you back."

"Well," said Kathy, abruptly, "I guess that's my signal to leave."

"No, Kathy," Trish protested. "Don't go."

But she continued to get up and collect her souvenirs and purse. "No, no. That's okay," she continued, feigning hurt feelings. "I can take a hint. A ton of bricks doesn't have to fall on *me*."

Trish walked to the door with Kathy. When they hugged good-bye, Kathy said, with uncharacteristic sincerity, "I'm really glad you enjoyed yourself on this trip. You're in a lot better shape than you were the last time."

"Maybe I'm starting to get things right for a change."

"We'll get together and talk about it some more later." Then Kathy addressed Jimmy, who was still in the living room, "I'm leaving now. Don't bother to get up. I'm not one to stick around when they're not wanted."

He shook his head and snickered.

She turned back to Trish and added, with a mischievous grin, "Sleep tight tonight." And then she was out the door.

• • •

The next morning, as Trish unpacked and stacked her notes beside the computer, Jimmy offered to take her rolls of film to be developed when he went downtown.

After he left, she settled into the easy chair in her computer room, with her feet propped on an ottoman, and called Max. For almost half an hour she filled him in on the trip and the sightseeing. Then she talked about her experiences with the Aborigines in Kadadu. "The thing is," she began, "I can't understand how primitive people could have that kind of knowledge about radioactive hot spots for thousands of years. It's too sophisticated."

"Sophisticated from your viewpoint perhaps, but it may well be very basic to them."

"How so?"

"Perhaps it's an innate knowledge."

"Like something you're born with?"

"Of course. Aren't animals and even insects born with their instincts?"

"Sure, but…"

"Patty," he interjected, "Excuse me a moment; I have to get my pipe." He chuckled. "Can't seem to even talk without it." When he returned to the phone, he explained how some insects and fish never saw their adult counterparts, because they were long gone before the offspring hatched. "Still, they know how to live and what their purpose is. No one teaches them. They know intuitively when to mate, where to lay eggs, what constitutes dangers for them and so on. It has to be some kind of genetic imprinting." He asked her how else they could know how to migrate to a place they'd never been before when there was no member of a previous generation to tell or show them.

She shrugged. "I don't know, Max, but it sounds like you're saying that memory and instinct are cellular."

"Who knows? Maybe that's all instinct and memory are: genetically encoded data." He reminded her of recent stories of people with organ transplants developing traits, as well as what appeared to be the memories of their donors. "That certainly suggests cellular memory. At any rate, should man have any less access to instinct than animals? I believe primitive people use infinitely more of their access to instincts than modern."

"Why?"

"Simply because native cultures always live closer to the earth, just like the animal kingdom, and they're much more sensitive to it and its signals and messages."

"Hmm," she muttered. "Jenny said something like that, too."

He told Trish that because modern people had cut themselves off from the weather with air conditioning and heating, staying indoors most of their lives, they no longer got the sense of earth changes. "We don't feel the earth anymore. And, consequently, we don't seem to feel much of anything anymore. We've come to rely on authority figures to tell us how to think and live instead of trusting our own instincts."

Trish cocked her head to the side. "Max, everybody keeps saying this to me, but are we really that disconnected from our instincts?"

She could hear him inhaling on his pipe. "I believe we are, Patty, and we really have given over entirely too much of our personal power to others in society." He said he thought it would be of great benefit for modern man to learn to listen to his own quiet inner voice instead of the loud, raucous, outer noises with which people were being bombarded in the modern world. "That's why I hardly ever watch television, anymore.

"You know," Max continued, "myth is the language of the soul. Maybe the Aborigines, with their stories of the Dreamtime, have simply learned to bypass the conscious mind when they need to speak directly to the soul." He reminded her that many myths and legends had become corrupted over the years, and that might be one reason she'd been frustrated studying them. He told her about a new trend in the previous few years that he found exciting. A number of authors had begun to reconstruct some of the old myths. "That may sound dull to most people, but the books on the subject are selling at a phenomenal rate. That alone should show there's a hunger out there for this type of knowledge. It should show the publishing houses, as well, though I'm not sure many of them are getting the message just yet." He inhaled on his pipe again. "We want to talk to our souls again, Patty."

Trish stared at the far wall. *Instincts, huh?*

"We speak of natural instincts in the animal world," Max continued, "and Jung talked about the collective unconscious in the psychological and spirit world of man. The Bible talks about the Holy Spirit that moves through us. Couldn't they all be the same thing, simply called by different names?"

Trish raised her eyebrows, and tilted her head. "Hmm. Interesting perspective. Can you think of any other possibility?"

He paused a moment and said, "Why don't *you* give that one some thought, and we can talk about it when you come up."

She smiled. He was always trying to get her to think for herself. "Well, I plan to come up Thursday morning, if it's all right. I've got some goodies I brought you from Australia, but I need a few days to get over the jet lag and catch up on some things."

"That'll be fine. I can't wait to see you."

"Thursday, then. Bye for now."

• • •

The next morning, after Trish picked up her developed pictures from the drugstore, she was walking slowly down the sidewalk, shuffling through them, when she heard her brother-in-law, Mack, calling out. "Patty, when did you get back?"

She turned toward him and grinned. "Hey, Mack. Day before yesterday." After they talked a little about her trip, he began telling her about a television program he'd just seen about Aboriginal rock art. Astronomers believed one particular piece of art was a celestial map of a distant star system. It was explained that the Aborigines couldn't possibly see it with the naked eye, and the astronomers believed that one of the planets in that system was able to support life.

Maybe it was another case of synchronicity, but Max *had* told her to think of another possible explanation for the Aborigine wisdom.

Chapter Thirty-Five

On Thursday morning, when Trish arrived at Max's cabin, he was sitting outside on his porch rocker. As she got out of her car, he walked over and hugged her. "Glad to see that none of those crocodiles took a liking to you," he teased.

She looked at him with a sober expression. "Max, those crocodiles were the biggest I've ever seen, and thank heavens most of them were in pens…or stuffed."

As she began gathering things, he said, "All of that can't be for me."

"Yes, it is. Let's go sit on the porch and sort it out."

After they got seated in Max's rockers, Trish presented him with a pipe with Aboriginal carvings on it. Then she gave him a hat, which he tried on. She was relieved that it was a perfect fit, and that he seemed delighted with it.

"And, of course, I brought you some books," she said with a flourish, as she stacked three of them together and set them in his lap. "They're all about Australia. I picked them up at a bookstore that you would have died for. They had everything there. I could have spent a whole day in just that one shop."

"Ah…mythology," he noted as he picked up one and scanned the cover. "Of course."

"Well, I know I'll enjoy them. What's that thing there?" he asked, pointing to an object on the floor.

She bent over and picked it up. "Oh, this. This is a bullroarer."

"A what?"

"A bull-roarer. The Aborigine use it."

"For what?"

"One shopkeeper said it's used in secret male initiation rite. I don't know if that was the standard tourist line or not, but I know how to use it. Watch." She walked out into the yard and started spinning the wooden object over her head from a couple of strings. As a deep rhythmic, whirring noise filled the air, Max's face lit up. "Like it?" she asked.

"I love it. Let me try." He walked over, got a brief instruction, and then Trish stood back while he spun the object over his head. Again, the humming, whirring noise filled the air. He reminded Trish of a kid with a new toy.

They walked back to the porch, and Max asked, "Are you ready to get into some of the subjects you mentioned?"

"You bet. Oh, Max, you would have just loved Australia."

"Well, I can see *you* certainly did," he beamed. "I don't know when

I've seen you more animated."

"Oh...speaking of which, I almost forgot my pictures." She hurried back to the car and returned with them. As Max went through the photographs, Trish provided the commentary that went along. Then they went inside the cabin, where he set his presents aside, sat down in his favorite chair and lit his pipe.

Trish settled into the chair beside him and immediately began questioning. "Okay, then, we talked about innate knowledge as a possible explanation for the Aborigines knowing the locations of radioactive spots. And you asked me to think about another. What about an ancient wisdom outside instead of inside ourselves?" She looked at him to gauge his reaction, then added, "Say from another galaxy."

He grinned. "So, we're really going to stretch our belief systems today, are we?"

"Why not, Max? This is exciting. Besides, you're the one who said that the bigger boat I needed to contain the monsters might be my belief system."

He inhaled on his pipe. "All right, then. An outside source."

"Outside of the galaxy," she added.

"All right. All right." As he held his pipe aloft, he said, "Well, first of all, I'd say that it was thoroughly arrogant for man not to accept the possibility of life on other planets. It would be kind of like the two-year old concept of 'the world revolves around me.' And you know," he continued, "I read once where one Nobel Prize winning professor said that life similar to ours is just bound to form under the same conditions that our planet evolved. His estimate of possible living planets runs into the trillions."

"Wow."

"Wow, indeed. And did you hear about the Hubble focusing its cameras for so long on the darkest spot in the universe...that spot near the handle of the Big Dipper?"

"I heard *something* about it."

"My dear, they came back with pictures simply full of galaxies." He told her that each of those galaxies contained millions of stars. "And this was one of the blackest points in the sky. They constantly find new planets that could sustain life, as *we* know it. And then I guess you'd always have to consider life forms that might exist in frequencies or dimensions that we don't quite grasp with our five senses."

"You mean like an inter-dimensional space?" she asked

"Possibly." He scratched his neck. "So you're suggesting the concept that others have of an alien source coming to earth many years ago and leaving primitive man warnings and wisdoms by which he could better live." He looked over at her. "Why are you going in this direction?"

She told Max about her encounter with her brother-in-law and reminded him about the ancient marks at the Nazca Plains in Peru, which couldn't be seen except from the sky—a perspective that ancient man didn't have.

"True. True," he responded.

She held out a hand. "And, too, how do we know that some of those supposed mythical beings in the different mythologies weren't just beings from another galaxy that visited here long ago?"

"That's possible, too, I suppose. I haven't done much studying in that field, really. So I'm afraid I can't be of much help to you here."

When Trish sighed audibly, Max looked at her and quickly added, "Now, don't let that discourage you. I've had some people ask me if I believe in astrology, and I say, 'I don't know, because I've never studied it.' I think it's foolish to come to a conclusion about any subject matter until you've taken the time to study it and give it a fair assessment."

He puffed on his pipe and added, "Besides, if a thing is true, it's true. It doesn't matter whether we believe in it or not." He reminded her that bacteria and viruses existed and performed their functions long before they were discovered by man. "It's also a fact that over half the world believes in reincarnation, but our culture doesn't. And I'll wager that the vast majority of people who reject it outright have never studied it. But if reincarnation—or some form of it—is real, it doesn't depend on our belief system to exist.

"They say," he continued, shifting in his seat, "that all references to reincarnation were expunged from the Bible some time after it was compiled, even though there were Christian sects who believed in it strongly. And I'll also wager that many Christians today are totally unaware of how their Bible was put together in the first place or how much editing was done to it over the years in that regard."

"You're right about that, because I sure didn't know anything about it till just now."

He waved his pipe. "Well, I didn't mean to digress. But there's something else on the subject I want to mention while I'm thinking about it."

"What's that?"

He told her that he'd read legends about Indian tribes in the Northeastern United States who told tales of a golden man—or man of light—who came down and left their tribes with a set of laws by which they should live.

She tilted her head. "I've never heard about that."

"Might sound like some kind of alien visitation."

Trish sat up straight in her chair. "And, there's something else. What about that face on Mars? Have you ever seen a picture of it?"

"As a matter of fact, I have."

"And what did you think when you saw it? Really."

"Well, I'd have to say that it looked like a face to me." He said that the first time he saw a picture of the object in a magazine, he thought that if it had been found on some remote spot on the earth, there wouldn't be any debate about whether it was a face or not. "We'd simply be trying to determine who constructed it, when and why. It'd become one of the mysteries of our own planet, like the Sphinx." Max turned toward Trish. "Tell me, Patty, why the sudden interest in extra-terrestrials?"

"It's something that hit me when I was at Kakadu, looking at some of those rock paintings."

"What was that?"

She slipped her shoes off and curled her legs up into the chair. "Well, something about a few of them seemed familiar, and I couldn't quite put my finger on it." She told him that sometime later it came to her that they looked eerily similar to the pictures people drew who claimed to have been abducted by aliens. She looked toward Max, again, trying to gauge his reaction. Before he could respond, however, she added, "I know. I know. My imagination runs away with me at times."

He chuckled. "Possibly. But, you seem to have this ability to see things that others don't when they look at the same thing."

"Really, I tried to dismiss it. But then the same day I ran into Mack, I was watching this cowboy movie…*Quigley Down Under,* about Australia in the 1800's…you know, because it was about Australia, and I'd just been there. And in one of the scenes, I noticed some more rock art with those creatures. Max, they really did look like those pictures of aliens."

Trish wrapped her arms around her legs. "Then I got to thinking about the rock art being off limits to the public because the Aborigines say spirits or dangerous beings are there sometimes that the uninitiated can't approach safely. And I thought, 'Maybe some alien race started coming to earth eons ago, communicating with them, and maybe the rest of us just can't understand those communications.'"

"That's thought provoking. Very thought provoking."

She tilted her head and shrugged her shoulders. "So, it's not easy to dismiss this aspect. Stuff keeps popping up about it—like synchronicity—and I can't help being curious."

Max wrinkled his forehead and raised an eyebrow. "My dear, don't apologize for your curiosity. It shows you're thinking. I'm delighted you're not ignoring the coincidences. If you pay attention to them, they can point the direction for you whenever you get stumped." He set his pipe down and laced his fingers together. "So…we've explored innate knowledge and knowledge from another planet as possible sources for the Aboriginal myths. Can you think of another?"

"Another?"

"Yes."

She looked across the room and back. "I don't know. I hadn't thought about anything else."

"Well, think about it a minute."

Trish rubbed the side of her head. "Look, I need a Coke or something before I can think any more."

"Good idea," Max replied. He looked at his watch, "Good heavens. I haven't even been thinking about the time. It's well past lunchtime." He turned toward Trish, "How about a salad and sandwich?"

"Sounds great."

• • •

In the kitchen, Max began pulling items from the refrigerator for lunch, while Trish set the table. As she filled a couple of glasses with ice and poured tea, she commented, "Max, you've got such a cozy place here."

"Thank you, Dear. I find it really suits me…the quiet…all the time in the world to read or write…places to walk in the woods. The setting up here is so inspiring. I've never regretted moving here for my retirement." He peered at her over the top of his glasses, and added, "And, of course, the company around here is quite nice."

"You mean, 'bothersome.'"

"Not at all. I find our conversations quite stimulating."

"You don't ever get lonesome?"

"Oh, I still miss Rachel. But I'd miss her wherever I was. No, all in all, I'm quite content here." He looked up. "Ham or turkey for your sandwich?"

"Turkey will be fine." She set the glasses on the table and sat down, while he continued preparing their lunch. "Max, why are people so threatened by new ideas?"

"I think that's perfectly natural." He explained that people had to have a basic belief system with which to function in life, a way to see their world. It shaped everything about them: their art, government, religion, science, their entire social structure. "When you challenge that belief system, you're challenging the whole structure of their lives, which can be quite unsettling."

Trish leaned onto the table. "Like saying the world is round, and then when you start to believe it, wondering why you don't fall off the bottom?"

He held up his knife for emphasis. "Exactly. And then that progression leads to the discovery of gravity, which, of course, was there all along before we discovered and began understanding it."

"But, Max, those kinds of shake-ups are the only way we can evolve."

"True," he responded, as he sliced the sandwiches. "But even though some may find it exciting whenever we take another step forward, others find it traumatic."

Trish laced her fingers together. "Why's that? And why do so many people view the world so differently?"

"Maybe some are just more comfortable on that cutting edge that we're always talking about, and some are simply more comfortable with things as they are. They don't want their belief systems challenged." He thought that, though humans tried to avoid changes like the plague, they inevitably found it quite stimulating. He stood up erect at the kitchen counter a moment, then turned toward her. "Have you ever seen any of those abstract pictures they make now...the ones with computer generated 3-D images implanted in them if you look just right?"

"I've seen them, but I've never been able to quite get the images in focus...and I've stared and stared at them for ages. Why?"

"Just a minute."

He wiped his hands on the kitchen towel and went to the den. When he returned a few moments later, he had a book. "Take this while I get the food on the table."

She took the book, thumbed through it quickly, looking at the collection of the abstract images, then turned back to the first page. "It just looks like a bunch of designs to me."

"You're not looking at it correctly. Look, pick out a picture and put it up to your nose."

After turning to one of butterflies, she pressed her nose to the page. "Okay."

"See how blurred everything is?"

She half laughed. "Yes."

"Now, move the picture back slowly from your face and don't refocus your eyes; maintain the blurring."

"Okay." She moved the picture slightly from her face.

"Slowly. Slowly," he cautioned.

"All right."

"Keep your vision blurred. Don't shift it. Don't lose it. Don't look at the designs. Just relax and focus on the blurring."

She moved the book out further, slowly, looking at the page and keeping her vision blurred. Then, as a three-dimensional image suddenly popped into view, she almost shouted, "Max! I've got it! I see it!" Once Trish had the desired perception, she was able to move her eyes and look all around the picture at a depth and clarity she hadn't seen before. "This is so neat, Max!"

"See, Patty, it was there all the time. The page hasn't changed at all, just your perception of it."

She peered over the top of the book. "I think I get your point."

"Well, and that is the point. Different people see entirely different things when they look at the same thing. They're all looking from their own per-spective, through their own lens. And consequently they may see a different depth or dimension."

Max set their plates on the table and sat down. Trish, however—still enchanted with the book—kept turning from page to page, trying out her new technique. "This is fun."

"I'm delighted you like it. And there may be another good reason you're so intrigued by your new toy…besides the obvious."

"What?" she asked as she closed the book, set it on the table and re-turned her attention to him.

"You're familiar with the saying that perception is everything?"

"Yeah."

"Well, in the process of shifting your visual perception, you may be opening up new neural pathways in your brain."

"Neural pathways?"

"Yes. You know we're only using a small percentage of our brain ca-pacity in everyday life."

"Yeah, I think they say around ten per cent."

He chuckled. "Personally, I think that's somewhat optimistic." He gestured with his hands as he explained the theory that, by shifting the way people perform everyday things, they were stimulating and opening up new neural pathways. "Simple things, like writing with our left hand instead of our right hand all of the time…trying new unfamiliar routes instead of our old well-worn ones. And…shifting our visual focus and having a whole new dimension coming into view. Changing and re-shifting our perception."

"Hmm." Trish picked up her sandwich and began eating.

"The vision you're using with this book is called 'soft focus.'" He explained that most often people saw with what was called sharp focus. Animals, however, used the blurred, soft focus most of the time. He said that it actually took much less energy to use that vision. "The only time animals use sharp focus is when they're in a predatory state or when they feel threat-ened."

"I've never heard of that before."

"It's all about perception." He placed his napkin on his lap as he con-tinued. "You see, if you go out in woods and sit down and shift into soft focus—like you were just using—you'll see that animals and insects will behave as though you're a tree or any other natural object around. Butterflies will light on you, and deer and squirrels will hardly notice your presence."

Max stopped long enough to drink some tea. "Then, if you shift back to sharp focus—and you don't have to move another muscle in your body—you'll see that the forest creatures will instantly scatter; they sense that you've shifted into a predatory state." Trish looked at him. She was beginning to understand why he enjoyed living alone in the woods. He told her that primitive cultures had used soft focus for eons, whereas modern cultures spent almost all of their waking time in sharp focus.

He began eating his lunch, when Trish said, "Max!"

He looked up "Yes?"

"What you just said…Old Tom…out in the bush…*he* looked at me like that right before he tapped me on the forehead. I didn't get it at the time, but it was a wild look. And I felt like he was looking right through me."

"It probably looked wild because wild animals use that vision most of the time."

"Yeah…maybe that was it."

"Well, if you read the instructions in the book more thoroughly at a later time, you'll see that the time for real discipline is when the depth image first begins to emerge. Our tendency is to re-shift our focus and start looking at it again instead of through and beyond it. Only when we do, the depth image disappears and we have to start again."

Trish looked up from her plate. "You're speaking metaphorically again, aren't you?"

"*Life* is a metaphor. Don't take it so literally. Look into it and through it, not at it."

"I wish I could, Max, but I *have* to take it literally. I actually saw mermaids and Cyclopes and all sorts of monsters with my own eyes. I can't treat life like a metaphor. It's real." She tapped her fist on the table for emphasis.

"I guess you think that table is real, too, don't you?"

"Huh?" she queried with a puzzled expression.

"Patty, when you break things down to their smallest components of matter, they're mostly just empty space. Everything—including us—is mostly whirling bits of energy. Basically we're all mostly energy. All matter in the Cosmos is basically tiny bits of energy filled with empty space."

"I've heard something like that before from Mary Ann Parker. But, I mean, it can't be."

"Why not?"

"Because, Max." She touched the palm of one hand with the fingers of the other. "I'm solid." She made a fist and tapped it on the top of the table again. "This is solid. If it was just energy, if there was mostly energy, my hand would pass right through it."

"Would it?"

"Of course, it would."

"Not if you were hypnotized."

"Hypnotized?"

"Yes" He leaned forward. "You see, a hypnotist can take a subject from his audience…and you've seen these kinds of demonstrations on TV before. Anyway, he hypnotizes a man and tells him that there's a wall in front of him. Then he tells the man to walk forward. The man bumps into that 'wall,' and he *can't* move forward. Again and again, he'll be told to move forward. And again and again, he'll bump into the invisible wall.

"The audience will be laughing, and even getting hysterical, because they know that nothing is there. But the subject takes it all quite seriously. He *can't* go through the wall that has been constructed in his mind. Our belief systems tell us that we live in a world of matter. Consequently we keep bumping into things."

"But, Max," she began in a tone still tinged with disbelief. Again, she hit the table with her fist, this time harder. "It feels solid."

"And that, my dear girl, is the awesome power of our beliefs. They quite literally shape our world and our experience of it."

Trish maintained the look of disbelief, and Max added, "I'm not sure I'm happy with this knowledge. And I'm quite sure I haven't fully accepted it, because the world still feels and looks solid to me, as well. But, intellectually, I think I may have a small grasp of it. I'm not sure I even want to embrace it fully, because to do that might de-mystify the very mystery of life I find so fascinating in the first place."

"And this hypnosis, where does it dome from? And who's doing it to us?" Trish asked, crossing her arms and leaning back.

"Oh, I believe it may well be some collective form of self-hypnosis…like a game that everyone is playing, and the rules have been previously set…unconsciously. Like Jung's collective unconscious."

"I don't know, Max. This is kind of weird."

"But, Patty, hasn't this whole experience you've been through been weird and mystifying and provocative?"

"Yeah, but…" She uncrossed her arms and slumped. "Oh, I don't know. It's just that it's been a lot of change to go through so fast."

"It has been something of a whirlwind, I have to admit, but you chose this route to get to whatever destination you're seeking, for whatever reason."

She held her hand out firmly. "But what I experienced was *real*."

"Of course, it was. It's also metaphorical. It's both. You need to relax your vision and step back from this a bit, Patty. You're up too close to it. The depth of it will appear when the time is right. You already have the tools you need to figure this thing out." He reminded her about the corruption of the myths, explaining that eons of editing would do that. He said that, in spite of that, he believed the true essence of all myths still rumbled around in each person's psyche. "It's only a matter of tapping into it."

"Well, I'm having one hell of a time tapping into it."

"Then keep practicing visually with your book, and other things might start popping out for you in your external world."

Maybe, Trish thought. But if anything more shocking than mermaids and Cyclopes came popping out of the external world, she wasn't sure she was ready for it.

● ● ●

After Trish and Max finished their meal Max said, "Something else I want to mention; you're familiar with left and right brain thinking, of course."

"Yes, we usually have a dominant side," she said, leaning back in her seat.

"Right," he responded, then leaned forward. He explained that while whole brain thinking was supposed to be a new concept, in actuality it was an ancient system of living on the planet. "You see, the left side of our brain thinks logically, linearly, numerically and verbally, while the right side thinks artistically, intuitively, spatially and emotionally. In the Western world, the logical hemisphere dominates. In the Eastern, it's the creative. Neither is good or bad; it's simply that by relying primarily on one side over the other, there's no balance. And life seeks balance—demands balance."

He said that thinking with both hemispheres of the brain could bring the cultures of two separate hemispheres of the world together in balance, as well as the two sides of man's psyche. "We need to stimulate our right brain in our society. We need art and music and dance as never before. We need rhythm.

"I believe the rash of crimes we see today is just a reflection of our disconnection from our emotions, or the more emotional, rhythmic side of right brain."

She looked puzzled at him, and he added, "Patty, if we can't feel life, we have no respect for it. If we can't truly feel our own emotions, we can't truly care about another person's feelings, and we do things that never take into account the effect of our actions on others."

"Hmm."

"We need that emotional, intuitive connection to be whole. And I believe rhythm is one of those connections." As he leaned back in his chair, a serene look came over his face. Trish instantly detected a subtle, but familiar shift in his demeanor. "Patty, our world is alive with rhythm and cycles. It permeates our very existence." He looked at the far wall of the kitchen. "Our hearts beat rhythmically. The moon constantly waxes and wanes, and the tides respond accordingly, ebbing and flowing. Season follows season. Rhythm. We breathe in and out, usually unconsciously. The sun rises and sets. Planets revolve, and galaxies spiral. The cat purrs softly on the sofa."

Max nodded toward his sleeping tabby cat in the next room. "Rhythm. It surrounds us and permeates us…a life force beyond our conscious understanding.

"The way we connect with unknown realms in our culture is through art, music, dance and dreams. Those are the things that trigger inspiration, creativity and imagination."

Trish resisted asking a question, not wanting to interrupt his train of thought. He'd lapsed into one of his rare, spellbinding and almost poetic streams of consciousness that she'd come to treasure over the years of their friendship.

"Our languages limit us; governments limit us. Music and art set us free. Art and music allow us to speak the truths that even our limited languages deny us. Music, art and dance are the only true universal languages. They allow us to escape cultural divides and communicate on a purely human and even spiritual level." He looked at her and held out his hand. "The universe is alive, Patty. The earth is alive. Even our scientists toying with their Gaia theory have begun to recognize this fact. To disconnect from the rhythms and cycles of the universe is to disconnect from our emotions. And a person totally disconnected from his emotions is the psychologist's worst nightmare." He nodded his head toward her. "Just read the front page of any newspaper."

He looked back across the room, almost through the walls. "The only real power in the universe is those cycles and rhythms. We may superimpose our own false powers on top of them in the form of boundary maps and laws, but those cycles and rhythms of the universe will continue in spite of what our governments do or don't do."

Trish sat silently, mesmerized.

"Each tornado, each flood, each volcano on the planet shows us who's really in charge, when all we can do is to simply get out of the way. Or we can learn to live in harmony with the planet, in balance with the earth and our own psyches. We can touch and stimulate that creative spark and ignite the creativity, imagination and vision that make us so uniquely human…humans intricately connected to our world, instead of separate from it."

When he stopped long enough to indicate that he was finished speaking, Trish folded her arms and said simply, "Max, you absolutely blow me away."

He tilted his head self-consciously, as though returning from some kind of trance state and waved his hand. "Ah! I still revert back to the classroom and lecturing, whenever I don't catch myself."

"Well, I'm glad you let yourself go, then. Being in one of your classes must have been an experience of a lifetime."

He picked up his utensils and plate. "Well, let's get this table cleared."

• • •

After Trish finished rinsing the dishes and putting them in the dish-washer, she returned to her chair and asked, "Max, were you suggesting earlier that I should spend time in an art museum or going to the opera?"

"Not necessarily," he answered, as he stood at the counter and refilled their glasses with tea. "Don't get me wrong; that would be divine if you had the time and opportunity. But just walking through the woods and viewing nature's own canvas might be even better. And dance your own dance. Sing your own song while you walk. There are thousands of ways to stimulate that right brain." He nodded in her direction and added, "And, believe me, television isn't one of them—at least, not most of the time."

"You know, Old Tom said that the white fellows don't have a song or dance or pictures that they pay attention to."

Max brought their glasses back to the table and sat back down. "Sounds like a smart fellow to me." He took a sip and told her about a group of people who had a condition called synesthesia, and that while talking about the whole brain thinking concept he'd been reminded of it. He said that, like the different visions, those people experienced all of their senses differently than most.

"Never heard of that. What is it?" Trish sipped her tea.

"It's my understanding that these people experience or perceive sounds and smells and other senses as colors and shapes...something like that. There are books about it, though I'm not that well versed on the subject. I've heard it once compared to that Walt Disney movie...you know, the one about danc-ing brooms and elephants?"

"Yeah."

Max crossed his arms. "It seems that their senses kind of merge or blend together, whereas, we experience each sense individually and sepa-rately. Quite remarkable people, really. Some of the ones who have it, think of it as a gift...another level of consciousness that others don't have." He leaned forward and took another sip of tea. "Who knows? Maybe Disney himself was one of them. But can you just imagine how that type of sensual merging would alter your view of the world? The only other place where I've read of a similar blending of senses was in a few of the accounts I've read about near death experiences."

He told Trish that he believed it was those types of phenomena that gave people their best chances of learning more about themselves. He also mentioned people with savant syndrome. He leaned back and draped his arm over the back of his chair. "I mean, think about people who can sit down at a piano and play Mozart—which they've never heard before and without the first lesson—yet some of them can't even tie their shoes. It's as though they've tapped into something, some level of genius. And if they can do it, why can't we? I really believe we all have access to genius; it's just that we're not tapping into it." He held a hand out. "How else do you explain savant syndrome?

Before she could respond, he said, "Patty, we posses the grandest computers in the world inside us, and we neglect them most of the time in favor of the toy computers we invented to play with."

She twisted her glass back and forth. "You're talking about our brains."

"Partially. Our minds, to be more precise. I believe we have other accesses, as well."

"Like what?"

"My dear, if the DNA in our bodies can link us all the way back to the first man and woman, then we bear the imprint of the entirety of humanity housed within our bodies. And, if that's true, shouldn't we even logically be able to access knowledge and memory from that lineage? Aren't we already programmed to do that?"

Trish shrugged. "I don't know. I never thought about anything like that before." She put her hand to her face. "Could that be what Old Tom was talking about when he tapped me on the forehead and talked about remembering?"

"I don't know. *Have* you started remembering things?"

She pushed her chair back from the table. "Well…on the way back to Darwin I had really clear memories of when I was a little girl, spinning around in the yard before a gathering storm." She looked at him. "But it wasn't so much the events I remembered as it was the feelings I had during them. I spun around and around as though I was gathering up energy. I mean, I really could feel that again."

Max smiled. "Ah…sounds like you were creating a vortex as a child."

"A what?"

"A vortex . It does just that…gathers energy."

Max drank more of his tea, then explained that vortices, gathered energy in one direction, as with a tornado, and dispersed it in another. Then he told Trish that he thought the real keys to other levels of knowledge and opportunities to evolve were the very mysteries and unexplained phenomena that didn't fit into the present world view. He said when people couldn't explain something with logic, they usually tried to deny, dismiss or ignore it—or ridicule it. In the natural progression of things, however, if enough of the inquisitive types focused their attention onto the extraordinary things in life—when they couldn't be ignored any longer—people were eventually forced to deal with them.

As Max finished the last of his tea, he wiped his mouth with his napkin and said, "Then once we accommodate them into a new belief system, they become ordinary—in fact, almost obvious. For instance, when people thought the world was flat, someone had to have started wondering why the sun always came up in the East and set in the West. That doesn't fit in a flat world concept. You see?"

"Yeah."

He talked about the people who for years were scoffed at because they claimed to see auras around people and objects, and that, with Kirlian photography, it was clear that those energy fields exist.

Trish and Max were talking about the phenomena of crop circles and ancient stone configurations, such as Stonehenge, when Trish abruptly sat up straight and said, "Max, I've got it."

"Got what?" Max asked, tilting his head.

"What you asked before, about another possible source of the Aboriginal myth."

"And what might that be?"

"Well, the first thought I had when I realized the connection between mythology and what was in the jars in that clinic was, *Oh, my God, we've done this before.* Then I meet Old Tom and I think the same thing." She held out a hand. "What if it was knowledge passed down from another ancient civilization that may have learned about the dangers of uranium when *they* experienced a catastrophe from messing around with it?"

"Hmm. You're speaking of former advanced cultures that may have disappeared without a trace?"

"Why not? If it's true that we could be totally wrong about the age of the earth and man's appearance on it, I don't see why not. What about the myths about Atlantis?"

"Well, I certainly believe we haven't scratched the surface of earth's history with our archeology. And Plato spoke of Atlantis. But, of course," he added with a nod of his head, "he had access to archives that we don't. He had the benefit of the great library at Alexandria before it burned down."

"I've read about the library of Alexandria," Trish interjected as she leaned back in her seat.

"That fire was probably one of our civilization's most terrible tragedies," Max continued, as he sat back and laced his fingers behind his head. "Historians today fairly weep at the thought of all the knowledge that was lost to mankind when it was destroyed. And I suppose if there was one advanced civilization, like Atlantis, there could have been more. That's certainly a possible explanation for the Aborigine myth."

"And I've read other myths about a civilization called Pacifica or Lemuria," Trish added.

Max lowered his arms. "It may just be coincidence," he began as he raised his eyebrows and then smiled and added, "but I doubt it." He inhaled deeply and said, "While you were in Australia, I was re-reading some ancient myths. There was one Indian text called the Mahabharata."

"Never heard of it."

"Well, it's probably the oldest existing text from that culture." He told Trish that it was filled with references to an entirely different cycle in the development of humanity. Some of the descriptions of events alluded to almost futuristic types of technology that could well be comparable to those of the modern world. He said that, however, the technology seemed to have disappeared abruptly, as might be expected from some major catastrophe. After that, man returned to a more primitive existence.

"Have archeologists ever found any evidence of it?" Trish asked.

"Oh, my dear, archeology isn't an exact science. It's ridiculous to treat it as such. It all hinges on subjective interpretations, and many in the archeological community will protect their own subjective bents with a vengeance." He told her that there were books written about finds that archeologists simply denied, ignored or buried in museum warehouses because they didn't fit into their current frames of reference.

"Really? Do you know the names of any of them off hand?"

"Oh, there's one that comes to mind called Forbidden Archeology."

Trish got up from the table. "Excuse me a minute, Max; I've got to get something to write on."

• • •

After Trish returned to the kitchen, and made a notation of the book title, Max told her about other articles and material he read about respected scientists who'd found objects and tools that pre-dated human history. "Mainstream science will attack the new finds as though the scientists presenting them were enemies of the state." He explained that while scientists used carbon dating to prove their ideas about the past, they weren't immune to ignoring it when it disproved their preconceived notions. "For archeology to be effective it has to be flexible enough to sometimes consider the impossible…and it simply isn't, at least not on the whole. There are thousands of objects that have been discovered that simply don't fit mainstream interpretation."

"Like what? Besides the tools," Trish asked as she perched her chin in the palm of her hand.

Max leaned back in his seat and told her about some of the finds and of one in particular called a stylized insect that he'd seen at the Smithsonian that seemed to be of ancient origin. He said that, though it was on display at one time, he wasn't sure if it was any longer. "It looked very much like a metal aircraft to me when I saw it." He smiled at her. "Of course, that's just *my* subjective interpretation of it—just as many of us saw a face on the surface of Mars, and many others didn't. But, I'm not aware of any insect or even fossilized insects that look that much like an aircraft." He pointed with his finger. "The point I'm trying to make, Patty, is that we've barely scratched the surface with archeology, and I do intend that as a pun."

He crossed his arms across his chest. "It makes me quite disillusioned with my fellow professionals and scientists when I see how close-minded some of them are about what constitutes the world around us and our experience of it." He uncrossed his arms and said, "Patty, you must continue thinking outside of the box, if you want to find answers to your questions. You can study the most ancient historical records in the world, and you won't find your answers there, either, because what you're looking for is pre-history. The only things that will be helpful to you right now are the myths, legends and oral histories. They dare to tell our truths...without threatening the scientific or left-brained communities because they've been written off as fairy tales." He smiled. "And, as you discovered in that clinic, they're not fairy tales."

Trish looked up. "What was the Mahabharata about?"

Max raised his eyebrows. "Oh, there were stories about battles that took place in the sky. To be perfectly honest, it may not have even involved people on earth. They may have simply been witnesses to some disconnected aerial event from ancient times. Even Inuit oral traditions feature stories of similar technologies in their ancient past."

"Like what?"

He told her about references to giant chariots in the sky and giant birds made of metal. "They sound a lot like Ezekiel's wheel from the Bible, which a lot of people believe is a description of a UFO encounter like some people have described today. But without the frame of reference we have, he may have interpreted it as God."

"So, we're back to the other theory now?"

"Possibly, and maybe not. It could even be that your Aborigines simply knew that normally radioactive hot spots were still cooling down on the earth, and that they still posed a danger."

Trish looked unsatisfied with his response. "Max, you frustrate me sometimes."

"How's that?" He got up from the table and started toward the refrigerator to put up the pitcher of tea.

"Well, I don't come here looking for any absolute answers..."

He turned and looked directly at her and said, "Good...because there aren't any." Then he turned back toward the refrigerator.

Trish looked at his back and mouthed his words mockingly and silently back at him. She hadn't realized that he could see her reflection in the kitchen window until he said very deliberately, "I saw that."

Trish winced at the comment, like a child caught in mischief.

Max walked back to the table and, in an authoritative tone, said, "Now that was something I would have expected from a sixth grade student."

They looked at each other, and the two of them burst into laughter.

Finally, still chuckling, Max asked, "Have we worked too long today?"

Trish put her hand over her face. "No. No. Really. I guess I just needed a little comic relief. I'm sorry."

"Apology accepted. Frankly, I think the conversation did need a little lightening. Now, why don't we go back into the den and get comfortable again?"

"Can't we stay in here to finish talking?"

"No," he answered with authority, "because I don't have comfortable chairs in here." He pointed his finger and added, "And because you act like you're at recess in here. Besides...I want to light up my pipe."

"Should I start the dishwasher?"

"No. I'll do that later. Can't stand the noise when I'm trying to concentrate."

Chapter Thirty-Six

After both of them took a bathroom break, Trish and Max got settled in their seats in the living room. Trish glanced at her watch. Their interchange had been going on for over two hours. Yet, it had been compelling and productive, and she wanted to stay with the rhythm as long as it continued. As Max retrieved his pipe from its holder and relit it, she asked, "Is this tiring you?"

He blew out his match and tossed it into the ashtray. "Not at all. I'm finding it quite stimulating." He looked toward her. "Besides, even when exploring a deep subject matter *gets* tiring, it helps to continue on. It can help break down the resistance of mental barriers that keep us trapped in old thought patterns. I've never understood why therapy sessions only last an hour. That's barely enough time to punch a few holes in defenses...and a week or month between those hours is plenty of time to reconstruct them." He waved his pipe. "If you're up to it, I say let's keep going."

"Okay, then." Trish leaned onto the arm of her chair. "I have to tell you, I just don't think we're going to be able to deal with environmental problems like we have in the past."

"Just what would you propose?" he asked, turning toward her.

"Well, I'm not sure exactly...but it's kind of like having a leaking kitchen sink, and all you're doing is mopping up the water from it, that's pooled on the floor. I mean, I think at some point you have to just let the water on the floor go, and go fix the damn sink."

"Interesting analogy."

"Think about it," she said, with her hand held out. "If we could clean up every polluted site—and that's not even possible with radioactive wastes— look what else is looming on the horizon: genetic engineering, nanotechnology, a thousand new chemicals every year, some with the same catastrophic side effects as dioxin and PCBs. We can't begin to reverse this process till we figure out why we're so bent on self-destruction in the first place."

She massaged her left temple with the tips of her fingers, lamenting the fact that so many modern religions lacked the same reverence for the earth that primitive cultures had. "Mark says that it's like something is missing, that it seems natural that people who profess to believe in God would revere his creation and try to protect it...and, it's in all the myths and legends world-wide. So, why don't we have it, too? I mean, the Bible even says that God will destroy those who destroy the earth."

Max took his pipe from his mouth. "Patty, have you ever heard of the lost gospels or the missing books of the Bible?"

"I've heard of them, but I have to admit to ignorance beyond that. Why?"

He leaned against the arm of his chair and explained that the New Testament wasn't put together until the fourth century—long after Christ's death—and that at the time, a lot of manipulation, control and outright force went into putting it together. "It certainly wasn't a democratic process, I can assure you. I've already told you about reincarnation. Other writings were left out or edited by the church during the Nicean Council in 325." He raised his eyebrows. "Not only that, but many texts that disagreed with the conclusions drawn by Emperor Constantine's council were labeled heretical and were systematically destroyed to keep them from coming to light."

"Why?"

"Because they didn't fit the image and the message that Constantine and leaders of the church wanted to project about Christianity." He inhaled from his pipe, then set it down. "For instance, we find references to a Book of Nathan and a Book of Gad, and we don't have any copies of those books. It's possible they were among the ones burned at the Library of Alexandria. However, so many writings were being destroyed that some of them were hidden away for protection. And other texts that were left out were kept in the vaults of the Catholic Church for centuries. Some of those weren't made public until this century. Many others are *still* kept from the public"

Trish wrinkled her brow. "What kind of writings were hidden?"

"Oh, the ones we know about contain more background on the childhood of Jesus, and more about Mary's life before he was born."

"Really? Who wrote them?"

"People who actually knew Jesus, like Peter and Nicodemus. And if things that important got left out, you can't help but wonder what else did." Max leaned toward her. "What I'm getting to is that back in the 1940s and 50s, discoveries were made of ancient texts in the Middle East. One set was the Dead Sea Scrolls that they found at Qumran near Jerusalem. You've heard of those."

"Yeah, sure."

"And there were sets of Gnostic writings from an early Christian sect that were found in the '40s at a place called Nag Hammadi in Egypt...over forty manuscripts."

"I'm not familiar with those."

He told her that even though the Dead Sea Scrolls eventually got a lot more press, for years, even those were kept under wraps by the Catholic Church. "Or maybe the public simply didn't know enough to *be* interested. Who knows? At any rate, the Scrolls were held for decades by a group of Catholic priests, mainly, who were supposed to be working on deciphering the scrolls. They weren't releasing anything to the public, however."

He laced his fingers together while explaining that experts, who were being denied access to the scrolls, began growing impatient and started complaining that the material should be made public, that the ones with control of it were hardly unbiased. The critics said that others, with different views, should be involved with viewing the artifacts and translating them. He talked about the controversy over it in the academic world, and, said that eventually, through public pressure mostly, other experts in the field were finally given access.

Max leaned back, took a deep breath and proceeded telling her that the Nag Hammadi texts were invaluable in providing information about unknown aspects of the life of Christ and the early days of the developing Christian world. "In fact, Carl Jung was so enthralled with the findings that the C.G. Jung Institute bought one of the codices and gave it to him on the occasion of his eightieth birthday."

"Really?

"Yes." He leaned forward again. "But what's important is that some of the material in these documents was new."

"How so?" she asked, curling her feet up under her and giving him her full attention.

"For instance, in the Gnostic writings there's a group of what has been called secret sayings of Jesus."

"What kind of secret sayings?"

"Well," he began, "I have a few books on this subject that you're welcome to study, but I suggest that you might want to look for more of them at the libraries. The thing of importance, though, is that some of the quotes…wait…let me get one of the books."

Max pulled himself up from his chair with some effort and went to a bookshelf at the end of the room, where he pulled out one of the books. "Can't trust my own memory on this one," he mumbled, as he adjusted his bifocals and turned to the index, then thumbed through the pages. "Here it is. Here's one where Jesus' disciples wonder how they will recognize him once he's gone. They say to him, 'Point out the place where thou art, because it is necessary for us to seek it.' And Jesus replies, 'I am the light that is above them all. I am the all, the all came forth from me, and the all became me. Cleave the wood, I am there; raise up the stone and you will find me.' "

"Holy Cow, Max," Trish responded, uncurling herself from her chair and leaning forward. "That sounds like he's telling them that he's in nature itself."

"Exactly." He closed the book and looked over at her. "The author of one of these books seems to think so, as well."

"Max, talk about a different perspective. Something like that could totally reshape religion today. It sure as hell might make people look at the earth with a new reverence."

"Exactly my point. And it might if people knew about it," he replied, as he returned to his seat with the book still in hand. "But I think many Christian religions today may be too entrenched to make such a drastic shift, no matter what might come to light from ancient texts. Conditioning can be very powerful, Trish." He handed her the book. "But there are references to other sayings you might find interesting, as well, in this and other books I have."

"Jeez, that 'cleave the wood, I am there' part might make people stop ridiculing tree-huggers."

"Perhaps. And perhaps *some* people might interpret the word 'cleave' as to cut, instead of to cling to."

Trish jutted her head back slightly. "I didn't think about that."

"The point I'm trying to make, Patty, is that when the Bible was first put together, we don't know what may have been left out...or for that matter, may have been put in for purely political reasons. There was a book written by Jesus' grandmother, Anna, and one by Mary Magdalene that is exquisitely beautiful. With the discovery of the Dead Sea Scrolls and the Nag Hammadi texts, some of these things are just beginning to filter into the public domain." He relit his pipe and inhaled several times, then pointed with it. "But the most valuable thing about those texts is that they *were* secreted away for hundreds upon hundreds of years, and weren't subjected to centuries of editing."

As Trish sat engrossed, Max told her that because the books in the Dead Sea Scrolls and the Nag Hammadi texts paralleled some of those in the Bible, their authenticity was fairly broadly accepted. "There are many people who now argue that some of those texts should be added to the Bible, that the work of Thomas, for instance, should be added to the Gospels. And frankly, I think it might be appropriate to begin asking whether we should leave the collection of texts in the Bible up to a long dead Roman Emperor or a bishop that no one ever heard of. We can only guess at King James' political agenda."

He puffed again on his pipe. "I think it's also important to ask why pockets of early Christians considered it necessary to secret away those priceless texts in the desert in the first place. What kinds of persecutions made that necessary? What was so threatening about the writings?" He pointed with his pipe. "Were the teachings of Christ being destroyed or manipulated after his death by people who could see their power and wanted to use it as a control mechanism for their own agendas?"

"Max," Trish began, shaking her head slowly from side to side, "I consider myself fairly well informed, but what you're telling me just isn't common knowledge."

"You're exactly right...just as the information you've accumulated about the atomic age isn't...and both *should* be part of the public debate." He told Trish it seemed only logical that any important or powerful texts would become corrupted, damaged or manipulated over a period of time, and because of that, it was the true essence of a message that needed to be retained. He said that, to be sure, there were people who'd always come at any subject with their own agendas, but that was part of the process, as well: having as many perspectives as possible in order to better see the whole. He reminded her of the Indian parable about the blind men all describing the elephant from their own point of view.

"They were all right, yet they were all wrong, because they couldn't get their ideas together into a complete whole. They just couldn't let go of their own individual perceptions. They clung to their own 'reality' too obsessively. That's what blinds all of us in the long run: clinging tenaciously to our own perceptions without considering other viewpoints."

Using his pipe with the finesse of a musical director as he spoke, he told her that there were a number of religions in the world that actually incorporated nature as a spiritual force, including some Catholic priests. He mentioned St. Francis of Assisi, then paused and asked Trish if she'd ever read about him.

"Not extensively. I know he began the order of Franciscan monks."

"That's the one." He told her that after a series of insights and visions that led Assisi to a form of enlightenment, he gave up his attraction to worldly goods. He developed a communion and a connection with all of nature, seeing God in every creature and plant. "They said that he could actually communicate with and summon the animals."

"Really?"

"So they say."

Trish smiled. "Maybe he used that soft focus you were talking about."

Max returned her smile. "Possibly." Then told her, "Anyway, I think we have to assume corruption of most religious beliefs, when you consider how many people have been killed over the years in the name of God by religions that preach a message of loving your brother—and even your enemy. It should be obvious we don't do a very good job at practicing even our most basic religious beliefs." He reminded her of the millions murdered by the Church during the Crusades, Inquisitions and witch hunts of Europe.

"You know, that's always bothered me. How can people murder in the name of God?" Trish asked.

He let out a short breath. "Oh, that's easy. It can happen whenever a person assumes a morally superior attitude to another person or group of people. If you're morally superior—if your position or belief system is better than anyone else's—then you can extrapolate that position to include *any* means to further your beliefs, including murder. And if you can justify murdering one person, what's to stop you from murdering millions, if you have the means?"

"Then the danger is in our basic attitudes?"

"I believe so…and our attitudes are shaped by our spiritual beliefs."

Trish sighed. "Max, what other bombshells are there in those Nag Hammadi texts? This is just phenomenal stuff."

"Well," he answered, pointing again with his pipe, "there are a number of new ideas and quotes that might interest you, but I'd like to tell you about one author who's studied them. He believes that throughout history, whenever humanity is in the worst crisis and needs the most help, some important tool or form of wisdom reveals itself to rescue us from destruction. He thinks the development of the atomic bomb and the discoveries of the Dead Sea Scrolls and Nag Hammadi texts all happening around the mid-1940s weren't coincidental."

"Well, you and Mark and Peggy, all three, have always maintained a belief about man's ability to pull himself out of crises."

"That particular author also points out that before his death Jung had visions of a great worldwide catastrophe."

"What kind of catastrophe?"

"Something along the lines of a fiery holocaust that would occur around 2010 or 2012."

"Really?" Trish asked, raising her eyebrows.

"Yes, and what's significant about that particular date is that it corresponds with the date that the Mayan calendar ends."

Trish propped her head on her fist. "What do you think about that?"

"Well, we've had warnings throughout the ages about the world coming to an end from some holocaust. I know a lot of them are obviously from kooks or opportunists…"

Trish interjected, "I'd hardly think of C.G. Jung as a kook or opportunist."

"Of course not. I think even the most cynical person would have to admit that he was on a sincere quest for wisdom and knowledge. I'm simply stating that an apocalyptic view is nothing new in history. That even Jung would have one, as well, seems significant to me."

Max stretched back in his seat and laced his fingers together behind his head. He speculated that Jung's belief might have been shaped by his seeing mankind develop the tool that could destroy his entire species along with others in a thermonuclear war. "Man has always been at war. Peace has only been the lull between wars throughout history. So the development of a weapon that could destroy our species might mean that it's only a matter of time before the winds of some future war would bring it about." He brought his hands back down. "It's only been in the last five decades that, when we decided to take up the sword, we risked falling on it ourselves for our entire race."

"We've all had that fear since the Cold War, Max," Trish said as she stood up and arched her back. "I think I need to stretch a little."

"I think I do, as well," he said, rising from his chair. "My old age talks to me whenever I sit too long."

● ● ●

After a short break, Max leaned onto the back of his chair and continued where he'd left off. "The best warnings in history are the ones that never came true, because we saw a possible disaster and consciously changed course."

Trish sat back down and crossed her arms. "Max, it sounds like this Nag Hammadi material might contain the missing part of the Sky Father/ Earth Mother reverence that primitive cultures have."

"Well, you're welcome to the book. And I have one or two others on the subject." He walked back to the bookshelf, looked around and pulled out two more. "These ought to do you for a while," he said as he approached her with the books in hand.

She took them, and asked, "Do *you* have an apocalyptic view?"

"Well," he said, as he retrieved his pipe from its holder and puffed on it while still standing, "it would be foolish not to entertain the very real possibility of it, but I still believe that man has control of his own destiny—that he has the power to change the future. One of my most ardent beliefs is free will. The book of Revelations certainly seems to herald an apocalyptic end." He looked at her, "So did your Aboriginal friend in his religion—which is much more ancient than the Bible."

"Speaking of Revelations," Trish broke in, tilting her head sideways, "you just reminded me of something I forgot to tell you about on the phone the other day." Max sat back down beside her as she explained that while in Hawaii on her way back from Australia, she wanted something to read on the plane. "I went to an airport shop, and couldn't find anything that really appealed to me. I was in a hurry, so I just grabbed a book with an interesting cover. It turned out that it was about a guy who'd had a near death experience back in the seventies. It's odd that I picked that one. I wouldn't have believed it had anything to do with the things I'd been working on. But, believe it or not, he said that he saw the accident at Chernobyl before it happened during his near death experience."

"Really?"

"Yeah. This happened in the seventies, and he said that he'd had several visions into the future—some that must have seemed impossible at the time, like the fall of communism.

"Anyway, one of the visions was of a huge concrete structure that blew up. He said that he knew it was a nuclear explosion, and that the name of the place was 'wormwood.' And you know what?"

"What?"

"Years later, when the Chernobyl accident happened, he found out that the name for Chernobyl is wormwood in English."

"Is that right?"

"Yes, it's the name of a plant of some kind that grows in the area."

"My, my…fascinating."

She told him about another nuclear accident the man saw in the future that would happen somewhere in a northern sea, and that the water would be so badly contaminated that fish would die, as well as people in the area. "*That* sounds pretty apocalyptic, don't you think?"

"I'd say so."

"Anyway, the thing is," she began, tapping her fingers on the arm of her seat, "something about wormwood kept gnawing at me. And then just yesterday I remembered something from the Bible, and I got it out and I'm reading Revelations—Revelations 8, as a matter of fact—and you know where it says that the angels will sound?"

"I remember."

"Well, it said that when the third angel sounded a great star would fall from heaven and it would fall on the third part of the rivers and on the fountain of waters. And guess what?"

"What?"

"The star was called 'Wormwood.'"

Max leaned forward. "Oh, my heavens, Patty…you're right. I *thought* that sounded familiar."

"And it goes on to say that the third part of the waters became wormwood and many men died when the waters were made bitter."

"I remember that, as well," Max said.

"Well," she continued, repositioning herself, "when I read that, I started to wonder about all the whales and porpoises beaching themselves, and I wondered if they weren't trying to tell us something…if some of the beachings weren't in areas where they've had nuclear ship accidents, because there were several incidents of whales beaching themselves after France's nuclear tests last year."

"Have there *been* many nuclear ship accidents?" he asked, surprised.

"Oh, my God, yes," she replied, nodding her head with deliberation. "But it's just like your Nag Hammadi texts; it's just not common knowledge." She slipped off her shoes, pulled her legs up in her chair and wrapped her arms around them. She told Max that it had been documented that around fifty nuclear weapons, as well as eight or nine nuclear reactors were lying at the bottom of the ocean. "With the kind of pressure and corrosion you have in the oceans, just how long do you think containment of those reactors and weapons is going to last?"

"My, Patty." Max's face was expressionless in disbelief.

"Then just a couple of months ago this scientist from Norway revealed that the Russians had dumped all kinds of radioactive wastes—including *seventeen* nuclear reactors into the Kara Sea." She related the scientist's fear that the radioactivity would be carried into the Atlantic Ocean in icebergs, where it would poison fish and become a health risk to humans. "Kind of sounds like a nuclear accident in a northern sea that the man with the near death experience predicted, huh?"

"You've got to be kidding, Patty. Why don't we *know* about these things?"

Trish motioned to her chest. "You're asking *me*? Even as a reporter, I didn't know about it till I started researching and interviewing people. The government and industry have done a thorough job of keeping some of these things under wraps. You know how Eisenhower warned the country about the military-industrial complex before he left office."

Max tilted his head. "Patty, was Chernobyl really that bad? I know people died there, but it doesn't seem it was *that* bad. Not biblically bad, at any rate."

She held out a hand. "That's the problem, Max. You haven't read much because the mainstream media didn't report much of the real news back then." She told him that while he'd probably read that a few dozen people died initially, the truth was that the Ukrainian Minister of Health was maintaining that 125,000 had died there since the accident, besides the immune diseases, congenital malformations and other problems. Thyroid cancers had increased anywhere from eighty to two hundred times normal levels.

Max raised his eyebrows. "Good heavens. I had no idea."

"Of course you didn't. At every anniversary of Chernobyl our media still reports that only 36 died. Eight thousand clean-up workers *alone* died." She tilted her head and added, "Come to think of it, that 125,000 death toll sounds remarkably close to the 133,000 dead that a university study estimated would die as a result of an accident at the Enrico Fermi plant in Detroit."

As Max sat transfixed, Trish repeated what Katrina had said about the things that took place during the aftermath of the accident. She leaned forward and added, "And that place is going to be radioactive for thousands of years to come. Who knows what the future will bring for the people there by the time a final casualty list is added up?" She leaned back again. "This tragedy is just beginning. You know how they talk about the gift that keeps on giving? This is the event that keeps on killing—not like a tidal wave or earthquake where you get a final total of casualties almost as soon as it happens."

She turned toward Max and told him about the relatively small number of research papers at Chernobyl. Then she added, "Besides, some researchers, journalists and scientists say the full truth *can't* come out because researchers aren't even following the basic nine steps of scientific research—the Rules of Research, they call them."

Max sighed. "Somehow that doesn't surprise me. I just wish *our* media were more thorough. Freedom of the press should give us a slight edge."

"Mark brought to my attention that the owners of two of the main television networks also *build* nuclear reactors. Talk about a conflict of interest…" she shook her head. "And there's the consolidation of the news media, where everyone is reporting the same thing. I tell you, as a former reporter, the level of public concealment of this topic staggers me."

Trish raised her right hand briefly and then lowered it. "Look, the worst thing about Chernobyl is that the danger may not even be over." She told him that ninety-five percent of the reactor core was still there and that the sarcophagus surrounding it was in danger of collapsing. She said the Ukrainian government was warning of another possible meltdown and wanted to close the whole complex down with the other reactors, but that they didn't have the money to do it. "They're begging the industrialized nations in the G-7 to help them fund a shutdown, and said that if they don't, they're going to have to upgrade the aging reactors and keep using them."

She stretched her legs out again and told Max that she believed the way governments had wielded nuclear power—the U.S. in particular—was in direct opposition to everything democracy was supposed to stand for. "And, hell," she continued, lifting her hand for emphasis, "democracy is supposed to be what the Cold War was about in the first place."

Trish exhaled deeply and leaned forward. She glanced over at Max. "This might be a good time for a little bit more of that comic relief. Got any handy?"

He smiled at her comment and inhaled from his pipe.

"Max, how have these things stayed hidden so well?"

He took the pipe from his mouth and said, "It's easy to manipulate recorded history once the victors have been determined. It's only when a conquered people refuse to be victimized on an intellectual and spiritual level that history begins to be rewritten. And there are many ways to be conquered. In our modern world, indoctrination is a much simpler method of controlling people than cutting off their heads…less messy, as well."

Trish smiled sideways. But he was going to have to do better than that for comic relief.

"It's easy to poison the planet hundreds of thousands of years into the future," he continued, "if you don't believe in reincarnation…if you don't

398

believe in karma. It's easy to give your power away to unknown forces if you've been convinced that you don't have any power…if you refuse to take responsibility for your own actions…or inactions."

"So why do we give our power away so carelessly to leaders and governments that don't act responsibly?"

"I believe power is scary to us. Therefore, we thrust it upon others. 'Let *them* take the responsibility if things go wrong. Let *them* do the dirty work I'm too moral or fearful to do myself. Then I can stand back and criticize when things go wrong.'" He looked directly at her. "The ones we give our power to, in turn, feel they have to live up to our expectations in order to maintain *their* illusions of control over others. That's fertile ground for abuse of power any way you divide it up."

"But, Max, it's not just indoctrination. Governments and religions, both, have killed millions in their quests for power and control.

"That's force, Patty, not power. The power to really change things can never be accomplished with force. Force is temporary illusion. Power is the ability to shape the external world from the internal workings of the heart and soul."

She looked over at him, moved by the profound nature of his comment. "So why do nations and governments and institutions keep repeating that history?" she asked.

"Repeating history is simply repeating patterns of behavior. Continual abuse of power is continuing to react out of fear to the exterior world instead of with love. If we always follow the same well-worn paths, we'll always end up with the same results. By changing the way we react to or behave toward external events, we open up those new neural pathways in our brains that we talked about before in the kitchen. When we open up those new routes, we open up new territories and quite literally change history."

Max leaned onto the arm of his chair. "What you saw in Clinic Number Four were the direct descendants of Cold War fear. What you experienced in that village with a little girl called Ilyani was the offspring of love. Seldom has anyone been shown so clearly the end results of two emotions, the destination of two separate paths: the profane and the divine."

Trish dropped her arm into her lap. "She *was* a divine child, Max…just like an archetype come to life." She stopped speaking as emotion welled up inside her and tears filled her eyes at the memory of the little girl. She lifted a hand and touched her face where Ilyani had touched it. In a whisper she said, "Max, she was magical. Sometimes I can still feel her touch. It was as though I'd been touched by God." She wiped the tears from beneath her eyes. "But, Max, how did it happen? How did she get that way?"

"Ah," he said, smiling, "*that's* what you *really* want to know. You know all too well how those babies in the clinic turned out the way they did.

But how did Ilyani? And are there others like her in this radiated world?" He leaned forward. "My dear, you've just shifted your path. You've just defined a new goal."

She looked at him. "You think it has something to do with the radiation, too, don't you?"

"Well, my dear, from what you told me, the little girl did have a small deformity on her hand, and she did live in the same area as the others. I think we can assume her mother had some kind of exposure to the radiation near Semipalatinsk."

"But, where did she get the magic? How did she avoid ending up in that clinic like the others?" Trish smiled sideways and let out a short breath. "Max, she was the happiest little kid you ever saw...all covered in mud. The other kids surrounded her at every step like a magnet." She let out another breath and added, "And after she touched me, I can see why."

He looked at her with tenderness. "Patty, I can see and hear and actually feel the shift in you." He set his head onto the back of his chair and then tilted it forward and said, "You said you wanted to figure out the why of the atomic age. Maybe it's simply because that's the way we've always done things. It's only the technology that's changed. Maybe, with the stakes so high now, we've never been more motivated to risk another course."

"Max, in the kitchen you talked about the need for archeologists to believe in the impossible." He nodded, and she continued. "Well, after those mutants and Ilyani, I believe in the impossible."

Max peered over his glasses. "Patty, you must believe in the impossible to discover what's possible. You must travel unknown territories to make them known." He held his pipe out. "You must experience the fog to recognize clarity." Leaning forward again, he continued, "I've watched you take several leaps of faith in the last few months. Maybe the greatest leap of faith can be a single step in a new direction." He looked at her very deliberately and asked, "Tell me. Why are you going to New Mexico?"

Trish looked at him, surprised, then glanced down. How could she begin to tell him? How could any man understand the depth of pain a woman would feel over being infertile? But Max was being uncharacteristically direct. She was going to have to tell him sooner or later.

Without warning, she began crying and cupped her hands over her face.

After Max had given Trish some tissues and comforted her, she raised her head and forced a smile. "I guess I'm getting in touch with my emotions again."

He chuckled. "Patty...it's such a lovely day. Would you like to go back out and sit on the porch?"

"Yeah...I think I would."

• • •

After Trish and Max went outside and got seated in the rockers, she began telling her story, still clutching her tissues. She reminded him about going to New Mexico as a child in the fifties, during the height of the atmospheric tests, then told him of her suspicions about her infertility. When she'd finished, they sat quietly several moments.

Max broke the silence. "Child, I don't know a damn thing about genetics, but you're the most fertile woman I've ever seen." He leaned forward. "I may not know what it *is* you're about to create, but I've watched you pulling back your power for months now, and you wouldn't be doing that if it wasn't for something big."

Looking over at him with a puzzled expression, she said, "Pulling back my power? Max, I've been a basket case a good chunk of the last year."

Max set his pipe in its holder by his rocker. "Patty, you can't dare to challenge the architecture of a structure that has supported the concept and experience of your entire life without feeling some pain or even guilt about it. The tears you've shed for yourself have come from a deep well within you...deeper than most are willing to go." He rested back against his rocker. "And they haven't been for you alone; they've gone deep enough to encompass the whole of humanity. That's how the fountain of compassion begins. And, believe me, those kinds of tears can quell the fires of *any* anger or fear."

She put her hand to the side of her red and swollen face. "Why has all this been so painful?"

"Because the birth of anything can be painful and because sometimes before the birth of something new, you first must go through the throes of death."

She looked at him, puzzled again, and he added, "Birth and death come in many forms, Patty: the death of ideas, beliefs, patterns of behavior, relationships...trust. Yet, that's part of the cycle, that rhythm of the universe." He let out a deep breath. "I just happen to believe that cycling is accelerating right now. And it has the look of chaos about it."

He looked over at her. "Remember what Nietzsche said about needing chaos to give birth to the dancing star?" She nodded. "Patty, we forget sometimes that we're made up of star dust. And you don't have to be a physicist to know that."

"Star dust, huh?" She smiled weakly. "You're going to have to explain that one. I didn't take physics."

He held out his hand. "Even the iron in our blood was created when a star exploded. All other heavier elements were created the same way."

"Hmm. I guess I've never really been aware of that before."

"It's just a simple thing. However, that simple awareness sometimes tends to shift the way we think and feel about life."

She wiped both her hands out across her face and took a deep breath. "Max, I don't have any regrets about getting personally involved in this story, even though it went against my training. I realize I had to. But...you know how you advise me not to take things personally?"

He nodded.

"Well, if the atomic age really is the cause of my infertility—like it was those mutants—then, damn it, Max, that's about as personal as it gets."

Max sat quietly for a moment, staring ahead. Then he said, "You feel betrayed, don't you?"

She wrinkled her face. "Of course, I do."

He sighed. "It's one thing to think this whole thing was a big mistake that nobody knows how to stop; it's quite another to think it was about greed and that the people you put your faith in—the ones you trusted to protect you—may have betrayed you in a most unseemly way." He nodded slightly several times. "That's pretty hard to swallow."

She nodded in assent, without looking up.

"It also may be the hardest obstacle you have to overcome in telling this story."

She looked at him, and he continued, "No one wants to feel betrayed. People don't want to admit they've put their faith in the wrong person or principle or institution. It makes them doubt their own judgment, wisdom and instincts." He leaned toward her onto the arm of the rocker. "Often when confronted with a reality like that, we simply slip into another layer of denial to keep from having to deal with the truth, because we don't know what to do with it, and because it's hard to feel vulnerable."

Trish shook her head back and forth. "Here, you're telling me how I have to get past psychological barriers to even tell the story, and the thing is, what difference will it make if no one is listening now to the warnings from these indigenous elders?"

She leaned closer to him on the arm of her rocker. "I guess I can see how the myths seemed so farfetched over the generations that people just couldn't understand them." She sighed heavily. "But the thing *I* can't understand is why these places are considered sacred. What does that mean? The forbidden part makes sense to me, but not the sacred. And what—or who—are the beings that the uninitiated can't approach safely?"

He shook his head. "I don't know, but I have a feeling that may be something else you're going to New Mexico to find out."

"Maybe." She tapped her fingers several times on the arm of her rocker, then stopped and turned toward him. "There's something else about Revelations."

"What's that?"

Trish pulled her legs up in her rocker and crossed them, then told him she'd read that some environmentalists were interpreting a portion of the book in an unconventional manner.

"What part is that?" he asked.

"It's the one that talks about the third part of the earth being burned up and the trees and grass and the mountain burning with fire from the other angels. They say that may be a symbol for the parts of the earth contaminated with pollution and nuclear fire."

"Well, I'd say that certainly seems reasonable at this point, wouldn't you?"

She wrinkled her brow, "Are you kidding? With all the dead zones in the sea and land?"

"Would you say it comes anywhere close to approaching a third of the earth?"

Trish smiled. "I get your point." She pulled herself forward and asked, "Can I go get your Bible a minute?"

"Certainly."

"I can't remember it verbatim," she added.

When Trish returned with the book, she sat back down, turned to Revelations and flipped through it. "Here it is. It says that when the plagues are sent upon man by the angels, God said that 'they should not hurt the grass of the earth, neither any green thing, neither any tree, but only those men who have not the seal of God on their foreheads.'"

"What do you think the seal was?" Max asked.

"I don't know," she answered, still looking at the page. "I was thinking about Old Tom touching me there. I had such a visceral reaction to it…but then while I was reading just now, I couldn't help but think about the 'Greens.'"

"The Greens?"

She looked up. "Yeah, you know, Max. Don't hurt any green thing…like the people who consider themselves part of the green movement…like Greenpeace, and like Gorbachev with his Green Cross, International. People who value the earth and have a relationship with it—like the primitive cultures…and St. Francis, and…I don't know, like people with green thumbs."

"But the mark was supposed to be on the *forehead*, Patty, not the *thumb*."

They both chuckled.

"Good," Trish said, "finally some levity." She closed the book.

"Did he leave a green mark on you?"

They both laughed again. Then Max said, "Well, Patty, I can see I'm probably going to be up all night reading those books of myth you brought me from Australia."

"Well, it's only tit for tat. I can't count the nights your ideas have had *me* up into the wee hours. And I will for the next few days again with this Nag Hammadi material." She tilted her head. "But, you know, speaking of Gorbachev and the green movement reminded me of something else that guy with the near death experience saw back in the 70s."

"What was that?" Max asked.

"That a Russian leader would become the head of an environmental movement. Sounds like Gorbachev, doesn't it?"

"It does at that."

Trish told Max she didn't know if it was possible to uncover everything Gorbachev talked about when he said Russia and the U.S. were still keeping secrets about the Cold War. She sighed. "These damn lies and secrets are poisoning us, Max."

"Secrets and lies always poison people, Patty. I firmly believe they may actually be toxic to our bodies." He stared out at the mountains for a moment, then tilted his head and said, "Come to think of it, radiation is probably a perfect metaphor for some of the secrets in our lives that we attempt to hide from the world." He looked at her. "Even lies designed simply to feed someone else's ego have an impact."

"How? If they don't hurt anyone."

"They set up patterns. They imprint and ingrain the habit of not speaking our truths. Then it becomes easier and easier to forget our truths."

Trish took and exhaled a deep breath. "I don't know if we'll ever know it all."

"Perhaps not, but I believe you and others have uncovered enough layers to alter the course of the atomic age."

"Oh, Max, so many people have collected so much hidden information, but it always gets back to the same thing: how do you get that information out against the wealth of the forces that are manipulating behind the scenes?"

Max pursed his lips and then said, "Patty, when the world is ready to know, it'll come out. It'll all come out. Our inner truths—the ones that sometimes stay hidden in the deepest recesses of our psyches—will always come out once we realize that the borrowed truths of the exterior world no longer feel right. Nothing is so secret that it can stay hidden once we're ready to know it." Leaning on the arm of his rocker, he asked. "Did you know that the word 'apocalypse' means a revelation…when the truth shall be revealed?"

"No…I didn't." She let his words sink in a moment before saying, "But, Max, this thing is so *big*."

"Of course, it is. It *has* to be. Heavens, crisis isn't all bad. It's a great motivator. It gets up off our duffs, and gets us in motion. Sometimes, I think when we most desperately need to change, it takes a crisis big enough—

monumental enough to truly motivate us to risk changing and finding solutions. We have to fear the problem more than the change. And if people can solve a problem of this magnitude...well, just look how much they will have learned in the process...and how much they will have evolved."

"But what lesson could possibly be so important for us to learn from this crisis?"

"Oh, maybe one of the ancient wisdoms—the one that says that we're all one." He said that people had been concentrating on their differences for a long time—their religions, their colors and their politics—and that they'd fought a lot of wars over those kinds of issues. "Maybe it's time for us to start concentrating on what we have in common for a change.

"Our truths surface when we're finally ready to know them. And who knows? Maybe this is the point when and where that Gaia principle you talk about kicks in and sets the wheels of survival of the planet into motion."

After several quiet moments of staring forward, Max added, "I was thinking about that author's belief that the development of the bomb and the discovery of the scrolls were connected. At that time in the mid-forties, I was at war, experiencing my own trauma...trying to stay alive, really.

"Well, back then I didn't even know about the discovery of the scrolls. And, frankly, I was up too close to world events at the time to see them clearly. It was all still a blur. It's only now, at a distance, that they start making sense to me...kind of like those 3-D abstract computer pictures"

He told Trish that over the previous year he'd felt fortunate to get glimpses of her abstract picture book from her own unique perception. He tapped his knee. "I think we may be getting far enough back from this period in history when it starts coming into focus. We may be on the cusp of seeing the real depth of it." He turned his head toward her. "Child, I think you really have stumbled onto the story of the millennium."

"Several millennia, Max. But I didn't stumble onto it; it's been there all along. I just wasn't seeing it. It's just like Old Tom said: we've got our stories and pictures and sources right before us. We just aren't paying attention."

Max's voice was gentle, as he said, "Well, I'm glad you've been paying attention." He picked up his pipe. "And I'm glad you're focusing on the earth, because I believe it's through the earth, through nature, through that grounding, if you will, to God's creation—this very life experience—that we make our connection to the spirit world. It's only when we have our feet firmly rooted in the earth that our spirits can truly lift to the heavens."

Trish propped her chin on her hand. "Max, I love to listen to you talk. One of the things I love about coming here is that no matter how deep or intense or depressing life gets for me, you always come up with a new perspective, or with something that sheds a new light on it."

"Like Psyche with her single candle?" Trish smiled, and he added, "It's you who's shining light on this thing, Patty."

Trish glanced at her watch. "Oh, gosh, look at the time. I almost forgot that Jimmy's coming over for dinner tonight. I've got to get to the grocery."

As she stood up, Max said, "Patty, you've come a long way since I saw you that day in the restaurant, looking so bewildered."

"Maybe so, but I'm afraid I've got longer to go still."

Looking up, he said, "Now, a determined woman like you will do fine. I'm sure of that." He shifted forward in his rocker and stood up and went inside to collect the books for Trish, including the book with the computer graphic images. When he returned and handed them to her, he asked her teasingly, "Which one do you think you're going to like most?"

"This one," she said, holding up the picture book.

He chuckled, and Trish asked him, "And which souvenir from Australia is *your* favorite?"

"The bull-roarer," he answered. They both laughed.

"I knew it," she said. "I guess we're both still just a couple of kids at heart." She looked at him and drew her head backward slightly. "Lord, we really had a marathon session today, didn't we?"

"That we did, Patty."

They hugged good-bye. Then Trish bounded down the steps with her books in hand.

Just before she reached the car, Max called to her from the porch, "Now, Patty, all these theories we've talked about today…don't think that any of them necessarily have to be mutually exclusive of each other."

"Now, Max," she responded sternly, "don't you dare throw me a curve now. I've got so much cerebral overload from this session already, that I'm going to have to do something purely mindless for the next few days…like reading one of those trashy gossip magazines."

They smiled at each other one last time and waved good-bye.

Chapter Thirty-Seven

The next week Trish was curled up in her living room chair, perusing one of Max's books, when Jimmy came through the door in a rush. When he saw her, he stopped almost frozen in mid step. She smiled at him. "Hey, Jimmy, what's up?"

Instead of returning her smile, his facial expression was blank, and he appeared to be searching for words.

"Jimmy. What is it? What's wrong?"

He stammered, and her face went blank, as well. "You're scaring me. What's going on?"

Jimmy came over to her chair and knelt down beside her. "Trish, Max has had a heart attack. I just heard about it. He's at the hospital, and it doesn't look good."

"*What*? No! No! It can't be. Jimmy...No!" As her mind began filling with unthinkable thoughts, tears began surfacing in her eyes. She covered her face with her hands.

"Oh, Baby, I'm so sorry," Jimmy said, caressing her on the shoulder for several moments.

Trish pulled her head up and wiped her face with her hands, then pulled them away. "He's alive, right?"

"That's what I heard."

Trish took a long breath. She couldn't allow herself to let go of any glimmer of hope. Her determination to go into action took over as she got up and rushed toward the bedroom. "I'll be ready in just a minute, Jimmy.'

He followed her to the door of the bedroom.

"Where did you hear about it?" she asked.

"Actually, I ran into Mack downtown at the hardware store. He was just about to phone me. He wanted me to come over here and tell you before you heard it from anyone else. Evidently, one of Max's neighbors went to see him and found him on the living room floor. They don't know how long he'd been unconscious."

Trish came back out of the room with her purse slung over her shoulder, carrying her shoes. As she sat down to put them on, she asked, "Have they contacted any of his relatives?"

"Honey, I'm afraid I don't know anymore than I just told you."

• • •

When they arrived at the hospital, and hurried to the ICU, the hospital staff would only confirm that Max was a patient there. Even after prolonged prodding by Trish, they wouldn't give out details about his condition. They went to the visitor's waiting room, where Trish recognized Max's neighbor, an older man named Henry sitting on a sofa in his coveralls, looking shaken. She walked over to him and put a hand on his shoulder.

He looked up. "Oh, hey, Patty."

"Henry, what happened?"

"I don't know exactly. I found him on the floor when he didn't answer the door. I knew he was home because his car was there. And he wasn't out, because his walking stick was still by the front door. I'd talked to him just last night. Anyway, when I went inside and found him, I called an ambulance. They were there pretty quick...but, I tell you, Trish, he looked bad...*real* bad."

"Has anyone called his relatives?"

"Well, he don't have many, you know. But I put in a call to a cousin of his in Marietta. She's on her way up now."

Trish looked at Jimmy in desperation. He put his arm around her and pulled her toward him. "It's going to be all right, Trish."

The rest of the afternoon passed uneventfully. They never got anything but the official status about Max's condition—which was "critical"—though Trish kept going to the nurses' station, trying to eke out any bits of information she could. The hospital wasn't allowing visitors, and after hours of waiting for the doctor to show up, Jimmy finally got Trish to agree to go home and wait, where she'd be more comfortable.

• • •

Later that evening when Trish called the hospital, she was able to reach Max's cousin in the waiting room. The woman had a calm and refined, but tired voice. After introducing herself as Evelyn Eubanks, she told Trish that the doctors had Max somewhat stabilized, but that they really wouldn't know much more about his prognosis until morning. She advised Trish to wait until then to come back to the hospital. She was going to a motel herself to get some rest after the long drive. When Trish suggested that Max's cousin stay with her, she said she preferred to be close to the hospital, and that she was leaving the hospital staff a number where she could be reached in a hurry, if needed.

Trish reluctantly agreed to follow everyone's advice about spending the night at home. Jimmy stayed with her. "God, Jimmy, I just feel like I have to *do* something."

The next morning, after a fitful night's sleep, she and Jimmy left for the hospital again. Upon entering the waiting room, Trish made eye contact with a woman she assumed to be Max's cousin. She was an older woman with white hair, dressed in a tailored green suit, and had the same dignified air about her that Max always did. She approached Trish with her hand out and said, "Hello, I'm Evelyn. You must be Patty."

Trish shook her hand. "I'm glad to meet you, Mrs. Eubanks. This is Jimmy Hartwell."

"Call me Evelyn. Glad to meet you, Jimmy." She turned and shook his hand, then looked back at Trish. "I hope you don't mind if I call you Patty. That's what Max always called you."

"Oh, sure, sure."

"I've heard a lot about you from Max over the years. He thinks very highly of you."

"He's something of a wonder to me, as well. How is he this morning? Have you heard anything?" she asked, clutching her fist to her chest.

"Yes, I saw him."

"You *did*?" For the first time Trish could feel her spirits lifting.

"Just for a short while. They really didn't want him to have visitors, but he's insisting on seeing you as soon as you get here…became quite agitated about it, in fact."

"How is he?"

"Weak, of course. But you'll see for yourself. Why don't you go on in?"

Trish took Jimmy's hand, and Evelyn walked with them to the door leading to the nurse's station. "Don't be too shocked at his condition," she cautioned, before turning to walk back to the waiting room.

As they walked into the cubicle Trish was bombarded by the antiseptic hospital smells. They made her weak and queasy. She focused on keeping her knees from buckling. Most of equipment in the room surrounded or was plugged into the motionless form on the bed. She approached softly. "Max?"

He opened his eyes and looked up, smiling weakly. His voice was equally weak. "Patty…Child…come on over."

With Jimmy at her side, she walked over and took his hand, trying to hide her shock at his helpless appearance. She'd never seen him like that before. He'd always been so dignified and stalwart. She'd always held an absolute belief in his strength, one that said nothing could ever touch him. That belief was shattered by the stark reality of the fragile, ashen form in the bed.

He was being administered oxygen through tubes in his nose, and when he spoke it was quietly, and with obvious difficulty. "Don't look so scared," he told Trish. "You know how I can always read your face."

"Oh, Max," she whispered. "You really *have* given me a scare." She half expected him to comfort her.

"Patty, I saw Rachel," he confided in a whisper.

Trish looked at Jimmy pleadingly. She didn't understand.

"Oh, don't worry," Max assured her. "I haven't lost my mind. It's just my heart that's in trouble." His eyes lit up briefly, and he tightened his grip on Trish's hand. "I really did see her, Patty...yesterday. I talked to her, and it was simply grand...the grandest experience I've ever had." He stopped and caught his breath for a moment, then continued, "I'm not afraid. And you mustn't be afraid or sad, either." He took a few breaths and began again. "Listen to me. You know everything we've talked about and studied these last months?"

"Yes," she replied softly.

"Well, Girl, we may have only found another part of the elephant's body."

"What do you mean?"

"There's so much more, Patty...*so* much more."

Then he looked toward Jimmy, "Now you take care of our girl, young man."

"Max..." Trish said, as the tears she had been holding back began welling in her eyes.

"Now, don't you dare cry. I've had a *fine* time. My only regret is not being able to read your book." He let go of her hand. "Now, go on and get out of this dreadful, stuffy room, and get on with your lives."

He caught his breath again. Trish could see he was having more difficulty breathing. "Besides," he continued, "I don't think these nurses and doctors are through torturing me."

Trish gave a fragile smile, and leaned over and kissed him on the forehead. "We'll be back this evening. You get some rest and some sleep. Bye for now."

"Goodbye, Patty Girl."

When they got back to the waiting room Trish could feel her knees finally giving way. Jimmy slipped his arm around her and sat her down on the nearest seat. Evelyn walked over and knelt down beside Trish. "I know how bad he must have looked to you, but he was alone for a long time in that cabin after his attack. Truthfully, when they first brought him in, no one thought he'd make it through the night. They said he was clinically dead. So any improvement is miraculous."

Trish, barely able to comprehend Evelyn's words, looked up at her, "Did you say he was *dead*?"

"That's what the doctor told me. They aren't giving us any false hope." She lowered her eyes. "Really, I don't know how he's hung on this long."

"But why don't they move him to the medical center in Gainesville where they have better facilities?" she asked.

"Patty, I don't think he's in good enough shape to move." She stood up. "Besides, he's refused to be moved." Evelyn turned toward Jimmy and directed her comments to him. "It'll be hours before they'll let anyone else see him. Why don't you take her on home? I have your number, and I'll call if there's any change. There's no sense sitting around here."

Trish didn't put up any protest. All she wanted at that point was to be home. Somehow, she knew that Max wasn't going to make it.

And she knew that there wasn't a thing she could do about it.

• • •

It was a little after four o'clock when the call from Evelyn came. Max had just died peacefully in his sleep.

• • •

Trish insisted that Evelyn come and stay with her while they made arrangements for the funeral. It was comforting and easier to have her nearby. Jimmy relieved much of the pressures for both of them by driving them around town to the funeral home, the florist and the church. Jimmy confided to Trish how glad he was to be with her during her grieving, since he'd always regretted not being with her when her parents died.

She didn't know if it was from shock or denial, but Trish felt strangely calm through the viewing at the funeral home and through most of the funeral itself. Evelyn introduced her to family members and old friends of Max's that Trish hadn't known, and, in turn, Trish introduced Evelyn to his neighbors and colleagues that she had never met. Kathy, Mike and Peggy came to lend emotional support. It was only when they left the gravesite for the last time that Trish's composure broke. She hurried to the limousine and collapsed in a heap in the back seat, sobbing until she could hardly breathe.

After the funeral, Evelyn moved into Max's cabin temporarily to set his things in order. When they went through his desk, they found his safety deposit key exactly where he'd told Evelyn it would be. At the bank they retrieved his will and other financial papers. Even though Max had said he was leaving his cabin and books and everything to her, for some reason it surprised Trish that he had when they read the will.

"I don't know why he did that, Evelyn."

"Patty, you must realize how fond he was of you." She put her hand on Trish's shoulder. "You know, he and Rachel never had children; you were like a daughter to them. He always spoke of you with such pride. I found a personal letter for you in his desk, so when you get a moment to yourself, that may explain things better than I can. I *do* know it was important to him that you have his books—the books and a place on the mountain. That's what he told me in the hospital he wanted to leave you as a legacy."

Legacy? How could she ever have any greater legacy than the love he had lavished so generously on her over the years?

• • •

It was mid June when everything had been taken care of, and Max's attorney had been contacted to start probating his will. When it was time for Evelyn to return to Marietta, she had adopted Max's tabby cat, Franklin, and carried him home with her. Jimmy returned to work to catch up on a few things, which gave Trish the opportunity to be alone with her thoughts and memories. She sequestered herself in her house for several days, where she finally allowed herself the luxury of totally naked grieving.

Late one evening, when Jimmy came over, she confided in him, "You know, in all the years I knew Max, I don't think we ever had a cross word between us." She took a deep breath. "I honestly don't think I could have taken this if I hadn't talked to him at the hospital that day and seen the look of pure joy on his face when he talked about seeing Rachel. I know he was in some pain." She looked toward the ceiling. "But, Jimmy, he really wasn't scared or sad or anything, was he? He looked like someone at peace." She looked back at him. "I really don't think I could have gotten through this if I hadn't had that last bit of time with him."

"Trish, maybe that's why he hung on as long as he did."

Chapter Thirty-Eight

Weeks went by before Trish had the will to focus on the next leg of her journey. But it was already July, and she knew that, in spite of her diminished enthusiasm, she needed to continue. Max would have wanted it that way. Since she hadn't been able to bring herself to read the letter he'd left for her, she'd set it aside until later.

When she began her preparations to go out West, she decided to give herself two weeks for the trip, just as she had in Australia and Kazakhstan. Gladys Hartley O'Hara gave her the names and phone numbers of activists to contact in Grants, New Mexico. From the information Trish was able to glean about them from Gladys, she narrowed her interest to one activist in particular. After interviewing her, and possibly a few others, Trish planned to visit some of the Indian lands where uranium was mined.

Whenever Trish found herself losing her spirit to read any more research material, she practiced her new vision technique with Max's hologram book. Occasionally, when she needed other resources or began missing him, she drove up to his cabin. There his books surrounded her. Signs of his presence permeated the cabin itself. The smell of his pipe tobacco still hung in the air and seemed to penetrate everything she touched. The pictures of him with Rachel still smiled at her from their frames, as if in approval. It became a comforting cocoon.

She fell into a ritual of getting out the bull-roarer, taking it to the front yard and spinning it around, listening to the haunting echoes of Australia that Max so loved. It was as though she was summoning his spirit to the cabin to encourage her yet again with his words of wisdom. At those times she began to feel a sense of peace. Maybe it was simply shock, but even Max's death, as painful as it had been, began to seem like part of a total experience. It was as though he was still with her in a different dimension, as though she had incorporated his essence into her very being. She felt like she was beginning to know, almost intuitively, what he would have said to almost any question she would have asked him if he were still alive, as if she could hear his voice in her head still answering her questions.

Maybe she was being strengthened somehow by his death, made more whole, more alive. Life seemed more important...and yet, less so.

"Ah, there's that paradox again, girl," she heard him say.

• • •

One night after dinner at Trish's house, she curled up on the sofa next to Jimmy. Trish noticed that he'd been quieter than usual all evening. "Something's bothering you, Jimmy. What is it?"

"Oh, nothing."

She persisted. "Something sure seems to be on your mind."

Again he drew back. "It's nothing really."

She dropped the matter and returned to their former conversation, but after a while Jimmy seemed totally disengaged in it. "Jimmy, something's bothering you."

Then without any warning or build-up, he turned toward her. "Trish, I'm just going to tell you right out that I don't think you ought to be going to New Mexico right now."

She looked at him, surprised. "What do you mean?"

"It hasn't been that long since you got back from Australia, and it hasn't been long at all since Max died. You've had a pretty bad year, and, frankly, I think you're pushing it."

"Pushing it? Just how am I pushing it?"

"Physically...emotionally."

"Oh, Jimmy, physically I'm fine now. Never better. And, yeah, I've been on an emotional roller coaster this last year." She pursed her lips, then added, "But I'm finally starting to learn how to roll with the punches emotionally...and I just feel like I have to go to New Mexico right now." She sat up abruptly and raised her eyebrows. "Jimmy. Why don't you go with me?"

"I can't, Trish. You know this is rafting season."

She cocked her head to the side. "Well, just when *does* this business of yours practically run itself?"

"Oh, I can take a few days off now and again, but not for long stretches. Besides, how long will this take?"

"Well, I don't know. There's no way I *can* know right now."

"And where will you be going next?"

"I don't know that, either, Jimmy. If I had all the answers, I wouldn't have to go at all."

"Why *do* you have to go at all?"

She furrowed her brow. "You know, Jimmy. We've talked about this several times. It's research. Or maybe just a search...a personal search. I'm looking for the next piece of the puzzle. I'm trying to figure this thing out."

"Figure it out?" His voice was tinged with disbelief. "Why do you have to be the one who figures it out?" He crossed his arms. "Even if any one *could* figure it out."

When Trish realized that Jimmy's reservations about her trip had nothing to do with his concern for her physical and emotional well being, the conversation took a sudden turn. She turned her body fully toward him.

414

"Jimmy, what is all this about?"

"Look," he began, holding his hand palm up, "you've had this thing hanging over your head for months now, and…well, I just think it's time for us to get on with our lives. This doesn't have anything to do with us."

She wrinkled her brow and shifted away from him on the sofa. "Are you asking me to just walk away from this?"

"Well…yeah…maybe. I mean, what does all this have to do with our lives, anyway?" But before she could answer, he added, "If you could just forget about all of this morbid stuff, we could enjoy ourselves. Why can't you just let it go?"

"Let it go? Don't you think I've tried? God knows I've tried. But you can't know how it felt to see those mutants. I can't forget that." Her voice was growing audibly louder, and she was clenching her hand defiantly on her thigh in a fist. "You don't think any of this has anything to do with *us*? Oh, really? And just how many times have you and Mike Dunnigan gone hunting over in Dawson Forest? Did either one of you have any idea that you might be exposing yourselves to radioactive isotopes over there?"

"No, we didn't." His voice was equally stern. "And you can bet I won't ever go over there again. But I don't want to see you wasting your whole life chasing a wild goose and wallowing in this stuff."

"*Wallowing* in it? If I'm wallowing in anything, it's a truth I never saw before. And now that I *do* know about it, I can't just pretend like I don't— especially when there might be something I can do." She took just enough of a breath to continue. "Do you think that avoiding Dawson Forest is going to solve anything there? Hell, Jimmy, they're building apartments and condos and stores right on the edge of the thing right now. And those people over there don't know anything about the radiation experiments that went on…or that the thing hasn't been cleaned up properly. And there are places like that all over the country…and *those* people don't know anything about *those* contaminated spots, either."

She raised then set her fist down firmly on her thigh. "And damn it, I've known five people in the last year who've come down with leukemia, and three of them have died. I've never known anybody before in my *life* with leukemia, and now all of a sudden there's *five*? I know that's not any kind of scientific statistic, but it can't be just coincidence, either. I can't ignore that."

Jimmy looked away from her toward the ceiling, and she held out a hand. "Jimmy, there are seven, count 'em, *seven* atomic bombs somewhere in the U.S., that are unexploded." He looked back at her and she continued. "The government lost them on military maneuvers during the Cold War. They've been classified as unretrievable. And they're *armed*, for God's sake. And I for one would like to know where the hell they are." She held out both hands. "These things aren't like left over bombs from World War II. *These* bombs could wipe out entire chunks of the *country*. Hell, there's one off the coast of Savannah, and every time some reporter starts asking too many questions about it, they start re-classifying material and pretending that it's *not* armed."

She stood up and faced the opposite wall. "And the other six...who knows where the hell they are?" She held her arm out. "They're just lying dormant somewhere, waiting for a bulldozer or some dredging equipment or natural disaster to detonate them." She swung back toward him. "And we could be talking about wiping out a whole *city*.

"How do you know we're not sitting on top of one of them right now that could completely shatter your idea of the perfect life we're supposed to be living?"

"I don't want to know!" he responded, matching the force of her words. "I don't want to spend the rest of my life worrying about something that might never happen. I've always heard that the vast majority of things you worry about in life—like ninety per cent—never even happen. So what's the point of worrying about things like that?"

"Yeah...I've heard that, too. But they also say the things that *do* knock you off your feet are the things you never saw coming. And these...these are things no one would see coming, because nobody knows about them." Her voice softened. "Jimmy, these things *are* happening right now. The whole planet is being nuked...quietly, silently...without any fanfare. And the media...*God*." She stared up to the ceiling. "They tell you everything about what you *don't* need to know, and nothing about what you do."

She looked back at him. "I always knew it was a sham. I just never knew how much of one. A story like this should be headlines around the world for months...until something starts getting done about it. But it'll never even make it above the fold on page fifteen...if somebody doesn't start doing something. "

She sat back down on the sofa. "And now, after wasting all those years as a paid reporter, I guess I've finally got a chance to be a *real* reporter."

"But why do you have to be the one responsible for it?"

"Because I *know* about it." She emphasized the words with a hand held outward. "For whatever reason, I *know* about it. I didn't realize the story was going to take me where it did. But I'm *here*. And I can't pretend I'm not.

"Ánd somebody's got to tell about these things," she added.

"Why does it have to be you? Why do you have to be the one to save the world? Why can't we just live a normal life like everybody else?"

Trish could feel heat rising to the surface of her face. "I don't think about it as 'saving the world.' I just think about it as doing what I can.

And," she added, "when you talk about a 'normal' life, that just sounds to me like you're saying an 'ordinary' life…and I've *never* been satisfied with an ordinary life. I never will be. Not with you. Not with anybody." She let out a breath. "Not even by myself."

Jimmy lowered his head and ran his fingers through the sides of his hair, sighing heavily. Then he said almost calmly, "I don't understand why you have to run all over the world. There's only one place *I* need to go when I get confused or need to figure something out."

She looked up, and he added, "When I get out on the Tallulah River, I *know* who I am and what I want in life."

"I'm not like you, Jimmy."

"Well, your going from place to place looking for answers to the universe will be an issue for me, like my ex-wives are an issue for you." Then he added, "Oh, I don't know. Maybe I'm just afraid of being abandoned again."

Trish blurted out, "Abandoned? *You?* Hey, it wasn't me who married the first person that came along after I went to college."

As soon as the words left Trish's mouth, the pained look on Jimmy's face caused a sudden feeling of regret to run through her abdomen. The fire instantly drained from her body. He looked as though she had slapped him in the face.

"I'm sorry, Jimmy." She reached out to touch him, but he stood and backed up a step, holding up his hand.

"No. No. You're right. I've beaten myself up over my mistakes a lot more than you ever could, and I've made a lot of them…and, believe me, I'm still paying for some of them. And I may never finish paying for them. Maybe that's why you won't marry me…because I've been married so many times. Maybe this has nothing to do with the story you're after. I know I'm not a good marriage risk. But the truth is that you left *me* when you went away to college. You chose a career over *me*…and I wanted someone who'd chose me over anything and anybody else in the world. I needed that. Maybe I still do."

"I didn't choose a career over you. I just wanted you to wait for me. That's all. And is that what this is all about? If I abandon this story, then that proves I love you? Why do I have to prove it? Why do I have to give up everything else that's important to me for you to feel secure in our relationship?" Before he could answer, she asked, "Besides, did you ever find it?"

"Find what?"

"Someone who'd chose you over anything and anybody else." Then she added, "In all your years of searching."

Jimmy responded hesitantly, "I don't know. I guess not…maybe…"

Before he could finish his thought, she added, "Maybe we both have abandonment issues here, Jimmy, but I'm not the person I was twenty-five years ago. I'm not even sure *who* I am...or who you are. But I know I have to follow this story. Somebody *has* to do it."

Jimmy looked as though he'd been slapped a second time, as though he realized that his point hadn't even been debatable with her. "I think right now I'd just better go and give us time to cool down." He walked toward the kitchen door.

Trish followed him. "Don't go, Jimmy. Let's finish talking this out. Let's not leave it like this."

He turned toward her briefly. "It's all right, Trish. I just need some time to think. Maybe we both do."

Trish didn't make any further attempt at prolonging the discussion and gave a resigned look before replying simply to a presence that was no longer in the room, "Maybe..."

Before she had time to digest what had just happened, she heard his car door open and slam shut. He started his car and backed out of the driveway. She wondered in a corner of her mind if he was also backing out of her life.

Chapter Thirty-Nine

Two days passed after the argument between Jimmy and Trish; neither had made any attempt to contact the other. Trish felt torn about being the first to break the impasse. On the third day, however, she called him. His phone rang five times with no answer before she heard his recorded voice on the answering machine. "Hello, you've reached Jimmy Hartwell's. Can't come to the phone right now. Leave a message, and I'll get back to you."

Trish paused briefly, trying to decide whether to hang up or leave a message. Then, after the beeps, she said with some hesitancy, "It's Trish. Ah...I just wanted to talk. Call me when you get a chance."

Another two days passed, with no response. Trish was hoping to leave for New Mexico the next week, and felt an urgency to talk to Jimmy before then. In spite of the regret she was experiencing, a residual feeling of anger still lingered from their confrontation. He'd been right about one thing. She had been through a lot in the previous few months: the depression, being jobless and the sudden loss of Max. So, if he knew that, why was he adding to her burdens by throwing obstacles in her path and putting their relationship on the line?

And why was she the one making the first overtures toward mending the rift?

Her attempts at analyzing the situation weren't bringing Trish any clarity. The only thing she was absolutely clear about was that she was going to New Mexico. She simply knew something was there that would bring understanding about the odyssey she'd embarked on almost a year before. Still, no amount of analysis could explain that need or her determination to go, either to herself or to anyone else. Maybe it was what Max had said. Maybe it was simply intuition...or faith. And those were the kinds of things that couldn't be explained.

The activist in New Mexico that Gladys had told Trish about was named Jo Ann Richards. She lived just outside of Grants. When Trish telephoned her from Clayton, she learned that the woman was a young housewife with two small children. She related that she'd become an environmental activist several years before, after becoming aware of some unusual health problems in her community. After months and months of research, she discovered the full extent of the legacy left in her town from the uranium mining during the Cold War, and had been a dedicated activist since then.

As they talked, Trish became eager to meet her in person. After Jo Ann agreed to an interview, they arranged to meet at the latter part of the week at Jo Ann's home. With those plans in place, Trish busied herself making plane, hotel and car rental reservations for the trip to Albuquerque. From there she'd drive to Grants for the interview. Beyond that she'd let things fall where they would.

Several days later, after she finished packing one of her bags, memories of Max swept over her. It was time to go to his cabin again.

A half hour later, after the ride up the mountain, she sat rocking on the porch of the cabin, recycling parts of her past conversations with him. Since his death the recycling had brought moments of balance and rhythm, akin to a stream of divine consequence. At those times she felt more confident and more at peace. Even her current crisis with Jimmy seemed to have a softer edge than it would have just a few weeks earlier.

After a few minutes she stopped rocking and sat up straight.

Mirroring. That was it. That's what Max would have said. And it was why Jimmy's words had affected her so deeply. She simply wouldn't have reacted so strongly to his doubts if she weren't having doubts herself.

• • •

The day before leaving for New Mexico, Trish decided to try to contact Jimmy once more. She felt a need to talk to him before she left. After driving to his house and ringing the doorbell, she received no response. She walked to the other end of the porch and noticed that his truck wasn't there. No one around town had mentioned seeing him. Maybe he'd gone out of town. She'd call one last time before leaving and simply leave another message.

Later that evening she dialed his number. At the end of his recorded voice message she said, "Jimmy, it's Trish again. I'm catching a flight to Albuquerque in the morning, but before I left, I wanted to tell you how sorry I am our argument ended the way it did. I've been thinking about what you said…a lot, in fact, and what I finally realized out of the blue yesterday is that the reason I was so mad is because I have exactly the same doubts you expressed.

"I've been asking myself all along, 'Hey, who am *I* to be telling a story this big, anyway?' And *I'm* tempted all the time to just drop it and go on with my life…but I know I can't. And I don't think I can ever be happy if I don't…"

Trish's words were abruptly interrupted in mid-sentence by a loud beep on the phone. The time on the tape had run out.

She hung up the phone, took a deep breath and let out an equally deep sigh.

• • •

The next morning, Kathy drove Trish to the Atlanta airport. Trish had put up a protest initially, but Kathy had insisted that she needed to go into Atlanta anyway for some shopping. In truth, Trish appreciated her company on the trip down, so close on the heels of Max's death and her problems with Jimmy.

But if Kathy knew anything about the quarrel between her and Jimmy, she didn't mention it—or even Jimmy's name—during the entire trip, which was a noticeable change from Kathy's normally inquisitive and persistent meanders through her personal affairs. That convinced her that, somehow, Kathy knew. And because she wasn't pumping her with questions, she began wondering if the quarrel had been more serious than even she had thought.

When they pulled up to the curbside check-in at the airport, Kathy got out and helped unload Trish's bags. As they stood there, Kathy hesitated beside the car before saying good-bye. Almost sheepishly, she said, "I goaded you into going to Russia. And I goaded you into getting back with Jimmy. I'm not much of a friend, when you really think about it."

Trish sighed and shook her head with half a smile on her face. The thinly veiled ruse was finally over. "Kathy...Kathy..." Trish began, "What do you think? That I'm not mature enough and stubborn enough to make my own decisions about my life?"

Kathy stared at the pavement, like a child experiencing rare and genuine regret.

"Look," Trish continued, as she placed her hand on Kathy's shoulder, "when I get back, we'll sit down with a few good glasses of wine and talk about this. Maybe a few good *bottles*, and a *long* talk. But right now, I have a plane to catch, so..."

With the sentence hanging unfinished in midair, they hugged good-bye and Trish added, "Thanks for the ride." She secured her overnight bag on her shoulder and pulled her other suitcase up to the counter. They waved toward each other before Trish turned her attention to the ticket agent.

She briefly touched the side compartment of her purse, where she'd slipped Max's letter—in case she felt able to read it while in New Mexico.

• • •

After her flight arrived at the Albuquerque airport late that evening, Trish retrieved her luggage and picked up her rental car. By the time she got to her motel room, she felt emotionally drained and altogether lonely. She prepared for bed, turned on the television and ran the channels a few minutes, before turning it off. Then she went to her purse, picked it up and pulled out Max's letter. After fingering the envelope a few moments and staring at it, she said out loud, "What the hell?"

She sat down in a chair, opened it and retrieved two neatly folded pages. The date at the top of the letter surprised her. It was the day after her last visit with Max. She wondered why he'd written instead of calling her.

The letter began:

"My Dearest Patty,

I had a dream last night that at first unsettled me. In it, I found myself desperately trying to catch sand that was being poured out of a glass. I couldn't catch it all, or stop it. No matter how hard I tried, it kept slipping through my fingers. Then, suddenly, I realized that it wasn't a drinking glass, as I'd first thought, but rather an hourglass. I looked to see who was holding it, and saw Rachel's beautiful face smiling at me. I relaxed and stopped trying to catch the sand.

Patty, Rachel still is! We all still will be, and are and ever were!

I didn't need anyone to interpret the dream. I knew somehow that my time here is running out. I'm not sad about that fact, but I wanted to tell you good-bye without alarming you. So, I decided to write this letter. I wanted you to know how much I've enjoyed being the old man on the mountain in your life's journey, how much I've appreciated your company, how proud I am of you and how much my life has been enriched by your presence. I've especially enjoyed these years when you've been back in Clayton. It seems to be where you belong.

When I wondered about leaving you a legacy, my books were the first things that came to mind, but now I realize that you should be writing the books yourself. I wondered if I'd taught you enough to see you through your journey, but then I realized that at some point you had become the teacher.

So, what I wish most for you now, Dear Child, is the opportunity to teach others who will assuredly find their way to your door in the future.

My hope is that you find them as eager, bright-eyed, delightful and full of curiosity about the world as you have been, and I'm sure will continue to be. And, at some point when they become your teachers, perhaps you can take some pride in that fact, and say to yourself, as I did this morning, 'All is well.'

Thanks for the memories, Child."

It was signed simply, "Max."

Trish clutched the letter to her chest. "Oh, Max," she said out loud. Then she turned to the second page.

It read: "I wrote this down after the dream, and wanted to share it with you. Perhaps it's the ending for that third book I never got published."

Dreams! Glorious *dreams*!
Unbidden, unnoticed, unspoken.
Dreams! *Glorious* dreams!
From out of the depths of soul and song,
Sailing into my heart,
My mind, my soul, my movement;
Showering beams of now,
Of being, of knowing the All.
Lingering soft on my world,
Then *thrusting* my essence beyond,
Dreams! Glorious dreams!
Glimpses of All that I Am.

After Trish stopped crying, she felt only a sense of quiet peacefulness, and was able to fall asleep in the warmth of it.

Chapter Forty

The next morning, after a few stops to get her bearings and with the help of directions she had scribbled in her notebook, Trish found her way to Jo Ann Richard's home. The mailbox with the house number on it was situated in front of what appeared to be a large tract of land just at the outskirts of the small town of Grants. As she drove slowly down the long, dusty, gravel driveway, she noted the well-tended appearance of the yard immediately in front of a relatively new trailer.

Two small boys, surrounded by toys in the yard and shaded by the only few trees on the property, stopped playing long enough to squint curiously in her direction. As she got out of her car, her first impression of the boys, with their sandy colored, straight hair and blue eyes, was that they looked enough alike to be twins, though they were clearly two or three years apart in age. She smiled at them as she shut the car door. "Hi, there. How are you two doing this morning?"

"Fine," the older one replied, then tucked his head. They giggled and quickly turned their attention back to their play, with only a few sideways glimpses at her.

Trish paused a moment, scanning the wide, bleak landscape surrounding the home site. Not much had changed about the area since she'd been there as a child. The wind still whipped dust and sand around in little eddies and still chased tumbleweeds around the desert landscape like feral children. As she approached the door to the trailer, she looked down and noticed that a dusty halo had already settled on her bare ankles.

Before she reached the door a young woman opened it and descended the front steps with her hand extended. "You must be Trish."

"That's right," Trish replied as they shook hands. "Glad to finally meet you, Jo Ann." The young mother offered some obligatory words to her children about playing nicely together. It was clear to Trish that the children must have resembled their father, as they shared few physical similarities with Jo Ann. She had dark eyes, a clear, olive complexion and a round face. Her long straight, black hair was pulled back at the nape of her neck. Trish wondered if she had some Native American heritage.

She led Trish into her living room, which was tidy, though dusty around the front door from the windblown sand that had managed to infiltrate the edges of the interior of the trailer. The air conditioning was refreshing. Jo Ann offered her lemonade, and Trish declined. "Thanks, but I just had a fairly large breakfast, and I'm fine for now."

Trish sat down at one end of the living room sofa, and Jo Ann sat down on a chair opposite her and volunteered that her husband was a carpenter, and that she worked part time at night as a waitress.

While Jo Ann's children played just outside the trailer, she began sharing a wealth of local research with Trish. As she did, Trish quickly discovered that, despite her youth, the woman was thoroughly informed about environmental and nuclear issues.

After Trish related her own experiences in Kakadu and Kazakhstan, Jo Ann let out an audible breath. "I can't believe this. And I thought I knew a lot about the atomic age."

Trish chuckled. "That's the same reaction I've had. Of course, I haven't had years to get up to speed, like you."

She told Jo Ann how she continued to be puzzled over the lack of documented evidence of mutations in the U.S. like she'd seen in Kazakhstan.

"But there *have* been mutations, Trish."

"Documented?"

"Well, not any scientific studies...that I know of. But maybe no one was even doing any thorough documentation of those kinds of things. Why would they? You know the attitude: 'If we don't look for it, we won't find it.'" She reminded Trish that for decades the government and nuclear industry both denied there even was a problem, and that the entire time they were deliberately and secretly venting huge emissions into the atmosphere. "Why would they document the effects of things they were denying were happening in the first place?

"I work with people all over the West. South of Los Alamos, the people in the pueblos suffered tremendously. Women near the Savannah River Site testified at DOE hearings about their dead babies, and downwind from Hanford Reservation they had all kinds of mutations with their farm animals."

"What kinds?"

"The same as you're talking about: calves with two heads, or eight legs...all kinds of grotesque stuff. I've seen pictures of some of them. And it happened with some of the kids there, too. Not as dramatic as what you saw, but I doubt they were collecting specimens like the Russians. You sure as hell won't find any medical museum or anything." She arched her eyebrows and added, "Or, at least, I don't think you will." She suggested the possibility that the Russian government had simply been more careless about exposing more concentrated populations than the Americans had been.

Trish shifted her body to one side. "Jo Ann, have you ever studied about the fertility problems associated with nuclear exposures?" It was time to get straight to one of her main purposes for being there.

"Oh, sure. I've got all kinds of material on health consequences." The comment elicited a wave of anxiety that Trish felt physically in the area of her solar plexus. Jo Ann told her that while it wasn't always easy to find those kinds of materials, she had a professor friend who worked at a college

425

in Albuquerque who helped by generously supplying her with books and studies whenever she needed them. He did it because he couldn't speak out like Jo Ann could as a lay person.

"Why not?"

"Because he's not tenured yet."

"Oh."

"He believes in what I'm doing though, so he's helped educate me behind the scenes, so I'll be better informed when I do speak out publicly."

"Hmm. Must be quite a help in your work." She gave a slight smile. "I had a professor friend who helped me, too."

"Did you?"

"Yeah, but he died last month."

"Oh, I'm sorry to hear that."

Trish muttered a thank you, cleared her throat and asked, "So, tell me: what does your professor friend have to say about fertility problems?" She didn't mention her own infertility, lest the younger woman soften her information.

"Well," she began, "with men, it can lower sperm counts, of course. And that's exactly what's been happening to men worldwide...ever since World War II, as a matter of fact." Then she added, "Some coincidence, huh?"

Trish replied simply, "Right."

Jo Ann added that it wasn't only affecting humans. Low sperm counts were also being documented in some animals, such as male alligators in Florida. She related that some of them were being born with smaller sex organs or none at all. "Of course, the 'experts' will tell you that no one knows the cause for it, and that there's no cause for alarm, but I think the fact it's happening at all ought to be enough cause for alarm."

Trish glanced at Jo Ann at one point and asked in a level voice, "What about women?"

"Oh...well, you know that when a woman is born, she has all the eggs she'll release in her lifetime." Trish nodded, though she really hadn't given any thought to that fact before.

Jo Ann said that because of that, if a woman experienced radiation exposure—even as early as childhood—any or all of her eggs might be affected. As a result anything was possible, depending on the level of exposure, her own health or the timing of the exposure. She opened her hands outward and explained that if a woman was exposed during a pregnancy, the stage of the pregnancy or any number of factors might come into play. "She might even become sterile...or experience miscarriages. She might have a deformed or retarded child, either mildly or profoundly. If there's been a particularly heavy release, like some they emitted from Hanford, you might see clusters of these instances as evidence."

Trish felt a knot forming in her stomach, and she shifted again in her seat as Jo Ann continued. "See, it's hard to predetermine an exact cause and effect to any particular kind of exposure. It's too complex an issue, and there are so many factors involved—some we may not even understand. It's likely you wouldn't see any visible signs of exposure in the general population."

As unnerving as some of Jo Ann's information was, Trish couldn't help being impressed with the sophistication and the detail of it. Jo Ann Richard's professor friend had done a thorough job of educating her behind the scenes. And Jo Ann had been fertile soil for that education. "Where did you go to college, Jo Ann?" Trish asked.

Jo Ann lowered her eyes and smiled sideways. "I'm afraid I never went. I got married right out of high school. And my family couldn't have afforded it, anyway."

"Well, you could have fooled me. But, I didn't mean to interrupt. Keep going."

"See, it's not just fertility. It's cancer, too." She propped her arm on the side of the chair and explained that when the bombs were dropped on Hiroshima and Nagasaki, scientists accumulated a wealth of information about what happened when people were exposed to high levels of radiation. They weren't as well informed, however, about what would happen with low-level exposures. She said that recently it was suspected that long term, low level exposure might be even worse. "The National Academy of Sciences has put out the results of a major study that said that kind of exposure was much more likely to cause cancer than they'd thought before."

"Why do they think that?"

She explained that with high level doses, cells might be killed outright, as they were with cancer treatments. In that case, the cells were simply replaced with new ones. Jo Ann held her hand out in front of her, as she added that with lower level exposures, the cells might simply be damaged. In that case, the damaged cells could replicate themselves and multiply. "You could *get* cancer." She added that in addition there was no healing period with long term, low-level exposure.

Jo Ann leaned back and pointed, emphasizing her words, as she told Trish that if the cell damage was done to a reproductive cell, mutations might be produced. Genetic damage could also be passed down to future generations without any visible evidence of it. She propped her arm on the arm of the chair and added, "In a way, infertility might be a blessing."

The sound of a child's sudden squeal from outside caused Trish to jerk her head around before she had time to react to the comment. It was followed by loud sobbing, which brought Jo Ann immediately to her feet. "Well, I can see I'm going to have to referee the kids for a minute. It sounds like they're in Round 2 of the fight they started this morning."

• • •

Trish welcomed the chance to be alone. She felt as though she'd just been punched in the stomach. She had realized for some time that the children she had planned would never come. And she had suspected and, now, at last, she accepted the why of it. She didn't need any scientific verification. She knew it in her soul. And that was the only place she needed to know it.

After burying her face in her hands momentarily, she stood up and placed her hands at the small of her back and stretched her head and shoulders back slowly. She walked to the front door and watched as Jo Ann deftly mended the hurt feelings of her children and encouraged them to return to their play. The young mother joked with them until they both laughed, and the impasse was broken. It was something Trish realized she would never do with children of her own.

Maybe, unlike most people living in present day Grants, she received a larger initial dose back in the fifties. Why it had affected her and not her sisters, she didn't know. Maybe it was because she'd played longer on the school yard gravel. Or maybe it was because she'd kept the uranium rock in her room when they got home. She'd kept it right by her bed for months. She couldn't even recall what had happened to it. Who could possibly know at this late a date in time? Like Jo Ann had said, there were just so many variables involved with radiation exposures.

But she didn't feel blessed with her infertility, as Jo Ann had suggested, even though she'd thought the same thing in Kazakhstan. Instead, she felt an overwhelming sadness sweep over her: grief for children she would never have…grief for the future…and grief for Max.

Turning away from the door, she lowered her head in her hand. Why had she come to this place? It wasn't doing anything helpful for her. It wasn't solving anything. It wasn't helping her to find out the big why of it: why humanity was doing what it was during the atomic age. She'd had enough grief over her search. She wanted joy…joy and laughter and living. She wasn't going to step back into another abyss. She wouldn't allow herself to be swallowed up by useless, senseless regret or to let go of her last coin—whatever the hell that was.

When Jo Ann came back inside, Trish said, "If it's all right, I think I'll take you up on that drink now."

"Oh, yeah. I could use a break now, too."

The two of them went to the connecting kitchen and Trish sat at the kitchen counter, while Jo Ann got out the glasses.

"I'll just have water, if you don't mind," Trish said.

"Ice with it?"

"Please."

It was time for Trish to change the focus and get directly to the other purpose of her trip. "Do you know anything about Indian myths related to these sites where the uranium was mined?" she began abruptly.

"Indian myths? Why do you ask that?" Jo Ann asked, turning toward her with an expression of curiosity on her face and a slight, sideways smile.

"Well, this may sound crazy…" Trish began, leaning onto her forearms on the kitchen counter. She began sharing her theory about native, indigenous elders and medicine men worldwide and their oral warnings about radioactive hot spots. She explained that, because she couldn't understand why they also referred to the sites as sacred, she felt there must be something else about them that modern man simply wasn't seeing.

"Really?" Jo Ann asked, smiling a bit more noticeably. "It's weird you'd say that." She shut the cabinet door and looked directly at Trish. "And it's not so crazy at all."

Without changing her expression, Trish tilted her head. "What are you getting at?"

"Well, you know the Four Corners area where Arizona, New Mexico, Colorado and Utah all come together?"

"Yeah."

"It's supposed to be sacred to the Indians—some kind of power point or something—and it also happens to be rich in uranium all around there." Trish listened intently as Jo Ann told her about the Indian elders warning the miners not to dig into the uranium rich mountains at the beginning of the nuclear age in the forties. *Just like the shamans in Siberia and the elders in Australia*, Trish thought to herself. Jo Ann told her that when the Indians were offered jobs mining there, some of them took the jobs for the money. "They'd lived in poverty so long that the temptation was too great for some of them. They didn't understand the dangers, but the elders did. The whole thing was so tragic. They actually had Indians building their houses with uranium rocks."

"Jesus." Trish winced. "What happened to them?"

"Cancer—eventually. Some of the miners got thyroid cancer or leukemia from their exposure. There was even a tailing dam that collapsed." Jo Ann set Trish's glass of water down in front of her as she stood across the counter and took a sip from her lemonade. "You know what's so funny though?"

"No, what?" Trish asked. "I didn't know anything was."

"All along, the government and nuclear industry people have said, 'no immediate danger,' whenever folks get hyper about radiation exposures, like they did after the Three Mile Island accident. It's like a mantra or something now. And really, I guess they were telling the truth when you think about it."

She said that it was rare that anyone dropped dead instantly from exposure, as the thousands in Bhopal had in the 80s from the pesticide release. She explained that 250 to 600 rems were a lethal radioactive dose and that an immediate, "fry your brain" death from radiation would take around a thousand rems. In a case like that a direct and instant cause and effect would be undeniable. Nevertheless, a person could be exposed to ten to fifteen rems and experience genetic effects that would show no evidence at all. "And you might get cancer that wouldn't show up for decades."

"Or contaminate a place and make it dangerous for tens or hundreds of thousands of years," Trish finished.

"That's just it," Jo Ann agreed as she placed the palms of both hands on the counter. "That's why it's so damn hard to convince the public that these dangers are not only real, but profound. Nothing does happen immediately…at least not that you can see. But the Indians knew about it, and they still know a lot of things that we ought to be paying attention to."

"Like what?"

"Oh, I don't know."

Trish looked more closely at Jo Ann. She was holding something back. "Tell me, Jo Ann. Look, I'm not surprised by anything any more. And I really am interested in these native myths."

Jo Ann took a deep breath and released it quickly. "You know, some people think I've gone totally over the edge with some of my ideas. That's why I don't share them with many people. Even my husband gets upset with me at times."

"Look, some of the ideas I've come up with since Kazakhstan would put a lot of folks into a coma. I tell you, I've had some weird stuff happen to me since I started this research. I don't even know how to share it with some people."

Jo Ann raised her eyebrows. "Yeah?"

Trish nodded. "Yeah."

"All right, then. Just a minute." Jo Ann left the room.

When she came back, she had several books. "These tell how some medicine men from different tribes are making predictions about earth changes that are coming."

"Earth changes?"

"Yeah, major earth changes." She explained that, just as Trish had said, native elders worldwide had always understood the earth better than modern man. In more recent times they'd been predicting more droughts than ever before in some areas, while others would flood as never before. There would be wildly variant temperature changes in the seasons.

"Hell, we're seeing that right now," Trish commented.

"Exactly. But these books were written years ago—*before* the changes got so extreme. And they say it's going to get worse still, and that there will be increased earthquakes and volcanic activity."

Trish's eyes widened at the comment. "You're kidding."

"No. Why?"

"Well, I've been talking to sources who think the atomic explosions are actually triggering some of the earthquakes and volcanoes worldwide."

"Really?"

Trish nodded and Jo Ann said, "Well that fits right in with the prophecies then, because they say the earth has to go through a cleansing stage because of the atomic testing and pollution. And I've read other material that says the earth's tectonic plates are shattered like fractured glass around the tests sites, and it wouldn't take much—maybe even a natural quake—to crack whole areas."

Jo Ann explained that at times some of the older prophecies were very specific. She mentioned one from the Northwest that predicted a time in the future when Little Sister would speak, and Grandfather would answer. "Well, Little Sister is one of the Indian names for Mt. St. Helen's."

"Are you sure about that?"

"Yeah. It's all right here." Jo Ann held up the books.

"Jo Ann, I've been wondering if some of the atomic testing out West could have triggered the eruption of Mt. St. Helens."

"Yeah?" Jo Ann tapped on one of the books, while she told Trish that some of the Indians speculated the 'Grandfather answering' in the prophecy meant there would be another much larger eruption, since the rest of the prediction talked about the land being swept clean, all the way to the sea. "They say the Grandfather in the legend is actually Mt. Rainier."

By now Trish was focused completely on Jo Ann. "Do you realize that vulcanologists believe that Mount Rainier is the most dangerous mountain in the U.S., and that it could erupt at any time?"

"I didn't know that," she responded.

"And did you know that Mt. St. Helen's started rumbling again after they started the French nuclear tests in the South Pacific last year?"

"No."

"In fact, there were a lot of earthquakes around the world following each of those nuclear blasts."

"Somehow, none of this surprises me. It sure passes the old common sense test, when you think about it. Have you ever heard about the chaos theory?"

"Yeah." Trish half laughed and leaned back in her seat and crossed her arms. "One of my sources back in Georgia likes to throw that one at me every now and then. But it's been hard for me to grasp at times."

"I'm not sure I thoroughly understand it myself." She told Trish that if small, innocuous events on one side of the globe could affect weather patterns on the other side, it wasn't much of a stretch to think that something with the force of an atomic bomb could impact geologic conditions worldwide. Jo Ann propped her chin on her fist. "Come to think of it, Trish, you remember all that flooding in the Northwest earlier this year?"

"Yeah."

"They said it was caused by melting snows from warmer temperatures and warmer ocean currents."

"Yeah, I remember." Trish took another sip of her water, then set it down.

"Well, I wonder what a series of thermonuclear devices triggered under the ocean in the South Pacific would do to water temperatures," Jo Ann said.

Trish let out a short breath. "I don't know…but with all due respect to El Nino, those kinds of disruptions of temperatures anywhere on the planet are bound to have an effect." She detailed some of the earthquakes and volcanoes that followed each of the French blasts, adding, "It looked like a clear pattern to me."

"Hey, it makes sense to me, too, but you're talking to an easy audience here."

Trish smiled. "Tell me more about these legends. This thing has me by the throat."

"Well," Jo Ann began, as she picked up one of the books and fingered its edges, "they all have some kind of story saying there have actually been a number of different worlds." She told Trish that in the first world, man lived in harmony with the earth. When he got out of harmony, or balance, however, the Creator caused a great cleansing that destroyed a lot of people. Each time man got out of harmony, there was another great cleansing. She said that the predictions said the world was on the verge of another one. "They say we're about to enter the next world—at least those who are left after the cleansing."

"What kinds of cleansings preceded the changes?"

"Oh, they talk about volcanoes, polar shifts, floods. The last one was supposed to have been a worldwide flood."

"Well, I've read a lot of myths in the last few months, and there are loads of stories about some huge flood. People survived in a box or a log…"

"Or an ark," Jo Ann finished.

"Right."

Jo Ann stood up beside her seat. "I need to take the boys some more juice. Why don't you take your water back over to the sofa where it's more comfortable?"

Trish slid from the kitchen stool, and headed toward the sofa, while Jo Ann took a couple of packets of juice and straws from her cupboard and went outside for a few minutes.

• • •

When Jo Ann returned to her seat, she continued where she'd left off. "The Indians have prophecies that tell them when the next cleansing will happen. They talk about spider webs that people would talk through. You know what that sounds like."

"Telephone lines?" Trish asked.

"Could be. But lately I've been thinking more along the lines of web sites."

"Hmm."

"And, too, they say that the time would be marked by the eagle walking on the moon."

"An eagle on the moon?"

"Yeah. Some of the Hopi think that was signaled by the first moon landing, when Neil Armstrong said, 'The eagle has landed.'"

"Oh, my gosh."

"Yeah, and who would have even paid any attention to a myth about an eagle walking on the moon before the moon landing? It would have seemed like a fairy tale." Jo Ann half laughed. "I guess you can see why I don't talk about this to many people. They think I've gone totally bonkers."

"Well, you have some pretty respectable company, if you have, because no less than C. G. Jung predicted a worldwide catastrophe."

"He did?"

"Yeah. But, continue about the legends."

Jo Ann shifted around sideways in her seat and told Trish about one prophecy of a great war on the earth where two great powers would make the earth shake twice. She told Trish that the Hopi predicted that during this time a gourd of ashes would be poured on the earth that would boil the waters and make the fish go belly up. "They think this is a reference to the atomic bomb."

"Sure sounds like it. And it sounds a lot like Revelations, too, come to think of it." There were those similarities again that Max always told her to watch for.

Jo Ann told Trish that some of the Hopi tried to go to the United Nations to tell the other nations about the warnings, but that they weren't allowed to speak. She said that being denied the right to speak to world leaders was also part of the signal that the end would be near.

She explained that the legends said the end of the present world would come in two ways. One was a series of great natural disasters and the other would come in one day by a people whose color was red. "There's one particular author who thinks that might have been Chernobyl."

Trish looked up from her notepad. It was too much coincidence to ignore any longer. "Jo Ann, have you ever read Revelations?"

"Oh, sure…lots of times."

Trish reminded her about John's vision of the angel sounding and a great star falling from heaven and the waters becoming bitter. She told her about the near death predictions she'd read about on the way back from Hawaii and the similarities between wormwood and Chernobyl.

Jo Ann sat up erect in her seat, wide-eyed in disbelief. "You're kidding!"

"No, I'm not."

Jo Ann inhaled a deep breath. "My God." She let out a breath slowly. "You just reminded me of something, Trish," Jo Ann began. "I read an account once of the explosion at Chernobyl." She told Trish that when the people in the area heard a loud noise, they went out to see what it was. They thought it was some type of stellar event, because it looked like stars falling out of the sky and talked about how beautiful it was. They rode in elevators up to the top of the highest buildings so they could get a better view, and even called it a "beautiful shining."

"I've never read an account like that."

"And, come to think of it," she continued, slowly, "they also said that the water where the main rivers came together in the area was bitter tasting after the explosion."

Now Trish's eyes were widening. She held that expression motionless as she asked, "Would you happen to have a copy of that account?"

"As a matter of fact, I think I've got several. I keep copies of everything. And I think I can put my hands right on it." Jo Ann got up from her seat, went to the front door and glanced quickly at her children, then left the room. She came back holding a sheet of paper and handed it to Trish. "You can keep this."

"Thanks." Trish quickly scanned it as Jo Ann got settled again in her seat.

"It may seem strange," Jo Ann said, crossing her legs, "but I tend to get more inspiration from these Indian prophets than I do from any of the environmental groups I work with."

"Do you work with any *local* Indians?"

Jo Ann told Trish about some Western Shoshones she worked with who were fighting a proposed nuclear storage facility at one of their sacred areas. She told her that the U.S. government would be violating the Treaty of Peace and Friendship from the 1800's to site it there.

Trish scratched her forehead. "What the hell does sacred really mean, anyway?"

"I don't know," Jo Ann replied, shaking her head. "But your experience with the Aborigine elder is beginning to sound awfully familiar." She told Trish about an Indian she'd worked with once telling her that the mining had taken all of their precious sacredness and turned it into something deadly. She'd almost forgotten about it until Trish brought it up.

"What on earth could be sacred about uranium?"

Jo Ann shrugged her shoulders. "Beats me. But I don't think you're going to find your answers in any science books."

Trish leaned forward with her hand resting on her right thigh. "Jo Ann, remember when I talked earlier about the old man in Kakadu telling me that my job was to remember?"

"Yeah."

"Well, when he told me that, he tapped me on the forehead, and for some reason, that's stayed with me—like it's emblazoned on my forehead—like a mark, or something. I actually had a sense of time standing still...or at least that I lost awareness of it. Do you have any idea what he might have meant from your work with the Indians?"

"Well, maybe," she began slowly. "But it would be Eastern Indians, not Western."

"Yeah?"

"Yeah. It sounds like he was tapping your sixth chakra."

"Chakra? What's that?"

"Well, there's this belief in Eastern cultures about chakra centers." Jo Ann told her that chakras were whirling energy or emotional centers. There were supposed to be seven levels in the body.

"What are the seven levels?"

Jo Ann explained that the lower one was located at the base of the spine where people sat. It was called the root chakra. The second one was located at the sexual organs, and the third, at the solar plexus.

"Uh huh," Trish intoned.

"And the fourth is at the heart level. The fifth is at the throat. And the sixth is here at the level of the forehead—where the old man tapped you," she said, tapping her own forehead.

"What's the seventh?" Trish asked.

"That's the crown chakra." Jo Ann placed the palm of her hand slightly above her head, and explained that when a person reached that level, they were supposed to have reached the highest level of development. They were actually supposed to radiate at that level, and there was a belief that the reason Jesus and the other masters were pictured with glowing halos around their heads was because they had attained that level.

"What's supposed to be the significance of the chakra at the forehead where the old man tapped me?" Trish asked.

"That's supposed to be where you get your imagination," Jo Ann responded, gesturing with her hands. "It causes you to see and make a connection to the inner, as well as outer world...the inner being the spiritual. Some people call it the third eye chakra, because you have this inner vision."

"What's the significance of these energy centers? I mean, what are we supposed to know about them or learn from them?"

"Well," she began, leaning back in her seat and crossing her legs, "the theory goes that if all the chakras are perfectly aligned, opened and activated, you reach a level of peace, harmony and balance...wholeness."

"Aligned? Are we out of alignment?"

Jo Ann half laughed. "It sure seems like it sometimes, doesn't it? But, it's not like a car or anything." She uncrossed her legs and leaned forward again. "Look, you know how sometimes people will call a particular person an asshole?"

"Yeah...I've come across my share of them...especially in journalism."

Jo Ann smiled. "Well, if a *lot* of people call a person an asshole, it's probably because he's storing a lot of his energy at his lower level chakra."

"Kind of like when we call someone anal?"

"Yeah, that's it. It's like always operating from a survival mode."

"And you're saying the rest of us pick up on it subconsciously, and it comes out in our speech?"

"Something like that." She explained that languages were quite full of subtle and even direct references to an unconscious knowledge, but that people simply weren't hearing them or paying attention to them.

"The old Aborigine said that, too."

"And you know how some people are referred to as bleeding hearts?" Jo Ann continued.

"Yeah."

"Same thing. They're probably storing a lot of their energy at their heart chakra, or maybe losing it. I'm not all that well versed in this area, but I've read a couple of books about it." Jo Ann continued, "And you know how some people are real emotional and they always talk about one thing or another hitting them in the stomach?"

"Yeah, it happened to me just a while ago because of something you said."

"Well, I think it happens to most people on occasion. But when it happens to people a lot of time, it's probably because they're storing more energy at the solar plexus chakra...or losing it. And it's not like any one level is good or bad. It's just that when we keep them all open and activated and balanced, we can connect all the way from the base chakra to the crown chakra."

"Well, what's the purpose of reaching the crown chakra?"

"That's when we reach a state of living in harmony. It's where we're supposed to understand our divine purpose in life…self-realization. It's where we can actually see the future and get beyond the limits of time, space and substance."

"Like walking on water?"

"Yeah, you've got it. It's the divine, where miracles can happen, like healing and overcoming death…like Christ. Like I said, I think that's why the masters in the different religions had halos." Jo Ann rubbed her chin. "You know, Jesus never told us to worship him. He said that what he did, we could do. He told us, 'Ye are gods.' But if you suggest something like that today, it's almost considered sacrilegious. When everything else is taken so literally, why isn't that?"

"I don't know," Trish shrugged. "I've always had a little problem with organized religion…or at least with the way it's been practiced over the ages." She told Jo Ann that if it was true what the Bible said about the kingdom of heaven being within, it made sense to her that religion was supposed to be deeply personal, uncontrolled by any external, earthly hierarchies.

When Trish related her disappointments with modern religion because of their lack of reverence for the earth, Jo Ann told her about some religions that were in touch with an earthly reverence. She talked about a statement issued by the World Council of Churches about the use of nuclear energy and weapons. Then she told her about a group called Environmental Evangelicals who were working to reverse the anti-environmental political trends.

"I didn't know that," Trish commented.

"They've made up packets," Jo Ann added, "and sent them to other churches around the country and to politicians—Noah packets, I think they call them." She said that the packets asked that if the creatures of the earth were important enough to God to assign Noah the task of saving them—even when he was destroying most of humanity—then who were people to destroy and endanger his creatures for their own personal agendas.

"Sounds like a pretty powerful endorsement of the Endangered Species Act," Trish said. "But, Jo Ann," she continued, as she edged slightly forward on the sofa and crossed her ankles, "do you have any idea what the old Aborigine meant when he told me I'm supposed to remember? I can't seem to figure that one out."

"I don't know, but you were talking about near death experiences a while ago, and I've read about some of those accounts myself. They have a lot of similarities. Occasionally, you'll come across someone who's been through it saying something like, 'You know, all this knowledge I got on the other side…it wasn't like it was given to me or anything, but more like I was remembering it.'"

Trish became animated. "Now that you mention it, that guy I read about…the one who saw Chernobyl in the future…he said the same thing.

God!" she intoned as she looked toward the ceiling, "I read it right after I left Australia, and that connection never occurred to me at the time." Trish looked back at Jo Ann. "It amazes me how I keep missing things staring me right in the face."

Jo Ann asked, "Don't you think if we remember things over there, we could have access to that knowledge on this plane, too?"

"I don't know," she responded in an even tone. "But, Max—my professor friend—used to suggest that as humans, we hold the sum total of all human experience throughout human existence. I studied something like that back in college: the concept of the collective unconscious. But it's sort of hard for me to grasp."

"I don't know much about the collective unconscious, but I do believe that was what the different masters in the different religions—like Christ, Mohammed and Buddha—were trying to tell us." Trish tilted her head, and Jo Ann added. "I think they were trying to remind people of who they really are…like they were telling us that they were a prototype of what we could become and what our heritage is."

"If that's true, Jo Ann, why haven't we just accepted and started using all this heritage you say is ours for the taking?"

"Oh, Trish." Jo Ann lifted her hands and slapped them back on her thighs, "Just look at the mess we've made of things with the little power that we've *been* using. If we'd used more, with our attitudes and lack of spirituality—my, gosh—there's no telling what we would have done to the planet and each other…or even to other planets."

"Then you don't think we're spiritually *ready* to evolve to another level?"

"Not quite yet. But, for some reason, I've started believing we're close—really close."

Trish glanced sideways at Jo Ann. She thought about how the younger woman balanced a life of raising children and waiting on tables at night, and, in between, had probably studied the equivalent of several college courses on the environment, and even dabbled in Eastern mysticism.

Jo Ann looked up at her. "I guess I've surprised you with some of my outlandish ideas."

"Not at all. We can't learn anything with a closed mind, can we?"

Jo Ann shrugged. "So they say." She propped herself sideways on her arm. "It's just that I'm convinced there's so much more to life than we detect with our five senses…so much more out there for us to learn and discover about life and about ourselves…and I just can't wait to get out there and find out what it's all really about. You know?"

Trish grinned. "It's strange that you'd say that, because my professor friend said something very similar when he was literally on his death bed."

"He did?"

"Yeah, he said, 'There's so much more…so much more.' Thing is, I think he'd had one of those near death experiences just the previous day."

"Really?"

Trish looked straight ahead. "I think so." She looked down. "Anyway, he looked so peaceful when he talked about it, that I've found it a lot easier to deal with his death." She turned toward Jo Ann. "Tell me something, if you don't mind. Just how did you get interested in these kinds of issues?"

"Oh, well," she replied, shrugging, "I guess the real turning point came one night after I'd put my older son to bed. It was about three in the morning, and I heard one of his little musical toys playing—just a bit of a song, really. So I got up and went to his room, thinking he'd gotten up and was playing with his toys."

She said that when she got to his room and turned on the light, he was sound asleep. Thinking he was pretending to be asleep, since she'd heard the music so clearly, she looked for the toy, under the covers. When she finally found it, though, it was on the top shelf of his closet, where he couldn't possibly have reached it.

"Yeah?" Trish asked.

"Yeah. I mean—it really had me stumped. I knew I'd heard the thing, but how did it start playing by itself?" she asked rhetorically. "Then I started back to my bedroom wondering what the hell all that was about, and all of a sudden, it hit me."

"What?"

"The music I'd heard. It was a line from the child's song that went, 'merrily, merrily, merrily, merrily, life is but a dream.'

"I tell you it blew my mind." She told Trish that the next few days, she began seeing the same idea pop up in several different places and in different things she read, from authors past and present: the idea that essentially life was the dream and reality was something else, and it was time for people to wake up. "And I thought, 'Man, something else is going on here."

Yeah, Trish thought, placing her curved index finger over her lips to cover a smile. *It's called synchronicity. Had a few doses of that myself.*

Jo Ann said that when she told her husband and some friends about it, they tried to explain it logically, but that she simply knew better. "Those logical explanations just don't work for me anymore." She nodded her head forcefully once. "I knew in my soul there was something else to it, and I was determined to find out what." Jo Ann sat back and relaxed, adding, "So there you have it: the reason I'm crazy."

Trish smiled. "Not so crazy. Not at all. In fact, that's a beautiful story." *Familiar, too.* Synchronicity was like that. It couldn't be explained. It had to be experienced.

Jo Ann said, "I've got to check the boys again, and get them some more juice."

Chapter Forty-One

While Jo Ann was gone, Trish reflected on the general optimism she maintained in spite of her work in the nuclear field. When she returned, Trish asked her about it.

"Well, Trish, some people say that because we live in a cause and effect world, we're just going to have to experience the consequences of the things we've already set in motion." Jo Ann said, however, that she had a strong belief, maybe even a faith, that man had the power to change even the dramatic consequences of the atomic age, if he could simply have a change of heart and mind, and will it to be.

"You think it's that simple?" Trish asked non-plussed.

"Simple?" Jo Ann asked, wide-eyed. "You've got to be kidding. *That's* not simple. Most people would literally rather *die* than change their minds. Oh, I think they can do it. I guess I just don't have that much confidence in the speed it's going to take for them to get there." She shrugged her shoulders slightly. "Maybe it'll take a few more crises like Chernobyl or Bhopal to wake us up. Who knows?"

Jo Ann turned and faced Trish more directly and tilted her head slightly. "Look, I'm enjoying talking to you and exchanging information. But honestly, I don't feel like I'm helping you with what you're really looking for. I mean, we're both just preaching to the choir here. What are you really trying to figure out?"

"Oh, I don't know," she replied, shaking her head. "You have given me a lot of information that I wasn't aware of, and maybe I've given you some, too, but...well, it's still just the 'what' of it. It piques my interest, but I want to know *why* it all happened. If we could clean up every radiated spot on the planet, what would be the point if we don't know why we did it in the first place? We'd just do it all over again."

Trish gestured toward Jo Ann with her open hands and continued. "Look, we're intelligent creatures. I know we don't always act like it, but deep down, we are, or we wouldn't have come as far as we have technologically. We wouldn't have made it to the moon or orbiting Mars. So, why are we doing this?" She told her that the atomic age was looking more and more like slow suicide of the species. She didn't believe the same people who were smart enough to invent the atomic bomb were dumb enough not to realize at some point they were endangering the entire planet for eons into the future. She leaned back. "So, yeah, why are we doing it? That's what I'm after now."

"Mm," Jo Ann intoned. "I've asked myself that a lot of times before, too, and all I've come up with is that I just don't know."

Trish sifted forward again, "Well, that's not good enough for me. I told my friend Max, that I just couldn't deal with the things I was finding out if I couldn't figure out why we did it. I know there's some kind of connection to the myths, and some kind of answers there, but I can't get a handle on it. And he said I could look till I was blue in the face, and go all the way back to the oldest texts on earth, and I'd never figure it out there, because it's pre-history—that I'd have to find it out somehow without the books.

"What could be the connection to those creatures and mythology?" she continued. "I looked at those things in the jars, and I just couldn't get my mind around it. I just thought, 'Shit, we've done this before.' But then I thought, 'It couldn't be. We haven't been on the planet that long.'"

Jo Ann stood up and picked up their glasses. "Let me get us something else to drink." She walked to the counter, set the glasses down, and looked back at Trish. "Have you ever heard of Edgar Cayce?"

"Isn't that the guy who channeled back in the thirties and forties?"

"Yeah, he did it over a long period of time during his adult life." She told Trish that Cayce went into a deep trance state during the channeling and had no recall of it afterwards. His secretary dictated the material, volumes and volumes of which were now housed in an institute in Virginia Beach, devoted to the study of the information.

"Wasn't it about healing people?"

"A lot of it was, but there were other readings that pertained to ancient civilizations, like Atlantis."

Trish perked up. "Really?"

Jo Ann refilled their glasses. "Yeah. I've read several books about him, and I remember those readings in particular."

"You know, I've been curious about that legend lately. What did his readings say about it?"

Jo Ann brought the glasses back, set them on the coffee table, then got seated again in her chair. There she explained that in Cayce's channeling, he didn't refer to simply one civilization, but rather several that had flourished and reached high levels of technological advances, including ships that sailed on land and in the water. She said that for some unknown reason the technology went awry, and the civilizations collapsed. She took a drink from her glass. "He channeled information that the destruction of Atlantis was caused by some kind of manmade explosions that got out of hand and triggered earthquakes and volcanic eruptions."

"Jesus. You're kidding."

"No. They said that the technology was supposed to have a beneficial purpose—like in transportation and communications or something—but that the ruling class turned it into something destructive. That's when catastrophe hit."

"Good God, *that* sounds familiar." Trish picked up her glass and sipped some water.

"Well, there's more," Jo Ann added. "He even talked about radioactive forces that were used in these ancient civilizations."

Trish stared at her. "Holy Shit."

Jo Ann told Trish that Cayce even talked about what sounded very much like atomic power plants, and that he channeled all of this in the thirties, before the invention of atomic power. "He channeled that some of the same forces in Atlantis were being rediscovered."

Trish was almost afraid to breathe. With a deadpan expression, she said, "I'd be interested in reading some of that material."

"I'll give you the names of some of the books. I don't have them anymore. I only started thinking about them when you told me about the earthquakes and volcanic activity with the French nuclear tests...*and* because of what you saw in that clinic."

"What about the clinic? Don't tell me there are similarities there, too."

Jo Ann took another drink from her glass and set it down, as Trish sat literally on the edge of her seat. "Well, actually there are. He channeled that after one of the destructions of one civilization—I don't remember which one—they had hospitals where people could go and have what he called appendages of animal characteristics removed."

Trish dropped her right hand and almost whispered, "Good God."

"He said that those people had body parts like tails and fins," Jo Ann continued. She said that the readings definitely talked about humanoid creatures with animal looking parts, and that they appeared after at least one of what Cayce called "the destructions."

Trish put her hand to her head. "Man. I wish I'd heard about this sooner. I got so frustrated because the most ancient texts don't address this. There's just the mythology, and most of it just confused the hell out of me."

"Well, some people believe that mythologies are just jumbled, confused recollections of prehistory that have been passed down through oral story tellers...like your Aboriginal friend." Jo Ann held her hands out, palms up and asked, "What if that's all mythology is?"

"But, Jo Ann, why would radiation cause some hybrids with *animal* parts? I don't get that."

Jo Ann shrugged her shoulders. "I don't know." She exhaled and added, "But you talked earlier about the collective unconscious. Cayce talked about universal memory, like it's something that's locked in us genetically. Couldn't they be the same thing?"

"Yeah, Max suggested cellular memory is what accounts for instinctive behavior."

Jo Ann leaned back. "Well, if there *is* universal memory in our genes, what if the reintroduction of radiation to the planet and our bodies just reactivates the ancient cellular memory in our DNA? What if a developing fetus gets a huge dose of that exposure and it triggers an ancient gene that was abandoned in our evolution eons ago? I've heard of throwbacks of those kinds before. You must have, too: kids in Mexico with Werewolf syndrome, with hair all over their bodies. And I've heard of kids in the Appalachians being born with an extension of their tailbones."

"A little tail?"

"Yeah."

"God, Jo Ann. Oak Ridge is in the Appalachians."

Jo Ann didn't seem surprised and reminded Trish that likely the ones closest to facilities like Oak Ridge—the ones downwind or downstream—would be the most affected, like the ones nearest the testing sites. "And it's common sense that developing fetuses are going to be more visibly affected than mature adults."

Trish took another drink, then closed her eyes and took two deep breaths. It felt similar to trying to catch her breath that day in the clinic. *Breathe, Trish, breathe.* She opened her eyes. "Jo Ann, this may be what I've been looking for."

"What? The Cayce information?"

"Yeah." Then she took another deep breath and sighed. "But I still have a hard time believing man has been on the planet that long. And it's still channeling. I need proof. I need to access ancient wisdom and ancient information. I thought I was getting somewhere with Old Tom in Australia, but he just turned around and left…just disappeared with his 'remembering' comment, as if I had the answers. But, I don't. That's why I'm here, trying to figure out why."

Jo Ann laced her fingers. "What if you don't need ancient texts? We have the equivalent of an ancient genetic library stored in our DNA, and as far as worldwide devastations are concerned, we know from mitochondrial studies that the human population has crashed almost to the point of extinction at least twice. There has to be a way for us to access the genetic library inside us." She leaned forward in her chair and looked at the floor for a moment and uttered a low "Hmm." She looked up and spoke, almost sheepishly to Trish. "Look, I don't know exactly how to approach this." She hesitated.

Trish prodded, "I'm ready for anything at this point, so fire away. You're talking to someone who's seen some pretty unbelievable stuff…impossible stuff."

"All right, then. Here goes." Jo Ann cleared her throat and repositioned herself. "The last few years I've been meeting with a group that's studying…and practicing shamanism."

"Shamanism?"

"Yeah, you know how you were talking earlier about the shamans in the Soviet Union?"

"Yeah."

"I almost fell off my seat when you mentioned it." She took a breath. "This group does some pretty incredible stuff. They drum and rattle to produce a mild trance state. I thought I was pretty open to those kinds of things, but this was just weird when I first heard about it."

Trish nodded. *That's why it was a death sentence to own a drum in Stalin's time.*

"They do healing work, and they go and talk to what they call spirits throughout the universe. The few times I've worked with them I've pulled up things that blow *me* away. If I hadn't experienced it myself, I wouldn't believe it."

"Like?"

"It's hard to explain. Let me think a second." She squinted her eyes and looked at the ceiling and then back again. "Like talking to dead spirits."

Trish pulled her head back slightly. "Dead spirits?"

Jo Ann explained that the people in the circle didn't seem to have boundaries like time or space when they went on what they called "journeys."

"If someone comes to them and wants closure with a dead loved one, they'll journey for them and maybe bring back an answer to a question they have. It may not make any sense to the shamans, but it can blow the client away."

"Client? Do they charge a fee?"

"No...at least not the group I've worked with. But when they bring back information from wherever it is they go, it always hits you in your solar plexus—or chakra we talked about. And it's because they know the shamans couldn't possibly have any previous knowledge about it. It sounds like the universal memory Cayce talked about."

"Yeah, it does. Has any of this happened to you?"

"Well, I haven't gone to any dead relatives, or anything, but I have seen them do it with other people, and they did healing work on me once. They told me the emotional reason behind my physical problem." She shook her head. "I tell you, they really hit the nail on the head. I can't explain it to you, but they absolutely could not have known or guessed the information they came back with. No way."

"Hmm." Trish felt a twinge of skepticism, along with a simultaneously sense of intrigue.

"The reason I'm telling you this is because there's this one woman in the group, Stephanie Carter, who connected one night with this ancient goddess called Freya."

"Freya?"

"Yeah. She's a Norse goddess...supposed to be the keeper of ancient wisdom."

"Really?" Trish perked up at the reference.

"I thought that might get your attention. Anyway, she connected on a deep level with this entity, and it stayed with her. Now she does readings at her home for people who want to ask this Freya questions."

"You mean channeling again?"

"I'm not sure how to categorize it. But, Trish, I think some of these things we've talked about...channeling, healing, miracles and shamanism are all basically physics. Quantum physics, scientific facts that we don't understand yet." She speculated that what people called mysticism was simply right brained knowing based on faith, without having to have proof, without demanding proof. "It reminds me of holograms." She squinted. "Have you ever seen one?"

"I've seen some, but I certainly don't understand how they work."

"Who does? But I saw one in a jewelry store once. Thought it was real and wondered why the jewelers were leaving this expensive diamond, sapphire watch out in the open, and, as if he was reading my mind, the jeweler walked over and ran his hand right through it. I thought, 'Holy Cow!' Then I started to run *my* hand through it. Kept thinking if I touched the edges just right I'd feel them. But, of course, I didn't. I couldn't. It wasn't there. And yet there it was."

"Holograms, huh?"

"Yeah. As if any piece of it contains the whole. As if there's no separation between you and me." She looked around. "Or that lamp. We're each aspects of a greater whole. We each contain a connection to all memory, Cayce's 'universal memory.' When you look at it like that, this weird stuff begins making perfect sense." She speculated that Western culture might have developed the logical mind just long enough and far enough that it could begin integrating it with Eastern mysticism to be more whole. She posed the possibility that the re-introduction of an ancient system like shamanism into a modern culture was the beginning of that process.

"God, Jo Ann, Max, talked about whole brain thinking the last time I was at his place."

"Yeah?"

"Yeah."

"Well, my friend, Stephanie, has developed a connection to this Freya, that's lingered beyond the circle meetings, and she's able access it whenever she needs to." Again, Jo Ann seemed sheepish. "Would you be interested in meeting with her?"

"I don't know. I mean, why not? I'm game for just about anything at this point. Sure. Let's give it a shot."

"Well, then…" Jo Ann smiled and rubbed her hands together, as though she had just concocted a potion. "How about tomorrow? Or day after?"

"Sure. Either would work for me."

"Okay." Jo Ann got up from her seat. "Let me give her a call and see if she's home and available."

As Jo Ann left the room and went back to her bedroom, Trish couldn't believe how quickly her itinerary had shifted.

When Jo Ann returned, her demeanor was bubbly. "Stephanie said her calendar is clear for both days, so you're set up for tomorrow morning."

"Jeez, that was quick." Trish raised her eyebrows and grinned. "I wonder what I'm getting into here?"

Jo Ann snickered. "I know what you mean. That's what I said the first time I went to the drumming circle."

"Will you be going with me?"

"Oh, you don't need me. I'll write down her address and phone number in Albuquerque. You'll be fine. I promise, you'll have the time of your life." Jo Ann scribbled the information and handed it to Trish. "It's easy to find her, but give her a call if you have any trouble."

Trish was about to ask Jo Ann another question, when she heard loud, unhappy squeals from the boys outside the trailer.

"Uh, oh," Jo Ann said. "I think it's time for lunch and a nap."

"Listen, I've taken enough of your time, anyway," Trish said, as she picked up her purse. "Get back to your kids, and I'll call you tomorrow."

"Yeah, it's about that time," Jo Ann agreed, rising to her feet.

As they walked to the door, Jo Ann said, "Do let me know how things work out on this."

"I will. Jo Ann, I don't know how to thank you for all your help. It means a lot to me. You've helped more than you know."

"I hope Stephanie can help you with what you're really looking for."

There was another scream, and the two of them exited the trailer. Outside Jo Ann scooped up the crying child in her arms and comforted him in a singing tone. "Shhh, shhh, now. It's Okay."

Trish patted the little boy's back, as he nestled on his mother's shoulder, rubbing his eyes.

"Take care of these little fellas."

"Don't worry about that. They manage to get all the attention they need."

"Jo Ann, it's been a real pleasure." She stuck out her hand, and Jo Ann smiled, and—instead of shaking Trish's hand—she reached over and hugged her with her left arm, while still cradling her child in the other. Trish smiled, got in her car and backed out of the driveway.

Chapter Forty-Two

The next morning, when Trish turned onto Stephanie Carter's street, she noticed how stylish the neighborhood was. She pulled into the driveway and got out and scanned the large adobe home with its terra cotta tile roof and immaculate landscaping.

Trish thought the woman who answered the door could easily have been a movie star. "You must be Trish," she said as they shook hands. Stephanie's large, dark eyes, full cheeks and flawless complexion had an exotic quality to them. Her coloring was fairer than one would expect in someone with such dark hair, making it difficult to determine her heritage. Trish judged her age to be in the mid to late thirties.

After their greeting, Stephanie led the way into a large, sunny room with an abundance of plants and windows. Stephanie said that since her husband—a pilot—was away on a trip and her children were at school, they'd have the house to themselves for the day. Before she sat down, Stephanie asked if she could get Trish something to drink.

"Not right now. But thank you."

After the women got seated across from each other on matching sofas, Stephanie said, "Trish, whenever I work with someone, the first thing I do is try to explain a little about the process—at least, what I know about it." She crossed her legs. "All of this began a couple of years ago when I started working with a shaman group."

She placed her hands in her lap and explained that shamanism had been around for untold thousands of years. Not only did it have an indefinite time frame, it was also used by virtually every culture in the world. "This was long before advent of any modern forms of communication. It was even used by Aborigines, who were completely cut off from the rest of the world for many thousands of years."

Trish didn't mention her recent visit to Australia or that she had met an elder there.

Stephanie continued, "Modern anthropologists have studied it for quite some time, as well as people interested in spiritual and alternative healing." She told Trish that years ago, when a number of anthropologists became intrigued by the practice on a personal level, they subsequently began studying with shaman teachers. They practiced with a number of primitive tribes in the jungles of South America, with Inuit people in the tundra and Native Americans in the States. "All over the world, really. But often they couldn't grasp the concept of shamanism."

Trish could tell that, not only was the information coming at a rapid pace, it was full of detail. "Stephanie," she interrupted, "will you mind if I use a tape recorder later during the session?"

"No. In fact, I usually use one for a session myself because I get pretty out of it."

Stephanie continued. "The shamans were probably as frustrated explaining it to them as the men were in trying to grasp the concepts. Sometimes the shamans would use local hallucinogenic plants, like peyote or ayahausca, to facilitate a journey and teach them.

"Eventually a number of the ones who'd experienced shamanism personally were so affected by it that they began introducing it into our culture." Stephanie picked up a pillow from the side of the sofa and placed it precisely behind the small of her back, as though she had done it a thousand times before. She told Trish that most of the modern shamanic teachers used a drum to induce the shamanic state, since many of them didn't need or want the influence of drugs. She explained that the drum was beaten at a rate that would induce an Alpha or deeper Theta state, and that the rhythm of the beat corresponded with what scientists had found to be the electromagnetic energy emanating from the earth. "They call it the Schuman Resonance."

Stephanie crossed her legs. "When you journey, you tune in to the earth. I don't pretend to know the science behind it, but the brain waves will actually shift during the journey. I think the Aborigine use their didgeridoos and bullroarers, instead of drums, to break through the ethers and call the spirits in."

Trish smiled to herself, as the image of Max spinning the bull-roarer came to mind, as well as Old Tom's story about the didgeridoo.

Stephanie continued, "This journeying is such a life changing experience for so many people that it has really taken on a life of its own. Several years ago I was going through a serious crisis…no longer happy with my life and looking for…well, *something*. I didn't really know what. But I heard from a friend about this workshop on shamanism they were having and decided, 'What the hell. I'll give it a shot.' At that point, I would have tried anything."

Trish looked up and smiled. "I understand that feeling."

Stephanie smiled back. "Desperation, I think they call it. We all identify with it at some point in our lives." She looked up at the ceiling and then back again. "At any rate, my friend and I went together and took the course, and the long and the short of it is that my life hasn't been the same since. We started a little circle of our own when we got back." She explained that the circle grew and was constant. They were all dedicated to and fascinated by it. What they discovered was never quite what they expected to find, and yet always had the ring of truth. "I think it's changed all of our lives.

"Anybody can do it. In fact, everyone does it on a daily basis; they just aren't conscious of it."

448

"How's that?" Trish asked.

"Well, when we get tired or distracted, we'll shift into an Alpha state without knowing it. Say, we might be driving down the street and we get deep in thought and the next thing we know we're miles ahead of where we thought we were, and we don't even remember how we got there."

Trish propped her arm on the arm of the sofa and rested her chin on her hand. "Now that you say that, it happened to me some months ago when I returned from Russia. I was driving home and was so deep in thought that the next thing I knew I was in town, and couldn't remember anything about the drive...like being on automatic or something."

"That's just what I'm talking about," Stephanie responded with enthusiasm, as her eyes lit up. "We do things like that every day. We'll be watching television, thinking about something else so hard that when we shift back into focus to the events on the TV, we don't remember a thing about what we were just watching. Something else has taken over—the 'automatic.' Some people call it daydreaming...but it's an Alpha state we slip into unconsciously. In shamanism we slip into it with consciousness."

She explained that all anyone had to do to access that type of consciousness was to get a few basic instructions about going to the lower world to find their power animal and then to the upper world to find their teacher. "And they're in business." Stephanie smiled and said that even though it might sound crazy, it wasn't unlike remote viewing that the government had secretly done for years for spying purposes. "They still do it, I'm sure, because, just like shamanism, it works."

"You know, I've seen a program or two on remote viewing," Trish commented. "After they teach these guys to remote view, they have them sit in a room and give them a fixed point of some kind. I think they called it a...a...a..."

"A target."

Trish pointed with her finger. "That's it."

"In remote viewing," Stephanie continued, "a specific geographical target would be selected, and by using some kind of co-ordinate they went there in their minds and reported everything they saw—even to some place on the other side of the globe—without ever leaving the room." She said that in the Army program they were only looking at the physical world—or what shamans refer to as the middle world, ordinary reality. "In shamanism we also journey to the spirit of a thing...a person, an idea or a disease. We believe there is spirit behind everything, and that's the only place you can truly connect and understand what's behind the physical world or events that we see and experience in everyday life."

Trish was trying to absorb what she was hearing, when Stephanie said, "I know it's a difficult concept. It was for me, too. But after a couple of years of actually doing it, I realized how powerful it is. I realized, too, that anyone can do it."

"Anyone?"

"Yes, in the Army they originally thought only psychics could remote view. But they found that almost anyone could be trained to do it. At that point they started bringing guys in off the streets, so to speak, and training them. After all, psychics—and in particular willing psychics—were in short supply.

Stephanie repositioned in her seat and gestured with her hand. "Part of the trouble they had with it, though, was that some of the men were so intrigued by the remote viewing, that they started traveling on their own and finding—I guess—some of the same things we were—tapping into other dimensions, or whatever. Then they didn't want to mess around with spying anymore…thought it was a corruption of the power, because intention is everything in this work."

Trish looked up. "Intention?"

"Yes. Remote viewing was sometimes used for questionable purposes. Whereas, shamanism is used to gain insight into your life or helping other people to learn about themselves…spiritual growth…bringing back advice, divining, doing healing work and so forth. In shamanism intention is everything," she repeated.

"I'm a little confused. You're talking about shamanism, and I thought Jo Ann said you channeled. Is that the same thing?"

"Honestly, I don't know. I suppose on some level it is. I just know that one night our circle leader for the night said, 'Tonight let's journey to the spirit of the goddess, Freya.'" Stephanie's eyes grew large as she said, "Well, I popped right up and said, 'Who's that?' I'd never heard of her.

"Turns out she was an ancient Norse goddess—keeper of ancient wisdom." Stephanie tilted her head. "Anyway, this wasn't unusual. We'd journeyed to a lot of spirits before." She talked about journeying to find the source behind certain holidays or the true nature of healing. She told about journeying for people who were ill or in pain. She said they'd been all over the universe, swimming with fish and walking on the moon. "Nothing was too miniscule or unreachable."

When Trish smiled, Stephanie added, "I know how crazy this must sound, but shamans in primitive cultures just experience the world differently than we do. And I tell you, it wouldn't have been around for thousands of years if it didn't work. Besides, I don't try to convince anyone anymore," she said with a wave of her hand. "If someone asks for help or information, I give it. That's all. It's something people have to experience to believe in."

Trish smiled. *Yeah, as with synchronicity and mermaids.*

"And," Stephanie quickly added, "I never work on anyone without permission. That's a basic we abide by."

Trish looked up. "Why not? Couldn't you do healing work on someone who may not even know about shamanism—much less believe in it—but might need help anyway."

Stephanie tilted her head. "Oh, I was tempted in the beginning—like when my aunt came down with breast cancer. I went to her and explained what I did and offered her help, but she just couldn't open up to the possibility and wanted to stick with modern medicine. It was something she knew and was comfortable with."

"Couldn't you try to help her without her knowledge? What harm would it have done?"

Stephanie held out a hand. "I don't know...and that's the point." She told Trish that, since no one could presume to know another person's soul purpose in life, they shouldn't interfere. "My aunt may have had an important lesson she needed to learn from her breast cancer. It might have been an opportunity rather than a tragedy. We help where we can, but we can't make decisions for someone else." Stephanie smiled and shook her head. "Look, I don't know how this works. I just know it does. I think what might happen in healing is that the person decides to get well, and he comes to us with that intention, and we just facilitate what is already decided. We're the vehicle; the real power is theirs all along."

"You say you know it works. How?"

"Well..." Stephanie leaned forward, then said, "In circle we have someone come to us, or even not come to us. They may have just sent their name to us and asked us to work on them..."

"You mean they don't have to physically be there?" Trish interjected, raising her eyebrows.

"That's right. We're just working with energy. Anyway, we might have only the person's name to work with. In fact, we've gotten to the point that we don't even want any more information than that. It just muddies the water and gives us preconceived ideas. And we don't know if they've got bad knees or cancer or what...or even maybe a broken heart...and when we journey, we'll always come up with the same things."

"Like what?"

She told Trish that everyone journeying might see trouble in the left side of a person's chest, and they would each work on it in their own way. Then later they'd find out that the person had lung cancer in his left lung.

Trish raised her eyebrows. "Yeah?"

"Yeah. Or we might be working on a person and we're all getting this heavy, grieving feeling, and we find out later that a family member has just died." Stephanie told of one woman in their group who actually saw the people they worked on in her mind—from hair color to scars or birthmarks, and she always turned out to be accurate. "I don't get concrete images of the person, unless they're in the room. I guess—knowing myself—I'd probably focus on it and be distracted from the work.

"That's how I know Jo Ann. She came one night after hearing about us from a friend. We worked on physical problems. We also work on each other from time to time."

"Has anyone you've worked on ever died? Have you ever had failures?"

"Sure, some have died, but we don't consider it a failure."

Trish wrinkled her forehead. "What do you mean?"

Stephanie draped her arm across the back of the sofa. "Well, the first time it happened, I was devastated, thought we must have done something wrong." She said it had shaken her faith. She was at the point of walking away. Then, in desperation, she journeyed to her power animal to ask about it, and was told, "In the healing work that you do, you must never confuse death with failure." She leaned forward and held a hand out. "See, Trish, healing is healing, on whatever level it takes place. And not dying isn't one of the options. We all die. Our only choice is whether or not we die healed. When someone makes a choice on a soul level to die, we assist that person in making the process smoother."

Stephanie said that at about that time she was studying Eastern religions in a continuing education course, and came across an account of a Buddhist who went to the Visage of Death to learn about life. She said it sounded like shamanism to her. Then she wondered why anyone would go to death to learn about life. She decided to journey to the Visage of Death herself. Stephanie smiled at the recall. "He was this big hulking, imposing character, sitting cross-legged, laughing this big bellied laugh. And I asked him to tell me about life. He showed me, with his hands pushing together, like this." Stephanie gestured, as she repeated his words. "'Death *propels* you into life. You must have death to have life. It would be as if you stopped up the exhaust of your car and expected the engine to keep running.' It was an image I could relate to."

She told Trish that they would never tell anyone to abandon traditional medicine. She thought of energy work only as paralleling or complimenting modern medicine. "I think in the future we're going to see more and more of this kind of work done because people will see that it works." She thought the medical world was going to have to go through an incredible shift from disease management to actual healing, if they wanted to stay in business. "Being a doctor doesn't necessarily make you a healer." She'd heard that some hospitals were presently even using Reiki masters with some of their patients before and after surgery.

Stephanie looked at her watch. "I didn't mean to get so deep into this explanation."

Trish raised her hand. "Don't apologize. I have this effect. I never know when to stop." She raised her eyebrows. "Unless you're in a hurry or have something you need to get to."

"No. I blocked out the day for this session. Jo Ann indicated it might be a long one. Besides, you've tapped into one of my favorite topics."

"So, back to…Freya."

"Yes, Freya. Among other things, she *was* the keeper of ancient wisdom. I think that's why Jo Ann sent you to me, because part of what you're working on is pre-history. Right?"

"That's right, particularly Greek mythology—though I actually think it may apply to all mythologies."

"Don't tell me too much," Stephanie cautioned with her hand outstretched in front of her. "I'm having a hard time holding back information already."

Trish uttered an inquisitive snicker. "Okay."

"Well, I have to tell you," Stephanie continued, "that my first encounter with Freya was incredible." She said their teacher told them only to look for her in the upper world, but that when she got there she saw the goddess with earth things all around her—water, stones, grass and trees. She was surrounded by the most incredible mixture of earth and sky energy Stephanie had ever seen. "She was very seductive, with this sheer drape around her. You could see her nude body underneath, and she had starlight in her long, blond hair.

"I began by asking her the question we'd been told to ask, and I connected with her in a way I hadn't with any other spirit. I don't know why, but I couldn't wait to journey to her again. The information she gave was meaningful, and given with such love." She crossed her legs. "One day I decided to get out my drum and rattle, candles and sweet grass so I could do ceremony and journey to her, and I heard her voice before I got started. I'll never forget what she said."

Stephanie smiled. "She said, 'You do not have to use elaborate ways to come to me. I will come to you in dreams, on the wind, along the wooded path, in the words of others…and you will know that they are my words. For I *live* in your dreams, on the wind, along your wooded paths, in the words of others…and I live in you.'"

"Wow," Trish commented. "Beautiful."

"I think everything she says is beautiful. Anyway, since that time, I've been talking to her, and sometimes I do it for other people. You could call it channeling. I try not to label it. But I know it sprang from shamanism." She didn't even know or care anymore where it came from. "Whatever it is, it's available if you need it."

"Would you categorize shamanism as a religion?"

"No. I've only heard it defined as a method."

"A method?"

"Just one of many methods for reaching spirit. I just think it's the easiest and most rewarding...and the most illuminating I've ever come across...that's all. And the method I learned is core shamanism...sort of like a basic form of it."

"Stephanie, I know how much time I'm taking. How much do you charge for a session?"

"I don't charge anything. I've never even considered it."

Stephanie set her hands on her thighs. "Now, I think I'll get us both a glass of water to have handy in case we need it during the session."

When she returned from the kitchen, Trish said, "This should be interesting. Can't say I've ever interviewed a goddess before."

Chapter Forty-Three

As they began their session, Stephanie repositioned herself on the sofa with her pillow at her back, shifted her body and straightened her clothes. She pivoted her head and neck around slowly and deliberately and said, "All right." She closed her eyes a few moments, as though in prayer, then opened them and turned to Trish, seated on the sofa across from her and asked, "Are you ready? Got your tape going?"

"Yeah. At least I think I'm ready."

Stephanie nodded toward the note pad in Trish's lap. "I see you've got questions prepared."

"I worked on them for two hours last night," she responded, smiling.

"Well, that's great, but…hmm. Well, you might start out with them, but…"

"But?"

"Oh, I don't know. Let's just say that this may not go where you intend. You may do better winging it. Why don't you just follow her lead?" The comment sounded more like a suggestion than a question.

Damn, Trish thought to herself, *I guess interviewing a goddess isn't any different than interviewing anyone else. They all try to take you where they want to go.*

"I'm ready whenever you are," Trish said out loud.

"Ask your first question."

Trish wondered if the session had started. Then she saw that Stephanie's eyes were already closed and her breathing had noticeably slowed.

"All right, then," Trish began.

"Is there a connection between mythology and the appearance of mythological creatures during this atomic age?"

"Yes, indeed, there is."

Trish was surprised by the response and by the gentle, yet vibrant tone in Stephanie's voice. She continued. *"Have we radiated the earth before?"*

"Many times."

"Why?"

"You know the razor's edge—the one upon which your life exists—the one of which you have spoken?"

"Yes."

"Your world has danced on that razor's edge many times. You like it. You, Trish Cagle, have danced on that edge many times."

Trish knew this to be true. She let out a breath, then lowered her prepared questions to her lap and took the path in front of her. *"Why do we do that?"*

"It is exciting because it is perilous. You are never more alive than when you are taking the greatest risk. Then when you make what you perceive as mistakes, you attempt to bury them in the earth and in your memory and assign them to the gods of the underworld to transmute them."

"Are they transmuted?"

"In what you perceive as your time—your ages."

"Are we transmuted, in time, as well?"

"As human beings you change your molecular structure all of your time, or what you perceive as time."

Trish wasn't grasping the meaning of the answers she was receiving and so returned to her original train of thought. *"Why are the mutants appearing now?"*

"They have waited for such a time as this. They are harbingers. They have sacrificed their lives on Earth to bring humanity a message. The message is that your world is out of balance. Because they have sacrificed so much, they are sacred. They are gods, as they have always been gods."

"What about the time line thing? It isn't possible that what you're talking about happened in our time frame—our history."

"The past is present. The future is now. All depends on your point of view."

"That just sounds like a riddle to me," Trish replied.

"You like your riddles. You, Trish Cagle, like your riddles. You like to play with them—to try to figure them out. Is that not so?"

"How do you know that?"

"I observe."

Trish became frustrated. She didn't understand the answers and momentarily thought about abandoning the session. Something about the information, however, compelled her to keep going.

"Is one of the purposes of my research to help find and encourage a new source of energy for mankind?"

"Everything in your world, your plane, can be used for energy, for everything in your world *is* energy—sound, sun, stones—anything that vibrates. And everything vibrates. Everything in your world can be used for great healing. And everything in your world can also be used for great destruction. The choice is always yours.

"What you infuse into that element is what you get out of it. *You* are the creator. You are truly creators of your own realities—as you have so often heard before. If you put greed into the sun, greed is what you will receive. If you put fear into stones, fear is what will be produced. If you put love into sounds, love will be your reward. It is the same with every experience and every relationship.

"That is the only true cause and effect in *your* world."

"Well, if we don't use nuclear or coal powered energy, how do we get

energy?"

"Why do you think you must depend on others to produce energy? You already have all of the internal energy you need. You do not have to depend on someone else to give you power—or sell you power. You *are* energy. You have all the energy you need in a lifetime and more—much more—right now. You are surrounded by universal energy."

"But how do we heat and cool our homes?"

"You do not need to. You only need to heat and cool your own bodies, and you already have the power to do that."

"How?"

"You start by disconnecting from all of the false sources of power and *re*-connecting with true power—the source power. And you begin by redis-covering your own true personal power."

"But how will we build our homes and cities without electric tools?"

"Why do you need elaborate homes and cities? To discover the answers to your questions, you must question your concepts of what you need and desire in your lives.

"Many of you spend your holidays and free times in parks and in your woods and on mountaintops and along rivers and shorelines, enjoying the beauty and sounds of nature. That is what you do at what you call special times. Why limit your daily lives to elaborate houses or cities?"

"But we have to live in cities to be close to work and shopping."

"Why? Again, dare to question your basic concepts, if you want an-swers to your questions. Dare to see the world with different eyes.

"Are your people who live in cities chasing a career, really doing what their hearts desire and what brings them genuine joy?"

"Fewer and fewer of them," she responded with resignation.

Trish didn't quite know where to go or how to proceed with her line of questioning, so she shifted gears yet again. *"You said the mythical beings are appearing now because the world is out of balance. Why is that happen-ing?"*

"Many of you have forgotten a connection to your source."

"How did that happen?" she pressed.

"You speak of your beginnings, but you have forgotten your beginning—or what you speak of as your beginning—on this Earth plane for a time. In *your* beginning your God wed your Goddess. And that sacred union of your Earth Mother and your Sky Father produced offspring: the children of the Earth and Sky. The seed, the sacred idea, the inspiration—for that is all inspiration is—was united in sacred union with your Earth plane to produce a vibrational field upon which your life could materialize—at least in your minds—for there is no matter. But no matter—you may believe what you will.

"You are the products, the children, of an idea—a sacred thought—an inspiration. And in truth, you are thought forms. You have assumed the form you have taken for your own purposes."

"I don't know about this. This is way out there."

"Yes, it is 'way out there'." Stephanie pointed to the center of her chest. "And it is also 'way in here.' Do your myths not speak of these things?"

"Some of them do."

"And some of them are true in parts. Did you not think they were *all* fairy tales before you saw your Cyclops and mermaid with your own eyes?"

"I guess I did at that."

"Is that not 'way out there?'"

"I guess it would be for most people."

"For the ones who have not seen with your vision. For you were truly seeking and you are truly finding."

"But it keeps confusing me. I don't understand."

"That is why you sought me out."

"Sought you out?"

"Yes, you summoned me."

"Summoned you? I did?"

"From the very depths and heights of your soul. You knocked on the door, and it is opening for you. Nothing would stop you from your quest. You gave up everything. And because you made that sacrifice, because you have risked it all in faith, all shall be returned to you in full measure."

Trish felt tears welling in her eyes and was unable to speak for a moment.

"I love you well, my child," Freya added.

Emotions began welling up even more in Trish. So much had transpired in the previous months that she'd begun trying to hold many of her emotions below the surface of her consciousness. But an intense feeling of pure love from the entity she was communicating with began enveloping her and penetrating those barriers she had erected. It felt like being with Ilyani.

"I have always loved you well—even when you did not know it. You were not contaminated when you came to this place as a child. You were kissed by the gods. And you were kissed by the goddess, as well."

"I . . . I . . ." Trish stammered as she tried to speak, but her resistance was cracking.

"My child, do not try to push away your emotions. They are part of who you truly are. Do you not feel it?"

"Yes, I think I do," she answered, still choking back tears. She pulled a tissue from the table beside her and wiped her eyes.

"You are that thought form—that sacred idea...and you are also emotion—feelings. You are that thought—that seed—that energy of your Father, combined with your Mother's feeling. That is *all* that you are: manifested thought forms of energy.

"The feelings truly move you. Thought has energy. Thought *is* energy. When you wed it with the energy of emotion—feeling—you become alive. You become what you experience as 'real'…materialized. You are energy in motion."

Trish continued to wipe her eyes and then clutched the tissue in her hand as she tried to regain her composure.

● ● ●

After a few moments, Trish continued. *"Well, if all this is true…about our sacredness, then why are we so destructive?"*

"That is who you are, as well. You *are* destroyers. You are made in the image—the imagination—of God. You are sacred beings, thus, anything you feel or manifest—anger, depression, pain, fear or destruction—is sacred, as well. They serve you as much as love and joy, kindness and patience…and creation. You are made of both of what you perceive as negative and positive aspects. You need them both. You should embrace them both. Did your Max not tell you how he needed his pain?"

"Yes, but, I'm sorry, you're talking about things I've always thought of as good and bad."

"Ah, the darkness and the light."

"Yes!"

"The right and wrong."

"Yes."

"The right and the left."

"Yes…" she said it with some hesitancy.

"The feminine and the masculine."

"Now, wait a minute…"

"Does your world not dishonor the feminine? Does your world not dishonor the Earth? Does your world not teach that men should rule over women?"

"I guess on the whole…but that's not the same as creation and destruction."

"Is it not? How can you experience creation without destruction? How can you experience rebirth without death? How can you know who you are unless you have seen who you have been? How can you know the light unless you have experienced darkness? To know and see and experience the sacredness in yourself, you must know and see and experience the sacredness in all others, as well—even those you consider to be wrong—especially in those

459

that you consider to be wrong."

"But, what about murderers?"

"There are many ways to kill, and there are many weapons to use for killing. You can kill a person's enthusiasm, a person's joy and even a person's love. Is this no less real? And you may do it with no less a weapon than words or no more subtle a gesture than a look, and, yes, even a thought. And these can be no less destructive than even your atomic weapons, for they can be spirit killers. *That* is the nature of the power you possess.

"The razor's edge, upon which you live, is merely your specific field vibration—your Earth plane. Your thoughts and words and feelings have a vibration that resonates outward into the universe. Those vibrations are no less real than the chair upon which you are sitting, that you believe to be solid or 'real.'

Trish wrinkled her forehead. *"But you can't tell me murdering someone isn't wrong."*

"It *would* be what you know as 'wrong', in your reality, for you do not require that experience."

"Does a murderer require that experience?"

"If he chooses."

"Then what about the victim? Are you telling me the victim also chooses to be a victim?"

"Indeed."

"That's hard to swallow. That sounds like' blame the victim' to me."

"There is no blame. You are creatures of love at your core. You know that unconsciously. You are trying to remember who you truly are—to bring that knowing to your conscious level. You may choose to do it in pain, or you may choose to do it in joy."

"Why would anyone choose pain?"

"It gets your attention…like the monsters in your dreams—like the monsters in the place called Clinic Number Four. As your Max once told you, they are not meant to frighten you. They are meant to get your attention. If you pay attention—if you honor them—and simply ask them what they are trying to tell you, then you will see that they will be transformed before your eyes."

"You said that we are sacred, but if we cause another person pain, I don't see how that's sacred?"

"It is both sacred and a great sacrifice. You are creatures of love. To provide an environment of pain for another, you are providing that soul with an environment he needs or desires to experience whatever feeling he needs to feel, for whatever may be his soul's purpose. Just as water is shaped by its environment, so you shape the environment, the classroom, for the other soul to experience *his* growth."

"Water is shaped by its environment?"

"Indeed. Water—the energy, the mood, the appearance of water is shaped and defined by the environment, the elements, which surround it. In the air it falls as raindrops. In the bowl of a lake it becomes still and tranquil and placid. If it chooses the rocky downward surface of a river, it becomes rapids with energy thrusting itself forward with vibrance.

"It changes its structure completely as heat allows it to transmute into vapor as it ascends back to the heavens. It transmutes to the touch of frigid temperatures into the solidity of ice. So, as with water, you also are shaped— your energies, your moods, your very appearances are shaped—by the environment, the experiences, the relationships, the very life that surrounds you."

"You make it sound as though the water has the consciousness controlling its surroundings."

"It does. Like you, it has a consciousness...and like you, it also has what you term unconsciousness and supra-consciousness. At those levels you connect with water. That is what this one is doing now." Stephanie pointed to herself. "She is connecting with all things. There is no separation between your self and all others. You only maintain the illusion of separateness for your purposes in this reality—in this experience. If you looked *beyond* your present experience instead of at it, you would see and feel this blending with all things. You could move through your universe without a need for your elaborate and expensive and sometimes faulty machines."

"You mean in our minds?"

"In an entirely different form. It is the same form you use when you travel in your dreams. Only you may do it with consciousness, if you will." Again, Stephanie pointed to herself. "This one is doing that now. Some of your scientists are even beginning to see some of these things, but they have no words within their framework to express what they are seeing and finding. It is a new world for some of them, as it is becoming a new world for others.

"Glory in your anger, when it truly serves you. Revel in your joy. Merge with the music of the spheres. Celebrate your beingness. Blend with the universe. It is 'all' there, if you would but see it or hear it—if you would but feel it and know it—if you would but choose it."

"You make it sound as though we are completely in charge."

"Indeed. You constantly shift your relationships and environment in order to experience whatever feeling or energy you need to feel...whether it be the surging force of rage or the tranquility of love or the depression of a backwater swampy region of living."

"And do we also have the ability to transmute ourselves?"

"Of course. As I said, you change your molecular structure all of the time. You are intimately involved in your evolutionary process."

"Were you saying a minute ago that growth has to be painful?"

"It *may* be. It also may be joyful…and at those times you may shape the environment that gives another soul joy, as other sacred souls shape your environment and experiences on this vibrational plane you call Earth.

"There is no good or bad in your growth processes. They simply express. They simply are. There are no judgements of them from the universe—nor of you."

"Even if what you do causes another person pain?"

"Even then. All of your relationships and experiences come from love."

"To cause pain is an act of love?"

"If it is what another chooses to experience. Your soul does not judge, either. It merely supports the experiences another chooses and experiences itself."

"This totally goes against everything I've ever believed."

"What you believed before shaped your world before. What you believe tomorrow will shape your world tomorrow. The truth you always speak of is your *illusion* of truth. If you hold firm to one, unchangeable truth, then you are denying all other possibilities in life—all of the discoveries that you could make about yourselves, your world and your universe. Can you possibly know everything from that one unchangeable and inflexible viewpoint?

"You would be like the man who said that you should shut down your patent offices because everything that *could* be invented, had already been invented. Would he not be staggered by your world today?"

Trish smiled.

"You also would be staggered if you could view your existence from my vantage point. The real 'truth' is beyond your imaginings from your viewpoint. You must get beyond your false perceptions—your false boundaries and limits of truth—to see and know who you truly are.

"Would you have known the moon if you had stayed fixed on your planet Earth? Would you have been able to truly see yourselves—your world— if you had refused to leave the fixed point of a flat world?

"Change your perception and you change your world. Move your point of perception and you shift your vision of yourself and all that surrounds you.

"If you could look *through* your life and your experiences instead of at them, you might choose less pain and more joy…and so might others…but it would still be a matter of choice."

"You make it sound like I have—like we all have—total control of our lives."

"You do."

"It doesn't feel like it. I feel out of control a lot of the time. Things rarely go the way I plan or hope they will."

"That is only on the conscious level. Your unconscious and your supraconscious—or your soul—or whatever you choose to call your pure essence—knows your true desires. But you fight it. You do not surrender to it and trust it, and, thus, the illusion of being out of control.

"If you *feel* out of control, then you need to *be* out of control, to stop trying to control. If you would but allow your desires—your true desires—to manifest, you would see how much less energy it would take."

"When you say surrender it sounds to me like giving up—like putting yourself in the role of a victim."

"Again, that is your illusion of surrender. True surrender is not forced. It is a willful giving over, not a giving up. In true surrender you give up nothing of true value. You only gain. The things you do give up are the false parts of yourself—the things you no longer need—the things you have struggled to hold onto for so long that your energies are drained."

"Like what?"

"False beliefs, false personal power, false boundaries and limits—a false perception of your life and your world."

"And what do you gain? A new set of false boundaries and limits and beliefs?"

"That would not be true surrender. That would be false surrender. That *would* put you in your role of victim."

"Then what do you gain in true surrender?"

"All."

"All?"

"Yes. All. All of yourself—every aspect of your being…and that is also who you surrender to."

"Then, if we are the all and we surrender to ourselves, then… Wait a minute… Wait a minute…I can't seem to grasp this."

"To grasp it will make it slip away. If you loosen your mind's grasp, you will allow it to come. You give it permission. You do not force it. This thought will not truly surrender unless it comes willingly, also.

"You can never hold on to what truly is not yours…and nothing can truly be yours unless it is given willingly. False captivity will never last. It will always slip away. Like the idea, you gain nothing by conquering."

"So I just allow the thought?"

"Indeed, by letting go of your control of it…by loosening your mind. Loose your mind, and then fully lose your mind. In that moment the thought will come."

"Lose my mind?"

"Is that not a fair price to pay for gaining your heart and your soul?"

"But we don't need all of them? Our hearts and souls and our minds?"

"That is what you term 'very good.' You do need all of your aspects to become what you, Trish Cagle, desire to be. But it is about balance. Always, it is balance. 'Being' is your center point. It is not one side of the other. It is not up or down. It is not mind or soul, male or female. It is All—in balance. The All coming from your center point."

"Doesn't everyone have a center point?"

"Yes. That is the center point of *their* world, *their* life, *their* business, *their* perspective."

"But if we are ' all'—as you say—then wouldn't that be our center point, too?"

"Did I not tell you how much beyond your imaginings this would be?"

"But I don't get it." Trish rubbed her temple.

"You cannot get it. You cannot grasp it. You cannot capture it. You can only allow it. You surrender to it in love and in joy and allow it to surrender to you. That is your feminine side—your receptive side. It is your masculine side that wants to penetrate the thought, the idea.

"To attain your quest for wisdom, you must have both: the penetrating aspect that wants to know, that questions, that probes...the side of you that you have nurtured so well as a reporter. But, if you truly want answers, you must also have the receptive side that attracts, that allows the knowledge—or whatever you desire—to come forth.

"Do you know how you sometimes try to think of a name and you cannot?"

"Yes."

"You say that it is on the tip of your tongue, but you just cannot remember it?"

"Yes."

"And then later in your day, when you have stopped trying, it will pop into your head?"

"Yeah, it happens all the time."

"You remember because you have stopped trying. You have stopped trying to control. You have stopped trying to force, and you have allowed the information to come forth.

"You have surrendered."

Trish stopped and smiled and took several deep breaths. Then she took a drink of water, as Stephanie sat silently for a few moments. Trish took advantage of the quiet time to try to absorb what she had just heard and to try and reframe more questions.

• • •

Finally Trish smiled. *"You know, you sound a lot like a female version of my old friend, Max."*

"Your friend, Max, had accessed a great deal of his feminine energy. It was a lack of full acceptance of that aspect of his being that kept him from experiencing his full grandeur on this Earth plane. When he lost his wife, he tried to push his pain away. If he had embraced it—as he had learned to embrace the pain of his wartime experiences—he would have been better able to accept his feminine energies and power and, thus, restored a measure of his beloved wife's love and presence back into his life."

"I feel that you're implying I haven't embraced the pain of my experiences in Kazakhstan, yet."

"You have not even embraced the joy in your life, yet."

"What do you mean by that?"

"You have not surrendered to the love and joy that have returned to your life in full measure. If you would give yourself over to it completely, you would quench the flames of doubt that plague your beloved and that also plague the masculine side of your own being.

"You would heal the wounds between you."

Trish hadn't expected the interview to take such a personal turn, and she felt a little wary and self-conscious. She wondered just how much this Freya—this Stephanie—knew about her. Still, somehow, she knew the words she was hearing were words of truth—her truth.

Stephanie continued, "To experience the fullness of your relationship, you must honor the conflict between you and your beloved as much as you honor the love between you. It is merely a mirror—a reflection—of your own inner conflict. It has simply been brought out into the open so that you may deal with it consciously."

Trish let out a breath and said, *"I don't think I understand anything about relationships. What am I not seeing about them?"*

"Now you are getting to the 'heart of the matter.' Relationship is always about you. Experience is always about you. It is all about realizing that you are part of the ALL that is, whether it is stones or galaxies or long-eared rabbits. It is you reflecting you. Source reflecting source. The seeker realizing that what he seeks is the self. Coming home. Being home wherever and whenever you are. Needing nothing, for you already are all that you desire outside of yourself. You are an aspect of all that is. When you 'get' that you *become* the person you desire in your life. You become the comforter you seek outside yourself, the healer, the companion, the lover, the compassionate and passionate mate. For you *are* all of those things and so much more than you have dreamed in all of your philosophies. You are boundless creation in a time- and space-, emotion- and thought-bound universe, which exists in a multi-verse of possibility and potential.

"Believe in the impossible, and the impossible unfolds before you."

Trish moved her head slowly from side to side. *"Well, I've gotta' tell you, I want it all. That's what I want. I admit it."*

"You already have it. You simply do not know it. For it is your propensity to possess which keeps you from knowing it. If you think you possess a house, control a person or own a piece of land with a deed, a marriage license, a ring or a promise, you are limiting and fooling yourself. And if you are attempting to find your Spirit while clinging to those beliefs, you may find how quickly they slip away. Possession may be nine-tenths of *your* law, but it is a fool's law. It limits you. It impedes your dance of life. For it controls and possesses *you*.

"When you resolve your inner conflict, that which seems to separate you and your mate will evaporate like morning mist.

"Is that not a beautiful gift that your beloved has given you? Is that not selfless sacrifice? He has put himself in pain to help you deal with your conflict—to move forward and to grow in Spirit.

"Honor it."

"How do you know so much about me?"

"I *am* you. And you are me. There are no delineations—except in the world you have chosen to experience."

"You make this sound like co-dependency...and I've always tried to avoid co-dependency."

"Indeed, you have...but your very existence is co-dependent. It is interconnected with every person, every plant, every animal, every relationship and every event that in any way affects your life.

"And it *All* affects your life.

"There are no delineations—no boundaries, no separations—except those which you create for your purposes."

"Nothing, no one, no spirit of anyone or anything exists without everything else. Life expands and implodes, inhales and exhales, dies and is reborn in each moment, in each NOW."

Trish put her hand to her face, took a deep breath, then lowered it and returned to a previous thought. *"So, in the context of my experiences in Kazakhstan, I think you're saying they weren't really bad, and that those mutations weren't bad. But I have to tell you that looking at them... it just seemed wrong to me. It hit me like a ton of bricks when I saw them. They looked so...so... foreign—like aliens—like something evil had happened. But, you say they're gods instead of monsters."*

"They were meant to bring those feelings forth when you gazed upon them. Their appearance triggered a remembrance from deep within your psyche, of a time long past—an ancient memory of another time, and that remembering has come from within your genes—your DNA—your basic structure. Your remembering altered your basic structure—your own personal DNA, if you will. For it began to bring your unconscious up to your conscious level, and you will never see your world in the same way again in this lifetime."

"How do I get over this lingering depression I've been feeling?" Trish asked, as she tilted her head and rubbed her temple.

"You have needed this depression—this backwater stillness—for though it is dark, it is also rich with nutrients to germinate the new growth within you, the new birth of who you are becoming.

"You are dying to your old self. The depression is an acknowledgement of that death."

She lowered her hand. *"But I also have this fear of where I'm heading—of what I might find in my search. I don't want to lose who I am in the process."*

"What do you fear?"

"I think...I'm afraid of becoming cynical...or of dying." She paused a moment before adding, *"I tell you that for a short time right after I got back from Russia, I was actually contemplating suicide."* She paused again. *"I've never said those words before now."*

"But you thought them."

"I guess I just felt so hopeless—like no matter what I tried to do to get this story out—it wasn't really going to make any difference in the end. We were just going to nuke ourselves and our planet to smithereens, anyway."

"And now?"

"Well, now, I feel a little differently—a little more hopeful." Then she quickly added, *"But I still believe it's wrong when I see or hear about clusters of babies born without eyes—like in England, or about babies born without brains in Mexico, or without spines, like the jellyfish babies in the Pacific Islands."*

"The babies in England are born without eyes so the rest of humanity will see. The babies in Mexico are born without brains so the rest of humanity will think...and the babies in the islands are born without spines so the rest of humanity will have courage."

"And what about the mutants in Kazakhstan? Why do they look like the myths?"

"Your genes, your DNA, are a library of the past of all mankind. Your mutants are reawakening from your ancient past. There are things that have occurred during your atomic age which have reawakened ancient memories. Most of you are consciously unaware of them at this time. You became aware of it when you viewed the Cyclops, mermaid and Janus in Clinic Number Four.

"Max was correct when he spoke of memory being cellular. Indeed, just as he suggested, the memory of everything that has ever happened in your vibrational plane is held within every cell of your body. You are beginning to access those memories to which you believed you had no access, and in so doing, you are awakening or enlivening certain access points inside and outside of your body, which many of you call chakras. They are different vibrations of energy, some of which have lain dormant or little used both within and without your body.

"They have lain dormant for such a time as this, when you are ready to access them. You have drawn to you certain people and certain events because you are ready to awaken these sleeping memories—to awaken your access to them and thus your own sleeping energies.

"The genetic symbols, or blueprints, of your Cyclops and mermaid and Janus were called forth from the unconscious aspect of your species from a time and a place that you call myth because your unconscious knows that your conscious is ready to meet it…that you are ready to become self aware."

"Are we at the beginning of this catastrophe?"

"You are, indeed, at the beginning of what you label catastrophe. There will be more gods born as more and more people are exposed to pockets of radiation. The gods *will* walk your Earth again. And when their work is done—when mankind hears and receives the message of the gods—then they will retreat from the Earth again and return to their source, leaving behind only myths and legends of their presence…only stories that you will call fairy tales."

Trish rubbed her forehead and again tried to gather her thoughts. Stephanie sat silently while Trish tried to regroup enough to ask more questions.

● ● ●

After a few more quiet moments, Trish finally asked, *"Then, I guess if I'm following you correctly, if I want to grow spiritually—I'm not supposed to fight or resist the whole atomic age and the radiation it's produced, but embrace it?"*

"Is anything more dark or sinister in your eyes?"

"No…but, now, are you saying that I'm not to embrace the atomic radiation itself, but the illusion of it?"

"Is there anything more invisible to your naked eye? Is that not what you call illusion?"

"Yes, but it produced some very real monsters in its wake. I saw them. They're real."

"Yes, and are they not wondrous to sacrifice themselves to bring you and mankind to an awakening of who you truly are?

"You *are* the ones who produced atomic weapons and atomic energy, as well as the ones who fight it. You *are* humanity. There is no separation."

Trish relaxed her body, as well as her hold on her beliefs long enough to ask, with resignation and sadness, *"Why did we do it?"*

"You did it collectively for the experience. You risked everything in your world, as you know it, to come to this point. Is that not courageous? Is that not sacrifice?"

"What do courage and sacrifice have to do with the atomic age? What is the atomic age really about?"

"You *exist* at the atomic level. And you are intimately connected to every other thing in your world that exists at the atomic level. You only see an exterior world with delineations between yourselves and every other thing or person because you have held on to that illusion, and have been attached to it for so long, that you are afraid to let go of it. You still see your world with sharp focus instead of soft focus."

"You know about that?"

"I observe many things. If *you* could but see with different vision, your delineations would disappear before your very eyes."

"You make it sound as though there are no boundaries between anything, and yet, we're told to respect each other's boundaries. Is that wrong?"

"There is no wrong or right…but as long as you *believe* in boundaries, it would be well to respect each other's *perception* of boundaries"

"Well, what about when peoples' perceptions of boundaries are in conflict—like in the Middle East?"

"Where there is conflict of boundaries, you are already breaking them down. For, even in conflict, you are already inter-mingling your energies one with another…and in so doing, you are exchanging your essences. You are *involved* one with the other, and, in the process of eliminating your perceptions of boundaries and separations."

"Even when you're killing one another?"

"Is that not sacrifice? Is that not a wondrous price for a soul to pay to help his fellow man to see his connection with all of the rest of humanity and beyond?"

"But does it always have to be so violent?"

"There are many paths. Some may be long or short, straight or winding, painful or joyful, and they may also change at any time. But *all* paths are sacred, for *you* walk your paths of life, and *you* are sacred souls. You are Children of God."

"And if we chose to see our world without the 'delineations,' what would we see?"

"The choice would still be yours. You always create your own world."

"But it seems like it was wrong to produce atomic bombs and atomic energy."

"That is your perception. The developments you speak of were the result of the splitting of some of the tiniest of your elements—your atom.

Look at the display of sheer power and energy from that tiny part of your world's essence."

Trish gave a resigned half grin. *"I have to admit those films of atomic blasts were pretty awesome to watch."*

"They were indeed...to us, as well...but you do not have to split your atoms or split yourselves apart or blow yourselves up to discover or create energy. You already have it, more than you will ever need. It is a gathering together of your atoms, of yourselves, that is the true source of your power."

"You're talking about fission and fusion."

"Whatever term you choose. It is a joining together in love, not a splitting apart in fear at your very basic level that is where the rest of your true power lies. Just as destructive as you have been, you may be healing, as well."

Trish tried to gather her thoughts for a moment, searching for her next question. Then she asked, *"Am I supposed to write the book that Max was talking about?"*

"You already *are* writing your book. Only the book you are writing is called your Book of Life. Everyone is already writing his own book called his life, and that is a very hard thing for you to bring to your conscious level, is it not?"

"I'm not sure," she said with some hesitancy, *"but what I'm talking about is the literal book that Max talked about."*

"Ah, yes, *the* book. That book already exists in Spirit. It is already in the 'out there' you like to call 'space.' Again, it is your choice to decide whether to give birth to *this* book...to accept the seed of inspiration and nurture it and give it life on your plane.

"For *this* book will come into your vibration of Earth through your mind and heart and soul instead of through your womb...and it is your choice to decide what form it will take. For it will bear *your* genetic blueprint...*your* DNA ...your *idea* of yourself and your experiences and your feelings about them.

"It will have *your* fingerprints all over it."

"But I'm afraid, I think, to relive some of my experiences...or at least some of the feelings and emotions I went through... and I'm having a hard time putting it all together... in focus."

"Do you remember your toy? The book you like to play with visually?"

"You know about that, too?

"I observe.

"To see beyond the one dimensional, flat picture, you have to keep your vision blurred and then slowly step back. Out of the blurring, the chaos, the *confusion* of your dimension, a New World will emerge for those who seek the vision."

"What about those who don't?"

"They may choose whatever they wish. They may start over, or they may not."

"What about those who don't even want to see a new image of the world and are satisfied to just see it in this dimension?"

"Then for them it will simply be a curious puzzle."

Trish noticed Stephanie's breathing shifting. Then slowly her eyes began to open, her movements matching those of someone rousing from sleep. When she seemed fully present again, Trish asked, "Do you remember anything about what was just said?"

"Just bits and pieces. Sometimes I remember most of it quite vividly...and at others I just get snatches of it...like...sort of like when you wake up from sleep and mostly remember the last part of your dream." After a few minutes, she stood up slowly. "Trish, let's go to the kitchen. You'll need to drink lots of water during this session. Your body is going to start shifting and releasing things, and you're going to need to flush out your system. In fact, we both need some water."

Trish raised her eyebrows slightly, and Stephanie added, "It has something to do with the electromagnetic energies in your body. Water is just a good conductor for it."

Chapter Forty-Four

After the break, Trish returned to the dialogue.

"Can we get back for a moment to the part about what you call delineations?"

"Indeed, All are truly One, as the ancients told you. You only make distinctions, delineations, separations, for your own purposes of coming to realization. You think you can draw boundaries on the land and possess it because it seems stable and you can mark it. But in your heart you know you cannot draw boundaries on Mother Nature. You cannot own the wind, and you cannot own the Spirit of Lightning. For they are aware that they belong to the All.

"Instead of standing humbled in the face of your Mother Earth, your feminine side, you continue to stand in your arrogance—your illusions—again and again. You may build your elaborate homes and mighty cities, and the cleansing, purifying Spirit of your Hurricane can come and wipe it away in minutes. The cleansing Spirit of Flood wipes clean everything in its path. You believe that you can superimpose false boundaries on yourselves and on your Earth, but those laws of your Nature, as you like to call them—and which you like to ignore—will continue in spite of what your governments and your people do or do not do in their unconscious states."

"But you make it sound like punishment if someone has his house destroyed."

"There is no punishment. There is no judgement. Nature does not judge. There is no separation. You *are* nature…and nature, the Earth, your special plane of vibration, is *you*. You may choose to experience the awesome power of nature, because it is but a reflection of your own true power. You become more alive when you face that power—your power. You experience fear to its fullest, excitement, awe and wonder. You come face to face with who you really are."

"Even if it kills you?"

"You cannot die. You are safe, always. You merely move to another vibration."

"I think I believe that on some level, but how does it happen?"

"Again, you change your molecular structure. You 'die' and are reborn with each breath and in each moment, dying to who you are and reborn to a new you. You are becoming. Nothing—no one—is constant, and the only thing constant is change, as you have heard many times."

"That's always sounded contradictory to me."

"It is meant to. It is a puzzle…and you like puzzles. You like to figure them out. Your curiosity is also a sacred gift."

"Look, if we have all this choice about our lives that you talk about, then why don't we just make our own lives easier?"

"Oh, you would be bored."

Trish grinned, knowing she'd always had a low threshold for boredom.

"You like challenges. Challenge is the exercise of spiritual growth for you. The greater the challenge, the greater the opportunity for spiritual strides. You call it 'crisis,' and if you do not have one handy, you will invent one. You like stretching your boundaries, your spiritual powers. Even a seeming ordinary and uneventful life may bring great inner conflict that challenges you. You are all on the verge...the verge of something magnificent, and it can be painful at times.

"The moments before any birth may be the most painful. That is why you call that birthing stage 'transition.' It is intense, but it is also short in duration. And then comes the time that a woman comes into her full power. Her body—the body of the Earth—your feminine side—brings her normally dormant state to the fore of her being to force the new birth that she has already dreamed to reality.

"And she dies a little to her old self as she gives herself new life, for she is both mother and child, father and midwife. She is the book you write. The beginning and the end. She is All. Always. You are mighty spiritual beings, and you give birth to mighty spiritual beings—whatever form they take— whether they be gods or monsters or whether you call them good or evil, Christ or anti-Christ, right or wrong, male or female, dark or light."

"If I do write this book—the one I'm thinking about—how will I know if I get it right?"

"There is no right or wrong...but it is not for you to worry. You may be patient. You have no need for rushing. You do not require what you perceive as perfection. Always you are seeking perfection...but it is only your illusion of perfection that you seek. You maintain your illusion of perfection just as you maintain your illusions about darkness—just as you seek a perfect world— or your illusion of a perfect world."

"So, how do we find perfection?"

"You already *are* perfect. Every act, every breath, every word, every fiber of your being is perfect. You are God's children, and God is love. *You* are love. Though you do not know it consciously."

"And the perfect world?"

"You create your world every day, and it, too, is perfect. Look at your world from your outer space. Is that not perfection? Are you not beautiful? Do you not take your breath away?"

"You make it sound as though we don't have to strive for anything—to do anything."

"You do not. You do not have to do anything. All choice, as always, is yours…and your world may not change at all, only your perception of it. You might go about your life as you did before—only you might be a little happier, more joyful, as you begin to discover yourself—to know who you truly are. Or you may change your life—your world—completely, and that, too, you may be doing in joy."

"So what keeps us from enjoying our lives completely now?"

"Your lack of love for yourselves. If you could but see yourselves as *I* see you, you would experience the greatest 'falling in love' that you could imagine. You speak of bells ringing when you fall in love with another. Well, you would hear the music of the spheres, if you would only give yourself permission to love yourselves—if you could only enjoy the pleasure of your own company. *Then* you would live in joy and love."

"Mm," Trish responded with skepticism. *"I don't know about that."*

"That is because you do not think you deserve joy. So you push it away when you think you have had your share. There is no share. There is no limit…not for you…not for anyone. You do not deprive any other of their share, if you take too much. There is no limit to any feeling you feel.

"When you have rested and grown enough in your rich backwater depression, you may choose to surge forward again at whatever speed you choose. You may leap the waterfall or just *be* as in the stillness of the lake. You may even choose to change your form completely, seeming to ascend into vapor toward the clouds to join other souls. And the world, your world—your friends, your enemies, your weather, your environment—will arrange itself to support you in the moods, the experiences, the life you choose to have."

"And if we lived in joy and love, our choices might change?"

"They might. And they might not. You might go to your work or school or play as you did before and look and seem exactly the same.

"But the divine in the people around you would notice the twinkle in your eye."

"Then if we are children of God, and God is love, and we are love, then are you saying we are gods?"

"Did your Christed one not say, 'Ye are gods'? Did he not sacrifice to bring you that message? As your Jo Ann asked, when you take so much of your Bible so literally, why do you not take that part literally, as well?"

"I don't take the Bible literally."

"I know…but you take your life literally."

"Not as much as I used to."

"I know."

Trish sat a moment, staring at Stephanie.

"Ah…I don't know where to go from here."

"The choice is yours."

She continued to sit quietly.

"Why do you hesitate? You may ask me anything."

"I know. I guess I'm afraid of what you might answer."

Stephanie—or Freya—laughed a lusty laugh.

The impasse was broken, as Trish joined in the laughter.

• • •

"Okay, okay," Trish finally began when she'd regained her composure, *"Then we're children of God. So are we also children of the goddess?"*

"Indeed, you are...though you have forgotten that for a time, for an age."

"People aren't going to find that very palatable."

"That is because they have been thinking with their left brain so long—their masculine side—as you already know."

"Yeah, Max and I talked about that."

"Well, for logical creatures who enjoy your left brain, you have not been very logical."

"How so?"

"Does it fit your logic to think that only male can give birth? Do you know many male creatures in your world that can give birth alone? Even your creatures that *can* birth alone have both male and female parts. If God is your creator, and you are his children, would he have produced offspring that suddenly required female to produce? Why would he have need of female? Where is your logic in that? Where is your science in that? Where is your 'reality' in that?"

"I...I don't know. I never thought about it like that before."

"Well, think about it, if you will...and, if you will, you might discover that you are using your right brain a little more." Trish smiled. "That is all right. You use yours more than others."

After a pause, Freya added, "But take care not to be *all* right, if you seek balance in your life."

"Huh?"

"If you seek balance, take care not to *re*act by sacrificing your left brain—your masculine side. You need both your masculine and feminine energies to be in balance as the creatures you truly are. Your Max was correct on that one. Have you not sacrificed enough of yourselves already—enough of your women?"

"Sacrificed our women?"

"Yes, by burning them and attempting to sacrifice that part of yourselves at the stakes."

"Yes. We did that, didn't we? Trish glanced across the room and back again. *"Why did we do that?"*

"You did it for the experience. You wanted to explore that region—that masculine side of yourselves completely...and to do so required cutting off yourselves, and so, your God, from the feminine...forgetting for a time that part of yourselves. You had to demonize your Eve...your Goddess...your female.

"In other times you have sacrificed and demonized and cut yourselves off from your masculine, as well."

"Well, if we're so perfect like you say, how is that perfect?"

"There is no judgement. You did it for the experience—to experience the depth and breadth of each of the sides that you perceive as your duality. It was part of the journey. It has brought you to this point, your center point, if you chose."

"But I'm not sure people today would believe in a goddess. For sure, some don't believe in God."

"That is all right with me. Is it not all right with you?"

"Well, yeah, sure. I mean, I don't care whether people believe in God or not."

"Indeed. At one time you did not believe in your God."

"Oh, yeah, in college," she said with a little embarrassment.

"That is 'all right' with me, as well. It is your free will to believe what you choose. Your doubts—or what you considered your loss of faith—were merely doubts and a loss of faith in your world's *perception* of your God. You were beginning, even then, to see your divinity with new eyes.

"As Freya, I continue to 'be,' whether any choose to believe in me or not...for that is also their choice. It might make their existence more pleasant, however, if they truly believed in themselves—and not just their illusions of who they are. For one cannot truly 'be,' unless he believes in himself."

"You make it sound like we can't make any mistakes no matter what we do... like our choices don't really matter."

"Of course, your choices matter. 'Matter' is the only thing that does not matter...but in your minds it is the only thing that does matter.

"Your thoughts, your ideas, your decisions are the form—or imprint—of what you think of as matter. Those choices carry you on your life's path, and that path can lead in an unlimited number of directions at any point. They give form to what you think of as reality. But, however straight or winding or short or long or easy or circuitous that path is, it always brings you back to yourself. Your destination is always your starting point. The journey is merely the adventure of your free will.

"Do you remember how enchanted some of your people became with the movie you called 'Free Willy'?"

"Yes, but, now, I didn't see it."

"It does not matter." Trish picked up on the pun and smiled. "Ah, you 'caught' that one. It was indeed a big one." Trish grinned wider.

"Well, you 'caught' enough of your whale story to know that he symbolized free will in the subconscious of your people. Your free will has been locked up. *You* have locked it up…and you cheered—we all cheered—when the whale escaped his bonds. The reason you were so emotional was because he symbolized the breaching of the bonds of the most sacred of all the gifts of humanity—free will!"

"I never thought of that analogy before."

"Well, curious thing—the real whale from your movie is still held captive by humanity. Some of you believe that humanity still cannot be trusted with free will…that you still need bonds to restrain you. You can never fully experience the sacred gift of free will until you honor that gift for everyone else—for all of the aspects of who you are.

"You said we are gods. But if that's true, we've done some pretty ungodly things during the atomic age with the atomic bomb."

"Do your scientists not talk about your 'Big Bang?"

"Yeah."

"They are merely attempting to recreate what is in their unconscious remembering—from their beginnings—their source on this plane. In a sense it was a sacred desire."

"Yeah? Well, they nuked the whole friggin' planet in the process."

"They did. And, indeed at one time your radiation was used for healing purposes, rather than destruction."

"Are you talking about fission and fusion again?"

"In your sense."

"I'm lost here… and I'm not a scientist, but they say they haven't had any real success in creating fusion in the labs, as yet."

"What is their intention? Remember your true cause and effect in your plane. What you infuse into a thing is what you get out. Are they working in their laboratories from love or from greed or from frustration? In your deeds, if you consciously came from love, you would not even need your laboratories or your scientists to create what you term 'fusion.' The ancients used uranium—your radiation—for great healing, renewal of energy and information at their sacred spots—long before your scientists ever appeared on your plane."

"How did they do it?"

"They willed it through intention, and allowed it. It was manifested through them. At one time only your priests or shamans or medicine men conducted these ceremonies. But all of you may do it—as you will—for All are One…and All are mighty spirits."

"So was the Big Bang theory really the beginning of the earth?"

"The All was the One. And the One suffered in a great loneliness, a void and a darkness. It split itself apart in a brilliant explosion of separation—your 'Big Bang'—and created galaxies, worlds, all peopled with beings, and on many levels of what you term 'space.' You think you are alone because you have chosen to feel alone in your plane for your purposes."

"But we're not?"

"Indeed not."

Trish smiled. *"I didn't think so."*

"Some of you have begun to allow this knowing to enter your consciousness—for it no longer serves your purpose to feel alone."

"And the purpose?"

"To remember who you truly are. For how may you remember unless first you forget?"

She let out a breath. She was back to Old Tom's words again. Full circle. It was time to pause and orient herself again. The dialogue was moving rapidly. Maybe that was the point.

• • •

After a few moments, Trish looked at the pad beside her with the totally abandoned questions on it, then looked up and said, *"Okay, then. Let me pick this up again. We're creators of our world..."*

"*Many* worlds—the ones you dream, the ones you imagine, the ones you desire and the ones you run from."

"Now, that sounds like the Dreamtime the Aborigines talk about. But, if we create so many worlds, how does it go on?" I mean, it has to end somewhere."

"Do your scientists not speculate about your expanding universe?"

"Will it all come back together again at some point?"

"Just as there is an expansion outward, there is also the breathing in—the returning to source. Some call it a black hole. Others call it darkness and void...but there is breathing in and breathing out. There is death and there is birth. There is creation and there is destruction."

"Can we heal the radioactive wounds on the earth from all the bombings and the wastes?"

"I have said, as destructive as you have been, you may be healing, as well."

"If we have all this ability to heal, how do we go about healing the earth?"

"To access your abilities to heal the Earth—for they are many—you must first access your feminine nature. Because your intellect and your technologies have brought your Earth plane to such a wounded state, you believe

478

that your intellect and technologies alone may heal those wounds. But your Earth plane now requires an entirely different level of cleansings for her massive wounds. For her massive wounds are but a reflection of your own *in*ternal and sometimes *ex*ternal wounds that have been inflicted as a result of ignoring and denying an aspect of your Spiritual nature; therefore, you have brought yourselves unconsciously to the point of requiring your Spiritual nature to heal your Earth plane, and in so doing, bringing yourself more fully to your consciousness, or awareness.

"It is a method you have employed, a path you have chosen unconsciously to lead you to who you truly are. The path is one of love for nature, and thus, love for your own nature…for your 'nature' is merely your nature. Your Earth reflects you as the moon reflects the Sun. To look upon the Sun is too bright for your Earth eyes, but your moon behaves as a 'transducer' so you may look upon it in awe and wonder with ease. To look upon your God self is also too bright for your Earth eyes at this time, so you may look upon your reflection of nature in awe and wonder with ease, and you may glimpse your own nature.

"You have brought yourselves to the point of requiring spiritual development in order to save your physical environment. You have—as you say—painted your self into that corner unconsciously…and you may not walk out of it. You may *levitate* your way out of it. For, indeed, you have always had that ability and many others, though you have not been aware of it consciously."

Trish squirmed in her seat. *"So, how do we start accessing these abilities you say we have, like healing the earth?"*

"By recognizing and honoring the Goddess that lives inside each of you. To heal and nurture that neglected side of yourselves is to heal and nurture your Earth. To heal the neglected side of your Earth is to heal and nurture yourselves.

"Your nurturing, creative, mystical aspects of your nature, in balance with your probing, logical, destructive aspects of your nature will bring back balance to the forces of your Earth nature…the harmony and exquisite balance that your spiritual nature seeks."

"I guess I'm asking more for specifics," she said.

"You have a difficult time accepting and acknowledging your powers. You fear that if you use them in an unaware state, you will misuse them and create what you see as havoc in your world. But, have you not already created what you see as havoc in your world? Have you not already brought your world to your brinks of 'disaster?' Have you anything left to lose?

"To become aware of what you call your 'specifics' for healing your Earth, you must allow that awareness to come into your consciousness. First invite it in to your conscious levels, and then allow it to enter. Knock on the door, and it will open. Put forth your desire into the universe and the universe will respond.

"If you will, use the method this one uses. Stephanie pointed to herself. "For there are many methods...many 'specifics'...many paths. There are those on your Earth who are already consciously using their powers to heal it and its people. If it were not so, you would have already wiped out *vast* numbers of your race. If you seek out these teachers, they will come into your lives in a variety of ways to assist you...for as long as you require their assistance...for as long as it takes you to accept the power that is already yours.

"You are focused on physical healing, but there is much more at stake here than your physical survival. Because you are so focused on physical survival, because it has your attention, you are forcing yourselves to use your spiritual aspects—to develop your spiritual nature—in order to salvage your physical bodies. And in the process of that awakening, your physical bodies will also awaken, evolve and mutate to a more spiritual form...one that will both give and receive on a spiritual level...one that will communicate with Spirit...one that will be One with Spirit...the Holy—Wholly Spirit."

"How many people would it take to heal the earth?"

"One."

"Just one?"

"One person with consciousness.

"One person with his finger on what you call 'the button' may *destroy* your world as you know it, in *un*consciousness. Is that not one person? There is much that you have not discovered with your research—many more 'accidents' in your atomic age."

"That doesn't surprise me in the least."

"And there have been many more of what you term 'rescues' or 'salvations' in your atomic age, as well. There have been many individuals who have stepped forward in your time and saved your world...again, as you know it. They are not in your awareness at this time, but you will see them in time, and you will know the full power of 'one' through their eyes and their experiences."

Trish's curiosity was piqued. *"Then there were some real heroes during the Cold War?"*

"Indeed. And how may you *be* heroes—experience yourselves at your best—if you do not have what you call villains to reflect you? This, too, is a great sacrifice.

"You have more power in one of your little fingers than in all your atomic bombs. 'One' with consciousness is powerful beyond imagination. Two are more powerful...and a circle of 'ones' is powerful beyond comprehension in the space you think you inhabit. *This* is the nature of the power you possess.

"Already a 'one' has come forward in your history, and he has sacrificed himself, both for his comrades and for his enemies—for his world—for *your* world. He believed consciously that his actions were the result of an order he had to obey—that he had no choice. But, in truth, he was born—he *chose* to be born—at an exact point of time and place in order to fulfill his mission of sacrifice. In an act of love, that one has already saved your world from your 'mutually assured destruction.' Several 'ones' have already saved your world, though you do not know it.

"You may, indeed, be healers. You have *been* healers. You *are* healers, as well as destroyers—for that, too, is your nature."

"But how do we do it? How do we become healers?"

"You dream it. You drum it. You draw it. You shape it. You sing it. You dance it. And you sculpt it. *That* will make it come alive for you, as well as for others."

"How does that work?"

"Water is what you call your symbol for emotions...and just as water provides a barrier to your radiation, so, too, may your emotions provide a shield, or protection, from what you consider to be detrimental effects of radiation."

"Hmm. A good motivation for getting in touch with your emotions, huh?"

"With the intensity of your emotions, or, as your friend Max called it, the depth of emotion."

"Wait a minute. You said 'what we consider to be detrimental effects of radiation.' What are the positive effects of radiation exposure?"

"Your world was *bathed* in radiation at its beginning. It was immersed in unbelievable amounts of radiation—much more than in all of your atomic bombs together. It is your breeding ground. You—all of you—*sprang* from it. You could not have existed without it.

"Even now, during your cooling period, it still shapes your evolution. You are constantly evolving—or 'mutating.' Intricately measured amounts of radiation have constantly entered your Earth bodies for all of your eons. It is your Father's power—your Sun god—tempered by your Mother's grounding—your Earth Mother.

"On your Earth plane there is knowledge held in stone. Your stones have stories to tell. One stone in particular holds ancient memory and power. You call it Uranium. It is rich with the blood of the god, Uranus, from the beginning of your creation. It is through the process of intention that one accesses the ancient knowledge held in this stone. Again, as a child you were not contaminated by that stone you kept by your bed. You loved it. Because you did, your dormant ancient memories, or genes, were implanted with an activation which could awaken it at an appropriate time in your future. Your trigger point for activation was at the clinic."

"An activation was implanted in me from the rock? How?"

"Parts of your nature are represented in nature. As air represents ideas and water represents emotions, so parts of your body correspond or align with parts of the body of the Earth. Stones are the bones of the Earth."

"Yeah, now that you mention it, I read that once in a Greek myth."

"Medicine men and women from your world perform rock grinding initiations in which the rock speaks to them, sings to them, answers questions, shows them glimpses of the past, or of other realities. This is ancient wisdom. Stones are as a library in the sands of time. And so, the stones—or bones of the body of the Earth—align with the bones of your own body. There, too, in your bones, knowledge—or what you call 'data'—is held."

"Interesting concept."

"Do some of you not say, 'I just know it in my bones'?"

"We do, don't we?"

"Indeed. You just know in your bones that you know in your bones." Trish smiled.

"It is through the process of intention that one accesses ancient information or knowledge held in stone and bone. Certain isotopes from your uranium have been taken up into your bones through your food chain and are also activated by a process known as intention. Your altar of intention resides at a place you call your thymus gland, between your heart and throat. Drum it lightly, again, with intention, to activate this process within you. With focus on your intention, you transmute the original intent of using uranium to war against your other selves—or fellow man—into an intention of loving your other selves, of informing and awakening within the birthright of your human species.

"You are transmuted into a cosmic species with access to, not only your Earthly plane of existence, but other realms, or kingdoms, or dimensions of existence that you have only dreamed of. The Christ consciousness within you is not a kingdom of the Earth plane until you bring your heaven to Earth. This is ancient wisdom. You have done this before, for you have dreamed it into your future. Look at the feast you have set before yourselves. Partake of it. Savor it. All of it. What you call dark and light, feminine and masculine, left and right, yin and yang, good and bad, all of it. For you are, indeed, all one. Aspects of all that is…omnipresent, omniperfect. All truth is held in paradox so that you may know who you are. Ye are gods."

Stephanie fell silent, and Trish simply stared at her. All she could think was, *My God.* She felt like a miner who'd just come upon a huge vein of gold. Or in this case, uranium. But what to do with it? Where did she go from here? She took a few moments again to catch her breath.

• • •

When she had the presence to formulate another question, Trish asked, *"But aren't some of us getting too much radiation now?"*

"You are still 'getting' exactly as much as you need. You are getting enough to bring forth the message that you need or desire to hear at such a time as this."

"The message of the gods, huh?" She paused. *"Will we hear it?"*

"If you will. For all is your will. For you are both the messenger and the receiver of that message. And you are the message."

"But, in large enough dose, radiation kills people, for Christ's sake."

"People may indeed be killed for Christ's sake. But they—their spirits—may never be harmed. They—you—are safe always."

"Okay, but in the physical state we can be hurt."

"In the physical state, if you are in true balance with the love of your universe—your being—you may receive any amount of radiation with no harm. You may drink poisons and take up deadly snakes and come to no harm."

"I find that hard to believe."

"As do most of you. That is why it would be well not to attempt such things in your present states of disbelief."

"Do you think people want to give birth to mutated, deformed babies because of radiation exposure?"

"Not consciously. And I do not think anything. I merely reflect, as all others around you reflect you, as the moon reflects the sun. The people you speak of have chosen their path on a spiritual level. It is not for you or me or even for them to judge from an unconscious state. All things become clear in their time."

"You say not to be in judgment. And I know the Bible says, 'Judge not, lest ye be judged.' But what about Judgment Day? We were raised on this concept."

"Your perceptions of 'Judgment Day' will shift as your vision becomes clearer—your focus softer…and what you perceived as bad—or good—will come into balance.

"What you perceive as positive and negative—and what you judge as good and bad is no more good or bad than the positive and negative polarities of your world that hold it in balance. They are merely the opposing forces that, in truth, hold your world—your lives together."

"I want to get back to something you said about 'intricately received…'"

"measured…"

"Okay…measured amounts of radiation in order to evolve to a certain point?"

"To a point of receiving a message."

"Explain that."

"You are constantly evolving on many levels, and you are intimately involved in this process. You—many of you—have chosen to be at a point of your Second Coming, when the Christ consciousness will enter your bodies. One way for this to happen may be through radiation exposure. The exact amount of what you call radiation—or sun energy—can allow this process to occur on the physical level in an accelerated manner, if that is your intention.

"At one time you communicated with the Spirit world—what your scientists call 'waves'—on a constant basis. This communication took place through your fontanel—your soft spot. It never closed. But when you chose to forget, to lose faith, you physically hardened your fontanel. You became 'hardheaded', stubborn, and you denied the World of Spirit.

"To reconnect your physical with your Spirit—to understand what your scientists call wave *and* particle, you must soften, both your heart *and* your head, your thoughts *and* your emotions. This change will occur on your spirit level through increased levels of sun energy, and will be manifested on your physical level in the restructuring of your DNA or genetic codes."

"Will this happen to everyone?"

"Only those who choose."

"And the rest?"

"Those may sacrifice themselves—their lineage, their blood lines and their blueprints—if their genetic materials will not conform to the necessary *physical* requirements of the new human species that is evolving."

"That sounds awfully grim."

"It is not as you think 'grim.' Is there any greater love than this: to lay down one's life for one's fellow man? And this is not the only existence that they may choose. It only seems like the only existence because you have forgotten all else save this. You—all of you—are safe always. And all of you have choices."

"But do other existences also have free will?"

"If you chose to gift yourselves with it. You may also choose a very structured existence with no chance for variation—one without 'bumps in the road,' or challenges or crises."

"That sounds somehow dull to me."

"Then you probably would choose otherwise."

"If we stay here on earth, and we choose to begin communicating directly with spirit, what will it be like?"

"It also will be as you choose. You may choose to experience the individual mind, as you do at this time. You may also choose to experience the group mind. What Jung called the 'collective unconscious,' may become the 'collective awareness.' And it may not be limited to your present belief of boundaries of the human mind.

"For, if you choose, you may become as birds flying through the air as one, turning and soaring in unison on the wind. You may become as fish flowing and darting together with the currents of your oceans. And you may encompass more—much more. For you may become the very waters flowing over smooth pebbles. You may be the sound of it and the force of it. You may be the lightness of the air on cloudless, warm days and the power of a cleansing, spiraling hurricane.

"You may become the joy of flames, dancing, collapsing and then reaching again and again from source to source. You may be the silence of the still dawn that listens and watches as the autumn leaves sing their colors to the world.

"You may be the warm Earth that cradles the seed in its womb for whatever cycle the seed wishes to become. And you may be the very stars and the star light, the fragrance of the lily, and the color of the violet, the sound of the moon rising and of a single raindrop on a single leaf."

Trish let out a slow breath and said, *"That was beautiful."*

"It will be, indeed. And all that is required of you is to knock at the door…and it will be opened."

"How do we knock?"

"Listen. Do you hear it? It is the sound of your heart beating in your chest."

Trish sat for a moment and became aware of the pulsing in her heart. The pulsing sound grew slowly stronger and louder. The force of it extended into her veins and into her fingertips and her toes—into the top of her head and her ears—stronger and stronger. It seemed to penetrate into the sofa, even into the earth below the floor of the house. She felt as though she was pulsating in unison with the earth.

And then almost as quickly as she felt it, the surprise of it made it slip away. Trish took a deep breath. *"Wow! What was that?"*

"It was a glimpse of your connection to the universe—a promise and a hope of greater things than you have ever dreamed in this life."

"How do I get that feeling back?"

There was a stillness in the room. Then Freya said, "As I have said, water is your symbol for emotions, for your feelings, your feminine. When water is flowing freely on the Earth, there are no straight lines. Its nature is to meander—to turn back on itself. But always it moves forward, as your emotional life moves forward. You may damn up the nature of your emotions, as you damn up your water. And you may re-channel it. But always it returns to its own nature—to the true Spirit of water.

"It may take a long time, in the way you measure time; however—as with emotion that has been held back for too long—it will burst forth, as your feminine aspect will burst forth when it has been held back for too long.

"To reconnect with that feminine energy into your whole, holy being, you must allow it—your emotions—to flow freely...and forward, ever forward. When the energy of your emotions takes you somewhere you must allow yourself to follow it, if you choose this path.

"You must remember this aspect of your goddess nature in order to move into conscious co-creation."

It was time for another "breather," and, as if sensing it, Stephanie sat quietly as Trish tried to absorb the previous comments.

● ● ●

After a few more moments, Trish picked up with her spontaneous questions again.

"When you talk about our merging with water and about our being energy..."

"Streams of energy."

"Okay, streams of energy."

"That is your energy in motion—your thoughts with your feelings—your E-motion, your energy *and* your emotion. That is who you are."

"If that's true, then theoretically shouldn't we be able to walk through walls?"

"You *do* in other realities. In other realities you walk through mountains."

Trish thought of the various world myths about spirits living in mountains.

"For in other realities you do not experience your mountains as solid. You see them as an extension of the same energy of which you are composed. You make no distinctions, no delineations. So you move through them."

"Then how do you keep your energy from merging with, say, the mountain or wall?"

"You *may* merge with the mountains and walls...and you do that, as well, at times. But you may also hold your form—your energy—together in a thought form. For thought *is* energy. You are holding yourself together and yet apart from your surroundings with a thought form now—in this moment, in this lifetime—with your beliefs."

"But if spirit is everywhere, why do we have doors for it to enter? Isn't it already everywhere?"

"Spirit does not require doors. *You* require doors to accommodate your present belief systems. And Spirit honors your beliefs of separation, which you have adopted with your free will."

"So, if we just changed our beliefs we could walk through doors and

mountains."

"To change your belief is a scary thought for you. Your current beliefs have held your world as you know it together."

"But the world is out of balance now."

"It is. And your mythical beings are a sign of that time."

"So, why did we do it?"

"You did it to 'shake things up'—as you say—to challenge your ideas about your world. You took great risk to be more alive, to feel more alive, to experience yourselves as more than you have believed you were."

Trish felt like a small child. *"It's hard to imagine walking through mountains."*

"You are 'imagining' the world you live in now, and it is more of a fairy tale than what you call fairy tales. It is a beautiful tale, and you have enjoyed it—as we have enjoyed it. But when you are no longer living in joy, you begin to risk your beliefs—your world, as you know it and experience it—in order to discover a new world, a new you…the Christ consciousness of which we speak.

"And as that prototype emerges in you, you may, indeed, walk through mountains and walk on water. You may even move mountains."

"With the faith of a mustard seed?"

"The seed, the idea, combined with feeling—emotion—your energy revealed—your faith."

"Blind faith?"

"True faith is anything but blind. It merely refuses to see with the vision you have chosen for your existence on this plane. Its sight is guided by the vision of trust that sees *no* obstacles in its path, that knows *no* boundaries to its goal, that does not even limit *itself* to the destination it believes it seeks.

"You all have this vision. Most of you only let it come up in times of chaos or crisis or extraordinary loss, and sometimes not even then. A few of you allow it to come up in moments of great joy. But whenever you allow it, and however you glimpse it, it is also always your choice."

"You talk about all this control we have over our lives. But if we do, why do we feel so out of control so much of the time?"

"You *are* in control. It is your illusion of control that brings you frustration."

"So what is the illusion of control?"

"It is the illusion that you can make things happen. You cannot force anything to happen. Much of the time when you cannot force a thing to happen, you simply give up and move on—change your direction. But at other times when your determination carries you further, you try to force harder. You push with all of your seeming might, all of your conscious thought. And the harder you try, the further the goal slips away. The goal becomes unreachable—the object unmovable."

"So if we want something, how do we get it, if we really are in control?"

"You allow it."

"But how do we allow it? I'm not sure I know what that means."

"That is the easiest part. It is to do nothing. It is simply to receive."

"Receive?"

"Indeed. How do you receive a gift from a friend?"

"Well, I just accept it."

"And you have choice about accepting it, do you not?"

"I guess so. But how do I accept the kinds of gifts we're talking about?"

"By creating an opening for the gift to be received."

"What kind of an opening?"

"An opening of the heart—an opening of feeling—a gratitude, an acceptance, an allowing. To receive your gifts, you both give and receive them. You allow. You know how to put your desires forth. You have honed your masculine side very well, indeed. But you are still struggling. You are not what you call happy, fulfilled, because you still deny much of your feminine, receptive side. Even your females deny much of their feminine side.

"Your answers, your desires will come if you allow them. You release your false control—you allow it to leave—for you even try to control your control. Then you put forth your desire, your goal, your question. Know that it will be received, fulfilled, answered. Forget about it, if you will. Let it go. Allow.

"Nothing happens without your will. You *are* in control—the Spirit of you—the All of you."

"Is it really that easy?"

"It is easy, but not within the framework of your ideas about your life. If you allow your old frameworks or support systems to expand beyond their present constructs, you will see just how easy it can be."

"If we're so powerful... if I'm so powerful, why can't I just blink my eyes and suddenly create a beautiful mansion or luxury car out of thin air?"

"You can. You create *worlds* out of what you call thin air. But *your* world would not seem real to you if you suddenly defied your 'laws of nature' and 'laws of science,' your self-constructed boundaries that support your particular world of illusion.

"But you may, indeed, 'create' a beautiful mansion or luxury car *within* the framework of your laws of time and effort. If you suddenly bypassed your laws of science and created them in one of your 'instants,' you might have trouble explaining them to your IRS, which you have also created."

"But we can do it, right?"

"You can do anything you truly believe you can. And you do much more than you know. As I said, you have more power—more energy—in one of your little fingers than in all of your atomic bombs, though you do not know it."

Trish rubbed the side of her face. Where did she go from here? She sensed she was experiencing the chance of a lifetime, but wasn't sure if she was taking proper advantage of it. She rested her chin on her hand and thought.

• • •

After a few moments, Trish asked, *"Why are we so destructive?"*

"That, too, is part of your nature. As *human* beings, you must tear down in order to build anew. You must bear pain in order to give new life. As human beings, you must destroy who you *are,* in order to become a new being. You cannot escape your self-constructed bonds—your idea frameworks—without breaking them."

"But all destruction can't be good."

"Always, you are in judgment. This is who you were and are…and are becoming. You are a process—not a thing. As many have said, you are a verb, not a noun.

"You have gone to that razor's edge and danced on it many times before. You have risked that dance of destruction—going to the edge of who you think you are—the edge of the world, which once you believed to be flat and now believe to be round, because you are ready to explore the new regions of who you truly are.

"Would you leave the idea of your nice, warm womb of Earth without labor, without pain, without transition?"

"But do we have to destroy the earth in the process?"

"You will not destroy your Earth…only the Earth as you know and experience it in your particular vibrational field. Your Earth—your Mother—has choice, has consciousness, as well as you. And in her consciousness she would not allow her children—her species of children—to be completely annihilated. All of her creatures from all of your 'time' live in Spirit—a vibrational world, or frequency, of Spirit—from her dinosaurs to the species of plants and animals that you believe you are destroying en masse, at this period of 'time.'

"Your Noah's Ark is a safe harbor for the genetic blueprints of all of your Earth's creatures.

"Just as your body will send the tiniest of its creatures to fight any part of it that threatens the whole, so the body of your Earth will fight and destroy any part of it that threatens its whole.

"Earth is creative as well as destructive. *It* has feminine and masculine aspects, as well."

"You make it sound as though the Earth and humanity are separate now."

"You *believe* you are separate, but just as the viruses and bacteria and white corpuscles and red corpuscles of your body, work to protect *your* whole, with creative and destructive aspects, so those aspects work silently and unseen to protect your species."

"The earth's destructive aspects... Is that what we're seeing now? Are we at the end of one world and the beginning of another, like the Indian prophecies say?"

"You are, indeed, at the end of one vibrational existence and the beginning of another. That is why your mutants—your gods—are appearing at this time. This is their message. They always appear at such a time as this."

"Will there be massive deaths during this period? Are we talking about... well, Armageddon type deaths?"

"In the world as you know it—it may require massive 'deaths' to protect your species—though no one truly dies. Your Armageddon has many names and it will be, it *is,* many things to many people. Many of your myths speak of these times. You are correct in your belief that your atomic age was prophesied in your myths and legends and Bible. But you have been limited in your understanding of it.

"One of your Indian myths speaks of a red serpent and a white serpent fighting until they can fight no more—until the rivers boil with dead fish. Then a black serpent comes and defeats them both. He then turns to the people who are left, but is frightened away by the Light of the Great Teacher.

"These myths are both internal and external. The red and white corpuscles of your bodies may fight amongst themselves until dis-ease overtakes them both. The ones who are left, the ones who seek—the ones who knock at the door will be shielded from these dis-eases by the Light—by the blood of the Lamb—by the mutated DNA of the Cosmic Man—by the blood of your Christed One—the Enlightenment—the IN-LIGHT-IN-MEN—of *All* of your Enlightened Ones who have come before, from the four corners of your Earth— to show you the way, the truth and the Light.

"However, there are many ways to die. You may only have to die to who you think you are in order to be reborn. Or you may choose to die to the physical life, as you know it. It is your choice."

"You said we don't really die, and I think I believe that on some level, but this idea of just changing your minds to change your world. You make it sound so easy, in one way... "

"As your Jo Ann told you, changing your minds is not what you call 'easy.' Some would rather 'die' than change their minds. And some *are* risking death to change their minds, their brains. But, it is not necessary to do so. You may simply change your heart—your emotions—and your mind—your thoughts and your perceptions—will follow."

"How do you change your heart?"

"Open it."

"Open it?"

"Open the door to your heart. *That* is the door your Christed one spoke of when he said, 'Behold, I stand at the door and knock.'

"And many of you are also 'dying' to open the door—the heart. That is why you are having so many open-heart surgeries. You are attacking your own hearts—risking your own deaths—in order to open the heart. The body is merely the physical manifestation of the soul. It is truly the temple of the soul.

"But you may open your heart without surgery, if you choose. It *may* require pain—pain of loss, or *fear* of loss. For you can lose nothing. You are part of the All.

"You may also choose to open your heart without pain."

"Without pain? How?"

"Open it in love."

"I don't know. Sometimes love hurts."

"Not true love. Only your *idea* of love hurts"

"So, what is true love? And how do you find it?"

"By accepting all of life as sacred—all of it—and not judging what you call good and bad, light and dark. Knowing yourselves as sacred beings. Knowing your *self* as sacred, as well as human, and loving yourself. For if you love yourself, then you have *found* love, for you *are* love. God is love, and you are Children of God, Beings of Light and Love, mighty spiritual beings.

"You open your heart to your Christed being, willingly. And he—your Christed self—will enter. This is what you speak of with your Second Coming. You thought he would come as a conqueror into your physical plane with sword in hand at the head of an army of men to slay your enemies—or those you perceived as enemies. But He only enters your consciousness through your will, through your allowing, through your feminine, receptive, emotional side. He does not force himself on any one—as many of your religions seek to do. He (you) do not conquer; you only surrender yourself."

"If the Christ consciousness is already within us, why does it have to enter through a door? Wouldn't it just be awakened in us, if we make that choice to accept it?"

"If you make that choice to accept—or allow—your Cosmic birthright, you will *become* the portal through which you enter...*after* you have created the empty space—the void—in your lives for the gift of yourselves. The *concept* you have of your lives is one which still includes doors, windows, boundaries. And your concepts must be honored throughout your unfolding as long as they serve your purposes…as long as you require them.

"Certainly, the people of the day of your Christed One, the Buddha, Krishna, Mohammed and all of your Enlightened Ones perceived boundaries and limits and delineations, just as they perceived a flat world with edges. Therefore, their messages were framed within those perceptions; their gifts were wrapped within those idea constructions. As your perceptions expand, so, too, will your internal messages, or rememberings.

"Your Cosmic DNA may *well* be awakened, as the sleeping seed that awakens in the warm Earth after a season of winter dormancy. It may fully blossom from within in the twinkling of an eye. But, as within, so without. As without, so within. You are your inner being , and you are your outer being. You are the 'you' you perceive, and you are those you perceive as others. If you perceive your Christ(ed Being) as other than yourself, then he (you) may, indeed, enter into you. If you can perceive your Christ(ed DNA) as an aspect of yourself, and not separate, then you may awaken from within to who you truly are."

"Then can we heal the earth?"

"You may heal your Earth, as well as yourselves, for, as I said, as destructive as you have been, you may be as healing, as well…for the nature of healing is focused love. You may turn your beam onto whatever pain you perceive, and you may heal. For pain is only your *perception* of a lack of love. In reality, there is no lack of love…for God is love…and love is everywhere.

"The Buddha was once threatened with death by a bandit, but he requested a dying wish. He asked the bandit to sever a branch from a nearby tree. The bandit drew his sword and complied. He then asked, 'Now, what?' And the Buddha replied, 'Now, put it back.'

"The bandit laughed and said that he must think him crazy, to which the Buddha replied that he must *be* crazy to believe that it was mighty to wound and destroy—that *that* was the task of children. He said that the *mighty* know how to create and to heal.

"As a Cosmic Being you may create and heal and restore beyond your imaginings as God's creatures. You have always had this power. You have simply chosen to separate yourselves from the All—from God—by creating your perceptions of pain and time and bodies and worlds.

"You did this to see yourselves from different eyes. How else may you see yourself and know yourself and appreciate the grandeur of who you truly are? You are the mirror you hold up to you. You are your own reflection. You hold up your mirror to those you perceive to be others, as well…for you are *their* reflection, as they are yours. You support each other's perceptions for your purposes—your intentions."

"And we can return to our source at any time we wish."

"It is so. And you may journey to other of your worlds, as well, at any time. And you do. As I said and say again, you change your molecular structures all of your 'time'...by simply shifting your perceptions. You do this in what you call your Dreamtime. And that, too, seems 'real'—as this world seems real."

"Is this world real?"

"As real as you believe it to be. Look to your children's song that your Jo Ann heard at one of her awakenings: 'Merrily, merrily, merrily, merrily, life is but a dream.'"

Stephanie gave an audible exhalation of air and began to stir, then slowly began opening her eyes.

Trish was grateful.

Since it was approaching lunchtime, Stephanie suggested they have a light meal. "First of all, though, we need to go take a walk. You're getting a lot of information, evidently. And the best way to integrate it is to do something physical. I think we *both* need it."

Chapter Forty-Five

After the walk and lunch, the two returned to the sunroom and resumed their positions.

"Okay," Trish began, *"I want to talk about this time thing. I know it's supposed to be an illusion, but I just don't get it."*

"It, too, is a puzzle you have created. There was time when there was no time. All simply was and is and will be.

"Completing your illusion of separateness also required an illusion of time. You began putting things in boxes, frameworks, boundaries. To experience yourselves as separated parts of your whole, you had to create a framework—a form—a body to 'be' in, a *space* in which to move…and a time, which you could measure. Any 'time' you measure something, you limit it— give it boundaries. These are the boundaries of your known world."

"It's still confusing."

"That is because you have done your job well with your creation of time.

"Do you know how some will speak of experiencing a serious trauma or meaningful event, and say it was as though time stood still?"

Trish immediately recalled Old Tom's finger on her forehead. *"Yes."*

"That is a sacred moment, for in that moment you are so fully 'into' the emotion that no other thing exists for you, and you have escaped the bonds of time."

"Are you saying that if we were always fully into our emotions, we could 'escape' the bonds of time?"

"*And* of space, *and* of bodies."

She grinned. *"I'm having trouble wrapping my mind around this."*

"That is because this explanation is trying to be expressed within your limits of words…and your words are limited by your limits of ideas."

"Well, that's all I have to deal with right now."

"In truth, it is not, for even now, on a conscious level, you are struggling with these boundaries—stretching and chafing at these idea forms— these limits. It is not the words themselves that matter; it is the power behind them…the emotion and intent…the Spirit. This dialogue, as it is expressed, is being tempered by the way your thought processes work, by the way you interpret or define your words and your world. It is only an approximation of the depth of answers which you seek. It is a process, a journey. Each step of it brings you closer and closer to your destiny, but no one step *is* the destiny. And no one answer you receive is absolute.

"Yet the power behind your quest, and the longing you sense within, are conveyed in a manner by the stories you tell. The story that you have sought so desperately around your world and throughout your life is a story as old as time itself. It is a story of when there was no time, and will be no more. It is a story that has been crying to be told from the depths of the soul of man. It is a story that was told and retold by Christ, Mohammed, the Buddha, Krishna—the story that *all* of your enlightened ones have told throughout your ages and before and beyond.

"The words of your enlightened ones have been manipulated throughout your times. They have been used for purposes of control. Even in their pure forms, they were being spoken with the sometimes inadequate forms of words, such as these words are. Your words do not encompass, nor *can* they encompass the human heart or the human Spirit. Therefore, do not attempt to hold onto these words if you desire a connection to the living word, for the Spirit of life is as fluid as water in a stream. You cannot capture truth within words any more than you can capture water from a flowing stream in a fish net, for again, it is not the words that matter, but the power behind them. When you 'get' that you will not even need words."

"*Why did we do all this? This time, this space, these words, these stories, this life you say we've created?*"

"You did it for the experience, to play with, to learn from."

"*Well, sometimes it doesn't seem like fun.*"

"*How* you experience depends upon your motivation—your intention. Do your movie actors not say before a scene, 'What is my motivation?'"

"*Yes.*"

"How well they know their motivation—their intention—determines their ability to play their part. The better they 'get into' their emotions, the better their performance, whether it be tragedy or comedy. Sometimes they are so 'into' their emotions that they forget they are acting, and that, too, is a sacred moment. It is the play within the play. You recognize those sacred, holy moments with annual celebrations and statues and awards.

"You should celebrate *all* of your moments every day of your lives—for, indeed, you are 'into' your lives so well that you have forgotten almost completely, on a conscious level, who you truly are. You are the finest of actors that you could imagine…and you are playing your parts with such grace, beauty and realism.

"Each of you and all of you should be honored…for without a villain, you would have no hero. Without your student, there would be no teacher. Without your male, you would have no female. Without your darkness, you would have no light. Without your yin, you would have no yang.

"Without your dualities, how would you know yourselves? How would you be able to recognize yourself?

"All of your moments are sacred in this lifetime, because you have allowed yourselves to forget who you truly are, in order to play your part."

"Then Shakespeare was right: we're all actors on the stage."

"His was a good analogy. *Your* stage—your particular vibration—has a particular essence of time and space and form. And is it not glorious?"

"Some of the time."

"Ah. Without your time, your emotions could not change, could they?"

"I guess not." Trish thought a moment. *"Then time serves a vital purpose."*

"*Your* purpose."

"And when it doesn't serve our purpose anymore?"

"Then you will discard it...and that will be your end of time. It will not be the end of your world—only the world as you know it—and as you experience it at *this* time...for there will be a new Heaven and a new Earth, and, consequently, a new you."

"Then we do it all over again?"

"If you choose. It is always your choice, as is your choice of free will. You gave yourself that gift...and it is sacred because you are sacred, as your life is sacred. Because you do not know this, you are always trying to escape to some where else...but always you come back to 'where' you are."

"Then these riddles—if we solve them—like who we are...and where we're going...then we're back where we began. If we 'escape' this life, we're still who we are."

"No matter what you discover or what riddles you solve about yourselves, you are still who you are."

● ● ●

Trish rubbed her face and stretched her arms. Then she said, *"I want to ask something here, and this seems as good a time as any. You talk about 'the end of time,' but that it's not the end of the world. It seems like we're killing the world, poisoning it. And lately I've been wondering if poisons kill off the weaker of the species of bugs and bacteria, and those that survive become stronger—more resistant—then couldn't that be what's happening to us? Could the weakest of us be dying off while others are becoming stronger—more resistant to, say, radiation or poisonous chemicals?"*

"That is what *is* happening."

"And we're in control of this?"

"You are. The weaker are sacrificing themselves for this process to occur. Your DNA is changing. It is changing for your species to be able to survive the coming Earth changes. The new world will require a new DNA—a new genetic code—in order for the new species you will become to survive, and, at some point, to *thrive* in your coming growth, or expansion process."

"Some of us are becoming physically stronger?"

"And more importantly, *spiritually*, for you *are* mighty spiritual beings. That is your heritage. That is what you are struggling to remember."

"So, it's the same with us as it is with bugs and viruses and bacteria?"

"Your bugs and bacteria and viruses 'mutate,' as you call it, with consciousness. They have the faith of the mustard seed. And in their conscious mutation, they are assisting you in your unconscious mutation, just as you unconsciously assist them with theirs by providing them with a host environment within which to alter *their* genetic codes.

"And you may do it with consciousness, as well. Indeed, you *will* do it with consciousness—if you so choose—for that is how it is done.

"Mutations are the manifestations of genetic predispositions brought about by a spiritual process that *you* know as intention and purpose. These mutations have been subtle to your naked, or 'veiled,' eye during your period of historical recording, but the more dramatic forms—which you saw in the clinic—harken back to a time when you were more aware of the Spirit *behind* those manifestations. During *this* historical period you see everything as a physical manifestation and every process as a physical materialization. But evolution is brought about by a spiritual process; else, from what source would materialization occur? From what source would manifestation occur? It is all reflection. All that you see and experience in your physical world is reflection. But reflection of what? Reflection from where?

"In the land and time of Mu you knew these sources. You worked with these sources. And the more dramatic Mu-tations—or manifestations from the time of Mu—you saw as messengers. The mutations you saw in the clinic have come from another time when you lost your balance and slipped into the abyss of chaos. Many of your kind died to your physical world during those times and transcended back to the Spirit world."

"So, you're saying that what looks like a disaster of biblical proportions, is simply our species mutating to a stronger, more spiritual form?"

"It is."

"The divine order behind the chaos?"

"It is."

"And who will survive the disaster, if that's what it is?"

"*All* will survive. There is no death. It is the play. It is the drama. It is your creation."

"Okay, Okay. So, who will survive physically?"

"Those who have consciously chosen to survive physically…those with the faith of a mustard seed. They will carry the new DNA—the new genetic code—into the New World that will emerge—that *is* emerging."

"Did your Christed One not remind you of the consequences of putting new wine into old bottles? Old bottles burst forth with the power of new wine…the new wisdom. Your old bodies cannot contain the new wisdom, therefore, your old bodies must be transformed—or transmuted—in order to receive the new wisdom—to hear the new word—and to see the New World. You are being transmuted by the power of your atom. Your kingdom of heaven is at hand. The temple—your body—will be rent asunder or it will be rebuilt. You will change or you will be changed. You have left yourselves no other choice—at this point. It is your plan—your divine plan—come to fulfillment.

"The time is at hand. The choice is yours. And your choice must be conscious to reach your state of awareness. You are beyond the time of unconscious choice."

"Will the earth changes come dramatically?"

"They will if you choose...and you *are* choosing some changes now, and some are, indeed, 'dramatic.' But they may also come as your thief in the night."

"And the mark on the forehead. What will that be?"

"There is no outward sign. It is all internal. It is the point where your Old Tom touched you. It is what you call your third eye—your consciousness awakened."

"Is that what they call the eye of God?"

"It is."

"Is it also the eye that appears at the apex of the pyramid on the dollar bill?"

"It is a symbol...and it was a conscious attempt by your founding fathers to put the symbol into the hands of every person in your country every day. In their attempt to transfer a desire for the glory of the Light, they *unconsciously* transferred that power into a desire for money."

Trish tapped her thigh with the palm of her hand. *"So, that's how it happened. That's why we're so greedy.*

"Was that a mistake? Wait...Okay, so it wasn't a mistake... but it seems like one."

"It was a pathway to your now point. It has served its purpose. And the image will begin to disappear from your dollars, for it, too, has served its purpose...for there is purpose in all you experience, in all you create.

"You like your chaos theory because there seems to be order in it—order behind your seeming chaos. And, indeed, there *is* order behind it. And it *is* what you call 'divine order.' For there is, indeed, 'method' to what you define as 'madness.'

"All of you are seeing through the eyes or the eye of God unconsciously...and this you may do with consciousness, as well. For what you see and what you experience, even *unconsciously*, is shared with the All that are One.

"You have chosen a wondrous time to be 'alive' on your plane."

"It doesn't always seem like it."

"But it '*is*.' And *that* is the wondrousness of it—the 'isness'—the beingness. For you are human beings, mighty spiritual beings. To know this—to remember this—is the peace that surpasses all understanding."

"I don't know... the idea of spirituality seems so formal to me, so somber and serious, somehow. Like there isn't any fun in it."

"It may be, as you say 'formal,' if you choose. But you have taught us much with your humor."

"We have taught you?"

"Indeed. In the pain of your forgetfulness, you have created humor to sustain you—to enable you to endure. And it, too, is a sacred gift that you have created and shared. You may bring your humor—your 'fun'—along with you if you choose your spiritual path of awakening."

Humor, Trish thought. *I hope so. I think I'm going to need it.*

• • •

After Trish had taken time to reflect on what had been said, she took up the pace again, asking, *"If there really is a third eye, are there also energy chakras like Jo Ann was talking about?"*

"There are; however, you have limited your conscious use of your energy centers to seven for your purposes on the Earth plane at this time."

"Are there more?"

"There are."

"How many?"

"As many as the stars."

"How do we access this energy...consciously?"

"You must first consciously destroy your concept of a *limit* of seven—your self-set boundaries."

"How?"

"With your destroyer angels—your powers of destruction."

"We wipe out our seven energy chakras?"

"It is unnecessary to do so. To access your other energies consciously you must only destroy your concept of those limits. You may, indeed, destroy them and start over—your fission. But you may also blend them gently into the unconscious, unused energies you possess by fusing them."

"Why did we limit them to seven in the first place?"

"Again, for the experience. You might say, 'Let me experience a life without eyesight and see how that feels.' Or, 'Let us together create a tidal wave and see how that affects our being, both as the wave, and as the shore upon which it smashes.' Or, 'Let us smash our atoms and see what happens,' 'Let us experience a world based on seven notes of music and seven colors of the rainbow and seven energy chakras.

"Now, read your Revelations with your new eyes and see if you find some revelations. Read your *life* with your new eyes and see if *it* becomes more revealing. See where your battle of Armageddon truly takes place. It is in your mind and your heart and your soul. It is your different aspects warring amongst themselves. It takes place on your physical plane.

"Or it is simply a myth told by a crazy man. It is all things to all people."

"And what about the angels sounding?"

"They are the trigger points that each and all of you have programmed into your DNA to awaken at such a time as they may choose. Some of you call them your 'defining moments.' But each moment is a defining moment, and they are all different; yet they are all the same."

"What about 'wormwood?' Was that really Chernobyl?"

"Indeed. It was 'Chernobyl'…and it was a thousand wormwoods in a thousand worlds. It served its purpose. It awakened some souls, as your alarm clocks waken you from sleep.

"Just as certain things that you do in your ordinary waking state will trigger memories of the previous night's dreams, so certain world events and personal experiences will trigger memories from the unconscious. You may experience these events as feelings of déjà vu, or as what you call 'real attention getters.' They are your wake-up calls, your trigger points, your defining moments, your angel soundings.

"The mutants in the jars were *your* wake up call, *your* angel sounding. You knew in your soul that you were supposed to pay attention.

"You pre-set these alarm systems before you entered this Earth plane, as you pre-set your alarm clocks every night. Then, when you slipped into your forgetful state, there were alarms, triggers, soundings that *could* awaken you from your forgetful state, if you chose. All humans have these trigger points pre-set into their memory banks. For many they are ignored. Chernobyl was a trigger point for many.

"How do you like your puzzles now?"

She smiled. *"I think I'm more confused than ever."*

"Even your confusion serves you."

"How?"

"When it reaches a point of 'critical mass'—as you call it in your nuclear age—it is a magical moment.

"You say, 'Oh, to hell with it,' and send your confusion to the netherworld of what you call 'hell,' and start anew.

"You surrender your energy to a new beginning, a new direction, because the old path—which once served you—no longer does.

"*All* of your emotions—your disillusionment, jealously, guilt, anger, depression and confusion serve you. All were created *by* you and *for* you to assist in your experiences as separated beings—your *illusion* of separated beings. They were created as tools to assist on your path, just as your ego was created for that purpose, but you judge them in your now point to be good or bad. They are neither. They simply are. They are energy.

"When you deny them—your tools, your creations, your children—you bring them forth. And sometimes they overwhelm and rule over you. If you *allow* them, instead of resisting your *illusions* of them as monsters and demons, you may again experience them as tools—children—instead of masters."

"So how does disillusion serve me?"

"It is a breaking down—a destroying of your illusions—a *dis*-illusion."

"Well, it doesn't feel like it serves me. It just makes me feel angry and... and empty."

"Indeed. For it takes the *passion* of your anger to help you to destroy that which serves you no longer. It takes the *intensity* of that passion to bring you to the point of releasing an illusion that brought you so much comfort and felt so familiar in your past.

"The emptiness you feel is the space created by the releasing of the illusion. You have not yet replaced your illusion with a new idea framework; therefore, you feel adrift, lost, empty and abandoned by what helped support your *idea* of yourself—your illusion. However, you require that empty space, in order to allow new ideas, new perceptions, new possibilities in life to enter your consciousness.

"Much of your world is entering a collective phase of disillusionment with the structures that supported it in *its* past—its reliance on its government, its social structures, its religions, medicine and industry—just as Max and Jo Ann recognized. And this is well, for this is your world's now choice."

"How is it well?"

"For much of your time you have 'externalized' your power. You have been able to see it in other people and institutions. You have projected it *onto* others, but you have felt and thought that it was somehow missing in yourselves. When you lose your illusions of those structures that once served you, but that no longer do, then you will create space—a void, a darkness—that requires filling. Some of you experience it as depression."

"So what do we fill it with? Another illusion?"

"Perhaps, or you may choose to fill your empty space with your *own* power—your source power...for source power is not an illusion of power. It is a force beyond your imaginings.

"Jealously and guilt—and not your *illusions* of them—also have purpose.

"You believe consciously that to be too emotional, to show too much emotion, is weakness—just as you think the female is your weaker sex…but your soul knows that you *need* your emotions…for you *are* your emotions— or thought in motion.

"Do you not use art and music and dance to stir up your emotions?"

"Sometimes."

"You also like to use scary movies and confrontations to stir up your emotions of fear and anger."

"And that's okay?"

"It is with me.

"I say again that you *need* your emotions for you *are* your thoughts in motion. If you have tried to push them down and control them too much, your unconscious will create what you think of as a crisis—or even a tragedy—to make you come into your feeling again. You cannot deny your feelings, for they will not be denied. They are part of you, whether you honor or acknowledge them or not."

"Honor fear and anger?"

"Fear and anger are part of your being. You are sacred creatures. How can any part of you be less than sacred? Fear and anger are blessed gifts…but, like joy and surrender, you have many false ideas about them."

"Like?"

"You see them as aspects of the dark side, but true and honest anger can be used as a tool to motivate. It can get you moving. It can even be used to heal—to release pains and memories and thought patterns that no longer serve you. True fear can be used to get your attention, if you will but honor it and ask it, 'What are you trying to tell me?' And sometimes fear can make you move quickly before you have time to think. At *those* times, if you ignore it, you may do so at the risk of your survival on your Earth plane."

"How do jealously and guilt serve us?"

"Without the jealousy of Venus, and her attempts at manipulation, your Psyche would never have been set on a path that would ultimately bring her to immortality. So did not her seeming negative intention *support* Psyche along her path and give her opportunity to attain her quest?"

"How does guilt serve us? What is the purpose of guilt?

"Much of the time your guilt has *not* served you, for you have allowed your *illusion* of it to rule over you. It does, however, have purpose. You live in a forgetful state, and at times you forget the very large reminders that have already presented themselves in your daily lives. Your guilt is a reminder of the things that have already entered into your conscious awareness. It may be saying, 'You have already been down this path. It is not necessary to go there again.'

"When you do not pay attention to it and it begins to 'nag' at you, then you are allowing it to rule over you. If you ask the *Spirit* of the guilt what it is trying to tell you when you first feel it, and if you allow its message to enter into your consciousness, then its purpose is served…the one you created it for. It is transformed. And you may bless it. Then it will evaporate like morning mist."

"If you find that the *illusions* of your emotions no longer serve you, you may ask them to leave and allow them to leave. But, first, you must fully embrace these illusions, for they, too, are your creations.

"If you treat your pure emotions of fear, anger and jealousy as your creatures—your children—instead of your illusions of monsters and demons, you may ask them for the messages they are trying to convey to you under your veils of illusion and forgetfulness.

"And you may ask your monsters in Clinic Number Four what they are trying to tell you…for they, too, are your creations."

Trish thought some of the comments were getting a little redundant, and, as if her thought were being read, Freya said,

"If you hear redundancy in these words as they are expressed, then you may appreciate the redundancy of what you regard as your mistakes, as well…what you refer to as 'same song, second verse.'"

Trish was surprised by the comment. She pursed her lips, then said, *"Well, we do seem to repeat the same processes over and over again. It must be frustrating for you to watch. Is it?"*

"It is the song. It is the dance. It is *your* song, *your* dance…and there is intricate, exquisite beauty in it—beyond your knowing."

Trish tilted her head and asked, *"Are we at a point where we can use some of that extra energy you talked about? You know, so we won't misuse it, or, I guess, so we can use it in balance like you said?"*

"Indeed, some of you are. And in *your* fact, you have resisted it for such a time as you were ready. The time—your time—is now. That is why you are here."

"What will happen when these energies enter our physical bodies?"

"When the power of the awakening energies enters into you or emerges from within, it may feel overwhelming. It may be accompanied by much chattering of teeth, shaking and crying with emotion. You may feel internal vibrations that seem to rock you noticeably, usually at night, during sleep or in the early morning upon waking…though no one else may be able to feel them if they touch you. It may be as subtle or as strong as is required by your own entity.

"But there is no danger in power. Your use of it is all that matters in your evolutionary process."

• • •

After a pause to change the tape in her recorder and readjust her position, Trish took a few deep breaths and said, *"I'd like to shift gears a bit here and ask you something I've always been curious about. Are there extra-terrestrials?"*

"Indeed. There are what you term *extra*-terrestrials, and there are also what you would term *inter*-terrestrials. Who do you think populates your worlds within and your worlds without?"

"I don't know. Why do they have to be populated? Can't they be deserted?"

"Many are. Do you believe *all* of them are deserted? Do you believe that you alone have been selected as the only intelligent life forms to inhabit your galaxies?"

"Well, no."

"That would be like believing you were the only species on your planet. On your planet it *requires* other living creatures both within and without your bodies to support the functions of your bodies. Your bacteria and viruses, plants and animals all live together in an interconnected system of life. It is the same throughout your galaxies and beyond. Would this interconnected system of balances and support suddenly stop at your world's boundaries? At the edge of your flat world?"

"There is no edge of a flat world."

"And there are no boundaries to the world as you view it now, at *this* evolutionary stage, in *this* moment of time."

"Then why can't we see them—the extra-terrestrials and inter-terrestrials—with the naked eye?"

"You *may* see them with your naked eye. It is your veiled eye that you may not see them with."

"Okay, okay. So inter-terrestrials?"

"Your world within. Did not your bacteria and viruses exist for eons—supporting you and helping you to evolve—long before you 'saw' them with your 'naked' eyes? Your awareness is limited only by the limits of your perceptions—your beliefs. Many human beings interact with extra-terrestrials and inter-terrestrials on a conscious level, and many of you also interact with them on an unconscious level, as well. In *their* world, *you* may be the extra-terrestrial or the inter-terrestrial. But you continue to support each other, though you are not always aware of the balances and supports that exist between you."

"So why can't we see them with our veiled eyes?"

"Just as you may receive many different frequencies—or stations—on your radios, there are many frequencies—or vibrations—of existence in your world and beyond. If you never attempted to change your radio station, you would swear that your neighbor was lying if he told you that he was hearing strange voices on other stations of *his* radio…but it would simply be that he was expanding his range of choices with his control knobs.

"There are 'rules'—spoken and unspoken—in your vibrational plane. The more you allow yourselves to challenge these rules, boundaries, controls and these ideas about who you are, where you are and when you are, the more expansive your existence will become. You all have control knobs, but many of you have chosen not to exercise that free will of tuning them consciously."

"But some of us are 'tuning in' unconsciously to those other frequencies?"

"Indeed. But, again, nothing is done without your will. You have both conscious and unconscious will. And it is with your unconscious will that you do most of your 'behind-the-scenes' work and play—that determine the direction of your daily conscious waking states."

"So what is going on then? Is it our sleep state you're talking about?"

"It is your sleep state…but you do not leave your unconscious state at your bedroom door, either. Your unconscious is always conscious. It is only your conscious that is unconscious. When your unconscious reaches your conscious level—that is a state of awareness. You are always in control. You do not exist at the whims of fate, or even the gods, as you once believed.

"You like your Greek myths, as you like your puzzles. Your Greek myths say that Jupiter himself bestowed Psyche with the gift of immortality. You read that she was the first mortal to be given that status."

"Yeah, I read it in several books."

"Who do you think the gods were?"

Trish shrugged her shoulders. *"I don't know. Do you mean the Greek idea of gods?"*

"Ah…you are seeing with your new vision now…the *idea* of their gods."

"Were they extra-terrestrials?" she posed.

"They were your present *idea* of extra-terrestrials. Psyche was given the gift of immortality merely because she became self-aware. She 'woke up,' just as Sleeping Beauty was awakened by the kiss of her beloved. She joined her dualities as one—her male and her female—her darkness and her light—her positive and her negative—and, indeed, her heart and her soul. And she did it with consciousness. In so doing, she found her joy. She exists today—not only in your books of myth—but also in your world of Spirit. She is also a prototype—as real as your Christed One, the Buddha, Mary and Eve.

"She journeyed to the Land of the Dead because one must always die to oneself before becoming self-aware—before seeing one's connection to the All—before becoming the All…fusion, as you like to call it."

"But isn't it dangerous to go to the land of the dead?"

"There is no danger, for there is no death. There is only your fear of death. She risked all she knew to enter that realm—that place in your minds that mortals have believed into reality—and she returned from that place by remembering to keep her last coin for her passage back."

"What was her last coin?"

"Her love for her beloved—the other half of her self. For to love yourself, is to love the All. And to love the All is to love God. You cannot truly love your idea of God, if you do not truly love the idea of yourself."

• • •

Trish mulled over the words she had just heard a while. Then in a soft voice, she asked, *"Freya?"*

"I am here."

"What is my last coin? I feel as though I've been to the land of the dead, and I want to get back now."

"It is for each 'one' to determine what his last coin is. It is that which you value above all else, that which you will hang on to when you have allowed all else to slip away. But ultimately you must also give up that which you value most in order to become self-aware—to come truly and ultimately to your joy."

Trish hesitated for a long moment.

"I think my last coin is my identity. I'm scared to death of losing my identity—the me that I am—the Trish Cagle that I've known all my life."

"You are so caught up in your identity—your play—that your heart has felt betrayed by your identity. For what you call your I.D.—or your 'id'-entity, the unconscious aspect of your psyche, your mortal, forgetful aspect—failed to recognize, in faith, its sacred connection to the heart, your Cupid. So your heart withdrew, closed itself off from your reach for a time…such a time as this, when you have journeyed to the Land of the Dead—your dark side—your descent into the abyss of chaos. And you are now ready to return to your emotional, loving aspect.

"You had to risk all, in faith, in order to retrieve the beauty that is rightfully yours as sacred creatures. The faith you lose in your relationship with your heart is retrieved when you risk going to darkness in faith. You *return* in faith by giving up your last coin."

"If we're these mighty creatures, I don't understand why we've forgotten it."

"You have chosen to experience this particular forgetful frequency for a purpose…the purpose of focusing exclusively through the lens of individual and collective self-reflection. You are quite literally mirroring a world of your thoughts and intentions. Your experience of your world *is* a physical manifestation of your beliefs.

"Thoughts *are* energy. You are energy. Your quantum physics will catch up to this one day. And it will 'blow your minds away'."

"Then will our thoughts change?"

"So dramatically that it cannot be expressed in these words and on that tape in a way that you can fathom."

"Try, please," Trish asked.

"Do you have your seat belt fastened?"

"No, but I'm ready."

"When you finally fully realize that you create your world and your experience of it with your thoughts, you will 'shape shift' with animals, plants, the wind and waterfalls. You will 'journey' to unnamed galaxies. You will *create* galaxies. You will explore the feelings of 'being' ALL THAT IS. And anything...*anything* that can be thought or believed or imagined or dreamed or wondered with that incredible Spirit and mind of yours already is or was, or can or will be again."

"You're right; that's hard to fathom."

"Then simply consider the possibility."

Trish let out a breath. *"Well, it certainly puts my life in a different perspective."*

"Do not diminish the experiences you are having in this particular time and place. It is a field of vibration that is your particular field of vibration to experience, feel and explore. For you are simply 'remembering' it and making other choices."

"Well, now that does blow my mind. And the other choices I could have made?"

"They are being played out in another field of vibration. You are simply focused on this one at this 'time' and 'place.'"

"Then what is the point of all this?"

"It is the play...playing in the fields of the Lord."

"Who is the Lord?"

"All That Is. The Glorious Infinite. Your universe, your multi-verses, ever expanding."

"And contracting, too."

"Indeed. There is breathing in and breathing out. For all we have spoken of—the galaxies and possibilities and experiences—are also within you. Those vast regions of being are within you. Now breathe, and 'be' with these thoughts for a moment."

Trish began breathing deeply.

• • •

After Trish had taken a few moments for deep breathing, Freya said,

"This journey into forgetfulness is for the purpose of self-discovery. Can you imagine the joy of coming from such a depth back to such a height? It would put your bungee jumps to such shame."

"No, I can't imagine that."

"Not in this moment. But, you may if you choose. And, you do and have. Have many of you not spoken of going to hell and back?"

"Yes."

"Did what you experienced as hell in Clinic Number Four, not bring you to *this* point of discovering yourself?"

"I guess it did."

"And do you not find heaven on your Earth plane, as well, at moments in time?"

"I guess we do."

"Could you begin to experience that intensity of joy without your intensity of pain?"

"I guess not."

"Could you appreciate your satisfactions with clarity or even understanding, if you did not have disappointments? If all of your moments were the same, could you have a sense of range? If all of your notes were high, could you have music in your world? If you only had mountaintops, could you appreciate your valleys?

"No."

"If you did not have hell on Earth, could you appreciate your heaven on Earth?"

"No, I don't think I could."

"Are you not wondrous creatures to dream up such an idea?"

Trish chuckled and shook her head from side to side, and lifted her hand to cover her face.

"That is all right. You may blush, if you choose."

She laughed out loud. *"It's my choice, isn't it?"*

"Indeed."

Trish allowed herself to laugh fully, then asked, *"Who would have thought that hell could be such a hilarious subject?"*

"Not your saints."

At that Trish started laughing even harder.

"Oh...oh... I can't believe it. You've got a sense of humor!"

"I cannot believe it, either."

With that Trish doubled over in her chair with laughter that filled every corner of the room, and even Stephanie was beginning to smile.

"God! I can't believe how good this feels!"

Stephanie remained silent, but Trish continued laughing. When her laughter finally subsided, somewhat, she straightened back in her seat and wiped the tears from her cheeks. *"Oh, my gosh. Oh, my. Oh..."*

Freya finally spoke. "If you are not careful, you may bring your Stephanie back and send me on my way."

"But it's my choice, right?"

Stephanie pointed to her chest. "It may be time for this one to have her space back before you get us all into what you call 'trouble.'"

"Okay, okay. Hmm... But then can we get back to some of this?"

There was a pause; then Stephanie's eyes opened slowly. She shifted in her seat and ran her hands up and down her face.

"Whew! Well, I don't know what all *that* was about, but I sure do feel refreshed. What *was* that all about?"

"I don't know if I can explain it," Trish responded, still smiling. "I guess you just had to have been there."

Chapter Forty-Six

After a quick break, which included a lot of water, the two women settled into their seats once again. After Trish checked the tape in her recorder, she continued the session where she had left off.

"I think we were talking about forgetfulness," Trish began.

"Ah, yes. How else may you 'discover' your own glory, unless you forget it?"

"Then it's a rediscovery."

"A remembering, a bringing back together the parts of yourself—your members—into one whole body...the One—the All—the God force that lives in each of you—the God that is everywhere. If your God is everywhere, how can he not be where you are? How can he not be in every one?

"You *say* that you believe your God is everywhere. But you do not truly consciously believe it. For if God is everywhere, there would be no place for evil or devil in your belief system.

"You have created *that* belief for your purposes—a belief that there is separateness from God, so that your consciousness could be lost from its Oneness. Only if your consciousness was lost in your state of forgetfulness, could you experience the joy of returning home—to the Source—the One—the All.

"As long as you keep alive your belief in evil, you will do your best to create it. As long as you fail to see the divine in all others, you will project your *idea* of evil *on* to others. The divine is in the All—in all others, as well as yourself. You may awaken the divine in yourself, as well as in others, if you recognize and treat yourself and your other selves as divine parts of the whole—Holy One.

"If you speak to your neighbor, speak to him as God. If you speak to your enemy, speak to him as God. Do not wait for them to achieve your *illusion* of perfection. They already *are* perfect...as *you* are perfect. They may still be asleep, but that is beautiful, as well. They are as beautiful as the curly-haired babe that sleeps peacefully in its crib. *Then* you recognize the perfection of the child who brought you to such frustration just minutes before with its curiosity, vibrancy and abandon."

"But I think the real thing is what I said before...that I'm afraid that if I remember—like you say—I'll lose myself, the Trish Cagle I am."

"How could you ever lose yourself? All roads lead to you, as all roads lead to God. You will always be Trish Cagle—and, oh, so much more than you ever dreamed you were in your wildest imaginings. You may be Trish Cagle for as long as you like. You may slip into and out of her clothes at any 'time,'—as you may slip into and out of other consciousnesses, as you will,

510

as you *do*…though you may not realize it at this time.

"As Freya, I have chosen to dwell in the upper world…but I have also chosen to live with my beloved Earth surrounding me—my stones, my water, my grounding—for it is my choice to do so."

"And you can choose to leave at any time, too?"

"There is no time where I dwell…but, indeed, at this moment—at this 'time'—I have slipped into the body of *this* one." Stephanie pointed to herself. "For, you have summoned me. And she has allowed my spirit in.

"You may ever be Trish Cagle, for she is your creation. You created her for your intentions.

"I love you, Trish Cagle."

Trish again began feeling an overwhelming sense of pure love and couldn't speak. It was a feeling she hadn't felt since she was with Ilyani. And she wept from her soul.

Freya sat quietly as Trish gave herself over to her emotions.

Then, after the crying stopped, Freya said, "If you begin accepting or allowing this love, you will begin to truly love yourself. You will become. You will come into your being."

Trish continued to compose herself and smiled slightly. *"I know I said it before, but this is all so 'way out there.' "*

"Did your Christed one not say that the Holy (Wholly) Spirit would bring all things to your remembrance in his name? How may you remember, if you have not first forgotten—if you have not first known?

"There are many ghosts and many spirits. It is through your Wholly Ghost—your Wholly Spirit—that you will find what you seek. The Holy Grail—the blood of Christ—that so many before you have sought throughout your world and throughout your stars—is within you. It is in your DNA. Did your Christed one not say that the kingdom of heaven is within? Did he not also say that his kingdom was not of this Earth? Is that not 'way out there?' And is that not 'way in here?'" Stephanie pointed to the center of her chest with both hands. "Did your Christed one not also say that he and the Father are as One? Did he not say that what he did, you may do and more?

"You are beginning to 'move' into new dimensions. It is 'simply' a vibrational shift, and it is 'simply' logical that beings from other past and future dimensions will visit your reality from time to time in order to help awaken you to this fact. Myths and mythical beings explain the unexplainable. They help you glimpse other dimensions that you cannot comprehend from a third dimensional perspective, that you cannot measure with 3D tools, or fathom with 3D senses. They make no sense from a 3D perspective.

"However, if you can believe that all things are possible, if you can believe that you can 'dream your world into being,' if you can believe in a larger reality, you can make this vibrational shift that has been prophesied in countless legends throughout your ages. The Age of Light, the Great Purification, the Dawning of a New Day is upon you. Dip your finger in it. Pierce the veil. Allow what is possible to be, and be aware of who you truly are. "Ye are gods. And that is not what you call sacrilege. It is sacrilege to believe that you are less."

"Honestly, I'm still having a little difficulty with this destructive aspect."

"Is not your God a wrathful God, as well as a God of love?"

"You know, now that you mention it...I never 'got' that. In one book of the Bible it says, 'Thou shalt not kill.' And in another it commands people to go out and slaughter their enemies. What's that about?"

"You are creators and you are destroyers. You are opposite ends of your spectrum. You are your opposing forces—your polarities—that, in truth, hold your world together. The more you deny one of your opposing forces, the stronger it becomes. If you deny your dark side—externalize it by calling it 'evil'—the more you will bring it forth. In truth, 'evil' is simply your E-veil, your emotional veil—your hidden potentiality. You think of it as the Dark Force—the devil—because it repulses and repels you.

"There *are* angels of Light, *and* angels of Darkness, just as there are dark stars and dark energy, and they each serve their purpose in the divine order. You may run from your shadow, but you will never escape it. The more you run from it, the brighter your light will shine and the more visible it will become."

"Is that why there's so much chaos and violence in the world today?"

"Indeed. You may deny your protons and electrons—your opposing forces—which hold your bodies and your galaxies together...but they will still exist and still give each other balance. Deny your destructive forces and you will call them forth.

"*Acknowledge* your dark side—your energies which repel—as *well* as your light side which attracts, and you may hold your lives, your world together in harmony and balance in a conscious, aware state.

"Darkness has been your perception of 'evil' for eons."

"And it's not?"

"What do you think darkness is?"

"I don't know." She thought a moment. *"Nothing?"*

"There is no 'nothing.' What you *perceive* as nothing is also part of the 'All That Is.' You negate it. You deny it. You call it 'evil,' and fear it. But it is and ever was and ever shall be."

"Then what is darkness?"

"Darkness is the edge of your world. It is the edge of what you have allowed yourself to see and to know...to be aware of. You define yourself and your experience of your world in a certain way, and you do not see beyond that. It may not be altogether comfortable to you, yet it is familiar. You can see it. You know it. Darkness, however, is what you term the 'boogey man,' who will 'get' you, and do unspeakable things to you."

"That's just childish."

"Is it not? You have used some very imaginative ways to define your darkness, those aspects of your world and yourselves that you have not allowed yourselves to see and to know and to remember. In your beginnings there was darkness and void. Darkness is the womb from which creation is dreamed into being.

"Do you remember how Max spoke of Galileo?"

Trish nodded.

"Do you not see how wise and courageous he was to speak his truth...to dare to present another view of your universe beyond the perceptions of his day?"

"I guess so," she agreed.

"He shined light on what before had been darkness...the edge of *his* world. He walked boldly into darkness and saw that there was something else there...beyond the limits of what his world's religions, governments and cultures had said there were. Then *he* was labeled 'evil.' *He* was persecuted, just as your Christed One was. Now you look back and say how obvious everything he said was. How could the people of his day have been so stupid, so arrogant, so 'childish,' as you say?

"Darkness is always the edge of the world as you know it and believe it to be. But, as Max said, 'There is more...so much more.' Whenever some of you shine light on what has been darkness, many of you cover your eyes and remain in darkness, and say, 'No, no, it's too bright. Turn it off. It hurts my eyes...my 'perceptions.'

"But do not fear. Your eyes may become accustomed to darkness after a time.

"Dare to walk into the darkness—that which you do not know—and shine your light wherever you set your foot. There are worlds and galaxies beyond even the limits of your powerful telescopes; and there are worlds within, beyond the limits of your microscopes. You have dared to shine light into darkness, and you have had a glimpse. And because of that, you will keep searching again and again. And, if you are truly seeking, you will keep finding it again and again...until you realize that *everything* that you see and hear and feel and experience and witness and, yes, dream and wonder...*all* of it is a part of that glimpse.

"As you risk going into what you perceive as darkness—those things you have labeled death and evil and boogey men—you illuminate other worlds that you have only dreamed of, wondered about, imagined. And you begin bringing them into being.

"In the beginning 'all' was darkness and void, and God said, "Let there be light." Spread your sparks of light as you walk into darkness, *beyond* the vibrations of the Earth plane, as you experience it. Bring your kingdom of Heaven to your Earth plane. Why do you hide your light under the mask of your present belief systems? Where are the words you speak of with your lips? Search for them in your heart…faith, trust, courage, joy. You may not illuminate the darkness by avoiding it, hiding from it or cursing it. It is, and ever shall be, the edges of your awareness."

"This is a totally different concept for me."

"Indeed. There are vast regions beyond and within the speck of creation that you inhabit and of which you are aware. These worlds, these vibrations, do no always behave in the manner to which you are accustomed. You say that they are not real, if you cannot measure or define them with your third dimensional tools, but they exist beyond the boundaries of these limitations. Your innate tools of awareness *can* perceive and encompass them, if you would but allow it.

"Yea, though you walk through the shadows of what you perceive as death and evil, you need not fear death or evil, for your Christ consciousness is with you and within you, and will not forsake you. Lift the veil from you eyes to the wonder of All of your God's creation…that which you see with your third dimensional perceptions and that which you see but through a veil dimly.

"You must die to who you believe you are in order to be reborn into a new you. You must walk into the darkness of the unknown to make known. If you have the courage to light even the tiniest flame of faith and trust and hope, you may illuminate galaxies. And the cup of your life will run over and nurture all around you with the joy of truly living. You must embrace all of life to truly live…what you perceive as darkness, as well as what you perceive as light. The edges of your perception, the edges of your five and even six senses, the edges of your three dimensional plane of experience are the darkness you fear. They are the edges of the world as you know it and experience it. As you illuminate your in-light, you illuminate and enlighten the world around you."

Trish sat speechless for a few moments. Unable to grasp what she had heard with her logical mind, she sat with the feeling.

● ● ●

After a few more moments, Trish said, *"I'm not sure I even know what to ask next."* She sat a moment longer and said, *"Explain this destroyer business a little more."*

"Would you ever harm another?"

"Not intentionally..."

"But you do it unconsciously much of your time."

Trish raised an eyebrow. *"How so?"*

"You hurt your beloved, did you not?"

The argument between her and Jimmy instantly came to mind. *"Yeah...I did, at that. But that was wrong, and I'm sorry for it."*

"Do not regret...for by destroying a mental barrier that *he* held in place, you have provided *him* with an opportunity to face *his* demons, *his* fears and *his* inner turmoil—which he would not have had without your tender tongue lashing. Some times you have to destroy in order to heal.

"You have to destroy the lineage of old patterns and old pains that have been passed down through your genetic make-up in order to become the healthy, whole, aware person you desire to be. You must mutate. You must change. You must transform—if you choose. Always, it is your choice. And in that process, you are actually altering your DNA—what you call your 'genetic predisposition.'"

"Your physical evolution is inseparably linked to your spiritual evolution...and your spiritual evolution is inseparably linked to your physical evolution."

"How does this process take place?"

"Your physical bodies are a manifestation of what you think and feel about yourselves. In one respect, you are a reflection of your beliefs about yourselves. This physical appearance is shaped on your cellular level. Your very DNA—the strands, or streams of it, mirror your beliefs about yourselves—your beings. By unconsciously choosing to negate aspects of your feminine for a time, you have essentially short-circuited certain aspects of your DNA. You have mutated yourselves at your basic cellular level.

"Your physical appearance has not changed dramatically, but the change has been basic—yet subtle. It has been hormonal, chemical, electric. There are markers to the new genetic code that is evolving, which your scientists have not yet deciphered...and they may not decipher them if they are looking for them simply through their instruments, instead of through their hearts.

"You *appear* much the same—for that is all your physical bodies are— physical appearances. You *appear* to be what you think of as solid. You are simply and exquisitely a certain vibrational level of apparition.

"By reconnecting with the emotional aspect of your being on a conscious level, you are reawakening those aspects of your genetic materials and mutating to a more spiritual Cosmic Being, one that will be able to do the things of which we have spoken. Telepathic communication will replace speech in some instances. It will *transcend* speech, for you will transfer, not only the thoughts your words represent, but also the feeling—the empathy— the telepathic emotions that accompany them.

"You already *are* telepathic. You simply do it on an unconscious level most of the time. You will do it with awareness when your mutation to a cosmic species is complete.

"The radiating of your planet is taking place, not only on the Earthly, but on the intergalactic level, as well. You have assisted this process by opening up your shield of ozone. It is no accident that this process is taking place at the Southern Pole. Much of the intergalactic radiation is entering at the Northern Pole. Your magnetic, feminine side is attracting this force, as it always has…and it is manifested in the spectacular auric displays of your Northern Lights. This attraction is merely happening at an accelerated pace at this point in time.

"For, as you open your heart to this process, so your thoughts will be opened, as well. The most masculine, destroying aspects of your species have assisted in opening up the ozone, while your awakening feminine aspects have attracted the force of intergalactic radiation that will create, or give birth to, the new cosmic species you are becoming.

"You will still be products of your Mother and your Father. Just as Eve, Pandora, the Goddess awakened man to his *present* state of *un*consciousness that you chose with free will, so the feminine will awaken the new human being to a cosmic, aware state.

"You speak of gene manipulation as though it was a new concept, but you have been involved in gene manipulation for eons. What do you think your plagues were? What do you think your wars were? Your famines? Your Great Flood? What do you think of your atomic age?

"It was your destroyer aspect guiding your species to this point. Have not your great 'calamities' and 'disasters' been followed by periods of great renaissance? This, your greatest calamity and disaster may, indeed, be followed by your greatest renaissance. Your world of 'chaos' may evolve to your world of divine order."

"You say 'may'."

"I *must* say 'may,' for I must honor your free will, always—even when it is unconscious."

"Are the changes in species and DNA you're talking about along the order of what they call Spontaneous Generation? Because a lot of scientists say that's not possible."

"Then for them it may *be* impossible…but for those who choose, it can happen in the twinkle of an eye. For others, it may be slower. For still others, it may not happen at all."

"But what if my—my personal self—chooses differently than, say, the majority of people. Will I suffer the consequences of their choices?"

"All decisions are made both collectively and individually in your vibration. If you choose individually a separate path from the collective, then your experiences will be experienced differently from those of the collective. You will *interpret* your experience from a different perception."

"I don't see how it can be good for us to be opening up the ozone hole and letting in radiation on the planet or digging it up from the earth."

"In opening up your ozone hole, you are opening yourselves up to cosmic forces—Sun energy. Have you not spoken for decades about your need for solar power? This process is facilitating your spiritual evolution. It is awakening your consciousness, Christ consciousness. Your ozone hole is opening in direct proportion to the softening of the soft spot on the top of your head—your fontanel—through which you will allow yourself to receive direct contact with Spirit again. This is not necessarily what you recognize as a physical process.

"A few of you have never forgotten how to communicate directly with Spirit. Now more have that opportunity. This is a glorious time that you have chosen to be alive."

"Maybe so. But it's a little unsettling to think of people dying from this 'glorious' exposure you're talking about."

"They are sacrificing their existence on this Earth plane on an unconscious level, so that the blood lines of the new species may emerge. And they *do not die.* They merely shift to other levels…and as the new species you are becoming evolves, you will be able to communicate with them at will and *see* that they are still very much alive.

"You are, indeed, Children of Gaia and Uranus—the Sky and the Earth. Your uranium—as you so sacredly and unconsciously named it—is as much a part of your heritage—your bloodline—as it is a bloodline that runs through the veins of your Earth. Uranium is a powerful being. It chooses to live in stone in specific places, places the ancients called sacred. It is, indeed, a sacred being. Information is held in stone and is now held in your bones. This powerful being and the information and mysteries it can impart, can awaken within you."

"How do we awaken it?"

"Through the vibration of love. Love will be the spiritual evolution of your species."

"But these deaths, these diseases, these mutations—it seems so grim."

"You have mutated, always. You have died, always. You have born diseases, always. It is just at an accelerated pace that some of you have chosen now. Uranium amplifies intention. It accelerates, magnifies and heightens. Through it, you begin to see the monsters within yourselves. You begin to see the healing abilities within yourselves, the divine children, as well. You begin to see *all* of the aspects of yourselves, those you deny and hide from, as well as those you think too grand to accept as your own. The entire spectrum of your being is emerging. The wounded, dark, hidden aspects within you are emerging to be healed by the divine within you. Not all of your mutating is as profound as those in the clinic. Some of it is subtle and undetectable. It is coming as your thief in the night."

"Why were the mutants so dramatic?"

"To get your attention. To teach you more about yourselves. They have chosen to be here at this time, as I first told you, to act as harbingers. They are gods, as they have always been gods. And they are monsters, as they have always been monsters. How you perceive or experience them or what you call them is your choice."

"This is still a little fuzzy."

"There are cardinal points throughout your evolutionary process when your species, humankind, can evolve, or a better word might be 'become' transmuted to forms other than the one you experience in this particular vibrational field. As there are countless vibrational fields of existence upon which you may play, it might be well for you to know that those other forms exist in other dimensions.

"In *some* dimension your dinosaurs still walk your planet. Your dead still live. And as there is no time, your Earth is still forming from molten matter. Because you have limited your perceptions to this single vibrational frequency, you experience many of these *possible* realities as ancient history, fairy tales, myths and legends. But I tell you that anything that is possible *is*. Anything that you can dream or imagine *is*. What you call reality is merely the limiting factor—the boundaries—of those who lack imagination, dreams and wonder.

"Your limited perceptions conceive of a division of good or bad with such intensity that you categorize *all* of creation in like manner. Your 'past' has been visited by creatures from your 'future,' and without a frame of reference, you have labeled these beings either good or evil—gods or monsters. Your thought-forms and your feelings create worlds, all existing simultaneously with the one you experience as real. You have glimpses of other realities throughout your lifetimes, but more often you dismiss them. Your children have *many* glimpses of them, but you have taught them to dismiss them as daydreams and to forget or ignore them."

"Like kids who talk about their invisible friends?"

"Indeed. And there are beings from other dimensions among you, who have agreed to be born into your vibrational Earth plane as human beings to assist humans in their spiritual development. Their kingdoms are not of this Earth plane. They are *in* the Earth plane, but not *of* it, though their experiences as humans help them to understand your thought patterns and feelings.

"In reality there are numerous realities…many fields upon which you may experience. Simply open your heart and your perceptions to these possibilities, and they will unfold before you as morning glories opening their petals at the warm touch of sunlight. Let your own light shine before you, and behold the wonders of the universe."

Trish let out a breath. *"Wow. This sure puts a different spin on things."*

"As a species you have experienced yourselves in such a limited fashion for so long that you find it difficult to accept and believe in all that you are. You take baby steps when your Now cries out for giant leaps of faith into the unknown realms of being. You are electromagnetic entities in a multiverse of beings and being.

"At the point of your perfect balance—at the point of your Second Coming—when you have reached your most exquisite state of equilibrium and harmony, time will stand still...for all of your time. It will be a moment when you recognize the perfection in all that is."

"The appearance of your mythical beings at this time is an omen of these times. These are sacred times, transitional times, times of great loss, and also of great potential."

"So, who is Janus, really?"

"Ah, Janus...the *children* of Janus. Janus—or your DNA that calls *forth* Janus—is appearing now because he *always* appears at times as these. His image has been placed at doorways because he stands at portals, always. He is the god of beginnings and endings. He stands posed at the ending of old worlds and ages and the beginning of new worlds and ages. He holds the key to what lies ahead, because he lives in the now and can simultaneously sees what has been and will be. How may you see your future, lest you know and understand your past?"

"The mermaid, the children in Moscow missing their left arms, and the Cyclops—what truths or meanings do these souls have to tell us?"

"You are thought and you are emotion. The spirit of water represents the spirit of emotions. If you attempt to cut yourself off from part of your emotional being, that part of you will emerge in dramatic ways. That part of you may, indeed, swim in the oceans of your emotions on a physical plane.

"Your myths speak of these times as times when the gods showed themselves as both human and animal.

"You weep for the children without arms. Yet, in your arms race, you have cut yourselves off from half of the energy and the power you possess. Arms are the extension of your power to both give and receive. With your right arm—or hand—you give, and with your left arm—or hand—you receive. If you have lost—or ignored—your ability to receive, you may lose or damage your left arm.

"To receive is not weakness.

"Your feminine side receives—allows. Your masculine side has been in the fore of your being—your penetrating, destroying, positive side—throughout the arms race. This has resulted in a cause and effect that you see in your children in Moscow. When you lose a part of yourself as a species, part of your species will demonstrate that loss on the physical plane.

"To see through the eye of the Cyclops is to see the world anew with your magic eye. Were you not told in your Bible that the light of the body is the eye, that when your eye is single, your whole body is also full of light? What *you* are beginning to see with your new vision you may share with others, if you will."

"Why are some of the mutants hybrids with animal looking features?"

"When you fail to recognize your connection to the animal kingdom, your animal characteristics will begin emerging on the physical plane to get your attention. When you fail to recognize your connection to the stone kingdom—through the minerals you require to stay alive—your hearts will begin to turn to stone.

"When you refer to yourselves as mankind, you are negating one half of your being.

"Look to your sacred manatee. Do you remember the one in your news who was wounded by a propeller and rescued?"

"Yes."

"He was named 'Hugh' by his rescuers. And hugh-manatee has given you a new name to wear, for humanity encompasses all of your race. If you deny the sacredness of one aspect of your world, you will never fully accept your own sacred being.

"You may think of this as spirituality, or as quantum physics, if you chose. But all things are connected in a way that you cannot fathom at your present level of understanding.

"Begin to love yourself, and you will begin to understand."

"Tell me about Ilyani."

"Ilyani lives inside you."

"How is that possible?"

"Because you experienced her, she is part of you. Everyone you meet, everything you experience, imagine, dream and wonder is part of you—aspects of yourself that you have acknowledged and are mirroring."

"How am I like Ilyani?"

"You were correct that she was 'contaminated,' or seeded, before her birth, just as you were 'contaminated,' or seeded, in this desert as a child. You were both exposed to the blood of your father, Uranus, through the uranium veins which run in the Earth. Uranium is a vibration. Ilyani is a vibration. You are a vibration. The vibration of what you know as uranium was carried into your bones through the milk of your Earth Mother. Through the process of intention, through the magic and alchemy of love, your blood is being crystallized—a concept you call transubstantiation. You are the vessel, and you are being Christed.

"In this state, you may, indeed, heal with a touch, as Ilyani did. You may transform, transmute and transfigure. You may bi-locate and disappear, walk on water and move mountains. You are all mutating now. You *have* been throughout this atomic age. It is a time prophesied in legends, myths and in the Great Pyramid.

"Ilyani and others like her are simply harbingers, heralders, of the Divine Child within all of you."

"But you said the mutants were harbingers."

"They are heralders, as well. The divine children and the monster children come to the surface at the same time to allow you to see two extremes of your spectrum, two extreme effects of the causes you have put in place in your world. They show you possible futures, offer you clear choices about the paths you take, and tell you something about your destinations. They both come to be acknowledged.

"All you call sin, demons, monsters and darkness, are creations or creatures of your making, birthed from a place of fear. They are surfacing for healing to take place, for enlightenment to take place. For healing and enlightenment are products of focused love. Love will be the evolutionary catalyst of your age—unconditional, compassionate, forgiving, giving and receiving.

"Do not deny any part of yourself, if you desire enlightenment, for as long as there is sun, there will be shadow. As long as there is pain, there will be love to heal it. And you are creatures of love and light, dust of the Earth, and magic of Starlight.

"You all seek love so desperately outside of yourselves, yet it exists in unlimited measure within you. If you seek this source within you and give it freely, if you become the cup that runs over, you will experience a joy more exquisite than any of your imaginings."

"I know that little girl seemed happier than any kid I've ever seen."

"She had pain, as well. All of you have pain from time to time. You are in transition, the final stages of a birthing process. The pain you experience is the dying of the old self. However, it is not the releasing of the old self that pains you; it is holding on to it.

"Many of you are holding on desperately. And many are releasing, as well, surrendering to that knock at the door. Listen. Do you hear it?

"It is the sound of your own heart, beating inside your chest."

Trish let out a breath. *"You know, a lot is reaching me, yet I feel so inadequate to tell this story. What if I decide not to write the book?"*

"It is your choice. And it does not matter what choice you make, for even in *viewing* your world anew, you are already sharing your vision with others on a level that you are unaware—unconscious. You are already changing your world—as others have and are in their way...providing possible ways or probable worlds to evolve.

"As I said, you are intimately involved in your evolutionary process.

"Just as the words of a book symbolize the ideas and emotions that give it body, or substance, so the DNA of your body is symbolic of the thoughts and emotions that give you form—or what you *perceive* as substance. Your genetic coding follows the same set of rules as your languages, and vice versus. Change one word in your book and you may change the whole meaning in the sentence where the word is located. That change in one sentence may alter the chapter, and the chapter may change the entire book. Then the title of the book may require changing, as well, for it may be an entirely different book than it was before.

"In the same way, mutations occur. Your thoughts and your emotions may alter one 'word'—or symbol—of your DNA blueprints. That change may alter the whole of your body. Some changes in your DNA symbols may be subtle, in that they may exhibit no outward changes in your physical appearances, but they may have a *profound* effect on your spiritual body—your 'words behind your words.' Other changes in your DNA may have dramatic effects on your physical body, and you may have to change the title of your body. You may have the body of your Cyclops or your Mermaid. You may have the body of Janus.

"With your books of Janus and the Mermaid and the Cyclops, you may have altered your entire library—your entire species. Change your library and you may alter your city. Your city may alter your country…and your country, your world. Your change in your world may alter your solar system. And the change in your solar system may alter your galaxies and beyond.

"Such is the power of your thoughts and emotions. In the beginning was the word. When you *say* your words, their vibrations are felt in your beyond."

Trish took a breath. *"God… That's almost too awesome to contemplate for someone who used to be a reporter, and is considering becoming a writer."*

"You already are a writer. Every soul is the author of his book, his library, his world and his galaxies. Every thought he has, every emotion he feels, every word he speaks, every sacred breath he takes affects the All."

"That's…that's just too much power to contemplate."

"You have been wielding that power *un*consciously for your eons.

"You are the architect of your house—your temple. You design your blueprints with your chapters of chromosomes and with your 'designer genes.' You are the builder, as well as the dweller in your temple—your physical body.

"You know, Max said that I was dying to write a book about my experiences."

"You are. You are dying to the person you were in order to become the person who will write the book. And if you choose to write this book, there will be those who will be 'dying' to read it...dying to who *they* once were and awakening to another level of consciousness...if they choose.

"You would not even be aware of the possibility of this book if you were not meant to have the choice of writing it."

"Now that you're saying this, I have to say that I feel like I was meant to write about this story—as though I was born to write it."

"You were. You chose your entry point on this plane. You sat above your 33rd ᴾarallel and watched an atomic bomb explode at Alamogordo. It was your signal—your trigger point—to enter into this particular vibrational field—as all others have recognized their signals and entered this particular vibrational field at a time suited for their purposes."

"But I don't know how to go about writing this story. People even fight over religious texts, so I don't know how to write about these kinds of new ideas."

"These are not new ideas. And it is their choice if people choose to fight. You cannot control them. They are creatures of free will, as well. They may choose to read or not to read, to believe or not to believe—to see or not to see. To truly see the divine in your self, you must recognize it in others.

"If they choose death and destruction in their lives, they may war over a comic book...or a color."

"But how on earth is that divine?"

"This is *not* the only pathway. There are untold numbers of pathways. If one chooses to find himself—his God—he may, indeed, find it in the Bible or the Koran or the Torah. He may even find it on a bloody battlefield—or in a walk through the woods in a drop of dew—or in a subway train at rush hour.

"*All* paths lead to God...for God is everywhere."

"Maybe my ego is keeping me from fully grasping this."

"Your ego is simply a tool. Many of you judge it to be bad and think you must discard it...but you created it also for your purposes. It is your specific, individual filtering system. It filters *out* what your conscious self is *not* ready to know. It allows in the parts of the unconscious that your conscious mind *is* ready to know. And your filter—your ego—is a constantly changing, shifting alive energy.

"You worry about those who may not believe in your book, but for those who choose to, their egos will allow in what they desire on *their* conscious level and filter out the rest. For still others, they may read these words—and more—much more. They may read between *your* lines—*your* boundaries—*your* filtering system."

"What is my filtering system?"

"The questions you are asking—the directions they are taking. It is merely *your* pathway at this point. It is not *the* pathway. Truth—*your* truth is only what you now know…and you only know now what you are ready to know.

"Max once told you that there are no absolute truths. He recognized that in a multifaceted, constantly changing world, truth would necessarily shift as the shifting sands of *any* time. Indeed, truth has a thousand faces—as many facets as there are ways to perceive it…and they are all valid. Do not invalidate the truth of any one soul, if you wish to be true to your own soul, for each is a part of the whole of which you are comprised—each a living cell of the living body. There is, indeed, no one absolute truth. All that is projected and perceived is true…for All are magnificent aspects of the Glorious Infinite.

"Max also said he thought we were ready for the Dead Sea Scrolls and the Nag Hammadi texts because they appeared about the same time as the atomic bomb. Was that true…or I guess I should say valid? "

"Were you not told that there were many other things that were not written in your Bible? You were ready for the message of the secreted texts, but, like your myths, they have already become corrupted. You are translating them in the context of *your* world and *your* understanding…and parts of them have already been literally and figuratively blown away with the winds."

"Why did a particular sect of Christians feel as though they had to secret them away in the first place?"

"They were hidden for a reason. It is not important here, but is seemed like a good reason at the time. However, when those of you buried them in the caves and deserts, you began to forget them, so you also buried the wisdom they held into the recesses of your minds. And, therefore, they were lost to mankind both literally and symbolically.

"Now the ancient texts have reappeared, and they are fragmented, damaged, worded for another time. Thus it is important to commit this information that you are being given to your memory and to preserve it—not merely on paper, but in your heart and mind—not in a stone cave. And it is passed along in that way. And in that way, no one can destroy its value. It can never be lost again. It will stay alive…a living force—beyond the grasp of language, time and decay.

"This is your purpose. This is your mission. This is your last coin. *This* is what you will hold on to when you have let go of all else."

"This book?"

"Your connection to your own inner awareness that you have accessed through the *process* of this book…the unlocking of the door to your kingdom within…and your kingdom that is not of this world, not of this particular vibrational plane."

Trish was trying to think of her next question, when Freya asked, "Do you recall the day you became aware of this story?"

Trish closed her eyes for a moment, remembering the day she saw the television program. *"I remember," she replied.*

"You believe that the inspiration for your story came from the airways on a television screen, do you not?"

"Yes."

"The airways of what you call telecommunication are not the only forms of communication carried on the air in your world. There are other messages—sometimes subtle, sometimes forceful—carried on the air, the wind and even strange, ghostly puffs of wind."

Trish looked up, surprised.

"Ah. You remember the mysterious drafts from that day in your garden.

"Years before that day in your time frame, a woman in the place called Kazakhstan gave birth to one of the harbinger gods of which we spoke. She felt the same horror that you felt in the clinic that day, and at a time when she should have been experiencing great joy. In her pain, she cried out from the depths of her soul to the universe, as had others before her. Her plea for help was sent out with such pain, intensity, sincerity and depth of emotion that it transcended the bonds of time and space that you experience on your Earth plane.

"That sincere plea—that prayer—went out into the universe with such force it was as a seed driven into the Earth by a great whirlwind. That seed, that prayer, traveled the realms of the universe on the wind until it found fertile ground. It lodged itself in your feelings that day in your garden. You were struggling to protect your plants, to keep them alive, and you provided the ground for the seed she sent to be sown. You nurtured that seed as a woman with child, and your time for birthing is upon you."

Trish almost whispered, *"I remember that day.."*

"Indeed. And on the day you fainted in your clinic, you had just gazed upon the woman's harbinger child."

"Oh..." she whispered again, remembering the sight. Her eyes began filling, and tears began running down her face.

"At times you must be still enough to hear those messages. Even in the midst of frenzy, you must have a still place inside you that is ready to hear. There are messages imprinted on the ethers if you can listen with other ears. And, if you learned to do this, you might not need your media to provide you with information. That day is upon you. One day you will find so much information and adventure and entertainment even in a walk through the woods that you will forget to turn on your television screens, for they will pale in comparison.

"Your electronic gadgetry, which you now find so entertaining, will never be as fascinating as your own selves, for you are the creators of those gadgets, and you will always be greater than they. That is why your awesome powers are greater—many times greater—than your atomic bombs. The power of those bombs is held within the power of your atoms. Now, look at your little finger and tell me: how many atoms do you see? Look at your body and tell me if you need a lie detector machine to know your truth."

Trish took in a deep breath and let it out.

"Your truth was even carried on your breath just now. It is in your body, in your goose bumps, which you felt the day you breathed in the strange waft of air in your garden. Your body knows *all* truth, and it speaks to you often, if you will only take time to listen. Your heart is speaking to you now. Can you hear it? It knocks at the door of your consciousness dozens of times each minute.

"Is that not loyalty? Is that not love?"

As tears continued to roll down Trish's cheeks, she wiped them with her hand.

"Even your tears know your truth. You searched throughout your adult life to find the truth, and all the time it was within you as well as without.

"Now, speak it. Sing it. Give it a new vibration that shares with the world. For in the myriad of truths being spoken and sung, is a celestial chorus waiting to be heard on your Earth plane. This truth does not say 'yes' when it means 'no.' It does not sing happiness when it feels sorrow. It expresses what it is from the heart.

"Listen to your beating heart. Feel it. Express it."

Trish sat in silence for a moment, then asked, *"But what happened when I fainted in the clinic? Where did I go? I felt like I went somewhere I'd been before, but I can't remember what happened."*

"You, too, had escaped the bonds of time and space. That place is always there, when your conscious mind can no longer deal with those boundaries. Some experience that place as what you call deep coma and stay for a longer time. Others never return. It is as another vibrational plane. You were being prepared for the journey ahead of you.

"This journey has been about you. The atomic age is about you."

Trish wiped the last of her tears from her face and looked up.

"And if all that you see and experience and feel and remember *is* you, what does your atomic age say about you?"

"I don't know what you mean."

"Are your atomic bombs and hydrogen bombs and neutron bombs not the most powerful forces you can imagine of your manmade inventions?"

"Yes, I guess so."

"And are they not your creations?"

"Yeah...they are."

"They *are* part of you—an aspect of you—as are your uranium cartels. And if your bombs and cartels and governments and news media are aspects of all that you are, then what is it that they—you—don't want you to know about yourselves?"

Trish paused a moment, and then her eyes widened, as she responded with surprise, *"How much power we have?"*

Stephanie let out a sigh. "Yes! More in your little finger than in all of your atomic or hydrogen or neutron bombs. For how may you feel empowered, lest you are able to face what you perceive as the most powerful force on your Earth plane? How may you face your fears unless you feel as though you have no other choice? Unless you feel as though you are facing your physical death? You have brought yourselves to this point with your creations. And your powerful creations are bringing you to awareness...if you choose this awareness...if you choose to begin experiencing the true power of your Spiritual heritage."

"Then if just one of us knows this..."

"And *feels* it..."

"... and feels it, then will everyone else begin becoming aware of it?"

"It is as the one mustard seed which *knows*...and it will become fruitful and multiply."

"Even in the face of so much opposition?"

"The seed of ideas...the Light of your Being may never be extinguished, for its Source will ever be."

"And the knowledge the seed contains?"

"What you call 'knowledge' is not what you call wisdom. Knowledge is learned; wisdom is known. It is known in the depths of the soul, rather than limited to the mind. It is known also in the heart.

"It is born of stillness, rather than of agitation. It is not a reward for hard work, but a gift ever present. It does not have to be broken into, but only allowed in.

"It must come in, not only through the head, but also through the heart and the breath.

"Wisdom is love. Love is power. All are One.

"If you choose to enter into or allow your Christ consciousness, you may move beyond your knowledge of good and evil, into an aware state of wisdom. And it will be a glorious awakening. You will feel as though you have made many exciting discoveries, but these 'discoveries' will simply be the aspects of yourselves that were always there—hidden behind your veil of forgetfulness...for you create *worlds*. Every thought, every image, every daydream you have ever dreamed, sprinkles stars upon your heavens. *That* is the power you possess."

"Just like Old Tom said about remembering?"

"Indeed."

Trish paused. *"Sometimes, I think I should have eaten that Witchetty grub he offered me."*

"You would not have like it."

Trish laughed out loud.

"Let us pause now for this one's sake."

Chapter Forty-Seven

After another break, Trish resumed. *"Maybe I shouldn't, but I still get a little frustrated when I see how governments and multi-national corporations treat indigenous people like Old Tom and the others."*

"They have stolen none of the true power of the people, for you are never less than you are. To follow the path that you, Trish Cagle, have chosen, you must see the divinity in all others—including the entities of your governments and your corporations—for they are your mirrors—as you are theirs. What you see as separate is but a reflection of yourself. And in that moment of recognizing the divinity in all there is and was and shall be, you are in a holy, wholly moment.

"Even your news media—which you have left because you have judged it to be corrupt—is a divine entity."

"I don't know how you figure that."

"Did you not learn about your Cyclops and Mermaid from your news media?"

"Yeah, but...but they didn't intend for it to affect me the way it did or to find what I did. They just saw it as another interesting story they could make money on."

"Ah...intentions...and, indeed, that may have been their *conscious* intention, but look to your puzzles—your stories behind the stories—the intention behind the intention. Did not even their conscious intention get *your* attention? Did it not bring you ultimately to this point? Do you not feel blessed by what you considered your nemesis?"

Trish focused on the words and tried to breathe them in. She sat with that feeling for a moment, as the intensity of her former feeling toward her profession began melting into a strange sensation of warmth and realization.

"Is this what you mean by transformation?"

"You are trying it on for size. How does it feel?"

She laughed out loud. *"Actually, it feels pretty damn good!"*

"Beyond your 'transformations' may come transfigurations."

"What's that?"

"The transfiguration that you speak of with your Christed Being was a remembrance—a reminder—of the processes that you have employed in times from your ancient past. There will come a time in your not too distant future when many of you will begin experiencing transformation, transmutation, transfiguration and transcension. The only differences in these processes are your levels of awareness.

"Some of your indigenous people of ancient and present times, as well as your holy men and shamans, experience some of these processes as what you call shape shifting, invisibility and bi-location—various states brought about by conscious and even unconscious molecular and vibrational shifting. From what source do you believe words like 'transfiguration' and 'transcension,' are derived? You have a knowing beyond your arcane educational systems that keep you locked in boxes of third dimensional perceptions. You may feel and language yourselves back to these ancient wisdoms and begin to re-experience the *true* freedoms you seek so desperately that your lives are in turmoil, and you don't even know why. You are chafing at your 3D boundaries.

"These processes are merely consciousness shifted to other aspects of yourselves that you experience as separate. You are no more separate than any cell of your body is separate from your whole body. It is the functioning of your body, the purpose of it that you experience as materialized. When it no longer serves your purpose, your intention, you 'die' to it. It drops away, and you return to your source. You are approaching a time when death, as you experience it, is not your only option, or you will become aware of the other options which you have, and which you have employed in your past— or other levels of awareness. This is what you have referred to as a time of your Second Coming. It is upon you. Your time is at hand. It has always been at hand—at the tips of your fingers—the tip of your tongue—the edges of your memory—the boundaries of your consciousness.

"Opportunity after opportunity presents itself every day of your life in a myriad of forms and events that make up your daily experiences. Experience them. Recognize them. Become aware of them. They come as gentle breezes of coolness on a hot summer day; as joy at the birth of any new living creature; as shock at anything that disrupts your everyday sleeping existence. They may be gentle or forceful. They are breakthroughs, breakdowns, cracks in your perceptions that lead to transcensions and awareness.

"You are the atomic generation. You have all been 'nuked,' as you say. It is a golden age, a golden opportunity. A door has opened. Do not judge who opened that door for you."

"You said we could feel and language ourselves back to the ancient wisdoms. How do we language ourselves?"

"You create your state of mind with your words.

"You define your words, and your words, in turn, define you. You *spell* your words, and your words, in turn, spell *you*. They put you under a spell of limits of time, space and bodies—frameworks, beliefs and ideas.

"The spell your words have cast on you is one of a limit of seven. It shapes your present world and how you experience it. It is the limit of your time, colors, sounds and energies. It is the edge of your present world."

"I know you said earlier there are an infinite number of energies or chakras. But for the next level of our evolutionary progression as more

spiritual beings, what number is optimum for our present use?"

"Your questions are becoming more direct and conscious."

Stephanie sat quietly for a moment, then…"It is difficult for you to let go of your linear beliefs at this point. But a natural, more balanced number of chakras would be the number twelve. This number provides a portal into untold numbers of chakras for future spiritual development."

"Why twelve?"

"Twelve is a number associated with your sacred geometry. And your sacred geometry is that which is built into your bodies and your nature. It is the number of the Disciples with which the Christed Being encircled himself to fulfill his mission.

"Look also to the number of sections on many of your turtle shells. The center section of the shell is encircled with twelve, which support it in *its* life cycle. The turtle is the symbol for Mother Earth in many native myths. It symbolizes the Goddess of the Great Spirit. Many native cultures keep that Spirit alive in ceremony with consciousness, as they sweat in a circular, purification lodge around a central flame encircled with twelve poles.

"Twelve is the number of your signs of your Zodiac—the totality of your circular patterning of your time measurements of Earth and Sky. It is the number of your tribes of Israel. It is the number of angels after Armageddon. It is the number of foundations of the new city that descends from heaven—the New Jerusalem that follows Armageddon. It is the number of the fruits of the Tree of Life and from which fruit are yielded every month…again, after Armageddon.

"It is the age your Christed Being came into his fullness. *Your* species is entering *its* age of twelve, as well. This is, indeed, your dawning of your Age of Twelve, your Age of Aquarius. It is there for your taking…and you may doubt and you may deny and prophesy and betray and tempt and heal, as did the twelve apostles. But until *all* of your energies of denial, doubt, treachery, prophecy, healing, learning, teaching, creating, nurturing, destroying, supporting and surrendering are in balance, they cannot awaken to the thirteenth consciousness of your Christed Being. When you gather *all* of your aspects together in balance, they provide your center of gravity—the point of perfect equilibrium…the awakening of the Christ consciousness.

"Behold! He (you) stands at the door (of your heart) and knocks. Do you hear him (you)? Do you hear the beating of his heart inside your chest?

"It is a cellular coming. It is a cellular memory that will awaken your birthright. The new wine is creating new bottles, new temples, new bodies—that can contain the new wine that will be poured into your being.

"If you have encircled your being with the sacred support of twelve, then you may reach a perfect balance of your center now-point, and you will gift yourself with your Christ consciousness—your thirteenth being. None may reach the Father/Mother except through this consciousness.

"The seven colors of your rainbow are the present edge of your world. The seven notes of the sound of your music, the seven energy centers from which you operate, the seven days of creation—all—are the edges of your world. Your seven wonders of your world are the edges of your wonders. And even your seven heavens are the edges of your heavens. Seven years are your cycles of death and rebirth. The number seven has been your vibrational limit of time, sight and sound. It is your creation.

"You are, indeed, gods. You are both creators and destroyers—for there is a time for building up and a time for tearing down.

"The day after your Trinity—which you called your day at Alamogordo—a new cycle began for your planet. It is a cycle of death and rebirth."

"If we're moving from a vibration of seven to one of twelve, what new levels of energies—or chakras—will be awakened at this time?"

"There are many diverse disciplines about chakras in your cultures, and there is no one truth about them. It is all true within the context in which they are understood and worked with.

"One of the new awakenings of energy that may take place in the temples of your bodies is the one of which we spoke...the one described as your fontanel—the soft spot that has become hardened. To receive the new wine, a new opening must emerge on your head. This is the allowance of your feminine energy.

"You may experience tingling at this portal when it begins opening for you, or loss of hair."

"And the other chakras?"

"Your Zeal point rests at the base of your skull, the top of your spine, the place where the energies of your head and heart come together. It is what has been called your 'old brain,' your reptilian brain. It controls your very breath. It is the house of ancient memory.

"It is the point that was jolted into wakefulness when you viewed the mutants in Clinic Number Four. It is why you slipped suddenly into 'unconsciousness'—but which, in fact, was consciousness—for it was a timelessness.

"At that point, or chakra, you were 'hooked,' committed. A door had opened, an ancient portal into your temple. You glimpsed an ancient truth—a prophecy and a wisdom."

"Is that why I'm here...talking to the goddess who's supposed to be the keeper of ancient wisdom?"

"*Someone* has to remember." Stephanie pointed to herself. "I am that aspect of your self and of this one, and of all aspects of all others—even in those where I sleep, waiting to be awakened.

"You were awakened at the clinic, and began the process of remembering who you truly are."

"When Stephanie said 'the keeper of ancient wisdom,' I was puzzled. Is there only one keeper of ancient wisdom?"

"Any one who keeps ancient wisdom is a keeper of those wisdoms. Your present belief system supports an idea framework of 'one' God—'the' God—and that is your truth, just as others in their times believed in many gods, and that was their truth in their time. For there are, indeed, many gods and there is one—just as there are many goddesses, and there is one. All *are* one, and the One is many...many aspects, which you experience as separate and apart. That perception, which you hold for your present purposes, has served you. When it no longer serves your purposes, you may begin releasing it, and thus your hold on your perceptions of 'the' and 'a' and 'one'...and, yes, even 'many.'"

"After the Zeal Point, what level is next?"

"It is the Thymus Chakra we spoke of earlier."

"Thymus, huh?"

"It is called that. Some call these points 'sub-chakras.' The thymus is called a gland, and it resides between your heart and your throat chakra. When your heart is opened—through whatever manner you chose, your thymus chakra awakened allows the joining of the energies of your heart and your throat. It allows the expression of the heart to manifest through the throat. It is where you set your intentions, imprint your gratitude and formulate your desires. It is the altar of your temple, from which flow the prayers of your sincerity, or your incense to the gods—*all* gods—the One and the All."

"Where are the other three located?"

"They reside below your heart chakra. They reside among the other chakras below your heart.

"Once you begin feeling your truth from your heart center and speaking it through your intention from your throat center, you must stand in it, if you are to continue in your progression of awakening as Spiritual Beings. Once you stand in your truth, you must walk in it to continue forward motion. You are mobile beings, and entropy is a powerful energy to keep you set in your ways. There is a time for the stillness of meditation and there is a time for walking meditation.

"Your feet are the entryways from the vibration of the Earth. They keep you rooted whenever you need the support of the Earth, and they provide support for you to walk your path. If you focus on the energy at this connection point between your body and the Earth and allow it to enter your body, you can feel the energy manifesting in tingling or warmth and then pull it into your body. Walk barefoot to feel that power of the Earth Mother. She is

533

waiting for your touch.

"You touch the Earth through your feet and you touch that which is around you with your hands. Your hands and your feet are your animating principles. Again, when they awaken, they may begin to heat or tingle. You may pull in the energies of the Sky through your fontanel and the energies of the Earth through your feet and out through your hands. You may do this to heal. Some call it therapeutic touch or laying-on-of-hands, as the Christed One did. Hippocrates referred to it as the heat that oozes through the hands in his healing work. Some call it Reiki. It is all the same.

"Your feet and your hands moving in the Earth plane form the circle that you see in the DaVinci sketch. It forms the sacred geometry of your bodies. It is your extension from the interior world to the exterior."

When Stephanie paused, Trish asked, *"And then?"*

"Another chakra where energy and awareness are awakening is a place that runs along a line in your body referred to as the Hara Line. It is well known in some cultures, and for good reason. When you walk in your truth, you must have balance. The center of gravity that resides on your Hara Line, when awakened, will provide the more exquisite balance needed for the newly awakened Cosmic Beings that walk the Earth plane. You speak of the center of gravity in your bodies. This center is your mixing bowl or storage center for Sky energy and Earth energy, also called Chi or prana.

"Your organs and glands in the belly chakra are influenced by this center. When the new wine enters your vessel, that which enters into your energy field must be digested and absorbed...and that which no longer serves you at any particular point of this evolutionary process must be released.

"It is difficult for you to think of thought-forms being processed through your body, as though they were food products. But this is the function of your mind, body and soul connection. You are energy. Food is energy. Thought is energy. What you experience in your *spiritual* field of energy is manifested in your *physical* field of energy. Energy moves through you. It must move through you, for you to continue to exist in this vibrational field."

"And the other chakra?"

"It is sometimes called the diaphragm chakra. The Breath of Life lives here. Focusing on your breath brings awareness of your source. You can exercise with your breath. Some of you call this 'breath work,' and, with awareness, you can pull in much energy and information that lies within and without you. There is no need to point out the importance of this unconscious energy, for without it you would not survive long on this Earth plane. However, by focusing on it with consciousness—even on occasion through your day—you bring an awareness to your life that can take your breath away.

"When you begin entering into this new dimension of evolution, your spiritual and physical connection is stronger. The delineations you have maintained with your mind are less defined. The vibrations that enter your body in the form of food, and the spiritual vibrations that enter your consciousness, are of utmost importance.

"The vibrations you take *in* to your personal field will be what you give out. And what you give *out* will be what you receive. That is the nature of electromagnetic beings."

"So, if I'm understanding this correctly, there are twelve energies—or chakras—in our bodies required for the next level of awareness. And the thirteenth is above our bodies, termed the crown chakra, or Christ consciousness."

"Yes. There are infinite numbers of energies outside of your bodies…but they must be accessed through your Christ consciousness. None come to the Creator, but through this energy.

"Hmm. I'm going to have to think about this a while."

"Instead of thinking, try feeling. Some of these minor chakras are already awakening in people; they can feel it. Simple awareness of them is powerful, indeed."

Stephanie sat quietly a few moments, while Trish examined her feelings. Trish focused on several of the discussed locations in her body. In her hands and the top of her head, she began feeling tingling.

● ● ●

While Stephanie drank some water, Trish gathered her thoughts. Then Freya continued.

"Your DNA takes the form of a double helix, like the symbol of your medical community, where the serpents twine around a staff. That is an ancient symbol.

The staff symbolizes your spine, and the serpents symbolize your DNA. When these twelve chakras open, or activate, your DNA will take on a new and ancient form. You will have twelve points bound together in the spiral. This DNA may be referred to as junk DNA. However, the animating principle of the universal energy field, the very spirit of creation, was much wiser than to produce 'junk.'

"Your body is your temple where you meet your God. Be ye therefore wise as serpents, if you are truly seeking. For if you are truly seeking, you shall find. If you truly knock, it will be opened unto you. No one other than your self holds the key for you, for you live in a vibrational plane of free will."

"I'm having a different perception of this free will thing…how it may work into some kind of plan."

"Ah, your plan...the divine plan. Is it not divine?"

"I'm not sure. I haven't had much time to think about it, yet. I know you said to try to feel about it, but I guess I'm not even sure how I feel about it."

"That is because you try to *define* your feelings—to put them in your words, to judge them and control them, instead of simply allowing them...allowing them to move you forward...toward the thing you seek in the deepest and highest part of your Spirit."

"But is that it? The Great Mystery? The divine plan?"

"It is but one of a million mysteries and a million wonders in a million worlds, beyond your conscious awareness."

"But that makes it sound so simple...and yet so unreachable."

"What would your Max have said about that?"

Trish grinned. *"He would have said, 'There's that paradox again.'"* Trish raised her hand up and propped her chin in it. *"He was really something, wasn't he?"*

"Do you know how much you loved him?"

Trish brought her hand down. *"Yes,"* she replied, with emotion welling inside her.

"Love yourself that much."

Again, Trish wept, while Stephanie sat quietly.

● ● ●

Trish regained her composure after a time and returned to the conversation.

"Tell me more about this Christ consciousness that's supposed to be awakening in us."

"Your Christed One—your Christed self—came to bring fire, ancient fire, nuclear fire, radiation, that you may radiate with the Light that is within you.

"He came not to bring peace, but division—or fission—to disperse what you *think* of as yourselves. Only when your ideas of yourselves have been *dis*membered with the sword of the Christed Being, may you *re*member your atoms, your fusion, who you truly are.

"Your other selves may often bring what you perceive as frustration, treachery and temptation, as you, your self may bring these to your own being. You may also experience what you perceive as great love, healing, prophecy and knowing from yourself and your other selves. But it is all of these aspects in balance—all of these energies in balance—that bring your Christed being to your consciousness—your awareness.

"You believed that Judas was evil. But treachery was necessary for the divine plan to be fulfilled. You betray your *selves* when it is necessary to fulfill *your* destiny—as your other selves betray you to fulfill theirs, as well as yours.

"When all your selves are remembered as One—*then* you may realize and remember the Light that is within you. Then you may walk, as your Bible says, without stumbling in the twelve hours of the day in the Light of the world. Then you may sing a new song. Then you may see through the single eye that brings Light throughout your whole—holy—body.

"Your Christed One had many things to say to you in his physical time on your Earth, but he told you that you could not hear them at that time…and there were many other things that were not written in his physical time. Yet, he sent Spirit to teach you and to guide you and to help you to remember.

"If you open yourself to your Christ consciousness, you wed the Spirit and the Bride. Then the marriage of the Lamb and his Wife, spoken of in the Bible, is come. Then you enter the New Heaven and New Earth."

"Tell me more about the twined serpents."

"It is not only an ancient symbol; it is an ancient wisdom. The serpents were not always twined. They could lie coiled at the base of the spine. When the Kundalini energy rose up the spine, it was a time of awakening.

"In ancient times…in times reflected in hieroglyphics…those of the throne did not wear golden *crowns* of cobras. They wore *live* cobras coiled in majesty on their heads. They had achieved a level of initiation into the Great Mystery that was symbolized by the coiled serpent—their vortex awakened. Cobras today still remember the role they played in those ancient times.

"And in those ancient times, those of the throne symbolized what the masses could achieve in another lifetime. They could aspire to that majesty as long as they kept their symbol alive.

"Then Masters came *among* the people—not *above* them—as other Masters had before—to show them that they could achieve states of consciousness such as theirs' in *this* lifetime…that they could do even greater works than they…that they could be, therefore, wise as serpents.

"There are moments of great and sudden emotion that cause you to recoil. You may think some of these moments are horrid or physically shocking, but, in fact, these are sacred moments. For in those moments, your energies are brought back into their natural state of the coiled serpent. That is also what happened to you at Clinic Number Four. The horror you felt— the trigger you sensed—caused your energies to unconsciously, involuntarily and momentarily retreat to a primal ancient, natural state.

"This is also what happened to Max at Dachau…though, like you, he was consciously unaware of it."

"So these things we think of as crises and trauma really do serve a vital purpose in our growth?"

"Yes."

"And they come when we don't realize it, if we experience them while we're on a sacred path?"

"*All* paths are sacred...but when you risk the world as you know it, you bring yourself to the edge of life as you know it. And when you bring yourself to that point and make your desires known to the universe, there is an expansion...first in vortex areas on Earth, then in yourself. You may only sense these expansions—for you may not measure them with your Old World instruments."

"Have I been in one of these areas in the last few months?"

"Several times."

"Where?"

"Can you think of one where you felt it?"

Trish closed her eyes and thought a moment. *"In the front yard of Max's cabin when I was spinning the bull-roarer?"*

"That is the spot where you summoned me."

"I don't remember consciously doing that."

"You were summoning the wisdom that you felt had left you...the wisdom that Max represented. Your desire, your prayer, at that time of the spinning energies, broke through the vibrations of your Earth plane and was heard throughout the galaxies."

"You created that vortex. You created them as a child when you spun the energies of the rising storms around with your body. When you spoke to Old Tom, when you had your 'epiphany,' and time stood still, this, too, was a vortex. He summoned you from the shade of the billabong out to that sacred spot.

"Though some of these vortices may lie unseen and unfelt on the Earth plane, they are sensed by spiritual seekers, and are enhanced by those who use them. You make them come alive, and they, in turn, enliven you. When you enter these areas, they help align, or re-awaken, the sleeping vortex, the sleeping serpent, of your own body. And when you make your true desires known in these vortex areas, the universe will respond with manifestation.

"The ancients knew these sacred spots. They are portals, centers of communication with Spirit, and they radiate sacred energies."

"Aren't all spots sacred?"

"All spots *are* sacred...but in your unaware states, it is difficult for many of you to accept that *any* spot is sacred. You are somewhat able to accept that there are—or were—Enlightened Ones among you. As you become aware that all of you are sacred, you will also become aware that all places are sacred, and you will no longer require pilgrimages to far away places or studies of long ago saints to find the enlightenment or sacredness that is at each of your fingertips, or at each spot where you set your foot.

"Because the Earth is alive, these power points are shifting. They only remain in areas where they are appreciated, loved, energized. Those on a spiritual path are being drawn to these areas. They are leading the way to the edges of your world, as you know it.

"Your scientists—your 1500—were correct with the prophecy they made known to your world. Their prophecy *is* being fulfilled; for your world—as you know it—*is* being destroyed. It is being destroyed by your Destroyer Angels."

Trish let out a long, slow breath. *"You know, I started this out by asking about the mermaids and Cyclopes and mythology and the atomic age. And it didn't go at all where I intended."*

"The answers you sought could not be understood within the framework of your conscious understanding."

"I think I'm beginning to understand some of this, to believe it. I'm not sure how I feel about all of it, but some of it does resonate with me. On some level it makes sense, and sort of feels right. You know?"

"I am aware of your feelings."

"But now I'm kind of sorry that I wasted so much of the last year going in some wrong directions in my search for answers."

"You were not going in wrong directions. A chrysalis must break free from its shell to become the creature of its nature…when the shell no longer serves its desired level of becoming. It was necessary for your destroyer aspects to de-construct your previously held beliefs in a power only outside of yourself. You had to eliminate your faith in institutions which supported your belief systems in your past, but which no longer do. You had to shatter these illusions about your existence on this Earth plane before you could accept, or allow, the new but ancient truths of your being, your world and your galaxies.

"If you had not created that empty space in your belief system—that depression and void—you would not have had a place for the new wine to begin entering into your vessel. It was a necessary process for your evolutionary path to continue its movement forward. It was required for your evolutionary destiny to begin being fulfilled. Darkness *is* the womb from which creation is thought into being…just as night is the cocoon from which your day emerges.

"When starlight was breathed into the darkness, night became day…and when you are come into your Being, you absorb that Light, and you reflect it…for you *are* the Light of your Being.

"And, as your Max told you in your last conversation, 'There is more…*so* much more…'"

"I was going to ask if I could come back sometime at a future date and talk to you again, but…"

"But, as I told this one," Stephanie pointed to her chest. "'You do not have to use elaborate ways to come to me. I will come to you in dreams, along the wooded path and in the words of others...and you will know that they are my words...for I live in your dreams and along your wooded path...and I live in you, as I live in others.'"

"I think I'm ready to go home now."

"You already are."

Chapter Forty-Eight

After Stephanie opened her eyes and took a few moments to clear her head, she said, "I don't know what you got in this channeling, but I know you're going to have to take some time to let it integrate."

Trish shook her head from side to side. "I guess I will. I feel a little shell shocked right now, to tell the truth."

They talked a while longer about what had transpired over the previous hours. Then Trish gathered her things. As they made their way to the front door, Trish thanked her graciously for her time, patience and hospitality.

"It was my pleasure," Stephanie assured her. "I hope it's been some help."

"I'm not sure I can even tell you how much. And you're right; it's been a lot to absorb. I feel like a sponge...like I'm so saturated that, if you touch me, I'll just drip tears."

Stephanie smiled. "Well, don't do that, because I intended to hug you good-bye."

Trish smiled back and the two of them embraced. When they released each other, both had tears streaming down their faces. Trish laughed self-consciously.

"Don't worry, Trish. These are cleansing tears. I think they might be helping you release some blockages and baggage."

As she backed out of the driveway, Trish caught one last glimpse of Stephanie, leaning against the frame of her front door with her arms crossed, beaming a broad smile.

After returning to her hotel, Trish cancelled the rest of her reservations there and called and booked a flight back to Atlanta for the next day. Later that evening she packed her bags, then called Jimmy's house once more. And, once again, the answering machine clicked on. When the tone at the end of the recording came on, she spoke thoughtfully. "Jimmy, it's Trish again. I'm calling from New Mexico. I've just been out here a few days...but I've discovered something here that's caused me to cut my trip short. I'm coming home. I'm catching the 308 flight on Delta tomorrow morning, and I hope we'll have a chance to talk when I get back.

"I love you, Jimmy. I've always loved you. Even with all the pain I've experienced this last year, these have been the happiest months of my entire life—because you were part of it."

• • •

When the Delta jet began its descent into the Atlanta area, Trish felt excitement and tension coursing through her body at the thought of getting back home. She even imagined for a moment that Jimmy might be there at the terminal, waiting for her. On approach, she watched from the window as the streets and cars streaked by. By the time she felt the wheels touch down on the runway, the anticipation had built to a level that made her want to cheer.

Though it seemed to take an eternity for the jet to taxi to the terminal, at last, it came to a stop at the gate. When it did, Trish hurriedly retrieved her carry-on luggage and stood, waiting impatiently for the door to be opened. What if Jimmy didn't want to see her? What if it was too late for the two of them to work things out? She couldn't think like that. She had to believe in the impossible. She let out a breath and felt her body relax. And she had to surrender to life. Everything would be all right...somehow...no matter what happened.

As the doors opened, she wedged into the slowly moving line and out toward the gate. Inside the terminal she looked around. People were everywhere. Just past the gate, away from the worst of the congestion, she stopped to take another look around. Was he there—somewhere in the crowd? Was she just being silly to think that?

She ran her hand through her hair nervously. *Oh, well, I'll just pick up my bag and call Kathy to meet me at the train station.* She started walking down the concourse toward the train and baggage claim.

As she continued reminding herself that everything would work out no matter what happened, she saw Jimmy off at a distance, scanning the crowd. She waved to him, and their eyes met. As he walked toward her, she couldn't believe how good he looked, with that sideways grin and that unruly strand of hair bouncing with each step. For just a moment, she thought she was going to cry. But before she had a chance, he reached her, embraced her tightly and unexpectedly lifted her off the floor, spinning her around in his arms.

When he lowered her back to the floor and released her, she looked up at him. Did this even come close to how Max felt when he got back from the war into Rachel's arms? "Jimmy, it's so good to see you. You just don't know."

"Oh, I think I might," he responded, grinning broadly. Then, with a heave of his chest, he said, "So tell me, Miss Trish, have you found the meaning of life, yet?"

She lowered her eyes and smiled, surveying the floor briefly. How could she ever tell him? "Oh, I don't know, Jimmy...and honestly I don't know if I'll ever even stop searching for it." She looked back up at him, "But there's one thing in this life I *am* absolutely certain about. I'm supposed to love you. I'm supposed to be with you...and grow old with you."

He drew his head back slightly, raising his eyebrows. Then he smiled and drew her to him, as he whispered in her ear, "That's what I've been waiting to hear, Lady." Trish was unaccustomed to hearing that kind of sincerity in his voice. And she liked it.

After Jimmy took her carry-on bag from her shoulder, and they started walking down the concourse, he said, "Baby, there's something I have to tell you about."

He glanced over at an airport concession area along the concourse. "Here…wait a minute." Jimmy quickly guided her to an empty table, where she sat down. He asked if she wanted something to drink.

"A diet drink would be great."

He deposited her bag on the floor and left for the counter. As he stood in line, Trish watched him, noting how appealing he still was to her. As he chatted with another man in line, she noticed how quickly he broke into that enticing smile that had first captivated her so many years before. She felt what seemed like a surge of love reaching out to him from somewhere in her chest area, and—as though he had sensed it—Jimmy turned instantly toward her and beamed that smile directly at her. To Trish it felt as if it all happened in slow motion—as though she was suspending the moment in time.

When he came back to the table with their drinks, he was almost bubbly with enthusiasm. "Trish, I've got to tell you what happened to me while you were gone."

She wondered if he'd had a few doses of synchronicity.

"I got your message this morning," he continued. "In fact, I picked up *all* of your messages this morning…but when I called your hotel, you'd already left for the airport. So I decided to just drive down here and take a chance that I'd meet your flight in time."

"You just got my messages this morning?"

"Yeah."

"Where have you been all this time?"

"Well, after our little spat," he began, as Trish sipped on her soft drink, "I was so down and so confused and frustrated that I just had to get away for a while—from the business, from town and from everybody…to just think. You know?"

She nodded sideways.

"Well, I grabbed my camping gear and headed over to the Tallulah River. Those big boulders and that clear water always get me centered when I need it. I'd rather camp out there than anywhere else in the world." He leaned back and continued. "Anyway, when I got there the weather was great…not too many other folks around. But I was miserable without you…and I wondered where the hell my life was going and what was going to happen to us. I wasn't having much luck with the trout, either," he added.

"But I'd made up my mind I was going to stay as long as it took to figure out what I was going to do. So, last night, after I settled down at my campfire, this old guy who'd been camping nearby came over. I wasn't real eager to have company or strike up any conversations when he asked if he could join me...but I was being polite. You know?"

"Yeah."

Jimmy turned sideways in his chair and draped his arm over the back of it. "He was going on about how his life hadn't turned out like he'd planned and how he was near the end of it now and how he really regretted some of the choices he'd made...how he wished he had a chance to make some of his choices over again." He held out his hand. "I felt sorry for the guy, but I'm thinking, 'Look, Man, I've got problems of my *own* here. Why don't you just go back to your tent and give me a chance to work them out?' But I'm still being polite—even though I'm starting to get annoyed. And he keeps on and on.

"Then all of a sudden it just hits me out of the blue."

"What?"

He leaned onto the table. "He's pouring his heart out to me, talking about how he'd done all these things in his life to let happiness slip through his fingers, and now he was all alone with nothing to do but regret it all...and it just dawns on me. 'Hey, that could be *me* thirty years or so from now. *I* could be the one sitting across from some guy on the Tallulah River telling him how I'd wasted *my* chances at happiness.'" He took a long breath. "Then the guy went back to his campsite, and I started feeling sorry for him instead of annoyed." He tapped his fingers on the table. "Then I started thinking about what you asked me that day...about whether I'd ever found someone who'd choose me over everything and everybody else..."

She nodded.

"And I realized I had. In fact, in my last marriage to Deidre, she practically gave up everything in her life for me. She stayed home, cleaned house, cooked. She was a great cook. She didn't really maintain any close relationships with anybody else—but me. Hardly ever went anywhere without me. Wasn't even really interested in having children. She didn't act like she cared about much of anything, but me and our marriage. And you know what?"

"What?"

"I eventually felt smothered by her. I mean, it was great at first. But then I started feeling trapped...like she was dependent on me for everything—even her emotional stability. I didn't feel like I had a chance to be myself with her. She didn't want us to associate with other couples...or me with any of my old friends...and by the time we got divorced, I was so relieved to be out of the marriage that I felt like some animal that had been let out of a cage."

Trish was listening intently, with only occasional, absent-minded sips on her drink.

"Then something else dawned on me...sitting there on that river," he continued.

"What was that?"

He smiled at her. "I realized the *passion* you have for the things you do is exactly what attracted me to you." He leaned back again. "I mean, I've always had this thing about people from Atlanta who go up to Rabun County and buy a piece of land because it's natural and wild and beautiful. Right off the bat, they start cutting down trees and mountain laurel, and planting grass that they'll have to mow and flowers they'll have to tend. I always think, 'Hell, if you want Atlanta, then stay the hell in Atlanta. If you want mountains and wilderness, then let it alone...and just *enjoy* it. What you saw when you got here, is why you fell in love with it in the first place.

"Now, I realize that was exactly what I'd been doing with you, Trish: not appreciating you for what you are...trying to change you into one of those kinds of women I *thought* I wanted, instead of just enjoying you for who you are. Who you are, is why I fell in love with you in the first place." He wagged his head and gave a slight snicker. "Besides, I don't think I ever *could* change you if I tried. I don't think anyone could. It's like those folks from Atlanta—the ones who try to change the mountains, instead of enjoying them for what they are—they don't last. They don't belong there. The first ice storm—without water and electricity for a few days—and that 'for sale' sign goes up, and they're gone.

"The mountains will always go back wild...eventually. They won't tolerate someone who doesn't have a taste—a *passion*—for the wild in them."

Jimmy looked down at the floor a moment...and Trish allowed the moment to linger without interruption.

He looked back up. "Anyway, I went to sleep last night, and then this morning I packed up my gear and went back home. I decided then and there that whatever it took, we were going to have a life together...if you'd still have me, that is...however you wanted it. If you *never* wanted to get married, that'd be fine with me. If you wanted to go to the Arctic Pole or to the *moon* looking for whatever it is you're looking for, that'd be fine, too. I know I said it before, but I really mean it now. I think I've finally grown into the words I said. I even figured I'd go with you on some of your searches...if you wanted me along...even if I need to sell the business."

He stretched back in the seat. "Hell, I need to start focusing on my life and what I really want out of it instead of chasing a buck all the time, anyway. I need to spend more time with my horses and fishing." He chuckled. "It didn't matter that the fish weren't biting the last few days; I realized at some point that I was just meditating. My head got so clear out there...always does."

He looked directly at her. "I need to figure out a *lot* of things about myself, Trish: why I run from one relationship to the other when things get tough; why I let you get out of my life instead of confronting what I thought was going on. I don't think I'll ever be able to be whole in a relationship until I can be whole with myself, like I was out there on the Tallulah. I started really *feeling* things for a change."

Trish felt tears welling in her eyes, but she blinked them away and continued to focus on Jimmy.

"So, I get home and see I've got messages on the machine, and I punch the button, and there's your voice telling me what you're thinking and feeling. And I realize that everything's going to be okay." He finished his drink, then stared at his glass.

Trish finally broke the silence. "Jimmy, that's probably the most beautiful story I've ever heard."

He twisted the glass back and forth. "Well, I thought I'd really blown it this time. And, all of a sudden, I felt like I'd gotten a reprieve from the governor or something." He looked up at her. "So, tell me, what happened out in New Mexico that brought you home in such a hurry?"

Trish shrugged her shoulders. "Oh, I don't know if it was as dramatic as your story." She grinned sideways. "But it'll take me a little longer to tell you about it. Why don't we go pick up my other bag? And we'll talk about it on the way back to Clayton."

He leaned forward, put his hand behind her neck and kissed her on the forehead.

"Jimmy?"

"Yeah?" he asked, leaning back.

"I like the man who came back from the Tallulah River this morning. I've never seen him before. And I'd like to get to know him better, while he starts discovering himself."

He threw his head back and laughed. "Do you think you're ready for that?"

"Jimmy, I'm ready for *anything*. I always was a risk-taker."

As Trish and Jimmy got up from their seats and started walking back down the concourse, she said, "I hope you'll be able to put up with me now."

"Why? What *has* been going on with you?" He stopped a moment. "And why did you cut your trip short?"

"Well...I've been going through some discoveries about myself, too." Looking ahead as they continued walking, she asked, "What would you think if I wrote a book and you were one of the characters in it?"

"*Me*? Hell, I'd *sue* you."

She laughed. "But what if I made a lot of money at it?"

"Then I'd sue you for a lot of money."

She laughed again. "Well, after the wedding, I think I might be spending a *lot* of time around the house writing that book."

Jimmy stopped abruptly, and she took one more step before she stopped, too, and turned to face him. Without saying a word, he shot her that sideways smile again.

"Do you think you can find time to fit that into your schedule?" she asked, tilting her head to the side.

"Well..." He grinned. "I *think* I could squeeze you in."

They took up their pace walking again and Jimmy added, "But now, I'm planning to go hunting with Mack next week..."

Trish jabbed him in the ribs with her elbow.

"...and I'm planning to go trout fishing again with Mike after *that*..."

Trish broke out into an open laugh.

"...and then *next* month I'm..."

As they continued down the concourse, the sound of their voices trailed off into the din of other voices and noises that surrounded them, and just for a second, Trish felt as though she was watching herself and Jimmy from a distance, as their tiny images—like drops of water—faded into the stream of activity and bustle around them...and their pathway merged into that stream, like any stream that merges with others into mighty rivers and ultimately to their source.

Chapter Forty-Nine

Fourth Millennium
Desert region of the Southwest Quadrant

When Evonna de los Legionnites pulled up to the domed edifice where the sightseeing tour was to begin, she parked her hoverlette at one of the posts, then ran her wrist over its scanner. The familiar bleep sounded, signaling that her implant coder had charged her account and secured her vehicle. The first to arrive, she decided to wait outside for the others. The warm sun and the light breezes were too inviting to waste.

She straightened her prism necklace and dusted her lavender tunic. That morning she'd selected the color to match her aura. Even though a lot of people still didn't see auras, it didn't matter; she only dressed for herself. The prism, however, was selected for others; whenever the sunlight hit it at the just the right angle, it would bounce off someone else's aura, creating a dazzling light display—but only for those who could see it, and it was easy to gauge from people's reactions just who saw it and who didn't.

Evonna was taking the tour that day with her friend, Belina de los Terralites. Belina was going through a marked change in her life, having applied for and received a license for a birthing experience. Accordingly, her implant coder had been reprogrammed to allow her body to release eggs. She had been allotted two years to try for a natural impregnation with her male counter-partner, and if unsuccessful, she had received a credit for two implant tries. Her friend had been full of expectation at the prospect of having a baby.

Though Evonna, herself, had at least five more years to decide whether to apply, she felt no pressure to make a hurried decision. She was quite content working with the primitives who lived in the commune near the ancient pyramid mountain on the outskirts of her city. Similar mysterious mounds also dotted landscapes all over the world, and she felt fortunate to be able to devote her career to studying the people who lived near them.

She'd begun her professional life as a transcriber. When the worldwide plague viruses had incapacitated the computers many years before, much of the knowledge of the past had been lost. In retrospect, it seemed ironic that most of the world's databases on history, archeology, technology and medicine had been stored in computer banks, since when the plagues hit, almost all of it had been wiped out. What was left and what was reprogrammed, had to be backed up now by Scribes, who transferred the remaining computer data into books made with lisolite pages, and which in turn were stored in secure vaults.

For a long time Evonna had enjoyed the work. It was fulfilling to complete a book and be able to hold a tangible object that could be read without an energy source. But when she started becoming bored with her work, she went for a career re-evaluation, and just as she'd suspected, she had evolved to another level.

Eventually she was assigned to work with people who hadn't yet learned to communicate psychically. It was rewarding work. She, along with more and more others, had been born with telepathic abilities, and she found it enjoyable to teach some of those who had been born without the talent already awakened. Whenever one of her mostly older students finally mastered mind telepathy, the look in their eyes and the surprise and joy they radiated at that moment of revelation was one of the most rewarding experiences she'd had in her working life.

Then unexpectedly one day, she was asked if she wanted to transfer to an assignment working on communication with the primitives. She agreed, and immediately found the assignment to be interesting and challenging. She developed a satisfactory rapport with the primitives, although she faced the same problem with them that everyone else had: an inability to communicate with them fully on any level.

The systems leader thought it was useless to continue trying to communicate with them through telepathy, believing it might be more useful to first teach them Universalis and then the telepathy. Though the universal language that had developed out of a need to communicate universally had been helpful to humanity, it had also been extremely limiting. It was impossible to fit all human emotions and thoughts into the constraints of the language, as comprehensive as it was.

A virtually unsuccessful program had begun years before to teach the elder primitives the language, and Evonna quickly came to the conclusion that it might never be successful. Even though the primitives made only grunting and clicking sounds as well as hums to each other, observations led her to believe they had their own system of telepathic communication. That no one had tapped into it yet didn't dampen her belief. And because she held so fervently to that belief, she had been allowed to pursue her theory.

● ● ●

Evonna's studies of the primitives—or mound builders, as they were sometimes called—painted a picture of an unusual people, complex and even mystical. Worldwide, they lived in close proximity to the various strange pyramid-shaped mound mountains, and they all performed the same strange religious rituals. Though the rituals were well documented, they were not at all understood. One of those daily rituals involved their flowers, which the primitive mound builders called spiders. Great care was taken to tend the flowers, which were considered sacred. Some researchers even referred to them as "the flower worshippers."

Numerous picture symbols of the flowers were drawn around the pyramids, which always had a circular black center with three black petals radiating from there into a larger outer circle. It puzzled Trish that the petals were drawn in straight lines and wider at the outside—not at all like the shape of the real flower. And instead of purple, blue or pink, they were always colored black with a golden yellow background.

Once in a great while, after one of their daily flower rituals—no one knew why—the primitives went into a frenzy of piling stones, dirt and debris—anything they could find—onto the mound. One historian had described one of those infrequent events as looking like ants building an anthill. The work would go on for weeks, and sometimes months on end. Then, after one of the morning flower rituals, the work would suddenly stop as mysteriously as it had begun.

Evonna had never witnessed one of these events in the vicinity of the pyramid mounds in her quadrant, but she had flown to another part of the world in time to observe one in the Western Tropic. It was an awesome sight. Even though there was an obvious urgency about their work, the primitives worked together effectively, diligently and relentlessly, as a single unit, intent on one objective: piling material on the mound. But for what purpose, no one knew. Some speculated that they were trying to make the mound tall enough to reach their gods in the heavens.

Evonna knew a system leader who had begun another program to teach some of the younger primitive children Universalis. Like her, he believed it was pointless to try to teach the elders. Since the primitives appeared to have some form of traditions that they passed down to their children, he'd hoped to learn from those children as they grew. Perhaps they'd be able, through them, to reconstruct some of their own history that had been lost during the plagues. In addition, there was that basic curiosity about the primitive obsession with the mounds and the flowers.

The primitive children learned the language quickly enough, but there was still some kind of barrier or blockage to understanding what they were saying. What they did glean from the children was that theirs was an ancient culture. Yet, the stories they told about their history and religion, which they told in myths, seemed more confusing than enlightening. It was assumed that they were either speaking in riddles or symbolism.

They worshipped at least two ancient gods called Uranus and Pluto, who were said to live on two planets in the sky. Their sons, whom they called Uranium and Plutonium, were believed to live in the mounds. The mounds were considered sacred because the primitives believed they had been touched by the gods. Their myths were replete with stories of ancient heroes and gods. There was one god who breathed fire and stomped the earth and shook it whenever he walked. He was called Zilla, the god of earthquakes and volcanoes. It appeared that an ancient warrior named Shima had once tried to fight Zilla, but in the end he was killed. Still, many worshipped the hero Shima for his bravery, and they marked his death with reverence. Many others fought and lost to the god Zilla over the centuries, but Shima was worshipped because he was the first to defy the god.

Though the primitives appeared totally peaceful, Evonna concluded that their ancestors must have been savage indeed, for they talked about sacrificing not only individuals to their gods in their past, but entire cities were wiped out in their names. For many years there was no evidence that these cities ever existed, but their legends called them by names such as Savana, Navada, Huragua, Lop Nur and Novaya Zemlya. What any of these cities or gods had to do with the flowers they worshipped or its symbol or the work on the pyramid mounds, no one knew. Some even thought that the aroma from the flowers might have hallucinogenic properties, though there was no evidence to prove this.

There was much that Evonna couldn't grasp about the myths by communicating with the younger primitives. Even the ones who'd grown up learning Universalis confused her. She wasn't sure if they thought the gods and their sons they worshipped were real and actually lived in the mounds and the sky, or if they were symbolic—or if they worshipped the mountains themselves—or if they were simply monuments to their gods. She struggled with trying to understand what would make an entire race of people so focused and so dedicated to the single purpose of building and maintaining and continually enlarging a structure like the ones that existed around the world. What was it about their religion that held such a powerful force over their lives?

They made dire predictions about what would happen if the son-gods were disturbed, but the predictions were about natural phenomena—such as earthquakes and volcanoes and fires that Zilla would unleash on mankind. They even said that monsters lived in the mounds. She didn't understand the part about monsters. Did they live there along with the son-gods? Pictures of the monsters showed up in some of the primitive art, with animal and human-looking parts, two heads or one eye. Frustrated by her inability to grasp the meaning of the myths, Evonna even began wondering if the primitive children meant "Sun Gods" instead of "Son Gods."

Researchers and archeologists had recently located two areas on the planet that they believed to be the Lop Nur and Novaya Zemlya from primitive myths. Though they might have been cities at one time, there was no evidence to confirm this. The areas were all pock-marked with craters, and it had been confirmed by scientists that at some time in the ancient past, a cluster of powerful meteorites had struck both areas—all at about the same time. But, if there had been cities there, they had been wiped out without a trace.

The children of the primitives in those two locales told tales about giant, poisonous mushrooms which once grew in the craters. The primitives in other parts of the world told myths about these giant mushrooms, as well, and their primitive art was filled with pictures of the oddly-shaped fungi. It was a species unknown to man. The primitives said that the earth had swallowed them up and belched them out again. Though they were considered extinct, there were still warnings about growing or eating the mushrooms. It was said that only the initiated had the power to transmute their poison. Like the flowers, many researchers believed the mushrooms had been powerfully hallucinogenic.

It appeared that the primitives believed the gods, Uranus and Pluto, made the craters. From that, Evonna reasoned they attributed natural events like meteor showers to some kind of sky gods simply because they came from the sky—or they believed they had come from those planets. Still, she couldn't understand why they believed the sons of the sky gods lived underneath the mountain mounds.

Her system leader, Maximillian de los Medicios, suggested at one point that she was trying to interpret the myths too literally.

During her work she had established a relationship with an older priest named Radja Bullah, who lived by the mound mountain near her city. The two of them had a primitive way of communicating and, though it was unsatisfactory in collecting data, she was quite fond of the old man. Occasionally, she'd be so deep in thought with him that she'd think she was about to tap into his mind stream. But always, it would slip away. Still, she thought that she was close—very close.

One day after Evonna felt as though she had won Radja Bullah's confidence, he agreed to share the meaning behind the myths with her through a young primitive interpreter who would translate to her in Universalis. The prospect of unraveling more of the primitive mysteries left her excited and expectant.

• • •

When the time finally felt right to the elder man, he, the young interpreter and Evonna set out one day, traveling to the edge of a large plateau overlooking the desert. There they sat in a circle and began what she realized was a truly historic session. She thought how appropriate it was for a Scribe to be writing down the myths for prosperity.

Through the young interpreter, the elder said that the tale he was about to tell was not for everyone. It was only meant for those who had the wisdom to understand it, and he entreated her not to write the material down, but rather to entrust it to her memory. The young interpreter was only there because he had recently remembered his duty to tell the stories, as well. Then he told of creation—of a time of blackness and chaos and how out of that chaos, great dreamers, or gods, gave life and form to the chaos. That was the beginning of the earth. One god, called Uranus, who shared the dream, wed the goddess of the earth, Gaia, to create life and to produce the first men. Some of those first men were monsters, which Uranus buried in the earth in the hope that they would never again see the light of day. This made some of his other sons—some of whom were known as titans—angry, and with their mother's encouragement, they waged war against their father, Uranus. He was gravely wounded by his offspring. His rich and powerful blood fell onto the earth, where it seeped into the earth in veins. It was called Uranium, and each place where it fell became sacred.

Eventually the sons of the earth became so greedy and power hungry that they decided to dig up their father's blood heritage from the earth so they could be as powerful as he had been. They were warned not to, for to do so would unleash plagues upon the planet. But in their blindness, they did it anyway; and what man unleashed on the face of the earth were the Furies. The Furies were the daughters of the earth who punished the sins that the greedy men had carried out against their fellow man. Even though their punishment was merciless, it was, nevertheless, just.

When the Furies were unleashed, men produced and began to eat the giant mushrooms. Many were poisoned by them, and a great war and rumors of wars erupted. Plagues, famine, fire and flood spread across the land as man grew colder and more merciless. The colder men grew, the colder the Great War grew. It lasted four score years. The war was so cold that the earth grew heated and made men sick. The first battle of the war took place in a desert, which was called Alamogordo, but to the Hebrew was known as Armageddon.

When Evonna asked about the Hero Shima, the old man said that he fought in the first battle which was waged by a true man. Only a True-Man was worthy to fight the Hero Shima. Shima had a brother called Nag Hasaki. The True-man decided that he must destroy the brothers. He would not go to battle himself, but sent his son, a little boy with his large, fat teacher as a companion. Together the Little Boy and the Fat Man killed the Hero Shima and his brother, Nag Hasaki—along with all of their families—with a weapon given to them by the god Zilla. It was ten times brighter than the sun. However, when the Little Boy saw the damage the weapon had inflicted on the earth and mankind, he became remorseful and said, "My god, what have we done?"

Other nations, impressed with, and yet fearful of the powerful weapon, however, took it up and continued to wage war on the earth and on mankind. They did not realize that the power of the sun would ultimately rain destruction on all, those who used the weapon as well as those upon whom the weapon was directed.

Evonna asked about Plutonium. Radja Bullah told her that the sons of Pluto wore invisible helmets in the great battle, which were called war helmets or warheads. They were clad in metal armor and lived silently in the earth until such time as they were called into battle by the sons of man. They were joined by some of Uranus' children who were called Titans.

Some of the weapons of war were marked with the sign of Plutonium and Uranium. When the elder drew one of the signs in the sand, Evonna noted with surprise that it was a picture of the flower symbols that the primitives drew so often. He said that the weapons were carried on the wings of eagles clad in metal armor and that they were dropped on both those who waged war and those who were peaceful, and sometimes they were thrown into the very bowels of the earth. No one was safe from the battle. The whole earth shook from its force.

During that cold war some of Uranus' monster children from the beginning of time came back to life to roam the earth again. Each time the greedy men dug their father's blood from the earth, they released powerful forces—forces that were meant to stay in the bosom of the earth mother, Gaia, and she turned over on her side and shook the earth to show her displeasure at being robbed of her bounty.

Radja told Evonna that some of the places on the earth had been so damaged by all the battles, diseases and plagues that Gaia returned them to the healing waters of the sea to become pure again, and that thousands upon thousands of men died during those days.

Then, after the turning and shaking, there came a new wisdom which was more powerful than any weapon and with it a new heaven and a new earth, and all was peaceful for a long time.

After the shaking of the earth, men realized what they had done and tried to return their father's blood back to the earth. But they had poisoned the sacred blood for the time that it was unleashed upon the earth, and there was no way to return it to its purity, and there was no way to ensure that man would not dig it up again one day in his greed. So it was sealed in the earth with giant gates that were guarded for all time by the "anointed"—priests and priestesses of the highest order, whose sacred duty it was to stand guard at the gates of hell for all time to warn others. Radja Bullah was one of those sacred priests.

After the elder had finished telling his story, however, Evonna didn't feel any more enlightened. She was only confused further, and she knew she still had a long way to go in her studies of the myths to understand them.

• • •

The purpose of the tour Evonna was taking that day to the local mound was to give a select group of people a chance to witness the penetration of it. Scientists had recently developed a new technology for probing the contents of the mounds without doing too much damage to them.

Evonna was somewhat uncomfortable with this attempt to learn more about the mysterious mound builders. She felt it was an unnecessary intrusion into their lives. But those few who had opposed it were overruled by the tug of curiosity that many scientists, governmental agencies and others were feeling. Some even thought the mounds held treasures of some kind, that they were actually tombs which held the remains of former kings—along with treasures that may have been buried along with them.

With the help of the young primitive who spoke Universalis, Evonna had been able to explain to Radja Bullah the purpose of the equipment that was being assembled near their mound. He became quite agitated when he began to understand the meaning of what she was trying to communicate to him. In fact, the understanding they had of the project had created quite a stir among all of the primitives, not just the ones with whom she worked. Simultaneously, there were reports of primitives from around the world becoming distraught. That fact convinced Evonna even further of their ability to communicate with their own form of mind telepathy.

• • •

While Evonna had been deep in her thoughts about the mounds, people had been gathering in and around the domed building waiting to leave for the tour. Finally, her friend Belina appeared, rosy-cheeked and bubbly. Evonna knew instantly that she was pregnant. Without saying a word, they embraced and shared in the joy of the moment. Even if both of them had not had telepathic abilities, Evonna could have guessed her friend's news; she was that obvious. Some of the other people standing around smiled, knowing what was happening, and they, too, shared in the joy of the moment, and silently communicated their congratulations.

At the proper time they all boarded the larger communal hovercraft and traversed the distance to the mound mountain quickly, across the dry, dusty desert. On the way, Evonna shared her feelings about the penetration of the mounds to those who were able to read her thoughts. The others listened to the pre-recorded commentary about the tour on their individual listening sets.

As the mound appeared in the distance, it became clear that something was amiss. They could see the equipment ready at the site with the media people, government officials, scientists and historians crowded around the area in preparation for the impending event. The primitives, however, were in a high state of agitation—almost a frenzy—a frenzy, Evonna thought, very similar to the one she had witnessed at the mound covering ritual she'd witnessed years before...except that this frenzy was much more pronounced.

When they exited the hovercraft, Evonna immediately headed toward the commotion, hoping she could assist somehow with interpretations. As she approached the crowd, she could see some of the primitive women weeping uncontrollably. Even she had underestimated the level to which the primitives were being affected by the project. As the machine was being set in position for the penetration, the commotion and wailing grew increasingly louder. Some of the younger ones who recognized Evonna, approached and kept repeating in Universalis, "No, you mustn't. You mustn't do this."

Just then her eyes met Radja Bullah's in the distance. The panic she saw in them was obvious, and it was uncharacteristic for the old man. But she saw something else in them she had never seen before...pure fear.

She almost ran toward him, dodging people along the way, never taking her eyes off his. Then suddenly they both stopped. She had a strange sensation, similar to the feeling she got each time she was about to tap into his mind stream. She froze in mid step, as he did. With their eyes locked, a flood of information, along with emotions, suddenly came barreling at her and crashed into her consciousness like an invisible bolt of lightening. She could almost see it and feel it and taste it. It almost knocked her off her feet.

Instantly she knew. She understood the myths. Finally.

And then as the same panic gripped her that had gripped Radja Bullah, she turned in what felt like slow motion toward the people operating the equipment to breach the mound seal, threw out her arm and screamed from the depths of her soul...

• • •

"NO...O...O...O!"

Jimmy Hartwell was jolted from his sleep by the sound of his wife, Trish, screaming beside him in the bed. He jerked upright, put his hand to his head and blinked his eyes. In the dim light, he could see her arm outstretched in the air and still hear the echo from her scream in his head. "Trish, what's wrong? You're all right. It was just another nightmare."

As he leaned back onto his pillow, he drew her toward him. She clutched at him almost frantically, whimpering like a wounded animal.

"Shhh...Shhh. Now, now. You're fine," he reassured her. "You're with me now. Everything's all right. You were just dreaming. You had another nightmare."

The soothing tone in his voice was beginning to work. She was calming—but slowly. Her heart still raced in her chest like a jackhammer, as she attempted to orient herself.

"Oh, Jimmy, it wasn't like a dream at *all*. It was so *real!*"

"I know. I know. But, you're doing better. The nightmares are getting farther apart now." He brushed the hair from her forehead and looked at her. "Maybe they'll go away for good before much longer."

"I hope so."

But she didn't sound convinced.

• • •

In many ways, Trish Hartwell's life with her new husband had been even happier than she'd hoped it would be. Still, her sleep had become saturated with nightmares in the previous few months, even though Jimmy was right that they were getting farther apart. Her therapy sessions were helping. And her writing—what little she was able to do—was helping, as well, though she felt unable to stay focused on it.

While attempting to work on the book, she continued to keep up with world events. She wasn't surprised by the discovery of the possibility of ancient life on the planet Mars, nor by the archeological discovery that suggested the Aborigine culture was at least 100,000 years older than previously believed. She wasn't surprised when astronomers reported evidence of a mysterious "negative gravity force" called "dark energy" in the universe, that repels objects that are usually attracted to each other by gravity.

The revelations that thousands of children from Chernobyl were quietly being sent to Cuba for treatment for their diseases didn't surprise her, nor did the fact that the American media continued to report only 36 deaths due to the accident at Chernobyl. And, since Mark Matheson had identified China as one of the last new frontier markets for the uranium cartel, she wasn't surprised that China was embracing a program of building new nuclear power plants at the same time other countries were rejecting the technology.

When the report by the European Commission on Radiation Risk came out, she wasn't surprised that they predicted 61,600,000 deaths worldwide from the nuclear project since 1945, 1,600,000 infantile deaths and 1,900,000 fetal deaths.

She wasn't even shocked about revelations that on October 3, 1986 a Soviet nuclear submarine called K219, carrying 16 ballistic missiles, and an American nuclear submarine had collided off the East coast of the United States during one of many Cold War military games of cat and mouse. The

557

collision caused a catastrophic fire on board the Soviet submarine, threatening to launch missiles on major cities: New York, Boston, Philadelphia, Washington, D.C., Miami, Atlanta and others. After the fire was put out on the sub, its two nuclear reactors almost melted down off the coast threatening to release a radioactive cloud seven miles across. The captain of K219 guided his wounded vessel out into the open waters of the North Atlantic, as far away from land as possible in case of a meltdown.

That submarine, with its reactors and missiles on board, sank and came to rest at the bottom of the Atlantic Ocean, along with the body of a nineteen year-old Russian sailor named Sergei Preminin. After lowering the last of four control rods into the reactors, successfully shutting them down and preventing a meltdown, the heat and pressure in the reactor room increased to the point of trapping the young sailor inside. Though Preminin went down with the submarine to his death, his actions had spared the Eastern coast of the U.S from a nuclear holocaust.

Trish wasn't surprised that most Americans were totally unaware of the name or even the existence of the Russian sailor who had saved the lives of several million Americans during the Cold War. She wasn't surprised that the U.S. government was still denying that one of their submarines was involved in the event, or that they had refused to warn the American public when the danger was imminent, fearing that they might jeopardize the upcoming summit at Reykjavik, Iceland between then President Reagan and Soviet leader Gorbachev. And she especially wasn't astonished that many of the revelations about the secret incident were uncovered years later by the entertainment industry and a foreign news agency instead of the mainstream U. S. news media, or that, even then, it was given scant attention in the U.S.

She wondered if that was one of the incidents that Gorbachev was talking about when he said that Americans and Russians were still unaware of the things their countries had done and were still doing, and if it was one of the incidents that Freya had referenced in New Mexico.

In fact, nothing much surprised her anymore. She was concerned that she couldn't quite shake the sense of foreboding she'd felt since her return from Kazakhstan, before she and Jimmy got married. Though the events in New Mexico proved to be a comfort in her life, she still felt incapable of dealing with what she had seen and experienced in Clinic Number Four on an emotional level.

• • •

"Look, Trish," Jimmy finally said as he continued holding her, "I think the reason you're having these recurring dreams might be because you really need to finish the book. I've noticed they seem to be worse when you're *not* writing. I think…"

"These aren't recurring dreams, Jimmy," she interrupted. "They're recurring *nightmares* …and besides, I've *tried* to finish the book…time and time again…at least a hundred times. Some of it's easy; I just transcribe it from the tape recordings. But in journalism, it was like a mantra: Never *become* the story. I don't know *how* to write in the first person. And I don't know how to get back to my feelings. Every time I try to write about the clinic, I freeze up. The writer's block comes back. I keep hitting that wall. I just can't go back to that place…not even in my mind. It just brings up too much pain."

"But, didn't Max say something to you about the monsters in your dreams just trying to get your attention?"

"Yeah…well it's got my attention…but I don't have a clue what it's trying to tell me. And on top of that, I think I'm starting my change of life. I haven't had a period for two months…and, that's all I need right now."

Jimmy rubbed the top of her head with his chin. "Look," he finally said. "Go to the doctor tomorrow and get an exam, and if you need some pills or something, just get them. That ought to take care of any hormone problems.

"As for the book…well…why not try writing it in the third person…you know, like fiction, or something? *That* might get you over the emotional hump you're feeling."

After digesting his comments a moment, she sat upright in the bed, then turned and stared at him in the dim light. The suggestion was so simple and so obvious. Even Max had suggested that at one point, but she had casually dismissed it.

A smile came over her face, as she lay back down and snuggled into the warm safety of her husband's embrace, certain that she would be able to sleep undisturbed for the rest the night with an idea of how she might navigate her way through a book.

Chapter Fifty

The navigation took years with many distractions. During that navigation, on September 11th, 2001, two commercial jets crashed into the Twin Towers of the World Trade Center in New York City, leveling them in minutes. In the hours and days of national and international chaos that followed, Trish thought of Stephanie. She couldn't remember what airlines her husband worked for and called her in Albuquerque to make sure he was safe. When she reached her, the strain in Stephanie's voice was evident.

"He was home on vacation when it happened." Trish let out a breath, and Stephanie's voice cracked, as she added, "But I don't know how I'm going to be able to watch him leave on his next trip." There was a long pause, as Trish heard her choking back tears. Then Stephanie said, "I've been thinking about you, Trish. Freya said that there's some more dialogue for you to add to the book, but that you didn't have to come here for it. She said for you to just start writing on your computer—typing questions or anything—and it would start coming. She said it would be like pulling a loose thread on a sweater; it'll just come."

They talked a while longer, before saying good-bye. Trish went straight to her computer room and started typing. She wanted answers, and she wanted them now. But her questions wouldn't formulate. They were scattered, frustrated, angry, rambling. She turned the computer off and turned on the television. At times she couldn't watch the news, and at others, she had to.

A few nights later she awoke from another nightmare, and got out of bed to try again. She sat down at her computer and typed: *"I just had a horrible nightmare. What does it mean?"*

"It means that you have been letting too much horror seep into your every day waking state. You need to see with different eyes if you wish to transmute the effects of that horror you witnessed over and over. What has been implanted in your brain will affect all that you love if you do not allow the true wisdom to emerge from within and beyond it. Look to your heart for the deeper and higher meanings of the world events and transmute them. For with understanding comes healing."

"Why did this awful thing happen?"

"The event that has impacted so many in a single day has marked the end of an era. Your world did, indeed, change on what you mark as 9-11-01 on your calendar. There is meaning to everything that happened. All of it. Each story woven within the fabric of the event moves you to tears and inspires: the firemen running into chaos, the instant spiritual connections between strangers and the many stories of miracles. There are hundreds of these stories being shared, and it is opening your hearts—your heart chakras.

The pain, courage and sacrifice of family members left behind touches you. You will all go through what they have: death and rebirth of old paradigms, relationships and cultural conditioning. Their courage will give you the strength to walk through your own personal fires when they come. And they will. This is a collective event. You are not separate from it.

"Even the seemingly unfathomable and immovable amount of entangled debris is serving a purpose. It is protection. It is 'holding the space' long enough for people to come to view it as meaningful beyond the value a culture once put upon it as real estate. It is beginning to be recognized as sacred space, a symbol of sacrifice to the altars of duality and separation. What a perfect symbol. Towers of duality: male/female, right/left, hard/soft, light/dark. It all collapsed before your very eyes: the solidity of your structures—your belief systems—everything you had put your faith in…gone in minutes. When they were shattered into dust, it began a process within you of shattering your own illusions of solidity, financial power, material dependence and security. You do not recognize these illusions as traps. However, these illusions are being shattered both without and within you.

"And amidst all that rubble, a miracle, a sign, another symbol appeared in the rubble of the old symbols of duality. Two steel beams were left standing, forming the sign of the cross, the symbol of your Christ consciousness. There is death, and there is rebirth. Now you may become as the Phoenix rising…that exquisite point where cold meets hot, pain meets joy, peace meets chaos, male meets female, old meets new and villain meets hero. Where flesh merges with Spirit, Heaven touches Earth. Your dualities merged as One. As All. Balance. Now. That is your moment where your time stands still.

"Could you not see the beauty amidst the horror? Did it not move you? Did it not turn your hearts of stone into flesh again? Did everything without meaning in your lives not melt away?"

"Yes, it really did."

"What sacrifice. What inspiration. What opportunity played out on your world stage. Rarely is so much given to so many so clearly.

"And, indeed, you may go about your daily lives as you did before, but you will feel differently—vastly differently. You will live your life as *in* the world, but not *of* the world. Your Christ consciousness enters—or awakens—only through your will, and that consciousness is not of this world. It is beyond and within a kingdom—a frequency, if you will—that you have only dreamed about in your mortal states, or frequencies."

"Is it necessary for us to go to war over this?"

"Not if you are able to do the work internally."

"I don't understand."

"Do you not study Projection 101 in your psychology classes?"

"Well...yeah."

"What you do not work on within yourselves, you project onto others. Where do you think your front lines are? On some battlefield? You are externalizing issues that you are not able to work on *internally*—just as Max said about your Cold War."

"So, do we have to go to war?"

"Again, only if you are unable to do it internally. If you are not, then you may do it externally, but the result will be the same in time. What you experience as male and female, friend and foe, black and white, good and evil—the polarities of your being will become one. You may sacrifice yourselves on this cross, or you may joyfully blend all of the aspects of who you are: office worker, terrorist, hero, pilot, abused woman across the globe. Ah, can you not see how it happened? Can you not see how it *all* affects you? Like cells of your body, the diseased 'cells' reach out and strike at healthy cells. When and where there is lack of ease—lack of love—it affects the all. For all are one—one with Spirit.

"Your terrorists do not all come in the form of foreign terrorist cells like viruses and bacteria. They come from within you, as well. You and your children kill each other every day. You and they die to who you truly are every day. Little aspects of you and them are dying in each moment that you turn from the riches that lie within you to those illusions of riches that you amass to make you feel secure in your material plane. But there is no material security. There are no material guarantees in your material world, for there is no matter in your material world. It is *all* illusion. It is the play, the drama that is playing itself out with props that you have 'materialized' from within your own grand being.

"You *are* mighty Spiritual beings. Accept that. Feel that. Know that. Act upon that to become the being that you have sought throughout your life and throughout your ages and throughout your galaxies.

"It is the Holy Grail. Drink from it from your own source, in joy and wonder and awe."

Trish sat and read what her hands had just typed.

"Those are beautiful words."

"Words and dreams and reason cannot contain the enormity of what you have experienced and will experience. Many will choose *not* to experience it. Be not concerned about those who make that choice. For no one may truly judge another's path from unconscious states."

"How is it that the site of the Twin Towers will become sacred?"

"Each event, each collapse of skyscrapers, each flap of a bird's wing that moves you reinforces and yet challenges your beliefs about the world around you. You feel 'in' your world, yet somehow apart. Your emotional responses to *any* experience—whether those experiences are subtle or dramatic—bring you closer and closer to your true identity—make you feel more 'real,' more alive. The more you *feel,* the more you are.

"If the objectified world of materialization you experience is comprised of thought patterns, then each object in it is necessarily imbued with the Spirit of all who have touched it, created it and even noticed or thought about it. When many individuals have focused on a place or an object with awe and wonder and feeling long enough or intently enough, that place, that thing becomes 'sacred.' That is, the place, the object, is saturated with the thought patterns combined with the emotions of the collective Spirit, which in turn 'feeds' the individual and collective Spirit—causes it to think, to feel more fully...become more alive.

"Objects hold memory. Places hold memory. Thus objects and places feel, as well...*and* they respond. They respond to your presence and to your very thoughts. Indeed, they can communicate with you. The 'language' through which they communicate can be as confusing or unrecognizable as what you experience as a foreign language, or it may be as clear as what you experience as crystal. Your receptions of these communications are dependent only upon how much your filtering system—or ego—allows into your consciousness.

"As more and more of you visit a 'sacred' site, the faith and hope that you bring with you empowers it more and more, and it becomes more and more healing. You are experiencing a collective healing right now—a great purification."

"It doesn't feel like it."

"Healing takes time. Do not judge what form or time or process healing takes."

Trish put her hand to her mouth for a moment and then typed, *"If we truly understood our world, would it 'disappear' before our eyes?"*

"The world as you know it would vanish, and the universe as it *also* is would *re-*'appear' through perceptions which you can now only dream of in an 'altered state.' Your world truly changed on September the 11th. And each time you recall that event, you re-arrange your cellular components momentarily to predispose yourself to 're-act' or 're-enact' or recall your feelings at that time. That memory stimulation keeps your cellular components reverting back to that moment until your cells 'lock' into that configuration long enough to change you both collectively and individually. Your cellular arrangement is shifted. Your world changes.

"You have chosen to be on this Earth plane at this time. We beseech you to fulfill your mission. Open you hearts to all of your emotions and *feel* what you already know deep within the structure of your cells. You are mutating on a cellular level so that the 'new wine' may enter your 'new bottles.' Those who choose not to transform may not be able to contain the new wine—the new wisdom that is entering your plane of existence. The atomic structure of your physical vehicles will adapt to the conditions and the events that lie ahead, if you choose to experience the New Heaven and the New Earth that await your coming—the Second Coming of the Christ consciousness that is at hand in this moment of your time."

"Wow. This thing is even bigger than I thought, isn't it?"

"In time you will come to view this as a blessed event. Even now you are beginning to recognize how it is changing and challenging and shaping your lives for the better. In that moment of recoil that you experienced collectively and individually—your re-coil to shock and disbelief—all else fell away. All things unimportant in your life, you saw with new perspective. Your relationships are changing. Some become stronger. Some collapse. There is a great shifting of energies within your culture and throughout your world.

"What made you feel safe disappeared before your eyes. You felt vulnerable, yet in that vulnerability, you opened your hearts. Your ability to keep your hearts open in the very face of vulnerability is the source of your true power—not that which you *perceive* as power."

"When you talk about Christ consciousness, could we just as easily say Buddha, Mohammed or Krishna consciousness?"

"Indeed. This awakening consciousness within you is not confined to any one entity or to any one culture. There is no duality here—no right or wrong, black or white. It is merely that perfect point of balance of *both* aspects of your dualities. When they are crossed at your center point, you will find harmony in your lives and in your world. Do you not recognize the number of the place of your twin towers—the one you call your zip code, 10084? It numbers 13...as does your 13th consciousness. It is a vibration, a frequency, a kingdom not of this 3-Dimensional plane.

"The consciousness, the rebirth, is coming for all who choose it from the death of old ideas, assumptions, beliefs and conditioning. Some things must die inside you in order for other things to live and thrive and grow. That is the nature of life. New plants thrive in the decomposed richness of the death of other plants. Death is the very ground from which new life springs. Your culture has forgotten to appreciate this fact, and instead focuses only on grief.

"Many things in your world must break down in order for others to build up."

"Sometimes I feel like what happened is being used and manipulated again to cling to old beliefs and ways of doing things—old patterns. I get caught up in it myself."

"To enhance your own spiritual evolution do not expend a lot of your energies trying to control the reactions of others to the paradigm shift, which is occurring in your country. There are many who have a vested interest in maintaining the status quo. Economic, social, religious and political interests all feel threatened by the changes they have seen and felt. They feel their illusions of power slipping away, just as they saw their illusions of safety crumble before their eyes. They are desperately trying to cling to a belief that is dissolving in their grasp. And the more tightly they cling, the faster the illusions will dissolve.

"Do not be in judgment of their reactions, for they are fear-based. Rather, focus your attentions and intuitions on your own responses. Look from your perspective of overview to the deeper and higher observations of the event. Then send those vibrations out into your universe to help break up old patterns. Cry if you must. Feel what you feel. Allow your emotions, and through them come into your being.

"Be a light—a beacon—in a world of darkness and fear. If you do not walk into darkness—the unknown—because of fear, then you may already be in it. Do not feed on the daily fears of your culture. Begin your slate anew. Leave your 'news,' or fear, behind. It is an old tale, told over and over again by those who dare not live the life that is possible.

"Can you not already see the love brought forth from your sacrifice of September the 11th? Can you not see how many lives have been changed for the better…how it gave opportunity to so many to feel strongly and deeply and to examine their lives and make changes, take new directions, to swim in the currents of their emotions and live life more fully, more deeply, more spontaneously and passionately, without the rigidity of their past? Could any of this have been possible without your sacrificial lambs, without your heroes, your villains, your Christed Consciousness and your betraying Judas— your opposite poles, your range of being human, and yet, at the same time, gods among men? You *are* gods and goddesses who walk among humanity. You have simply been sleep walking through your experiences, and are awakening to your birthright—to the source *behind* your very being. *This* is the 'who you are' and 'why you are here.' *This* is your purpose in this life…to be here at this exact point in the human experience when you awaken human unconsciousness into the fullness of Spiritual being—human beings aware, being and knowing who they truly are behind the masks of unconsciousness. Ah, the grand experiences and discoveries that await you!"

"What do you know, Trish Cagle?"

Without hesitation, she typed, *"We are all God."*

"Can you love your enemy?"

"I feel mostly non-feeling…no, anger…and regret, like why didn't I know? Why couldn't I stop it?"

"Do you wish to control others? *Can you love your enemy?"*

"I could if I could understand him—why it happened. I thought it was

religious zealotry. But now that doesn't seem to be the case. So what was it?"

"People commit suicide every day. The entire atomic age has been a form of slow suicide for many. Did suicide not bother you before?"

"I always thought it was their business unless they took someone else with them when they killed themselves."

"They always take someone with them. They always destroy little pieces of others when they go. People kill little pieces of *themselves* every day and kill little pieces of others when they do. It is no different with your Twin Towers. It has just been brought out into the open for all to see. Much is surfacing now in the personal lives of all who have been affected by this event, which was prophesied in your ancient histories. It is, indeed, a period of Great Purification. It is a glorious time to be alive.

"Can you love your enemy?"

"Well, I know that a lot of people have opened their hearts as a result of this event...and it happened very quickly. And I know that ultimately we are in control of everything that happens to us—whether we accept that responsibility or not. So the people involved must have agreed to be participants in these events on some spiritual or unconscious level before they happened...all of them, including the terrorists. And it has opened our hearts. And it is our choice whether we keep them open at a time of vulnerability. And, yes, I feel that is our true strength and our true power. And, yes, I know that someone had to be the Judas in order for the purpose of the Christ consciousness to be fulfilled. And, yes, I know that we even betray ourselves when it serves our higher purpose."

Trish sighed forcefully. *"Yes, I guess from that standpoint I can love my enemy."*

"Blessings."

Trish smiled and let out a lighter sigh. *"It is a blessing, isn't it?"*

"Indeed. Now...can you love yourself? For *that* is the greatest blessing of all."

Trish's face contorted, as her eyes filled with tears. She raised her hand to her mouth and started to shake. Then she typed, *"Thank you,"* shut down her computer, and wept.

Epilogue

In time Trish finished the book, as Max and her husband had suggested, by writing it in the third person. It was easier that way, somehow.

It still is . . .

And I still find it easier at times to write my book of life in the third person, for sometimes I still forget who I truly am. And at other times...at other times...I remember.

I try to keep my life moving forward—ever forward—and free...free flowing, like my husband's raging, wild river. I have given up trying to find an explanation for life—for I believe we may never be able to explain life... for to explain it, we must limit it, and life is as limitless as the "out there" that we can only dream about. Maybe it has always been our purpose to simply experience life—to experience it and to feel it—to be it—as human beings and as humans being.

I have learned to honor the mystery. I still probe and question from time to time, as is my nature, but there is a certain peace even in that—not quite the "peace that passeth all understanding"—but I am getting there. I am becoming, as we all are becoming. And I have learned to be gentle with myself.

Our lives—Jimmy's and mine—can still be maddening at times. I still get angry or frustrated with my husband, my government, my neighbor, myself. At those times I have learned to simply allow myself to experience those feelings—all of my feelings—for they are part of who I am. And in that way they are transformed. And I am still touched by people. Some still leave a mark on me.

At times our lives can be quite sweet. The menopause I thought I was experiencing turned out to be a pregnancy. Freya—or whomever it was I spoke to that day in New Mexico—had been right. I wasn't contaminated there as a child. I was just waiting for the right moment. And five years ago we welcomed a baby girl into our lives. We named her Kristen Joy.

She is a happy child, and she runs around our house and around our lives constantly chanting, "Why? Why? Why?" She wants to figure everything out. It is her nature. She is her mother's daughter. Sometimes I think she's just trying to figure out what planet she's landed on. And sometimes she can be a real handful. Her limitless curiosity, vitality and determination test Jimmy's and my physical, mental and emotional limits to their breaking points—their boundaries. And then she breaks them. She can be quite a little devil. That is also her nature.

Then there are those moments when she's playing with her new puppy or giggling wide-eyed at the candles lit on her birthday cake or napping peacefully in the crook of my arm, while I twist a strand of her blond ringlets in my fingers. At those times I know—I truly know in my heart—that she is a divine child.

And I simply bask in her reflection.

There is an order and a harmony to the universe. We can feel it at times. We may not be able to describe it or name it, but we sense it whenever we experience it. And we know it whenever it touches us. I could have stayed in my garden that summer day in 1995 and learned what I have known deep down all along. But I chose to venture outside of my garden, and despite the pain, the trauma and the fear that came with that journey, in the end I found my joy...what I had been born for...my purpose in life...a glimpse of who I am.

I believe in myths now, or at least some form of them—perhaps more than I believe in the "borrowed truths" of history and science books. And I believe in fairy tales again—just as I did as a little girl. I know in my heart that wherever my path takes me, and whatever I experience in my future life, I can live happily ever after.

At times I remember my old friend, Max's last poem.

Dreams! Glorious *dreams!*
Unbidden, unnoticed, unspoken.
Dreams! *Glorious* dreams*!*
From out of the depths of soul and song,
Sailing into my heart,
My mind, my soul, my movement;
Showering beams of now...
Of being, of knowing the All.
Lingering soft on my world,
Then *thrusting* my essence beyond.
Dreams! *Glorious* dreams!
Glimpses of ALL that I AM.

That's when I wonder: Was it all—is it all—just a dream?

Merrily...

Merrily...

Merrily...

Merrily...

Suggested Reading

No Immediate Danger - Rosalie Bertell

Chernobyl - The Forbidden Truth - Alla Yaroshinskaya

No Breathing Room - Grigori Medvedev

We Almost Lost Detroit - John G. Fuller

The Woman Who Knew Too Much - Gail Green - The life of Alice Stewart

Chaos - James Gleick

The Hot Zone - Richard Preston

The Lost Books of the Bible - Gramercy Books

Mythology - Edith Hamilton

The Power of Myth - Joseph Campbell

Women Who Run With the Wolves - Clarissa Pinkola Estes, Ph.D.

Voices of the First Day - Robert Lawlor

Medicine for the Earth - Sandra Ingerman

The Way of the Shaman - Michael Harner

Soul Retrieval - Sandra Ingerman

Shamanic Journeying - Sandra Ingerman - A Beginner's Guide

Black Dawn, Bright Day - Sun Bear, with Wabun Wind

Magic Eye - A New Way of Looking at the World - 3-D Illusions - by N. E. Thing Enterprises

Saved by the Light - Dannion Brinkley

Cosmic Voyage - Courtney Brown, Ph.D.

Psychic Warrior - David Morehouse

The State of Native Americans - Edited by M. Annette Jaimes

National Geographic Magazine - "Living with Radiation" April 1989
"Lethal Danger" By Mike Edwards, August, 1994

Time Magazine - "Blowing the Whistle on Nuclear Safety" By Eric Pooley
March 4, 1996

60 Minutes - "Semipalatinsk" Ed Bradley, August 28, 1994

The Nation Magazine - "Nuclear Shadow" by Helen Caldicott, April 29,
1996; "In the Dead Zone: Aftermath of the Apocalypse" By Harvey
Wasserman, April 29, 1996

The Bulletin of the Atomic Scientists - "Truth Was an Early Casualty"
By Alexander R. Sich, May/June, 1996

The Holographic Universe - Michael Talbot

False Profits - Peter Truell and Larry Gurwin, a book about the BCCI
scandal and how U.S. policy in the Middle East was influenced

Spider's Web - Alan Friedman, a book about the BNL scandal and how the
Bush White House armed Iraq

Gulliver File - Roger Moody, Mindwatch

"The European Commission on Radiation Risk - 2003, Health Effects of
Ionizing Radiation Exposures at Low Doses" - www.euradcom.org

Code Red Alert - www.cleanenergy.org

Nuclear Information and Resource Service - www.nirs.org